Agatha Christie Crime Collection

A 19

Agatha Christie

CRIME COLLECTION

A Caribbean Mystery

Taken at the Flood

The Seven Dials Mystery

PAUL HAMLYN · LONDON

A Caribbean Mystery; *Taken at the Flood*; *The Seven Dials Mystery*; all originally published by William Collins, Sons & Co. Ltd, and copyright by Agatha Christie, 1964, 1948, 1929

Photoset in Malta by St Paul's Press Ltd
Printed in England by International Printers Limited
SBN 6007 66 195

CONTENTS

A Caribbean Mystery

To my old friend
JOHN CRUIKSHANK ROSE
with happy memories of my visit
to the West Indies

1. *Major Palgrave tells a story*

'TAKE ALL THIS BUSINESS about Kenya,' said Major Palgrave. 'Lots of chaps gabbing away who know nothing about the place! Now *I* spent fourteen years of my life there. Some of the best years of my life, too——'

Old Miss Marple inclined her head.

It was a gentle gesture of courtesy. Whilst Major Palgrave proceeded with the somewhat uninteresting recollections of a lifetime, Miss Marple peacefully pursued her own thoughts. It was a routine with which she was well acquainted. The locale varied. In the past, it had been predominantly India. Majors, Colonels, Lieutenant-Generals—and a familiar series of words: *Simla. Bearers. Tigers. Chota Hazri—Tiffin. Khitmagars*, and so on. With Major Palgrave the terms were slightly different. *Safari. Kikuyu. Elephants. Swahili*. But the pattern was essentially the same. An elderly man who needed a listener so that he could, in memory, relive days in which he had been happy. Days when his back had been straight, his eyesight keen, his hearing acute. Some of these talkers had been handsome soldierly old boys, some again had been regrettably unattractive; and Major Palgrave, purple of face, with a glass eye, and the general appearance of a stuffed frog, belonged in the latter category.

Miss Marple had bestowed on all of them the same gentle charity. She had sat attentively, inclining her head from time to time in gentle agreement, thinking her own thoughts and enjoying what there was to enjoy: in this case the deep blue of a Caribbean Sea.

So kind of dear Raymond,—she was thinking gratefully, so really and truly kind . . . Why he should take so much trouble about his old aunt, she really did not know. Conscience, perhaps; family feeling? Or possibly he was truly fond of her . . .

She thought, on the whole, that he *was* fond of her—he always had been—in a slightly exasperated and contemptuous way! Always trying to bring her up to date. Sending her books to read. Modern novels. So difficult—all about such unpleasant people, doing such very odd things and not, apparently, even enjoying them. 'Sex' as a word had not been much mentioned in Miss Marple's young days; but there had been plenty of it—not talked about so much—but enjoyed far more than nowadays, or so it seemed to her. Though usually labelled Sin, she couldn't help feeling that that was preferable to what it seemed to be nowadays—a kind of Duty.

Her glance strayed for a moment to the book on her lap lying open at page twenty-three which was as far as she had got (and indeed as far as she felt like getting!).

"'Do you mean that you've had no sexual experience at ALL?' demanded the young man incredulously. 'At *nineteen*? But you *must*. It's vital.'

The girl hung her head unhappily, her straight greasy hair fell forward over her face.

'I know,' she muttered, 'I know.'

He looked at her, stained old jersey, the bare feet, the dirty toe nails, the smell of rancid fat . . . He wondered why he found her so maddeningly attractive."

Miss Marple wondered too! And really! To have sex experience urged on you exactly as though it was an iron tonic! Poor young things . . .

'My dear Aunt Jane, why must you bury your head in the sand like a very delightful ostrich? All bound up in this idyllic rural life of yours. REAL LIFE—that's what matters.'

Thus Raymond—and his Aunt Jane had looked properly abashed—and said 'Yes,' she was afraid she *was* rather old-fashioned.

Though really rural life was far from idyllic. People like Raymond were so ignorant. In the course of her duties in a country parish, Jane Marple had acquired quite a comprehensive knowledge of the facts of rural life. She had no urge to *talk* about them, far less to *write* about them—but she knew them. Plenty of sex, natural and unnatural. Rape, incest, perversions of all kinds. (Some kinds, indeed, that even the clever young men from Oxford who wrote books didn't seem to have heard about.)

Miss Marple came back to the Caribbean and took up the thread of what Major Palgrave was saying . . .

'A very unusual experience,' she said encouragingly. '*Most* interesting.'

'I could tell you a lot more. Some of the things, of course, not fit for a lady's ears——'

With the ease of long practice, Miss Marple dropped her eyelids in a fluttery fashion, and Major Palgrave continued his bowdlerised version of tribal customs whilst Miss Marple resumed her thoughts of her affectionate nephew.

Raymond West was a very successful novelist and made a large income, and he conscientiously and kindly did all he could to alleviate the life of his elderly aunt. The preceding winter she had had a bad go of pneumonia, and medical opinion had advised sunshine. In lordly fashion Raymond had suggested a trip to the West Indies. Miss Marple had demurred—at the expense, the distance, the difficulties of travel, and at abandoning her house in St. Mary Mead. Raymond had dealt with everything. A friend who was writing a book wanted a quiet place in the country. 'He'll look after the house all right. He's very house proud. He's a queer. I mean——'

He had paused, slightly embarrassed—but surely even dear old Aunt Jane must have heard of queers.

He went on to deal with the next points. Travel was nothing nowadays. She would go by air—another friend, Diana Horrocks, was going out to Trinidad and would see Aunt Jane was all right as far as there, and at St. Honoré she would stay at the Golden Palm Hotel which was run by the Sandersons. Nicest couple in the world. They'd see she was all right. He'd write to them straightaway.

As it happened the Sandersons had returned to England. But their successors, the Kendals, had been very nice and friendly and had assured Raymond that he need have no qualms about his aunt. There was a very good doctor on the island in case of emergency and they themselves would keep an eye on her and see to her comfort.

They had been as good as their word, too. Molly Kendal was an ingenuous blonde of twenty odd, always apparently in good spirits. She had greeted the old lady warmly and did everything to make her comfortable. Tim Kendal, her husband, lean, dark and in his thirties, had also been kindness itself.

So there she was, thought Miss Marple, far from the rigours of the English climate, with a nice little bungalow of her own, with friendly smiling West Indian girls to wait on her, Tim Kendal to meet her in the dining-room and crack a joke as he advised her about the day's menu, and an easy path from her bungalow to the sea front and the bathing beach where she could sit in a comfortable basket chair and watch the bathing. There were even a few elderly guests for company. Old Mr. Rafiel, Dr. Graham, Canon Prescott and his sister, and her present cavalier Major Palgrave.

What more could an elderly lady want?

It is deeply to be regretted, and Miss Marple felt guilty even admitting it to herself, but she was not as satisfied as she ought to be.

Lovely and warm, yes—and *so* good for her rheumatism—and beautiful scenery, though perhaps—a trifle monotonous? So *many* palm trees. Everything the same every day—never anything *happening*. Not like St. Mary Mead where something was always happening. Her nephew had once compared life in St. Mary Mead to scum on a pond, and she had indignantly pointed out that smeared on a slide under the microscope there would be plenty of life to be observed. Yes, indeed, in St. Mary Mead, there was always something going on. Incident after incident flashed through Miss Marple's mind, the mistake in old Mrs. Linnett's cough mixture—that very odd behaviour of young Polegate—the time when Georgy Wood's mother had come down to see him—(but *was* she his mother—?) the real cause of the quarrel between Joe Arden and his wife. So many interesting human problems—giving rise to endless pleasurable hours of speculation. If only there were something here that she could—well—get her teeth into.

With a start she realised that Major Palgrave had abandoned Kenya for the North West Frontier and was relating his experiences as a subaltern. Unfortunately he was asking her with great earnestness: 'Now don't you agree?'

Long practice had made Miss Marple quite an adept at dealing with that one.

'I don't really feel that I've got sufficient experience to judge. I'm afraid I've led rather a sheltered life.'

'And so you should, dear lady, so you should,' cried Major Palgrave gallantly.

'You've had such a very varied life,' went on Miss Marple, determined to make amends for her former pleasurable inattention.

'Not bad,' said Major Palgrave, complacently. 'Not bad at all.' He looked round him appreciatively. 'Lovely place, this.'

'Yes, indeed,' said Miss Marple and was then unable to stop herself going on: 'Does anything ever happen here, I wonder?'

Major Palgrave stared.

'Oh rather. Plenty of scandals—eh what? Why, I could tell you——'

But it wasn't really scandals Miss Marple wanted. Nothing to get your teeth into in scandals nowadays. Just men and women changing partners, and calling attention to it, instead of trying decently to hush it up and be properly ashamed of themselves.

'There was even a murder here a couple of years ago. Man called Harry Western. Made a big splash in the papers. Daresay you remember it.'

Miss Marple nodded without enthusiasm. It had not been her kind of murder. It had made a big splash mainly because everyone concerned had been very rich. It had seemed likely enough that Harry Western had shot the Count de Ferrari, his wife's lover, and equally likely that his well-arranged alibi had been bought and paid for. Everyone seemed to have been drunk, and there was a fine scattering of dope addicts. Not really interesting people, thought Miss Marple—although no doubt very spectacular and attractive to *look* at. But definitely not *her* cup of tea.

'And if you ask me, that wasn't the only murder about that time.' He nodded and winked. 'I had my suspicions—oh!—well——'

Miss Marple dropped her ball of wool, and the Major stooped and picked it up for her.

'Talking of murder,' he went on. 'I once came across a very curious case—not exactly personally.'

Miss Marple smiled encouragingly.

'Lot of chaps talking at the club one day, you know, and a chap began telling a story. Medical man he was. One of his cases. Young fellow came and knocked him up in the middle of the night. His wife had hanged herself. They hadn't got a telephone, so after the chap had cut her down and done what he could, he'd got out his car and hared off looking for a doctor. Well, she wasn't dead but pretty far gone. Anyway, she pulled through. Young fellow seemed devoted to her. Cried like a child. He'd noticed that she'd been odd for some time, fits of depression and all that. Well, that was that. Everything seemed all right. But actually, about a month later, the wife took an overdose of sleeping stuff and passed out. Sad case.'

Major Palgrave paused, and nodded his head several times. Since there was obviously more to come Miss Marple waited.

'And that's that, you might say. Nothing there. Neurotic woman, nothing out of the usual. But about a year later, this medical chap was swapping yarns with a fellow medico, and the other chap told him about a woman who'd tried to drown herself, husband got her out, got a doctor, they pulled her round—and then a few weeks later she gassed herself.

'Well, a bit of a coincidence—eh? Same sort of story. My chap said—"I had a case rather like that. Name of Jones (or whatever the name was)—What was your man's name?" "Can't remember. Robinson I think. Certainly not Jones."

'Well, the chaps looked at each other and said it was pretty odd. And then my chap pulled out a snapshot. He showed it to the second chap. "That's the fellow," he said—"I'd gone along the next day to check up on the particulars, and I noticed a magnificent species of hibiscus just by the front door, a variety I'd never seen before in this country. My camera was in the car and I took a photo. Just as I snapped the shutter the husband came out of the front door so I got him as well. Don't think he realised it. I asked him about the hibiscus but he couldn't tell me its name." Second medico looked at the snap. He said: "It's a bit out of focus—But I could swear—at any rate I'm almost sure—*it's the same man*."

'Don't know if they followed it up. But if so they didn't get anywhere. Expect Mr. Jones or Robinson covered his tracks too well. But queer story, isn't it? Wouldn't think things like that could happen.'

'Oh yes, I would,' said Miss Marple placidly. 'Practically every day.'

'Oh, come, come. That's a bit fantastic.'

'If a man gets a formula that works—he won't stop. He'll go on.'

'Brides in the bath—eh?'

'That kind of thing, yes.'

'Doctor let me have that snap just as a curiosity——'

Major Palgrave began fumbling through an overstuffed wallet murmuring to himself: 'Lots of things in here—don't know why I keep all these things . . .'

Miss Marple thought she did know. They were part of the Major's stock-in-trade. They illustrated his repertoire of stories. The story he had just told, or so she suspected, had not been originally like that—it had been worked up a good deal in repeated telling.

The Major was still shuffling and muttering—'Forgotten all about *that* business. Good-looking woman *she* was, you'd never suspect—Now *where*—Ah—that takes my mind back—what tusks! I must show you——'

He stopped—sorted out a small photographic print and peered down at it.

'Like to see the picture of a murderer?'

He was about to pass it to her when his movement was suddenly arrested. Looking more like a stuffed frog than ever, Major Palgrave appeared to be staring fixedly over her right shoulder—from whence came the sound of approaching footsteps and voices.

'Well, I'm damned—I mean——' He stuffed everything back into his wallet and crammed it into his pocket.

His face went an even deeper shade of purplish red. He exclaimed in a loud, artificial voice:

'As I was saying—I'd like to have shown you those elephant tusks—biggest elephant I've ever shot—— Ah, hallo!' His voice took on a somewhat spurious hearty note.

'Look who's here! The great quartette—Flora and Fauna—— What luck have you had to-day— Eh?'

The approaching footsteps resolved themselves into four hotel guests whom Miss Marple already knew by sight. They consisted of two married couples and though Miss Marple was not as yet acquainted with their surnames, she knew that the big man with the upstanding bush of thick grey hair was addressed as 'Greg', that the golden blonde woman, his wife, was known as Lucky—and that the other married couple, the dark lean man and the handsome but rather weather-beaten woman, were Edward and Evelyn. They were botanists, she understood, and also interested in birds.

'No luck at all,' said Greg—'At least no luck in getting what we were after.'

'Don't know if you know Miss Marple? Colonel and Mrs. Hillingdon and Greg and Lucky Dyson.'

They greeted her pleasantly and Lucky said loudly that she'd die if she didn't have a drink at once or sooner.

Greg hailed Tim Kendal who was sitting a little way away with his wife poring over account books.

'Hi, Tim. Get us some drinks.' He addressed the others. 'Planters Punch?'

They agreed.

'Same for you, Miss Marple?'

Miss Marple said Thank you, but she would prefer fresh lime.

'Fresh lime it is,' said Tim Kendal 'and five Planters Punches.'

'Join us, Tim?'

'Wish I could. But I've got to fix up these accounts. Can't leave Molly to cope with everything. Steel band to-night, by the way.'

'Good,' cried Lucky. 'Damn it,' she winced, 'I'm all over thorns. Ouch! Edward deliberately rammed me into a thorn bush!'

'Lovely pink flowers,' said Hillingdon.

'And lovely long thorns. Sadistic brute, aren't you, Edward?'

'Not like me,' said Greg, grinning. 'Full of the milk of human kindness.'

Evelyn Hillingdon sat down by Miss Marple and started talking to her in an easy pleasant way.

Miss Marple put her knitting down on her lap. Slowly and with some difficulty, owing to rheumatism in the neck, she turned her head over her right shoulder to look behind her. At some little distance there was the large bungalow occupied by the rich Mr. Rafiel. But it showed no sign of life.

She replied suitably to Evelyn's remarks (really, how kind people were to her!) but her eyes scanned thoughtfully the faces of the two men.

Edward Hillingdon looked a nice man. Quiet but with a lot of charm . . . And Greg—big, boisterous, happy-looking. He and Lucky were Canadian or American, she thought.

She looked at Major Palgrave, still acting a *bonhomie* a little larger than life.

Interesting . . .

2. *Miss Marple makes comparisons*

IT WAS VERY GAY that evening at the Golden Palm Hotel.

Seated at her little corner table, Miss Marple looked round her in an interested fashion. The dining-room was a large room open on three sides to the soft warm scented air of the West Indies. There were small table lamps, all softly coloured. Most of the women were in evening dress; light cotton prints out of which bronzed shoulders and arms emerged. Miss Marple herself had been urged by her nephew's wife, Joan, in the sweetest way possible, to accept 'a small cheque'.

'Because, Aunt Jane, it will be rather hot out there, and I don't expect you have any very thin clothes.'

Jane Marple had thanked her and had accepted the cheque. She came of the age when it was natural for the old to support and finance the young, but also for the middle-aged to look after the old.

She could not, however, force herself to buy anything very *thin*! At her age she seldom felt more than pleasantly warm even in the hottest weather, and the temperature of St. Honoré was not really what is referred to as 'tropical heat'. This evening she was attired in the best traditions of the provincial gentlewomen of England—grey lace.

Not that she was the only elderly person present. There were representatives of all ages in the room. There were elderly tycoons with young third or fourth wives. There were middle-aged couples from the North of England. There was a gay family from Caracas complete with children. The various countries of South America were well represented, all chattering loudly in Spanish or Portuguese. There was a solid English background of two clergymen, one doctor and one retired judge. There was even a family of Chinese. The dining-room service was mainly done by women, tall black girls of proud carriage, dressed in crisp white; but there was an experienced Italian head waiter in charge, and a French wine waiter, and there was the attentive eye of Tim Kendal watching over everything, pausing here and there to have a social word with people at their tables. His wife seconded him ably. She was a good-looking girl. Her hair was a natural golden blonde and she had a wide generous mouth that laughed easily. It was very seldom that Molly Kendal was out of temper. Her staff worked for her enthusiastically, and she adapted her manner carefully to suit her different guests. With the elderly men she laughed and flirted; she congratulated the younger women on their clothes.

'Oh what a smashing dress you've got on to-night, Mrs. Dyson. I'm so jealous I could tear it off your back.' But she looked very well in her own dress, or so Miss Marple thought; a white sheath, with a pale green embroidered silk shawl thrown over her shoulders. Lucky was fingering the shawl. 'Lovely colour! I'd like one like it.'

'You can get them at the shop here,' Molly told her and passed on. She did not pause by Miss Marple's table. Elderly ladies she usually left to her husband. 'The old dears like a man much better,' she used to say.

Tim Kendal came and bent over Miss Marple.

'Nothing special you want, is there?' he asked. 'Because you've only got to tell me—and I could get it specially cooked for you. Hotel food, and semitropical at that, isn't quite what you're used to at home, I expect?'

Miss Marple smiled and said that that was one of the pleasures of coming abroad.

'That's all right, then. But if there *is* anything——'

'Such as?'

'Well—' Tim Kendal looked a little doubtful—'Bread and butter pudding?' he hazarded.

Miss Marple smiled and said that she thought she could do without bread and butter pudding very nicely for the present.

She picked up her spoon and began to eat her passion fruit sundae with cheerful appreciation.

Then the steel band began to play. The steel bands were one of the main attractions of the islands. Truth to tell, Miss Marple could have done very well without them. She considered that they made a hideous noise, unnecessarily loud. The pleasure that everyone else took in them was undeniable, however, and Miss Marple, in the true spirit of her youth, decided that as they had to be, she must manage somehow to learn to like them. She could hardly request Tim Kendal to conjure up from somewhere the muted strains of the 'Blue Danube.' (So graceful—waltzing.) Most peculiar, the way people danced nowadays. Flinging themselves about, seeming quite *contorted*. Oh well, young people must enjoy—— Her thoughts were arrested. Because, now she came to think of it, very few of these people *were* young. Dancing, lights, the music of a band (even a steel band) all that surely was for *youth*. But where was youth? Studying, she supposed, at universities, or doing a job—with a fortnight's holiday a year. A place like this was too far away and too expensive. This gay and carefree life was all for the thirties and the forties—and the old men who were trying to live up (or down) to their young wives. It seemed, somehow, a *pity*.

Miss Marple sighed for youth. There was Mrs. Kendal, of course. She wasn't more than twenty-two or three, probably, and she seemed to be enjoying herself—but even so, it was a *job* she was doing.

At a table nearby Canon Prescott and his sister were sitting. They motioned to Miss Marple to join them for coffee and she did so. Miss Prescott was a thin severe-looking woman, the Canon was a round, rubicund man, breathing geniality.

Coffee was brought, and chairs were pushed a little way away from the tables. Miss Prescott opened a work bag and took out some frankly hideous table mats that she was hemming. She told Miss Marple all about the day's events. They had visited a new Girls' School in the morning. After an afternoon's rest, they had walked through a cane plantation to have tea at a *pension* where some friends of theirs were staying.

Since the Prescotts had been at the Golden Palm longer than Miss Marple, they were able to enlighten her as to some of her fellow guests.

That very old man, Mr. Rafiel. He came every year. Fantastically rich! Owned an enormous chain of supermarkets in the North of England. The young woman with him was his secretary, Esther Walters—a widow. (Quite all *right*, of course. Nothing improper. After all, he was nearly eighty!)

Miss Marple accepted the propriety of the relationship with an understanding nod and the Canon remarked:

'A very nice young woman; her mother, I understand, is a widow and lives in Chichester.'

'Mr. Rafiel has a valet with him, too. Or rather a kind of Nurse Attendant—he's a qualified masseur, I believe. Jackson, his name is. Poor Mr. Rafiel is practically paralysed. So sad—with all that money, too.'

'A generous and cheerful giver,' said Canon Prescott approvingly.

People were regrouping themselves round about, some going farther from the steel band, others crowding up to it. Major Palgrave had joined the Hillingdon-Dyson quartette.

'Now those people——' said Miss Prescott, lowering her voice quite unnecessarily since the steel band easily drowned it.

'Yes, I was going to ask you about them.'

'They were here last year. They spend three months every year in the West Indies, going round the different islands. The tall thin man is Colonel Hillingdon and the dark woman is his wife—they are botanists. The other two, Mr. and Mrs. Gregory Dyson—they're American. He writes on butterflies, I believe. And all of them are interested in birds.'

'So nice for people to have open-air hobbies,' said Canon Prescott genially.

'I don't think they'd like to hear you call it hobbies, Jeremy,' said his sister. 'They have articles printed in the *National Geographic* and in the *Royal Horticultural Journal*. They take themselves very seriously.'

A loud outburst of laughter came from the table they had been observing. It was loud enough to overcome the steel band. Gregory Dyson was leaning back in his chair and thumping the table, his wife was protesting, and Major Palgrave emptied his glass and seemed to be applauding.

They hardly qualified for the moment as people who took themselves seriously.

'Major Palgrave should not drink so much,' said Miss Prescott acidly. 'He has blood pressure.'

A fresh supply of Planters Punches were brought to the table.

'It's so nice to get people sorted out,' said Miss Marple. 'When I met them this afternoon I wasn't sure which was married to which.'

There was a slight pause. Miss Prescott coughed a small dry cough, and said—'Well, as to that——'

'Joan,' said the Canon in an admonitory voice. 'Perhaps it would be wise to say no more.'

'Really, Jeremy, I wasn't going to say *anything*. Only that last year, for some reason or other—I really don't know *why*—we got the idea that Mrs. Dyson was Mrs. Hillingdon until someone told us she wasn't.'

'It's odd how one gets impressions, isn't it?' said Miss Marple innocently. Her eyes met Miss Prescott's for a moment. A flash of womanly understanding passed between them.

A more sensitive man than Canon Prescott might have felt that he was *de trop*.

Another signal passed between the women. It said as clearly as if the words had been spoken: '*Some other time . . .*'

'Mr. Dyson calls his wife "Lucky". Is that her real name or a nickname?' asked Miss Marple.

'It can hardly be her real name, I should think.'

'I happened to ask him,' said the Canon. 'He said he called her Lucky because she was his good luck piece. If he lost her, he said, he'd lose his luck. Very nicely put, I thought.'

'He's very fond of joking,' said Miss Prescott.

The Canon looked at his sister doubtfully.

The steel band outdid itself with a wild burst of cacophony and a troupe of dancers came racing on to the floor.

Miss Marple and the others turned their chairs to watch. Miss Marple enjoyed the dancing better than the music; she liked the shuffling feet and the rhythmic sway of the bodies. It seemed, she thought, very *real*. It had a kind of power of understatement.

To-night, for the first time, she began to feel slightly at home in her new environment. . . . Up to now, she had missed what she usually found so easily, points of resemblance in the people she met, to various people known to her personally. She had, possibly, been dazzled by the gay clothes and the exotic colouring; but soon, she felt, she would be able to make some interesting comparisons.

Molly Kendal, for instance, was like that nice girl whose name she couldn't remember, but who was a conductress on the Market Basing bus. Helped you in, and never rang the bus on until she was sure you'd sat down safely. Tim Kendal was just a little like the head waiter at the Royal George in Medchester. Self-confident, and yet, at the same time, worried. (He had had an ulcer, she remembered.) As for Major Palgrave, he was indistinguishable from General Leroy, Captain Felmming, Admiral Wicklow and Commander Richardson. She went on to someone more interesting. Greg for instance? Greg was difficult because he was American. A dash of Sir George Trollope, perhaps, always so full of jokes at the Civil Defence meetings—or perhaps Mr. Murdoch the butcher. Mr. Murdoch had had rather a bad reputation, but some people said it was just gossip, and that Mr. Murdoch himself liked to encourage the rumours! 'Lucky' now? Well, that was easy—Marleen at the Three Crowns. Evelyn Hillingdon? She couldn't fit Evelyn in precisely. In appearance she fitted many roles—tall thin weather-beaten Englishwomen were plentiful. Lady Caroline Wolfe, Peter Wolfe's first wife, who had committed suicide? Or there was Leslie James—that quiet woman who seldom showed what she felt and who had sold up her house and left without ever telling anyone she was going. Colonel Hillingdon? No immediate clue there. She'd have to get to know him a little first. One of those quiet men with good manners. You never knew what they were thinking about. Sometimes they surprised you. Major Harper, she remembered, had quietly cut his throat one day. Nobody had ever known why. Miss Marple thought that she did know—but she'd never been quite sure. . . .

Her eyes strayed to Mr. Rafiel's table. The principal thing known about Mr. Rafiel was that he was incredibly rich, he came every year to the West Indies, he was semi-paralysed and looked like a wrinkled old bird of prey. His clothes hung loosely on his shrunken form. He might have been seventy or eighty, or even ninety. His eyes were shrewd and he was frequently rude, but people seldom took offence, partly because he was so rich, and partly because of his overwhelming personality which hypnotised you into feeling that somehow, Mr. Rafiel had the right to be rude if he wanted to.

With him sat his secretary, Mrs. Walters. She had corn-coloured hair, and a pleasant face. Mr. Rafiel was frequently very rude to her, but she never seemed to notice it—— She was not so much subservient, as oblivious. She behaved like a well-trained hospital nurse. Possibly, thought Miss Marple, she had been a hospital nurse.

A young man, tall and good-looking, in a white jacket, came to stand by Mr. Rafiel's chair. The old man looked up at him, nodded, then motioned him to a chair. The young man sat down as bidden. 'Mr. Jackson, I presume,' said Miss Marple to herself—'His valet-attendant.'

She studied Mr. Jackson with some attention.

2

In the bar, Molly Kendal stretched her back, and slipped off her high-heeled shoes. Tim came in from the terrace to join her. They had the bar to themselves for the moment.

'Tired, darling?' he asked.

'Just a bit. I seem to be feeling my feet to-night.'

'Not too much for you, is it? All this? I know it's hard work.' He looked at her anxiously.

She laughed. 'Oh Tim, don't be ridiculous. I love it here. It's gorgeous. The kind of dream I've always had, come true.'

'Yes, it would be all right—if one was just a guest. But running the show—that's work.'

'Well, you can't have anything for nothing, can you?' said Molly Kendal reasonably.

Tim Kendal frowned.

'You think it's going all right? A success? We're making a go of it?'

'Of course we are.'

'You don't think people are saying, "It's not the same as when the Sandersons were here".'

'Of course *someone* will be saying that—they always do! But only some old stick-in-the-mud. I'm sure that we're far better at the job than they were. We're more glamorous. You charm the old pussies and manage to look as though you'd like to make love to the desperate forties and fifties, and I ogle the old gentlemen and make them feel sexy dogs—or play the sweet little daughter the sentimental ones would love to have had. Oh, we've got it all taped splendidly.'

Tim's frown vanished.

'As long as *you* think so. I get scared. We've risked everything on making a job of this. I chucked my job——'

'And quite right to do so,' Molly put in quickly. 'It was soul-destroying.'

He laughed and kissed the tip of her nose.

'I tell you we've got it taped,' she repeated. 'Why do you always worry?'

'Made that way, I suppose. I'm always thinking—suppose something should go wrong.'

'What sort of thing——'

'Oh I don't know. Somebody might get drowned.'

'Not they. It's one of the safest of all the beaches. And we've got that hulking Swede always on guard.'

'I'm a fool,' said Tim Kendal. He hesitated—and then said, 'You—haven't had any more of those dreams, have you?'

'That was shellfish,' said Molly, and laughed.

3. *A Death in the Hotel*

MISS MARPLE had her breakfast brought to her in bed as usual. Tea, a boiled egg, and a slice of paw-paw.

The fruit on the island, thought Miss Marple, was rather disappointing. It seemed always to be paw-paw. If she could have a nice apple now—but apples seemed to be unknown.

Now that she had been here a week, Miss Marple had cured herself of the impulse to ask what the weather was like. The weather was always the same—fine. No interesting variations.

'The many splendoured weather of an English day' she murmured to herself and wondered if it was a quotation, or whether she had made it up.

There were, of course, hurricanes, or so she understood. But hurricanes were not weather in Miss Marple's sense of the word. They were more in the nature of an Act of God. There was rain, short violent rainfall that lasted five minutes and stopped abruptly. Everything and everyone was wringing wet, but in another five minutes they were dry again.

The black West Indian girl smiled and said Good Morning as she placed the tray on Miss Marple's knees. Such lovely white teeth and so happy and smiling. Nice natures, all these girls, and a pity they were so averse to getting married. It worried Canon Prescott a good deal. Plenty of christenings, he said, trying to console himself, but no weddings.

Miss Marple ate her breakfast and decided how she would spend her day. It didn't really take much deciding. She would get up at her leisure, moving slowly because it was rather hot and her fingers weren't as nimble as they used to be. Then she would rest for ten minutes or so, and she would take her knitting and walk slowly along towards the hotel and decide where she would settle herself. On the terrace overlooking the sea? Or should she go on to the bathing beach to watch the bathers and the children? Usually it was the latter. In the afternoon, after her rest, she might take a drive. It really didn't matter very much.

To-day would be a day like any other day, she said to herself.

Only, of course, it wasn't.

Miss Marple carried out her programme as planned and was slowly making her way along the path towards the hotel when she met Molly Kendal. For once that sunny young woman was not smiling. Her air of distress was so unlike her that Miss Marple said immediately:

'My dear, is anything wrong?'

Molly nodded. She hesitated and then said: 'Well, you'll have to know—everyone will have to know. It's Major Palgrave. He's dead.'

'Dead?'

'Yes. He died in the night.'

'Oh dear, I *am* sorry.'

'Yes, it's horrid having a death here. It makes everyone depressed. Of course—he *was* quite old.'

'He seemed quite well and cheerful yesterday,' said Miss Marple, slightly resenting this calm assumption that everyone of advanced years was liable to die at any minute.

'He seemed quite healthy,' she added.

'He had high blood pressure,' said Molly.

'But surely there are things one takes nowadays—some kind of pill. Science is so wonderful.'

'Oh yes, but perhaps he forgot to take his pills, or took too many of them. Like insulin, you know.'

Miss Marple did not think that diabetes and high blood pressure were at all the same kind of thing. She asked:

'What does the doctor say?'

'Oh, Dr. Graham, who's practically retired now, and lives in the hotel, took a look at him, and the local people came officially, of course, to give a death certificate, but it all seems quite straightforward. This kind of thing is quite liable to happen when you have high blood pressure, especially if you overdo the alcohol, and Major Palgrave was really very naughty that way. Last night, for instance.'

'Yes, I noticed,' said Miss Marple.

'He probably forgot to take his pills. It is bad luck for the old boy—but people can't live for ever, can they? But it's terribly worrying—for me and Tim, I mean. People might suggest it was something in the food.'

'But surely the symptoms of food poisoning and of blood pressure are *quite* different?'

'Yes. But people do *say* things so easily. And if people decided the food was bad—and left—or told their friends——'

'I really don't think you need worry,' said Miss Marple kindly. 'As you say, an elderly man like Major Palgrave—he must have been over seventy—is quite liable to die. To most people it will seem quite an ordinary occurrence—sad, but not out of the way at all.'

'If only,' said Molly unhappily, 'it hadn't been so *sudden.*'

Yes, it had been very sudden, Miss Marple thought as she walked slowly on. There he had been last night, laughing and talking in the best of spirits with the Hillingdons and the Dysons.

The Hillingdons and the Dysons. . . . Miss Marple walked more slowly still . . . Finally she stopped abruptly. Instead of going to the bathing beach she settled herself in a shady corner of the terrace. She took out her knitting and the needles clicked rapidly as though they were trying to match the speed of her thoughts. *She didn't like it—no she didn't like it. It came so pat.*

She went over the occurrences of yesterday in her mind.

Major Palgrave and his stories . . .

That was all as usual and one didn't need to listen very closely . . . Perhaps, though, it would have been better if she had.

Kenya—he had talked about Kenya and then India—the North West Frontier—and then—for some reason they had got on to murder—— And even *then* she hadn't really been listening . . .

Some famous case that had taken place out here—that had been in the newspapers——

It was after that—when he picked up her ball of wool—that he had begun telling her about a snapshot—*A snapshot of a murderer*—that is what he had said.

Miss Marple closed her eyes and tried to remember just exactly how that story had gone.

It had been rather a confused story—told to the Major in his Club—or in somebody else's club—told him by a doctor—who had heard it from another doctor—and one doctor had taken a snapshot of someone coming through a front door—someone who was a murderer——

Yes, that was it—the various details were coming back to her now——

And he had offered to show her that snapshot—— He had got out his wallet and begun hunting through its contents—talking all the time——

And then still talking, he had looked up—had looked—not at her—but at something behind her—behind her right shoulder to be accurate. And he had stopped talking, his face had gone purple—and he had started stuffing back everything into his wallet with slightly shaky hands and had begun talking in a loud unnatural voice about elephant tusks!

A moment or two later the Hillingdons and the Dysons had joined them. . . .

It was then that she had turned her head over her right shoulder to look . . . But there had been nothing and nobody to see. To her left, some distance away, in the direction of the hotel, there had been Tim Kendal and his wife; and beyond them a family group of Venezuelans. But Major Palgrave had not been looking in that direction . . .

Miss Marple meditated until lunch time.

After lunch she did not go for a drive.

Instead she sent a message to say that she was not feeling very well, and to ask if Dr. Graham would be kind enough to come and see her.

4. *Miss Marple seeks medical attention*

DR. GRAHAM was a kindly elderly man of about sixty-five. He had practised in the West Indies for many years, but was now semi-retired, and left most of his work to his West Indian partners. He greeted Miss Marple pleasantly and asked her what the trouble was.

Fortunately at Miss Marple's age, there was always some ailment that could be discussed with slight exaggerations on the patient's part. Miss Marple hesitated between 'her shoulder' and 'her knee', but finally decided upon the knee. Miss Marple's knee, as she would have put it to herself, was always with her.

Dr. Graham was exceedingly kindly but he refrained from putting into words the fact that at her time of life such troubles were only to be expected. He prescribed for her one of the brands of useful little pills that form the basis of a doctor's prescriptions. Since he knew by experience that many elderly people could be lonely when they first came to St. Honoré, he remained for a while gently chatting.

'A very nice man,' thought Miss Marple to herself, 'and I really feel rather ashamed of having to tell him lies. But I don't quite see what else I can do.'

Miss Marple had been brought up to have a proper regard for truth and was indeed by nature a very truthful person. But on certain occasions, when she considered it her duty so to do, she could tell lies with a really astonishing verisimilitude.

She cleared her throat, uttered an apologetic little cough, and said, in an old ladyish and slightly twittering manner:

'There is something, Dr. Graham, I would like to ask you. I don't really like mentioning it—but I don't quite see what else I am to do—although of course it's *quite* unimportant really. But you see, it's important to *me*. And I hope you will understand and not think what I am asking is tiresome or—or unpardonable in any way.'

To this opening Dr. Graham replied kindly: 'Something is worrying you? Do let me help.'

'It's connected with Major Palgrave. *So* sad about his dying. It was quite a shock when I heard it this morning.'

'Yes,' said Dr. Graham, 'it was very sudden, I'm afraid. He seemed in such good spirits yesterday.' He spoke kindly, but conventionally. To him, clearly, Major Palgrave's death was nothing out of the way. Miss Marple wondered whether she was really making something out of nothing. Was this suspicious habit of mind growing on her? Perhaps she could no longer trust her own judgment. Not that it was judgment really, only suspicion. Anyway she was in for it now! She must go ahead.

'We were sitting talking together yesterday afternoon,' she said. 'He was telling me about his very varied and interesting life. So many strange parts of the globe.'

'Yes indeed,' said Dr. Graham, who had been bored many times by the Major's reminiscences.

'And then he spoke of his family, boyhood rather, and I told him a little about my own nephews and nieces and he listened very sympathetically. And I showed him a snapshot I had with me of one of my nephews. Such a dear boy—at least not exactly a boy now, but always a boy to *me* if you understand.'

'Quite so,' said Dr. Graham, wondering how long it would be before the old lady was going to come to the point.

'I had handed it to him and he was examining it when quite suddenly those people—those very nice people—who collect wild flowers and butterflies, Colonel and Mrs. Hillingdon I think the name is——'

'Oh yes? The Hillingdons and the Dysons.'

'Yes, that's right. They came suddenly along laughing and talking. They sat down and ordered drinks and we all talked together. Very pleasant it was. But without thinking, Major Palgrave must have put back my snapshot into his wallet and returned it to his pocket. I wasn't paying very much attention at the time but I remembered afterward and I said to myself—"I mustn't forget to ask the Major to give me back my picture of Denzil." I *did* think of it last night while the dancing and the band was going on, but I didn't like to interrupt him just then, because they were having such a merry party together and I thought "I will remember to ask him for it in the morning". Only this morning——' Miss Marple paused—out of breath.

'Yes, yes,' said Dr. Graham, 'I quite understand. And you—well, naturally you want the snapshot back. Is that it?'

Miss Marple nodded her head in eager agreement.

'Yes. That's it. You see, it is the only one I have got and I haven't got the negative. And I would hate to lose that snapshot, because poor Denzil died some five or six years ago and he was my favourite nephew. This is the only picture I have to remind me of him. I wondered—I hoped—it is rather tiresome of me to ask—whether you could possibly manage to get hold of it for me? I don't really know who else to ask, you see. I don't know who'll attend to all his belongings and things like that. It is all so difficult. They would think it such a nuisance of me. You see, they don't understand. Nobody could quite understand what this snapshot means to me.'

'Of course, of course,' said Dr. Graham. 'I quite understand. A most natural feeling on your part. Actually, I am meeting the local authorities shortly—the funeral is to-morrow, and someone will be coming from the Administrator's office to look over his papers and effects before communicating with the next of kin—all that sort of thing—— If you could describe this snapshot.'

'It was just the front of a house,' said Miss Marple. 'And someone —Denzil, I mean—was just coming out of the front door. As I say it was taken by one of my other nephews who is very keen on flower shows—and he was photographing a hibiscus, I think, or one of those beautiful—something like antipasto—lilies. Denzil just happened to come out of the front door at that time. It wasn't a very good photograph of him—just a trifle blurred—— But I liked it and have always kept it.'

'Well,' said Dr. Graham, 'that seems clear enough. I think we'll have no difficulty in getting back your picture for you, Miss Marple.'

He rose from his chair. Miss Marple smiled up at him.

'You are very kind, Dr. Graham, very kind *indeed*. You do understand, don't you?'

'Of course I do, of course I do,' said Dr. Graham, shaking her warmly by the hand. 'Now don't you worry. Exercise that knee every day gently but not too much, and I'll send you round these tablets. Take one three times a day.'

5. *Miss Marple makes a decision*

THE FUNERAL SERVICE was said over the body of the late Major Palgrave on the following day. Miss Marple attended in company with Miss Prescott. The Canon read the service—after that life went on as usual.

Major Palgrave's death was already only an incident, a slightly unpleasant incident, but one that was soon forgotten. Life here was sunshine, sea, and social pleasures. A grim visitor had interrupted these activities, casting a momentary shadow, but the shadow was now gone. After all, nobody had known the deceased very well. He had been rather a garrulous elderly man of the club-bore type, always telling you personal reminiscences that you had no particular desire to hear. He had had little to anchor himself to any particular part of the world. His wife had died many years ago. He had had a lonely life and a lonely death. But it had been the kind of loneliness that spends itself in living amongst people, and in passing the time that way not unpleasantly. Major Palgrave might have been a lonely man, he had also been quite a cheerful one. He had enjoyed himself in his own particular way. And now he was dead, buried, and nobody cared very much, and in another week's time nobody would even remember him or spare him a passing thought.

The only person who could possibly be said to miss him was Miss Marple. Not indeed out of any personal affection, but he represented a kind of life that she knew. As one grew older, so she reflected to herself, one got more and more into the habit of listening; listening possibly without any great interest, but there had been between her and the Major the gentle give and take of two old people. It had had a cheerful, human quality. She did not actually mourn Major Palgrave but she missed him.

On the afternoon of the funeral, as she was sitting knitting in her favourite spot, Dr. Graham came and joined her. She put her needles down and greeted him. He said at once, rather apologetically:

'I am afraid I have rather disappointing news, Miss Marple.'

'Indeed? About my——'

'Yes. We haven't found that precious snapshot of yours. I'm afraid that will be a disappointment to you.'

'Yes. Yes it is. But of course it does not *really* matter. It was a sentimentality. I do realise that now. It wasn't in Major Palgrave's wallet?'

'No. Nor anywhere else among his things. There were a few letters and newspaper clippings and odds and ends, and a few old photographs, but no sign of a snapshot such as you mentioned.'

'Oh dear,' said Miss Marple. 'Well, it can't be helped . . . Thank you very much, Dr. Graham, for the trouble you've taken.'

'Oh it was no trouble, indeed. But I know quite well from my own experience how much family trifles mean to one, especially as one is getting older.'

The old lady was really taking it very well, he thought. Major Palgrave, he presumed, had probably come across the snapshot when taking something out of his wallet, and not even realising how it had come there, had torn it up as something of no importance. But of course it was of great importance to this old lady. Still, she seemed quite cheerful and philosophical about it.

Internally, however, Miss Marple was far from being either cheerful or philosophical. She wanted a little time in which to think things out, but she was also determined to use her present opportunities to the fullest effect.

She engaged Dr. Graham in conversation with an eagerness which she did not attempt to conceal. That kindly man, putting down her flow of talk to the natural loneliness of an old lady, exerted himself to divert her mind from the loss of the snapshot, by conversing easily and pleasantly about life in St. Honoré, and the various interesting places perhaps Miss Marple might like to visit. He hardly knew himself how the conversation drifted back to Major Palgrave's decease.

'It seems so sad,' said Miss Marple, 'to think of anyone dying like this away from home. Though I gather, from what he himself told me, that he had no immediate family. It seems he lived by himself in London.'

'He travelled a fair amount, I believe,' said Dr. Graham. 'At any rate in the winters. He didn't carc for our English winters. Can't say I blame him.'

'No, indeed,' said Miss Marple. 'And perhaps he had some special reason like a weakness of the lungs or something which made it necessary for him to winter abroad?'

'Oh no, I don't think so.'

'He had high blood pressure, I believe. So sad nowadays. One hears so much of it.'

'He spoke about it to you, did he?'

'Oh no. No, *he* never mentioned it. It was somebody else who told me.'

'Ah, really.'

'I suppose,' went on Miss Marple, 'that death was to be expected under those circumstances.'

'Not necessarily,' said Dr. Graham. 'There are methods of controlling blood pressure nowadays.'

'His death *seemed* very sudden—but I suppose *you* weren't surprised.'

'Well I wasn't particularly surprised in a man of that age. But I certainly didn't expect it. Frankly, he always seemed to me in very good form, but I hadn't ever attended him professionally. I'd never taken his blood pressure or anything like that.'

'Does one know—I mean, does a doctor know—when a man has high blood pressure just by looking at him?' Miss Marple inquired with a kind of dewy innocence.

'Not just by looking,' said the doctor, smiling. 'One has to do a bit of testing.'

'Oh I see. That dreadful thing when you put a rubber band round somebody's arm and blow it up—I dislike it *so* much. But my doctor said that my blood pressure was really very good for my age.'

'Well that's good hearing,' said Dr. Graham.

'Of course, the Major *was* rather fond of Planters Punch,' said Miss Marple thoughtfully.

'Yes. Not the best thing with blood pressure—alcohol.'

'One takes tablets, doesn't one, or so I have heard?'

'Yes. There are several on the market. There was a bottle of one of them in his room—Serenite.'

'How wonderful science is nowadays,' said Miss Marple. 'Doctors can do so much, can't they?'

'We all have one great competitor,' said Dr. Graham. 'Nature, you know. And some of the good old-fashioned home remedies come back from time to time.'

'Like putting cobwebs on a cut?' said Miss Marple. 'We always used to do that when I was a child.'

'Very sensible,' said Dr. Graham.

'And a linseed poultice on the chest and rubbing in camphorated oil for a bad cough.'

'I see you know it all!' said Dr. Graham laughing. He got up. 'How's the knee? Not been too troublesome?'

'No, it seems much, much better.'

'Well, we won't say whether that's Nature or my pills,' said Dr. Graham. 'Sorry I couldn't have been of more help to you.'

'But you have been most kind—I am really ashamed of taking up your time—— Did you say that there were no photographs in the Major's wallet?'

'Oh yes—a very old one of the Major himself as quite a young man on a polo pony—and one of a dead tiger——He was standing with his foot on it. Snaps of that sort—memories of his younger days—— But I looked very carefully, I assure you, and the one you describe of your nephew was definitely not there——'

'Oh I'm sure you looked carefully—I didn't mean that—I was just interested—— We all tend to keep such very odd things——'

'Treasures from the past,' said the doctor smiling.

He said good-bye and departed.

Miss Marple remained looking thoughtfully at the palm trees and the sea. She did not pick up her knitting again for some minutes. She had a fact now. She had to think about that fact and what it meant. The snapshot that the Major had brought out of his wallet and replaced so hurriedly was *not there after he died.* It was not the sort of thing the Major would throw away. He had replaced it in his wallet and it ought to have been in his wallet after his death. Money might have been stolen, but no one would want to steal a snapshot. Unless, that is, they had a special reason for so doing. . . .

Miss Marple's face was grave. She had to take a decision. Was she, or was she not, going to allow Major Palgrave to remain quietly in his grave? Might it not be better to do just that? She quoted under her breath. 'Duncan is dead. After Life's fitful fever he sleeps well!' Nothing could hurt Major Palgrave now. He had gone where danger could not touch him. Was it just a coincidence that he should have died on that particular night? Or was it just possibly *not* a coincidence? Doctors accepted the deaths of elderly men so easily. Especially since in his room there had been a bottle of the tablets that people with high blood pressure had to take every day of their lives. But if someone had taken the snapshot from the Major's wallet, that same person could have put that bottle of tablets in the Major's room. She herself never remembered *seeing* the Major take tablets; he had never spoken about his blood pressure to her. The only thing he had ever said about his health was the admission—'Not as young as I was'. He had been occasionally a little short of breath, a trifle asthmatic, nothing else. But someone had mentioned that Major Palgrave had high blood pressure—Molly? Miss Prescott? She couldn't remember.

Miss Marple sighed, then admonished herself in words, though she did not speak those words aloud.

'Now, Jane, what are you suggesting or thinking? Are you, perhaps, just making the whole thing up? Have you *really* got anything to build on?'

She went over, step by step, as nearly as she could, the conversation between herself and the Major on the subject of murder and murderers.

'Oh dear,' said Miss Marple. 'Even if—really, I *don't* see how I *can* do anything about it——'

But she knew that she meant to try.

6. *In the small hours*

MISS MARPLE woke early. Like many old people she slept lightly and had periods of wakefulness which she used for the planning of some action or actions to be carried out on the next or following days. Usually, of course, these were of a wholly private or domestic nature, of little interest to anybody but herself. But this morning Miss Marple lay thinking soberly and constructively of murder, and what, if her suspicions were correct, she could do about it. It wasn't going to be easy. She had one weapon and one weapon only, and that was conversation.

Old ladies were given to a good deal of rambling conversation. People were bored by this, but certainly did not suspect them of ulterior motives. It would not be a case of asking direct questions. (Indeed, she would have found it difficult to know what questions to ask!) It would be a question of finding out a little more about certain people. She reviewed these certain people in her mind.

She could find out, possibly, a little more about Major Palgrave, but would that really help her? She doubted if it would. If Major Palgrave had been killed it was not because of secrets in his life or to inherit his money or for revenge upon him. In fact, although he was the victim, it was one of those rare cases where a greater knowledge of the victim does not help you or lead you in any way to his murderer. The point, it seemed to her, and the sole point, was that Major Palgrave talked too much!

She had learnt one rather interesting fact from Dr. Graham. He had had in his wallet various photographs; one of himself in company with a polo pony, one of a dead tiger, also one or two other shots of the same nature. Now why did Major Palgrave carry these about with him? Obviously, thought Miss Marple, with long experience of old Admirals, Brigadier-Generals and mere Majors behind her, because he had certain stories which he enjoyed telling to people. Starting off with 'Curious thing happened once when I was out tiger shooting in India . . .' Or a reminiscence of himself and a polo pony. Therefore this story about a suspected murderer would in due course be illustrated by the production of the snapshot from his wallet.

He had been following that pattern in his conversation with her. The subject of murder having come up, and to focus interest on his story, he had done what he no doubt usually did, produced his snapshot and said something in the nature of 'Wouldn't think this chap was a murderer, would you?'

The point was that it had been a *habit* of his. This murderer story was one of his regular repertoire. If any reference to murder came up, then away went the Major, full steam ahead.

In that case reflected Miss Marple, he might *already* have told his story to someone else here. Or to more than one person—— If that were so, then she herself might learn from that person what the further details of the story had been, possibly what the person in the snapshot had looked like.

She nodded her head in satisfaction—— That would be a beginning.

And, of course, there were the people she called in her mind the 'Four Suspects'. Though really, since Major Palgrave had been talking about a *man*—there were only two. Colonel Hillingdon or Mr. Dyson, very unlikely looking murderers, but then murderers so often *were* unlikely. Could there have been anyone else? She had seen no one when she turned her head to look. There was the bungalow of course. Mr. Rafiel's bungalow. Could somebody have come out of the bungalow and gone in again before she had had time to turn her head? If so, it could only have been the valet-attendant. What was his name? Oh yes, Jackson. Could it have been *Jackson* who had come out of the door? That would have been the same pose as the photograph. *A man coming out of a door*. Recognition might have struck suddenly. Up till then, Major Palgrave would not have looked at Arthur Jackson, valet-attendant, with any interest. His roving and curious eye was essentially a snobbish eye—Arthur Jackson was not a *pukka sahib*—Major Palgrave would not have glanced at him twice.

Until, perhaps, he had had the snapshot in his hand, and had looked over Miss Marple's right shoulder and had seen a man coming out of a door . . . ?

Miss Marple turned over on her pillow—Programme for to-morrow—or rather for to-day—Further investigation of the Hillingdons, the Dysons and Arthur Jackson, valet-attendant.

2

Dr. Graham also woke early. Usually he turned over and went to sleep again. But to-day he was uneasy and sleep failed to come. This anxiety that made it so difficult to go to sleep again was a thing he had not suffered from for a long time. What was causing this anxiety? Really, he couldn't make it out. He lay there thinking it over. Something to do with—something to do with—yes, Major Palgrave. Major Palgrave's death? He didn't see, though, what there could be to make him uneasy there. Was it something that that twittery old lady had said? Bad luck for her about her snapshot. She'd taken it very well. But now what was it she had said, what chance word of hers had it been, that had given him this funny feeling of uneasiness? After all, there was nothing *odd* about the Major's death. Nothing at all. At least he supposed there was nothing at all.

It was quite clear that in the Major's state of health—a faint check came in his thought process. Did he really know much *about* Major Palgrave's state of health? Everybody *said* that he'd suffered from high blood pressure. But he himself had never had any conversation with the Major about it. But then he'd never had much conversation with Major Palgrave anyway. Palgrave was an old bore and he avoided old bores. Why on earth should he have this idea that perhaps everything *mightn't* be all right? Was it that old woman? But after all she hadn't *said* anything. Anyway, it was none of his business. The local authorities were quite satisfied. There had been that bottle of Serenite tablets, and the old boy had apparently talked to people about his blood pressure quite freely.

Dr. Graham turned over in bed and soon went to sleep again.

3

Outside the hotel grounds, in one of a row of shanty cabins beside a creek, the girl Victoria Johnson rolled over and sat up in bed. The St. Honoré girl was a magnificent creature with a torso of black marble such as a sculptor would have enjoyed. She ran her fingers through her dark, tightly curling hair. With her foot she nudged her sleeping companion in the ribs.

'Wake up, man.'

The man grunted and turned.

'What you want? It's not morning.'

'Wake up, man. I want to talk to you.'

The man sat up, stretched, showed a wide mouth and beautiful teeth.

'What's worrying you, woman?'

'That Major man who died. Something I don't like. Something wrong about it.'

'Ah, what d'you want to worry about that? He was old. He died.'

'Listen, man. It's them pills. Them pills the doctor asked me about.'

'Well, what about them? He took too many maybe.'

'No. It's not that. Listen.' She leant towards him, talking vehemently. He yawned and lay down again.

'There's nothing in that. What're you talking about?'

'All the same, I'll speak to Mrs. Kendal about it in the morning. I think there's something wrong there somewhere.'

'Shouldn't bother,' said the man who, without benefit of ceremony she considered as her present husband. 'Don't let's look for trouble,' he said and rolled over on his side yawning.

7. *Morning on the beach*

IT WAS MID MORNING on the beach below the hotel.

Evelyn Hillingdon came out of the water and dropped on the warm golden sand. She took off her bathing cap and shook her dark head vigorously. The beach was not a very big one. People tended to congregate there in the mornings and about 11.30 there was always something of a social reunion. To Evelyn's left in one of the exotic-looking modern basket chairs lay Señora de Caspearo, a handsome woman from Venezuela. Next to her was old Mr. Rafiel who was by now the doyen of the Golden Palm Hotel and held the sway that only an elderly invalid of great wealth could attain. Esther Walters was in attendance on him. She usually had her shorthand notebook and pencil with her in case Mr. Rafiel should suddenly think of urgent business cables which must be got off at once. Mr. Rafiel in beach attire was incredibly desiccated, his bones draped with festoons of dry skin. Though looking like a man on the point of death, he had looked exactly the same for at least the last eight years—or so it was said in the islands. Sharp blue eyes peered out of his wrinkled cheeks, and his principal pleasure in life was denying robustly anything that anyone else said.

Miss Marple was also present. As usual she sat and knitted and listened to what went on, and very occasionally joined in the conversation. When she did so, everyone was surprised because they had usually forgotten that she was there! Evelyn Hillingdon looked at her indulgently, and thought that she was a nice old pussy.

Señora de Caspearo rubbed some more oil on her long beautiful legs and hummed to herself. She was not a woman who spoke much. She looked discontentedly at the flask of sun oil.

'This is not so good as Frangipanio,' she said, sadly. 'One cannot get it here. A pity.' Her eyelids drooped again.

'Are you going in for your dip now, Mr. Rafiel?' asked Esther Walters.

'I'll go in when I'm ready,' said Mr. Rafiel, snappishly.

'It's half past eleven,' said Mrs. Walters.

'What of it?' said Mr. Rafiel. 'Think I'm the kind of man to be tied by the clock? Do this at the hour, do this at twenty minutes past, do that at twenty to—bah!'

Mrs. Walters had been in attendance on Mr. Rafiel long enough to have adopted her own formula for dealing with him. She knew that he liked a good space of time in which to recover from the exertion of bathing and she had therefore reminded him of the time, allowing a good ten minutes for him to rebut her suggestion and then be able to adopt it without seeming to do so.

'I don't like these espadrilles,' said Mr. Rafiel raising a foot and looking at it. 'I told that fool Jackson so. The man never pays attention to a word I say.'

'I'll fetch you some others, shall I, Mr. Rafiel?'

'No, you won't, you'll sit here and keep quiet. I hate people rushing about like clucking hens.'

Evelyn shifted slightly in the warm sand, stretching out her arms.

Miss Marple, intent on her knitting—or so it seemed—stretched out a foot, then hastily she apologised.

'I'm so sorry, so very sorry, Mrs. Hillingdon. I'm afraid I kicked you.'

'Oh, it's quite all right,' said Evelyn. 'This beach gets rather crowded.'

'Oh, please don't move. Please. I'll move my chair a little back so that I won't do it again.'

As Miss Marple resettled herself, she went on talking in a childish and garrulous manner.

'It still seems so wonderful to be *here*! I've never been to the

West Indies before, you know. I thought it was the kind of place I never should come to and here I am. All by the kindness of my dear nephew. I suppose you know this part of the world very well, don't you, Mrs. Hillingdon?'

'I have been in this island once or twice before and of course in most of the others.'

'Oh yes. Butterflies isn't it, and wild flowers? You and your—your friends—or are they relations?'

'Friends. Nothing more.'

'And I suppose you go about together a great deal because of your interests being the same?'

'Yes. We've travelled together for some years now.'

'I suppose you must have had some rather exciting adventures sometimes?'

'I don't think so,' said Evelyn. Her voice was unaccentuated, slightly bored. 'Adventures always seem to happen to other people.' She yawned.

'No dangerous encounters with snakes or with wild animals or with natives gone berserk?'

('What a fool I sound,') thought Miss Marple.

'Nothing worse than insect bites,' Evelyn assured her.

'Poor Major Palgrave, you know, was bitten by a snake once,' said Miss Marple, making a purely fictitious statement.

'Was he?'

'Did he never tell you about it?'

'Perhaps. I don't remember.'

'I suppose you knew him quite well, didn't you?'

'Major Palgrave? No, hardly at all.'

'He always had so many interesting stories to tell.'

'Ghastly old bore,' said Mr. Rafiel. 'Silly fool, too. He needn't have died if he'd looked after himself properly.'

'Oh come now, Mr. Rafiel,' said Mrs. Walters.

'I know what I'm talking about. If you look after your health properly you're all right anywhere. Look at me. The doctors gave *me* up years ago. All right, I said, I've got my own rules of health and I shall keep to them. And here I am.'

He looked round proudly.

It did indeed seem rather a miracle that he should be there.

'Poor Major Palgrave had high blood pressure,' said Mrs. Walters.

'Nonsense,' said Mr. Rafiel.

'Oh, but he did,' said Evelyn Hillingdon. She spoke with sudden, unexpected authority.

'Who says so?' said Mr. Rafiel. 'Did he tell you so?'

'Somebody said so.'

'He looked very red in the face,' Miss Marple contributed.

'Can't go by that,' said Mr. Rafiel. 'And anyway he *didn't* have high blood pressure because he told me so.'

'What do you mean, he told you so?' said Mrs. Walters. 'I mean, you can't exactly tell people you *haven't* got a thing.'

'Yes you can. I said to him once when he was downing all those Planters Punches, and eating too much, I said, "You ought to watch your diet and your drink. You've got to think of your blood pressure at your age." And he said he'd nothing to look out for in that line, that his blood pressure was very good for his age.'

'But he took some stuff for it, I believe,' said Miss Marple, entering the conversation once more. 'Some stuff called—oh, something like—was it Serenite?'

'If you ask me,' said Evelyn Hillingdon, 'I don't think he ever liked to admit that there could be anything the matter with him or that he could be ill. I think he was one of those people who are afraid of illness and therefore deny there's ever anything wrong with them.'

It was a long speech for her. Miss Marple looked thoughtfully down at the top of her dark head.

'The trouble is,' said Mr. Rafiel dictatorially 'everybody's too fond of knowing other people's ailments. They think everybody over fifty is going to die of hypertension or coronary thrombosis or one of those things—poppycock! If a man says there's nothing much wrong with him I don't suppose there is. A man ought to know about his own health. What's the time? Quarter to twelve? I ought to have had my dip long ago. Why can't you remind me about these things, Esther?'

Mrs. Walters made no protest. She rose to her feet and with some deftness assisted Mr. Rafiel to his. Together they went down the beach, she supporting him carefully. Together they stepped into the sea.

Señora de Caspearo opened her eyes and murmured: 'How ugly are old men! Oh how they are ugly! They should all be put to death at forty, or perhaps thirty-five would be better. Yes?'

Edward Hillingdon and Gregory Dyson came crunching down the beach.

'What's the water like, Evelyn?'

'Just the same as always.'

'Never much variation, is there? Where's Lucky?'

'I don't know,' said Evelyn.

Again Miss Marple looked down thoughtfully at the dark head.

'Well, now I give my imitation of a whale,' said Gregory. He threw off his gaily patterned Bermuda shirt and tore down the beach, flinging himself, puffing and panting, into the sea, doing a fast crawl. Edward Hillingdon sat down on the beach by his wife. Presently he asked, 'Coming in again?'

She smiled—put on her cap—and they went down the beach together in a much less spectacular manner.

Señora de Caspearo opened her eyes again.

'I think at first those two they are on their honeymoon, he is so charming to her, but I hear they have been married eight—nine years. It is incredible, is it not?'

'I wonder where Mrs. Dyson is?' said Miss Marple.

'That Lucky? She is with some man.'

'You—you think so?'

'It is certain,' said Señora de Caspearo. 'She is that type. But she is not so young any longer—Her husband—already his eyes go elsewhere—He makes passes—here, there, all the time. I know.'

'Yes,' said Miss Marple, 'I expect you would know.'

Señora de Caspearo shot a surprised glance at her. It was clearly not what she had expected from that quarter.

Miss Marple, however, was looking at the waves with an air of gentle innocence.

2

'May I speak to you, ma'am, Mrs. Kendal?'

'Yes, of course,' said Molly. She was sitting at her desk in the office.

Victoria Johnson tall, and buoyant in her crisp white uniform came in farther and shut the door behind her with a somewhat mysterious air.

'I like to tell you something, please, Mrs. Kendal.'

'Yes, what is it. Is anything wrong?'

'I don't know that. Not for sure. It's the old gentleman who died. The Major gentleman. He die in his sleep.'

'Yes, yes. What about it?'

'There was a bottle of pills in his room. Doctor, he asked me about them.'

'Yes?'

'The doctor said—"Let me see what he has here on the bathroom shelf," and he looked, you see. He see there was tooth powder and indigestion pills and aspirin and cascara pills and then these pills in a bottle called Serenite.'

'Yes,' repeated Molly yet again.

'And the doctor looked at them. He seemed quite satisfied, and nodded his head. But I get to thinking afterwards. Those pills weren't there before. I've not seen them in his bathroom before. The others, yes. The tooth powder and the aspirin and the after shave lotion and all the rest. But those pills, those Serenite pills, I never noticed them before.'

'So you think——' Molly looked puzzled.

'I don't know what to think,' said Victoria. 'I just think it's not right, so I think I better tell you about it. Perhaps you tell doctor? Perhaps it means something. Perhaps *someone* put those pills there so he take them and he died.'

'Oh, I don't think that's likely at all,' said Molly.

Victoria shook her dark head. 'You never know. People do bad things.'

Molly glanced out of the window. The place looked like an earthly paradise. With its sunshine, its sea, its coral reef, its music, its dancing, it seemed a Garden of Eden. But even in the Garden of Eden, there had been a shadow—the shadow of the Serpent—*Bad things*—how hateful to hear those words.

'I'll make inquiries, Victoria,' she said sharply. 'Don't worry. And above all don't go starting a lot of silly rumours.'

Tim Kendal came in, just as Victoria was, somewhat unwillingly, leaving.

'Anything wrong, Molly?'

She hesitated—but Victoria might go to him—— She told him what the girl had said.

'I don't see what all this rigmarole—what *were* these pills anyway?'

'Well, I don't really know, Tim. Dr. Robertson when he came said they—were something to do with blood pressure, I think.'

'Well, that would be all right, wouldn't it? I mean, he *had* high blood pressure, and he *would* be taking things for it, wouldn't he? People do. I've seen them, lots of times.'

'Yes,' Molly hesitated, 'but Victoria seemed to think that he might have taken one of these pills and it would have killed him.'

'Oh darling, that is a bit *too* melodramatic! You mean that somebody might have changed his blood pressure pills for something else, and that they poisoned him?'

'It does sound absurd,' said Molly apologetically, 'when you say it like that. But that seemed to be what Victoria thought!'

'Silly girl! We *could* go and ask Dr. Graham about it, I suppose he'd know. But really it's such nonsense that it's not worth bothering him.'

'That's what I think.'

'What on earth made the girl think anybody would have changed the pills. You mean, put different pills into the same bottle?'

'I didn't quite gather,' said Molly, looking rather helpless. 'Victoria seemed to think that was the first time that Serenite bottle had been there.'

'Oh but that's nonsense,' said Tim Kendal. 'He had to take those pills all the time to keep his blood pressure down.' And he went off cheerfully to consult with Fernando the *maître d'hôtel*.

But Molly could not dismiss the matter so lightly. After the stress of lunch was over she said to her husband:

'Tim—I've been thinking—— If Victoria is going around talking about this perhaps we ought just to ask someone about it?'

'My dear girl! Robertson and all the rest of them came and looked at everything and asked all the questions they wanted at the time.'

'Yes, but you know how they work themselves up, these girls—'

'Oh, all right! I'll tell you what—we'll go and ask Graham—he'll know.'

Dr. Graham was sitting on his loggia with a book. The young couple came in and Molly plunged into her recital. It was a little incoherent and Tim took over.

'Sounds rather idiotic,' he said apologetically, 'but as far as I can make out, this girl has got it into her head that someone put some poison tablets in the—what's the name of the stuff—Sera—something bottle.'

'But why should she get this idea into her head?' asked Dr. Graham. 'Did she see anything or hear anything or—I mean, why should she think so?'

'I don't know,' said Tim rather helplessly. 'Was it a different bottle? Was that it, Molly?'

'No,' said Molly. 'I think what she said was that there was a bottle there labelled—Seven—Seren——'

'Serenite,' said the doctor. 'That's quite right. A well-known preparation. He'd been taking it regularly.'

'Victoria said she'd never seen it in his room before.'

'Never seen it in his room before?' said Graham sharply. 'What does she mean by that?'

'Well, that's what she *said*. She said there were all sorts of things on the bathroom shelf. You know, tooth powder, aspirin and after shave and—oh—she rattled them off gaily. I suppose she's always cleaning them and so she knows them all off by heart. But this one—the Serenite—she hadn't seen it there until the day after he died.'

'That's very odd,' said Dr. Graham, rather sharply. 'Is she sure?'

The unusual sharpness of his tone made both of the Kendals look at him. They had not expected Dr. Graham to take up quite this attitude.

'She sounded sure,' said Molly slowly.

'Perhaps she just wanted to be sensational,' suggested Tim.

'I think perhaps,' said Dr. Graham, 'I'd better have a few words with the girl myself.'

Victoria displayed a distinct pleasure at being allowed to tell her story.

'I don't want to get in no trouble,' she said. '*I* didn't put that bottle there and I don't know who did.'

'But you think it *was* put there?' asked Graham.

'Well, you see, Doctor, it *must* have been put there if it wasn't there before.'

'Major Palgrave could have kept it in a drawer—or a dispatch-case, something like that.'

Victoria shook her head shrewdly.

'Wouldn't do that if he was taking it all the time, would he?'

'No,' said Graham reluctantly. 'No, it was stuff he would have to take several times a day. You never saw him taking it or anything of that kind?'

'He didn't have it there before. I just thought—word got round as that stuff had something to do with his death, poisoned his blood or something, and I thought maybe he had an enemy put it there so as to kill him.'

'Nonsense, my girl,' said the doctor robustly. 'Sheer nonsense.'

Victoria looked shaken.

'You say as this stuff was medicine, good medicine?' she asked doubtfully.

'Good medicine, and what is more, *necessary* medicine,' said Dr. Graham. 'So you needn't worry, Victoria. I can assure you there was nothing wrong with that medicine. It was the proper thing for a man to take who had his complaint.'

'Surely you've taken a load off my mind,' said Victoria. She showed white teeth at him in a cheerful smile.

But the load was not taken off Dr. Graham's mind. That uneasiness of his that had been so nebulous was now becoming tangible.

8. *A talk with Esther Walters*

'THIS PLACE isn't what it used to be,' said Mr. Rafiel, irritably, as he observed Miss Marple approaching the spot where he and his secretary were sitting. 'Can't move a step without some old hen getting under your feet. What do old ladies want to come to the West Indies for?'

'Where do you suggest they should go?' asked Esther Walters.

'To Cheltenham,' said Mr. Rafiel promptly. 'Or Bournemouth,' he offered, 'or Torquay or Llandrindod Wells. Plenty of choice. They like it there—they're quite happy.'

'They can't often afford to come to the West Indies, I suppose,' said Esther. 'It isn't everyone who is as lucky as you are.'

'That's right,' said Mr. Rafiel. 'Rub it in. Here am I, a mass of aches and pains and disjoints. You grudge me any alleviation! And you don't do any work— Why haven't you typed out those letters yet?'

'I haven't had time.'

'Well, get on with it, can't you? I bring you out here to do a bit of work, not to sit about sunning yourself and showing off your figure.'

Some people would have considered Mr. Rafiel's remarks quite insupportable but Esther Walters had worked for him for some years and she knew well enough that Mr. Rafiel's bark was a great deal worse than his bite. He was a man who suffered almost continual pain, and making disagreeable remarks was one of his ways of letting off steam. No matter what he said she remained quite imperturbable.

'Such a lovely evening, isn't it?' said Miss Marple, pausing beside them.

'Why not?' said Mr. Rafiel. 'That's what we're here for, isn't it?'

Miss Marple gave a tinkly little laugh.

'You're so severe—of course the weather *is* a very English subject of conversation—one forgets— Oh dear—this is the wrong coloured wool.' She deposited her knitting bag on the garden table and trotted towards her own bungalow.

'Jackson!' yelled Mr. Rafiel.

Jackson appeared.

'Take me back inside,' said Mr. Rafiel. 'I'll have my massage now before that chattering hen comes back. Not that massage does me a bit of good,' he added. Having said which, he allowed himself to be deftly helped to his feet and went off with the masseur beside him into his bungalow.

Esther Walters looked after them and then turned her head as Miss Marple came back with a ball of wool to sit down near her.

'I hope I'm not disturbing you?' said Miss Marple.

'Of course not,' said Esther Walters, 'I've got to go off and do some typing in a minute, but I'm going to enjoy another ten minutes of the sunset first.'

Miss Marple sat down and in a gentle voice began to talk. As she talked, she summed up Esther Walters. Not at all glamorous, but could be attractive looking if she tried. Miss Marple wondered why she didn't try. It could be, of course, because Mr. Rafiel would not have liked it, but Miss Marple didn't think Mr. Rafiel would really mind in the least. He was so completely taken up with himself that so long as he was not personally neglected, his secretary might have got herself up like a houri in Paradise without his objecting. Besides, he usually went to bed early and in the evening hours of steel bands and dancing, Esther Walters might easily have—Miss Marple paused to select a word in her mind, at the same time conversing cheerfully about her visit to Jamestown.— Ah yes, *blossomed*. Esther Walters might have blossomed in the evening hours.

She led the conversation gently in the direction of Jackson.

On the subject of Jackson Esther Walters was rather vague.

'He's very competent,' she said. 'A fully trained masseur.'

'I suppose he's been with Mr. Rafiel a long time?'

'Oh no—about nine months, I think——'

'Is he married?' Miss Marple hazarded.

'Married? I don't think so,' said Esther slightly surprised. 'He's never mentioned it if so——

'No.' she added. 'Definitely *not* married, I should say.' And she showed amusement.

Miss Marple interpreted that by adding to it in her own mind the following sentence—'At any rate he doesn't behave as though he were married.'

But then, how many married men there were who behaved as though they weren't married!! Miss Marple could think of a dozen examples!

'He's quite good looking,' she said thoughtfully.

'Yes—I suppose he is,' said Esther without interest.

Miss Marple considered her thoughtfully. Uninterested in men? The kind of woman, perhaps, who was only interested in one man—— A widow, they had said.

She asked—'Have you worked for Mr. Rafiel long?'

'Four or five years. After my husband died, I had to take a job again. I've got a daughter at school and my husband left me very badly off.'

'Mr. Rafiel must be a difficult man to work for?' Miss Marple hazarded.

'Not really, when you get to know him. He flies into rages and is very contradictory. I think the real trouble is he gets tired of people. He's had five different valet-attendants in two years. He likes having someone new to bully. But he and I have always got on very well.'

'Mr. Jackson seems a very obliging young man?'

'He's very tactful and resourceful,' said Esther. 'Of course, he's sometimes a little——' She broke off.

Miss Marple considered. 'Rather a difficult position sometimes?' she suggested.

'Well, yes. Neither one thing nor the other. However—' she smiled—'I think he manages to have quite a good time.'

Miss Marple considered this also. It didn't help her much. She continued her twittering conversation and soon she was hearing a good deal about that nature-loving quartet, the Dysons and the Hillingdons.

'The Hillingdons have been here for the last three or four years at least,' said Esther, 'but Gregory Dyson has been here much longer than that. He knows the West Indies very well. He came here, originally, I believe, with his first wife. She was delicate and had to go abroad in the winters, or go somewhere warm, at any rate.'

'And she died? Or was it divorce?'

'No. She died. Out here, I believe. I don't mean this particular island but one of the West Indies islands. There was some sort of trouble, I believe, some kind of scandal or other. He never talks about her. Somebody else told me about it. They didn't, I gather, get on very well together.'

'And then he married this wife. "Lucky".' Miss Marple said the word with faint dissatisfaction as if to say 'Really, a most incredible name!'

'I believe she was a relation of his first wife.'

'Have they known the Hillingdons a great many years?'

'Oh, I think only since the Hillingdons came out here. Three or four years, not more.'

'The Hillingdons seem very pleasant,' said Miss Marple. 'Quiet, of course.'

'Yes. They're both quiet.'

'Everyone says they're very devoted to each other,' said Miss Marple. The tone of her voice was quite non-committal but Esther Walters looked at her sharply.

'But you don't think they are?' she said.

'You don't really think so yourself, do you, my dear?'

'Well, I've wondered sometimes . . .'

'Quiet men, like Colonel Hillingdon,' said Miss Marple 'are often attracted to flamboyant types.' And she added, after a significant pause 'Lucky—such a curious name. Do you think Mr. Dyson has any idea of—of what might be going on?'

'Old scandal-monger,' thought Esther Walters. 'Really, these old women!'

She said rather coldly, 'I've no idea.'

Miss Marple shifted to another subject. 'It's very sad about poor Major Palgrave isn't it?' she said.

Esther Walters agreed, though in a somewhat perfunctory fashion.

'The people I'm really sorry for are the Kendals,' she said.

'Yes, I suppose it is really rather unfortunate when something of that kind happens in a hotel.'

'People come here, you see, to enjoy themselves, don't they?'

said Esther. 'To forget about illnesses and deaths and income tax and frozen pipes and all the rest of it. They don't like—' she went on, with a sudden flash of an entirely different manner—'any reminders of mortality.'

Miss Marple laid down her knitting. 'Now that is very well put, my dear,' she said, 'very well put indeed. Yes, it is as you say.'

'And you see they're quite a young couple,' went on Esther Walters. 'They only just took over from the Sandersons six months ago and they're terribly worried about whether they're going to succeed or not, because they haven't had much experience.'

'And you think this might be really disadvantageous to them?'

'Well, no, I don't, frankly,' said Esther Walters. 'I don't think people remember anything for more than a day or two, not in this atmosphere of "we've-all-come-out-here-to-enjoy-ourselves-let's-get-on-with-it". I think a death just gives them a jolt for about twenty-four hours or so and then they don't think of it again once the funeral is over. Not unless they're reminded of it, that is. I've told Molly so, but of course she is a worrier.'

'Mrs. Kendal is a worrier? She always seems so carefree.'

'I think a lot of that is put on,' said Esther slowly. 'Actually, I think she's one of those anxious sort of people who can't help worrying all the time that things *may* go wrong.'

'I should have thought *he* worried more than she did.'

'No, I don't think so. I think she's the worrier and he worries because she worries if you know what I mean.'

'That is interesting,' said Miss Marple.

'I think Molly wants desperately to try and appear very gay and to be enjoying herself. She works at it very hard but the effort exhausts her. Then she has these odd fits of depression. She's not—well not really well-balanced.'

'Poor child,' said Miss Marple. 'There certainly are people like that, and very often outsiders don't suspect it.'

'No, they put on such a good show, don't they? However,' Esther added, 'I don't think Molly has really anything to worry about in this case. I mean, people are dying of coronary thrombosis or cerebral hæmorrhage or things of that kind all the time nowadays. Far more than they used to, as far as I can see. It's only food poisoning or typhoid or something like that, that makes people get het up.'

'Major Palgrave never mentioned to *me* that he had high blood pressure,' said Miss Marple. 'Did he to you?'

'He said so to somebody—I don't know who—It may have been to Mr. Rafiel. I know Mr. Rafiel says just the opposite—but then he's like that! Certainly Jackson mentioned it to me once. He said the Major ought to be more careful over the alcohol he took.'

'I see,' said Miss Marple, thoughtfully. She went on: 'I expect you found him rather a boring old man? He told a lot of stories and I expect repeated himself a good deal.'

'That's the worst of it,' said Esther. 'You do hear the same story again and again unless you can manage to be quick enough to fend it off.'

'Of course *I* didn't mind so much,' said Miss Marple, 'because I'm used to that sort of thing. If I get stories told to me rather often, I don't really mind hearing them again because I've usually forgotten them.'

'There is that,' said Esther and laughed cheerfully.

'There was one story he was very fond of telling,' said Miss Marple, 'about a murder. I expect he told you that, didn't he?'

Esther Walters opened her handbag and started searching through it. She drew out her lipstick saying, 'I thought I'd lost it.' Then she asked, 'I beg your pardon, what did you say?'

'I asked if Major Palgrave told you his favourite murder story?'

'I believe he did, now I come to think of it. Something about someone who gassed themselves, wasn't it? Only really it was the *wife* who gassed him. I mean she'd given him a sedative of some kind and then stuck his head in the gas oven. Was that it?'

'I don't think that was exactly it,' said Miss Marple. She looked at Esther Walters thoughtfully.

'He told such a lot of stories,' said Esther Walters, apologetically, 'and as I said, one didn't always listen.'

'He had a snapshot,' said Miss Marple, 'that he used to show people.'

'I believe he did . . . I can't remember what it was now. Did he show it to you?'

'No,' said Miss Marple. 'He didn't show it to me. We were interrupted——'

9. *Miss Prescott and others*

'THE STORY I heard,' began Miss Prescott, lowering her voice, and looking carefully around.

Miss Marple drew her chair a little closer. It had been some time before she had been able to get together with Miss Prescott for a heart-to-heart chat. This was owing to the fact that clergymen are very strong family men so that Miss Prescott was nearly always accompanied by her brother, and there was no doubt that Miss Marple and Miss Prescott found it less easy to take their back hair down in a good gossip when the jovial Canon was of their company.

'It seems,' said Miss Prescott, 'though of course I don't want to talk any scandal and I really know *nothing* about it——'

'Oh, I *quite* understand,' said Miss Marple.

'It seems there was some scandal when his first wife was still alive! Apparently this woman, Lucky—such a name!—who I think was a cousin of his first wife, came out here and joined them and I think did some work with him on flowers or butterflies or whatever it was. And people talked a lot because they got on so well together—if you know what I mean.'

'People do *notice* things so much, don't they,' said Miss Marple.

'And then of course, when his wife died rather suddenly——'

'She died here, on this island?'

'No. No, I think they were in Martinique or Tobago at the time.'

'I see.'

'But I gathered from some other people who were there at the time, and who came on here and talked about things, that the doctor wasn't very satisfied.'

'Indeed,' said Miss Marple, with interest.

'It was only *gossip*,' of course, 'but—well, Mr. Dyson certainly married again *very quickly*.' She lowered her voice again. 'Only a *month* I believe.'

'Only a month,' said Miss Marple.

The two women looked at each other. 'It seemed—unfeeling,' said Miss Prescott.

'Yes,' said Miss Marple. 'It certainly did.' She added delicately, 'Was there—any money?'

'I don't really know. He makes his little joke—perhaps you've heard him—about this wife being his "lucky piece"——'

'Yes, I've heard him,' said Miss Marple.

'And some people think that means that he was lucky to marry a rich wife. Though, of course,' said Miss Prescott with the air of one being entirely fair, 'she's very good-looking too, if you care for that type. And I think myself that it was the *first* wife who had the money.'

'Are the Hillingdons well off?'

'Well, I think they're *well off*. I don't mean fabulously rich, I just mean well off. They have two boys at Public School and a very nice place in England, I believe, and they travel most of the winter.'

The Canon appearing at this moment to suggest a brisk walk, Miss Prescott rose to join her brother. Miss Marple remained sitting there.

A few minutes later Gregory Dyson passed her striding along towards the hotel. He waved a cheerful hand as he passed.

'Penny for your thoughts,' he called out.

Miss Marple smiled gently, wondering how he would have reacted if she had replied:

'I was wondering if you were a murderer.'

It really seemed most probable that he was. It all fitted in so nicely—— This story about the death of the first Mrs. Dyson——Major Palgrave had certainly been talking about a wife killer—with special reference to the 'Brides in the Bath' case.

Yes—it fitted—the only objection was that it fitted almost too well. But Miss Marple reproved herself for this thought—— Who was she to demand Murders Made to Measure?

A voice made her jump—a somewhat raucous one.

'Seen Greg any place, Miss—er——'

Lucky, Miss Marple thought, was not in a good temper.

'He passed by just now—going towards the hotel.'

'I'll bet!' Lucky uttered an irritated ejaculation and hurried on.

'Forty, if she's a day, and looks it this morning,' thought Miss Marple.

Pity invaded her—Pity for the Luckys of the world—who were so vulnerable to Time.

At the sound of a noise behind her, she turned her chair round—

Mr. Rafiel, supported by Jackson, was making his morning appearance and coming out of his bungalow.

Jackson settled his employer in his wheel chair and fussed round him. Mr. Rafiel waved his attendant away impatiently and Jackson went off in the direction of the hotel.

Miss Marple lost no time—Mr. Rafiel was never left alone for long— Probably Esther Walters would come and join him. Miss Marple wanted a word alone with Mr. Rafiel and now, she thought, was her chance. She would have to be quick about what she wanted to say. There could be no leading up to things. Mr. Rafiel was not a man who cared for the idle twittering conversation of old ladies. He would probably retreat again into his bungalow, definitely regarding himself the victim of persecution. Miss Marple decided to plump for downrightness.

She made her way to where he was sitting, drew up a chair, sat down, and said:

'I want to ask you something, Mr. Rafiel.'

'All right, all right,' said Mr. Rafiel, 'let's have it. What do you want—a subscription, I suppose? Missions in Africa or repairing a church, something of that kind?'

'Yes,' said Miss Marple. 'I am interested in several objects of that nature, and I shall be delighted if you will give me a subscription for them. But that wasn't actually what I was going to ask you. What I was going to ask you was if Major Palgrave ever told you a story about a murder.'

'Oho,' said Mr. Rafiel. 'So he told it to you too, did he? And I suppose you fell for it, hook line and sinker.'

'I didn't really know what to think,' said Miss Marple. 'What exactly did he tell you?'

'He prattled on,' said Mr. Rafiel, 'about a lovely creature, Lucrezia Borgia reincarnated. Beautiful, young, golden-haired, everything.'

'Oh,' said Miss Marple slightly taken aback, 'and who did she murder?'

'Her husband, of course,' said Mr. Rafiel, 'who do you think?'

'Poison?'

'No, I think she gave him a sleeping draught and then stuck him in a gas oven. Resourceful female. Then she said it was suicide. She got off quite lightly. Diminished responsibility or something. That's what it's called nowadays if you're a good-looking woman, or some miserable young hooligan whose mother's been too fond of him. Bah!'

'Did the Major show you a snapshot?'

'What—a snapshot of the woman? No. Why should he?'

'Oh——' said Miss Marple.

She sat there, rather taken aback. Apparently Major Palgrave spent his life telling people not only about tigers he had shot and elephants he had hunted but also about murderers he had met. Perhaps he had a whole repertoire of murder stories. One had to face it—She was startled by Mr. Rafiel suddenly giving a roar of 'Jackson!' There was no response.

'Shall I find him for you?' said Miss Marple rising.

'You won't find him. Tom-catting somewhere, that's what he does. No good, that fellow. Bad character. But he suits me all right.'

'I'll go and look for him,' said Miss Marple.

Miss Marple found Jackson sitting on the far side of the hotel terrace having a drink with Tim Kendal.

'Mr. Rafiel is asking for you,' she said.

Jackson made an expressive grimace, drained his glass, and rose to his feet.

'Here we go again,' he said. 'No peace for the wicked—— Two telephone calls and a special diet order—I thought that might give me a quarter of an hour's alibi——Apparently not! Thank you, Miss Marple. Thanks for the drink, Mr. Kendal.'

He strode away.

'I feel sorry for that chap,' said Tim. 'I have to stand him a drink now and then, just to cheer him up—— Can I offer you something, Miss Marple— How about fresh lime? I know you're fond of that.'

'Not just now, thank you—I suppose looking after someone like Mr. Rafiel must always be rather exacting. Invalids are frequently difficult——'

'I didn't mean only that—— It's very well paid and you expect to put up with a good deal of crotchetiness—old Rafiel's not really a bad sort. I meant more that——' he hesitated.

Miss Marple looked inquiring.

'Well—how shall I put it—it's difficult for him socially. People are so damned snobbish—there's no one here of his class. He's better than a servant—and below the average visitor—or they think he is. Rather like the Victorian governess. Even the secretary woman, Mrs. Walters—feels she's a cut above him. Makes things difficult.' Tim paused, then said with feeling: 'It's really awful the amount of social problems there are in a place like this.'

Dr. Graham passed them. He had a book in his hand. He went and sat at a table overlooking the sea.

'Dr. Graham looks rather worried,' remarked Miss Marple.

'Oh! We're all worried.'

'You too? Because of Major Palgrave's death?'

'I've left off worrying about that. People seem to have forgotten it—taken it in their stride. No—it's my wife—Molly—— Do you know anything about dreams?'

'Dreams?' Miss Marple was surprised.

'Yes—bad dreams—nightmares, I suppose. Oh, we all get that sort of thing sometimes. But Molly—she seems to have them nearly all the time. They frighten her. Is there anything one can do about them? Take for them? She's got some sleeping pills, but she says they make it worse—she struggles to wake up and can't.'

'What are the dreams about?'

'Oh, something or someone chasing her—— Or watching her and spying on her—she can't shake off the feeling even when she's awake.'

'Surely a doctor——'

'She's got a thing against doctors. Won't hear of it—— Oh well—I daresay it will all pass off—— But we were so happy. It was all such fun—— And now, just lately—— Perhaps old Palgrave's death upset her. She seems like a different person since . . .'

He got up.

'Must get on with the daily chores—are you sure you won't have that fresh lime?'

Miss Marple shook her head.

She sat there, thinking. Her face was grave and anxious.

She glanced over at Dr. Graham.

Presently she came to a decision.

She rose and went across to his table.

'I have got to apologise to you, Dr. Graham,' she said.

'Indeed?' The doctor looked at her in kindly surprise. He pulled forward a chair and she sat down.

'I am afraid I have done the most disgraceful thing,' said Miss Marple. 'I told you, Dr. Graham, a deliberate lie.'

She looked at him apprehensively.

Dr. Graham did not look at all shattered, but he did look a little surprised.

'Really?' he said. 'Ah well, you mustn't let that worry you too much.'

What had the dear old thing been telling lies about, he wondered; her age? Though as far as he could remember she hadn't mentioned her age. 'Well, let's hear about it,' he said, since she clearly wished to confess.

'You remember my speaking to you about a snapshot of my nephew, one that I showed to Major Palgrave, and that he didn't give back to me?'

'Yes, yes, of course I remember. Sorry we couldn't find it for you.'

'There wasn't any such thing,' said Miss Marple, in a small, frightened voice.

'I beg your pardon?'

'There wasn't any such thing. I made up that story, I'm afraid.'

'You made it up?' Dr. Graham looked slightly annoyed. 'Why?'

Miss Marple told him. She told him quite clearly, without twittering. She told him about Major Palgrave's murder story and how he'd been about to show her this particular snapshot and his sudden confusion and then she went on to her own anxiety and to her final decision to try somehow to obtain a view of it.

'And really, I couldn't see *any* way of doing so without telling you something that was quite untrue,' she said, 'I do hope you will forgive me.'

'You thought that what he had been about to show you was a picture of a murderer?'

'That's what he said it was,' said Miss Marple. 'At least he said it was given him by this acquaintance who had told him the story about a man who was a murderer.'

'Yes, yes. And—excuse me—you believed him?'

'I don't know if I really believed him or not at the time,' said Miss Marple. 'But then, you see, the next day he died.'

'Yes,' said Dr. Graham, struck suddenly by the clarity of that one sentence. *The next day he died. . . .*

'And the snapshot had disappeared.'

Dr. Graham looked at her. He didn't know quite what to say.

'Excuse me, Miss Marple,' he said at last, 'but is what you're telling me now—is it really true this time?'

'I don't wonder your doubting me,' said Miss Marple. 'I should, in your place. Yes, it is true what I am telling you now, but I quite realise that you have only my word for it. Still, even if you don't believe me, I thought I ought to tell you.'

'Why?'

'I realised that you ought to have the fullest information possible—— In case——'

'In case what?'

'In case you decided to take any steps about it.'

10. *A decision in Jamestown*

DR. GRAHAM was in Jamestown, in the Adminstrator's office; sitting at a table opposite his friend Daventry, a grave young man of thirty-five.

'You sounded rather mysterious on the phone, Graham,' said Daventry. 'Anything special the matter?'

'I don't know,' said Dr. Graham, 'but I'm worried.'

Daventry looked at the other's face, then he nodded as drinks were brought in. He spoke lightly of a fishing expedition he had made lately. Then when the servant had gone away, he sat back in his chair and looked at the other man.

'Now then,' he said, 'let's have it.'

Dr. Graham recounted the facts that had worried him. Daventry gave a slow long whistle.

'I see. You think maybe there's something funny about old Palgrave's death? You're no longer sure that it was just natural causes? Who certified the death? Robertson, I suppose. He didn't have any doubts, did he?'

'No, but I think he may have been influenced in giving the certificate by the fact of the Serenite tablets in the bathroom. He asked me if Palgrave had mentioned that he suffered from hypertension, and I said No, I'd never had any medical conversation with him myself, but apparently he had talked about it to other people in the hotel. The whole thing—the bottle of tablets, and what Palgrave had said to people—it all fitted in—no earthly reason to suspect anything else. It was a perfectly natural inference to make—but I think now it may not have been correct. If it had been my business to give the certificate, I'd have given it without a second thought. The appearances are quite consistent with his having died from that cause. I'd never have thought about it since if it hadn't been for the odd disappearance of that snapshot . . .'

'But look here, Graham,' said Daventry, 'if you will allow me to say so, aren't you relying a little too much on a rather fanciful story told you by an elderly lady. You know what these elderly ladies are like. They magnify some small detail and work the whole thing up.'

'Yes, I know,' said Dr. Graham, unhappily. 'I know that. I've said to myself that it may be so, that it probably *is* so. But I can't quite convince myself. She was so very clear and detailed in her statement.'

'The whole thing seems wildly improbable to me,' said Daventry. 'Some old lady tells a story about a snapshot that ought not to be there—no I'm getting mixed myself—I mean the other way about don't I?—but the only thing you've really got to go on is that a chambermaid says that a bottle of pills which the authorities had relied on for evidence, wasn't in the Major's room the day before his death. But there are a hundred explanations for that. He might always have carried those pills about in his pocket.'

'It's possible, I suppose, yes.'

'Or the chambermaid may have made a mistake and she simply hadn't noticed them before——'

'That's possible, too.'

'Well, then.'

Graham said slowly:

'The girl was very positive.'

'Well, the St. Honoré people are very excitable, you know. Emotional. Work themselves up easily. Are you thinking that she knows—a little more than she has said?'

'I think it might be so,' said Dr. Graham slowly.

'You'd better try and get it out of her, if so. We don't want to make an unnecessary fuss—unless we've something definite to go on. If he didn't die of blood pressure, what do you think it was?'

'There are too many things it might be nowadays,' said Dr. Graham.

'You mean things that don't leave recognisable traces?'

'Not everyone,' said Dr. Graham dryly, 'is so considerate as to use arsenic.'

'Now let's get things quite clear—what's the suggestion? That a bottle of pills was substituted for the real ones? And that Major Palgrave was poisoned in that way?'

'No—it's not like that. That's what the girl—Victoria Something thinks—— But she's got it all wrong—— If it was decided to get rid of the Major—quickly—he would have been given something—most likely in a drink of some kind. Then to make it appear a natural death, a bottle of the tablets prescribed to relieve blood pressure was put in his room. And the rumour was put about that he suffered from high blood pressure.'

'Who put the rumour about?'

'I've tried to find out—with no success—— It's been too cleverly done. A says "I *think* B told me"—B, asked, says "No, I didn't say so but I do remember C mentioning it one day". C says "Several people talked about it—one of them, I think, was A". And there we are, back again.'

'Someone was clever?'

'Yes. As soon as the death was discovered, everybody seemed to be talking about the Major's high blood pressure and repeating round what other people had said.'

'Wouldn't it have been simpler just to poison him and let it go at that?'

'No. That might have meant inquiry—possibly an autopsy. This way, a doctor would accept the death and give a certificate—as he did.'

'What do you want me to do? Go to the C.I.D.? Suggest they dig the chap up? It'd make a lot of stink——'

'It could be kept quite quiet.'

'Could it? In St. Honoré? Think again! The grapevine would be on to it before it had happened. All the same,' Daventry sighed— 'I suppose we'll have to do something. But if you ask me, it's all a mare's nest!'

'I devoutly hope it is,' said Dr. Graham.

11. *Evening at the Golden Palm*

MOLLY rearranged a few of the table decorations in the dining-room, removed an extra knife, straightened a fork, reset a glass or two, stood back to look at the effect and then walked out on to the terrace outside. There was no one about just at present and she strolled to the far corner and stood by the balustrade. Soon another evening would begin. Chattering, talking, drinking, all so gay and carefree, the sort of life she had longed for and, up to a few days ago, had enjoyed so much. Now even Tim seemed anxious and worried. Natural, perhaps, that he should worry a little. It was important that this venture of theirs should turn out all right. After all, he had sunk all he had in it.

But that, thought Molly, is not *really* what's worrying him. It's *me*. But I don't see, said Molly to herself, why he should worry about *me*. Because he did worry about her. That she was quite sure of. The questions he put, the quick nervous glance he shot at her from time to time. But why? thought Molly. 'I've been very careful,' she summed up things in her mind. She didn't understand it really herself. She couldn't remember when it had begun. She wasn't even very sure what it was. She'd begun to be frightened of people. She didn't know why. What could they do to her? What should they want to do to her?

She nodded her head, then started violently as a hand touched her arm. She spum round to find Gregory Dyson, slightly taken aback, looking apologetic.

'Ever so sorry. Did I startle you, little girl?'

Molly hated being called 'little girl'. She said quickly and brightly: 'I didn't hear you coming, Mr. Dyson, so it made me jump.'

'Mr. Dyson? We're very formal to-night. Aren't we all one great happy family here? Ed and me and Lucky and Evelyn and you and Tim and Esther Walters and old Rafiel. All the lot of us one happy family.'

'He's had plenty to drink already,' thought Molly. She smiled at him pleasantly.

'Oh! I come over the heavy hostess sometimes,' she said, lightly. 'Tim and I think it's more polite not to be too handy with Christian names.'

'Aw! we don't want any of that stuffed-shirt business. Now then, Molly my lovely, have a drink with me.'

'Ask me later,' said Molly. 'I have a few things to get on with.'

'Now don't run away.' His arm fastened round her arm. 'You're a lovely girl, Molly. I hope Tim appreciates his good luck.'

'Oh, I see to it that he does,' said Molly cheerfully.

'I could go for you, you know, in a big way.' He leered at her—'though I wouldn't let my wife hear me say so.'

'Did you have a good trip this afternoon?'

'I suppose so. Between you and me I get a bit fed up sometimes.

You can get tired of the birds and butterflies. What say you and I go for a little picnic on our own one day?'

'We'll have to see about that,' said Molly gaily. 'I'll be looking forward to it.'

With a light laugh she escaped, and went back into the bar.

'Hallo, Molly,' said Tim, 'you seem in a hurry. Who's that you've been with out there?'

He peered out.

'Gregory Dyson.'

'What does he want?'

'Wanted to make a pass at me,' said Molly.

'Blast him,' said Tim.

'Don't worry,' said Molly, 'I can do all the blasting necessary.'

Tim started to answer her, caught sight of Fernando and went over to him shouting out some directions. Molly slipped away through the kitchen, out through the kitchen door and down the steps to the beach.

Gregory Dyson swore under his breath. Then he walked slowly back in the direction of his bungalow. He had nearly got there when a voice spoke to him from the shadow of one of the bushes. He turned his head, startled. In the gathering dusk he thought for a moment that it was a ghostly figure that stood there. Then he laughed. It had looked like a faceless apparition but that was because, though the dress was white, the face was black.

Victoria stepped out of the bushes on to the path.

'Mr. Dyson, please?'

'Yes. What is it?'

Ashamed of being startled, he spoke with a touch of impatience.

'I brought you this, sir.' She held out her hand. In it was a bottle of tablets. 'This belongs to you, doesn't it. Yes?'

'Oh, my bottle of Serenite tablets. Yes, of course. Where did you find it?'

'I found it where it had been put. In the gentleman's room.'

'What do you mean—in the gentleman's room?'

'The gentleman who is dead,' she added gravely. 'I do not think he sleeps very well in his grave.'

'Why the devil not?' asked Dyson.

Victoria stood looking at him.

'I still don't know what you're talking about. You mean you found this bottle of tablets in Major Palgrave's bungalow?'

'That is right, yes. After the doctor and the Jamestown people go away, they give me all the things in his bathroom to throw away. The toothpaste and the lotions, and all the other things—including this.'

'Well, why didn't you throw it away?'

'Because these are yours. You missed them. You remember, you asked about them?'

'Yes—well—yes, I did. I—I thought I'd just mislaid them.'

'No, you did not mislay them. They were taken from your bungalow and put in Major Palgrave's bungalow.'

'How do you know?' He spoke roughly.

'I know. I saw.' She smiled at him in a sudden flash of white teeth. 'Someone put them in the dead gentleman's room. Now I give them back to you.'

'Here—wait. What do you mean? What—who did you see?'

She hurried away, back into the darkness of the bushes. Greg made as if to move after her and then stopped. He stood stroking his chin.

'What's the matter, Greg? Seen a ghost?' asked Mrs. Dyson, as she came along the path from their bungalow.

'Thought I had for a minute or two.'

'Who was that you were talking to?'

'The coloured girl who does our place. Victoria, her name is, isn't it?'

'What did she want? Making a pass at you?'

'Don't be stupid, Lucky. That girl's got some idiotic idea into her head.'

'Idea about what?'

'You remember I couldn't find my Serenite the other day?'

'You said you couldn't.'

'What do you mean "I said I couldn't"?'

'Oh, for heck's sake, have you got to take me up on everything?'

'I'm sorry,' said Greg. 'Everybody goes about being so damn' mysterious.' He held out his hand with the bottle in it. 'That girl brought them back to me.'

'Had she pinched them?'

'No. She—found them somewhere I think.'

'Well, what of it? What's the mystery about?'

'Oh nothing,' said Greg. 'She just riled me, that's all.'

'Look here, Greg, what is this stuff all about? Come along and have a drink before dinner.'

2

Molly had gone down to the beach. She pulled out one of the old basket chairs, one of the more rickety ones that were seldom used. She sat in it for a while looking at the sea, then suddenly she dropped her head in her hands and burst into tears. She sat there sobbing unrestrainedly for some time. Then she heard a rustle close by her and glanced up sharply to see Mrs. Hillingdon looking down at her.

'Hallo, Evelyn, I didn't hear you. I—I'm sorry.'

'What's the matter, child?' said Evelyn. 'Something gone wrong?' She pulled another chair forward and sat down. 'Tell me.'

'There's nothing wrong,' said Molly. 'Nothing at all.'

'Of course there is. You wouldn't sit and cry here for nothing. Can't you tell me? Is it—some trouble between you and Tim?'

'Oh *no*.'

'I'm glad of that. You always look so happy together.'

'Not more than you do,' said Molly. 'Tim and I always think how wonderful it is that you and Edward should seem so happy together after being married so many years.'

'Oh, that,' said Evelyn. Her voice was sharp as she spoke but Molly hardly noticed.

'People bicker so,' she said, 'and have such rows. Even if they're quite fond of each other they still seem to have rows and not to mind a bit whether they have them in public or not.'

'Some people like living that way,' said Evelyn. 'It doesn't really mean anything.'

'Well, I think it's horrid,' said Molly.

'So do I, really,' said Evelyn.

'But to see you and Edward——'

'Oh it's no good, Molly. I can't let you go on thinking things of that kind. Edward and I—' she paused. 'If you want to know the truth, we've hardly said a word to each other in private for the last three years.'

'What!' Molly stared at her, appalled. 'I—I can't believe it.'

'Oh, we both put up quite a good show,' said Evelyn. 'We're neither of us the kind that like having rows in public. And anyway there's nothing really to have a row about.'

'But what went wrong?' asked Molly.

'Just the usual.'

'What do you mean by the usual? Another——'

'Yes, another woman in the case, and I don't suppose it will be difficult for you to guess who the woman is.'

'Do you mean Mrs. Dyson—Lucky?'

Evelyn nodded.

'I know they always flirt together a lot,' said Molly, 'but I thought that was just . . .'

'Just high spirits?' said Evelyn. 'Nothing behind it?'

'But why—' Molly paused and tried again. 'But didn't you—oh I mean, well I suppose I oughtn't to ask.'

'Ask anything you like,' said Evelyn. 'I'm tired of never saying a word, tired of being a well-bred happy wife. Edward just lost his head completely about Lucky. He was stupid enough to come and tell me about it. It made him feel better I suppose. Truthful. Honourable. All that sort of stuff. It didn't occur to him to think that it wouldn't make *me* feel better.'

'Did he want to leave you?'

Evelyn shook her head. 'We've got two children, you know,' she said. 'Children whom we're both very fond of. They're at school in England. We didn't want to break up the home. And then of course, Lucky didn't want a divorce either. Greg's a very rich man. His first wife left a lot of money. So we agreed to live and let live—Edward and Lucky in happy immorality, Greg in blissful ignorance, and Edward and I just good friends.' She spoke with scalding bitterness.

'How—how can you bear it?'

'One gets used to anything. But sometimes——'

'Yes?' said Molly.

'Sometimes I'd like to kill that woman.'

The passion behind her voice startled Molly.

'Don't let's talk any more about me,' said Evelyn. 'Let's talk about you. I want to know what's the matter.'

Molly was silent for some moments and then she said, 'It's only—it's only that I think there's something wrong about me.'

'Wrong? What do you mean?'

Molly shook her head unhappily. 'I'm frightened,' she said. 'I'm terribly frightened.'

'Frightened of what?'

'Everything,' said Molly. 'It's—growing on me. Voices in the bushes, footsteps—or things that people say. As though someone were watching me all the time, spying on me. Somebody hates me. That's what I keep feeling. Somebody hates me.'

'My dear child.' Evelyn was shocked and startled. 'How long has this been going on?'

'I don't know. It came—it started by degrees. And there have been other things too.'

'What sort of things?'

'There are times,' said Molly slowly, 'that I can't account for, that I can't remember.'

'Do you mean you have blackouts—that sort of thing.'

'I suppose so. I mean sometimes it's—oh, say it's five o'clock—and I can't remember anything since about half past one or two.'

'Oh my dear, but that's just that you've been asleep. Had a doze.'

'No,' said Molly, 'it's not like that at all. Because you see, at the end of the time it's not as though I'd just dozed off. I'm in a different *place*. Sometimes I'm wearing different clothes and sometimes I seem to have been doing things—even saying things to people, talking to someone, and not remembering that I've done so.'

Evelyn looked shocked. 'But, Molly, my dear, if this is so, then you ought to see a doctor.'

'I won't see a doctor! I don't want to. I wouldn't go *near* a doctor.'

Evelyn looked sharply down into her face, then she took the girl's hand in hers.

'You may be frightening yourself for nothing, Molly. You know there are all kinds of nervous disorders that aren't really serious at all. A doctor would soon reassure you.'

'He mightn't. He might say that there was something really wrong with me.'

'Why should there be anything wrong with you?'

'Because—' Molly spoke and then was silent,—'—no reason, I suppose,' she said.

'Couldn't your family—haven't you any family, any mother or sisters or someone who could come out here?'

'I don't get on with my mother. I never have. I've got sisters. They're married but I suppose—I suppose they could come if I wanted them. But I don't want them. I don't want anyone—anyone except Tim.'

'Does Tim know about this? Have you told him?'

'Not really,' said Molly. 'But he's anxious about me and he watches me. It's as though he were trying to—to help me or to shield me. But if he does that it means I want shielding, doesn't it?'

'I think a lot of it may be imagination but I still think you ought to see a doctor.'

'Old Dr. Graham? He wouldn't be any good.'

'There are other doctors on the island.'

'It's all right, really,' said Molly. 'I just—mustn't think of it. I expect, as you say, it's all imagination. Good gracious, it's getting frightfully late. I ought to be on duty now in the dining-room. I—I must go back.'

She looked sharply and almost offensively at Evelyn Hillingdon, and then hurried off. Evelyn stared after her.

12. *Old sins cast long shadows*

'I THINK as I am on to something, man.'

'What's that you say, Victoria?'

'I think I'm on to something. It may mean money. Big money.'

'Now look, girl, you be careful, you'll not tangle yourself up in something. Maybe I'd better tackle what it is.'

Victoria laughed, a deep rich chuckle.

'You wait and see,' she said. 'I know how to play this hand. It's money, man, it's big money. Something I see, and something I guess. I think I guess right.'

And again the soft rich chuckle rolled out on the night.

2

'Evelyn . . .'

'Yes?'

Evelyn Hillingdon spoke mechanically, without interest. She did not look at her husband.

'Evelyn, would you mind if we chucked all this and went home to England?'

She had been combing her short dark hair. Now her hands came down from her head sharply. She turned towards him.

'You mean—but we've only just come. We've not been out here in the islands for more than three weeks.'

'I know. But—would you mind?'

Her eyes searched him incredulously.

'You really want to go back to England. Back home?'

'Yes.'

'Leaving—Lucky.'

He winced.

'You've known all the time, I suppose, that—that it was still going on?'

'Pretty well. Yes.'

'You've never said anything.'

'Why should I? We had the whole thing out years ago. Neither of us wanted to make a break. So we agreed to go our separate ways—but keep up the show in public.' Then she added before he could speak, 'But why are you so set on going back to England *now*?'

'Because I'm at breaking point. I can't stick it any longer, Evelyn. I can't.' The quiet Edward Hillingdon was transformed. His hands shook, he swallowed, his calm unemotional face seemed distorted by pain.

'For God's sake, Edward, what's the *matter*?'

'Nothing's the matter except that I want to get out of here——'

'You fell wildly in love with Lucky. And now you've got over it. Is that what you're telling me?'

'Yes. I don't suppose you'll ever feel the same.'

'Oh let's not go into that now! I want to understand what's upsetting you so much, Edward.'

'I'm not particularly upset.'

'But you are. Why?'

'Isn't it obvious?'

'No, it isn't,' said Evelyn. 'Let's put it in plain concrete terms. You've had an affair with a woman. That happens often enough. And now it's over. Or isn't it over? Perhaps it isn't over on *her* side. Is that it? Does Greg know about it? I've often wondered.'

'I don't know,' said Edward. 'He's never said anything. He always seems friendly enough.'

'Men can be extraordinarily obtuse,' said Evelyn thoughtfully. 'Or else—— Perhaps Greg has got an outside interest of his own!'

'He's made passes at you, hasn't he?' said Edward. 'Answer me—I know he has——'

'Oh yes,' said Evelyn, carelessly, 'but he makes passes at everybody.

That's just Greg. It doesn't ever really mean much, I imagine. It's just part of the Greg he-man act.'

'Do you care for him, Evelyn? I'd rather know the truth.'

'Greg? I'm quite fond of him—he amuses me. He's a good friend.'

'And that's all? I wish I could believe you.'

'I can't really see how it can possibly matter to you,' said Evelyn dryly.

'I suppose I deserve that.'

Evelyn walked to the window, looked out across the veranda and came back again.

'I wish you would tell me what's *really* upsetting you, Edward.'

'I've told you.'

'I wonder.'

'You can't understand, I suppose, how extraordinary a temporary madness of this kind can seem to you after you've got over it.'

'I can try, I suppose. But what's worrying me now is that Lucky seems to have got some kind of stranglehold upon you. She's not just a discarded mistress. She's a tigress with claws. You *must* tell me the truth, Edward. It's the only way if you want me to stand by you.'

Edward said in a low voice: 'If I don't get away from her soon—I shall kill her.'

'Kill Lucky? Why?'

'Because of what she made me do . . .'

'What did she make you do?'

'I helped her to commit a murder——'

The words were out. There was silence. Evelyn stared at him. 'Do you know what you are saying?'

'Yes. I didn't know I was doing it. There were things she asked me to get for her—at the chemist's. I didn't know—I hadn't the least idea what she wanted them for—— She got me to copy out a prescription she had . . .'

'When was this?'

'Four years ago. When we were in Martinique. When—when Greg's wife——'

'You mean Greg's first wife—Gail? You mean Lucky poisoned her?'

'Yes—and I helped her. When I realised——'

Evelyn interrupted him.

'When you realised what had happened, Lucky pointed out to you that *you* had written out the prescription, that *you* had got the drugs, that you and she were in it together? Is that right?'

'Yes. She said she had done it out of pity—that Gail was suffering —that she had begged Lucky to get something that would end it all.'

'A mercy killing! I see. And you believed *that*?'

Edward Hillingdon was silent a moment—then he said:

'No—I didn't really—not deep down—I accepted it because I *wanted* to believe it—because I was infatuated with Lucky.'

'And afterwards—when she married Greg—did you still believe it?'

'I'd made myself believe it by then.'

'And Greg—how much did he know about it all?'

'Nothing at all.'

'That I find hard to believe!'

Edward Hillingdon broke out——

'Evelyn, I've *got* to get free of it all! That woman taunts me still with what I did. She knows I don't care for her any longer. Care for her?—— I've come to hate her—— But she makes me feel I'm tied to her—by the thing we did together——'

Evelyn walked up and down the room—then she stopped and faced him.

'The entire trouble with you, Edward, is that you are ridiculously sensitive—and also incredibly suggestible. That devil of a woman has got you just where she wants you by playing on your sense of guilt—— And I'll tell you this in plain Bible terms, the guilt that weighs on you is the guilt of adultery—not murder—— You were guilt-stricken about your affair with Lucky—and then she made a cat's-paw of you for her murder scheme, and managed to make you feel you shared her guilt. You *don't*.'

'Evelyn' . . . He stepped towards her.

She stepped back a little—and looked at him searchingly.

'Is this all true, Edward—— *Is* it? Or are you making it up?'

'Evelyn! Why on earth should I do such a thing?'

'I don't know,' said Evelyn Hillingdon slowly——'It's just perhaps —because I find it hard to trust—anybody. And because—— Oh! I don't know—— I've got, I suppose, so that I don't know the truth when I hear it.'

'Let's chuck all this—— Go back home to England.'

'Yes—— We will—— But not now.'

'Why not?'

'We must carry on as usual—just for the present. It's important. Do you understand, Edward? Don't let Lucky have an inkling of what we're up to——'

13. *Exit Victoria Johnson*

THE EVENING was drawing to a close. The steel band was at last relaxing its efforts. Tim stood by the dining-room looking over the terrace. He extinguished a few lights on tables that had been vacated.

A voice spoke behind him. 'Tim, can I speak to you a moment?'

Tim Kendal started.

'Hallo, Evelyn, is there anything I can do for you?'

Evelyn looked round.

'Come to this table here, and let's sit down a minute.'

She led the way to a table at the extreme end of the terrace. There were no other people near them.

'Tim, you must forgive me talking to you, but I'm worried about Molly.'

His face changed at once.

'What about Molly?' he said stiffly.

'I don't think she's awfully well. She seems upset.'

'Things do seem to upset her rather easily just lately.'

'She ought to see a doctor, I think.'

'Yes, I know, but she doesn't want to. She'd hate it.'

'Why?'

'Eh? What d'you mean?'

'I said why? Why should she hate seeing a doctor?'

'Well,' said Tim rather vaguely, 'people do sometimes, you know. It's—well, it sort of makes them feel frightened about themselves.'

'You're worried about her yourself, aren't you, Tim?'

'Yes. Yes, I am rather.'

'Isn't there anyone of her family who could come out here to be with her?'

'No. That'd make things worse, far worse.'

'What *is* the trouble—with her family, I mean?'

'Oh, just one of those things. I suppose she's just highly strung and—she didn't get on with them—particularly her mother. She never has. They're—they're rather an odd family in some ways and she cut loose from them. Good thing she did, I think.'

Evelyn said hesitantly—'She seems to have had blackouts, from what she told me, and to be frightened of people. Almost like persecution mania.'

'Don't say that,' said Tim angrily. 'Persecution mania! People always say that about people. Just because she—well—maybe she's a bit nervy. Coming out here to the West Indies. All the dark faces. You know, people are rather queer, sometimes, about the West Indies and coloured people.'

'Surely not girls like Molly?'

'Oh, how does one know the things people are frightened of? There are people who can't be in the room with cats. And other people who faint if a caterpillar drops on them.'

'I hate suggesting it—but don't you think perhaps she ought to see a—well, a psychiatrist?'

'*No!*' said Tim explosively. 'I won't have people like that monkeying about with her. I don't believe in them. They make people worse. If her mother had left psychiatrists alone . . .'

'So there *was* trouble of that kind in her family—was there? I mean a history of—' she chose the word carefully—'instability.'

'I don't want to talk about it—— I took her away from it all and she was all right, quite all right. She has just got into a nervous state. . . . But these things aren't hereditary. Everybody knows that nowadays. It's an exploded idea. Molly's perfectly sane. It's just that—oh! I believe it was that wretched old Palgrave dying that started it all off.'

'I see,' said Evelyn thoughtfully. 'But there was nothing really to worry anyone in Major Palgrave's death, was there?'

'No of course there wasn't. But it's a kind of shock when somebody dies suddenly.'

He looked so desperate and defeated that Evelyn's heart smote her. She put her hand on his arm.

'Well, I hope you know what you're doing, Tim, but if I could help in any way—I mean if I could go with Molly to New York—I could fly with her there or Miami or somewhere where she could get really first-class medical advice.'

'It's very good of you, Evelyn, but Molly's all right. She's getting over it, anyway.'

Evelyn shook her head in doubt. She turned away slowly and looked along the line of the terrace. Most people had gone by now to their bungalows. Evelyn was walking towards her table to see if she'd left anything behind there, when she heard Tim give an exclamation. She looked up sharply. He was staring towards the steps at the end of the terrace and she followed his gaze. Then she too caught her breath.

Molly was coming up the steps from the beach. She was breathing with deep, sobbing breaths, her body swayed to and fro as she came, in a curious directionless run. Tim cried,

'*Molly!* What's the matter?'

He ran towards her and Evelyn followed him. Molly was at the top of the steps now and she stood there, both hands behind her back. She said in sobbing breaths:

'I found her. . . . She's there in the bushes . . . There in the bushes . . . And look at my hands—look at my *hands*.' She held them out and Evelyn caught her breath as she saw the queer dark stains. They looked dark in the subdued lighting but she knew well enough that their real colour was red.

'What's happened, Molly?' cried Tim.

'Down there,' said Molly. She swayed on her feet. 'In the bushes . . .'

Tim hesitated, looked at Evelyn, then shoved Molly a little towards Evelyn and ran down the steps. Evelyn put her arm round the girl.

'Come. Sit down, Molly. Here. You'd better have something to drink.'

Molly collapsed in a chair and leaned forward on the table, her forehead on her crossed arms. Evelyn did not question her any more. She thought it better to leave her time to recover.

'It'll be all right, you know,' said Evelyn gently. 'It'll be all right.'

'I don't know,' said Molly. 'I don't know what happened. I don't know anything. I can't remember. I—' she raised her head suddenly. 'What's the matter with me? What's the *matter* with me?'

'It's all right, child. It's all right.'

Tim was coming slowly up the steps. His face was ghastly. Evelyn looked up at him, raising her eyebrows in a query.

'It's one of our girls,' he said. 'What's-her-name—Victoria. Somebody's put a knife in her.'

14. *Inquiry*

MOLLY lay on her bed. Dr. Graham and Dr. Robertson, the West Indian police doctor stood on one side—Tim on the other. Robertson had his hand on Molly's pulse. He nodded to the man at the foot of the bed, a slender dark man in police uniform, Inspector Weston of the St. Honoré Police Force.

'A bare statement—no more,' the doctor said.

The other nodded.

'Now, Mrs. Kendal—just tell us how you came to find this girl.'

For a moment or two it was as though the figure on the bed had not heard. Then she spoke in a faint, far-away voice.

'In the bushes—white. . . .'

'You saw something white—and you looked to see what it was? Is that it?'

'Yes—white—lying there—I tried—tried to lift—she—it—blood—blood all over my hands.'

She began to tremble.

Dr. Graham shook his head at them. Robertson whispered—'She can't stand much more.'

'What were you doing on the beach path, Mrs. Kendal?'

'Warm—nice—by the sea——'

'You knew who the girl was?'

'Victoria—nice—nice girl—laughs—she used to laugh—oh! and now she won't—— She won't ever laugh again. I'll never forget it—I'll never forget it——' Her voice rose hysterically.

'Molly—don't.' It was Tim.

'Quiet—Quiet—.' Dr. Robertson spoke with a soothing authority—'Just relax—relax—— Now just a small prick——'

He withdrew the hypodermic.

'She'll be in no fit condition to be questioned for at least twenty-four hours,' he said—'I'll let you know when.'

2

The big handsome negro looked from one to the other of the men sitting at the table.

'Ah declare to God,' he said. 'That's all I know. I don't know nothing but what Ah've told you.'

The perspiration stood out on his forehead. Daventry sighed. The man presiding at the table, Inspector Weston of the St. Honoré C.I.D., made a gesture of dismissal. Big Jim Ellis shuffled out of the room.

'It's not all he knows, of course,' Weston said. He had the soft Island voice. 'But it's all we shall learn from him.'

'You think he's in the clear himself?' asked Daventry.

'Yes. They seem to have been on good terms together.'

'They weren't married?'

A faint smile appeared on Lieutenant Weston's lips. 'No,' he said, 'they weren't married. We don't have so many marriages on the Island. They christen the children, though. He's had two children by Victoria.'

'Do you think he was in it, whatever it was, with her?'

'Probably not. I think he'd have been nervous of anything of that kind. And I'd say, too, that what she did know wasn't very much.'

'But enough for blackmail?'

'I don't know that I'd even call it that. I doubt if the girl would even understand that word. Payment for being discreet isn't thought of as blackmail. You see, some of the people who stay here are the rich playboy lot and their morals won't bear much investigation.' His voice was slightly scathing.

'We get all kinds, I agree,' said Daventry. 'A woman, maybe, doesn't want it known that she's sleeping around, so she gives a present to the girl who waits on her. It's tacitly understood that the payment's for discretion.'

'Exactly.'

'But this,' objected Daventry, 'wasn't anything of *that* kind. It was murder.'

'I should doubt, though, if the girl knew it was serious. She saw something, some puzzling incident, something to do presumably with this bottle of pills. It belonged to Mr. Dyson, I understand. We'd better see him next.'

Gregory came in with his usual hearty air.

'Here I am,' he said, 'what can I do to help? Too bad about this girl. She was a nice girl. We both liked her. I suppose it was some sort of quarrel or other with a man, but she seemed quite happy and no signs of being in trouble about anything. I was kidding her only last night.'

'I believe you take a preparation, Mr. Dyson, called Serenite?'

'Quite right. Little pink tablets.'

'You have them on prescription from a physician?'

'Yes. I can show it to you if you like. Suffer a bit from high blood pressure, like so many people do nowadays.'

'Very few people seem to be aware of that fact.'

'Well, I don't go talking about it. I—well, I've always been well and hearty and I never like people who talk about their ailments all the time.'

'How many of the pills do you take?'

'Two, three times a day.'

'Do you have a fairly large stock with you?'

'Yes. I've got about half a dozen bottles. But they're locked up, you know, in a suitcase. I only keep out one, the one that's in current use.'

'And you missed this bottle a short time ago, so I hear?'

'Quite right.'

'And you asked this girl, Victoria Johnson, whether she'd seen it?'

'Yes, I did.'

'And what did she say?'

'She said the last time she'd seen it was on the shelf in our bathroom. She said she'd look around.'

'And after that?'

'She came and returned the bottle to me some time later. She said was this the bottle that was missing?'

'And you said?'

'I said "that's it, all right, where did you find it?" And she said it was in old Major Palgrave's room. I said "how on earth did it get there?"'

'And what did she answer to that?'

'She said she didn't know, but——' he hesitated.

'Yes, Mr. Dyson?'

'Well, she gave me the feeling that she did know a little more than she was saying, but I didn't pay much attention. After all, it wasn't very important. As I say, I've got other bottles of the pills with me. I thought perhaps I'd left it around in the restaurant or somewhere and old Palgrave picked it up for some reason. Perhaps he put it in his pocket meaning to return it to me, then forgot.'

'And that's all you know about it, Mr. Dyson?'

'That's all I know. Sorry to be so unhelpful. Is it important? Why?'

Weston shrugged his shoulders. 'As things are, anything may be important.'

'I don't see where pills come in. I thought you'd want to know about what my movements were when this wretched girl was stabbed. I've written them all down as carefully as I can.'

Weston looked at him thoughtfully.

'Indeed? That was very helpful of you, Mr. Dyson.'

'Save everybody trouble, I thought,' said Greg. He shoved a piece of paper across the table.

Weston studied it and Daventry drew his chair a little closer and looked over his shoulder.

'That seems very clear,' said Weston, after a moment or two. 'You and your wife were together changing for dinner in your bungalow until ten minutes to nine. You then went along to the terrace where you had drinks with Señora de Caspearo. At quarter past nine Colonel and Mrs. Hillingdon joined you and you went in to dine. As far as you can remember, you went off to bed at about half past eleven.'

'Of course,' said Greg. 'I don't know what time the girl was actually killed——?'

There was a faint semblance of a question in the words. Lieutenant Weston, however, did not appear to notice it.

'Mrs. Kendal found her, I understand? Must have been a very nasty shock for her.'

'Yes. Dr. Robertson had to give her a sedative.'

'This was quite late, wasn't it, when most people had trundled off to bed?'

'Yes.'

'Had she been dead long? When Mrs. Kendal found her, I mean?'

'We're not quite certain of the exact time yet,' said Weston smoothly.

'Poor little Molly. It must have been a nasty shock for her. Matter of fact, I didn't notice *her* about last night. Thought she might have had a headache or something and was lying down.'

'When was the last time you *did* see Mrs. Kendal?'

'Oh, quite early, before I went to change. She was playing about with some of the table decorations and things. Rearranging the knives.'

'I see.'

'She was quite cheerful then,' said Greg. 'Kidding and all that. She's a great girl. We're all very fond of her. Tim's a lucky fellow.'

'Well, thank you, Mr. Dyson. You can't remember anything more than you've told us about what the girl Victoria said when she returned the tablets?'

'No . . . It was just as I say. Asked me were these the tablets I'd been asking for. Said she'd found them in old Palgrave's room.'

'She'd no idea who put them there?'

'Don't think so—can't remember, really.'

'Thank you, Mr. Dyson.'

Gregory went out.

'Very thoughtful of him,' said Weston, gently tapping the paper with his fingernail, 'to be so anxious to want us to know for sure exactly where he was last night.'

'A little over-anxious do you think?' asked Daventry.

'That's very difficult to tell. There are people, you know, who are naturally nervous about their own safety, about being mixed up with anything. It isn't necessarily because they have any guilty knowledge. On the other hand it might be just that.'

'What about opportunity? Nobody's really got much of an alibi, what with the band and the dancing and the coming and going. People are getting up, leaving their tables, coming back. Women go to powder their noses. Men take a stroll. Dyson could have slipped away. Anybody could have slipped away. But he does seem rather anxious to prove that *he* didn't.' He looked thoughtfully down at the paper. 'So Mrs. Kendal was rearranging knives on the table,' he said. 'I rather wonder if he dragged that in on purpose.'

'Did it sound like it to you?'

The other considered. 'I think it's possible.'

Outside the room where the two men were sitting, a noise had arisen. A high voice was demanding admittance shrilly.

'I've got something to tell. I've got something to tell. You take me in to where the gentlemen are. You take me in to where the policeman is.'

A uniformed policeman pushed open the door.

'It's one of the cooks here,' he said, 'very anxious to see you. Says he's got something you ought to know.'

A frightened dark man in a cook's cap pushed past him and came into the room. It was one of the minor cooks. A Cuban, not a native of St. Honoré.

'I tell you something. I tell you,' he said. 'She come through my kitchen, she did, and she had a knife with her. A knife, I tell you. She had a knife in her hand. She come through my kitchen and out the door. Out into the garden. I saw her.'

'Now calm down,' said Daventry, 'calm down. Who are you talking about?'

'I tell you who I'm talking about. I'm talking about the boss's wife. Mrs. Kendal. I'm talking about her. She have a knife in her hand and she go out into the dark. Before dinner that was—and *she didn't come back.*'

15. *Inquiry continued*

'CAN WE HAVE a word with you, Mr. Kendal?'

'Of course.' Tim looked up from his desk. He pushed some papers aside and indicated chairs. His face was drawn and miserable. 'How are you getting on? Got any forwarder? There seems to be a doom in this place. People are wanting to leave, you know, asking about air passages. Just when it seemed everything was being a success. Oh lord, you don't know what it means, this place, to me and to Molly. We staked everything on it.'

'It's very hard on you, I know,' said Inspector Weston. 'Don't think that we don't sympathise.'

'If it all could be cleared up quickly,' said Tim. 'This wretched girl Victoria—Oh! I oughtn't to talk about her like that. She was quite a good sort, Victoria was. But—but there must be some quite simple reason, some—kind of intrigue, or love affair she had. Perhaps her husband——'

'Jim Ellis wasn't her husband, and they seemed a settled sort of couple.'

'If it could only be cleared up *quickly*,' said Tim again. 'I'm sorry. You wanted to talk to me about something, ask me something.'

'Yes. It was about last night. According to medical evidence Victoria was killed some time between 10.30 p.m. and midnight. Alibis under the circumstances that prevail here, are not very easy to prove. People are moving about, dancing, walking away from the terrace, coming back. It's all very difficult.'

'I suppose so. But does that mean that you definitely consider Victoria was killed by one of the guests here?'

'Well, we have to examine that possibility, Mr. Kendal. What I want to ask you particularly about, is a statement made by one of your cooks.'

'Oh? Which one? What does he say?'

'He's a Cuban, I understand.'

'We've got two Cubans and a Puerto Rican.'

'This man Enrico states that your wife passed through the kitchen on her way from the dining-room, and went out into the garden and that she was carrying a knife.'

Tim stared at him.

'Molly, carrying a knife? Well, why shouldn't she? I mean—why—you don't think—what are you trying to suggest?'

'I am talking of the time before people had come into the dining-room. It would be, I suppose, some time about 8.30. You yourself were in the dining-room talking to the head waiter, Fernando, I believe.'

'Yes.' Tim cast his mind back. 'Yes, I remember.'

'And your wife came in from the terrace?'

'Yes, she did,' Tim agreed. 'She always went out to look over the tables. Sometimes the boys set things wrong, forgot some of the cutlery, things like that. Very likely that's what it was. She may have been rearranging cutlery or something. She might have had a spare knife or a spoon, something like that in her hand.'

'And she came from the terrace into the dining-room. Did she speak to you?'

'Yes, we had a word or two together.'

'What did she say? Can you remember?'

'I think I asked her who she'd been talking to. I heard her voice out there.'

'And who did she say she'd been talking to?'

'Gregory Dyson.'

'Ah. Yes. That is what *he* said.'

Tim went on, 'He'd been making a pass at her, I understand. He was a bit given to that kind of thing. It annoyed me and I said "Blast him" and Molly laughed and said she could do all the blasting that needed to be done. Molly's a very clever girl that way. It's not always an easy position, you know. You can't offend guests, and so an attractive girl like Molly has to pass things off with a laugh and a shrug. Gregory Dyson finds it difficult to keep his hands off any good-looking woman.'

'Had there been any altercation between them?'

'No, I don't think so. I think, as I say, she just laughed it off as usual.'

'You can't say definitely whether she had a knife in her hand or not?'

'I can't remember—I'm almost sure she didn't—In fact quite sure she didn't.'

'But you said just now . . .'

'Look here, what I meant was that if she was in the dining-room or in the kitchen it's quite likely she might have picked up a knife or had one in her hand. Matter of fact I can remember quite well, she came in from the dining-room and she had *nothing* in her hand. *Nothing at all*. That's definite.'

'I see,' said Weston.

Tim looked at him uneasily.

'What on earth is this you're getting at? What did that damn' fool Enrico—Manuel—whichever it was—say?'

'He said your wife came out into the kitchen, that she looked upset, that she had a knife in her hand.'

'He's just dramatising.'

'Did you have any further conversation with your wife during dinner or after?'

'No, I don't think I did really. Matter of fact I was rather busy.'

'Was your wife there in the dining-room during the meal?'

'I—oh—yes, we always move about among the guests and things like that. See how things are going on.'

'Did you speak to her at all?'

'No, I don't think I did . . . We're usually fairly busy. We don't always notice what the other one's doing and we certainly haven't got time to talk to each other.'

'Actually you don't remember speaking to her until she came up the steps three hours later, after finding the body?'

'It was an awful shock for her. It upset her terribly.'

'I know. A very unpleasant experience. How did she come to be walking along the beach path?'

'After the stress of dinner being served, she often does go for a turn. You know, get away from the guests for a minute or two, get a breather.'

'When she came back, I understand you were talking to Mrs. Hillingdon.'

'Yes. Practically everyone else had gone to bed.'

'What was the subject of your conversation with Mrs. Hillingdon?'

'Nothing particular. Why? What's she been saying?'

'So far she hasn't said anything. We haven't asked her.'

'We were just talking of this and that. Molly, and hotel running, and one thing and another.'

'And then—your wife came up the steps of the terrace and told you what had happened?'

'Yes.'

'There was blood on her hands?'

'Of course there was! She'd bent over the girl, tried to lift her, couldn't understand what had happened, what was the matter with her. Of course there was blood on her hands! Look here, what the hell are you suggesting? You *are* suggesting something?'

'Please calm down,' said Daventry. 'It's all a great strain on you I know, Tim, but we have to get the facts clear. I understand your wife hasn't been feeling very well lately?'

'Nonsense—she's all right. Major Palgrave's death upset her a bit. Naturally. She's a sensitive girl.'

'We shall have to ask her a few questions as soon as she's fit enough,' said Weston.

'Well, you can't now. The doctor gave her a sedative and said she wasn't to be disturbed. I won't have her upset and brow-beaten, d'you hear?'

'We're not going to do any brow-beating,' said Weston. 'We've just got to get the facts clear. We won't disturb her at present, but as soon as the doctor allows us, we'll have to see her.' His voice was gentle—inflexible.

Tim looked at him, opened his mouth, but said nothing.

2

Evelyn Hillingdon, calm and composed as usual, sat down in the chair indicated. She considered the few questions asked her, taking her time over it. Her dark, intelligent eyes looked at Weston thoughtfully.

'Yes,' she said, 'I was talking to Mr. Kendal on the terrace when his wife came up the steps and told us about the murder.'

'Your husband wasn't there?'

'No, he had gone to bed.'

'Had you any special reason for your conversation with Mr. Kendal?'

Evelyn raised her finely pencilled eyebrows—— It was a definite rebuke.

She said coldly:

'What a very odd question. No—there was nothing special about our conversation.'

'Did you discuss the matter of his wife's health?'

Again Evelyn took her time.

'I really can't remember,' she said at last.

'Are you sure of that?'

'Sure that I can't remember? What a curious way of putting it—one talks about so many things at different times.'

'Mrs. Kendal has not been in good health lately, I understand.'

'She looked quite all right—a little tired perhaps. Of course running a place like this means a lot of worries, and she is quite inexperienced. Naturally, she gets flustered now and then.'

'Flustered.' Weston repeated the word. 'That was the way you would describe it?'

'It's an old-fashioned word, perhaps, but just as good as the modern jargon we use for everything—A "virus infection" for a bilious attack—an "anxiety neurosis" for the minor bothers of daily life——'

Her smile made Weston feel slightly ridiculous. He thought to himself that Evelyn Hillingdon was a clever woman. He looked at Daventry whose face remained unmoved and wondered what he thought.

'Thank you, Mrs. Hillingdon,' said Weston.

3

'We don't want to worry you, Mrs. Kendal, but we have to have your account of just how you came to find this girl. Dr. Graham says you are sufficiently recovered to talk about it now.'

'Oh yes,' said Molly, 'I'm really quite all right again.' She gave them a small nervous smile. 'It was just the shock—— It *was* rather awful, you know.'

'Yes, indeed it must have been—I understand you went for a walk after dinner.'

'Yes—I—often do.'

Her eyes shifted, Daventry noticed, and the fingers of her hands twined and untwined about each other.

'What time would that have been, Mrs. Kendal?' asked Weston.

'Well, I don't really know—we don't go much by the time.'

'The steel band was still playing?'

'Yes—at least—I think so—I can't really remember.'

'And you walked—which way?'

'Oh, along the beach path.'

'To the left or the right?'

'Oh! First one way—and then the other—I—I—really didn't notice.'

'Why didn't you notice, Mrs. Kendal?'

She frowned.

'I suppose I was—well—thinking of things.'

'Thinking of anything particular?'

'No—No—Nothing particular—— Just things that had to be done—seen to—in the hotel.' Again that nervous twining and untwining of fingers. 'And then—I noticed something white—in a clump of hibiscus bushes—and I wondered what it was. I stopped and—and pulled——' She swallowed convulsively. 'And it was her—Victoria—all huddled up—and I tried to raise her head up and I got—blood—on my hands.'

She looked at them and repeated wonderingly as though recalling something impossible:

'Blood—on my hands.'

'Yes—Yes—— A very dreadful experience. There is no need for you to tell us more about that part of it—— How long had you been walking, do you think, when you found her——?'

'I don't know—I have no idea.'

'An hour? Half an hour? Or more than an hour——'

'I don't know,' Molly repeated.

Daventry asked in a quiet everyday voice:

'Did you take a knife with you on your—walk?'

'A knife?' Molly sounded surprised. 'Why should I take a knife?'

'I only ask because one of the kitchen staff mentioned that you had a knife in your hand when you went out of the kitchen into the garden.'

Molly frowned.

'But I didn't go out of the kitchen—oh you mean earlier—before dinner—I—I don't *think* so——'

'You had been rearranging the cutlery on the tables, perhaps.'

'I have to, sometimes. They lay things wrong—not enough

knives—or too many. The wrong number of forks and spoons—that sort of thing.'

'And did that happen on this particular evening?'

'It may have done—something like that—— It's really automatic. One doesn't think, or remember——'

'So you may have gone out of the kitchen that evening carrying a knife in your hand?'

'I don't think I did—I'm sure I didn't—' She added— 'Tim was there—he would know. Ask him.'

'Did you like this girl—Victoria—was she good at her work?' asked Weston.

'Yes—she was a very nice girl.'

'You had had no dispute with her?'

'Dispute? No.'

'She had never threatened you—in any way?'

'Threatened me? What do you mean?'

'It doesn't matter—— You have no idea of who could have killed her? No idea at all?'

'None.' She spoke positively.

'Well, thank you, Mrs. Kendal.' He smiled. 'It wasn't so terrible, was it?'

'That's all?'

'That's all for now.'

Daventry got up, opened the door for her, and watched her go out.

'Tim would know,' he quoted as he returned to his chair. 'And Tim says definitely that she *didn't* have a knife.'

Weston said gravely:

'I think that that is what any husband would feel called upon to say.'

'A table knife seems a very poor type of knife to use for murder.'

'But it was a *steak* knife, Mr. Daventry. Steaks were on the menu that evening. Steak knives are kept sharp.'

'I really can't bring myself to believe that that girl we've just been talking to is a red-handed murderess, Weston.'

'It is not necessary to believe it yet. It could be that Mrs. Kendal went out into the garden before dinner, clasping a knife she had taken off one of the tables because it was superfluous—she might not even have noticed she was holding it, and she could have put it down somewhere—or dropped it—— It could have been found and used by someone else—— I, too, think her an unlikely murderess.'

'All the same,' said Daventry thoughtfully, 'I'm pretty sure she is not telling all she knows. Her vagueness over time is odd—where was she—what was she doing out there? Nobody, so far, seems to have noticed her in the dining-room that evening.'

'The husband was about as usual—but not the wife——'

'You think she went to meet someone—Victoria Johnson?'

'Perhaps—or perhaps she saw whoever it was who did go to meet Victoria.'

'You're thinking of Gregory Dyson?'

'We know he was talking to Victoria earlier—— He may have arranged to meet her again later—everyone moved around freely on the terrace, remember—dancing, drinking—in and out of the bar.'

'No alibi like a steel band,' said Daventry wryly.

16. *Miss Marple seeks assistance*

IF ANYBODY had been there to observe the gentle-looking elderly lady who stood meditatively on the loggia outside her bungalow, they would have thought she had nothing more on her mind than deliberation on how to arrange her time that day—— An expedition, perhaps, to Castle Cliff—a visit to Jamestown—a nice drive and lunch at Pelican Point—or just a quiet morning on the beach——

But the gentle old lady was deliberating quite other matters—she was in militant mood.

'*Something has got to be done*,' said Miss Marple to herself.

Moreover, she was convinced that there was no time to be lost—There was urgency.

But who was there that she could convince of that fact? Given time, she thought she could find out the truth by herself.

She had found out a good deal. But not enough—not nearly enough. And time was short.

She realised, bitterly, that here on this Paradise of an island, she had none of her usual allies.

She thought regretfully of her friends in England—Sir Henry Clithering—always willing to listen indulgently—his godson Dermot, who in spite of his increased status at Scotland Yard, was still ready to believe that when Miss Marple voiced an opinion there was usually something behind it.

But would that soft-voiced native police officer pay any attention to an old lady's urgency? Dr. Graham? But Dr. Graham was not what she needed—too gentle and hesitant, certainly not a man of quick decisions and rapid actions.

Miss Marple, feeling rather like a humble deputy of the Almighty, almost cried aloud her need in Biblical phrasing.

Who will go for me?

Whom shall I send?

The sound that reached her ears a moment later was not instantly recognised by her as an answer to prayer—far from it——At the back of her mind it registered only as a man possibly calling his dog.

'Hi!'

Miss Marple, lost in perplexity, paid no attention.

'Hi!' The volume thus increased, Miss Marple looked vaguely round.

'HI!' called Mr. Rafiel impatiently. He added—'You—there——'

Miss Marple had not at first realised that Mr. Rafiel's 'Hi You' was addressed to her. It was not a method that anyone had ever used before to summon her. It was certainly not a gentlemanly mode of address. Miss Marple did not resent it, because people seldom did resent Mr. Rafiel's somewhat arbitrary method of doing things. He was a law unto himself and people accepted him as such. Miss Marple looked across the intervening space between her bungalow and his. Mr. Rafiel was sitting outside on his loggia and he beckoned her.

'You were calling me?' she asked.

'Of course I was calling you,' said Mr. Rafiel. 'Who did you think I was calling—a cat? Come over here.'

Miss Marple looked round for her handbag, picked it up, and crossed the intervening space.

'I can't come to you unless someone helps me,' explained Mr. Rafiel, 'so you've got to come to me.'

'Oh yes,' said Miss Marple, 'I quite understand *that*.'

Mr. Rafiel pointed to an adjacent chair. 'Sit down,' he said, 'I want to talk to you. Something damned odd is going on in this island.'

'Yes, indeed,' agreed Miss Marple, taking the chair as indicated. By sheer habit she drew her knitting out of her bag.

'Don't start knitting again,' said Mr. Rafiel, 'I can't stand it. I hate women knitting. It irritates me.'

Miss Marple returned her knitting to her bag. She did this with no undue air of meekness, rather with the air of one who makes allowances for a fractious patient.

'There's a lot of chit-chat going on,' said Mr. Rafiel, 'and I bet you're in the forefront of it. You and the parson and his sister.'

'It is, perhaps, only natural that there should be chit-chat,' said Miss Marple with spirit, 'given the circumstances.'

'This Island girl gets herself knifed. Found in the bushes. *Might* be ordinary enough. That chap she was living with might have got jealous of another man—or he's got himself another girl and she got jealous and they had a row. Sex in the tropics. That sort of stuff. What do you say?'

'No,' said Miss Marple, shaking her head.

'The authorities don't think so, either.'

'They would say more to you,' pointed out Miss Marple, 'than they would say to me.'

'All the same, I bet you know more about it than I do. You've listened to the tittle-tattle.'

'Certainly I have,' said Miss Marple.

'Nothing much else to do, have you, except listen to tittle-tattle?'

'It is often informative and useful.'

'D'you know,' said Mr. Rafiel, studying her attentively, 'I made a mistake about you. I don't often make mistakes about people. There's a lot more to you than I thought there was. All these rumours about Major Palgrave and the stories he told. You think he was bumped off, don't you?'

'I very much fear so,' said Miss Marple.

'Well, he was,' said Mr. Rafiel.

Miss Marple drew a deep breath. 'That is definite, is it?' she asked.

'Yes, it's definite enough. I had it from Daventry. I'm not breaking a confidence because the facts of the autopsy will have to come out. You told Graham something, he went to Daventry, Daventry went to the Administrator, the C.I.D. were informed, and between them they agreed that things looked fishy, so they dug up old Palgrave and had a look.'

'And they found?' Miss Marple paused interrogatively.

'They found he'd had a lethal dose of something that only a doctor could pronounce properly. As far as I remember it sounds vaguely like di-flor, hexagonal-ethylcarbenzol. That's not the right name. But that's roughly what it *sounds* like. The police doctor put it that way so that nobody should know, I suppose, what it really *was*. The stuff's probably got some quite simple nice easy name like Evipan or Veronal or Easton's Syrup or something of that kind. This is its official name to baffle laymen with. Anyway, a sizeable dose of it, I gather, would produce death, and the signs would be much the same as those of high blood pressure aggravated by over indulgence in alcohol on a gay evening. In fact, it all looked perfectly natural and nobody questioned it for a moment. Just said "poor old chap" and buried him quick. Now they wonder if he ever had high blood pressure at all. Did he ever say he had to you?'

'No.'

'Exactly! And yet everyone seems to have taken it as a fact.'

'Apparently he told people he had.'

'It's like seeing ghosts,' said Mr. Rafiel. 'You never meet the chap who's seen the ghost himself. It's always the second cousin of his aunt, or a friend, or a friend of a friend. But leave that for a moment. They thought he had blood pressure, because there was a bottle of tablets controlling blood pressure found in his room but—and now we're coming to the point—I gather that this girl who was killed went about saying that that bottle was put there by somebody else, and that *actually* it belonged to that fellow Greg.'

'Mr. Dyson *has* got blood pressure. His wife mentioned it,' said Miss Marple.

'So it was put in Palgrave's room to suggest that he suffered from blood pressure and to make his death seem natural.'

'Exactly,' said Miss Marple. 'And the story was put about, very cleverly, that he had frequently mentioned to people that he had high blood pressure. But you know, it's very easy to put about a story. Very easy. I've seen a lot of it in my time.'

'I bet you have,' said Mr. Rafiel.

'It only needs a murmur here and there,' said Miss Marple. 'You don't say it of your own knowledge, you just say that Mrs. B. told you that Colonel C. told her. It's always at second hand or third hand or fourth hand and it's very difficult to find out who was the original whisperer. Oh yes, it can be done. And the people you say it to go on and repeat it to others as if they know it of their own knowledge.'

'Somebody's been clever,' said Mr. Rafiel thoughtfully.

'Yes,' said Miss Marple, 'I think somebody's been quite clever.'

'This girl saw something, or knew something and tried blackmail, I suppose,' said Mr. Rafiel.

'She mayn't have thought of it as blackmail,' said Miss Marple. 'In these large hotels, there are often things the maids know that some people would rather not have repeated. And so they hand out a larger tip or a little present of money. The girl possibly didn't realise at first the importance of what she knew.'

'Still, she got a knife in her back all right,' said Mr. Rafiel brutally.

'Yes. Evidently someone couldn't afford to let her talk.'

'Well? Let's hear what you think about it all.'

Miss Marple looked at him thoughtfully.

'Why should you think I know any more than you do, Mr. Rafiel?'

'Probably you don't,' said Mr. Rafiel, 'but I'm interested to hear your ideas about what you do know.'

'But why?'

'There's not very much to do out here,' said Mr. Rafiel, 'except make money.'

Miss Marple looked slightly surprised.

'Make money? Out here?'

'You can send out half a dozen cables in code every day if you like,' said Mr. Rafiel. 'That's how I amuse myself.'

'Take-over bids?' Miss Marple asked doubtfully, in the tone of one who speaks a foreign language.

'That kind of thing,' agreed Mr. Rafiel. 'Pitting your wits against other people's wits. The trouble is it doesn't occupy enough time, so I've got interested in this business. It's aroused my curiosity. Palgrave spent a good deal of his time talking to you. Nobody else would be bothered with him, I expect. What did he say?'

'He told me a good many stories,' said Miss Marple.

'I know he did. Damn' boring, most of them. And you hadn't only got to hear them once. If you got anywhere within range you heard them three or four times over.'

'I know,' said Miss Marple. 'I'm afraid that does happen when gentlemen get older.'

Mr. Rafiel looked at her very sharply.

'I don't tell stories,' he said. 'Go on. It started with one of Palgrave's stories, did it?'

'He said he knew a murderer,' said Miss Marple. 'There's nothing really special about that,' she added in her gentle voice, 'because I suppose it happens to nearly everybody.'

'I don't follow you,' said Mr. Rafiel.

'I don't mean specifically,' said Miss Marple, 'but surely, Mr. Rafiel, if you cast over in your mind your recollections of various events in your life, hasn't there nearly always been an occasion when somebody has made some careless reference such as "Oh yes I knew the So-and-So's quite well—he died very suddenly and they always say his wife did him in, but I daresay that's just gossip". You've heard people say something like that, haven't you?'

'Well, I suppose so—yes, something of the kind. But not—well, not seriously.'

'Exactly,' said Miss Marple, 'but Major Palgrave was a very serious man. I think he enjoyed telling this story. He said he had a snapshot of the murderer. He was going to show it to me but—actually—he didn't.'

'Why?'

'Because he saw something,' said Miss Marple. 'Saw someone, I suspect. His face got very red and he shoved back the snapshot into his wallet and began talking on another subject.'

'Who did he see?'

'I've thought about that a good deal,' said Miss Marple. 'I was sitting outside my bungalow, and he was sitting nearly opposite me and—whatever he saw, he saw over my right shoulder.'

'Someone coming along the path then from behind you on the right, the path from the creek and the car park——'

'Yes.'

'*Was* anyone coming along the path?'

'Mr. and Mrs. Dyson and Colonel and Mrs. Hillingdon.'

'Anybody else?'

'Not that I can find out. Of course, your bungalow would also be in his line of vision. . . .'

'Ah. Then we include—shall we say—Esther Walters and my chap, Jackson. Is that right? Either of them, I suppose, *might* have come out of the bungalow and gone back inside again without your seeing them.'

'They might have,' said Miss Marple, 'I didn't turn my head at once.'

'The Dysons, the Hillingdons, Esther, Jackson. One of them's a murderer. Or of course, myself,' he added; obviously as an afterthought.

Miss Marple smiled faintly.

'And he spoke of the murderer as a *man*?'

'Yes.'

'Right. That cuts out Evelyn Hillingdon, Lucky and Esther Walters. So your murderer, allowing that all this far-fetched nonsense is true, your murderer is Dyson, Hillingdon or my smooth-tongued Jackson.'

'Or yourself,' said Miss Marple.

Mr. Rafiel ignored this last point.

'Don't say things to irritate me,' he said. 'I'll tell you the first thing that strikes me, and which you don't seem to have thought of. *If* it's one of those three, why the devil didn't old Palgrave recognise him before? Dash it all, they've all been sitting round looking at each other for the last two weeks. That doesn't seem to make sense.'

'I think it could,' said Miss Marple.

'Well, tell me how.'

'You see, in Major Palgrave's story he hadn't seen this man *himself* at any time. It was a story told to him by a doctor. The doctor gave him the snapshot as a curiosity. Major Palgrave may have looked at the snapshot fairly closely at the time but after that he'd just stack it away in his wallet and keep it as a souvenir. Occasionally, perhaps, he'd take it out and show it to someone he was telling the story to. And another thing, Mr. Rafiel, we don't know how long ago this happened. He didn't give me any indication of that when he was telling the story. I mean this may have been a story he's been telling to people for *years*. Five years—ten years—longer still perhaps. Some of his tiger stories go back about twenty years.'

'They would!' said Mr. Rafiel.

'So I don't suppose for a moment that Major Palgrave would recognise the face in the snapshot if he came across the man casually. What I think happened, what I'm almost sure *must* have happened, is that as he told his story he fumbled for the snapshot, took it out, looked down at it studying the face and then looked up to see *the same face*, or one with a strong resemblance coming towards him from a distance of about ten or twelve feet away.'

'Yes,' said Mr. Rafiel consideringly, 'Yes, that's possible.'

'He was taken aback,' said Miss Marple, 'and he shoved it back in his wallet and began to talk loudly about something else.'

'He couldn't have been sure,' said Mr. Rafiel, shrewdly.

'No,' said Miss Marple, 'he couldn't have been sure. But of course afterwards he would have studied the snapshot very carefully and would have looked at the man and tried to make up his mind whether it was just a likeness or whether it could actually be the same person.'

Mr. Rafiel reflected a moment or two, then he shook his head.

'There's something wrong here. The motive's inadequate. Absolutely inadequate. He was speaking to you loudly, was he?'

'Yes,' said Miss Marple, 'quite loudly. He always did.'

'True enough. Yes, he did shout. So whoever was approaching would hear what he said?'

'I should imagine you could hear it for quite a good radius round.'

Mr. Rafiel shook his head again. He said, 'It's fantastic, too fantastic. Anybody would laugh at such a story. Here's an old booby telling a story about another story somebody told him, and showing a snapshot, and all of it centring round a murder which had taken place years ago! Or at any rate, a year or two. How on earth can *that* worry the man in question. No evidence, just a bit of hearsay, a story at third hand. He could even admit a likeness, he could say: "Yes, I *do* look rather like that fellow, don't I! Ha, ha!" Nobody's going to take old Palgrave's identification seriously. Don't tell me so, because I won't believe it. No, the chap, if it *was* the chap, had nothing to fear—nothing whatever. It's the kind of accusation he can just laugh off. Why on earth should he proceed to murder old Palgrave? It's absolutely unnecessary. You must see that.'

'Oh I do see that,' said Miss Marple. 'I couldn't agree with you more. That's what makes me uneasy. So very uneasy that I really couldn't sleep last night.'

Mr. Rafiel stared at her. 'Let's hear what's on your mind,' he said quietly.

'I may be entirely wrong,' said Miss Marple hesitantly.

'Probably you are,' said Mr. Rafiel with his usual lack of courtesy, 'but at any rate let's hear what you've thought up in the small hours.'

'There could be a very powerful motive if——'

'If what?'

'If there was going to be—quite soon—*another murder*.'

Mr. Rafiel stared at her. He tried to pull himself up a little in his chair.

'Let's get this clear,' he said.

'I am so bad at explaining.' Miss Marple spoke rapidly and rather incoherently. A pink flush rose to her cheeks. 'Supposing there was a murder planned. If you remember, the story Major Palgrave told me concerned a man whose wife died under suspicious circumstances.

Then, after a certain lapse of time, there was another murder under exactly the same circumstances. A man of a different name had a wife who died in much the same way and the doctor who was telling it recognised him as the same man, although he'd changed his name. Well, it does look, doesn't it, as though this murderer might be the kind of murderer who made a habit of the thing?'

'You mean like Smith, *Brides in the Bath*, that kind of thing. Yes.'

'As far as I can make out,' said Miss Marple, 'and from what I have heard and read, a man who does a wicked thing like this and gets away with it the first time, is, alas, *encouraged*. He thinks it's easy, he thinks he's clever. And so he repeats it. And in the end, as you say, like Smith and the Brides in the Bath, it becomes a *habit*. Each time in a different place and each time the man changes his name. But the crimes themselves are all very much alike. So it seems to me, although I may be quite wrong——'

'But you don't think you are wrong, do you?' Mr. Rafiel put in shrewdly.

Miss Marple went on without answering. '—that if that *were* so and if this—this person had got things all lined up for a murder out here, for getting rid of *another* wife, say, and if this is crime three or four, well then, the Major's story *would* matter because the murderer couldn't afford to have any similarity pointed out. If you remember, that was exactly the way Smith got caught. The circumstances of a crime attracted the attention of somebody who compared it with a newspaper clipping of some other case. So you do see, don't you, that if this wicked person has got a crime planned, arranged, and shortly about to take place, he couldn't afford to let Major Palgrave go about telling this story and showing that snapshot.'

She stopped and looked appealingly at Mr. Rafiel.

'So you see he had to do something very quickly, as quickly as possible.'

Mr. Rafiel spoke, 'In fact, that very same night, eh?'

'Yes,' said Miss Marple.

'Quick work,' said Mr. Rafiel, 'but it could be done. Put the tablets in old Palgrave's room, spread the blood pressure rumour about and add a little of our fourteen syllable drug to a Planters Punch. Is that it?'

'Yes— But that's all over—we needn't worry about it. It's the *future*. It's now. With Major Palgrave out of the way and the snapshot destroyed, *this man will go on with his murder as planned*.'

Mr. Rafiel whistled.

'You've got it all worked out, haven't you?'

Miss Marple nodded. She said in a most unaccustomed voice, firm and almost dictatorial, 'And we've got to stop it. *You've* got to stop it, Mr. Rafiel.'

'Me?' said Mr. Rafiel, astonished, 'why me?'

'Because you're rich and important,' said Miss Marple, simply. 'People will take notice of what you say or suggest. They wouldn't listen to me for a moment. They would say that I was an old lady imagining things.'

'They might at that,' said Mr. Rafiel. 'More fools if they did. I must say, though, that nobody would think you had any brains in your head to hear your usual line of talk. Actually, you've got a logical mind. Very few women have.' He shifted himself uncomfortably in his chair. 'Where the hell's Esther or Jackson?' he said. 'I need resettling. No, it's no good your doing it. You're not strong enough. I don't know what they mean, leaving me alone like this.'

'I'll go and find them.'

'No, you won't. You'll stay here—and thrash this out. Which of them is it? The egregious Greg? The quiet Edward Hillingdon or my fellow Jackson? It's got to be one of the three, hasn't it?'

17. *Mr. Rafiel takes charge*

'I DON'T KNOW,' said Miss Marple.

'What do you mean? What have we been talking about for the last twenty minutes?'

'It has occurred to me that I may have been wrong.'

Mr. Rafiel stared at her.

'Scatty after all!' he said disgustedly. 'And you sounded so sure of yourself.'

'Oh, I am sure—about the *murder*. It's the *murderer* I'm not sure about. You see I've found out that Major Palgrave had more than one murder story—you told me yourself he'd told you one about a kind of Lucrezia Borgia——'

'So he did—at that. But that was quite a different kind of story.'

'I know. And Mrs. Walters said he had one about someone being gassed in a gas oven——'

'But the story he told you——'

Miss Marple allowed herself to interrupt—a thing that did not often happen to Mr. Rafiel.

She spoke with desperate earnestness and only moderate incoherence.

'Don't you see—it's so difficult to be *sure*. The whole point is that—so often—one doesn't *listen*. Ask Mrs. Walters—she said the same thing—you listen to begin with—and then your attention flags—your mind wanders—and suddenly you find you've missed a bit. I just wonder if possibly there may have been a gap—a very small one—between the story he was telling me—about a *man*—and the moment when he was getting out his wallet and saying—"Like to see a picture of a murderer".'

'But you thought it was a picture of the man he had been talking about?'

'I thought so—yes. It never occurred to me that it mightn't have been. But now—how can I be *sure*?'

Mr. Rafiel looked at her very thoughtfully. . . .

'The trouble with you is,' he said, 'that you're too conscientious. Great mistake— Make up your mind and don't shilly shally. You didn't shilly shally to begin with. If you ask me, in all this chit-chat you've been having with the parson's sister and the rest of them, you've got hold of something that's unsettled you.'

'Perhaps you're right.'

'Well, cut it out for the moment. Let's go ahead with what you had to begin with. Because, nine times out of ten, one's original judgments are right—or so I've found. We've got three suspects. Let's take 'em out and have a good look at them. Any preference?'

'I really haven't,' said Miss Marple, 'all three of them seem so very unlikely.'

'We'll take Greg first,' said Mr. Rafiel. 'Can't stand the fellow. Doesn't make him a murderer, though. Still, there *are* one or two points against him. Those blood pressure tablets belonged to him. Nice and handy to make use of.'

'That would be a little obvious, wouldn't it?' Miss Marple objected.

'I don't know that it would,' said Mr. Rafiel. 'After all, the main thing was to do something *quickly*, and he'd got the tablets. Hadn't much time to go looking round for tablets that somebody else might have. Let's say it's Greg. All right. *If* he wanted to put his dear wife Lucky out of the way—(Good job, too, I'd say. In fact I'm in sympathy with him) I can't actually see his motive. From all accounts he's rich. Inherited money from his first wife who had pots of it. He qualifies on that as a possible wife murderer all right. But that's over and done with. He got away with it. But Lucky was his first wife's poor relation. No money there, so if he wants to put *her* out of the way it must be in order to marry somebody else. Any gossip going around about that?'

Miss Marple shook her head.

'Not that I have heard. He—er—has a very gallant manner with *all* the ladies.'

'Well, that's a nice, old-fashioned way of putting it,' said Mr. Rafiel. 'All right, he's a stoat. He makes passes. Not enough! We want more than that. Let's go on to Edward Hillingdon. Now there's a dark horse, if ever there was one.'

'He is not, I think, a happy man,' offered Miss Marple.

Mr. Rafiel looked at her thoughtfully.

'Do you think a murderer ought to be a happy man?'

Miss Marple coughed.

'Well, they usually have been in my experience.'

'I don't suppose your experience has gone very far,' said Mr. Rafiel.

In this assumption, as Miss Marple could have told him, he was wrong. But she forbore to contest his statement. Gentlemen, she knew, did not like to be put right in their facts.

'I rather fancy Hillingdon myself,' said Mr. Rafiel. 'I've an idea that there is something a bit odd going on between him and his wife. You noticed it at all?'

'Oh yes,' said Miss Marple, 'I have noticed it. Their behaviour is perfect in public, of course, but that one would expect.'

'You probably know more about those sort of people than I would,' said Mr. Rafiel. 'Very well, then, everything is in perfectly good taste but it's a probability that, in a gentlemanly way, Edward Hillingdon is contemplating doing away with Evelyn Hillingdon. Do you agree?'

'If so,' said Miss Marple, 'there must be another woman.'

'But what woman?'

Miss Marple shook her head in a dissatisfied manner.

'I can't help feeling—I really can't—that it's not all quite as simple as that.'

'Well, who shall we consider next—Jackson? We leave me out of it.'

Miss Marple smiled for the first time.

'And why do we leave you out of it, Mr. Rafiel?'

'Because if you want to discuss the possibilities of my being a murderer you'd have to do it with somebody else. Waste of time talking about it to me. And anyway, I ask you, am I cut out for the part? Helpless, hauled out of bed like a dummy, dressed, wheeled about in a chair, shuffled along for a walk. What earthly chance have *I* of going and murdering anyone?'

'Probably as good a chance as anyone else,' said Miss Marple vigorously.

'And how do you make that out?'

'Well, you would agree yourself, I think, that you have brains?'

'Of course I've got brains,' declared Mr. Rafiel. 'A good deal more than anybody else in this community, I'd say.'

'And having brains,' went on Miss Marple, 'would enable you to overcome the physical difficulties of being a murderer.'

'It would take some doing!'

'Yes,' said Miss Marple, 'it would take some doing. But then, I think, Mr. Rafiel, you would enjoy that.'

Mr. Rafiel stared at her for quite a long time and then he suddenly laughed.

'You've got a nerve!' he said. 'Not quite the gentle fluffy old lady you look, are you? So you really think I'm a murderer?'

'No,' said Miss Marple, 'I do not.'

'And why?'

'Well, really, I think just *because* you have got brains. Having brains, you can get most things you want without having recourse to murder. Murder is stupid.'

'And anyway who the devil should I want to murder?'

'That would be a very interesting question,' said Miss Marple. 'I have not yet had the pleasure of sufficient conversation with you to evolve a theory as to that.'

Mr. Rafiel's smile broadened.

'Conversations with you might be dangerous,' he said.

'Conversations are always dangerous, if you have something to hide,' said Miss Marple.

'You may be right. Let's get on to Jackson. What do you think of Jackson?'

'It is difficult for me to say. I have not had the opportunity really of *any* conversation with him.'

'So you've no views on the subject?'

'He reminds me a little,' said Miss Marple reflectively, 'of a young man in the Town Clerk's office near where I live, Jonas Parry.'

'And?' Mr. Rafiel asked and paused.

'He was not,' said Miss Marple, 'very satisfactory.'

'Jackson's not wholly satisfactory either. He suits me all right. He's first class at his job, and he doesn't mind being sworn at. He knows he's damn' well paid and so he puts up with things. I wouldn't employ him in a position of trust, but I don't have to trust him. Maybe his past is blameless, maybe it isn't. His references were all right but I discern—shall I say, a note of reserve. Fortunately, I'm not a man who has any guilty secrets, so I'm not a subject for blackmail.'

'No secrets?' said Miss Marple, thoughtfully. 'Surely, Mr. Rafiel, you have business secrets?'

'Not where Jackson can get at them. No. Jackson is a smooth article, one might say, but I really don't see him as a murderer. I'd say that wasn't his line at all.'

He paused a minute and then said suddenly, 'Do you know, if one stands back and takes a good look at all this fantastic business, Major Palgrave and his ridiculous stories and all the rest of it, the *emphasis* is entirely wrong. *I'm* the person who ought to be murdered.'

Miss Marple looked at him in some surprise.

'Proper type casting,' explained Mr. Rafiel. 'Who's the victim in murder stories? Elderly men with lots of money.'

'And lots of people with a good reason for wishing him out of the way, so as to get that money,' said Miss Marple. 'Is that true also?'

'Well——' Mr. Rafiel considered, 'I can count up to five or six men in London who wouldn't burst into tears if they read my obituary in *The Times*. But they wouldn't go so far as to do anything to bring about my demise. After all, why should they? I'm expected to die any day. In fact the bug—blighters are astonished that I've lasted so long. The doctors are surprised too.'

'You have of course, a great will to live,' said Miss Marple.

'You think that's odd, I suppose,' said Mr. Rafiel.

Miss Marple shook her head.

'Oh no,' she said, 'I think it's quite natural. Life is more worth living, more full of interest when you are likely to lose it. It shouldn't be, perhaps, but it is. When you're young and strong and healthy, and life stretches ahead of you, living isn't really important at all. It's young people who commit suicide easily, out of despair from love, sometimes from sheer anxiety and worry. But old people know how valuable life is and how interesting.'

'Hah!' said Mr. Rafiel, snorting. 'Listen to a couple of old crocks.'

'Well, what I said is true, isn't it?' demanded Miss Marple.

'Oh, yes,' said Mr. Rafiel, 'it's true enough. But don't you think I'm right when I say that I ought to be cast as the victim?'

'It depends on who has reason to gain by your death,' said Miss Marple.

'Nobody, really,' said Mr. Rafiel. 'Apart, as I've said, from my competitors in the business world who, as I have also said, can count comfortably on my being out of it before very long. I'm not such a fool as to leave a lot of money divided up among my relations. Precious little they'd get of it after the Government had taken practically the lot. Oh no, I've attended to all that years ago. Settlements, trusts and all the rest of it.'

'Jackson, for instance, wouldn't profit by your death?'

'He wouldn't get a penny,' said Mr. Rafiel cheerfully. 'I pay him double the salary that he'd get from anyone else. That's because he has to put up with my bad temper; and he knows quite well that he will be the loser when I die.'

'And Mrs. Walters?'

'The same goes for Esther. She's a good girl. First-class secretary, intelligent, good-tempered, understands my ways, doesn't turn a hair if I fly off the handle, couldn't care less if I insult her. Behaves like a nice nursery governess in charge of an outrageous and obstreperous child. She irritates me a bit sometimes, but who doesn't? There's nothing outstanding about her. She's rather a commonplace young woman in many ways, but I couldn't have anyone who suited me better. She's had a lot of trouble in her life. Married a man who wasn't much good. I'd say she never had much judgment when it came to men. Some women haven't. They fall for anyone who tells them a hard luck story. Always convinced that all the man needs is proper female understanding. That, once married to her, he'll pull up his socks and make a go of life! But of course that type of man never does. Anyway, fortunately her unsatisfactory husband died; drank too much at a party one night and stepped in front of a bus. Esther had a daughter to support and she went back to her secretarial job. She's been with me five years. I made it quite clear to her from the start that she need have no expectations from me in the event of my death. I paid her from the start a very large salary, and that salary I've augmented by as much as a quarter as much again each year. However decent and honest people are, one should never trust *anybody*—that's why I told Esther quite clearly that she'd nothing to hope for from my death. Every year I live she'll get a bigger salary. If she puts most of that aside every year—and that's what I think she has done—she'll be quite a well-to-do woman by the time I kick the bucket. I've made myself responsible for her daughter's schooling and I've put a sum in trust for the daughter which she'll get when she comes of age. So Mrs. Esther Walters is very comfortably placed. My death, let me tell you, would mean a serious financial loss to her.' He looked very hard at Miss Marple. 'She fully realises all that. She's very sensible, Esther is.'

'Do she and Jackson get on?' asked Miss Marple.

Mr. Rafiel shot a quick glance at her.

'Noticed something, have you?' he said. 'Yes, I think Jackson's done a bit of tom-catting around, with an eye in her direction, especially lately. He's a good-looking chap, of course, but he hasn't cut any ice in that direction. For one thing, there's class distinction. She's just a cut above him. Not very much. If she was *really* a cut above him it wouldn't matter, but the lower middle class—they're very particular. Her mother was a school teacher and her father a bank clerk. No, she won't make a fool of herself about Jackson. Dare say he's after her little nest egg, but he won't get it.'

'Hush—she's coming now!' said Miss Marple.

They both looked at Esther Walters as she came along the hotel path towards them.

'She's quite a good-looking girl, you know,' said Mr. Rafiel, 'but not an atom of glamour. I don't know why, she's quite nicely turned out.'

Miss Marple sighed, a sigh that any woman will give however old at what might be considered wasted opportunities. What was lacking in Esther had been called by so many names during Miss Marple's span of existence. 'Not really attractive to men.' 'No S.A.' 'Lacks Come-hither in her eye.' Fair hair, good complexion, hazel eyes, quite a good figure, pleasant smile, but lacking that something that makes a man's head turn when he passes a woman in the street.

'She ought to get married again,' said Miss Marple, lowering her voice.

'Of course she ought. She'd make a man a good wife.'

Esther Walters joined them and Mr. Rafiel said, in a slightly artificial voice:

'So there you are at last! What's been keeping you?'

'Everyone seemed to be sending cables this morning,' said Esther. 'What with that, and people trying to check out——'

'Trying to check out, are they? A result of this murder business?'

'I suppose so. Poor Tim Kendal is worried to death.'

'And well he might be. Bad luck for that young couple, I must say.'

'I know. I gather it was rather a big undertaking for them to take on this place. They've been worried about making a success of it. They were doing very well, too.'

'They were doing a good job,' agreed Mr. Rafiel. 'He's very capable and a damned hard worker. She's a very nice girl—attractive too. They've both worked like blacks, though that's an odd term to use out here, for blacks don't work themselves to death at all, so far as I can see. Was looking at a fellow shinning up a coconut tree to get his breakfast, then he goes to sleep for the rest of the day. Nice life.'

He added, 'We've been discussing the murder here.'

Esther Walters looked slightly startled. She turned her head towards Miss Marple.

'I've been wrong about her,' said Mr. Rafiel, with characteristic frankness. 'Never been much of a one for the old pussies. All knitting wool and tittle-tattle. But this one's got something. Eyes and ears, and she uses them.'

Esther Walters looked apologetically at Miss Marple, but Miss Marple did not appear to take offence.

'That's really meant to be a compliment, you know,' Esther explained.

'I quite realise that,' said Miss Marple. 'I realise, too, that Mr. Rafiel is privileged, or thinks he is.'

'What do you mean—privileged?' asked Mr. Rafiel.

'To be rude if you want to be rude,' said Miss Marple.

'Have I been rude?' said Mr. Rafiel, surprised. 'I'm sorry if I've offended you.'

'You haven't offended me,' said Miss Marple, 'I make allowances.'

'Now, don't be nasty. Esther, get a chair and bring it here. Maybe you can help.'

Esther walked a few steps to the balcony of the bungalow and brought over a light basket chair.

'We'll go on with our consultation,' said Mr. Rafiel. 'We started with old Palgrave, deceased, and his eternal stories.'

'Oh dear,' sighed Esther. 'I'm afraid I used to escape from him whenever I could.'

'Miss Marple was more patient,' said Mr. Rafiel. 'Tell me, Esther, did he ever tell you a story about a murderer?'

'Oh yes,' said Esther. 'Several times.'

'What was it exactly? Let's have *your* recollection.'

'Well——' Esther paused to think. 'The trouble is,' she said apologetically, 'I didn't really listen very closely. You see, it was rather like that terrible story about the lion in Rhodesia which used to go on and on. One did get rather in the habit of not listening.'

'Well, tell us what you *do* remember.'

'I think it arose out of some murder case that had been in the papers. Major Palgrave said that he'd had an experience not every person had had. He'd actually met a murderer face to face.'

'Met?' Mr. Rafiel exclaimed. 'Did he actually use the word "Met"?'

Esther looked confused.

'I think so.' She was doubtful. 'Or he may have said, "I can point you out a murderer".'

'Well, which was it? There's a difference.'

'I can't really be sure . . . I *think* he said he'd show me a picture of someone.'

'That's better.'

'And then he talked a lot about Lucrezia Borgia.'

'Never mind Lucrezia Borgia. We know all about her.'

'He talked about poisoners and that Lucrezia was very beautiful and had red hair. He said there were probably far more women poisoners going about the world than anyone knew.'

'That I fear is *quite* likely,' said Miss Marple.

'And he talked about poison being a woman's weapon.'

'Seems to have been wandering from the point a bit,' said Mr. Rafiel.

'Well, of course, he always did wander from the point in his stories. And then one used to stop listening and just say "Yes" and "Really?" and "You don't say so".'

'What about this picture he was going to show you?'

'I don't remember. It may have been something he'd seen in the paper——'

'He didn't actually show you a snapshot?'

'A snapshot? No.' She shook her head. 'I'm quite sure of that. He did say that she was a good-looking woman, and you'd never think she was a murderer to look at her.'

'She?'

'There you are,' exclaimed Miss Marple. 'It makes it all so confusing.'

'He was talking about a woman?' Mr. Rafiel asked.

'Oh yes.'

'The snapshot was a snapshot of a woman?'

'Yes.'

'It can't have been!'

'But it was,' Esther persisted. 'He said "She's here in this island. I'll point her out to you, and then I'll tell you the whole story".'

Mr. Rafiel swore. In saying what he thought of the late Major Palgrave he did not mince his words.

'The probabilities are,' he finished, 'that not a word of anything he said was true!'

'One does begin to wonder,' Miss Marple murmured.

'So there we are,' said Mr. Rafiel. 'The old booby started telling you hunting tales. Pig sticking, tiger shooting, elephant hunting, narrow escapes from lions. One or two of them might have been fact. Several of them were fiction, and others had happened to somebody else! Then he gets on to the subject of murder and he tells one murder story to cap another murder story. And what's more he tells them all as if they'd happened to *him*. Ten to one most of them were a hash up of what he'd read in the paper, or seen on T.V.'

He turned accusingly on Esther. 'You admit that you weren't listening closely. Perhaps you misunderstood what he was saying.'

'I'm certain he was talking about a woman,' said Esther obstinately, 'because of course I wondered who it was.'

'Who do you think it was?' asked Miss Marple.

Esther flushed and looked slightly embarrassed.

'Oh, I didn't really—I mean, I wouldn't like to——'

Miss Marple did not insist. The presence of Mr. Rafiel, she thought, was inimical to her finding out exactly what suppositions Esther Walters had made. That could only be cosily brought out in a tête-à-tête between two women. And there was, of course, the possibility that Esther Walters was lying. Naturally, Miss Marple did not suggest this aloud. She registered it as a possibility but she was not inclined to believe in it. For one thing she did not think that Esther Walters was a liar (though one never knew) and for another, she could see no point in such a lie.

'But *you* say,' Mr. Rafiel was now turning upon Miss Marple, '*you* say that he told you this yarn about a murderer and that he then said he had a picture of him which he was going to show you.'

'I thought so, yes.'

'You thought so? You were sure enough to begin with!'

Miss Marple retorted with spirit.

'It is never easy to repeat a conversation and be entirely accurate in what the other party to it has said. One is always inclined to jump at what you think they *meant*. Then, afterwards, you put actual words into their mouths. Major Palgrave told me this story, yes. He told me that the man who told it to him, this doctor, had shown him a snapshot of the murderer; but if I am to be quite honest I must admit that what he actually said to me was "Would you like to see a snapshot of a murderer?" and naturally I assumed that it was the same snapshot he had been talking about. That it was the snapshot of that particular murderer. But I have to admit that it is possible—only remotely possible, but still possible—that by an association of ideas in his mind he leaped from the snapshot he had been shown in the past, to a snapshot he had taken recently of someone here whom he was convinced was a murderer.'

'Women!' snorted Mr. Rafiel, in exasperation, 'You're all the same, the whole blinking lot of you! Can't be accurate. You're never exactly *sure* of what a thing was. And now,' he added irritably, 'where does *that* leave us?' He snorted. 'Evelyn Hillingdon, or Greg's wife, Lucky? The whole thing is a mess.'

There was a slight apologetic cough. Arthur Jackson was standing at Mr. Rafiel's elbow. He had come so noiselessly that nobody had noticed him.

'Time for your massage, sir,' he said.

Mr. Rafiel displayed immediate temper.

'What do you mean by sneaking up on me in that way and making me jump? I never heard you.'

'Very sorry, sir.'

'I don't think I'll have any massage to-day. It never does me a damn' bit of good.'

'Oh come sir, you mustn't say that.' Jackson was full of professional cheerfulness. 'You'd soon notice it if you left it off.'

He wheeled the chair deftly round.

Miss Marple rose to her feet, smiled at Esther and went down to the beach.

18. *Without benefit of clergy*

THE BEACH was rather empty this morning. Greg was splashing in the water in his usual noisy style, Lucky was lying on her face on the beach with a sun-tanned back well oiled and her blonde hair splayed over her shoulders. The Hillingdons were not there. Señora de Caspearo, with an assorted bag of gentlemen in attendance was lying face upwards and talking deep-throated, happy Spanish. Some French and Italian children were playing at the water's edge and laughing. Canon and Miss Prescott were sitting in beach chairs observing the scene. The Canon had his hat tilted forward over his eyes and seemed half asleep. There was a convenient chair next to Miss Prescott and Miss Marple made for it and sat down.

'Oh dear,' she said, with a deep sigh.

'I know,' said Miss Prescott.

It was their joint tribute to violent death.

'That poor girl,' said Miss Marple.

'Very sad,' said the Canon. 'Most deplorable.'

'For a moment or two,' said Miss Prescott, 'we really thought of leaving, Jeremy and I. But then we decided against it. It would not really be fair, I felt, on the Kendals. After all, it's not *their* fault—— It might have happened anywhere.'

'In the midst of life we are in death,' said the Canon solemnly.

'It's very important, you know,' said Miss Prescott, 'that they should make a go of this place. They have sunk all their capital in it.'

'A very sweet girl,' said Miss Marple, 'but not looking at all well lately.'

'Very nervy,' agreed Miss Prescott. 'Of course her family——' she shook her head.

'I really think, Joan,' said the Canon in mild reproof, 'that there are some things——'

'Everybody knows about it,' said Miss Prescott. 'Her family live in our part of the world. A great-aunt—most peculiar—and one of her uncles took off all his clothes in one of the tube stations. Green Park, I believe it was.'

'Joan, that is a thing that should *not* be repeated.'

'Very sad,' said Miss Marple, shaking her head, 'though I believe not an uncommon form of madness. I know when we were working for the Armenian relief, a most respectable elderly clergyman was afflicted the same way. They telephoned his wife and she came along at once and took him home in a cab, wrapped in a blanket.'

'Of course, Molly's immediate family's all right,' said Miss Prescott. 'She never got on very well with her mother, but then so few girls seem to get on with their mothers nowadays.'

'Such a pity,' said Miss Marple, shaking her head, 'because really a young girl needs her mother's knowledge of the world and experience.'

'Exactly,' said Miss Prescott with emphasis. 'Molly, you know, took up with some man—*quite* unsuitable, I understand.'

'It so often happens,' said Miss Marple.

'Her family disapproved, naturally. *She* didn't tell them about it. They heard about it from a complete outsider. Of course her mother said she must bring him along so that they met him properly. This, I understand, the girl refused to do. She said it was humiliating to him. Most insulting to be made to come and meet her family and be looked over. Just as though you were a horse, she said.'

Miss Marple sighed. 'One does need so much *tact* when dealing with the young,' she murmured.

'Anyway there it was! They forbade her to see him.'

'But you can't *do* that nowadays,' said Miss Marple. 'Girls have jobs and they meet people whether anyone forbids them or not.'

'But then, very fortunately,' went on Miss Prescott, 'she met Tim Kendal, and the other man sort of faded out of the picture. I can't *tell* you how relieved the family was.'

'I hope they didn't show it too plainly,' said Miss Marple.

'That so often puts girls off from forming suitable attachments.'

'Yes, indeed.'

'One remembers oneself——' murmured Miss Marple, her mind going back to the past. A young man she had met at a croquet party. He had seemed so nice—rather gay, almost *Bohemian* in his views. And then he had been unexpectedly warmly welcomed by her father. He had been suitable, eligible; he had been asked freely to the house more than once, and Miss Marple had found that, after all, he was *dull*. Very dull.

The Canon seemed safely comatose and Miss Marple advanced tentatively to the subject she was anxious to pursue.

'Of course you know so much about this place,' she murmured. 'You have been here several years running, have you not?'

'Well, last year and two years before that. We like St. Honoré very much. Always such nice people here. Not the flashy, ultra-rich set.'

'So I suppose you know the Hillingdons and the Dysons well?'

'Yes, fairly well.'

Miss Marple coughed and lowered her voice slightly.

'Major Palgrave told me such an interesting story,' she said.

'He had a great repertoire of stories, hadn't he? Of course he had travelled very widely. Africa, India, even China I believe.'

'Yes indeed,' said Miss Marple. 'But I didn't mean one of *those* stories. This was a story concerned with—well, with one of the people I have just mentioned.'

'Oh!' said Miss Prescott. Her voice held meaning.

'Yes. Now I wonder——' Miss Marple allowed her eyes to travel gently round the beach to where Lucky lay sunning her back. 'Very beautifully tanned, isn't she,' remarked Miss Marple. 'And her hair. Most attractive. Practically the same colour as Molly Kendal's, isn't it?'

'The only difference,' said Miss Prescott, 'is that Molly's is natural and Lucky's comes out of a bottle!'

'Really, Joan,' the Canon protested, unexpectedly awake again. 'Don't you think that is *rather* an uncharitable thing to say?'

'It's not uncharitable,' said Miss Prescott, acidly. 'Merely a *fact*.'

'It looks very nice to *me*,' said the Canon.

'Of course. That's why she does it. But I assure you, my dear Jeremy, it wouldn't deceive any *woman* for a moment. Would it?' She appealed to Miss Marple.

'Well, I'm afraid—' said Miss Marple, 'of course I haven't the experience that you have—but I'm afraid—yes I should say definitely *not natural*. The appearance at the roots every fifth or sixth day——' She looked at Miss Prescott and they both nodded with quiet female assurance.

The Canon appeared to be dropping off again.

'Major Palgrave told me a really extraordinary story,' murmured Miss Marple, 'about—well I couldn't quite make out. I am a little deaf sometimes. He appeared to be saying or hinting——' she paused.

'I know what you mean. There was a great deal of talk at the time——'

'You mean at the time that——'

'When the first Mrs. Dyson died. Her death was quite unexpected. In fact, everybody thought she was a *malade imaginaire*—a hypochondriac. So when she had this attack and died so unexpectedly, well, of course, people did talk.'

'There wasn't—any—trouble at the time?'

'The doctor was puzzled. He was quite a young man and he hadn't had much experience. He was what I call one of those antibiotics-for-all men. You know, the kind that doesn't bother to look at the patient much, or worry what's the matter with him. They just give them some kind of pill out of a bottle and if they don't get better, then they try a different pill. Yes, I believe he *was* puzzled, but it seemed she had had gastric trouble before. At least her husband said so, and there seemed no reason for believing anything was *wrong*.'

'But you yourself think——'

'Well, I always try to keep an open mind, but one does *wonder*, you know. And what with various things people said——'

'Joan!' The Canon sat up. He looked belligerent. 'I don't like—I really don't like to hear this kind of ill-natured gossip being repeated. We've always set our faces against that kind of thing. See no evil, hear no evil, speak no evil—and what is more, *think* no evil! That should be the motto of every Christian man and woman.'

The two women sat in silence. They were rebuked, and in deference to their training they deferred to the criticism of a man. But inwardly they were frustrated, irritated and quite unrepentant. Miss Prescott threw a frank glance of irritation towards her brother. Miss Marple took out her knitting and looked at it. Fortunately for them Chance was on their side.

'*Mon père*,' said a small shrill voice. It was one of the French children who had been playing at the water's edge. She had come up unnoticed, and was standing by Canon Prescott's chair.

'*Mon père*,' she fluted.

'Eh? Yes, my dear? *Oui, qu'est-ce qu'il y a, ma petite?*'

The child explained. There had been a dispute about who should have the water-wings next and also other matters of seaside etiquette. Canon Prescott was extremely fond of children, especially small girls. He was always delighted to be summoned to act as arbiter in their disputes. He rose willingly now and accompanied the child to the water's edge. Miss Marple and Miss Prescott breathed deep sighs and turned avidly towards each other.

'Jeremy, of course rightly, is very against ill-natured gossip,' said Miss Prescott, 'but one cannot really ignore what people are saying. And there was, as I say, a great deal of talk at the time.'

'Yes?' Miss Marple's tone urged her forward.

'This young woman, you see, Miss Greatorex I think her name was then, I can't remember now, was a kind of cousin and she looked after Mrs. Dyson. Gave her all her medicines and things like that.' There was a short, meaningful pause. 'And of course there had, I understand'—Miss Prescott's voice was lowered—'been goings-on between Mr. Dyson and Miss Greatorex. A lot of people had noticed them. I mean things like that are quickly observed in a place like this. Then there was some curious story about some stuff that Edward Hillingdon got for her at a chemist.'

'Oh, Edward Hillingdon came into it?'

'Oh yes, he was very much attracted. People noticed it. And Lucky—Miss Greatorex—played them off against each other. Gregory Dyson and Edward Hillingdon. One has to face it, she has always been an attractive woman.'

'Though not as young as she was,' Miss Marple replied.

'Exactly. But she was always very well turned out and made up. Of course not so flamboyant when she was just the poor relation. She always *seemed* very devoted to the invalid. But, well, you see how it was.'

'What was this story about the chemist—how did that get known?'

'Well, it wasn't in Jamestown, I think it was when they were in Martinique. The French, I believe, are more lax than we are in the matter of drugs—— This chemist talked to someone, and the story got around—— Well, you know how these things happen.'

Miss Marple did. None better.

'He said something about Colonel Hillingdon asking for something and not seeming to know what it was he was asking for. Consulting a piece of paper, you know, on which it was written down. Anyway, as I say, there was *talk*.'

'But I don't see quite why Colonel Hillingdon——' Miss Marple frowned in perplexity.

'I suppose he was just being used as a *cat's-paw*. Anyway, Gregory Dyson married again in an almost indecently short time. Barely a month later, I understand.'

They looked at each other.

'But there was no *real* suspicion?' Miss Marple asked.

'Oh no, it was just—well, *talk*. Of course there may have been absolutely nothing in it.'

'Major Palgrave thought there was.'

'Did he say so to you?'

'I wasn't really listening very closely,' confessed Miss Marple. 'I just wondered if—er—well, if he'd said the same things to you?'

'He did point her out to me one day,' said Miss Prescott.

'Really? He actually pointed her out?'

'Yes. As a matter of fact, I thought at first it was Mrs. Hillingdon he was pointing out. He wheezed and chuckled a bit and said "Look at that woman over there. In my opinion that's a woman who's done murder and got away with it." I was very shocked, of course. I said, "surely you're joking, Major Palgrave," and he said "Yes, yes, dear lady, let's call it joking." The Dysons and the Hillingdons were sitting at a table quite near to us, and I was afraid they'd overhear. He chuckled and said "Wouldn't care to go to a drink party and have a certain person mix me a cocktail. Too much like supper with the Borgias."'

'How *very* interesting,' said Miss Marple. 'Did he mention a—a photograph?'

'I don't remember. . . . Was it some newspaper cutting?'

Miss Marple, about to speak, shut her lips. The sun was momentarily obscured by a shadow. Evelyn Hillingdon paused beside them.

'Good morning,' she said.

'I was wondering where you were,' said Miss Prescott, looking up brightly.

'I've been to Jamestown, shopping.'

'Oh, I see.'

Miss Prescott looked round vaguely and Evelyn Hillingdon said:

'Oh, I didn't take Edward with me. Men hate shopping.'

'Did you find anything of interest?'

'It wasn't that sort of shopping. I just had to go to the chemist.'

With a smile and a slight nod she went on down the beach.

'Such nice people, the Hillingdons,' said Miss Prescott, 'though she's not really very easy to know, is she? I mean, she's always very pleasant and all that, but one never seems to get to know her any better.'

Miss Marple agreed thoughtfully.

'One never knows what she is thinking,' said Miss Prescott.

'Perhaps that is just as well,' said Miss Marple.

'I beg your pardon?'

'Oh nothing really, only that I've always had the feeling that perhaps her thoughts might be rather disconcerting.'

'Oh,' said Miss Prescott, looking puzzled. 'I see what you mean.' She went on with a slight change of subject. 'I believe they have a very charming place in Hampshire, and a boy—or is it two boys—who have just gone—or one of them—to Winchester.'

'Do you know Hampshire well?'

'No. Hardly at all. I believe their house is somewhere near Alton.'

'I see.' Miss Marple paused and then said, 'And where do the Dysons live?'

'California,' said Miss Prescott. 'When they are at home, that is. They are great travellers.'

'One really knows so little about the people one meets when one is travelling,' said Miss Marple. 'I mean—how shall I put it—— One only knows, doesn't one, what they choose to tell you about themselves. For instance, you don't *really* know that the Dysons live in California.'

Miss Prescott looked startled.

'I'm sure Mr. Dyson mentioned it.'

'Yes. Yes, exactly. That's what I mean. And the same thing perhaps with the Hillingdons. I mean when you say that they live in Hampshire, you're really repeating what *they* told *you*, aren't you?'

Miss Prescott looked slightly alarmed. 'Do you mean that they don't live in Hampshire?' she asked.

'No, no, not for one moment,' said Miss Marple, quickly apologetic. 'I was only using them as an instance as to what one knows or doesn't know about people.' She added, '*I* have told you that I live at St.

Mary Mead, which is a place, no doubt, of which you have never heard. But you don't, if I may say so, know it of your *own* knowledge, do you?'

Miss Prescott forbore from saying that she really couldn't care less *where* Miss Marple lived. It was somewhere in the country and in the south of England and that is all she knew. 'Oh, I do see what you mean,' she agreed hastily, 'and I know that one can't possibly be too careful when one is abroad.'

'I didn't exactly mean *that*,' said Miss Marple.

There were some odd thoughts going through Miss Marple's mind. Did she really know, she was asking herself, that Canon Prescott and Miss Prescott were really Canon Prescott and Miss Prescott? They said so. There was no evidence to contradict them. It would really be easy, would it not, to put on a dog-collar, to wear the appropriate clothes, to make the appropriate conversation. If there was a motive . . .

Miss Marple was fairly knowledgeable about the clergy in her part of the world, but the Prescotts came from the north. Durham, wasn't it? She had no doubt they were the Prescotts, but still, it came back to the same thing—one believed what people said to one.

Perhaps one ought to be on one's guard against that. Perhaps. . . . She shook her head thoughtfully.

19. *Uses of a shoe*

CANON PRESCOTT came back from the water's edge slightly short of breath (playing with children is always exhausting).

Presently he and his sister went back to the hotel, finding the beach a little too hot.

'But,' said Señora de Caspearo scornfully as they walked away—'How can a beach be too hot? It is nonsense that——And look what she wears—her arms and her neck are all covered up. Perhaps it is as well, that. Her skin it is hideous, like a plucked chicken!'

Miss Marple drew a deep breath. Now or never was the time for conversation with Señora de Caspearo. Unfortunately she did not know what to say. There seemed to be no common ground on which they could meet.

'You have children, Señora?' she inquired.

'I have three angels,' said Señora de Caspearo, kissing her fingertips.

Miss Marple was rather uncertain as to whether this meant that Señora de Caspearo's offspring were in Heaven or whether it merely referred to their characters.

One of the gentlemen in attendance made a remark in Spanish and Señora de Caspearo flung back her head appreciatively and laughed loudly and melodiously.

'You understand what he said?' she inquired of Miss Marple.

'I'm afraid not,' said Miss Marple apologetically.

'It is just as well. He is a wicked man.'

A rapid and spirited interchange of Spanish badinage followed.

'It is infamous—infamous,' said Señora de Caspearo, reverting to English with sudden gravity, 'that the police do not let us go from this island. I storm, I scream, I stamp my foot—but all they say is No—No. You know how it will end—we shall all be killed.'

Her bodyguard attempted to reassure her.

'But yes—I tell you it is unlucky here. I knew it from the first—— That old Major, the ugly one—he had the Evil Eye—you remember? His eyes they crossed—— It is bad, that! I make the Sign of the Horns every time when he looks my way.' She made it in illustration. 'Though since he is cross-eyed I am not always sure when he does look my way——'

'He had a glass eye,' said Miss Marple in an explanatory voice. 'An accident, I understand, when he was quite young. It was not his fault.'

'I tell you he brought bad luck—— I say it is the evil eye he had.'

Her hand shot out again in the well-known Latin gesture—the first finger and the little finger sticking out, the two middle ones doubled in. 'Anyway,' she said cheerfully, 'he is dead—I do not have to look at him any more. I do not like to look at things that are ugly.'

It was, Miss Marple thought, a somewhat cruel epitaph on Major Palgrave.

Farther down the beach Gregory Dyson had come out of the sea. Lucky had turned herself over on the sand. Evelyn Hillingdon was looking at Lucky, and her expression, for some reason, made Miss Marple shiver.

'Surely I can't be cold—in this hot sun,' she thought.

What was the old phrase—'*A goose walking over your grave*——'

She got up and went slowly back to her bungalow.

On the way she passed Mr. Rafiel and Esther Walters coming down the beach. Mr. Rafiel winked at her. Miss Marple did not wink back. She looked disapproving.

She went into her bungalow and lay down on her bed. She felt old and tired and worried.

She was quite certain that there was no time to be lost—no time—to—be lost. . . . It was getting late. . . . The sun was going to set—the sun—one must always look at the sun through smoked glass——Where was that piece of smoked glass that someone had given her? . . .

No, she wouldn't need it after all. A shadow had come over the sun blotting it out. A shadow. Evelyn Hillingdon's shadow——No, not Evelyn Hillingdon—— The Shadow (what were the words) the *Shadow of the Valley of Death.* That was it. She must—what was it? Make the Sign of the Horns—to avert the Evil Eye—Major Palgrave's Evil Eye.

Her eyelids flickered open—she had been asleep. But there *was* a shadow—someone peering in at her window.

The shadow moved away—and Miss Marple saw who it was—It was Jackson.

'Impertinence—peering in like that,' she thought—and added parenthetically 'Just like Jonas Parry.'

The comparison reflected no credit on Jackson.

Then she wondered *why* Jackson had been peering into her bedroom. To see if she was there? Or to note that she was there, but was asleep?

She got up, went into the bathroom and peered cautiously through the window.

Arthur Jackson was standing by the door of the bungalow next door. Mr. Rafiel's bungalow. She saw him give a rapid glance round and then slip quickly inside. Interesting, thought Miss Marple. Why did he have to look round in that furtive manner. Nothing in the world could have been more natural than his going into Mr. Rafiel's bungalow since he himself had a room at the back of it. He was always going in and out of it on some errand or other. So why that quick, guilty glance round? 'Only one reason,' said Miss Marple answering her own question, 'he wanted to be sure that nobody was observing him enter at this particular moment because of something he was going to do in there.'

Everybody, of course, was on the beach at this moment except those who had gone for expeditions. In about twenty minutes or so, Jackson himself would arrive on the beach in the course of his duties to aid Mr. Rafiel to take his sea dip. If he wanted to do anything in the bungalow unobserved, now was a very good time. He had satisfied himself that Miss Marple was asleep on her bed, he had satisfied himself that there was nobody near at hand to observe his movements. Well, she must do her best to do exactly that.

Sitting down on her bed, Miss Marple removed her neat sandal shoes and replaced them with a pair of plimsolls. Then she shook her head, removed the plimsolls, burrowed in her suitcase and took out a pair of shoes the heel on one of which she had recently caught on a hook by the door. It was now in a slightly precarious state and Miss Marple adroitly rendered it even more precarious by attention with a nail file. Then she emerged with due precaution from her door walking in stockinged feet. With all the care of a Big Game Hunter approaching up-wind of a herd of antelope, Miss Marple gently circumnavigated Mr. Rafiel's bungalow.

Cautiously she manœuvred her way around the corner of the house. She put on one of the shoes she was carrying, gave a final wrench to the heel of the other, sank gently to her knees and lay prone under the window. If Jackson heard anything, if he came to the window to look out, an old lady would have had a fall owing to the heel coming off her shoe. But evidently Jackson had heard nothing.

Very, very gently Miss Marple raised her head. The windows of the bungalow were low. Shielding herself slightly with a festoon of creeper she peered inside. . . .

Jackson was on his knees before a suitcase. The lid of the suitcase was up and Miss Marple could see that it was a specially fitted affair containing compartments filled with various kinds of papers. Jackson was looking through the papers, occasionally drawing documents out of long envelopes. Miss Marple did not remain at her observation post for long. All she wanted was to know what Jackson was doing. She knew now. Jackson was snooping. Whether he was looking for something in particular, or whether he was just indulging his natural instincts, she had no means of judging. But it confirmed her in her belief that Arthur Jackson and Jonas Parry had strong affinities in other things than facial resemblance.

Her problem was now to withdraw. Very carefully she dropped down again and crept along the flower-bed until she was clear of the window. She returned to her bungalow and carefully put away the shoe and the heel that she had detached from it. She looked at them with affection. A good device which she could use on another day if necessary. She resumed her own sandal shoes, and went thoughtfully down to the beach again.

Choosing a moment when Esther Walters was in the water, Miss Marple moved into the chair Esther had vacated.

Greg and Lucky were laughing and talking with Señora de Caspearo and making a good deal of noise.

Miss Marple spoke very quietly, almost under her breath, without looking at Mr. Rafiel.

'Do you know that Jackson snoops?'

'Doesn't surprise me,' said Mr. Rafiel. 'Caught him at it, did you?'

'I managed to observe him through a window. He had one of your suitcases open and was looking through your papers.'

'Must have managed to get hold of a key to it. Resourceful fellow. He'll be disappointed though. Nothing he gets hold of in that way will do him a mite of good.'

'He's coming down now,' said Miss Marple, glancing up towards the hotel.

'Time for that idiotic sea dip of mine.'

He spoke again—very quietly.

'As for you—don't be too enterprising. We don't want to be attending *your* funeral next. Remember your age, and be careful. There's somebody about who isn't too scrupulous, remember.'

20. *Night alarm*

EVENING CAME— The lights came up on the terrace—— People dined and talked and laughed, albeit less loudly and merrily than they had a day or two ago—— The steel band played.

But the dancing ended early. People yawned—went off to bed—— The lights went out—— There was darkness and stillness—— The Golden Palm Tree slept. . . .

'Evelyn. Evelyn!' The whisper came sharp and urgent.

Evelyn Hillingdon stirred and turned on her pillow.

'*Evelyn*. Please wake up.'

Evelyn Hillingdon sat up abruptly. Tim Kendal was standing in the doorway. She stared at him in surprise.

'Evelyn, *please*, could you come? It's—Molly. She's ill. I don't know what's the matter with her. I think she must have taken something.'

Evelyn was quick, decisive.

'All right, Tim. I'll come. You go back to her. I'll be with you in a moment.'

Tim Kendal disappeared. Evelyn slipped out of bed, threw on a dressing-gown and looked across at the other bed. Her husband, it seemed, had not been awakened. He lay there, his head turned away, breathing quietly. Evelyn hesitated for a moment, then decided not to disturb him. She went out of the door and walked rapidly to the main building and beyond it to the Kendals' bungalow. She caught up with Tim in the doorway.

Molly lay in bed. Her eyes were closed and her breathing was clearly not natural. Evelyn bent over her, rolled up an eyelid, felt her pulse and then looked at the bedside table. There was a glass there which had been used. Beside it was an empty phial of tablets. She picked it up.

'They were her sleeping pills,' said Tim, 'but that bottle was half full yesterday or the day before. I think she—must have taken the lot.'

'Go and get Dr. Graham,' said Evelyn, 'and on the way knock them up and tell them to make strong coffee. Strong as possible. Hurry.'

Tim dashed off. Just outside the doorway he collided with Edward Hillingdon.

'Oh, sorry, Edward.'

'What's happening here?' demanded Hillingdon. 'What's going on?'

'It's Molly. Evelyn's with her. I must get hold of the doctor. I suppose I ought've gone to him first but I—I wasn't sure and I thought Evelyn would know. Molly would have hated it if I'd fetched a doctor when it wasn't necessary.'

He went off, running. Edward Hillingdon looked after him for a moment and then he walked into the bedroom.

'What's happening?' he said. 'Is it serious?'

'Oh, there you are, Edward. I wondered if you'd woken up. This silly child has been taking things.'

'Is it bad?'

'One can't tell without knowing how much she's taken. I shouldn't think it was too bad if we get going in time. I've sent for coffee. If we can get some of that down her——'

'But why should she do such a thing? You don't think——' He stopped.

'What don't I think?' asked Evelyn.

'You don't think it's because of the inquiry—the police—all that?'

'It's possible, of course. That sort of thing could be very alarming to a nervous type.'

'Molly never used to seem a nervous type.'

'One can't really tell,' said Evelyn. 'It's the most unlikely people sometimes who lose their nerve.'

'Yes, I remember . . .' Again he stopped.

'The truth is,' said Evelyn, 'that one doesn't really know anything about anybody.' She added, 'Not even the people who are nearest to you. . . .'

'Isn't that going a little too far, Evelyn—exaggerating too much?'

'I don't think it is. When you think of people, it is in the image you have made of them for yourself.'

'I know you,' said Edward Hillingdon quietly.

'You think you do.'

'No. I'm sure.' He added, 'And you're sure of me.'

Evelyn looked at him then turned back to the bed. She took Molly by the shoulders and shook her.

'We ought to be doing something, but I suppose it's better to wait until Dr. Graham comes—— Oh, I think I hear them.'

2

'She'll do now.' Dr. Graham stepped back, wiped his forehead with a handkerchief and breathed a sigh of relief.

'You think she'll be all right, sir?' Tim demanded anxiously.

'Yes, yes. We got to her in good time. Anyway, she probably didn't take enough to kill her. A couple of days and she'll be as right as rain but she'll have a rather nasty day or two first.' He picked up the empty bottle. 'Who gave her these things anyway?'

'A doctor in New York. She wasn't sleeping well.'

'Well, well. I know all we medicos hand these things out freely nowadays. Nobody tells young women who can't sleep to count sheep, or get up and eat a biscuit, or write a couple of letters and then go back to bed. Instant remedies, that's what people demand nowadays. Sometimes I think it's a pity we give them to them. You've got to learn to put up with things in life. All very well to stuff a comforter into a baby's mouth to stop it crying. Can't go on doing that all a person's life.' He gave a small chuckle. 'I bet you, if you asked Miss Marple what she does if she can't sleep, she'd tell you she counted sheep going under a gate.' He turned back to the bed where Molly was stirring. Her eyes were open now. She looked at them without interest or recognition. Dr. Graham took her hand.

'Well, well, my dear, and what have you been doing to yourself?'

She blinked but did not reply.

'Why did you do it, Molly, why? Tell me why?' Tim took her other hand.

Still her eyes did not move. If they rested on anyone it was on Evelyn Hillingdon. There might have been even a faint question in them but it was hard to tell. Evelyn spoke as though there had been the question.

'Tim came and fetched me,' she said.

Her eyes went to Tim, then shifted to Dr. Graham.

'You're going to be all right now,' said Dr. Graham, 'but don't do it again.'

'She didn't mean to do it,' said Tim quietly. 'I'm sure she didn't mean to do it. She just wanted a good night's rest. Perhaps the pills didn't work at first and so she took more of them. Is that it, Molly?'

Her head moved very faintly in a negative motion.

'You mean—you took them on purpose?' said Tim.

Molly spoke then. 'Yes,' she said.

'But why, Molly, why?'

The eyelids faltered. 'Afraid.' The word was just heard.

'Afraid? Of what?'

But her eyelids closed down.

'Better let her be,' said Dr. Graham. Tim spoke impetuously.

'Afraid of what? The police? Because they've been hounding you, asking you questions? I don't wonder. Anyone might feel frightened. But it's just their way, that's all. Nobody thinks for one moment ——' he broke off.

Dr. Graham made him a decisive gesture.

'I want to go to sleep,' said Molly.

'The best thing for you,' said Dr. Graham.

He moved to the door and the others followed him.

'She'll sleep all right,' said Graham.

'Is there anything I ought to do?' asked Tim. He had the usual, slightly apprehensive attitude of a man in illness.

'I'll stay if you like,' said Evelyn kindly.

'Oh no. No, that's quite all right,' said Tim.

Evelyn went back towards the bed. 'Shall I stay with you, Molly?'

Molly's eyes opened again. She said, 'No,' and then after a pause, 'just Tim.'

Tim came back and sat down by the bed.

'I'm here, Molly,' he said and took her hand. 'Just go to sleep. I won't leave you.'

She sighed faintly and her eyes closed.

The doctor paused outside the bungalow and the Hillingdons stood with him.

'You're sure there's nothing more I can do?' asked Evelyn.

'I don't think so, thank you, Mrs. Hillingdon. She'll be better with her husband now. But possibly to-morrow—after all, he's got this hotel to run—I think someone should be with her.'

'D'you think she might—try again?' asked Hillingdon.

Graham rubbed his forehead irritably.

'One never knows in these cases. Actually, it's most unlikely. As you've seen for yourselves, the restorative treatment is extremely unpleasant. But of course one can never be absolutely certain. She may have more of this stuff hidden away somewhere.'

'I should never have thought of suicide in connection with a girl like Molly,' said Hillingdon.

Graham said dryly, 'It's not the people who are always talking of killing themselves, threatening to do so, who do it. They dramatise themselves that way and let off steam.'

'Molly always seemed such a happy girl. I think perhaps'—Evelyn hesitated—'I ought to tell you, Dr. Graham.'

She told him then about her interview with Molly on the beach the night that Victoria had been killed. Graham's face was very grave when she had finished.

'I'm glad you've told me, Mrs. Hillingdon. There are very definite indications there of some kind of deep-rooted trouble. Yes. I'll have a word with her husband in the morning.'

3

'I want to talk to you seriously, Kendal, about your wife.'

They were sitting in Tim's office. Evelyn Hillingdon had taken his place by Molly's bedside and Lucky had promised to come and, as she expressed it, "spell her" later. Miss Marple had also offered her services. Poor Tim was torn between his hotel commitments and his wife's condition.

'I can't understand it,' said Tim, 'I can't understand Molly any longer. She's changed. Changed out of all seeming.'

'I understand she's been having bad dreams?'

'Yes. Yes, she complained about them a good deal.'

'For how long?'

'Oh, I don't know. About—oh I suppose a month—perhaps longer. She—we—thought they were just—well, nightmares, you know.'

'Yes, yes, I quite understand. But what's a much more serious sign is the fact that she seems to have felt afraid of someone. Did she complain about that to you?'

'Well, yes. She said once or twice that—oh, people were following her.'

'Ah! Spying on her?'

'Yes, she did use that term once. She said they were her enemies and they'd followed her here.'

'Did she have enemies, Mr. Kendal?'

'No. Of course she didn't.'

'No incident in England, anything you know about before you were married?'

'Oh no, nothing of that kind. She didn't get on with her family very well, that was all. Her mother was rather an eccentric woman, difficult to live with perhaps, but. . . .'

'Any signs of mental instability in her family?'

Tim opened his mouth impulsively, then shut it again. He pushed a fountain pen about on the desk in front of him.

The doctor said:

'I must stress the fact that it would be better to tell me, Tim, if that is the case.'

'Well, yes, I believe so. Nothing serious, but I believe there was an aunt or something who was a bit batty. But that's nothing. I mean—well you get that in almost any family.'

'Oh yes, yes, that's quite true. I'm not trying to alarm you about that, but it just might show a tendency to—well to break down or imagine things if any stress arose.'

'I don't really know very much,' said Tim. 'After all, people don't pour out all their family histories to you, do they?'

'No, no. Quite so. She had no former friend—she was not engaged to anyone, anyone who might have threatened her or made jealous threats? That sort of thing?'

'I don't know. I don't think so. Molly *was* engaged to some other man before I came along. Her parents were very against it, I understand, and I think she really stuck to the chap more out of opposition and defiance than anything else.' He gave a sudden half-grin. 'You know what it is when you're young. If people cut up a fuss it makes you much keener on whoever it is.'

Dr. Graham smiled too. 'Ah yes, one often sees that. One should never take exception to one's children's objectionable friends. Usually they grow out of them naturally. This man, whoever he was, didn't make threats of any kind against Molly?'

'No, I'm sure he didn't. She would have told me. She said herself she just had a silly adolescent craze on him, mainly because he had such a bad reputation.'

'Yes, yes. Well, that doesn't sound serious. Now there's another thing. Apparently your wife has had what she describes as blackouts. Brief passages of time during which she can't account for her actions. Did you know about that, Tim?'

'No,' said Tim slowly. 'No. I didn't. She never told me. I did notice, you know, now you mention it, that she seemed rather vague sometimes and . . .' He paused, thinking. 'Yes, that explains it. I couldn't understand how she seemed to have forgotten the simplest things, or sometimes not to seem to know what time of day it was. I just thought she was absent-minded, I suppose.'

'What it amounts to, Tim, is just this. I advise you most strongly to take your wife to see a good specialist.'

Tim flushed angrily.

'You mean a mental specialist, I suppose?'

'Now, now, don't be upset by labels. A neurologist, a psychologist, someone who specialises in what the layman calls nervous breakdowns. There's a good man in Kingston. Or there's New York of course. There is something that is causing these nervous terrors of your wife's. Something perhaps for which she hardly knows the reason herself. Get advice about her, Tim. Get advice as soon as possible.'

He clapped his hand on the young man's shoulder and got up.

'There's no immediate worry. Your wife has good friends and we'll all be keeping an eye on her.'

'She won't—you don't think she'll try it again?'

'I think it most unlikely,' said Dr. Graham.

'You can't be sure,' said Tim.

'One can never be sure,' said Dr. Graham, 'that's one of the first things you learn in my profession.' Again he laid a hand on Tim's shoulder. 'Don't worry too much.'

'That's easy to say,' said Tim as the doctor went out of the door. 'Don't worry, indeed! What does he think I'm made of?'

21. *Jackson on cosmetics*

'YOU'RE SURE you don't mind, Miss Marple?' said Evelyn Hillingdon.

'No, indeed, my dear,' said Miss Marple. 'I'm only too delighted to be of use in any way. At my age, you know, one feels very useless in the world. Especially when I am in a place like this, just enjoying myself. No duties of any kind. No, I'll be delighted to sit with Molly. You go along on your expedition. Pelican Point, wasn't it?'

'Yes,' said Evelyn. 'Both Edward and I love it. I never get tired of seeing the birds diving down, catching up the fish. Tim's with Molly now. But he's got things to do and he doesn't seem to like her being left alone.'

'He's quite right,' said Miss Marple. 'I wouldn't in his place. One never knows, does one? when anyone has attempted anything of that kind—— Well, go along, my dear.'

Evelyn went off to join a little group that was waiting for her. Her husband, the Dysons and three or four other people. Miss Marple checked her knitting requirements, saw that she had all she wanted with her, and walked over towards the Kendals' bungalow.

As she came up on to the loggia she heard Tim's voice through the half-open french window.

'If you'd only tell me *why* you did it, Molly. What made you? Was it anything I did? There must be some reason. If you'd only tell me.'

Miss Marple paused. There was a little pause inside before Molly spoke. Her voice was flat and tired.

'I don't know, Tim, I really don't know. I suppose—something came over me.'

Miss Marple tapped on the window and walked in.

'Oh there you are, Miss Marple. It is very good of you.'

'Not at all,' said Miss Marple. 'I'm delighted to be of any help. Shall I sit here in this chair? You're looking much better, Molly. I'm so glad.'

'I'm all right,' said Molly. 'Quite all right. Just—oh, just sleepy.'

'I shan't talk,' said Miss Marple. 'You just lie quiet and rest. I'll get on with my knitting.'

Tim Kendal threw her a grateful glance and went out. Miss Marple established herself in her chair.

Molly was lying on her left side. She had a half-stupefied, exhausted look. She said in a voice that was almost a whisper:

'It's very kind of you, Miss Marple. I—I think I'll go to sleep.'

She half turned away on her pillows and closed her eyes. Her breathing grew more regular though it was still far from normal. Long experience of nursing made Miss Marple almost automatically straighten the sheet and tuck it under the mattress on her side of the bed. As she did so her hand encountered something hard and rectangular under the mattress. Rather surprised she took hold of this and pulled it out. It was a book. Miss Marple threw a quick glance at the girl in the bed, but she lay there utterly quiescent. She was evidently asleep. Miss Marple opened the book. It was, she saw, a current work on nervous diseases. It came open naturally at a certain place which gave a description of the onset of persecution mania and various other manifestations of schizophrenia and allied complaints.

It was not a highly technical book, but one that could be easily understood by a layman. Miss Marple's face grew very grave as she read. After a minute or two she closed the book and stayed thinking. Then she bent forward and with some care replaced the book where she had found it, under the mattress.

She shook her head in some perplexity. Noiselessly she rose from her chair. She walked the few steps towards the window, then turned her head sharply over her shoulder. Molly's eyes were open but even as Miss Marple turned the eyes shut again. For a minute or two Miss Marple was not quite certain whether she might not have imagined that quick, sharp glance. Was Molly then only pretending to be asleep? That might be natural enough. She might feel that Miss Marple would start talking to her if she showed herself awake. Yes, that could be all it was.

Was she reading into that glance of Molly's a kind of slyness that was somehow innately disagreeable? One doesn't know, Miss Marple thought to herself, one really doesn't know.

She decided that she would try to manage a little talk with Dr. Graham as soon as it could be managed. She came back to her chair by the bed. She decided after about five minutes or so that Molly was really asleep. No one could have lain so still, could have breathed so evenly. Miss Marple got up again. She was wearing her plimsolls to-day. Not perhaps very elegant, but admirably suited to this climate and comfortable and roomy for the feet.

She moved gently round the bedroom, pausing at both of the windows, which gave out in two different directions.

The hotel grounds seemed quiet and deserted. Miss Marple came back and was standing a little uncertainly before regaining her seat, when she thought she heard a faint sound outside. Like the scrape of a shoe on the loggia? She hesitated a moment then she went to the window, pushed it a little farther open, stepped out and turned her head back into the room as she spoke.

'I shall be gone only a very short time, dear,' she said, 'just back to my bungalow, to see where I could possibly have put that pattern. I was so sure I had brought it with me. You'll be quite all right till I come back, won't you?' Then turning her head back, she nodded to herself. 'Asleep, poor child. A good thing.'

She went quietly along the loggia, down the steps and turned sharp right to the path there. Passing along between the screen of some hibiscus bushes an observer might have been curious to see that Miss Marple veered sharply on to the flower-bed, passed round to the back of the bungalow and entered it again through the second door there. This led directly into a small room that Tim sometimes used as an unofficial office and from that into the sitting-room.

Here there were wide curtains semi-drawn to keep the room cool. Miss Marple slipped behind one of them. Then she waited. From the window here she had a good view of anyone who approached Molly's bedroom. It was some few minutes, four or five, before she saw anything.

The neat figure of Jackson in his white uniform went up the steps of the loggia. He paused for a minute at the balcony there, and then appeared to be giving a tiny discreet tap on the door of the window that was ajar. There was no response that Miss Marple could hear. Jackson looked around him, a quick furtive glance, then he slipped inside the open doors. Miss Marple moved to the door which led directly into the bedroom. She did not go through it but applied her eye to the hinge.

Jackson had walked into the room. He approached the bed and looked down for a minute on the sleeping girl. Then he turned away and walked not to the sitting-room door but to the far door which led into the adjoining bathroom. Miss Marple's eyebrows rose in slight surprise. She reflected a minute or two, then walked out into the passageway and into the bathroom by the other door.

Jackson spun round from examining the shelf over the wash-basin. He looked taken aback, which was not surprising.

'Oh,' he said, 'I—I didn't. . . .'

'Mr. Jackson,' said Miss Marple, in great surprise.

'I thought you'd be here somewhere,' said Jackson.

'Did you want anything?' inquired Miss Marple.

'Actually,' said Jackson, 'I was just looking at Mrs. Kendal's brand of face cream.'

Miss Marple appreciated the fact that as Jackson was standing with a jar of face cream in his hand he had been adroit in mentioning the fact at once.

'Nice smell,' he said, wrinkling up his nose. 'Fairly good stuff, as these preparations go. The cheaper brands don't suit every skin. Bring it out in a rash as likely as not. The same thing with face powders sometimes.'

'You seem to be very knowledgeable on the subject,' said Miss Marple.

'Worked in the pharmaceutical line for a bit,' said Jackson. 'One learns to know a good deal about cosmetics there. Put stuff in a fancy jar, package it expensively, and it's astonishing what you could rook women for.'

'Is that what you——?' Miss Marple broke off deliberately.

'Well no, I didn't come in here to talk about cosmetics,' Jackson agreed.

'You've not had much time to think up a lie,' thought Miss Marple to herself. 'Let's see what you'll come out with.'

'Matter of fact,' said Jackson, 'Mrs. Walters lent her lipstick to Mrs. Kendal the other day. I came in to get it back for her. I tapped on the window and then I saw Mrs. Kendal was fast asleep, so I thought it would be quite all right if I just walked across into the bathroom and looked for it.'

'I see,' said Miss Marple. 'And did you find it?'

Jackson shook his head. 'Probably in one of her handbags,' he said lightly. 'I won't bother. Mrs. Walters didn't make a point of it. She only just mentioned it casually.' He went on, surveying the toilet preparations: 'Doesn't have very much, does she? Ah well, doesn't need it at her age. Good natural skin.'

'You must look at women with quite a different eye from ordinary men,' said Miss Marple, smiling pleasantly.

'Yes. I suppose various jobs do alter one's angle.'

'You know a good deal about drugs?'

'Oh yes. Good working acquaintance with them. If you ask me, there are too many of them about nowadays. Too many tranquillisers and pep pills and miracle drugs and all the rest of it. All right if they're given on prescription, but there are too many of them you can get without prescription. Some of them can be dangerous.'

'I suppose so,' said Miss Marple. 'Yes, I suppose so.'

'They have a great effect, you know, on behaviour. A lot of this teenage hysteria you get from time to time. It's not natural causes. The kids've been taking things. Oh, there's nothing new about it. It's been known for ages. Out in the East—not that I've ever been there—all sorts of funny things used to happen. You'd be surprised at some of the things women gave their husbands. In India, for example, in the bad old days, a young wife who married an old husband. Didn't want to get rid of him, I suppose, because she'd have been burnt on the funeral pyre, or if she wasn't burnt she'd have been treated as an outcast by the family. No catch to have been a widow in India in those days. But she could keep an elderly husband under drugs, make him semi-imbecile, give him hallucinations, drive him more or less off his head.' He shook his head. 'Yes, lot of dirty work.'

He went on: 'And witches, you know. There's a lot of interesting things known now about witches. Why did they always confess, why did they admit so readily that they *were* witches, that they had flown on broomsticks to the Witches' Sabbath.'

'Torture,' said Miss Marple.

'Not always,' said Jackson. 'Oh yes, torture accounted for a lot of it, but they came out with some of those confessions almost before torture was mentioned. They didn't so much confess as boast about it.

Well, they rubbed themselves with ointments, you know. Anointing they used to call it. Some of the preparations, belladonna, atropine, all that sort of thing; if you rub them on the skin they give you hallucinations of levitation, of flying through the air. They thought it all was genuine, poor devils. And look at the Assassins—medieval people, out in Syria, the Lebanon, somewhere like that. They fed them Indian hemp, gave them hallucinations of paradise and houris, and endless time. They were told that that was what would happen to them after death, but to attain it they had to go and do a ritual killing. Oh, I'm not putting it in fancy language, but that's what it came to.'

'What it came to,' said Miss Marple, 'is in essence the fact that people are highly credulous.'

'Well yes, I suppose you could put it like that.'

'They believe what they are told,' said Miss Marple. 'Yes indeed, we're all inclined to do that,' she added. Then she said sharply, 'Who told you these stories about India, about the doping of husbands with datura,' and she added sharply, before he could answer, 'Was it Major Palgrave?'

Jackson looked slightly surprised. 'Well—yes, as a matter of fact, it was. He told me a lot of stories like that. Of course most of it must have been before his time, but he seemed to know all about it.

'Major Palgrave was under the impression that he knew a lot about everything,' said Miss Marple. 'He was often inaccurate in what he told people.' She shook her head thoughtfully. 'Major Palgrave,' she said, 'has a lot to answer for.'

There was a slight sound from the adjoining bedroom. Miss Marple turned her head sharply. She went quickly out of the bathroom into the bedroom. Lucky Dyson was standing just inside the window.

'I—oh! I didn't think you were here, Miss Marple.'

'I just stepped into the bathroom for a moment,' said Miss Marple, with dignity and a faint air of Victorian reserve.

In the bathroom, Jackson grinned broadly. Victorian modesty always amused him.

'I just wondered if you'd like me to sit with Molly for a bit,' said Lucky. She looked over towards the bed. 'She's asleep, isn't she?'

'I think so,' said Miss Marple. 'But it's really quite all right. You go and amuse yourself, my dear. I thought you'd gone on that expedition?'

'I was going,' said Lucky, 'but I had such a filthy headache that at the last moment I cried off. So I thought I might as well make myself useful.'

'That was very nice of you,' said Miss Marple. She reseated herself by the bed and resumed her knitting, 'but I'm *quite* happy here.'

Lucky hesitated for a moment or two and then turned away and went out. Miss Marple waited a moment then tiptoed back into the bathroom, but Jackson had departed, no doubt through the other door. Miss Marple picked up the jar of face cream he had been holding, and slipped it into her pocket.

22. *A man in her life?*

GETTING A LITTLE CHAT in a natural manner with Dr. Graham was not so easy as Miss Marple had hoped. She was particularly anxious not to approach him directly since she did not want to lend undue importance to the questions that she was going to ask him.

Tim was back, looking after Molly and Miss Marple had arranged that she should relieve him there during the time that dinner was served and he was needed in the dining-room. He had assured her that Mrs. Dyson was quite willing to take that on, or even Mrs. Hillingdon, but Miss Marple said firmly that they were both young women who liked enjoying themselves and that she herself preferred a light meal early and so that would suit everybody. Tim once again thanked her warmly. Hovering rather uncertainly round the hotel and on the pathway which connected with various bungalows, among them Dr. Graham's, Miss Marple tried to plan what she was going to do next.

She had a lot of confused and contradictory ideas in her head and if there was one thing that Miss Marple did not like, it was to have confused and contradictory ideas. This whole business had started out clearly enough. Major Palgrave with his regrettable capacity for telling stories, his indiscretion that had obviously been overheard and the corollary, his death within twenty-four hours. Nothing difficult about *that*, thought Miss Marple.

But afterwards, she was forced to admit, there was nothing *but* difficulty. Everything pointed in too many different directions at once. Once admit that you didn't believe a word that anybody had said to you, that nobody could be trusted, and that many of the persons with whom she had conversed here had had regrettable resemblances to certain persons at St. Mary Mead, and where did that lead you? Her mind was increasingly focused on the victim. Someone was going to be killed and she had the increasing feeling that she ought to know quite well who that someone was. There had been *something*. Something she had heard? Noticed? Seen?

Something someone had told her that had a bearing on the case. Joan Prescott? Joan Prescott had said a lot of things about a lot of people. Scandal? Gossip? What exactly *had* Joan Prescott said?

Gregory Dyson, Lucky—Miss Marple's mind hovered over Lucky. Lucky, she was convinced with a certainty born of her natural suspicions, had been actively concerned in the death of Gregory Dyson's first wife. Everything pointed to it. Could it be that the predestined victim over whom she was worrying was Gregory Dyson? That Lucky intended to try her luck again with another husband, and for that reason wanted not only freedom but the handsome inheritance that she would get as Gregory Dyson's widow?

'But really,' said Miss Marple to herself, 'this is all pure conjecture. I'm being stupid. I know I'm being stupid. The truth must be quite plain, if one could just clear away the litter. Too much litter, that's what's the matter.'

'Talking to yourself?' said Mr. Rafiel.

Miss Marple jumped. She had not noticed his approach. Esther Walters was supporting him and he was coming slowly down from his bungalow to the terrace.

'I really didn't notice you, Mr. Rafiel.'

'Your lips were moving. What's become of all this urgency of yours?'

'It's still urgent,' said Miss Marple, 'only I can't just see what must be perfectly plain——'

'I'm glad it's as simple as that—— Well, if you want any help, count on me.'

He turned his head as Jackson approached them along the path.

'So there you are, Jackson. Where the devil have you been? Never about when I want you.'

'Sorry, Mr. Rafiel.'

Dexterously he slipped his shoulder under Mr. Rafiel's. 'Down to the terrace, sir?'

'You can take me to the bar,' said Mr. Rafiel. 'All right, Esther, you can go now and change into your evening togs. Meet me on the terrace in half an hour.'

He and Jackson went off together. Mrs. Walters dropped into the chair by Miss Marple. She rubbed her arm gently.

'He *seems* a very light weight,' she observed, 'but at the moment my arm feels quite numb. I haven't seen you this afternoon at all Miss Marple.'

'No, I've been sitting with Molly Kendal,' Miss Marple explained. 'She seems really very much better.'

'If you ask me there was never very much wrong with her,' said Esther Walters.

Miss Marple raised her eyebrows. Esther Walters's tone had been decidedly dry.

'You mean—you think her suicide attempt . . .'

'I don't think there *was* any suicide attempt,' said Esther Walters. 'I don't believe for a moment she took a real overdose and I think Dr. Graham knows that perfectly well.'

'Now you interest me very much,' said Miss Marple. 'I wonder why you say that?'

'Because I'm almost certain that it's the case. Oh, it's a thing that happens very often. It's a way, I suppose, of calling attention to oneself,' went on Esther Walters.

'"You'll be sorry when I'm dead"?' quoted Miss Marple.

'That sort of thing,' agreed Esther Walters, 'though I don't think that was the motive in this particular instance. That's the sort of thing you feel like when your husband's playing you up and you're terribly fond of him.'

'You don't think Molly Kendal is fond of her husband?'

'Well,' said Esther Walters, 'do you?'

Miss Marple considered. 'I have,' she said, 'more or less assumed it.' She paused a moment before adding, 'perhaps wrongly.'

Esther was smiling her rather wry smile.

'I've heard a little about her, you know. About the whole business.'

'From Miss Prescott?'

'Oh,' said Esther, 'from one or two people. There's a man in the case. Someone she was keen on. Her people were dead against him.'

'Yes,' said Miss Marple, 'I did hear that.'

'And then she married Tim. Perhaps she was fond of him in a way. But the other man didn't give up. I've wondered once or twice if he didn't actually follow her out here.'

'Indeed. But—who?'

'I've no idea who,' said Esther, 'and I should imagine that they've been very careful.'

'You think she cares for this other man?'

Esther shrugged her shoulders. 'I dare say he's a bad lot,' she said, 'but that's very often the kind who knows how to get under a woman's skin and stay there.'

'You never heard what kind of a man—what he did—anything like that?'

Esther shook her head. 'No. People hazard guesses, but you can't go by that type of thing. He may have been a married man. That may have been why her people disliked it, or he may have been a real bad lot. Perhaps he drank. Perhaps he tangled with the law—I don't know. But she cares for him still. That I know positively.'

'You've seen something, heard something?' Miss Marple hazarded.

'I know what I'm talking about,' said Esther. Her voice was harsh and unfriendly.

'These murders——' began Miss Marple.

'Can't you forget murders?' said Esther. 'You've got Mr. Rafiel now all tangled up in them. Can't you just—let them be? You'll never find out any more, I'm sure of that.'

Miss Marple looked at her.

'You think you know, don't you?' she said.

'I think I do, yes. I'm fairly sure.'

'Then oughtn't you to tell what you know—do something about it?'

'Why should I? What good would it do? I couldn't prove anything. What would happen anyway? People get let off nowadays so easily. They call it diminished responsibility and things like that. A few years in prison and you're out again, as right as rain.'

'Supposing, because you don't tell what you know, somebody else gets killed—another victim?'

Esther shook her head with confidence. 'That won't happen,' she said.

'You can't be sure of it.'

'I am sure. And in any case I don't see who——' She frowned. 'Anyway,' she added, almost inconsequently, 'perhaps it *is*—diminished responsibility. Perhaps you can't help it—not if you are really mentally unbalanced. Oh, I don't know. By far the best thing would be if she went off with whoever it is, then we could all forget about things.'

She glanced at her watch, gave an exclamation of dismay and got up.

'I must go and change.'

Miss Marple sat looking after her. Pronouns, she thought, were always puzzling and women like Esther Walters were particularly prone to strew them about haphazard. Was Esther Walters for some reason convinced that a *woman* had been responsible for the deaths of Major Palgrave and Victoria? It sounded like it. Miss Marple considered.

'Ah, Miss Marple, sitting here all alone—and not even knitting?'

It was Dr. Graham for whom she had sought so long and so unsuccessfully. And here he was prepared of his own accord to sit down for a few minutes' chat. He wouldn't stay long, Miss Marple thought, because he too was bent on changing for dinner, and he usually dined fairly early. She explained that she had been sitting by Molly Kendal's bedside that afternoon.

'One can hardly believe she has made such a good recovery so quickly,' she said.

'Oh well,' said Dr. Graham, 'it's not very surprising. She didn't take a very heavy overdose, you know.'

'Oh, I understood she'd taken quite a half-bottle full of tablets.'

Dr. Graham was smiling indulgently.

'No,' he said, 'I don't think she took that amount. I dare say she meant to take them, then probably at the last moment she threw half of them away. People, even when they think they want to commit suicide, often don't *really* want to do it. They manage not to take a full overdose. It's not always deliberate deceit, it's just the subconscious looking after itself.'

'Or, I suppose it might be deliberate. I mean, wanting it to appear that . . .' Miss Marple paused.

'It's possible,' said Dr. Graham.

'If she and Tim had had a row, for instance?'

'They don't have rows, you know. They seem very fond of each other. Still, I suppose it can always happen once. No, I don't think there's very much wrong with her now. She could really get up and go about as usual. Still, it's safer to keep her where she is for a day or two——'

He got up, nodded cheerfully and went off towards the hotel. Miss Marple sat where she was a little while longer.

Various thoughts passed through her mind—— The book under Molly's mattress—— The way Molly had feigned sleep——

Things Joan Prescott and, later, Esther Walters, had said . . .

And then she went back to the beginning of it all—to Major Palgrave——

Something struggled in her mind. Something about Major Palgrave——

Something that if she could only remember——

23. *The last day*

'AND THE EVENING *and the morning were the last day*,' said Miss Marple to herself.

Then, slightly confused, she sat upright again in her chair. She had dozed off, an incredible thing to do because the steel band was playing and anyone who could doze off during the steel band——Well, it showed, thought Miss Marple, that she was getting used to this place! What was it she had been saying? Some quotation that she'd got wrong. Last day? *First* day. That's what it ought to be. This wasn't the first day. Presumably it wasn't the last day either.

She sat upright again. The fact was that she was extremely tired. All this anxiety, this feeling of having been shamefully inadequate in some way. . . . She remembered unpleasantly once more that queer sly look that Molly had given her from under her half-closed eyelids. What had been going on in that girl's head? How different, thought Miss Marple, everything had seemed at first. Tim Kendal and Molly, such a natural happy young couple. The Hillingdons so pleasant, so well-bred, such what is called 'nice' people. The gay hearty extrovert, Greg Dyson, and the gay strident Lucky, talking nineteen to the dozen, pleased with herself and the world . . . A quartet of people getting on so well together. Canon Prescott, that genial kindly man. Joan Prescott, an acid streak in her, but a very nice woman, and nice women have to have their gossipy distractions. They have to know what is going on, to know when two and two make four, and when it is possible to stretch them to five! There was no harm in such women. Their tongues wagged but they were kind if you were in misfortune. Mr. Rafiel, a personality, a man of character, a man that you would never by any chance forget. But Miss Marple thought she knew something else about Mr. Rafiel.

The doctors had often given him up, so he had said, but this time, she thought, they had been more certain in their pronouncements. Mr. Rafiel knew that his days were numbered.

Knowing this with certainty, was there any action he might have been likely to take?

Miss Marple considered the question.

It might, she thought, be important.

What was it exactly he had said, his voice a little too loud, a little too sure? Miss Marple was very skilful in tones of voice. She had done so much listening in her life.

Mr. Rafiel had been telling her something that wasn't true.

Miss Marple looked round her. The night air, the soft fragrance of flowers, the tables with their little lights, the women with their pretty dresses, Evelyn in a dark indigo and white print, Lucky in a white sheath, her golden hair shining. Everybody seemed gay and full of life to-night. Even Tim Kendal was smiling. He passed her table and said:

'Can't thank you enough for all you've done. Molly's practically herself again. The doc says she can get up to-morrow.'

Miss Marple smiled at him and said that that was good hearing. She found it, however, quite an effort to smile. Decidedly, she was tired . . .

She got up and walked slowly back to her bungalow. She would have liked to go on thinking, puzzling, trying to remember, trying to assemble various facts and words and glances. But she wasn't able to do it. The tired mind rebelled. It said 'Sleep! You've got to go to sleep!'

Miss Marple undressed, got into bed, read a few verses of the Thomas à Kempis which she kept by her bed, then she turned out the light. In the darkness she sent up a prayer. One couldn't do everything oneself. One had to have help. 'Nothing will happen to-night,' she murmured hopefully.

2

Miss Marple woke suddenly and sat up in bed. Her heart was beating. She switched on the light and looked at the little clock by her bedside. Two a.m. Two a.m. and outside activity of some kind was going on. She got up, put on her dressing-gown and slippers, and a woollen scarf round her head and went out to reconnoitre. There were people moving about with torches. Among them she saw Canon Prescott and went to him.

'What's happening?'

'Oh, Miss Marple? It's Mrs. Kendal. Her husband woke up, found she'd slipped out of bed and gone out. We're looking for her.'

He hurried on. Miss Marple walked more slowly after him. Where had Molly gone? Why? Had she planned this deliberately, planned to slip away as soon as the guard on her was relaxed, and while her husband was deep in sleep? Miss Marple thought it was probable. But why? What was the reason? Was there, as Esther Walters had so strongly hinted, some other man? If so, who could that man be? Or was there some more sinister reason?

Miss Marple walked on, looking around her, peering under bushes. Then suddenly she heard a faint call:

'Here. . . . This way. . . .'

The cry had come from some little distance beyond the hotel grounds. It must be, thought Miss Marple, near the creek of water that ran down to the sea. She went in that direction as briskly as she could.

There were not really so many searchers as it had seemed to her at first. Most people must still be asleep in their bungalows. She saw a place on the creek bank where there were people standing. Someone pushed past her, almost knocking her down, running in that direction. It was Tim Kendal. A minute or two later she heard his voice cry out: 'Molly! My God, Molly!'

It was a minute or two before Miss Marple was able to join the little group. It consisted of one of the Cuban waiters, Evelyn Hillingdon, and two of the native girls. They had parted to let Tim through. Miss Marple arrived as he was bending over to look.

'Molly . . .' He slowly dropped on to his knees. Miss Marple saw the girl's body clearly, lying there in the creek, her face below the level of the water, her golden hair spread over the pale green embroidered shawl that covered her shoulders. With the leaves and rushes of the creek, it seemed almost like a scene from *Hamlet* with Molly as the dead Ophelia. . . .

As Tim stretched out a hand to touch her, the quiet, common-sense Miss Marple took charge and spoke sharply and authoritatively.

'Don't move her, Mr. Kendal,' she said. 'She mustn't be moved.'

Tim turned a dazed face up to her.

'But—I must—it's Molly. I must . . .'

Evelyn Hillingdon touched his shoulder.

'She's dead, Tim. I didn't move her, but I did feel her pulse.'

'Dead?' said Tim unbelievingly. 'Dead? You mean she's—*drowned* herself?'

'I'm afraid so. It looks like it.'

'But *why?*' A great cry burst from the young man. '*Why?* She was so happy this evening. Talking about what we'd do to-morrow. Why should this terrible death wish come over her again. Why should she steal away as she did—rush out into the night, come down here and drown herself. What despair did she have—what misery—why couldn't she *tell* me anything?'

'I don't know, my dear,' said Evelyn gently. 'I don't know.'

Miss Marple said:

'Somebody had better get Dr. Graham. And someone will have to telephone the police.'

'The police?' Tim uttered a bitter laugh. 'What good will they be?'

'The police have to be notified in a case of suicide,' said Miss Marple.

Tim rose slowly to his feet.

'I'll get Graham,' he said heavily. 'Perhaps—even now—he could—do something.'

He stumbled away in the direction of the hotel.

Evelyn Hillingdon and Miss Marple stood side by side looking down at the dead girl.

Evelyn shook her head. 'It's too late. She's quite cold. She must have been dead at least an hour—perhaps more. What a tragedy it all is. Those two always seemed so happy. I suppose she was always unbalanced.'

'No,' said Miss Marple. 'I don't think she was unbalanced.'

Evelyn looked at her curiously. 'What do you mean?'

The moon had been behind a cloud, but now it came out into the open. It shone with a luminous silvery brightness on Molly's outspread hair . . .

Miss Marple gave a sudden ejaculation. She bent down, peering, then stretched out her hand and touched the golden head. She spoke to Evelyn Hillingdon, and her voice sounded quite different.

'I think,' she said, 'that we had better make sure.'

Evelyn Hillingdon stared at her in astonishment.

'But you yourself told Tim we mustn't touch anything?'

'I know. But the moon wasn't out. I hadn't seen——'

Her finger pointed. Then, very gently, she touched the blonde hair and parted it so that the roots were exposed . . .

Evelyn gave a sharp ejaculation.

'*Lucky!*'

And then after a moment she repeated:

'Not Molly. . . . Lucky.'

Miss Marple nodded. 'Their hair was of much the same colour—but hers, of course, was dark at the roots because it was dyed.'

'But she's wearing Molly's shawl?'

'She admired it. I heard her say she was going to get one like it. Evidently she did.'

'So that's why we were—deceived. . . .'

Evelyn broke off as she met Miss Marple's eyes watching her.

'Someone,' said Miss Marple, 'will have to tell her husband.'

There was a moment's pause, then Evelyn said:

'All right. I'll do it.'

She turned and walked away through the palm trees.

Miss Marple remained for a moment motionless, then she turned her head very slightly, and said: 'Yes, Colonel Hillingdon?'

Edward Hillingdon came from the trees behind her to stand by her side.

'You knew I was there?'

'You cast a shadow,' said Miss Marple.

They stood a moment in silence.

He said, more as though he were speaking to himself:

'So, in the end, she played her luck too far. . . .'

'You are, I think, glad that she is dead?'

'And that shocks you? Well, I will not deny it. I am glad she is dead.'

'Death is often a solution to problems.'

Edward Hillingdon turned his head slowly. Miss Marple met his eyes calmly and steadfastly.

'If you think——' he took a sharp step towards her.

There was a sudden menace in his tone.

Miss Marple said quietly:

'Your wife will be back with Mr. Dyson in a moment. Or Mr. Kendal will be here with Dr. Graham.'

Edward Hillingdon relaxed. He turned back to look down at the dead woman.

Miss Marple slipped away quietly. Presently her pace quickened.

Just before reaching her own bungalow, she paused. It was here that she had sat that day talking to Major Palgrave. It was here that he had fumbled in his wallet looking for the snapshot of a murderer. . . .

She remembered how he had looked up, and how his face had gone purple and red . . . 'So ugly,' as Señora de Caspearo had said. 'He has the Evil Eye.'

The Evil Eye . . . Eye . . . *Eye*. . . .

24. *Nemesis*

WHATEVER THE ALARMS and excursions of the night, Mr. Rafiel had not heard them.

He was fast asleep in bed, a faint thin snore coming from his nostrils, when he was taken by the shoulders and shaken violently.

'Eh—what—what the devil's this?'

'It's me,' said Miss Marple, for once ungrammatical, 'though I should put it a little more strongly than that. The Greeks, I believe, had a word for it. Nemesis, if I am not wrong.'

Mr. Rafiel raised himself on his pillows as far as he could. He stared at her. Miss Marple, standing there in the moonlight, her head encased in a fluffy scarf of pale pink wool, looked as unlike a figure of Nemesis as it was possible to imagine.

'So you're Nemesis, are you?' said Mr. Rafiel after a momentary pause.

'I hope to be—with your help.'

'Do you mind telling me quite plainly what you're talking about like this in the middle of the night.'

'I think we may have to act quickly. Very quickly. I have been foolish. Extremely foolish. I ought to have known from the very beginning what all this was about. It was so simple.'

'What was simple, and what are you talking about?'

'You slept through a good deal,' said Miss Marple. 'A body was found. We thought at first it was the body of Molly Kendal. It wasn't, it was Lucky Dyson. Drowned in the creek.'

'Lucky, eh?' said Mr. Rafiel. 'And drowned? In the creek. Did she drown herself or did somebody drown her?'

'Somebody drowned her,' said Miss Marple.

'I see. At least I think I see. That's what you mean by saying it's so simple, is it? Greg Dyson was always the first possibility, and he's the right one. Is that it? Is that what you're thinking? And what you're afraid of is that he may get away with it.'

Miss Marple took a deep breath.

'Mr. Rafiel, will you trust me. We have got to stop a murder being committed.'

'I thought you said it *had* been committed.'

'That murder was committed in error. Another murder may be committed any moment now. There's no time to lose. We must prevent it happening. We must go at once.'

'It's all very well to talk like that,' said Mr. Rafiel. '*We*, you say? What do you think *I* can do about it? I can't even walk without help. How can you and I set about preventing a murder? You're about a hundred and I'm a broken up old crock.'

'I was thinking of Jackson,' said Miss Marple. 'Jackson will do what you tell him, won't he?'

'He will indeed,' said Mr. Rafiel, 'especially if I add that I'll make it worth his while. Is that what you want?'

'Yes. Tell him to come with me and tell him to obey any orders I give him.'

Mr. Rafiel looked at her for about six seconds. Then he said:

'Done. I expect I'm taking the biggest risk of my life. Well, it won't be the first one.' He raised his voice. 'Jackson.' At the same time he picked up the electric bell that lay beside his hand and pressed the button.

Hardly thirty seconds passed before Jackson appeared through the connecting door to the adjoining room.

'You called and rang, sir? Anything wrong?' He broke off, staring at Miss Marple.

'Now Jackson, do as I tell you. You will go with this lady, Miss Marple. You'll go where she takes you and you'll do exactly as she says. You'll obey every order she gives you. Is that understood?'

'I——'

'*Is that understood?*'

'Yes, sir.'

'And for doing that,' said Mr. Rafiel, 'you won't be the loser. I'll make it worth your while.'

'Thank you, sir.'

'Come along, Mr. Jackson,' said Miss Marple. She spoke over her shoulder to Mr. Rafiel. 'We'll tell Mrs. Walters to come to you on our way. Get her to get you out of bed and bring you along.'

'Bring me along where?'

'To the Kendals' bungalow,' said Miss Marple. 'I think Molly will be coming back there.'

2

Molly came up the path from the sea. Her eyes stared fixedly ahead of her. Occasionally, under her breath, she gave a little whimper . . .

She went up the steps of the loggia, paused a moment, then pushed open the window and walked into the bedroom. The lights were on, but the room itself was empty. Molly went across to the bed and sat down. She sat for some minutes, now and again passing her hand over her forehead and frowning.

Then, after a quick surreptitious glance round, she slipped her hand under the mattress and brought out the book that was hidden there. She bent over it, turning the pages to find what she wanted.

Then she raised her head as a sound of running footsteps came from outside. With a quick guilty movement she pushed the book behind her back.

Tim Kendal, panting and out of breath, came in, and uttered a great sigh of relief at the sight of her.

'Thank God. Where have you been, Molly? I've been searching everywhere for you.'

'I went to the creek.'

'You went——' he stopped.

'Yes. I went to the creek. But I couldn't wait there. I couldn't. There was someone in the water—and she was dead.'

'You mean—— Do you know I thought it was *you*. I've only just found out it was Lucky.'

'I didn't kill her. Really, Tim, I didn't kill her. I'm sure I didn't. I mean—I'd remember if I did, wouldn't I?'

Tim sank slowly down on the end of the bed.

'You didn't—— Are you sure that——? No. No, of course you didn't!' He fairly shouted the words. 'Don't start thinking like that, Molly. Lucky drowned herself. Of course she drowned herself. Hillingdon was through with her. She went and lay down with her face in the water——'

'Lucky wouldn't do that. She'd never do that. But *I* didn't kill her. I swear I didn't.'

'Darling, of course you didn't!' He put his arms round her but she pulled herself away.

'I hate this place. It ought to be all sunlight. It seemed to be all sunlight. But it isn't. Instead there's a shadow—a big black shadow . . . And I'm in it—and I can't get out——'

Her voice had risen to a shout.

'Hush, Molly. For God's sake, hush! He went into the bathroom, came back with a glass.

'Look. Drink this. It'll steady you.'

'I—I can't drink anything. My teeth are chattering so.'

'Yes you can, darling. Sit down. Here, on the bed.' He put his arm round her. He approached the glass to her lips. 'There you are now. Drink it.'

A voice spoke from the window.

'Jackson,' said Miss Marple clearly. 'Go over. Take that glass from him and hold it tightly. Be careful. He's strong and he may be pretty desperate.'

There were certain points about Jackson. He was a man of training, trained to obey orders. He was a man with a great love for money, and money had been promised him by his employer, that employer being a man of stature and authority. He was also a man of extreme muscular development heightened by his training. His not to reason why, his but to do.

Swift as a flash he had crossed the room. His hand went over the glass that Tim was holding to Molly's lips, his other arm had fastened round Tim. A quick flick of the wrist and he had the glass. Tim turned on him wildly, but Jackson held him firmly.

'What the devil—let go of me. Let go of me. Have you gone mad? What are you doing?'

Tim struggled violently.

'Hold him, Jackson,' said Miss Marple.

'What's going on? What's the matter here?'

Supported by Esther Walters, Mr. Rafiel came through the window.

'You ask what's the matter?' shouted Tim. 'Your man's gone mad, stark, staring mad, that's what's the matter. Tell him to let go of me.'

'No,' said Miss Marple.

Mr. Rafiel turned to her.

'Speak up, Nemesis,' he said. 'We've got to have chapter and verse of some kind.'

'I've been stupid and a fool,' said Miss Marple, 'but I'm not being a fool now. When the contents of that glass that he was trying to make his wife drink, have been analysed, I'll wager—yes, I'll wager my immortal soul that you'll find it's got a lethal dose of narcotic in it. It's the same pattern, you see, the same pattern as in Major Palgrave's story. A wife in a depressed state, and she tries to do away with herself, husband saves her in time. Then the second time she succeeds. Yes, it's the right pattern. Major Palgrave told me the story and he took out a snapshot and then he looked up and saw——'

'Over your right shoulder——' continued Mr. Rafiel.

'No,' said Miss Marple, shaking her head. '*He didn't see anything over my right shoulder*.'

'What are you talking about? You told me . . .'

'I told you wrong. I was completely wrong. I was stupid beyond belief. Major Palgrave *appeared* to me to be looking over my right shoulder, glaring, in fact, at something—— But he couldn't have *seen* anything, because he was looking through his left eye and his left eye was his glass eye.'

'I remember—he *had* a glass eye,' said Mr. Rafiel. 'I'd forgotten —or I took it for granted. You mean he couldn't see anything?'

'Of course he could *see*,' said Miss Marple. 'He could *see* all right, but he could only see with one eye. The eye he *could* see with was his *right* eye. And so, you see, he must have been looking at something or someone not to the right of me but to the *left* of me.'

'Was there anyone on the left of you?'

'Yes,' said Miss Marple. 'Tim Kendal and his wife were sitting not far off. Sitting at a table just by a big hibiscus bush. They were doing accounts there. So you see the Major looked up. His glass left eye was glaring over my shoulder, but what he *saw* with his other eye was a man sitting by a hibiscus bush and the face was the same, only rather older, as the face in the snapshot. Also, by a hibiscus bush. Tim Kendal had heard the story the Major had been telling and he saw that the Major had recognised him. So, of course, he had to kill him. Later, he had to kill the girl, Victoria, because she'd seen him putting a bottle of tablets in the Major's room. She didn't think anything of it at first because of course it was quite natural on various occasions for Tim Kendal to go into the guests' bungalows. He might have just been returning something to it that had been left on a restaurant table. But she thought about it and then she asked him questions and so he had to get rid of her. But this is the real murder, the murder he's been planning all along. He's a wife-killer, you see.'

'What damned nonsense, what——' Tim Kendal shouted.

There was a sudden cry, a wild angry cry. Esther Walters detached herself from Mr. Rafiel, almost flinging him down and rushed across the room. She pulled vainly at Jackson.

'Let go of him—let go of him. It's not true. Not a word of it's true. Tim—Tim darling, it's not true. You could never kill anyone, I know you couldn't. I know you wouldn't. It's that horrible girl you married. She's been telling lies about you. They're not true. None of them are true. I believe in you. I love you and trust in you. I'll never believe a word anyone says. I'll——'

Then Tim Kendal lost control of himself.

'For God's sake, you damned bitch,' he said, 'shut up, can't you? D'you want to get me hanged? Shut up, I tell you. Shut that big, ugly mouth of yours.'

'Poor silly creature,' said Mr. Rafiel softly. 'So that's what's been going on, is it?'

25. *Miss Marple uses her imagination*

'SO THAT'S what had been going on?' said Mr. Rafiel.

He and Miss Marple were sitting together in a confidential manner.

'She'd been having an affair with Tim Kendal, had she?'

'Hardly an affair, I imagine,' said Miss Marple, primly. 'It was, I think, a romantic attachment with the prospect of marriage in the future.'

'What—after his wife was dead?'

'I don't think poor Esther Walters knew that Molly was going to die,' said Miss Marple. 'I just think she believed the story Tim Kendal told her about Molly having been in love with another man, and the man having followed her here, and I think she counted on Tim's getting a divorce. I think it was all quite proper and respectable. But she was very much in love with him.'

'Well, that's easily understood. He was an attractive chap. But what made *him* go for her—d'you know that too?'

'*You* know, don't you?' said Miss Marple.

'I dare say I've got a pretty fair idea, but I don't know how you should know about it. As far as that goes, I don't see how Tim Kendal could know about it.'

'Well, I really think I could explain all that with a little imagination, though it would be simpler if you told me.'

'I'm not going to tell you,' said Mr. Rafiel. 'You tell me, since you're being so clever.'

'Well, it seems to me possible,' said Miss Marple, 'that as I have already hinted to you, your man Jackson was in the habit of taking a good snoop through your various business papers from time to time.'

'Perfectly possible,' said Mr. Rafiel, 'but I shouldn't have said there was anything there that could do him much good. I took care of that.'

'I imagine,' said Miss Marple, 'he read your will.'

'Oh I see. Yes, yes, I did have a copy of my will along.'

'You told me,' said Miss Marple, 'you told me—(as Humpty Dumpty said—very loud and clear) that you had *not* left anything to Esther Walters in your will. You had impressed that fact upon her, and also upon Jackson. It was true in Jackson's case, I should imagine. You have not left *him* anything, but you *had* left Esther Walters money, though you weren't going to let her have any inkling of the fact. Isn't that right?'

'Yes, it's quite right, but I don't know how *you* knew.'

'Well, it's the way you insisted on the point,' said Miss Marple. 'I have a certain experience of the way people tell lies.'

'I give in,' said Mr. Rafiel. 'All right. I left Esther £50,000. It would come as a nice surprise to her when I died. I suppose that, knowing this, Tim Kendal decided to exterminate his present wife with a nice dose of something or other and marry £50,000 and Esther Walters. Possibly to dispose of her also in good time. But how did *he* know she was going to have £50,000?'

'Jackson told him, of course,' said Miss Marple. 'They were very friendly, those two. Tim Kendal was nice to Jackson and, quite, I should imagine, without ulterior motive. But amongst the bits of gossip that Jackson let slip I think Jackson told him that unbeknown to herself, Esther Walters was going to inherit a fat lot of money, and he may have said that he himself hoped to induce Esther Walters to marry him though he hadn't had much success so far in taking her fancy. Yes, I think that's how it happened.'

'The things you imagine always seem perfectly plausible,' said Mr. Rafiel.

'But I was stupid,' said Miss Marple, 'very stupid. Everything fitted in really, you see. Tim Kendal was a very clever man as well as being a very wicked one. He was particularly good at putting about rumours. Half the things I've been told here came from him originally, I imagine. There were stories going around about Molly wanting to marry an undesirable young man, but I rather fancy that the undesirable young man was actually Tim Kendal himself, though that wasn't the name he was using then. Her people had heard something, perhaps that his background was rather fishy. So he put on a high indignation act, refused to be taken by Molly to be "shown off" to her people and then he brewed up a little scheme with her which they both thought great fun. She pretended to sulk and pine for him. Then a Mr. Tim Kendal turned up, primed with the names of various old friends of Molly's people, and they welcomed him with open arms as being the sort of young man who would put the former delinquent one out of Molly's head. I am afraid Molly and he must have laughed over it a good deal. Anyway, he married her, and with her money he bought out the people who ran this place and they came out here. I should imagine that he ran through her money at a pretty fair rate. Then he came across Esther Walters and he saw a nice prospect of more money.'

'Why didn't he bump me off?' said Mr. Rafiel.

Miss Marple coughed.

'I expect he wanted to be fairly sure of Mrs. Walters first. Besides—I mean . . .' She stopped, a little confused.

'Besides, he realised he wouldn't have to wait long,' said Mr. Rafiel, 'and it would clearly be better for me to die a natural death. Being so rich. Deaths of millionaires are scrutinised rather carefully, aren't they, unlike mere wives?'

'Yes, you're quite right. Such a lot of lies as he told,' said Miss Marple. 'Look at the lies he got Molly herself to believe—putting that book on mental disorders in her way. Giving her drugs which would give her dreams and hallucinations. You know, your Jackson was rather clever over that. I think he recognised certain of Molly's symptoms as being the result of drugs. And he came into the bungalow that day to potter about a bit in the bathroom. That face cream he examined. He might have got some idea from the old tales of witches rubbing themselves with ointments that had belladonna in them. Belladonna in face cream could have produced just that result. Molly would have black-outs. Times she couldn't account for, dreams of flying through the air. No wonder she got frightened about herself. She had all the signs of mental illness, Jackson was on the right track. Maybe he got the idea from Major Palgrave's stories about the use of datura by Indian women on their husbands.'

'Major Palgrave' said Mr. Rafiel. 'Really, that man!'

'He brought about his own murder,' said Miss Marple, 'and that poor girl Victoria's murder, and he nearly brought about Molly's murder. But he recognised a murderer all right.'

'What made you suddenly remember about his glass eye?' asked Mr. Rafiel curiously.

'Something that Señora de Caspearo said. She talked some nonsense about his being ugly, and having the Evil Eye; and I said it was only a glass eye, and he couldn't help that, poor man, and she said his eyes looked different ways, they were cross-eyes—which, of course, they were. And she said it brought bad luck. I knew—I *knew* that I had heard something that day that was important. Last night, just after Lucky's death, it came to me what it was! And then I realised there was no time to waste . . .'

'How did Tim Kendal come to kill the wrong woman?'

'Sheer chance. I think his plan was this: Having convinced everybody—and that included Molly herself—that she was mentally unbalanced, and after giving her a sizeable dose of the drug he was using, he told her that between them they were going to clear up all these murder puzzles. But she had got to help him. After everyone was asleep, they would go separately and meet at an agreed spot by the creek.

'He said he had a very good idea who the murderer was, and they would trap him. Molly went off obediently—but she was confused and stupefied with the drug she had been given, and it slowed her up. Tim arrived there first and saw what he thought was Molly. Golden hair and pale green shawl. He came up behind her, put his hand over her mouth, and forced her down into the water and held her there.'

'Nice fellow! But wouldn't it have been easier just to give her an overdose of narcotic?'

'Much easier, of course. But that *might* have given rise to suspicion. All narcotics and sedatives had been very carefully removed from Molly's reach, remember. And if she *had* got hold of a fresh supply, who more likely to have supplied it than her husband? But if, in a fit of despair, she went out and drowned herself whilst her innocent husband slept, the whole thing would be a romantic tragedy, and no one would be likely to suggest that she had been drowned deliberately. Besides,' added Miss Marple, 'murderers always find it difficult to keep things simple. They can't keep themselves from elaborating.'

'You seem convinced you know all there is to be known about murderers! So you believe Tim didn't know he had killed the wrong woman?'

Miss Marple shook her head.

'He didn't even look at her face, just hurried off as quickly as he could, let an hour elapse, then started to organise a search for her, playing the part of a distracted husband.'

'But what the devil was Lucky doing hanging about the creek in the middle of the night?'

Miss Marple gave an embarrassed little cough.

'It is possible, I think, that she was—er—waiting to meet someone.'

'Edward Hillingdon?'

'Oh *no*,' said Miss Marple. 'That's all over. I wondered whether—just possibly—she might have been waiting for Jackson.'

'Waiting for *Jackson*?'

'I've noticed her—look at him once or twice,' murmured Miss Marple, averting her eyes.

Mr. Rafiel whistled.

'My Tom Cat Jackson! I wouldn't put it past him! Tim must have had a shock later when he found he'd killed the wrong woman.'

'Yes, indeed. He must have felt quite desperate. Here was Molly alive and wandering about. And the story he'd circulated so carefully about her mental condition wouldn't stand up for a moment once she got into the hands of competent mental specialists. And once she told her damning story of his having asked her to meet him at the creek, where would Tim Kendal be? He'd only one hope—to finish off Molly as quickly as possible. Then there was a very good chance that everyone would believe that Molly, in a fit of mania, had drowned Lucky, and had then, horrified by what she had done, taken her own life.'

'And it was then,' said Mr. Rafiel, 'that you decided to play Nemesis, eh?'

He leaned back suddenly and roared with laughter. 'It's a damned good joke,' he said. 'If you knew what you looked like that night with that fluffy pink wool all round your head, standing there and saying you were Nemesis! I'll never forget it!'

EPILOGUE

THE TIME HAD COME and Miss Marple was waiting at the airport for her plane. Quite a lot of people had come to see her off. The Hillingdons had left already. Gregory Dyson had flown to one of the other islands and the rumour had come that he was devoting himself to an Argentinian widow. Señora de Caspearo had returned to South America.

Molly had come to see Miss Marple off. She was pale and thin but she had weathered the shock of her discovery bravely and with the help of one of Mr. Rafiel's nominees whom he had wired for to England, she was carrying on with the running of the hotel.

'Do you good to be busy,' Mr. Rafiel observed. 'Keep you from thinking. Got a good thing here.'

'You don't think the murders——'

'People love murders when they're all cleared up,' Mr. Rafiel had assured her. 'You carry on, girl, and keep your heart up. Don't distrust all men because you've met one bad lot.'

'You sound like Miss Marple,' Molly had said, 'she's always telling me Mr. Right will come along one day.'

Mr. Rafiel grinned at this sentiment. So Molly was there and the two Prescotts and Mr. Rafiel, of course, and Esther—an Esther who looked older and sadder and to whom Mr. Rafiel was quite often unexpectedly kind. Jackson also was very much to the fore, pretending to be looking after Miss Marple's baggage. He was all smiles these days and let it be known that he had come into money.

There was a hum in the sky. The plane was arriving. Things were somewhat informal here. There was no 'taking your place by Channel 8' or Channel 9. You just walked out from the little flower-covered pavilion on to the tarmac.

'Good-bye, darling Miss Marple.' Molly kissed her.

'Good-bye. Do try and come and visit us.' Miss Prescott shook her warmly by the hand.

'It has been a great pleasure to know you,' said the Canon. 'I second my sister's invitation most warmly.'

'All the best, Madam,' said Jackson, 'and remember any time you want any massage free, just you send me a line and we'll make an appointment.'

Only Esther Walters turned slightly away when the time came for good-byes. Miss Marple did not force one upon her. Mr. Rafiel came last. He took her hand.

'*Ave Caesar, nos morituri te salutamus*,' he said.

'I'm afraid,' said Miss Marple, 'I don't know very much Latin.'

'But you understand that?'

'Yes.' She said no more. She knew quite well what he was telling her.

'It has been a great pleasure to know you,' she said.

Then she walked across the tarmac and got into the plane.

Taken at the Flood

There is a tide in the affairs of men,
Which, taken at the flood, leads on to fortune;
Omitted, all the voyage of their life
Is bound in shallows and in miseries.
On such a full sea are we now afloat,
And we must take the current when it serves,
Or lose our ventures.

SHAKESPEARE (*Julius Caesar*)

PROLOGUE

1

IN EVERY CLUB there is a club bore. The Coronation Club was no exception; and the fact that an Air Raid was in progress made no difference to normal procedure.

Major Porter, late Indian Army, rustled his newspaper and cleared his throat. Every one avoided his eye, but it was no use.

'I see they've got the announcement of Gordon Cloade's death in the *Times*,' he said. 'Discreetly put, of course. *On Oct. 5th, result of enemy action.* No address given. As a matter of fact it was just round the corner from my little place. One of those big houses on top of Campden Hill. I can tell you it shook me up a bit. I'm a Warden, you know. Cloade had only just got back from the States. He'd been over on that Government Purchase business. Got married while he was over there. A young widow—young enough to be his daughter. Mrs. Underhay. As a matter of fact I knew her first husband out in Nigeria.'

Major Porter paused. Nobody displayed any interest or asked him to continue. Newspapers were held up sedulously in front of faces, but it took more than that to discourage Major Porter. He always had long histories to relate, mostly about people whom nobody knew.

'Interesting,' said Major Porter, firmly, his eyes fixed absently on a pair of extremely pointed patent leather shoes—a type of footwear of which he profoundly disapproved. 'As I said, I'm a Warden. Funny business this blast. Never know what it's going to do. Blew the basement in and ripped off the roof. First floor practically wasn't touched. Six people in the house. Three servants; married couple and a housemaid, Gordon Cloade, his wife and the wife's brother. They were all down in the basement except the wife's brother—ex-Commando fellow—he preferred his own comfortable bedroom on the first floor—and by jove, he escaped with a few bruises. The three servants were all killed by blast—Gordon Cloade was buried, they dug him out but he died on the way to hospital. His wife was suffering from blast, hadn't got a stitch of clothing on her! but she was alive. They think she'll pull through. She'll be a rich widow—Gordon Cloade must have been worth well over a million.'

Again Major Porter paused. His eyes had travelled up from the patent leather shoes—striped trousers—black coat—egg-shaped head and colossal moustaches. Foreign, of course! That explained the shoes. 'Really,' thought Major Porter, 'what's the club coming to? Can't get away from foreigners even *here*.' This separate train of thought ran alongside his narrative.

The fact that the foreigner in question appeared to be giving him full attention did not abate Major Porter's prejudice in the slightest.

'She can't be more than about twenty-five,' he went on. 'And a widow for the second time. Or at any rate—that's what *she* thinks . . .'

He paused, hoping for curiosity—for comment. Not getting it, he nevertheless went doggedly on:

'Matter of fact I've got my own ideas about that. Queer business. As I told you, I knew her first husband, Underhay. Nice fellow—district commissioner in Nigeria at one time. Absolutely dead keen on his job—first-class chap. He married this girl in Capetown. She was out there with some touring company. Very down on her luck, and pretty and helpless and all that. Listened to poor old Underhay raving about his district and the great wide open spaces—and breathed out, "Wasn't it wonderful?" and how she wanted "to get away from everything." Well, she married him and got away from it. He was very much in love, poor fellow—but the thing didn't tick over from the first. She hated the bush and was terrified of the natives and was bored to death. Her idea of life was to go round to the local and meet the theatrical crowd and talk shop. Solitude à deux in the jungle wasn't at all her cup of tea. Mind you, I never met her myself—I heard all this from poor old Underhay. It hit him pretty hard. He did the decent thing, sent her home and agreed to give her a divorce. It was just after that that I met him. He was all on edge and in the mood when a man's got to talk. He was a funny old-fashioned kind of chap in some ways—an R.C., and he didn't care for divorce. He said to me, "There are other ways of giving a woman her freedom." "Now, look here, old boy," I said, "don't go doing anything foolish. No woman in the world is worth putting a bullet through your head."

'He said that that wasn't his idea at all. "But I'm a lonely man," he said. "Got no relations to bother about me. If a report of my death gets back that will make Rosaleen a widow, which is what she wants." "And what about you?" I said. "Well," he said, "maybe a Mr. Enoch Arden will turn up somewhere a thousand miles or so away and start life anew." "Might be awkward for her some day," I warned him. "Oh, no," he says, "I'd play the game. Robert Underhay would be dead all right."

'Well, I didn't think any more of it, but six months later I heard that Underhay had died of fever up in the bush somewhere. His natives were a trustworthy lot and they came back with a good circumstantial tale and a few last words scrawled in Underhay's writing saying they'd done all they could for him, and he was afraid he was pegging out, and praising up his headman. That man was devoted to him and so were all the others. Whatever he told them to swear to, they would swear to. So there it is . . . Maybe Underhay's buried up country in the midst of equatorial Africa but maybe he isn't—and if he isn't Mrs. Gordon Cloade may get a shock one day. And serve her right, I say. I never met her, but I know the sound of a little gold digger! She broke up poor old Underhay all right. It's an interesting story.'

Major Porter looked round rather wistfully for confirmation of this assertion. He met two bored and fishy stares, the half-averted gaze of young Mr. Mellon and the polite attention of M. Hercule Poirot.

Then the newspaper rustled and a grey-haired man with a singularly impassive face rose quietly from his arm-chair by the fire and went out.

Major Porter's jaw dropped, and young Mr. Mellon gave a faint whistle.

'Now you've done it!' he remarked. 'Know who that was?'

'God bless my soul,' said Major Porter in some agitation. 'Of course. I don't know him intimately but we are acquainted . . . Jeremy Cloade, isn't it, Gordon Cloade's brother? Upon my word, how extremely unfortunate! If I'd had any idea——'

'He's a solicitor,' said young Mr. Mellon. 'Bet he sues you for slander or defamation of character or something.'

For young Mr. Mellon enjoyed creating alarm and despondency in such places as it was not forbidden by the Defence of the Realm Act.

Major Porter continued to repeat in an agitated manner:

'Most unfortunate. *Most* unfortunate!'

'It will be all over Warmsley Heath by this evening,' said Mr.

Mellon. 'That's where all the Cloades hang out. They'll sit up late discussing what action to take.'

But at that moment the All Clear sounded, and young Mr. Mellon stopped being malicious, and tenderly piloted his friend Hercule Poirot out into the street.

'Terrible atmosphere, these clubs,' he said. 'The most crashing collection of old bores. Porter's easily the worst, though. His description of the Indian rope trick takes three quarters of an hour, and he knows everybody whose mother ever passed through Poona!'

This was in the Autumn of 1944. It was in late Spring, 1946, that Hercule Poirot received a visit.

2

Hercule Poirot was sitting at his neat writing-desk on a pleasant May morning when his manservant George approached him and murmured deferentially:

'There is a lady, sir, asking to see you.'

'What kind of a lady?' Poirot asked cautiously.

He always enjoyed the meticulous accuracy of George's descriptions.

'She would be aged between forty and fifty, I should say, sir. Untidy and somewhat artistic in appearance. Good walking-shoes, brogues. A tweed coat and skirt—but a lace blouse. Some questionable Egyptian beads and a blue chiffon scarf.'

Poirot shuddered slightly.

'I do not think,' he said, 'that I wish to see her.'

'Shall I tell her, sir, that you are indisposed?'

Poirot looked at him thoughtfully.

'You have already, I gather, told her that I am engaged on important business and cannot be disturbed?'

George coughed again.

'She said, sir, that she had come up from the country specially, and did not mind how long she waited.'

Poirot sighed.

'One should never struggle against the inevitable,' he said. 'If a middle-aged lady wearing sham Egyptian beads has made up her mind to see the famous Hercule Poirot, and has come up from the country to do so, nothing will deflect her. She will sit there in the hall till she gets her way. Show her in, George.'

George retreated, returning presently to announce formally:

'Mrs. Cloade.'

The figure in the worn tweeds and the floating scarf came in with a beaming face. She advanced to Poirot with an outstretched hand, all her bead necklaces swinging and clinking.

'M. Poirot,' she said, 'I have come to you under spirit guidance.'

Poirot blinked slightly.

'Indeed, Madame. Perhaps you will take a seat and tell me——'

He got no further.

'Both ways, M. Poirot. With the automatic writing *and* with the ouija board. It was the night before last. Madame Elvary (a wonderful woman she is) and I were using the board. We got the same initials repeatedly. H.P. H.P. H.P. Of course I did not get the true significance at once. It takes, you know, a little *time*. One cannot, on this earthly plane, see clearly. I racked my brains thinking of someone with those initials. I knew it must connect up with the last séance—really a most poignant one, but it was some time before I got it. And then I bought a copy of *Picture Post* (Spirit guidance again, you see, because usually I buy the *New Statesman*) and there you were—a picture of you, and described, and an account of what you had done. It is wonderful, don't you think, M. Poirot, how everything has a *purpose*? Clearly, you are the person appointed by the Guides to elucidate this matter.'

Poirot surveyed her thoughtfully. Strangely enough the thing that really caught his attention was that she had remarkably shrewd light-blue eyes. They gave point, as it were, to her rambling method of approach.

'And what, Mrs.—Cloade—is that right?' He frowned. 'I seem to have heard the name some time ago——'

She nodded vehemently.

'My poor brother-in-law—Gordon. Immensely rich and *often* mentioned in the press. He was killed in the Blitz over a year ago—a great blow to all of us. My husband is his younger brother. He is a doctor. Dr. Lionel Cloade. . . . Of course,' she added, lowering her voice, 'he has no idea that I am consulting you. He would not approve. Doctors, I find, have a very materialistic outlook. The spiritual seems to be strangely hidden from them. They pin their faith on Science—but what I say is . . . what *is* Science—what can it do?'

There seemed, to Hercule Poirot, to be no answer to the question other than a meticulous and painstaking description embracing Pasteur, Lister, Humphrey Davy's safety lamp—the convenience of electricity in the home and several hundred other kindred items. But that, naturally, was not the answer Mrs. Lionel Cloade wanted. In actual fact her question, like so many questions, was not really a question at all. It was a mere rhetorical gesture.

Hercule Poirot contented himself with inquiring in a practical manner:

'In what way do you believe I can help you, Mrs. Cloade?'

'Do you believe in the reality of the spirit world, M. Poirot?'

'I am a good Catholic,' said Poirot cautiously.

Mrs. Cloade waved aside the Catholic faith with a smile of pity.

'Blind! The Church is blind—prejudiced, foolish—not welcoming the reality and beauty of the world that lies behind this one.'

'At twelve o'clock,' said Hercule Poirot, 'I have an important appointment.'

It was a well-timed remark. Mrs. Cloade leaned forward.

'I must come to the point at once. Would it be possible for you, M. Poirot, to find a missing person?'

Poirot's eyebrows rose.

'It might be possible—yes,' he replied cautiously. 'But the police, my dear Mrs. Cloade, could do so a great deal more easily than I could. They have all the necessary machinery.'

Mrs. Cloade waved away the police as she had waved away the Catholic Church.

'No, M. Poirot—it is to you I have been guided—by those beyond the veil. Now listen. My brother Gordon married some weeks before his death, a young widow—a Mrs. Underhay. Her first husband (poor child, such a grief to her) was reported dead in Africa. A mysterious country—Africa.'

'A mysterious continent,' Poirot corrected her. 'Possibly. What part——'

She swept on.

'Central Africa. The home of voodoo, of the zhombie——'

'The zhombie is in the West Indies.'

Mrs. Cloade swept on:

'—of black magic—of strange and secret practices—a country where a man could disappear and never be heard of again.'

'Possibly, possibly,' said Poirot. 'But the same is true of Piccadilly Circus.'

Mrs. Cloade waved away Piccadilly Circus.

'Twice lately, M. Poirot, a communication has come through from a spirit who gives his name as Robert. The message was the same each time. *Not dead* . . . We were puzzled, we knew no Robert. Asking for further guidance we got this. "*R.U. R.U. R.U.*—then *Tell R. Tell R.*" "Tell Robert?" we asked. "No, *from* Robert. R.U." "What does the U. stand for?" Then, M. Poirot, the most significant answer came. "*Little Boy Blue. Little Boy Blue. Ha ha ha!*" You see?'

'No,' said Poirot, 'I do not.'

She looked at him pityingly.

'The nursery rhyme *Little Boy Blue*. "*Under* the *Hay*cock fast asleep" —*Underhay*—you see?'

Poirot nodded. He forbore to ask why, if the name Robert could be spelt out, the name Underhay could not have been treated the same way, and why it had been necessary to resort to a kind of cheap Secret Service spy jargon.

'And my sister-in-law's name is Rosaleen,' finished Mrs. Cloade triumphantly. 'You see? Confusing all these Rs. But the *meaning* is quite plain. "*Tell Rosaleen that Robert Underhay is not dead.*"'

'Aha, and did you tell her?'

Mrs. Cloade looked slightly taken aback.

'Er—well—no. You see, I mean—well, people are so *sceptical*. Rosaleen, I am sure, would be so. And then, poor child, it might upset her—wondering, you know, where he was—and what he was doing.'

'Besides projecting his voice through the ether? Quite so. A curious method, surely, of announcing his safety?'

'Ah, M. Poirot, you are not an initiate. And how do we know what the *circumstances* are? Poor Captain Underhay (or is it Major Underhay) may be a prisoner somewhere in the dark interior of Africa. But if he could be *found*, M. Poirot. If he could be restored to his dear young Rosaleen. Think of her happiness! Oh, M. Poirot, I have been *sent* to you—surely, *surely* you will not refuse the behest of the spiritual world.'

Poirot looked at her reflectively.

'My fees,' he said softly, 'are very expensive. I may say enormously expensive! And the task you suggest would not be easy.'

'Oh dear—but surely—it is most unfortunate. I and my husband are very badly off—very badly off indeed. Actually my own plight is worse than my dear husband knows. I bought some shares—under spirit guidance—and so far they have proved very disappointing—in fact, quite alarming. They have gone right down and are now, I gather, practically unsaleable.'

She looked at him with dismayed blue eyes.

'I have not dared to tell my husband. I simply tell *you* in order to explain how I am situated. But surely, dear M. Poirot, to reunite a young husband and wife—it is such a *noble* mission——'

'Nobility, *chère Madame*, will not pay steamer and railway and air travel fares. Nor will it cover the cost of long telegrams and cables, and the interrogations of witnesses.'

'But if he is found—if Captain Underhay is found alive and well—then—well, I think I may safely say that, once that was accomplished, there—there would be no difficulty about—er—reimbursing you.'

'Ah, he is rich, then, this Captain Underhay?'

'No. Well, no . . . But I can assure you—I can give you my *word*—that—that the money situation will not present difficulties.'

Slowly Poirot shook his head.

'I am sorry, Madame. The answer is No.'

He had a little difficulty in getting her to accept that answer.

When she had finally gone away, he stood lost in thought, frowning to himself. He remembered now why the name of Cloade was familiar to him. The conversation at the club the day of the Air Raid came back to him. The booming boring voice of Major Porter, going on and on, telling a story to which nobody wanted to listen.

He remembered the rustle of a newspaper and Major Porter's suddenly dropped jaw and expression of consternation.

But what worried him was trying to make up his mind about the eager middle-aged lady who had just left him. The glib spiritualistic patter, the vagueness, the floating scarves, the chains and amulets jingling round her neck—and finally, slightly at variance with all this, that sudden shrewd glint in a pair of pale-blue eyes.

'Just why exactly did she come to me?' he said to himself. 'And what, I wonder, has been going on in'—he looked down at the card on his desk—'Warmsley Vale?'

It was exactly five days later that he saw a small paragraph in an evening paper—it referred to the death of a man called Enoch Arden—at Warmsley Vale, a small old-world village about three miles from the popular Warmsley Heath Golf Course.

Hercule Poirot said to himself again:

'I wonder what has been going on in Warmsley Vale . . .'

BOOK ONE

CHAPTER I

WARMSLEY HEATH consists of a Golf Course, two Hotels, some very expensive modern villas giving on to the Golf Course, a row of what were, before the war, luxury shops, and a railway station.

Emerging from the railway station, a main road roars its way to London on your left—to your right a small path across a field is signposted *Footpath to Warmsley Vale*.

Warmsley Vale, tucked away amongst wooded hills, is as unlike Warmsley Heath as well can be. It is in essence a microscopic old-fashioned market town now degenerated into a village. It has a main street of Georgian houses, several pubs, a few unfashionable shops and a general air of being a hundred and fifty instead of twenty-eight miles from London.

Its occupants one and all unite in despising the mushroom growth of Warmsley Heath.

On the outskirts are some charming houses with pleasant old-world gardens. It was to one of these houses, the White House, that Lynn Marchmont returned in the early spring of 1946 when she was demobbed from the Wrens.

On her third morning she looked out of her bedroom window, across the untidy lawn to the elms in the meadow beyond, and sniffed the air happily. It was a gentle grey morning with a smell of soft wet earth. The kind of smell that she had been missing for the past two years and a half.

Wonderful to be home again, wonderful to be here in her own little bedroom which she had thought of so often and so nostalgically whilst she had been overseas. Wonderful to be out of uniform, to be able to get into a tweed skirt and a jumper—even if the moths *had* been rather too industrious during the war years!

It was good to be out of the Wrens and a free woman again, although she had really enjoyed her overseas service very much. The work had been reasonably interesting, there had been parties, plenty of fun, but there had also been the irksomeness of routine and the feeling of being herded together with her companions which had sometimes made her feel desperately anxious to escape.

It was then, during the long scorching summer out East, that she had thought so longingly of Warmsley Vale and the shabby cool pleasant house, and of dear Mums.

Lynn both loved her mother and was irritated by her. Far away from home, she had loved her still and had forgotten the irritation, or remembered it only with an additional homesick pang. Darling Mums, so completely maddening! What she would not have given to have heard Mums enunciate one cliché in her sweet complaining voice. Oh, to be at home again and never, *never* to have to leave home again!

And now here she was, out of the Service, free, and back at the White House. She had been back three days. And already a curious dissatisfied restlessness was creeping over her. It was all the same —almost too much all the same—the house and Mums and Rowley and the farm and the family. The thing that was different and that ought not to be different was herself . . .

'Darling . . .' Mrs. Marchmont's thin cry came up to the stairs. 'Shall I bring my girl a nice tray in bed?'

Lynn called out sharply:

'Of course not. I'm coming down.'

'And why,' she thought, 'has Mums got to say "my girl." It's so *silly*!'

She ran downstairs and entered the dining-room. It was not a very good breakfast. Already Lynn was realising the undue proportion of time and interest taken by the search for food. Except for a rather unreliable woman who came four mornings a week, Mrs. Marchmont was alone in the house, struggling with cooking and cleaning. She had been nearly forty when Lynn was born and her health was not good. Also Lynn realised with some dismay how their financial position had changed. The small but adequate fixed income which had kept them going comfortably before the war was now almost halved by taxation. Rates, expenses, wages had all gone up.

'Oh! brave new world,' thought Lynn grimly. Her eyes rested lightly on the columns of the daily paper. '*Ex-W.A.A.F. seeks post where initiative and drive will be appreciated.*' '*Former W.R.E.N. seeks post where organising ability and authority are needed.*'

Enterprise, initiative, command, those were the commodities offered. But what was wanted? People who could cook and clean, or write decent shorthand. Plodding people who knew a routine and could give good service.

Well, it didn't affect her. Her way ahead lay clear. Marriage to her cousin Rowley Cloade. They had got engaged seven years ago, just before the outbreak of war. Always as long as she could remember, she had meant to marry Rowley. His choice of a farming life had been acquiesced in readily by her. A good life—not exciting perhaps, and with plenty of hard work, but they both loved the open air and the care of animals.

Not that their prospects were quite what they had been—Uncle Gordon had always promised . . .

Mrs. Marchmont's voice broke in plaintively apposite:

'It's been the most dreadful blow to us all, Lynn darling, as I wrote you. Gordon had only been in England two days. We hadn't even *seen* him. If *only* he hadn't stayed in London. If he'd come straight down here.'

'Yes, if only . . .'

Far away, Lynn had been shocked and grieved by the news of her uncle's death, but the true significance of it was only now beginning to come home to her.

For as long as she could remember, her life, all their lives, had been dominated by Gorden Cloade. The rich, childless man had taken all his relatives completely under his wing.

Even Rowley . . . Rowley and his friend Johnnie Vavasour had started in partnership on the farm. Their capital was small, but they had been full of hope and energy. And Gordon Cloade had approved.

To her he had said more.

'You can't get anywhere in farming without capital. But the first thing to find out is whether these boys have really got the will and the energy to make a go of it. If I set them up now, I wouldn't know that—maybe for years. If they've got the right stuff in them, if I'm satisfied that their side of it is all right, well then, Lynn, you needn't worry. I'll finance them on the proper scale. So don't think badly of your prospects, my girl. You're just the wife Rowley needs. But keep what I've told you under your hat.'

Well, she had done that, but Rowley himself had sensed his uncle's benevolent interest. It was up to him to prove to the old boy that Rowley and Johnnie were a good investment for money.

Yes, they had all depended on Gordon Cloade. Not that any of the family had been spongers or idlers. Jeremy Cloade was senior partner in a firm of solicitors, Lionel Cloade was in practice as a doctor. But behind the workaday life was the comforting assurance of money in the background. There was never any need to stint or to save. The future was assured. Gordon Cloade, a childless widower, would see to that. He had told them all, more than once, that that was so.

His widowed sister, Adela Marchmont, had stayed on at the White House when she might, perhaps, have moved into a smaller, more labour-saving house. Lynn went to first-class schools. If the war had not come, she would have been able to take any kind of expensive training she had pleased. Cheques from Uncle Gordon flowed in with comfortable regularity to provide little luxuries.

Everything had been so *settled*, so *secure*. And then had come Gordon Cloade's wholly unexpected marriage.

'Of course, darling,' Adela went on, 'we were all flabbergasted. If there was one thing that seemed quite certain, it was that Gordon would never marry again. It wasn't, you see, as though he hadn't got plenty of family ties.'

Yes, thought Lynn, plenty of family. Sometimes, possibly, rather too much family?

'He was so kind always,' went on Mrs. Marchmont. 'Though perhaps just a weeny bit tyrannical on occasions. He never liked the habit of dining off a polished table. Always insisted on my sticking to the old-fashioned tablecloths. In fact, he sent me the most beautiful Venetian lace ones when he was in Italy.'

'It certainly paid to fall in with his wishes,' said Lynn dryly. She added with some curiosity, 'How did he meet this—second wife? You never told me in your letters.'

'Oh, my dear, on some boat or plane or other. Coming from South America to New York, I believe. After all those years! And after all those secretaries and typists and housekeepers and everything.'

Lynn smiled. Ever since she could remember, Gordon Cloade's secretaries, housekeepers and office staff had been subjected to the closest scrutiny and suspicion.

She asked curiously, 'She's good-looking, I suppose?'

'Well, dear,' said Adela, '*I* think myself she has rather a silly face.'

'You're not a man, Mums!'

'Of course,' Mrs. Marchmont went on, 'the poor girl was blitzed and had shock from blast and was really frightfully ill and all that, and it's my opinion she's never really quite recovered. She's a mass of nerves, if you know what I mean. And really, sometimes, she looks quite half-witted. I don't feel she could ever have made much of a companion for poor Gordon.'

Lynn smiled. She doubted whether Gordon Cloade had chosen to marry a woman years younger than himself for her intellectual companionship.

'And then, dear,' Mrs. Marchmont lowered her voice, 'I hate to say it, but of course she's *not* a lady!'

'What an expression, Mums! What does that matter nowadays?'

'It still matters in the country, dear,' said Adela placidly. 'I simply mean that she isn't exactly one of *us*!'

'Poor little devil!'

'Really, Lynn, I don't know what you mean. We have all been *most* careful to be kind and polite and to welcome her amongst us for Gordon's sake.'

'She's at Furrowbank, then?' Lynn asked curiously.

'Yes, naturally. Where else was there for her to go when she came out of the nursing home? The doctors said she must be out of London. She's at Furrowbank with her brother.'

'What's *he* like?' Lynn asked.

'A *dreadful* young man!' Mrs. Marchmont paused, and then added with a good deal of intensity: '*Rude*.'

A momentary flicker of sympathy crossed Lynn's mind. She thought: 'I bet *I'd* be rude in his place!'

She asked: 'What's his name?'

'Hunter. David Hunter. Irish, I believe. Of course they are not people one has ever heard of. She was a widow—a Mrs. Underhay. One doesn't wish to be *uncharitable*, but one can't help asking oneself —what *kind* of widow would be likely to be travelling about from South America in wartime? One can't help feeling, you know, that she was just *looking* for a rich husband.'

'In which case, she didn't look in vain,' remarked Lynn.

Mrs. Marchmont sighed.

'It seems so extraordinary. Gordon was such a shrewd man always. And it wasn't, I mean, that women hadn't *tried*. That last secretary but one, for instance. Really quite *blatant*. She was very efficient, I believe, but he had to get rid of her.'

Lynn said vaguely: 'I suppose there's always a Waterloo.'

'Sixty-two,' said Mrs. Marchmont. 'A very dangerous age. And a war, I imagine, is unsettling. But I can't tell you what a *shock* it was when we got his letter from New York.'

'What did it say exactly?'

'He wrote to Frances—I really can't *think* why. Perhaps he imagined that owing to her upbringing she might be more sympathetic. He said that we'd probably be surprised to hear that he was married. It had all been rather sudden, but he was sure we should all soon grow very fond of Rosaleen (such a very *theatrical* name, don't you think, dear? I mean definitely rather bogus). She had had a very sad life, he said, and had gone through a lot although she was so young. Really it was wonderful the plucky way she had stood up to life.'

'Quite a well-known gambit,' murmured Lynn.

'Oh, I know. I do agree. One has heard it so *many* times. But one would really think that *Gordon* with all his experience—still, there it is. She has the most enormous eyes—dark blue and what they call put in with a smutty finger.'

'Attractive?'

'Oh, yes, she is certainly very *pretty*. It's not the kind of prettiness *I* admire.'

'It never is,' said Lynn with a wry smile.

'No, dear. Really, *men*—but well, there's no accounting for men! Even the most well-balanced of them do the most incredibly foolish things! Gordon's letter went on to say that we mustn't think for a moment that this would mean any loosening of old ties. He still considered us all his special responsibility.'

'But he didn't,' said Lynn, 'make a will after his marriage?'

Mrs. Marchmont shook her head.

'The last will he made was in 1940. I don't know any details, but he gave us to understand at the time that we were all taken care of by it if anything should happen to him. That will, of course, was revoked by his marriage. I suppose he would have made a new will when he got home—but there just wasn't time. He was killed practically the day after he landed in this country.'

'And so she—Rosaleen—gets everything?'

'Yes. The old will was invalidated by his marriage.'

Lynn was silent. She was not more mercenary than most, but she would not have been human if she had not resented the new state of affairs. It was not, she felt, at all what Gordon Cloade himself would have envisaged. The bulk of his fortune he might have left to his young wife, but certain provisions he would certainly have made for the family he had encouraged to depend upon him. Again and again he had urged them not to save, not to make provision for the future. She had heard him say to Jeremy, 'You'll be a rich man when I die.' To her mother he had often said, 'Don't worry, Adela. I'll always look after Lynn—you know that, and I'd hate you to leave this house—it's your *home*. Send all the bills for repairs to me.' Rowley he had encouraged to take up farming. Antony, Jeremy's son, he had insisted should go into the Guards and he had always made him a handsome allowance. Lionel Cloade had been encouraged to follow up certain lines of medical research that were not immediately profitable and to let his practice run down.

Lynn's thoughts were broken into. Dramatically, and with a trembling lip, Mrs. Marchmont produced a sheaf of bills.

'And look at all these,' she wailed. 'What am I to *do*? What on earth am I to do, Lynn? The bank manager wrote me only this morning that I'm overdrawn. I don't see how I *can* be. I've been so careful. But it seems my investments just aren't producing what they used to. Increased taxation, he says. And all these yellow things, War Damage Insurance or something—one has to pay them whether one wants to or not.'

Lynn took the bills and glanced through them. There were no records of extravagance amongst them. They were for slates replaced on the roof; the mending of fences; replacement of a worn-out kitchen boiler—a new main water pipe. They amounted to a considerable sum.

Mrs. Marchmont said piteously:

'I suppose I ought to move from here. But where could I go? There isn't a small house anywhere—there just *isn't* such a thing. Oh, I don't want to worry you with all this, Lynn. Not just as soon as you've come home. But I don't know what to do. I really don't.'

Lynn looked at her mother. She was over sixty. She had never been a very strong woman. During the war she had taken in evacuees from London, had cooked and cleaned for them, had worked with the W.V.S., made jam, helped with school meals. She had worked fourteen hours a day in contrast to a pleasant easy life before the war. She was now, as Lynn saw, very near a breakdown. Tired out and frightened of the future.

A slow quiet anger rose in Lynn. She said slowly:

'Couldn't this Rosaleen—help?'

Mrs. Marchmont flushed.

'We've no right to anything—anything at all.'

Lynn demurred.

'I think you've a moral right. Uncle Gordon always helped.'

Mrs. Marchmont shook her head. She said:

'It wouldn't be very nice, dear, to ask favours—not of someone one doesn't like very much. And anyway that brother of hers would never let her give away a penny!'

And she added, heroism giving place to pure female cattiness: 'If he really *is* her brother, that is to say!'

CHAPTER II

FRANCES CLOADE looked thoughtfully across the dinner table at her husband.

Frances was forty-eight. She was one of those lean grey-hound women who look well in tweeds. There was a rather arrogant ravaged beauty about her face which had no make-up except a little carelessly applied lipstick. Jeremy Cloade was a spare grey-haired man of sixty-three, with a dry expressionless face.

It was, this evening, even more expressionless than usual.

His wife registered the fact with a swift flashing glance.

A fifteen year-old girl shuffled round the table, handing the dishes. Her agonised gaze was fixed on Frances. If Frances frowned, she nearly dropped something, a look of approval set her beaming.

It was noted enviously in Warmsley Vale that if any one had servants it would be Frances Cloade. She did not bribe them with extravagant wages, and she was exacting as to performance—but her warm approval of endeavour and her infectious energy and drive made of domestic service something creative and personal. She had been so used to being waited on all her life that she took it for granted without self-consciousness, and she had the same appreciation of a good cook or a good parlourmaid as she would have had for a good pianist.

Frances Cloade had been the only daughter of Lord Edward Trenton, who had trained his horses in the neighbourhood of Warmsley Heath. Lord Edward's final bankruptcy was realised by those in the know to be a merciful escape from worse things. There had been rumours of horses that had signally failed to stay at unexpected moments, other rumours of inquiries by the Stewards of the Jockey Club. But Lord Edward had escaped with his reputation only lightly tarnished and had reached an arrangement with his creditors which permitted him to live exceedingly comfortably in the South of France. And for these unexpected blessings he had to thank the shrewdness and special exertions of his solicitor, Jeremy Cloade. Cloade had done a good deal more than a solicitor usually does for a client, and had even advanced guarantees of his own. He had made it clear that he had a deep admiration for Frances Trenton, and in due course, when her father's affairs had been satisfactorily wound up, Frances became Mrs. Jeremy Cloade.

What she had felt about it no one had ever known. All that could be said was that she had kept her side of the bargain admirably. She had been an efficient and loyal wife to Jeremy, a careful mother to his son, had forwarded Jeremy's interests in every way and had never once suggested by word or deed that the match was anything but a freewill impulse on her part.

In response the Cloade family had an enormous respect and admiration for Frances. They were proud of her, they deferred to her judgment—but they never felt really quite intimate with her.

What Jeremy Cloade thought of his marriage nobody knew, because nobody ever did know what Jeremy Cloade thought or felt. 'A dry stick' was what people said about Jeremy. His reputation both as a man and a lawyer was very high. Cloade, Brunskill and Cloade never touched any questionable legal business. They were not supposed to be brilliant but were considered very sound. The firm prospered and the Jeremy Cloades lived in a handsome Georgian house just off the Market Place with a big old-fashioned walled garden behind it where the pear trees in Spring showed a sea of white blossom.

It was to a room overlooking the garden at the back of the house that the husband and wife went when they rose from the dinner table. Edna, the fifteen-year-old, brought in coffee, breathing excitedly and adenoidally.

Frances poured a little coffee into the cup. It was strong and hot. She said to Edna, crisply and approvingly:

'Excellent, Edna.'

Edna went crimson with pleasure and went out marvelling nevertheless at what some people liked. Coffee, in Edna's opinion, ought to be a pale cream colour, ever so sweet, with lots of milk! In the room overlooking the garden, the Cloades drank their coffee, black and without sugar. They had talked in a desultory way during dinner, of acquaintances met, of Lynn's return, of the prospects of farming in the near future, but now, alone together, they were silent.

Frances leaned back in her chair, watching her husband. He was quite oblivious of her regard. His right hand stroked his upper lip. Although Jeremy Cloade did not know it himself the gesture was a characteristic one and coincided with inner perturbation. Frances had not observed it very often. Once when Antony, their son, had been seriously ill as a child; once when waiting for a jury to consider their verdict; at the outbreak of war, waiting to hear the irrevocable words over the wireless; on the eve of Antony's departure after embarkation leave.

Frances thought a little while before she spoke. Their married life had been happy, but never intimate in so far as the spoken word went. She had respected Jeremy's reserves and he hers. Even when the telegram had come announcing Antony's death on active service, they had neither of them broken down.

He had opened it, then he had looked up at her. She had said, 'Is it——?'

He had bowed his head, then crossed and put the telegram into her outstretched hand.

They had stood there quite silently for a while. Then Jeremy had said: 'I wish I could help you, my dear.' And she had answered, her voice steady, her tears unshed, conscious only of the terrible emptiness and aching: 'It's just as bad for you.' He had patted her shoulder: 'Yes,' he said. 'Yes . . .' Then he had moved towards the door, walking a little awry, yet stiffly, suddenly an old man . . . saying as he did so, 'There's nothing to be said—nothing to be said. . . .'

She had been grateful to him, passionately grateful, for understanding so well, and had been torn with pity for him, seeing him suddenly turn into an old man. With the loss of her boy, something had hardened in her—some ordinary common kindness had dried up. She was more efficient, more energetic than ever—people became sometimes a little afraid of her ruthless common sense . . .

Jeremy Cloade's finger moved along his upper lip again—irresolutely, searching. And crisply, across the room, Frances spoke.

'Is anything the matter, Jeremy?'

He started. His coffee cup almost slipped from his hand. He

recovered himself, put it firmly down on the tray. Then he looked across at her.

'What do you mean, Frances?'

'I'm asking you if anything is the matter?'

'What should be the matter?'

'It would be foolish to guess. I would rather you told me.'

She spoke without emotion in a businesslike way.

He said unconvincingly:

'There is nothing the matter——'

She did not answer. She merely waited inquiringly. His denial, it seemed, she put aside as negligible. He looked at her uncertainly.

And just for a moment the imperturbable mask of his grey face slipped, and she caught a glimpse of such turbulent agony that she almost exclaimed aloud. It was only for a moment but she didn't doubt what she had seen.

She said quietly and unemotionally:

'I think you had better tell me——'

He sighed—a deep unhappy sigh.

'You will have to know, of course,' he said, 'sooner or later.'

And he added what was to her a very astonishing phrase.

'I'm afraid you've made a bad bargain, Frances.'

She went right past an implication she did not understand to attack hard facts.

'What is it,' she said; 'money?'

She did not know why she put money first. There had been no special signs of financial stringency other than were natural to the times. They were short-staffed at the office with more business than they could cope with, but that was the same everywhere and in the last month they had got back some of their people released from the Army. It might just as easily have been illness that he was concealing—his colour had been bad lately, and he had been overworked and overtired. But nevertheless Frances's instinct went towards money, and it seemed she was right.

Her husband nodded.

'I see.' She was silent a moment, thinking. She herself did not really care about money at all—but she knew that Jeremy was quite incapable of realising that. Money meant to him a four-square world—stability—obligations—a definite place and status in life. Money to her was a toy tossed into one's lap to play with. She had been born and bred in an atmosphere of financial instability.

There had been wonderful times when the horses had done what was expected of them. There had been difficult times when the tradesmen wouldn't give credit and Lord Edward had been forced to ignominious straits to avoid the bailiffs on the front-door step. Once they had lived on dry bread for a week and sent all the servants away. They had had the bailiffs in the house for three weeks once when Frances was a child. She had found the bum in question very agreeable to play with and full of stories of his own little girl.

If one had no money one simply scrounged, or went abroad, or lived on one's friends and relations for a bit. Or somebody tided you over with a loan . . .

But looking across at her husband Frances realised that in the Cloade world you didn't do that kind of thing. You didn't beg or borrow or live on other people. (And conversely you didn't expect them to beg or borrow or live off you!)

Frances felt terribly sorry for Jeremy and a little guilty about being so unperturbed herself. She took refuge in practicality.

'Shall we have to sell up everything? Is the firm going smash?'

Jeremy Cloade winced, and she realised she had been too matter-of-fact.

'My dear,' she said gently, 'do tell me. I can't go on guessing.'

Cloade said stiffly, 'We went through rather a bad crisis two years ago. Young Williams, you remember, absconded. We had some difficulty getting straight again. Then there were certain complications arising out of the position in the Far East after Singapore——'

She interrupted him.

'Never mind the whys—they are so unimportant. You were in a jam. And you haven't been able to snap out of it?'

He said, 'I relied on Gordon. Gordon would have put things straight.'

She gave a quick impatient sigh.

'Of course. I don't want to blame the poor man—after all, it's only human nature to lose your head about a pretty woman. And why on earth shouldn't he marry again if he wanted to? But it was unfortunate his being killed in that air raid before he'd settled anything or made a proper will or adjusted his affairs. The truth is that one never believes for a minute, no matter what danger you're in, that you yourself are going to be killed. The bomb is always going to hit the other person!'

'Apart from his loss, and I was very fond of Gordon—and proud of him too,' said Gordon Cloade's elder brother, 'his death was a catastrophe for me. It came at a moment——'

He stopped.

'Shall we be bankrupt?' Frances asked with intelligent interest.

Jeremy Cloade looked at her almost despairingly. Though she did not realise it, he could have coped much better with tears and alarm. This cool detached practical interest defeated him utterly.

He said harshly, 'It's a good deal worse than that . . .'

He watched her as she sat quite still, thinking over that. He said to himself, 'In another minute I shall have to tell her. She'll know what I am . . . She'll have to know. Perhaps she won't believe it at first.'

Frances Cloade sighed and sat up straight in her big armchair.

'I see,' she said. 'Embezzlement. Or if that isn't the right word, that kind of thing . . . Like young Williams.'

'Yes, but this time—you don't understand—*I'm* responsible. I've used trust funds that were committed to my charge. So far, I've covered my tracks——'

'But now it's all going to come out?'

'Unless I can get the necessary money—quickly.'

The shame he felt was the worst he had known in his life. How would she take it?

At the moment she was taking it very calmly. But then, he thought, Frances would never make a scene. Never reproach or upbraid.

Her hand to her cheek, she was frowning.

'It's so stupid,' she said, 'that I haven't got any money of my own at all . . .'

He said stiffly, 'There is your marriage settlement, but——'

She said absently, 'But I suppose that's gone too.'

He was silent. Then he said with difficulty, in his dry voice: 'I'm sorry, Frances. More sorry than I can say. You made a bad bargain.'

She looked up sharply.

'You said that before. What do you mean by that?'

Jeremy said stiffly:

'When you were good enough to marry me, you had the right to expect—well, integrity—and a life free from sordid anxieties.'

She was looking at him with complete astonishment.

'Really, Jeremy! What on earth do you think I married you for?'

He smiled slightly.

'You have always been a most loyal and devoted wife, my dear. But I can hardly flatter myself that you would have accepted me in—er—different circumstances.'

She stared at him and suddenly burst out laughing.

'You funny old stick! What a wonderful novelettish mind you must have behind that legal façade! Do you really think that I married you as the price of saving Father from the wolves—or the Stewards of the Jockey Club, et cetera?'

'You were very fond of your father, Frances.'

'I was devoted to Daddy! He was terribly attractive and the greatest fun to live with! But I always knew he was a bad hat. And if you think that I'd sell myself to the family solicitor in order to save him from getting what was always coming to him, then you've never understood the first thing about me. Never!'

She stared at him. Extraordinary, she thought, to have been married to someone for over twenty years and not have known what was going on in his mind. But how could one know when it was a mind so different from one's own? A romantic mind, of course, well camouflaged, but essentially romantic. She thought: 'All those old Stanley Weymans in his bedroom. I might have known from *them*! The poor idiotic darling!'

Aloud she said:

'I married you because I was in love with you, of course.'

'In love with me? But what could you see in me?'

'If you ask me that, Jeremy, I really don't know. You were such a *change* so different from all Father's crowd. You never talked about horses for one thing. You've no idea how *sick* I was of horses—and what the odds were likely to be for the Newmarket Cup! You came to dinner one night—do you remember?—and I sat next to you and asked you what bimetallism was, and you told me—really *told* me! It took the whole of dinner—six courses—we were in funds at the moment and had a French chef!'

'It must have been extremely boring,' said Jeremy.

'It was fascinating! Nobody had ever treated me seriously before. And you were so polite and yet never seemed to look at me or think I was nice or good looking or anything. It put me on my mettle. I *swore* I'd make you notice me.'

Jeremy Cloade said grimly: 'I noticed you all right. I went home that evening and didn't sleep a wink. You had a blue dress with cornflowers . . .'

There was silence for a moment or two, then Jeremy cleared his throat.

'Er—all that is a long time ago . . .'

She came quickly to the rescue of his embarrassment.

'And we're now a middle-aged married couple in difficulties, looking for the best way out.'

'After what you've just told me, Frances, it makes it a thousand times worse that this—this disgrace——'

She interrupted him.

'Let us please get things clear. You are being apologetic because you've fallen foul of the law. You may be prosecuted—go to prison.' (He winced.) 'I don't want that to happen. I'll fight like anything to stop it, but don't credit me with moral indignation. We're not a moral family, remember. Father, in spite of his attractiveness, was a bit of a crook. And there was Charles—my cousin. They hushed it up and he wasn't prosecuted, and they hustled him off to the Colonies. And there was my cousin Gerald—*he* forged a cheque at Oxford. But he went to fight and got a posthumous V.C. for complete bravery and devotion to his men and superhuman endurance. What I'm trying to say is people are *like* that—not quite bad or quite good. I don't suppose I'm particularly straight myself—I have been because there hasn't been any temptation to be otherwise. But what I have got is plenty of courage and' (she smiled at him) 'I'm *loyal*!'

'My dear!' He got up and came over to her. He stooped and put his lips to her hair.

'And now,' said Lord Edward Trenton's daughter, smiling up at him, 'what are we going to do? Raise money somehow?'

Jeremy's face stiffened.

'I don't see how.'

'A mortgage on this house. Oh, I see,' she was quick, 'that's been done. I'm stupid. Of course you've done all the obvious things. It's a question then, of a *touch*? Who *can* we touch? I suppose there's only one possibility. Gordon's widow—the dark Rosaleen!'

Jeremy shook his head dubiously.

'It would have to be a large sum . . . And it can't come out of capital. The money's only in trust for her for her life.'

'I hadn't realised that. I thought she had it absolutely. What happens when she dies?'

'It comes to Gordon's next of kin. That is to say it is divided between myself, Lionel, Adela, and Maurice's son, Rowley.'

'It comes to *us* . . .' said Frances slowly.

Something seemed to pass through the room—a cold air—the shadow of a thought . . .

Frances said: 'You didn't tell me that . . . I thought she got it for keeps—that she could leave it to any one she liked?'

'No. By the statute relating to intestacy of 1925 . . .'

It is doubtful whether Frances listened to his explanation. She said when his voice stopped:

'It hardly matters to us personally. We'll be dead and buried, long before she's middle-aged. How old is she? Twenty-five—twenty-six? She'll probably live to be seventy.'

Jeremy Cloade said doubtfully:

'We might ask her for a loan—putting it on family grounds? She may be a generous-minded girl—really we know so little of her——'

Frances said: 'At any rate we have been reasonably nice to her—not catty like Adela. She might respond.'

Her husband said warningly:

'There must be no hint of—er—real urgency.'

Frances said impatiently: 'Of course not! The trouble is that it's not the girl herself we shall have to deal with. She's completely under the thumb of that brother of hers.'

'A very unattractive young man,' said Jeremy Cloade.

Frances's sudden smile flashed out.

'Oh, no,' she said. 'He's attractive. *Most* attractive. Rather unscrupulous, too, I should imagine. But then as far as that goes, *I'm* unscrupulous too!'

Her smile hardened. She looked up at her husband.

'We're not going to be beaten, Jeremy,' she said. 'There's bound to be *some* way . . . if I have to rob a bank!'

CHAPTER III

'MONEY!' said Lynn.

Rowley Cloade nodded. He was a big square young man with a brick-red skin, thoughtful blue eyes and very fair hair. He had a slowness that seemed more purposeful than ingrained. He used deliberation as others use quickness of repartee.

'Yes,' he said, 'everything seems to boil down to money these days.'

'But I thought farmers had done so well during the war?'

'Oh, yes—but that doesn't do you any permanent good. In a year we'll be back where we were—with wages up, workers unwilling, everybody dissatisfied and nobody knowing where they are. Unless, of course, you can farm in a really big way. Old Gordon knew. That was where he was preparing to come in.'

'And now——' Lynn asked.

Rowley grinned.

'And now Mrs. Gordon goes to London and spends a couple of thousand on a nice mink coat.'

'It's—it's wicked!'

'Oh, no——' He paused and said: 'I'd rather like to give *you* a mink coat, Lynn——'

'What's she like, Rowley?' She wanted to get a contemporary judgment.

'You'll see her to-night. At Uncle Lionel's and Aunt Kathie's party.'

'Yes, I know. But I want *you* to tell me. Mums says she's half-witted?'

Rowley considered.

'Well—I shouldn't say intellect was her strong point. But I think really she only seems half-witted because she's being so frightfully careful.'

'Careful? Careful about what?'

'Oh, just careful. Mainly, I imagine, about her accent—she's got quite a brogue, you know, or else about the right fork, and any literary allusions that might be flying around.'

'Then she really is—quite—well, uneducated?'

Rowley grinned.

'Oh, she's not a lady, if that's what you mean. She's got lovely eyes, and a very good complexion—and I suppose old Gordon fell for that, with her extraordinary air of being quite unsophisticated. I don't *think* it's put on—though of course you never know. She just stands around looking dumb and letting David run her.'

'David?'

'That's the brother. I should say there's nothing much about sharp practice *he* doesn't know!' Rowley added: 'He doesn't like any of us much.'

'Why should he?' said Lynn sharply, and added as he looked at her, slightly surprised, 'I mean *you* don't like *him*.'

'I certainly don't. You won't either. He's not our sort.'

'You don't know who I like, Rowley, or who I don't! I've seen a lot of the world in the last three years. I—I think my outlook has broadened.'

'You've seen more of the world than I have, that's true.'

He said it quietly—but Lynn looked up sharply.

There had been something—behind those even tones.

He returned her glance squarely, his face unemotional. It had never, Lynn remembered, been easy to know exactly what Rowley was thinking.

What a queer topsy-turvy world it was, thought Lynn. It used to be the man who went to the wars, the woman who stayed at home. But here the positions were reversed.

Of the two young men, Rowley and Johnnie, one had had perforce to stay on the farm. They had tossed for it and Johnnie Vavasour had been the one to go. He had been killed almost at once—in Norway. All through the years of war Rowley had never been more than a mile or two from home.

And she, Lynn, had been to Egypt, to North Africa, to Sicily. She had been under fire more than once.

Here was Lynn Home-from-the-wars, and here was Rowley Stay-at-home.

She wondered, suddenly, if he minded . . .

She gave a nervous little half laugh. 'Things seem sometimes a bit upside down, don't they?'

'Oh, I don't know.' Rowley stared vacantly out over the country-side. 'Depends.'

'Rowley,' she hesitated, 'did you *mind*—I mean—Johnnie——'

His cold level gaze threw her back on herself.

'Let's leave Johnnie out of it! The war's over—and I've been lucky.'

'Lucky, you mean'—she paused doubtfully—'not to have had to—to go?'

'Wonderful luck, don't you think so?' She didn't know quite how to take that. His voice was smooth with hard edges. He added with a smile, 'But, of course, you service girls will find it hard to settle down at home.'

She said irritably, 'Oh, don't be stupid, Rowley.'

(But why be irritable? Why—unless because his words touched a raw nerve of truth somewhere.)

'Oh well,' said Rowley. 'I suppose we might as well consider getting married. Unless you've changed your mind?'

'Of course I haven't changed my mind. Why should I?'

He said vaguely:

'One never knows.'

'You mean you think I'm'—Lynn paused—'different?'

'Not particularly.'

'Perhaps *you've* changed your mind?'

'Oh, no, *I've* not changed. Very little change down on the farm, you know.'

'All right, then,' said Lynn—conscious, somehow, of anticlimax, 'let's get married. Whenever you like?'

'June or thereabouts?'

'Yes.'

They were silent. It was settled. In spite of herself, Lynn felt terribly depressed. Yet Rowley was Rowley—just as he always had been. Affectionate, unemotional, painstakingly given to understatement.

They loved each other. They had always loved each other. They had never talked about their love very much—so why should they begin now?

They would get married in June and live at Long Willows (a nice name, she had always thought) and she would never go away again. Go away, that is to say, in the sense that the words now held for her. The excitement of gang planks being pulled up, the racing of a ship's screw, the thrill as an aeroplane became airborne and soared up and over the earth beneath. Watching a strange coastline take form and shape. The smell of hot dust, and paraffin, and garlic—the clatter and gabble of foreign tongues. Strange flowers, red poinsettias rising proudly from a dusty garden . . . Packing, unpacking—where next?

All that was over. The war was over. Lynn Marchmont had come home. Home is the sailor, home from the sea . . . But I'm not the same Lynn who went away, she thought.

She looked up and saw Rowley watching her . . .

CHAPTER IV

AUNT KATHIE'S PARTIES were always much the same. They had a rather breathless amateurish quality about them characteristic of the hostess. Dr. Cloade had an air of holding irritability in check with difficulty. He was invariably courteous to his guests—but they were conscious of his courtesy being an effort.

In appearance Lionel Cloade was not unlike his brother Jeremy. He was spare and grey-haired—but he had not the lawyer's imperturbability. His manner was brusque and impatient—and his nervous irritability had affronted many of his patients and blinded them to his actual skill and kindliness. His real interests lay in research and his hobby was the use of medicinal herbs throughout history. He had a precise intellect and found it hard to be patient with his wife's vagaries.

Though Lynn and Rowley always called Mrs. Jeremy Cloade 'Frances,' Mrs. Lionel Cloade was invariably 'Aunt Kathie.' They were fond of her but found her rather ridiculous.

This 'party,' arranged ostensibly to celebrate Lynn's home-coming, was merely a family affair.

Aunt Kathie greeted her niece affectionately:

'So nice and *brown* you look, my dear. Egypt, I suppose. Did you read the book on the Pyramid prophecies I sent you? *So* interesting. Really explains everything, don't you think?'

Lynn was saved from replying by the entrance of Mrs. Gordon Cloade and her brother David.

'This is my niece, Lynn Marchmont, Rosaleen.'

Lynn looked at Gordon Cloade's widow with decorously veiled curiosity.

Yes, she *was* lovely, this girl who had married old Gordon Cloade for his money. And it was true what Rowley had said, that she had an air of innocence. Black hair, set in loose waves, Irish blue eyes put in with the smutty finger—half-parted lips.

The rest of her was predominantly expensive. Dress, jewels, manicured hands, fur cape. Quite a good figure, but she didn't, really, know how to wear expensive clothes. Didn't wear them as Lynn Marchmont could have worn them, given half a chance! (But you never *will* have a chance, said a voice in her brain.)

'How do you do,' said Rosaleen Cloade.

She turned hesitatingly to the man behind her.

She said: 'This—this is my brother.'

'How do you do,' said David Hunter.

He was a thin young man with dark hair and dark eyes. His face was unhappy and defiant and slightly insolent.

Lynn saw at once why all the Cloades disliked him so much. She had met men of that stamp abroad. Men who were reckless and slightly dangerous. Men whom you couldn't depend upon. Men who made their own laws and flouted the universe. Men who were worth their weight in gold in a push—and who drove their C.O.s to distraction out of the firing line!

Lynn said conversationally to Rosaleen:

'And how do you like living at Furrowbank?'

'I think it's a wonderful house,' said Rosaleen.

David Hunter gave a faint sneering laugh.

'Poor old Gordon did himself well,' he said. 'No expense spared.'

It was literally the truth. When Gordon had decided to settle down in Warmsley Vale—or rather had decided to spend a small portion of his busy life there, he had chosen to build. He was too much of an individualist to care for a house that was impregnated with other people's history.

He had employed a young modern architect and given him a free hand. Half Warmsley Vale thought Furrowbank a dreadful house, disliking its white squareness, its built-in furnishing, its sliding doors, and glass tables and chairs. The only parts of it they really admired wholeheartedly were the bathrooms.

There had been awe in Rosaleen's 'It's a wonderful house.' David's laugh made her flush.

'You're the returned Wren, aren't you?' said David to Lynn.

'Yes.'

His eyes swept over her appraisingly—and for some reason she flushed.

Aunt Katherine appeared again suddenly. She had a trick of seeming to materialise out of space. Perhaps she had caught the trick of it from many of the spiritualistic séances she attended.

'Supper,' she said, rather breathlessly, and added, parenthetically, 'I think it's better than calling it dinner. People don't *expect* so much. Everything's very difficult, isn't it? Mary Lewis tells me she slips the fishman ten shillings every other week. *I* think that's immoral.'

Dr. Lionel Cloade was giving his irritable nervous laugh as he talked to Frances Cloade. 'Oh, come, Frances,' he said. 'You can't expect me to believe you really think *that*—let's go in.'

They went into the shabby and rather ugly dining-room. Jeremy and Frances, Lionel and Katherine, Adela, Lynn and Rowley. A family party of Cloades—with two outsiders. For Rosaleen Cloade, though she bore the name, had not become a Cloade as Frances and Katherine had done.

She was the stranger, ill at ease, nervous. And David—David was the outlaw. By necessity, but also by choice. Lynn was thinking these things as she took her place at the table.

There were waves in the air of feeling—a strong electrical current of—what was it? Hate? Could it really be *hate*?

Something at any rate—*destructive*.

Lynn thought suddenly, 'But that's what's the matter everywhere. I've noticed it ever since I got home. It's the aftermath war has left. Ill will. Ill feeling. It's everywhere. On railways and buses and in shops and amongst workers and clerks and even agricultural labourers. And I suppose worse in mines and factories. Ill will. But here it's more than that. Here it's particular. It's *meant*!'

And she thought, shocked: '*Do* we hate them so much? These strangers who have taken what we think is ours?'

And then——'No, not yet. We might—but not yet. No, it's *they* who hate *us*.'

It seemed to her so overwhelming a discovery that she sat silent thinking about it and forgetting to talk to David Hunter who was sitting beside her.

Presently he said: 'Thinking out something?'

His voice was quite pleasant, slightly amused, but she felt conscience-stricken. He might think that she was going out of her way to be ill-mannered.

She said, 'I'm sorry. I was having thoughts about the state of the world.'

David said coolly, 'How extremely unoriginal!'

'Yes, it is rather. We are all so earnest nowadays. And it doesn't seem to do much good either.'

'It is usually more practical to wish to do harm. We've thought up one or two rather practical gadgets in that line during the last few years—including that *pièce de résistance*, the Atom Bomb.'

'That was what I was thinking about—oh, I don't mean the Atom Bomb. I meant ill will. Definite practical ill will.'

David said calmly:

'Ill will certainly—but I rather take issue to the word practical. They were more practical about it in the Middle Ages.'

'How do you mean?'

'Black magic generally. Ill wishing. Wax figures. Spells at the turn of the moon. Killing off your neighbour's cattle. Killing off your neighbour himself.'

'You don't really believe there *was* such a thing as black magic?' asked Lynn incredulously.

'Perhaps not. But at any rate people did *try* hard. Nowadays, well——' He shrugged his shoulders. 'With all the ill will in the world you and your family can't do much about Rosaleen and myself, can you?'

Lynn's head went back with a jerk. Suddenly she was enjoying herself.

'It's a little late in the day for that,' she said politely.

David Hunter laughed. He, too, sounded as though he were enjoying himself.

'Meaning we've got away with the booty? Yes, we're sitting pretty all right.'

'*And* you get a kick out of it!'

'Out of having a lot of money? I'll say we do.'

'I didn't mean only the money. I meant out of *us*.'

'Out of having scored off you? Well, perhaps. You'd all have been pretty smug and complacent about the old boy's cash. Looked upon it as practically in your pockets already.'

Lynn said: 'You must remember that we'd been taught to think so for years. Taught not to save, not to think of the future—encouraged to go ahead with all sorts of schemes and projects.'

(Rowley, she thought, Rowley and the farm.)

'Only one thing, in fact, that you hadn't learnt,' said David pleasantly.

'What's that?'

'That nothing's safe.'

'Lynn,' cried Aunt Katherine, leaning forward from the head of the table, 'one of Mrs. Lester's controls is a fourth dynasty priest. He's told us such wonderful things. You and I, Lynn, must have a long talk. Egypt, I feel, must have affected you psychically.'

Dr. Cloade said sharply:

'Lynn's had better things to do than play about with all this superstitious tomfoolery.'

'You are so biased, Lionel,' said his wife.

Lynn smiled at her aunt—then sat silent with the refrain of the words David had spoken swimming in her brain.

'*Nothing's safe* . . . .'

There were people who lived in such a world—people to whom everything was dangerous. David Hunter was such a person. . . . It was not the world that Lynn had been brought up in—but it was a world that held attractions for her nevertheless.

David said presently in the same low amused voice:

'Are we still on speaking terms?'

'Oh, yes.'

'Good. And do you still grudge Rosaleen and myself our ill-gotten access to wealth?'

'Yes,' said Lynn with spirit.

'Splendid. What are you going to do about it?'

'Buy some wax and practise black magic!'

He laughed.

'Oh, no, you won't do that. You aren't one of those who rely on old outmoded methods. Your methods will be modern and probably very efficient. But you won't win.'

'What makes you think there is going to be a fight? Haven't we all accepted the inevitable?'

'You all behave beautifully. It is very amusing.'

'Why,' said Lynn, in a low tone, 'do you hate us?'

Something flickered in those dark unfathomable eyes.

'I couldn't possibly make you understand.'

'I think you could,' said Lynn.

David was silent for a moment or two, then he asked in a light conversational tone:

'Why are you going to marry Rowley Cloade? He's an oaf.'

She said sharply:

'You know nothing about it—or about him. You couldn't begin to know!'

Without any air of changing the conversation David asked:

'What do you think of Rosaleen?'

'She's very lovely.'

'What else?'

'She doesn't seem to be enjoying herself.'

'Quite right,' said David, 'Rosaleen's rather stupid. She's scared. She always has been rather scared. She drifts into things and then doesn't know what it's all about. Shall I tell you about Rosaleen?'

'If you like,' said Lynn politely.

'I do like. She started by being stage-struck and drifted on to the stage. She wasn't any good, of course. She got into a third-rate touring company that was going out to South Africa. She liked the sound of South Africa. The company got stranded in Cape Town. Then she drifted into marriage with a Government official from Nigeria. She didn't like Nigeria—and I don't think she liked her husband much. If he'd been a hearty sort of fellow who drank and beat her, it would have been all right. But he was rather an intellectual man who kept a large library in the wilds and who liked to talk metaphysics. So she drifted back to Cape Town again. The fellow behaved very well and gave her an adequate allowance. He might have given her a divorce, but again he might not for he was a Catholic; but anyway he rather fortunately died of fever, and Rosaleen got a small pension. Then the war started and she drifted on to a boat for South America. She didn't like South America very much, so she drifted on to another boat and there she met Gordon Cloade and told him all about her sad life. So they got married in New York and lived happily for a fortnight, and a little later he was killed by a bomb and she was left a large house, a lot of expensive jewellery, and an immense income.'

'It's nice that the story has such a happy ending,' said Lynn.

'Yes,' said David Hunter. 'Possessing no intellect at all, Rosaleen has always been a lucky girl—which is just as well. Gordon Cloade was a strong old man. He was sixty-two. He might easily have lived for twenty years. He might have lived even longer. That wouldn't have been much fun for Rosaleen, would it? She was twenty-four when she married him. She's only twenty-six now.'

'She looks even younger,' said Lynn.

David looked across the table. Rosaleen Cloade was crumbling her bread. She looked like a nervous child.

'Yes,' he said thoughtfully. 'She does. Complete absence of thought, I suppose.'

'Poor thing,' said Lynn suddenly.

David frowned.

'Why the pity?' he said sharply. '*I'll* look after Rosaleen.'

'I expect you will.'

He scowled.

'Any one who tries to do down Rosaleen has got me to deal with! And I know a good many ways of making war—some of them not strictly orthodox.'

'Am I going to hear *your* life history now?' asked Lynn coldly.

'A very abridged edition.' He smiled. 'When the war broke out I saw no reason why I should fight for England. I'm Irish. But like all the Irish, I like fighting. The Commandos had an irresistible fascination for me. I had some fun but unfortunately I got knocked out with a bad leg wound. Then I went to Canada and did a job of training fellows there. I was at a loose end when I got Rosaleen's wire from New York saying she was getting married! She didn't actually announce that there would be pickings, but I'm quite sharp at reading between the lines. I flew there, tacked myself on to the happy pair and came back with them to London. And now'—he smiled insolently at her—'*Home is the sailor, home from the sea*. That's you! *And the Hunter home from the Hill*. What's the matter?'

'Nothing,' said Lynn.

She got up with the others. As they went into the drawing-room, Rowley said to her: 'You seemed to be getting on quite well with David Hunter. What were you talking about?'

'Nothing particular,' said Lynn.

CHAPTER V

'DAVID, when are we going back to London? When are we going to America?'

Across the breakfast table, David Hunter gave Rosaleen a quick surprised glance.

'There's no hurry, is there? What's wrong with this place?'

He gave a swift appreciative glance round the room where they were breakfasting. Furrowbank was built on the side of a hill and from the windows one had an unbroken panorama of sleepy English countryside. On the slope of the lawn thousands of daffodils had been planted. They were nearly over now, but a sheet of golden bloom still remained.

Crumbling the toast on her plate, Rosaleen murmured:

'You said we'd go to America—soon. As soon as it could be managed.'

'Yes—but actually it isn't managed so easily. There's priority. Neither you nor I have any business reasons to put forward. Things are always difficult after a war.'

He felt faintly irritated with himself as he spoke. The reasons he advanced, though genuine enough, had the sound of excuses. He wondered if they sounded that way to the girl who sat opposite him. And why was she suddenly so keen to go to America?

Rosaleen murmured: 'You said we'd only be here for a short time. You didn't say we were going to live here.'

'What's wrong with Warmsley Vale—and Furrowbank? Come now?'

'Nothing. It's *them*—all of them!'

'The Cloades?'

'Yes.'

'That's just what I get a kick out of,' said David. 'I like seeing their smug faces eaten up with envy and malice. Don't grudge me my fun, Rosaleen.'

She said in a low troubled voice:

'I wish you didn't feel like that. I don't like it.'

'Have some spirit, girl. We've been pushed around enough, you and I. The Cloades have lived soft—soft. Lived on big brother Gordon. Little fleas on a big flea. I hate their kind—I always have.'

She said, shocked:

'I don't like hating people. It's wicked.'

'Don't you think they hate you? Have they been kind to you—friendly?'

She said doubtfully:

'They haven't been unkind. They haven't done me any harm.'

'But they'd like to, babyface. They'd like to.' He laughed recklessly. 'If they weren't so careful of their own skins, you'd be found with a knife in your back one fine morning.'

She shivered.

'Don't say such dreadful things.'

'Well—perhaps not a knife. Strychnine in the soup.'

She stared at him, her mouth tremulous.

'You're joking . . .'

He became serious again.

'Don't worry, Rosaleen. I'll look after you. They've got me to deal with.'

She said, stumbling over the words, 'If it's true what you say—about their hating us—hating *me*—why don't we go to London? We'd be safe there—away from them all.'

'The country's good for you, my girl. You know it makes you ill being in London.'

'That was when the bombs were there—the bombs.' She shivered, closed her eyes. 'I'll never forget—*never* . . .'

'Yes, you will.' He took her gently by the shoulders, shook her slightly. 'Snap out of it, Rosaleen. You were badly shocked, but it's over now. There are no more bombs. Don't think about it. Don't remember. The doctor said country air and a country life for a long time to come. That's why I want to keep you away from London.'

'Is that really why? Is it, David? I thought—perhaps——'

'What did you think?'

Rosaleen said slowly:

'I thought perhaps it was because of *her* you wanted to be here . . .'

'Her?'

'You know the one I mean. The girl the other night. The one who was in the Wrens.'

His face was suddenly black and stern.

'Lynn? Lynn Marchmont.'

'She means something to you, David.'

'Lynn Marchmont? She's Rowley's girl. Good old stay-at-home Rowley. That bovine slow-witted good-looking ox.'

'I watched you talking to her the other night.'

'Oh, for Heaven's sake, Rosaleen.'

'And you've seen her since, haven't you?'

'I met her near the farm the other morning when I was out riding.'

'And you'll meet her again.'

'Of course I'll always be meeting her! This is a tiny place. You can't go two steps without falling over a Cloade. But if you think I've fallen for Lynn Marchmont, you're wrong. She's a proud stuck-up unpleasant girl without a civil tongue in her head. I wish old Rowley joy of her. No, Rosaleen, my girl, she's not my type.'

She said doubtfully, 'Are you sure, David?'

'Of course I'm sure.'

She said half-timidly:

'I know you don't like my laying out the cards . . . But they come true, they do indeed. There was a girl bringing trouble and sorrow—a girl would come from over the sea. There was a dark stranger, too, coming into our lives, and bringing danger with him. There was the death card, and——'

'You and your dark strangers!' David laughed. 'What a mass of superstition you are. Don't have any dealings with a dark stranger, that's my advice to you.'

He strolled out of the house laughing, but when he was away from the house, his face clouded over and he frowned to himself, murmuring:

'Bad luck to you, Lynn. Coming home from abroad and upsetting the apple cart.'

For he realised that at this very moment he was deliberately making a course on which he might hope to meet the girl he had just apostrophised so savagely.

Rosaleen watched him stroll away across the garden and out through the small gate that gave on to a public footpath across the fields. Then she went up to her bedroom and looked through the clothes in her wardrobe. She always enjoyed touching and feeling her new mink coat. To think she should own a coat like that—she could never quite get over the wonder of it. She was in her bedroom when the parlourmaid came up to tell her that Mrs. Marchmont had called.

Adela was sitting in the drawing-room with her lips set tightly together and her heart beating at twice its usual speed. She had been steeling herself for several days to make an appeal to Rosaleen but true to her nature had procrastinated. She had also been bewildered by finding that Lynn's attitude had unaccountably changed and that she was now rigidly opposed to her mother seeking relief from her anxieties by asking Gordon's widow for a loan.

However another letter from the Bank Manager that morning had driven Mrs. Marchmont into positive action. She could delay no longer. Lynn had gone out early, and Mrs. Marchmont had caught sight of David Hunter walking along the footpath—so the coast was clear. She particularly wanted to get Rosaleen alone, without David, rightly judging that Rosaleen alone would be a far easier proposition.

Nevertheless she felt dreadfully nervous as she waited in the sunny drawing-room, though she felt slightly better when Rosaleen came in with what Mrs. Marchmont always thought of as her 'half-witted look' more than usually marked.

'I wonder,' thought Adela to herself, 'if the blast did it or if she was always like that?'

Rosaleen stammered.

'Oh, g-g-ood morning. Is there anything? Do sit down.'

'Such a lovely morning,' said Mrs. Marchmont brightly. 'All my early tulips are out. Are yours?'

The girl stared at her vacantly.

'I don't know.'

What was one to do, thought Adela, with someone who didn't talk gardening or dogs—those standbyes of rural conversation.

Aloud she said, unable to help the tinge of acidity that crept into her tone:

'Of course you have so many gardeners—they attend to all that.'

'I believe we're shorthanded. Old Mullard wants two more men, he says. But there seems a terrible shortage still of labour.'

The words came out with a kind of glib parrot-like delivery—rather like a child who repeats what it has heard a grown-up person say.

Yes, she *was* like a child. Was that, Adela wondered, her charm? Was that what had attracted that hard-headed shrewd business man, Gordon Cloade, and blinded him to her stupidity and her lack of breeding? After all, it couldn't only be looks. Plenty of good-looking women had angled unsuccessfully to attract him.

But childishness, to a man of sixty-two, *might* be an attraction. Was it, could it be, real—or was it a pose—a pose that had paid and so had become second nature?

Rosaleen was saying, 'David's out, I'm afraid . . .' and the words recalled Mrs. Marchmont to herself. David might return. Now was her chance and she must not neglect it. The words stuck in her throat but she got them out.

'I wonder—if you could help me?'

'Help you?'

Rosaleen looked surprised, uncomprehending.

'I—things are very difficult—you see, Gordon's death has made a great difference to us all.'

'You silly idiot,' she thought. 'Must you go on gaping at me like that? You know what I mean! You *must* know what I mean. After all, you've been poor yourself . . .'

She hated Rosaleen at that moment. Hated her because she, Adela

Marchmont, was sitting here whining for money. She thought, 'I can't do it—I can't do it after all.'

In one brief instant all the long hours of thought and worry and vague planning flashed again across her brain.

Sell the house—(But move where? There weren't any small houses on the market—certainly not any cheap houses). Take paying guests —(But you couldn't get staff—and she simply couldn't—she just *couldn't* deal with all the cooking and housework involved. If Lynn helped—but Lynn was going to marry Rowley). Live with Rowley and Lynn herself? (No, she'd never do that!) Get a job. What job? Who wanted an untrained elderly tired-out woman?

She heard her voice, belligerent because she despised herself.

'I mean money,' she said.

'Money?' said Rosaleen.

She sounded ingenuously surprised, as though money was the last thing she expected to be mentioned.

Adela went on doggedly, tumbling the words out:

'I'm overdrawn at the bank, and I owe bills—repairs to the house—and the rates haven't been paid yet. You see, everything's halved—my income, I mean. I suppose it's taxation. Gordon, you see, used to help. With the house, I mean. He did all the repairs and the roof and painting and things like that. And an allowance as well. He paid it into the bank every quarter. He always said not to worry and of course I never did. I mean, it was all right when he was alive, but now——'

She stopped. She was ashamed—but at the same time relieved. After all, the worst was over. If the girl refused, she refused, and that was that.

Rosaleen was looking very uncomfortable.

'Oh, dear,' she said. 'I didn't know. I never thought . . . I—well, of course, I'll ask David . . .'

Grimly gripping the sides of her chair, Adela said, desperately; 'Couldn't you give me a cheque—now . . .'

'Yes—yes, I suppose I could.' Rosaleen, looking startled, got up, went to the desk. She hunted in various pigeon-holes and finally produced a cheque-book. 'Shall I—how much?'

"Would—would five hundred pounds——" Adela broke off.

'Five hundred pounds,' Rosaleen wrote obediently.

A load slipped off Adela's back. After all, it had been easy! She was dismayed as it occurred to her that it was less gratitude that she felt than a faint scorn for the easiness of her victory! Rosaleen was surely strangely simple.

The girl rose from the writing-desk and came across to her. She held out the cheque awkwardly. The embarrassment seemed now entirely on her side.

'I hope this is all right. I'm really so sorry——'

Adela took the cheque. The unformed childish hand straggled across the pink paper. Mrs. Marchmont. Five hundred pounds £500. Rosaleen Cloade.

'It's very good of you, Rosaleen. Thank you.'

'Oh please—I mean—I ought to have *thought*——'

'*Very* good of you, my dear.'

With the cheque in her handbag Adela Marchmont felt a different woman. The girl had really been very sweet about it. It would be embarrassing to prolong the interview. She said good-bye and departed. She passed David in the drive, said 'Good morning' pleasantly, and hurried on.

CHAPTER VI

'WHAT WAS the Marchmont woman doing here?' demanded David as soon as he got in.

'Oh, David. She wanted money dreadfully badly. I'd never thought——'

'And you gave it her, I suppose.'

He looked at her in half-humorous despair.

'You're not to be trusted alone, Rosaleen.'

'Oh, David, I couldn't refuse. After all——'

'After all—what? How much?'

In a small voice Rosaleen murmured, 'Five hundred pounds.'

To her relief David laughed.

'A mere fleabite!'

'Oh, David, it's a lot of money.'

'Not to us nowadays, Rosaleen. You never really seem to grasp that you're a very rich woman. All the same if she asked five hundred she'd have gone away perfectly satisfied with two-fifty. You must learn the language of borrowing!'

She murmured, 'I'm sorry, David.'

'My dear girl! After all, it's *your* money.'

'It isn't. Not really.'

'Now don't begin that all over again. Gordon Cloade died before he had time to make a will. That's what's called the luck of the game. We win, you and I. The others—lose.'

'It doesn't seem—right.'

'Come now, my lovely sister Rosaleen, aren't you enjoying all this? A big house, servants—jewellery? Isn't it a dream come true? Isn't it? Glory be to God, sometimes I think I'll wake up and find it *is* a dream.'

She laughed with him, and watching her narrowly, he was satisfied. He knew how to deal with his Rosaleen. It was inconvenient, he thought, that she should have a conscience, but there it was.

'It's quite true, David, it is like a dream—or like something on the Pictures. I do enjoy it all. I do really.'

'But what we have we hold,' he warned her. 'No more gifts to the Cloades, Rosaleen. Every one of them has got far more money than either you or I ever had.'

'Yes, I suppose that's true.'

'Where was Lynn this morning?' he asked.

'I think she'd gone to Long Willows.'

To Long Willows—to see Rowley—the oaf—the clodhopper! His good humour vanished. Set on marrying the fellow, was she?

Moodily he strolled out of the house, up through massed azaleas and out through the small gate on the top of the hill. From there the footpath dipped down the hill and past Rowley's farm.

As David stood there, he saw Lynn Marchmont coming up from the farm. He hesitated for a minute, then set his jaw pugnaciously and strolled down the hill to meet her. They met by a stile just half-way up the hill.

'Good morning,' said David. 'When's the wedding?'

'You've asked that before,' she retorted. 'You know well enough. It's in June.'

'You're going through with it?'

'I don't know what you mean, David.'

'Oh, yes, you do.' He have a contemptuous laugh. 'Rowley. What's Rowley?'

'A better man than you—touch him if you dare,' she said lightly.

'I've no doubt he's a better man than me—but I do dare. I'd dare anything for you, Lynn.'

She was silent for a moment or two. She said at last:

'What you don't understand is that I love Rowley.'

'I wonder.'

She said vehemently:

'I do, I tell you. I do.'

David looked at her searchingly.

'We all see pictures of ourselves—of ourselves as we want to be. You see yourself in love with Rowley, settling down with Rowley, living here contented with Rowley, never wanting to get away. But that's not the real you, is it, Lynn?'

'Oh, what is the real me? What's the real *you*, if it comes to that? What do *you* want?'

'I'd have said I wanted safety, peace after storm, ease after troubled seas. But I don't know. Sometimes I suspect, Lynn, that both you and I want—trouble.' He added moodily, 'I wish you'd never turned up here. I was remarkably happy until you came.'

'Aren't you happy now?'

He looked at her. She felt excitement rising in her. Her breath came faster. Never had she felt so strongly David's queer moody attraction. He shot out a hand, grasped her shoulder, swung her round . . .

Then as suddenly she felt his grasp slacken. He was staring over her shoulder up the hill. She twisted her head to see what it was that had caught his attention.

A woman was just going through the small gate above Furrowback. David said sharply: 'Who's that?'

Lynn said:

'It looks like Frances.'

'Frances?' He frowned. 'What does Frances want?'

'My dear Lynn! Only those who want something drop in to see Rosaleen. Your mother has already dropped in this morning.'

'*Mother?*' Lynn drew back. She frowned. 'What did she want?'

'Don't you know? Money!'

'Money?' Lynn stiffened.

'She got it all right,' said David. He was smiling now the cool cruel smile that fitted his face so well.

They had been near a moment or two ago, now they were miles apart, divided by a sharp antagonism.

Lynn cried out, 'Oh no, no, *no*!'

He mimicked her.

'Yes, yes, *yes*!'

'I don't believe it! How much?'

'Five hundred pounds.'

She drew her breath in sharply.

David said musingly:

'I wonder how much Frances is going to ask for? Really it's hardly safe to leave Rosaleen alone for five minutes! The poor girl doesn't know how to say No.'

'Have there been—who else?'

David smiled mockingly.

'Aunt Kathie had incurred certain debts—oh, nothing much, a mere two hundred and fifty covered them—but she was afraid it might get to the doctor's ears! Since they had been occasioned by payments to mediums, he might not have been sympathetic. She didn't know, of course,' added David, 'that the doctor himself had applied for a loan.'

Lynn said in a low voice, 'What you must think of us—what you must think of us!' Then, taking him by surprise, she turned and ran helter-skelter down the hill to the farm.

He frowned as he watched her go. She had gone to Rowley, flown there as a homing pigeon flies, and the fact disturbed him more than he cared to acknowledge.

He looked up the hill again and frowned.

'No, Frances,' he said under his breath. 'I think not. You've chosen a bad day,' and he strode purposefully up the hill.

He went through the gate and down through the azaleas—crossed the lawn, and came quietly in through the window of the drawing-room just as Frances Cloade was saying:

'—I wish I could make it all clearer. But you see, Rosaleen, it really is frightfully difficult to explain——'

A voice from behind her said:

'*Is it?*'

Frances Cloade turned sharply. Unlike Adela Marchmont she had not deliberately tried to find Rosaleen alone. The sum needed was sufficiently large to make it unlikely that Rosaleen would hand it over without consulting her brother. Actually, Frances would far rather have discussed the matter with David and Rosaleen together, than have David feel that she had tried to get money out of Rosaleen during his absence from the house.

She had not heard him come through the window, absorbed as she was in the presentation of a plausible case. The interruption startled her, and she realised also that David Hunter was, for some reason, in a particularly ugly mood.

'Oh, David,' she said easily, 'I'm glad you've come. I've just been telling Rosaleen. Gordon's death has left Jeremy in no end of a hole, and I'm wondering if she could possibly come to the rescue. It's like this——'

Her tongue flowed on swiftly—the large sum involved—Gordon's backing—promised verbally—Government restrictions and mortgages——

A certain admiration stirred in the darkness of David's mind. What a damned good liar the woman was! Plausible, the whole story. But not the truth. No, he'd take his oath on that. Not the truth! What, he wondered, *was* the truth? Jeremy been getting himself into Queer Street? It must be something pretty desperate, if he was allowing Frances to come and try this stunt. She was a proud woman, too——

He said, '*Ten thousand?*'

Rosaleen murmured in an awed voice:

'That's a lot of money.'

Frances said swiftly:

'Oh, I know it is. I wouldn't come to you if it wasn't such a difficult sum to raise. But Jeremy would never have gone into the deal if it hadn't been for Gordon's backing. It's so dreadfully unfortunate that Gordon should have died so suddenly——'

'Leaving you all out in the cold?' David's voice was unpleasant. 'After a sheltered life under his wing.'

There was a faint flash in Frances's eyes as she said:

'You put things so picturesquely!'

'Rosaleen can't touch the capital, you know. Only the income. And she pays about nineteen and six in the pound income tax.'

'Oh, I know. Taxation's dreadful these days. But it *could* be managed, couldn't it? We'd repay——'

He interrupted:

'It *could* be managed. *But it won't be!*'

Frances turned swiftly to Rosaleen.

'Rosaleen, you're such a generous——'

David's voice cut across her speech.

'What do you Cloades think Rosaleen is—a milch cow? All of you at her—hinting, asking, begging. And behind her back? Sneering at her, patronising her, resenting her, hating her, *wishing her dead*——'

'That's not true,' Frances cried.

'Isn't it? I tell you I'm sick of you all! *She's* sick of you all. You'll get no money out of us, so you can stop coming and whining for it? Understand?'

His face was black with fury.

Frances stood up. Her face was wooden and expressionless. She drew on a wash-leather glove absently, yet with attention, as though it was a significant action.

'You make your meaning quite plain, David,' she said.

Rosaleen murmured:

'I'm sorry. I'm really sorry . . . '

Frances paid no attention to her. Rosaleen might not have been in the room. She took a step towards the window and paused, facing David.

'You have said that I resent Rosaleen. That is not true. I have not resented Rosaleen—but I do resent—*you*!'

'What do you mean?'

He scowled at her.

'Women must live. Rosaleen married a very rich man, years older than herself. Why not? But *you*! You must live on your sister, live on the fat of the land, live softly—on *her*.'

'I stand between her and harpies.'

They stood looking at each other. He was aware of her anger and the thought flashed across him that Frances Cloade was a dangerous enemy, one who could be both unscrupulous and reckless.

When she opened her mouth to speak, he even felt a moment's apprehension. But what she said was singularly non-committal.

'I shall remember what you have said, David.'

Passing him, she went out of the window.

He wondered why he felt so strongly that the words had been a threat.

Rosaleen was crying.

'Oh, David, David—you oughtn't to have been saying those things to her. She's the one of them that's been the nicest to me.'

He said furiously: 'Shut up, you little fool. Do you want them to trample all over you and bleed you of every penny?'

'But the money—if—if it isn't rightfully mine——'

She quailed before his glance.

'I—I didn't mean that, David.'

'I should hope not.'

Conscience, he thought, was the devil!

He hadn't reckoned with the item of Rosaleen's conscience. It was going to make things awkward in the future.

The future? He frowned as he looked at her and let his thoughts race ahead. Rosaleen's future . . . His own . . . He'd always known what he wanted . . . he knew now . . . But Rosaleen? What future was there for Rosaleen?

As his face darkened—she cried out—suddenly shivering:

'Oh! Someone's walking over my grave.'

He said, looking at her curiously:

'So you realise it may come to that?'

'What do you mean, David?'

'I mean that five—six—seven people have every intention to hurry you into your grave before you're due there!'

'You don't mean—murder——' Her voice was horrified. 'You think these people would do murder—not nice people like the Cloades.'

'I'm not sure that it isn't just nice people like the Cloades who do do murder. But they won't succeed in murdering you while I'm here to look after you. They'd have to get me out of the way first. But if they did get me out of the way—well—look out for yourself!'

'David—don't say such awful things.'

'Listen,' he gripped her arm. 'If ever I'm not here, look after yourself, Rosaleen. Life isn't safe, remember—it's dangerous, damned dangerous. And I've an idea it's specially dangerous for you.'

CHAPTER VII

'ROWLEY, can you let me have five hundred pounds?'

Rowley stared at Lynn. She stood there, out of breath from running, her face pale, her mouth set.

He said soothingly and rather as he would speak to a horse:

'There, there, ease up, old girl. What's all this about?'

'I want five hundred pounds.'

'I could do with it myself, for that matter.'

'But Rowley, this is *serious*. Can't you lend me five hundred pounds?'

'I'm overdrawn as it is. That new tractor——'

'Yes, yes——' She pushed aside the farming details. 'But you could raise money somehow—if you had to, couldn't you?'

'What do you want it for, Lynn? Are you in some kind of a hole?'

'I want it for him——' She jerked her head backwards towards the big square house on the hill.

'Hunter? Why on earth——'

'It's Mums. She's been borrowing from him. She's—she's in a bit of a jam about money.'

'Yes, I expect she is.' Rowley sounded sympathetic. 'Damned hard lines on her. I wish I could help a bit—but I can't.'

'I can't stand her borrowing money from David!'

'Hold hard, old girl. It's Rosaleen who actually has to fork out the cash. And after all, why not?'

'Why not? You say, "*Why not*," Rowley?'

'I don't see why Rosaleen shouldn't come to the rescue once in a while. Old Gordon put us all in a spot by pegging out without a will. If the position is put clearly to Rosaleen she must see herself that a spot of help all round is indicated.'

'*You* haven't borrowed from her?'

'No—well—that's different. I can't very well go and ask a woman for money. Sort of thing you don't like doing.'

'Can't you see that I don't like being—being beholden to David Hunter?'

'But you're not. It isn't his money.'

'That's just what it is, actually. Rosaleen's completely under his thumb.'

'Oh, I dare say. But it isn't his legally.'

'And you won't, you can't—lend me some money?'

'Now look here, Lynn—if you were in some real jam—blackmail or debts—I might be able to sell land or stock—but it would be a pretty desperate proceeding. I'm only just keeping my head above water as it is. And what with not knowing what this damned Government is going to do next—hampered at every turn—snowed under with forms up to midnight trying to fill them in sometimes—it's too much for one man.'

Lynn said bitterly:

'Oh, I know! If only Johnnie hadn't been killed——'

He shouted out:

'Leave Johnnie out of it! Don't talk about that!'

She stared at him, astonished. His face was red and congested. He seemed beside himself with rage.

Lynn turned away and went slowly back to the White House.

'Can't you give it back, Mums?'

'Really, Lynn darling! I went straight to the bank with it. And then I paid Arthurs and Bodgham and Knebworth. Knebworth was getting quite abusive. Oh, my dear, the *relief*? I haven't been able to sleep for nights and nights. Really, Rosaleen was most understanding and nice about it.'

Lynn said bitterly:

'And I suppose you'll go to her again and again now.'

'I hope it won't be necessary, dear. I shall try to be very economical, you know that. But of course everything is so expensive nowadays. And it gets worse and worse.'

'Yes, and *we* shall get worse and worse. Going on cadging.'

Adela flushed.

'I don't think that's a nice way of putting it, Lynn. As I explained to Rosaleen, we had always depended on Gordon.'

'We shouldn't have. That's what's wrong, we shouldn't have.' Lynn added, 'He's right to despise us.'

'Who despises us?'

'That odious David Hunter.'

'Really,' said Mrs. Marchmont with dignity, 'I don't see that it can matter in the least *what* David Hunter thinks. Fortunately he wasn't at Furrowbank this morning—otherwise I dare say he would have influenced that girl. She's completely under his thumb, of course.'

Lynn shifted from one foot to the other.

'What did you mean, Mums, when you said—that first morning I was home—'*If* he *is* her brother?''

'Oh, *that*,' Mrs. Marchmont looked slightly embarrassed. 'Well, there's been a certain amount of gossip, you know.'

Lynn merely waited inquiringly. Mrs. Marchmont coughed.

'That type of young woman—the adventuress type (of course poor Gordon was completely taken in) they've usually got a—well, a young man of their own in the background. Suppose she says to Gordon she's got a brother—wires to him in Canada or wherever he was. This man turns up. How is *Gordon* to know whether he's her brother or not? Poor Gordon, absolutely infatuated no doubt, and believing everything she said. And so her 'brother' comes with them to England—poor Gordon quite unsuspecting.'

Lynn said fiercely: 'I don't believe it. I don't *believe* it!'

Mrs. Marchmont raised her eyebrows.

'Really, my dear——'

'He's not like that. And she—she isn't either. She's a fool perhaps, but she's sweet—yes, she's really sweet. It's just people's foul minds. I don't believe it, I tell you.'

Mrs. Marchmont said with dignity:

'There's really no need to *shout*.'

CHAPTER VIII

IT WAS A WEEK LATER that the 5.20 train drew into Warmsley Heath Station and a tall bronzed man with a knapsack got out.

On the opposite platform a cluster of golfers were waiting for the up train. The tall bearded man with the knapsack gave up his ticket and passed out of the station. He stood uncertainly for a minute or two—then he saw the signpost: *Footpath to Warmsley Vale*—and directed his steps that way with brisk determination.

At Long Willows, Rowley Cloade had just finished making himself a cup of tea when a shadow falling across the kitchen table made him look up.

If for just a moment he thought the girl standing just inside the door was Lynn, his disappointment turned to surprise when he saw it was Rosaleen Cloade.

She was wearing a frock of some peasant material in bright broad stripes of orange and green—the artificial simplicity of which had run into more money than Rowley could ever have imagined possible.

Up to now he had always seen her dressed in expensive and somewhat towny clothes which she wore with an artificial air—much, he had thought, as a mannequin might display dresses that did not belong to her but to the firm who employed her.

This afternoon in the broad peasant stripes of gay colour, he seemed to see a new Rosaleen Cloade. Her Irish origin was more noticeable, the dark curling hair and the lovely blue eyes put in with the smutty finger. Her voice, too, had a softer Irish sound instead of the careful rather mincing tones in which she usually spoke.

'It's such a lovely afternoon,' she said. 'So I came for a walk.'

She added:

'David's gone to London.'

She said it almost guiltily, then flushed and took a cigarette case out of her bag. She offered one to Rowley, who shook his head, then looked round for a match to light Rosaleen's cigarette. But she was flicking unsuccessfully at an expensive-looking small gold lighter. Rowley took it from her and with one sharp movement it lit. As she bent her head towards him to light her cigarette he noticed how long and dark the lashes were that lay on her cheek and he thought to himself:

'Old Gordon knew what he was doing . . .'

Rosaleen stepped back a pace and said admiringly:

'That's a lovely little heifer you've got in the top field.'

Astonished by her interest, Rowley began to talk to her about the farm. Her interest surprised him, but it was obviously genuine and not put on, and to his surprise he found that she was quite knowledgeable on farm matters. Butter-making and dairy produce she spoke of with familiarity.

'Why, you might be a farmer's wife, Rosaleen,' he said smiling.

The animation went out of her face.

She said:

'We had a farm—in Ireland—before I came over here—before——'

'Before you went on the stage?'

She said wistfully and a trifle, it seemed to him, guiltily:

'It's not so very long ago . . . I remember it all very well.' She added with a flash of spirit, 'I could milk your cows for you, Rowley, now.'

This was quite a new Rosaleen. Would David Hunter have approved these casual references to a farming past? Rowley thought not. Old Irish landed gentry, that was the impression David tried to put over. Rosaleen's version, he thought, was nearer the truth. Primitive farm life, then the lure of the stage, the touring company to South Africa, marriage—isolation in Central Africa—escape—hiatus—and finally marriage to a millionaire in New York . . .

Yes, Rosaleen Hunter had travelled a long way since milking a Kerry cow. Yet looking at her, he found it hard to believe that she had ever started. Her face had that innocent, slightly half-witted expression, the face of one who has no history. And she looked so young—much younger than her twenty-six years.

There was something appealing about her, she had the same pathetic quality as the little calves he had driven to the butcher that morning. He looked at her as he had looked at them. Poor little devils, he had thought, a pity that they had to be killed . . .

A look of alarm came into Rosaleen's eyes. She asked uneasily: 'What are you thinking of, Rowley?'

'Would you like to see over the farm and the dairy?'

'Oh, indeed, I would.'

Amused by her interest he took her all over the farm. But when he finally suggested making her a cup of tea, an alarmed expression came into her eyes.

'Oh, no—thank you, Rowley—I'd best be getting home.' She looked down at her watch. 'Oh! how late it is! David will be back by the 5.20 train. He'll wonder where I am. I—I must hurry.' She added shyly. 'I *have* enjoyed myself, Rowley.'

And that, he thought, was true. She *had* enjoyed herself. She had been able to be natural—to be her own raw unsophisticated self. She was afraid of her brother David, that was clear. David was the brains of the family. Well, for once, she'd had an afternoon out—yes, that was it, an afternoon out just like a servant! The rich Mrs. Gordon Cloade!

He smiled grimly as he stood by the gate watching her hurrying up the hill towards Furrowbank. Just before she reached the stile a man came over it—Rowley wondered if it was David but it was a bigger, heavier man. Rosaleen drew back to let him pass, then skipped lightly over the stile, her pace accentuating almost to a run.

Yes, she'd had an afternoon off—and he, Rowley, had wasted over an hour of valuable time! Well, perhaps it hadn't been wasted. Rosaleen, he thought, had seemed to like him. That might come in useful. A pretty thing—yes, and the calves this morning had been pretty . . . poor little devils.

Standing there, lost in thought, he was startled by a voice, and raised his head sharply.

A big man in a broad felt hat with a pack slung across his shoulders was standing on the footpath at the other side of the gate.

'Is this the way to Warmsley Vale?'

As Rowley stared he repeated his question. With an effort Rowley recalled his thoughts and answered:

'Yes, keep right along the path—across that next field. Turn to the left when you get to the road and about three minutes takes you right into the village.'

In the self-same words he had answered that particular question several hundred times. People took the footpath on leaving the station, followed it up over the hill, and lost faith in it as they came down the other side and saw no sign of their destination, for Blackwell Copse masked Warmsley Vale from sight. It was tucked away in a hollow there with only the tip of its church tower showing.

The next question was not quite so usual, but Rowley answered it without much thought.

'The Stag or the Bells and Motley. The Stag for choice. They're both equally good—or bad. I should think you'd get a room all right.'

The question made him look more attentively at his interlocutor. Nowadays people usually booked a room beforehand at any place they were going to . . .

The man was tall, with a bronzed face, a beard, and very blue eyes. He was about forty and not ill-looking in a tough and rather dare-devil style. It was not, perhaps, a wholly pleasant face.

Come from overseas somewhere, thought Rowley. Was there or was there not a faint Colonial twang in his accent? Curious, in some way, the face was not unfamiliar . . .

Where had he seen that face, or a face very like it, before?

Whilst he was puzzling unsuccessfully over that problem, the stranger startled him by asking:

'Can you tell me if there's a house called Furrowbank near here?'

Rowley answered slowly:

'Why, yes. Up there on the hill. You must have passed close by it —that is, if you've come along the footpath from the station.'

'Yes—that's what I did.' He turned, staring up the hill. 'So that was it—that big white new-looking house.'

'Yes, that's the one.'

'A big place to run,' said the man. 'Must cost a lot to keep up?'

A devil of a lot, thought Rowley. And *our* money . . . A stirring of anger made him forget for the moment where he was . . .

With a start he came back to himself to see the stranger staring up the hill with a curious speculative look in his eyes.

'Who lives there?' he said. 'Is it—a Mrs. Cloade?'

'That's right,' said Rowley. 'Mrs. Gordon Cloade.'

The stranger raised his eyebrows. He seemed gently amused.

'Oh,' he said, 'Mrs. Gordon Cloade. Very nice for her!'

Then he gave a short nod.

'Thanks, pal,' he said, and shifting the pack he carried he strode on towards Warmsley Vale.

Rowley turned slowly back into the farmyard. His mind was still puzzling over something.

Where the devil had he seen that fellow before?

About nine-thirty that night, Rowley pushed aside a heap of forms that had been littering the kitchen table and got up. He looked absentmindedly at the photograph of Lynn that stood on the mantelpiece, then frowning, he went out of the house.

Ten minutes later he pushed open the door of the Stag Saloon Bar. Beatrice Lippincott, behind the bar counter, smiled welcome at him. Mr. Rowley Cloade, she thought, was a fine figure of a man. Over a pint of bitter Rowley exchanged the usual observations with the company present, unfavourable comment was made upon the Government, the weather, and sundry particular crops.

Presently, moving up a little, Rowley was able to address Beatrice in a quiet voice:

'Got a stranger staying here? Big man? Slouch hat?'

'That's right, Mr. Rowley. Came along about six o'clock. That the one you mean?'

Rowley nodded.

'He passed my place. Asked his way.'

'That's right. Seems a stranger.'

'I wondered,' said Rowley, 'who he was.'

He looked at Beatrice and smiled. Beatrice smiled back.

'That's easy, Mr. Rowley, if you'd like to know.'

She dipped under the bar and out to return with a fat leather volume wherein were registered the arrivals.

She opened it at the page showing the most recent entries. The last of these ran as follows:

Enoch Arden. Cape Town. British.

CHAPTER IX

IT WAS A FINE MORNING. The birds were singing, and Rosaleen, coming down to breakfast in her expensive peasant dress felt happy.

The doubts and fears that had lately oppressed her seemed to have faded away. David was in a good temper, laughing and teasing her. His visit to London on the previous day had been satisfactory. Breakfast was well cooked and well served. They had just finished it when the post arrived.

There were seven or eight letters for Rosaleen. Bills, charitable appeals, some local invitations—nothing of any special interest.

David laid aside a couple of small bills and opened the third envelope. The enclosure, like the outside of the envelope, was written in printed characters.

DEAR MR. HUNTER,

I think it is best to approach you rather than your sister, 'Mrs. Cloade,' in case the contents of this letter might come as somewhat of a shock to her. Briefly, I have news of Captain Robert Underhay, which she may be glad to hear. I am staying at the Stag and if you will call there this evening, I shall be pleased to go into the matter with you.

Yours faithfully,
ENOCH ARDEN.

A strangled sound came from David's throat. Rosaleen looked up smiling, then her face changed to an expression of alarm.

'David—David—what is it?'

Mutely he held out the letter to her. She took it and read it.

'But—David—I don't understand—what does it mean?'

'You can read, can't you?'

She glanced up at him timorously.

'David—does it mean—what are we going to do?'

He was frowning—planning rapidly in his quick far-seeing mind.

'It's all right, Rosaleen, no need to be worried. I'll deal with it——'

'But does it mean that——'

'Don't worry, my dear girl. Leave it to me. Listen, this is what you've got to do. Pack a bag at once and go up to London. Go to the flat—and stay there until you hear from me? Understand?'

'Yes. Yes, of course I understand, but David——'

'Just do as I say, Rosaleen.' He smiled at her. He was kindly, reassuring. 'Go and pack. I'll drive you to the station. You can catch the 10.32. Tell the porter at the flats that you don't want to see any one. If any one calls and asks for you, he's to say you're out of town. Give him a quid. Understand? He's not to let any one up to see you except me.'

'Oh.' Her hands went up to her cheeks. She looked at him with scared lovely eyes.

'It's all right, Rosaleen—but it's tricky. You're not much hand at the tricky stuff? That's my look out. I want you out of the way so that I've got a free hand, that's all.'

'Can't I stay here, David?'

'No, of course you can't, Rosaleen. Do have some sense. I've got to have a free hand to deal with this fellow whoever he is——'

'Do you think that it's—that it's——'

He said with emphasis:

'I don't think anything at the moment. The first thing is to get you out of the way. Then I can find out where we stand. Go on—there's a good girl, don't argue.'

She turned and went out of the room.

David frowned down at the letter in his hand.

Very non-committal—polite—well phrased—might mean anything. It might be genuine solicitude in an awkward situation. Might be a veiled threat. He conned its phrases over and over—'I have news of Captain Robert Underhay' . . . 'Best to approach you' . . . 'I shall be pleased to go into the matter with you . . . ' 'Mrs. Cloade.' Damn it all, he didn't like those inverted commas—'*Mrs. Cloade* . . .'

He looked at the signature. Enoch Arden. Something stirred in his mind—some poetical memory . . . a line of verse.

When David strode into the hall of the Stag that evening, there was, as was usual, no one about. A door at the left was marked Coffee Room, a door on the right was marked Lounge. A door farther along was marked repressively 'For Resident Guests Only.' A passage on the right led along to the Bar, from whence a faint hum of voices could be heard. A small glass-encased box was labelled Office and had a push-bell placed conveniently on the side of its sliding window.

Sometimes, as David knew by experience, you had to ring four or five times before any one condescended to come and attend to you.

Except for the short period of meal times, the hall of the Stag was as deserted as Robinson Crusoe's island.

This time, David's third ring of the bell brought Miss Beatrice Lippincott along the passage from the bar, her hand patting her golden pompadour of hair into place. She slipped into the glass box and greeted him with a gracious smile.

'Good evening, Mr. Hunter. Rather cold weather for the time of year, isn't it?'

'Yes—I suppose it is. Have you got a Mr. Arden staying here?'

'Let me see now,' said Miss Lippincott, making rather a parade of not knowing exactly, a proceeding she always adopted as tending to increase the importance of the Stag. 'Oh, yes. Mr. *Enoch* Arden. No. 5. On the first floor. You can't miss it, Mr. Hunter. Up the stairs, and don't go along the gallery but round to the left and down three steps.'

Following these complicated directions, David tapped on the door of No. 5 and a voice said Come in.

He went in, closing the door behind him.

Coming out of the office, Beatrice Lippincott called, 'Lily.' An adenoidal girl with a giggle and pale boiled gooseberry eyes responded to the summons.

'Can you manage for a bit, Lily? I've got to see about some linen.'

Lily said, 'Oh, yes, Miss Lippincott,' gave a giggle and added, sighing gustily: 'I do think Mr. Hunter's *ever* so good-looking, don't you?'

'Ah, I've seen a lot of his type in the war,' said Miss Lippincott, with a world-weary air. 'Young pilots and such-like from the fighter station. Never could be sure about their cheques. Often had such a way with them that you'd cash the things against your better judgment. But, of course, I'm funny that way, Lily, what I like is *class*. Give me class every time. What I say is a gentleman's a gentleman even if he does drive a tractor.' With which enigmatic pronouncement Beatrice left Lily and went up the stairs.

Inside room No. 5, David Hunter paused inside the door and looked at the man who had signed himself Enoch Arden.

Fortyish, knocked about a bit, a suggestion of having come down in the world—on the whole a difficult customer. Such was David's summing up. Apart from that, not easy to fathom. A dark horse.

Arden said:

'Hallo—you Hunter? Good. Sit down. What'll you have? Whisky?'

He'd made himself comfortable, David noted that. A modest array of bottles—a fire burning in the grate on this chilly Spring evening. Clothes not English cut, but worn as an Englishman wears clothes. The man was the right age, too. . . .

'Thanks,' David said, 'I'll have a spot of whisky.'

'Say When.'

'When. Not too much soda.'

They were a little like dogs, manœuvring for position—circling round each other, backs stiff, hackles up, ready to be friendly or ready to snarl and snap.

'Cheerio,' said Arden.

'Cheerio.'

They set their glasses down, relaxed a little. Round One was over.

The man who called himself Enoch Arden said:

'You were surprised to get my letter?'

'Frankly,' said David, 'I don't understand it at all.'

'N-no—n-no—well, perhaps not.'

David said:

'I understand you knew my sister's first husband—Robert Underhay.'

'Yes, I knew Robert very well.' Arden was smiling, blowing clouds of smoke idly up in the air. 'As well, perhaps, as any one could know him. *You* never met him, did you, Hunter?'

'No.'

'Oh, perhaps that's as well.'

'What do you mean by that?' David asked sharply.

Arden said easily:

'My dear fellow, it makes everything much simpler—that's all. I apologise for asking you to come here, but I did think it was best to keep'—he paused—'Rosaleen out of it all. No need to give her unnecessary pain.'

'Do you mind coming to the point?'

'Of course, of course. Well now, did you ever suspect—how shall we say—that there was anything—well—*fishy*—about Underhay's death?'

'What on earth do you mean?'

'Well, Underhay had rather peculiar ideas, you know. It may have been chivalry—it may just possibly have been for quite a different reason—but let's say that, at a particular moment some years ago there were certain advantages to Underhay in being considered dead. He was good at managing natives—always had been. No trouble to him to get a probable story circulating with any amount of corroborative detail. All Underhay had to do was to turn up about a thousand miles away—with a new name.'

'It seems a most fantastic supposition to me,' said David.

'Does it? Does it really?' Arden smiled. He leaned forward, tapped David on the knee. 'Suppose it's true, Hunter? Eh? Suppose it's true?'

'I should require very definite proof of it.'

'Would you? Well, of course, there's no super-definite proof. Underhay himself could turn up here—in Warmsley Vale. How'd you like that for proof?'

'It would at least be conclusive,' said David dryly.

'Oh, yes, conclusive—but just a little embarrassing—for Mrs. Gordon Cloade, I mean. Because then, of course, she wouldn't *be* Mrs. Gordon Cloade. Awkward. You must admit, just a little bit awkward?'

'My sister,' said David, 'remarried in perfectly good faith.'

'Of course she did, my dear fellow. Of course she did. I'm not disputing that for a second. Any judge would say the same. No actual blame could attach to her.'

'Judge?' said David sharply.

The other said as though apologetically:

'I was thinking of bigamy.'

'Just what are you driving at?' asked David savagely.

'Now don't get excited, old boy. We just want to put our heads together and see what's best to be done—best for your sister, that's to say. Nobody wants a lot of dirty publicity. Underhay—well, Underhay was always a chivalrous kind of chap.' Arden paused. 'He still is . . . '

'*Is?*' asked David sharply.

'That's what I said.'

'You say Robert Underhay is alive. Where is he now?'

Arden leaned forward—his voice became confidential.

'*Do you really want to know, Hunter?* Wouldn't it be better if you *didn't* know? Put it that, as far as *you* know, and as far as Rosaleen knows, Underhay died in Africa. Very good, and *if* Underhay is alive, he doesn't know his wife has married again, he hasn't the least idea of it. Because, of course, if he *did* know he would have come forward . . . Rosaleen, you see, has inherited a good deal of money from her second husband—well, then, of course she isn't entitled to any of that money . . . Underhay is a man with a very sensitive sense of honour. He wouldn't like her inheriting money under false pretences.' He paused. 'But of course it's possible that Underhay doesn't know anything about her second marriage. He's in a bad way, poor fellow—in a very bad way.'

'What do you mean by in a bad way?'

Arden shook his head solemnly.

'Broken down in health. He needs medical attention—special treatments—all unfortunately rather *expensive*.'

The last word dropped delicately as though into a category of its own. It was the word for which David Hunter had been unconsciously waiting.

He said:

'Expensive?'

'Yes—unfortunately everything costs money. Underhay, poor devil, is practically destitute.' He added: 'He's got practically nothing but what he stands up in . . . '

Just for a moment David's eyes wandered round the room. He noted the pack slung on a chair. There was no suitcase to be seen.

'I wonder,' said David, and his voice was not pleasant, 'if Robert Underhay is quite the chivalrous gentleman you make him out to be.'

'He was once,' the other assured him. 'But life, you know, is inclined to make a fellow cynical.' He paused and added softly: 'Gordon Cloade was really an incredibly wealthy fellow. The spectacle of too much wealth arouses one's baser instincts.'

David Hunter got up.

'I've got an answer for you. Go to the devil.'

Unperturbed, Arden said, smiling:

'Yes, I thought you'd say that.'

'You're a damned blackmailer, neither more nor less. I've a good mind to call your bluff.'

'Publish and be damned? An admirable sentiment. But you wouldn't like it if I did "publish." Not that I shall. If you won't buy, I've another market.'

'What do you mean?'

'The Cloades. Suppose I go to them. "Excuse me, but would you be interested to learn that the late Robert Underhay is very much alive?" Why, man, they'll jump at it!'

David said scornfully:

'You won't get anything out of them. They're broke, every one of them.'

'Ah, but there's such a thing as a working arrangement. So much in cash on the day it's proved that Underhay is alive, that Mrs. Gordon Cloade is still Mrs. Robert Underhay and that consequently Gordon Cloade's will, made before his marriage, is good in law . . . '

For some few minutes David sat silent, then he asked bluntly:

'How much?'

The answer came as bluntly:

'Twenty thousand.'

'Out of the question! My sister can't touch the capital, she's only got a life interest.'

'Ten thousand, then. She can raise that, easily. There's jewellery, isn't there?'

David sat silent, then he said unexpectedly:

'All right.'

For a moment the other man seemed at a loss. It was as though the ease of his victory surprised him.

'No cheques,' he said. 'To be paid in notes!'

'You'll have to give us time—to get hold of the money.'

'I'll give you forty-eight hours.'

'Make it next Tuesday.'

'All right. You'll bring the money here.' He added before David could speak, 'I'm not meeting you at a lonely copse—or a deserted river bank, so don't you think so. You'll bring the money here—to the Stag—at nine o'clock next Tuesday evening.'

'Suspicious sort of chap, aren't you?'

'I know my way about. And I know your kind.'

'As you said, then.'

David went out of the room and down the stairs. His face was black with rage.

Beatrice Lippincott came out of the room marked No. 4. There was a communicating door between 4 and 5, though the fact could hardly be noted by an occupant in 5 since a wardrobe stood upright in front of it.

Miss Lippincott's cheeks were pink and her eyes bright with pleasurable excitement. She smoothed back her pompadour of hair with an agitated hand.

CHAPTER X

SHEPHERD'S COURT, MAYFAIR, was a large block of luxury service flats. Unharmed by the ravages of enemy action, they had nevertheless been unable to keep up quite their pre-war standard of ease. There was service still, although not very good service. Where there had been two uniformed porters there was now only one. The restaurant still served meals, but except for breakfast, meals were not sent up to the apartments.

The flat rented by Mrs. Gordon Cloade was on the third floor. It consisted of a sitting-room with a built-in cocktail bar, two bedrooms with built-in cupboards, and a superbly appointed bathroom, gleaming with tiles and chromium.

In the sitting-room David Hunter was striding up and down whilst Rosaleen sat on a big square-ended settee watching him. She looked pale and frightened.

'Blackmail!' he muttered. 'Blackmail! My God, am I the kind of man to let myself be blackmailed?'

She shook her head, bewildered, troubled.

'If I knew,' David was saying. 'If I only *knew*!'

From Rosaleen there came a small miserable sob.

He went on:

'It's this working in the dark—working blindfold——' He wheeled round suddenly. 'You took those emeralds round to Bond Street to old Greatorex?'

'Yes.'

'How much?'

Rosaleen's voice was stricken as she said:

'Four thousand. Four thousand *pounds*. He said if I didn't sell them they ought to be reinsured.'

'Yes—precious stones have doubled in value. Oh well, we *can* raise the money. But if we do, it's only the beginning—it means being bled to death—bled, Rosaleen, bled white!'

She cried:

'Oh, let's leave England—let's get away—couldn't we go to Ireland—America—*somewhere*?'

He turned and looked at her.

'You're not a fighter, are you, Rosaleen? Cut and run is your motto.'

She wailed: 'We're wrong—all this has been wrong—very wicked.'

'Don't turn pious on me just now! I can't stand it. We were sitting pretty, Rosaleen. For the first time in my life I was sitting pretty—and I'm not going to let it all go, do you hear? If only it wasn't this cursed fighting in the dark. You understand, don't you, that the whole thing may be bluff—nothing *but* bluff? Underhay's probably safely buried in Africa as we've always thought he was.'

She shivered.

'Don't, David. You make me afraid.'

He looked at her, saw the panic in her face, and at once his manner changed. He came over to her, sat down, took her cold hands in his.

'You're not to worry,' he said. 'Leave it all to me—and do as I tell you. You can manage that, can't you? Just do exactly as I tell you.'

'I always do, David.'

He laughed. 'Yes, you always do. We'll snap out of this, never you fear. I'll find a way of scotching Mr. Enoch Arden.'

'Wasn't there a poem, David—something about a man coming back——'

'Yes.' He cut her short. 'That's just what worries me . . . But I'll get to the bottom of things, never you fear.'

She said:

'It's Tuesday night you—take him the money?'

He nodded.

'Five thousand. I'll tell him I can't raise the rest all at once. But I *must* stop him going to the Cloades. I *think* that was only a threat, but I can't be *sure*.'

He stopped, his eyes became dreamy, far away. Behind them his mind worked, considering and rejecting possibilities.

Then he laughed. It was a gay reckless laugh. There were men, now dead, who would have recognised it . . .

It was the laugh of a man going into action on a hazardous and dangerous enterprise. There was enjoyment in it and defiance.

'I can trust you, Rosaleen,' he said. 'Thank goodness I can trust you absolutely!'

'Trust me?' She raised her big inquiring eyes. 'To do what?'

He smiled again.

'To do exactly as you are told. That's the secret, Rosaleen, of a successful operation.'

He laughed: 'Operation Enoch Arden.'

CHAPTER XI

ROWLEY opened the big mauve envelope with some surprise. Who on earth, he wondered, could be writing to him, using that kind of stationery—and how did they manage to get it, anyway. These fancy lines had surely gone right out during the war.

'DEAR MR. ROWLEY,' he read,

'I hope you won't think I'm taking a liberty in writing to you this way, but if you'll excuse me, I do think there are things going on that you *ought to know about*.'

He noted the underlining with a puzzled look.

'Arising out of our conversation the other evening when you came in asking about a *certain person*. If you could call in at the Stag I'd be very glad to tell you all about it. We've all of us felt down here what a wicked shame it was about your Uncle dying and his money going the way it did.

'Hoping you won't be angry with me, but I really do think you ought to know what's going on.

'Yours ever,

'BEATRICE LIPPINCOTT.'

Rowley stared down at this missive, his mind afire with speculation. What on earth was all this about? Good old Bee. He'd known Beatrice all his life. Bought tobacco from her father's shop and passed the time of day with her behind the counter. She'd been a good-looking girl. He remembered as a child hearing rumours about her during an absence of hers from Warmsley Vale. She'd been away about a year and everybody said she'd gone away to have an illegitimate baby. Perhaps she had, perhaps she hadn't. But she was certainly highly respectable and refined nowadays. Plenty of backchat and giggles, but an almost painful propriety.

Rowley glanced up at the clock. He'd go along to the Stag right away. To hell with all those forms. He wanted to know what it was that Beatrice was so anxious to tell him.

It was a little after eight when he pushed open the door of the saloon bar. There were the usual greetings, nods of the head, 'Evening, sir.' Rowley edged up to the bar and asked for a Guinness. Beatrice beamed upon him.

'Glad to see you, Mr. Rowley.'

'Evening, Beatrice. Thanks for your note.'

She gave him a quick glance.

'I'll be with you in a minute, Mr. Rowley.'

He nodded—and drank his half pint meditatively whilst he watched Beatrice finish serving out. She called over her shoulder and presently the girl Lily came in to relieve her. Beatrice murmured, 'If you'll come with me, Mr. Rowley?'

She led him along a passage and in through a door marked Private. Inside it was very small and overfurnished with plush arm-chairs, a blaring radio, a lot of china ornaments and a rather battered-looking pierrot doll thrown across the back of a chair.

Beatrice Lippincott turned off the radio and indicated a plush arm-chair.

'I'm ever so glad you came up, Mr. Rowley, and I hope you didn't mind my writing to you—but I've been turning it over in my mind all over the week-end—and as I said I really felt you ought to know what's going on.'

She was looking happy and important, clearly pleased with herself.

Rowley asked with mild curiosity: 'What is going on?'

'Well, Mr. Rowley, you know the gentleman who's staying here—Mr. Arden, the one you came and asked about.'

'Yes?'

'It was the very next evening. Mr. Hunter came along and asked for him.'

'Mr. Hunter?'

Rowley sat up interestedly.

'Yes, Mr. Rowley. No. 5, I said, and Mr. Hunter nodded and went straight up. I was surprised I must say, for this Mr. Arden hadn't said he knew any one in Warmsley Vale and I'd kind of taken it for granted he was a stranger here and didn't know any one in the place. Very out of temper Mr. Hunter looked, as though something had happened to upset him but of course I didn't make anything of it *then*.'

She paused for breath. Rowley said nothing, just listened. He never hurried people. If they liked to take their time it suited him.

Beatrice continued with dignity:

'It was just a little later I had occasion to go up to No. 4 to see to the towels and the bed linen. That's next door to No. 5, and as it happens there's a communicating door—not that you'd know it from No. 5 because the big wardrobe there stands right across it, so that you wouldn't know there *was* a door. Of course it's always kept shut but as it happened this time it was just a bit open—though *who* opened it I've no idea, I'm *sure*!'

Again Rowley said nothing, but just nodded his head.

Beatrice, he thought, had opened it. She had been curious and had gone up deliberately to No. 4 to find out what she could.

'And so you see, Mr. Rowley, I couldn't help hearing what was going on. Really, you could have knocked me over with a feather——'

A pretty substantial feather, thought Rowley, would be needed.

He listened, with an impassive, almost bovine face, to Beatrice's succinct account of the conversation she had overheard. When she had finished, she waited expectantly.

It was fully a couple of minutes before Rowley came out of his trance. Then he got up.

'Thanks, Beatrice,' he said. 'Thanks a lot.'

And with that he went straight out of the room. Beatrice felt somewhat deflated. She really *did* think, she said to herself, that Mr. Rowley might have said something.

CHAPTER XII

WHEN ROWLEY left the Stag his steps turned automatically in the direction of home, but after walking a few hundred yards, he pulled up short and retraced his steps.

His mind took things in slowly and his first astonishment over Beatrice's revelations was only now beginning to give way to a true appreciation of the significance. If her version of what she had overheard was correct, and he had no doubt that in substance it was so, then a situation had arisen which concerned every member of the Cloade family closely. The person most fitted to deal with this was clearly Rowley's Uncle Jeremy. As a solicitor, Jeremy Cloade would know what use could best be made of this surprising information, and exactly what steps to take.

Though Rowley would have liked to take action himself, he realised rather grudgingly that it would be far better to lay the matter before a shrewd and experienced lawyer. The sooner Jeremy was in possession of this information the better, and accordingly Rowley bent his footsteps straight to Jeremy's house in the High Street.

The little maid who opened the door informed him that Mr. and Mrs.

Cloade were still at the dinner table. She would have shown him in there, but Rowley negatived this and said he would wait in Jeremy's study till they had finished. He did not particularly want to include Frances in the colloquy. Indeed the fewer people who knew about it the better, until they should have determined on a definite course of action.

He wandered restlessly up and down Jeremy's study. On the flat-topped desk was a tin dispatch box labelled Sir William Jessamy Deceased. The shelves held a collection of legal tomes. There was an old photograph of Frances in evening dress and one of her father, Lord Edward Trenton, in riding kit. On the desk was the picture of a young man in uniform—Jeremy's son Antony, killed in the war.

Rowley winced and turned away. He sat down in a chair and stared at Lord Edward Trenton instead.

In the dining-room Frances said to her husband:

'I wonder what Rowley wants?'

Jeremy said wearily:

'Probably fallen foul of some Government regulation. No farmer understands more than a quarter of these forms they have to fill up. Rowley's a conscientious fellow. He gets worried.'

'He's nice,' said Frances, 'but terribly slow. I have a feeling, you know, that things aren't going too well between him and Lynn.'

Jeremy murmured vacantly:

'Lynn—oh, yes, of course. Forgive me, I—I don't seem able to concentrate. The strain——'

Frances said swiftly:

'Don't think about it. It's going to be all right, I tell you.'

'You frighten me sometimes, Frances. You're so terribly reckless. You don't realise——'

'I realise everything. I'm not afraid. Really, you know, Jeremy, I'm rather enjoying myself——'

'That, my dear,' said Jeremy, 'is just what causes me such anxiety.'

She smiled.

'Come,' she said. 'You mustn't keep that bucolic young man waiting too long. Go and help him to fill up form eleven hundred and ninety-nine, or whatever it is.'

But as they came out of the dining-room the front door banged shut. Edna came to tell them that Mr. Rowley had said he wouldn't wait and that it was nothing that really mattered.

CHAPTER XIII

ON THAT PARTICULAR Tuesday afternoon, Lynn Marchmont had gone for a long walk. Conscious of a growing restlessness and dissatisfaction with herself, she felt the need for thinking things out.

She had not seen Rowley for some days. After their somewhat stormy parting on the morning she had asked him to lend her five hundred pounds they had met as usual. Lynn realised that her demand had been unreasonable and that Rowley had been well within his rights in turning it down. Nevertheless reasonableness has never been a quality that appeals to lovers. Outwardly things were the same between her and Rowley, inwardly she was not so sure. The last few days she had found unbearably monotonous, yet hardly liked to acknowledge to herself that David Hunter's sudden departure to London with his sister might have something to do with their monotony. David, she admitted ruefully, was an exciting person . . .

As for her relations, at the moment she found them all unbearably trying. Her mother was in the best of spirits and had annoyed Lynn at lunch that day by announcing that she was going to try and find a second gardener. 'Old Tom really can't keep up with things here.'

'But, darling, we can't afford it,' Lynn had exclaimed.

'Nonsense, I really think, Lynn, that Gordon would be terribly upset if he could see how the garden has gone down. He was so particular always about the border, and the grass being kept mown, and the paths in good order—and just look at it now. I feel Gordon would want it put in order again.'

'Even if we have to borrow money from his widow to do it.'

'I told you, Lynn, Rosaleen couldn't have been nicer about it. I really think she quite saw my point of view. I have a nice balance at the bank after paying all the bills. And I really think a second gardener would be an *economy*. Think of the extra vegetables we could grow.'

'We could buy a lot of extra vegetables for a good deal less than another three pounds a week.'

'I think we could get someone for less than that, dear. There are men coming out of the Services now who *want* jobs. The paper says so.'

Lynn said dryly: 'I doubt if you'll find them in Warmsley Vale—or in Warmsley Heath.'

But although the matter was left like that, the tendency of her mother to count on Rosaleen as a regular source of support haunted Lynn. It revived the memory of David's sneering words.

So, feeling disgruntled and out of temper, she set out to walk her black mood off.

Her temper was not improved by a meeting with Aunt Kathie outside the post office. Aunt Kathie was in good spirits.

'I think Lynn dear, that we shall soon have good news.'

'What on earth do you mean, Aunt Kathie?'

Mrs. Cloade nodded and smiled and looked wise.

'I've had the most astonishing communications—really astonishing. A simple happy end to all our troubles. I had one setback, but since then I've got the message to Try try try again. If at first you don't succeed, etc. . . . I'm not going to betray my secrets, Lynn dear, and the last thing I should want to do would be to raise false hopes prematurely, but I have the strongest belief that things will very soon *be quite all right*. And quite time, too. I am really very worried about your uncle. He worked far too hard during the war. He really needs to retire and devote himself to his specialised studies—but of course he can't do that without an adequate income. And sometimes he has such queer nervous fits, I am really very worried about him. He is really quite odd.'

Lynn nodded thoughtfully. The change in Lionel Cloade had not escaped her notice, nor his curious alternation of moods. She suspected that he occasionally had recourse to drugs to stimulate himself, and she wondered whether he were not to a certain extent an addict. It would account for his extreme nervous irritability. She wondered how much Aunt Kathie knew or guessed. Aunt Kathie, thought Lynn, was not such a fool as she looked.

Going down the High Street, she caught a glimpse of her Uncle Jeremy letting himself into his front door. He looked, Lynn thought, very much older just in these last three weeks.

She quickened her pace. She wanted to get out of Warmsley Vale, up on to the hills and open spaces. Setting out at a brisk pace she soon felt better. She would go for a good tramp of six or seven miles—and really think things out. Always, all her life, she had been a resolute clear-headed person. She had known what she wanted and what she didn't want. Never, until now, had she been content just to drift along . . .

Yes, that was just what it was! Drifting along! An aimless, formless method of living. Ever since she had come out of the Service. A wave of nostalgia swept over her for those war days. Days when duties were clearly defined, when life was planned and orderly—when the weight of individual decisions had been lifted from her. But even as she formulated the idea, she was horrified at herself. Was that really and truly what people were secretly feeling everywhere? Was that what, ultimately, war did to you? It was not the physical dangers—the mines at sea, the bombs from the air, the crisp *ping* of a rifle bullet as you drove over a desert track. No, it was the spiritual danger of learning how much easier life was if you ceased to *think* . . . She, Lynn Marchmont, was no longer the clear-headed resolute intelligent girl who had joined up. Her intelligence had been specialised, directed in well-defined channels. Now mistress of herself and her life once more, she was appalled at the disinclination of her mind to seize and grapple with her own personal problems.

With a sudden wry smile, Lynn thought to herself: Odd if it's really that newspaper character 'the housewife' who has come into her own through war conditions. The women who, hindered by innumerable 'shall nots,' were not helped by any definite 'shalls.' Women who had to plan and think and improvise, who had to use every inch of the ingenuity they had been given, and to develop an ingenuity that they didn't know they had got! They alone, thought Lynn now, could stand upright without a crutch, responsible for themselves and others. And she, Lynn Marchmont, well educated, clever, having done a job that needed brains and close application, was now rudderless, devoid of resolution—yes, hateful word: *drifting* . . .

The people who had stayed at home; Rowley, for instance.

But at once Lynn's mind dropped from vague generalities to the immediate personal. *Herself and Rowley*. That was the problem, the real problem—the only problem. *Did she really want to marry Rowley?*

Slowly the shadows lengthened to twilight and dusk. Lynn sat motionless, her chin cupped in her hands on the outskirts of a small copse on the hillside, looking down over the valley. She had lost count of time, but she knew that she was strangely reluctant to go home to the White House. Below her, away to the left, was Long Willows. Long Willows, her home if she married Rowley.

If! It came back to that—if—if—if!

A bird flew out of the wood with a startled cry like the cry of an angry child. A billow of smoke from a train went eddying up in the sky forming as it did so a giant question mark:

? ? ?

Shall I marry Rowley? Do I *want* to marry Rowley? Did I ever want to marry Rowley? Could I bear *not* to marry Rowley?

The train puffed away up the valley, the smoke quivered and dispersed. But the question mark did not fade from Lynn's mind.

She had loved Rowley before she went away. 'But I've come home changed,' she thought. 'I'm not the same Lynn.'

A line of poetry floated into her mind.

'Life and the world and *mine own self* are changed . . . '

And Rowley? Rowley *hadn't* changed.

Yes, that was it. Rowley hadn't changed. Rowley was where she had left him four years ago.

Did she want to marry Rowley? If not, what did she want?

Twigs cracked in the copse behind her and a man's voice cursed as he pushed his way through.

She cried out, 'David!'

'Lynn!' He looked amazed as he came crashing through the undergrowth. 'What in the name of fortune are you doing here?'

He had been running and was slightly out of breath.

'I don't know. Just thinking—sitting and thinking.' She laughed uncertainly. 'I suppose—it's getting very late.'

'Haven't you any idea of the time?'

She looked down vaguely at her wrist-watch.

'It's stopped again. I disorganise watches.'

'More than watches!' David said. 'It's the electricity in you. The vitality. The *life*.'

He came up to her, and vaguely disturbed, she rose quickly to her feet.

'It's getting quite dark. I must hurry home. What time *is* it, David?'

'Quarter past nine. I must run like a hare. I simply must catch the 9.20 train to London.'

'I didn't know you had come back here!'

'I had to get some things from Furrowbank. But I must catch this train. Rosaleen's alone in the flat—and she gets the jitters if she's alone at night in London.'

'In a service flat?' Lynn's voice was scornful.

David said sharply:

'Fear isn't logical. When you've suffered from blast——'

Lynn was suddenly ashamed—contrite. She said:

'I'm sorry. I'd forgotten.'

With sudden bitterness David cried out:

'Yes, it's soon forgotten—all of it. Back to safety! Back to tameness! Back to where we were when the whole bloody show started! Creep into our rotten little holes and play safe again. You, too, Lynn—you're just the same as the rest of them!'

She cried, 'I'm not. I'm *not*, David. I was just thinking—now——'

'Of me?'

His quickness startled her. His arm was round her, holding him to her. He kissed her with hot angry lips.

'Rowley Cloade?' he said, 'that oaf? By God, Lynn, you belong to me.'

Then as suddenly as he had taken her, he released her, almost thrusting her away from him.

'I'll miss the train.'

He ran headlong down the hillside.

'David . . .'

He turned his head, calling back:

'I'll ring you when I get to London . . .'

She watched him running through the gathering gloom, light and athletic and full of natural grace.

Then, shaken, her heart strangely stirred, her mind chaotic, she walked slowly homeward.

She hesitated a little before going in. She shrank from her mother's affectionate welcome, her questions . . .

Her mother who had borrowed five hundred pounds from people whom she despised.

'We've no right to despise Rosaleen and David,' thought Lynn as she went very softly upstairs. 'We're just the same. We'd do anything—*anything* for money.'

She stood in her bedroom, looking curiously at her face in the mirror. It was, she thought, the face of a stranger . . .

And then, sharply, anger shook her.

'If Rowley really loved me,' she thought, 'he'd have got that five hundred pounds for me somehow. He would—he *would*. He wouldn't let me be humiliated by having to take it from David—David . . .'

David had said he would ring her when he got to London.

She went downstairs, walking in a dream . . .

Dreams, she thought, could be very dangerous things . . .

CHAPTER XIV

'OH, THERE YOU ARE, LYNN.' Adela's voice was brisk and relieved. 'I didn't hear you come in, darling. Have you been in long?'

'Oh, yes, ages. I was upstairs.'

'I wish you'd tell me when you come in, Lynn. I'm always nervous when you're out alone after dark.'

'Really, Mums, don't you think I can look after myself?'

'Well, there have been dreadful things in the papers lately. All these discharged soldiers—they attack girls.'

'I expect the girls ask for it.'

She smiled—rather a twisted smile.

Yes, girls did ask for danger . . . Who, after all, really wanted to be safe . . . ?

'Lynn, darling, are you listening?'

Lynn brought her mind back with a jerk.

Her mother had been talking.

'What did you say, Mums?'

'I was talking about your bridesmaids, dear. I suppose they'll be able to produce the coupons all right. It's very lucky for you having all your demob ones. I'm really terribly sorry for girls who get married nowadays on just their ordinary coupons. I mean they just can't have anything new at all. Not outside, I mean. What with the state all one's undies are in nowadays one just has to go for *them*. Yes, Lynn, you really are lucky.'

'Oh, very lucky.'

She was walking round the room—prowling, picking up things, putting them down.

'Must you be so terribly restless, dear? You make me feel quite jumpy!'

'Sorry, Mums.'

'There's nothing the matter, is there?'

'What should be the matter?' asked Lynn sharply.

'Well, don't jump down my throat, darling. Now about bridesmaids. I really think you ought to ask the Macrae girl. Her mother was my closest friend, remember, and I do think she'll be hurt if——'

'I loathe Joan Macrae and always have.'

'I know, darling, but does that really matter? Marjorie will, I'm sure, feel hurt——'

'Really, Mums, it's *my* wedding, isn't it?'

'Yes, I know, Lynn, but——'

'If there is a wedding at all!'

She hadn't meant to say that. The words slipped out without her having planned them. She would have caught them back, but it was too late. Mrs. Marchmont was staring at her daughter in alarm.

'Lynn, darling, what do you mean?'

'Oh, nothing, Mums.'

'You and Rowley haven't quarrelled?'

'No, of course not. Don't fuss, Mums, everything's all right.'

But Adela was looking at her daughter in real alarm, sensitive to the turmoil behind Lynn's frowning exterior.

'I've always felt you'd be so *safe* married to Rowley,' she said piteously.

'Who wants to be safe?' Lynn asked scornfully. She turned sharply. 'Was that the telephone?'

'No. Why? Are you expecting a call?'

Lynn shook her head. Humiliating to be waiting for the telephone to ring. He had said he would ring her to-night. He must. 'You're mad,' she told herself. 'Mad.'

Why did this man attract her so? The memory of his dark unhappy face rose up before her eyes. She tried to banish it, tried to replace it by Rowley's broad good-looking countenance. His slow smile, his affectionate glance. But did Rowley, she thought, *really* care about her? Surely if he'd really cared, he'd have understood that day when she came to him and begged for five hundred pounds. He'd have understood instead of being so maddeningly reasonable and matter-of-fact. Marry Rowley, live on the farm, never go away again, never see foreign skies, smell exotic smells—never again be free . . .

Sharply the telephone rang. Lynn took a deep breath, walked across the hall and picked up the receiver.

With the shock of a blow, Aunt Kathie's voice came thinly through the wire. 'Lynn? Is that you? Oh, I'm so glad. I'm afraid, you know, I've made rather a muddle—about the meeting at the Institute——'

The thin fluttering voice went on. Lynn listened, interpolated comments, uttered reassurances, received thanks.

'Such a comfort, dear Lynn, you are always so kind and so practical. I really can't imagine how I get things so muddled up.'

Lynn couldn't imagine either. Aunt Kathie's capacity for muddling the simplest issues amounted practically to genius.

'But I always do say,' finished Aunt Kathie, 'that everything goes wrong at once. Our telephone is out of order and I've had to go out to a call-box, and now I'm here I hadn't got twopence, only half-pennies—and I had to go and ask——'

It petered out at last. Lynn hung up and went back to the drawing-room.

Adela Marchmont, alert, asked: 'Was that——' and paused.

Lynn said quickly: 'Aunt Kathie.'

'What did she want?'

'Oh, just one of her usual muddles.'

Lynn sat down again with a book, glancing up at the clock. Yes—it had been too early. She couldn't expect her call yet. At five minutes past eleven the telephone rang again. She went slowly out to it. This time she wouldn't expect—it was probably Aunt Kathie again . . .'

But no. 'Warmsley Vale 34? Can Miss Lynn Marchmont take a personal call from London?'

Her heart missed a beat.

'This is Miss Lynn Marchmont speaking.'

'Hold on, please.'

She waited—confused noises—then silence. The telephone service was getting worse and worse. She waited. Finally she depressed the receiver angrily. Another woman's voice, indifferent, cold, spoke, was uninterested. 'Hang up, please. You'll be called later.'

She hung up, went back towards the drawing-room, the bell rang again as she had her hand on the door. She hurried back to the telephone.

'Hallo?'

A man's voice said: 'Warmsley Vale 34? Personal call from London for Miss Lynn Marchmont.'

'Speaking.'

'Just a minute please.' Then faintly, 'Speak up, London, you're through . . .'

And then, suddenly, David's voice:

'Lynn, is that you?'

'David!'

'I had to speak to you.'

'Yes . . .'

'Look here, Lynn, I think I'd better clear out——'

'What do you mean?'

'Clear out of England altogether. Oh, it's easy enough. I've pretended it wasn't to Rosaleen—simply because I didn't want to leave

Warmsley Vale. But what's the good of it all? You and I—it wouldn't work. You're a fine girl, Lynn—and as for me, I'm a bit of a crook, always have been. And don't flatter yourself that I'd go straight for your sake. I might mean to—but it wouldn't work. No, you'd better marry the plodding Rowley. He'll never give you a day's anxiety as long as you live. I should give you hell.'

She stood there, holding the receiver, saying nothing.

'Lynn, are you still there?'

'Yes, I'm here.'

'You didn't say anything.'

'What is there to say?'

'Lynn?'

'Well . . . ?'

Strange how clearly she could feel over all that distance, his excitement, the urgency of his mood . . .

He cursed softly, said explosively, 'Oh, to hell with everything!' and rang off.

Mrs. Marchmont, coming out of the drawing-room, said, 'Was that——?'

'A wrong number,' said Lynn and went quickly up the stairs.

CHAPTER XV

IT WAS THE CUSTOM at the Stag for guests to be called at whatever hour they named by the simple process of a loud bang on the door and the shouted information that it was 'eight-thirty, sir,' or 'eight o'clock' whatever the case might be. Early tea was produced if expressly stipulated, and was deposited with a rattle of crockery on the mat outside the door.

On this particular Wednesday morning, young Gladys went through the usual formula outside No. 5, yelling out, ' Eight-fifteen, sir,' and crashing down the tray with a bang that slopped the milk out of the jug. She then went on her way, calling more people and proceeding to her other duties.

It was ten o'clock before she took in the fact that No. 5's tea was still on the mat.

She beat a few heavy raps on the door, got no reply and thereupon walked in.

No. 5 was not the kind of gentleman who overslept himself, and she had just remembered that there was a convenient flat roof outside the window. It was just possible, thought Gladys, that No. 5 had done a bunk without paying his bill.

But the man registered as Enoch Arden had not done a bunk. He was lying on his face in the middle of the room and without any knowledge of medicine, Gladys had no doubt whatever that he was dead.

Gladys threw back her head and screamed, then rushed out of the room and down the stairs, still screaming.

'Ow, Miss Lippincott—Miss Lippincott—ow——'

Beatrice Lippincott was in her private room having a cut hand bandaged by Dr. Lionel Cloade—the latter dropped the bandage and turned irritably as the girl burst in.

'Ow, *Miss*!'

The doctor snapped: 'What is it? What is it?'

'What's the matter, Gladys?' asked Beatrice.

'It's the gentleman in No. 5, Miss. He's lying there on the floor, dead.'

The doctor stared at the girl and then at Miss Lippincott: the latter stared at Gladys and then at the doctor.

Finally, Dr. Cloade said uncertainly:

'Nonsense.'

'Dead as a doornail,' said Gladys, and added with a certain relish: ''Is 'ead's bashed in!'

The doctor looked towards Miss Lippincott.

'Perhaps I'd better——'

'Yes, please, Dr. Cloade. But really—I hardly think—it seems so impossible.'

They trooped upstairs, Gladys leading the way. Dr. Cloade took one look, knelt down and bent over the recumbent figure.

He looked up at Beatrice. His manner had changed. It was abrupt, authoritative.

'You'd better telephone through to the police station,' he said. Beatrice Lippincott went out, Gladys followed her.

Gladys said in an awed whisper:

'Ow, Miss, do you think it's *murder*?'

Beatrice smoothed back her golden pompadour with an agitated hand.

'You hold your tongue, Gladys,' she said sharply. 'Saying a thing's murder before you *know* it's murder is libel and you might be had up in court for it. It'll do the Stag no good to have a lot of gossip going about.' She added, as a gracious concession: 'You can go and make yourself a nice cup of tea. I dare say you need it.'

'Yes, indeed, Miss, I do. My inside's fair turning over! I'll bring you along a cup, too!'

To which Beatrice did not say No.

CHAPTER XVI

SUPERINTENDENT SPENCE looked thoughtfully across his table at Beatrice Lippincott, who was sitting with her lips compressed tightly together.

'Thank you, Miss Lippincott,' he said. 'That's all you can remember? I'll have it typed out for you to read and then if you wouldn't mind signing it——'

'Oh, dear—I shan't have to give evidence in a police court, I do hope.'

Superintendent Spence smiled appeasingly.

'Oh, we hope it mayn't come to that,' he said mendaciously.

'It may be suicide,' Beatrice suggested hopefully.

Superintendent Spence forebore to say that a suicide does not usually cave in the back of his skull with a pair of steel fire-tongs. Instead, he replied in the same easy manner:

'Never any good jumping to conclusions. Thank you, Miss Lippincott. Very good of you to come forward with this statement so promptly.'

When she had been ushered out, he ran over her statement in his mind. He knew all about Beatrice Lippincott, had a very good idea of how far her accuracy was to be depended upon. So much for a conversation genuinely overheard and remembered. A little extra embroidery for excitement's sake. A little extra still because murder had been done in bedroom No. 5. But take extras away and what remained was ugly and suggestive.

Superintendent Spence looked at the table in front of him. There was a wrist-watch with a smashed glass, a small gold lighter with initials on it, a lipstick in a gilt holder, and a pair of heavy steel fire-tongs, the heavy head of which was stained a rusty brown.

Sergeant Graves looked in and said that Mr. Rowley Cloade was waiting. Spence nodded and the Sergeant showed Rowley in.

Just as he knew all about Beatrice Lippincott, so the Superintendent knew all about Rowley Cloade. If Rowley had come to the police station, it was because Rowley had got something to say and that something would be solid, reliable and unimaginative. It would, in fact, be worth hearing. At the same time, Rowley being a deliberate type of person, it would take some time to say. And you couldn't hurry the Rowley Cloade type. If you did, they became rattled, repeated themselves, and generally took twice as long . . .

'Good morning, Mr. Cloade. Pleased to see you. Can you throw any light on this problem of ours? The man who was killed at the Stag.'

Rather to Spence's surprise, Rowley began with a question. He asked abruptly:

'Have you identified the fellow?'

'No,' said Spence slowly. 'I wouldn't say we had. He signed the register Enoch Arden. There's nothing in his possession to show he *was* Enoch Arden.'

Rowley frowned. 'Isn't that—rather odd?'

It was exceedingly odd, but Superintendent Spence did not propose to discuss with Rowley Cloade just how odd he thought it was. Instead he said pleasantly: 'Come now, Mr. Cloade, I'm the one who asks the questions. You went to see the dead man last night. Why?'

'You know Beatrice Lippincott, Superintendent? At the Stag.'

'Yes, of course. And,' said the Superintendent, taking what he hoped would be a short cut, 'I've heard her story. She came to me with it.'

Rowley looked relieved.

'Good. I was afraid she mightn't want to be mixed up with a police matter. These people are funny that way sometimes.' The Superintendent nodded. 'Well, then, Beatrice told me what she'd overheard and it seemed to me—I don't know if it does to you—decidedly fishy. What I mean is—we're, well, we're interested parties.'

Again the Superintendent nodded. He had taken a keen local interest in Gordon Cloade's death and in common with general local opinion he considered that Gordon's family had been badly treated. He endorsed the common opinion that Mrs. Gordon Cloade 'wasn't a lady,' and that Mrs. Gordon Cloade's brother was one of those young firebrand Commandos who, though they had had their uses in time of war, were to be looked at askance in peace-time.

'I don't suppose I need explain to you, Superintendent, that if Mrs. Gordon's first husband is still alive, it will make a big difference to us as a family. This story of Beatrice's was the first intimation I had that such a state of affairs might exist. I'd never dreamed of such a thing. Thought she was definitely a widow. And I may say it shook me up a lot. Took me a bit of time to realise it, as you might say. You know, I had to let it soak in.'

Spence nodded again. He could see Rowley slowly ruminating the matter, turning it over and over in his mind.

'First of all I thought I'd better get my uncle on to it—the lawyer one.'

'Mr. Jeremy Cloade?'

'Yes, so I went along there. Must have been some time after eight. They were still at dinner and I sat down in old Jeremy's study to wait for him, and I went on turning things over in my mind.'

'Yes?'

'And finally I came to the conclusion that I'd do a bit more myself before getting my uncle on to it. Lawyers, Superintendent, are all the same, I've found. Very slow, very cautious, and have to be absolutely sure of their facts before they'll move in a matter. The information I'd got had come to me in a rather hole-and-corner manner—and I wondered if old Jeremy might hem and haw a bit about acting on it. I decided I'd go along to the Stag and see this Johnnie for myself.'

'And you did so?'

'Yes. I went right back to the Stag——'

'At what time was this?'

Rowley pondered.

'Lemme see, I must have got to Jeremy's about twenty past eight or thereabouts—five minutes—well, I wouldn't like to say exactly, Spence—after half-past eight—perhaps about twenty to nine?'

'Yes, Mr. Cloade?'

'I knew where the bloke was—Bee had mentioned the number of his room—so I went right up and knocked at the door and he said, "Come in," and I went in.'

Rowley paused.

'Somehow I don't think I handled the business very well. I thought when I went in that *I* was the one who was on top. But the fellow must have been rather a clever fellow. I couldn't pin him down to anything definite. I thought he'd be frightened when I hinted he'd been doing a spot of blackmail, but it just seemed to amuse him. He asked me—damned cheek—if *I* was in the market too? "You can't play your dirty game with me," I said. "*I've* nothing to hide." And he said rather nastily that that wasn't his meaning. The point was, he said, that *he'd* got something to sell and was I a buyer? "What do you mean?" I said. He said: "How much will you—or the family generally—

pay me for the definite proof that Robert Underhay, reported dead in Africa, is really alive and kicking?" I asked him why the devil we should pay anything at all? And he laughed and said, "Because I've got a client coming this evening who certainly will pay a very substantial sum for proof positive that Robert Underhay is dead." Then—well, then, I'm afraid I rather lost my temper and told him that my family weren't used to doing that kind of dirty business. If Underhay was really alive, I said, the fact ought to be quite easy to establish. Upon that I was just stalking out when he laughed and said in what was really rather a queer tone, "I don't think you'll prove it without *my* co-operation." Funny sort of way he said that.'

'And then?'

'Well, frankly, I went home rather disturbed. Felt, you know, that I'd messed things up. Rather wished I'd left it to old Jeremy to tackle after all. I mean, dash it all, a lawyer's used to dealing with slippery customers.'

'What time did you leave the Stag?'

'I've no idea. Wait a sec. Must have been just before nine because I heard the pips for the news as I was going along the village—through one of the windows.'

'Did Arden say who it was he was expecting? The "client"?'

'No. I took it for granted it was David Hunter. Who else could it be?'

'He didn't seem in any way alarmed by the prospect?'

'I tell you the fellow was thoroughly pleased with himself and on top of the world!'

Spence indicated with a slight gesture the heavy steel tongs.

'Did you notice these in the grate, Mr. Cloade?'

'Those? No—I don't think so. The fire wasn't lit.' He frowned, trying to visualise the scene. 'There were fire-irons in the grate, I'm sure, but I can't say I noticed what they were.' He added, 'Was that what——'

Spence nodded.

'Smashed his skull in.'

Rowley frowned.

'Funny. Hunter's a lightly built chap—Arden was a big man—powerful.'

The Superintendent said in a colourless voice:

'The medical evidence is that he was struck down from behind and that the blows delivered with the head of the tongs were struck from above.'

Rowley said thoughtfully:

'Of course he was a cocksure sort of a bloke—but all the same I wouldn't have turned my back with a fellow in the room whom I was trying to bleed white and who'd done some pretty tough fighting in the war. Arden can't have been a very cautious sort of chap.'

'If he *had* been cautious very likely he'd be alive now,' said the Superintendent dryly.

'I wish to God he was,' said Rowley fervently. 'As it is I feel I've mucked things up thoroughly. If only I hadn't got on my high horse and stalked off, I might have got something useful out of him. I ought to have pretended that we *were* in the market, but the thing's so damned silly. I mean, who are we to bid against Rosaleen and David? They've got the cash. None of us could raise five hundred pounds between us.'

The Superintendent picked up the gold lighter. Seen this before?'

A crease appeared between Rowley's brows. He said slowly:

'I've seen it somewhere, yes, but I can't remember where. Not very long ago. No—I can't remember.'

Spence did not give the lighter into Rowley's outstretched hand. He put it down and picked up the lipstick, unsheathing it from its case.

'And this?'

Rowley grinned.

'Really, that's not in my line, Superintendent.'

Thoughtfully, Spence smeared a little on the back of his hand. He put his head on one side, studying it appreciatively.

'Brunette colouring, I should say,' he remarked.

'Funny things you policemen know,' said Rowley. He got up. 'And you don't—definitely do not—know *who* the dead man was?'

'Have you any idea yourself, Mr. Cloade?'

'I only wondered,' said Rowley slowly. 'I mean—this fellow was our only clue to Underhay. Now that he's dead—well, looking for Underhay is going to be like looking for a needle in a haystack.'

'There'll be publicity, Mr. Cloade,' said Spence. 'Remember that in due course a lot of this will appear in the press. If Underhay is alive and comes to read about it—well, he may come forward.'

'Yes,' said Rowley doubtfully. 'He may.'

'But you don't think so?'

'I think,' said Rowley Cloade, 'that Round One has gone to David Hunter.'

'I wonder,' said Spence. As Rowley went out, Spence picked up the gold lighter and looked at the initials D.H. on it. 'Expensive bit of work,' he said to Sergeant Graves. 'Not mass produced. Quite easily identified. Greatorex or one of those Bond Street places. Have it seen to!'

'Yes, sir.'

Then the Superintendent looked at the wrist-watch—the glass was smashed and the hands pointed to ten minutes past nine.

He looked at the Sergeant.

'Got the report on this, Graves?'

'Yes, sir. Mainspring's broken.'

'And the mechanism of the hands?'

'Quite all right, sir.'

'What, in your opinion, Graves, does the watch tell us?'

Graves murmured warily, 'Seems as though it might give us the time the crime was committed.'

'Ah,' said Spence, 'when you've been as long in the Force as I have, you'll be a leetle suspicious of anything so convenient as a smashed watch. It can be genuine—but it's a well-known hoary old trick. Turn the hands of a watch to a time that suits you—smash it—and out with some virtuous alibi. But you don't catch an old bird that way. I'm keeping a very open mind on the subject of the time this crime was committed. Medical evidence is: between 8 p.m. and 11 p.m.'

Sergeant Graves cleared his throat.

'Edwards, second gardener at Furrowbank, says he saw David Hunter coming out of a side door there about 7.30. The maids didn't know he was down here. They thought he was up in London with Mrs. Gordon. Shows he was in the neighbourhood all right.'

'Yes,' said Spence. 'I'll be interested to hear Hunter's own account of his doings.'

'Seems like a clear case, sir,' said Graves, looking at the initials on the lighter.

'H'm,' said the Superintendent. 'There's still this to account for.'

He indicated the lipstick.

'It had rolled under the chest of drawers, sir. Might have been there some time.'

'I've checked up,' said Spence. 'The last time a woman occupied that room was three weeks ago. I know service isn't up to much nowadays—but I still think they run a mop under the furniture once in three weeks. The Stag is kept pretty clean and tidy on the whole.'

'There's been no suggestion of a woman being mixed up with Arden.'

'I know,' said the Superintendent. 'That's why that lipstick is what I call the unknown quantity.'

Sergeant Graves refrained from saying 'Cherchez la femme.' He had a very good French accent and he knew better than to irritate Superintendent Spence by drawing attention to it. Sergeant Graves was a tactful young man.

CHAPTER XVII

SUPERINTENDENT SPENCE looked up at Shepherd's Court, Mayfair, before stepping inside its agreeable portal. Situated modestly in the vicinity of Shepherd's Market, it was discreet, expensive and inconspicuous.

Inside, Spence's feet sunk into soft pile carpet, there was a velvet covered settee and a jardinière full of flowering plants. A small automatic lift faced him, with a flight of stairs at one side of it. On the right of the hall was a door marked Office. Spence pushed it open and went through. He found himself in a small room with a counter, behind which was a table and a typewriter, and two chairs. One was drawn up to the table, the other, a more decorative one, was set at an angle to the window. There was no one visible.

Spying a bell inset on the mahogany counter, Spence pressed it. When nothing happened, he pressed it again. A minute or so later a door in the far wall was opened and a resplendent person in uniform appeared. His appearance was that of a foreign General or possibly Field Marshal, but his speech was of London and uneducated London at that.

'Yes, sir?'

'Mrs. Gordon Cloade.'

'Third floor, sir. Shall I ring through first?'

'She's here, is she?' said Spence. 'I had an idea she might be in the country.'

'No, sir, she's been here since Saturday last.'

'And Mr. David Hunter?'

'Mr. Hunter's been here, too.'

'He's not been away?'

'No, sir'

'Was he here last night?'

'Now then,' said the Field Marshal, suddenly becoming aggressive. 'What's all this about? Want to know every one's life history?'

Silently Spence displayed his warrant card. The Field Marshal was immediately deflated and became co-operative.

'Sorry, I'm sure,' he said. 'Couldn't tell, could I?'

'Now then, was Mr. Hunter here last night?'

'Yes, sir, he was. At least to the best of my belief he was. That is, he didn't say he was going away.'

'Would you know if he was away?'

'Well, generally speaking, no. I don't suppose I should. Gentlemen and ladies usually say if they're not going to be here. Leave word about letters or what they want said if any one rings up.'

'Do telephone calls go through this office?'

'No, most of the flats have their own lines. One or two prefer not to have a telephone and then we send up word on the house phone and the people come down and speak from the box in the hall.'

'But Mrs. Cloade's flat has its own phone?'

'Yes, sir.'

'And as far as you know they were both here last night?'

'That's right.'

'What about meals?'

'There's a restaurant, but Mrs. Cloade and Mr. Hunter don't very often use it. They usually go out to dinner.'

'Breakfast?'

'That's served in the flats.'

'Can you find out if breakfast was served this morning to them?'

'Yes, sir. I can find out from room service.'

Spence nodded. 'I'm going up now. Let me know about that when I come down.'

'Very good, sir.'

Spence entered the lift and pressed the button for the third floor. There were only two flats on each landing. Spence pushed the bell of No. 9.

David Hunter opened it. He did not know the Superintendent by sight and he spoke brusquely.

'Well, what is it?'

'Mr. Hunter?'

'Yes.'

'Superintendent Spence of the Oastshire County Police. Can I have a word with you?'

'I apologise, Superintendent.' He grinned. 'I thought you were a tout. Come in.'

He led the way into a modern and charming room. Rosaleen Cloade was standing by the window and turned at their entrance.

'Superintendent Spence, Rosaleen,' said Hunter. 'Sit down, Superintendent. Have a drink?'

'No, thank you, Mr. Hunter.'

Rosaleen had inclined her head slightly. She sat now, her back to the window, her hands clasped tightly on her lap.

'Smoke?' David proferred cigarettes.

'Thanks.' Spence took a cigarette, waited . . . watched David slide a hand into a pocket, slide it out, frown, look round and pick up a box of matches. He struck one and lit the Superintendent's cigarette.

'Thank you, sir.'

'Well,' said David, easily, as he lit his own cigarette. 'What's wrong at Warmsley Vale? Has our cook been dealing in the Black Market? She provides us with wonderful food, and I've always wondered if there was some sinister story behind it.'

'It's rather more serious than that,' said the Superintendent. 'A man died at the Stag Inn last night. Perhaps you saw it in the papers?'

David shook his head. 'No, I didn't notice it. What about him?'

'He didn't only die. He was killed. His head was stove in as a matter of fact.'

A half-choked exclamation came from Rosaleen. David said quickly:

'Please, Superintendent, don't enlarge on any details. My sister is delicate. She can't help it, but if you mention blood and horrors she'll probably faint.'

'Oh, I'm sorry,' said the Superintendent. 'But there wasn't any blood to speak of. It was murder right enough, though.'

He paused. David's eyebrows went up. He said gently:

'You interest me. Where do we come in?'

'We hoped you might be able to tell us something about this man, Mr. Hunter.'

'I?'

'You called to see him on Saturday evening last. His name—or the name he was registered under—was Enoch Arden.'

'Yes, of course. I remember now.'

David spoke quietly, without embarrassment.

'Well, Mr. Hunter?'

'Well, Superintendent, I'm afraid I can't help you. I know next to nothing about the man.'

'Was his name really Enoch Arden?'

'I should very much doubt it.'

'Why did you go to see him?'

'Just one of the usual hard luck stories. He mentioned certain places, war experiences, people——' David shrugged his shoulders. 'Just a touch, I'm afraid. The whole thing rather bogus.'

'Did you give him any money, sir?'

There was a fractional pause and then David said:

'Just a fiver—for luck. He'd been in the war all right.'

'He mentioned certain names that you—knew?'

'Yes.'

'Was one of those names Captain Robert Underhay?'

Now at last he got his effect. David stiffened. Behind him, Rosaleen gave a little frightened gasp.

'What makes you think that, Superintendent?' David asked at last. His eyes were cautious, probing.

'Information received,' said the Superintendent stolidly.

There was a short silence. The Superintendent was aware of David's eyes, studying him, sizing him up, striving to *know* . . . He himself waited quietly.

'Any idea who Robert Underhay was, Superintendent?' David asked.

'Suppose *you* tell me, sir.'

'Robert Underhay was my sister's first husband. He died in Africa some years ago.'

'Quite sure of that, Mr. Hunter?' Spence asked quickly.

'Quite sure. That's so, isn't it, Rosaleen?' He turned to her.

'Oh, yes.' She spoke quickly and breathlessly. 'Robert died of fever—blackwater fever. It was very sad.'

'Sometimes stories get about that aren't quite true, Mrs. Cloade.'

She said nothing. She was looking not at him, but at her brother. Then, after a moment, she said: 'Robert's dead.'

'From information in my possession,' said the Superintendent, 'I understand that this man, Enoch Arden, claimed to be a friend of the late Robert Underhay and at the same time informed you, Mr. Hunter, that Robert Underhay was alive.'

David shook his head.

'Nonsense,' he said. 'Absolute nonsense.'

'You state definitely that the name of Robert Underhay was not mentioned?'

'Oh,' David smiled charmingly, 'it was *mentioned*. This poor fellow had known Underhay.'

'There was no question of—blackmail, Mr. Hunter?'

'Blackmail? I don't understand you, Superintendent.'

'Don't you really, Mr. Hunter? By the way, just as a matter of form, where were you last night—between, shall we say, seven and eleven?'

'Just as a matter of form, Superintendent, suppose I refuse to answer?'

'Aren't you behaving rather childishly, Mr. Hunter?'

'I don't think so. I dislike—I always have disliked, being bullied.'

The Superintendent thought that was probably true.

He'd known witnesses of the David Hunter type before. Witnesses who were obstructive for the sake of being obstructive, and not in the least because they had anything to hide. The mere fact of being asked to account for their comings and goings seemed to raise a black pride and sullenness in them. They would make it a point to give the law all the trouble they could.

Superintendent Spence, though he prided himself on being a fair-minded man, had nevertheless come to Shepherd's Court with a very strong conviction that David Hunter was a murderer.

Now, for the first time, he was not so sure. The very puerility of David's defiance awoke doubts in him.

Spence looked at Rosaleen Cloade. She responded at once.

'David, why don't you tell him?'

'That's right, Mrs. Cloade. We only want to clear things up——'

David broke in savagely:

'You'll stop bullying my sister, do you hear? What is it to you where I may have been, here, or at Warmsley Vale or in Timbuctoo?'

Spence said warningly: 'You'll be subpœna'd for the Inquest, Mr. Hunter, and there you'll have to answer questions.'

'I'll wait for the Inquest, then! And now, Superintendent, will you get to hell out of here?'

'Very good, sir.' The Superintendent rose, imperturbable. 'But I've something to ask Mrs. Cloade first.'

'I don't want my sister worried.'

'Quite so. But I want her to look at the body and tell me if she can identify it. I'm within my rights there. It'll have to be done sooner or later. Why not let her come down with me now and get it over? The late Mr. Arden was heard by a witness to say that he knew Robert Underhay—*ergo* he may have known Mrs. Underhay—and therefore Mrs. Underhay may know him. If his name isn't Enoch Arden, we could do with knowing what it really is.'

Rather unexpectedly Rosaleen Cloade got up.

'I'll come, of course,' she said.

Spence expected a fresh outburst from David, but to his surprise the other grinned.

'Good for you, Rosaleen,' he said. 'I'll confess, I'm curious myself. After all, you *may* be able to put a name to the fellow.'

Spence said to her:

'You didn't see him yourself in Warmsley Vale?'

She shook her head.

'I've been in London since Saturday last.'

'And Arden arrived on Friday night—yes.'

Rosaleen asked: 'Do you want me to come *now*?'

She asked the question with something of the submissiveness of a little girl. In spite of himself the Superintendent was favourably impressed. There was a docility, a willingness about her which he had not expected.

'That would be very nice of you, Mrs. Cloade,' he said. 'The sooner we can get certain facts definitely established the better. I haven't got a police car here, I'm afraid.'

David crossed to the telephone.

'I'll ring up the Daimler Hire. It's beyond the legal limit—but I expect you can square that, Superintendent.'

'I think that can be arranged, Mr. Hunter.'

He got up. 'I'll be waiting for you downstairs.'

He went down in the lift and pushed open the office door once more.

The Field Marshal was awaiting him.

'Well?'

'Both beds slept in last night, sir. Baths and towels used. Breakfast was served to them in the flat at nine-thirty.'

'And you don't know what time Mr. Hunter came in yesterday evening?'

'I can't tell you anything further, I'm afraid, sir!'

Well, that was that, Spence thought. He wondered if there was anything behind David's refusal to speak except pure childlike defiance. He must realise that a charge of murder was hovering over him. Surely he must see that the sooner he told his story the better. Never a good thing to antagonise the police. But antagonising the police, he thought ruefully, was just what David Hunter would enjoy doing.

They talked very little on the way down. When they arrived at the mortuary Rosaleen Cloade was very pale. Her hands were shaking.

David looked concerned for her. He spoke to her as though she was a small child.

'It'll be only a minute or two, mavourneen. It's nothing at all, nothing at all now. Don't get worked up. You go in with the Superintendent and I'll wait for you. And there's nothing at all to mind about. Peaceful he'll look and just as though he were asleep.'

She gave him a little nod of the head and stretched out her hand. He gave it a little squeeze.

'Be a brave girl now, alanna.'

As she followed the Superintendent she said in her soft voice: 'You must think I'm a terrible coward, Superintendent. But when they've been all dead in the house—all dead but you—that awful night in London——'

He said gently: 'I understand, Mrs. Cloade. I know you went through a bad experience in the Blitz when your husband was killed. Really, it will be only a minute or two.'

At a sign from Spence the sheet was turned back. Rosaleen Cloade stood looking down at the man who had called himself Enoch Arden. Spence, unobtrusively standing to one side, was actually watching her closely.

She looked at the dead man curiously and as though wondering—she gave no start, no sign of emotion or recognition, just looked long and wonderingly at him. Then, very quietly, in an almost matter of fact way, she made the sign of the cross.

'God rest his soul,' she said. 'I've never seen that man in my life. I don't know who he is.'

Spence thought to himself:

'Either you're one of the finest actresses I've ever known or else you're speaking the truth.'

Later, Spence rang up Rowley Cloade.

'I've had the widow down,' he said. 'She says definitely that he's not Robert Underhay and that she's never seen him before. So that settles *that*!'

There was a pause. Then Rowley said slowly: *Does* it settle it?'

'I think a jury would believe her—in the absence of evidence to the contrary, of course.'

'Ye-es,' said Rowley and rang off.

Then, frowning, he picked up not the local telephone directory, but the London one. His forefinger ran methodically down the letter P. Presently he found what he wanted.

BOOK TWO

CHAPTER I

HERCULE POIROT carefully folded the last of the newspapers he had sent George out to purchase. The information they gave was somewhat meagre. Medical evidence was given that the man's skull was fractured by a series of heavy blows. The inquest had been adjourned for a fortnight. Anybody who could give information about a man named Enoch Arden believed to have lately arrived from Cape Town was asked to communicate with the Chief Constable of Oastshire.

Poirot laid the papers in a neat pile and gave himself up to meditation. He was interested. He might, perhaps, have passed the first small paragraph by without interest if it had not been for the recent visit of Mrs. Lionel Cloade. But that visit had recalled to him very clearly the incidents of that day at the Club during that Air Raid. He remembered, very distinctly, Major Porter's voice saying, 'Maybe a Mr. Enoch Arden will turn up somewhere a thousand miles away and start life anew.' He wanted now, rather badly, to know more about this man called Enoch Arden who had died by violence at Warmsley Vale.

He remembered that he was slightly acquainted with Superintendent Spence of the Oastshire police and he also remembered that young Mellon lived not very far from Warmsley Heath, and that young Mellon knew Jeremy Cloade.

It was while he was meditating a telephone call to young Mellon that George came in and announced that a Mr. Rowland Cloade would like to see him.

'Aha,' said Hercule Poirot with satisfaction. 'Show him in.'

A good-looking worried young man was shown in, and seemed rather at a loss how to begin.

'Well, Mr. Cloade,' said Poirot helpfully, 'and what can I do for you?'

Rowley Cloade was eyeing Poirot rather doubtfully. The flamboyant moustaches, the sartorial elegance, the white spats and the pointed patent leather shoes all filled this insular young man with distinct misgivings.

Poirot realised this perfectly well, and was somewhat amused.

Rowley Cloade began rather heavily:

'I'm afraid I'll have to explain who I am and all that. You won't know my name——'

Poirot interrupted him:

'But yes, I know your name perfectly. Your aunt, you see, came to see me last week.'

'My aunt?' Rowley's jaw dropped. He stared at Poirot with the utmost astonishment. This so clearly was news to him, that Poirot put aside his first surmise which was that the two visits were connected. For a moment it seemed to him a remarkable coincidence that two members of the Cloade family should choose to consult him within such a short period of time, but a second later he realised that there was no coincidence—merely a natural sequence proceeding from one initial cause.

Aloud he said:

'I assume that Mrs. Lionel Cloade *is* your aunt.'

If anything Rowley looked rather more astonished than before.

He said with the utmost incredulity:

'Aunt Kathie? Surely—don't you mean—Mrs. *Jeremy* Cloade?'

Poirot shook his head.

'But what on earth could Aunt Kathie——'

Poirot murmured discreetly:

'She was directed to me, I understand, by spirit guidance.'

'Oh Lord!' said Rowley. He looked relieved and amused. He said, as though reassuring Poirot, 'She's quite harmless, you know.'

'I wonder,' said Poirot.

'What do you mean?'

'Is anybody—ever—quite harmless?'

Rowley stared. Poirot sighed.

'You have come to me to ask me something?—Yes?' he prompted gently.

The worried look came back to Rowley's face.

'It's rather a long story, I'm afraid——'

Poirot was afraid of it, too. He had a very shrewd idea that Rowley Cloade was not the sort of person to come to the point quickly. He leaned back and half-closed his eyes as Rowley began:

'My uncle, you see, was Gordon Cloade——'

'I know all about Gordon Cloade,' said Poirot, helpfully.

'Good. Then I needn't explain. He married a few weeks before his death—a young widow called Underhay. Since his death she has been living at Warmsley Vale—she and a brother of hers. We all understood that her first husband had died of fever in Africa. But now it seems as though that mightn't be so.'

'Ah,' Poirot sat up. 'And what has led you to that surmise?'

Rowley described the advent of Mr. Enoch Arden in Warmsley Vale. 'Perhaps you have seen in the papers——'

'Yes, I have seen.' Poirot was again helpful.

Rowley went on. He described his first impression of the man Arden, his visit to the Stag, the letter he had received from Beatrice Lippincott and finally the conversation that Beatrice had overheard.

'Of course,' Rowley said, 'one can't be sure just what she *did* hear. She may have exaggerated it all a bit—or even got it wrong.'

'Has she told her story to the police?'

Rowley nodded. 'I told her she'd better.'

'I don't quite see—pardon me—why you come to *me*, Mr. Cloade? Do you want me to investigate this—murder? For it is murder, I assume.'

'Lord, no,' said Rowley. 'I don't want anything of that kind. That's a police job. He was bumped off all right. No, what I'm after is this. I want you to find out who the fellow *was*.'

Poirot's eyes narrowed.

'Who do you think he was, Mr. Cloade?'

'Well, I mean—Enoch Arden isn't a name. Dash it all, it's a quotation. Tennyson. I went and mugged it up. Fellow who comes back and finds out his wife has married another fellow.'

'So you think,' said Poirot quietly, 'that Enoch Arden was Robert Underhay himself?'

Rowley said slowly:

'Well, he might have been—I mean, about the right age and appearance and all that. Of course I've gone over it all with Beatrice again and again. She can't naturally remember *exactly* what they both said. The chap said Robert Underhay had come down in the world and was in bad health and needed money. Well, he might have been talking about himself, mightn't he? He seems to have said something about it wouldn't suit David Hunter's book if Underhay turned up in Warmsley Vale—sounding a bit as though he *was* there under an assumed name.'

'What evidence of identification was there at the Inquest?'

Rowley shook his head.

'Nothing definite. Only the Stag people saying he was the man who'd come there and registered as Enoch Arden.'

'What about his papers?'

'He hadn't any.'

'What?' Poirot sat up in surprise. 'No papers of any kind?'

'Nothing at all. Some spare socks and a shirt and a toothbrush, etc.—but no papers.'

'No passport? No letters? Not even a ration card?'

'Nothing at all.'

'That,' said Poirot, 'is very interesting. Yes, very interesting.'

Rowley went on: 'David Hunter, that's Rosaleen Cloade's brother, had called to see him the evening after he arrived. His story to the police is that he'd had a letter from the chap saying he had been a friend of Robert Underhay's and was down and out. At his sister's request he went to the Stag and saw the fellow and gave him a fiver. That's *his* story and you bet he means to stick to it! Of course the police are keeping dark about what Beatrice heard.'

'David Hunter says he had no previous acquaintance with the man?'

'That's what he says. Anyway, I gather Hunter never met Underhay.'

'And what about Rosaleen Cloade?'

'The police asked her to look at the body in case she knew the man. She told them that he was a complete stranger to her.'

'*Eh bien*,' said Poirot. 'Then that answers your question!'

'Does it?' said Rowley bluntly. 'I think not. If the dead man *is* Underhay then Rosaleen was never my uncle's wife and she's not entitled to a penny of his money. Do you think she *would* recognise him under those circumstances?'

'You don't trust her?'

'I don't trust either of them.'

'Surely there are plenty of people who could say for certain that the dead man is or is not Underhay?'

'It doesn't seem to be so easy. That's what I want you to do. Find someone who knows Underhay. Apparently he has no living relations in this country—and he was always an unsociable lonely sort of chap. I suppose there must be old servants—friends—*someone*—but the war's broken up everything and shifted people round. *I* wouldn't know how to begin to tackle the job—anyway I haven't the time. I'm a farmer—and I'm short-handed.'

'Why me?' said Hercule Poirot.

Rowley looked embarrassed.

A faint twinkle came into Poirot's eye.

'Spirit guidance?' he murmured.

'Good Lord, no,' said Rowley horrified. 'Matter of fact,' he hesitated, 'I heard a fellow I know talk about you—said you were a wizard at these sort of things. I don't know about your fees—expensive, I expect—we're rather a stony-broke lot, but I dare say we could cough it up amongst the lot of us. That is, if you'll take it on.'

Hercule Poirot said slowly:

'Yes, I think perhaps I can help you.'

His memory, a very precise and definite memory, went back. The club bore, the rustling newspapers, the monotonous voice.

The name—he had heard the name—it would come back to him presently. If not, he could always ask Mellon . . . No, he had got it. Porter. Major Porter.

Hercule Poirot rose to his feet.

'Will you come back here this afternoon, Mr. Cloade?'

'Well—I don't know. Yes, I suppose I could. But surely you can't do anything in that short time?'

He looked at Poirot with awe and incredulity. Poirot would have been less than human if he could have resisted the temptation to show off. With memories of a brilliant predecessor in his mind, he said solemnly:

'I have my methods, Mr. Cloade.'

It was clearly the right thing to say. Rowley's expression became respectful in the extreme.

'Yes—of course—really—I don't know how you people do these things.'

Poirot did not enlighten him. When Rowley had gone, he sat down and wrote a short note. Giving it to George he instructed him to take it to the Coronation Club and wait for an answer.

The answer was highly satisfactory. Major Porter presented his compliments to M. Hercule Poirot and would be happy to see him and his friend at 79 Edgeway Street, Campden Hill, that afternoon at five o'clock.

At four-thirty Rowley Cloade reappeared.

'Any luck, M. Poirot?'

'But yes, Mr. Cloade, we go now to see an old friend of Captain Robert Underhay's.'

'*What?*' Rowley's mouth fell open. He stared at Poirot with the amazement a small boy shows when a conjurer produces rabbits out of a hat. 'But it's *incredible*! I don't understand how you can do these things—why, it's only a few hours.'

Poirot waved a deprecating hand and tried to look modest. He had no intention of revealing the simplicity with which his conjuring trick had been done. His vanity was pleased to impress this simple Rowley.

The two men went out together, and hailing a taxi they drove to Campden Hill.

Major Porter had the first floor of a small shabby house. They were admitted by a cheerful blowsy-looking woman who took them up. It was a square room with bookshelves round it and some rather bad sporting prints. There were two rugs on the floor—good rugs with lovely dim colour but very worn. Poirot noticed that the centre of the floor was covered with a new heavy varnish whereas the varnish round the edge was old and rubbed. He realised then that there had been other better rugs until recently—rugs that were worth good money in these days. He looked up at the man standing erect by the fireplace in his well-cut shabby suit. Poirot guessed that for Major Porter, retired Army officer, life was lived very near the bone. Taxation and increased cost of living struck hardest at the old war-horses. Some things, he guessed, Major Porter would cling to until the end. His club subscription, for instance.

Major Porter was speaking jerkily.

''Fraid I don't remember meeting you, M. Poirot. At the club, you say? Couple of years ago? Know your *name* of course.'

'This,' said Poirot, 'is Mr. Rowland Cloade.'

Major Porter jerked his head in honour of the introduction.

'How d'ye do?' he said. ''Fraid I can't ask you to have a glass of sherry. Matter of fact my wine merchant has lost his stock in the Blitz. Got some gin. Filthy stuff, *I* always think. Or what about some beer?'

They accepted beer. Major Porter produced a cigarette case. 'Smoke?' Poirot accepted a cigarette. The Major struck a match and lighted Poirot's cigarette.

'*You* don't, I know,' said the Major to Rowley. 'Mind if I light my pipe?' He did so with a good deal of sucking and blowing.

'Now then,' he said when all these preliminaries had been accomplished. 'What's all this about?'

He looked from one to the other of them.

Poirot said: 'You may have read in the paper of the death of a man at Warmsley Vale?'

Porter shook his head.

'May have. Don't think so.'

'His name was Arden. Enoch Arden?'

Porter still shook his head.

'He was found at the Stag Inn with the back of his head smashed in.'

Porter frowned.

'Let me see—yes, did see something about it, I believe—some days ago.'

'Yes. I have here a photograph—it is a press photograph and not very clear, I'm afraid! What we should like to know, Major Porter, is whether you have ever seen this man before?'

He handed over the best reproduction of the dead man's face he had been able to find.

Major Porter took it and frowned at it.

'Wait a sec.' The Major took out his spectacles, adjusted them on his nose and studied the photograph more closely—then he gave a sudden start.

'God bless my soul!' he said. 'Well, I'm damned!'

'You know the man, Major?'

'Of course I know him. It's Underhay—Robert Underhay.'

'You're sure of that?' There was triumph in Rowley's voice.

'Of course I'm sure. Robert Underhay! I'd swear to it anywhere.'

CHAPTER II

THE TELEPHONE RANG and Lynn went to answer it.

Rowley's voice spoke.

'Lynn?'

'Rowley?'

Her voice sounded depressed. He said:

'What are you up to? I never see you these days.'

'Oh, well—it's all chores—you know. Running round with a basket, waiting for fish and queueing up for a bit of quite disgusting cake. All that sort of thing. Home life.'

'I want to see you. I've got something to tell you.'

'What sort of thing?'

He gave a chuckle.

'Good news. Meet me by Rolland Copse. We're ploughing up there.'

Good news? Lynn put the receiver down. What to Rowley Cloade would be good news? Finance? Had he sold that young bull at a better price than he had hoped to get?

No, she thought, it must be more than that. As she walked up the field to Rolland Copse, Rowley left the tractor and came to meet her.

'Hallo, Lynn.'

'Why, Rowley—you look—*different*, somehow?'

He laughed.

'I should think I do. *Our luck's turned*, Lynn!'

'What *do* you mean?'

'Do you remember old Jeremy mentioning a chap called Hercule Poirot?'

'Hercule Poirot?' Lynn frowned. 'Yes, I do remember *something*——'

'Quite a long time ago. When the war was on. They were in that mausoleum of a club of his and there was an Air Raid.'

'Well?' Lynn demanded impatiently.

'Fellow has the wrong clothes and all that. French chap—or Belgian. Queer fellow but he's the goods all right.'

Lynn knit her brows.

'Wasn't he—a *detective*?'

'That's right. Well, you know, this fellow who was done in at the Stag. I didn't tell you but an idea was getting around that he might just possibly be Rosaleen Cloade's first husband.'

Lynn laughed.

'Simply because he called himself Enoch Arden? What an absurd idea!'

'Not so absurd, my girl. Old Spence got Rosaleen down to have a look at him. And she swore quite firmly that he *wasn't* her husband.'

'So that finished it?'

'It might have,' said Rowley. 'But for *me*!'

'For you? What did *you* do?'

'I went to this fellow Hercule Poirot. I told him we wanted another opinion. Could be rustle up someone who had actually known Robert Underhay? My word, but he's absolutely wizard that chap! Just like rabbits out of a hat. He produced a fellow who was Underhay's best friend in a few hours. Old boy called Porter.' Rowley stopped. Then he chuckled again with that note of excitement that had surprised and startled Lynn. 'Now *keep this under your hat*, Lynn. The Super swore me to secrecy—but I'd like *you* to know. The dead man is Robert Underhay.'

'What?' Lynn took a step back. She stared at Rowley blankly.

'Robert Underhay himself. Porter hadn't the least doubt. So you see, Lynn'—Rowley's voice rose excitedly—'*we've won*! After all, we've *won*! We've beaten those damned crooks!'

'What damned crooks?'

'Hunter and his sister. They're licked—out of it. Rosaleen doesn't get Gordon's money. *We* get it. It's *ours*! Gordon's will that he made before he married Rosaleen holds good and that divides it amongst us. I get a fourth share. See? *If* her first husband was alive when she married Gordon, *she was never married to Gordon at all*!'

'Are you—are you *sure* of what you're saying?'

He stared at her, for the first time he looked faintly puzzled.

'Of course I'm sure! It's elementary. Everything's all right now. It's the same as Gordon meant it to be. Everthing's the same as if that precious pair had never butted in.'

Everything's the same . . . But you couldn't, Lynn thought, wash out like that something that had happened. You couldn't pretend that it had never been. She said slowly:

'What will they do?'

'Eh?' She saw that until that moment Rowley had hardly considered that question. 'I don't know. Go back where they came from, I suppose. I think, you know——' She could see him slowly following it out. 'Yes, I think we ought to do something for *her*. I mean, she married Gordon in all good faith. I gather she really believed her first husband was dead. It's not *her* fault. Yes, we must do something about her—give her a decent allowance. Make it up between us all.'

'You like her, don't you?' said Lynn.

'Well, yes.' He considered. 'I do in a way. She's a nice kid. She knows a cow when she sees it.'

'I don't,' said Lynn.

'Oh, you'll learn,' said Rowley kindly.

'And what about—David?' asked Lynn.

Rowley scowled.

'To hell with David! It was never *his* money anyway. He just came along and sponged on his sister.'

'No, Rowley, it wasn't like that—it wasn't. He's *not* a sponger. He's—he's an adventurer, perhaps——'

'*And* a ruddy murderer!'

She said breathlessly:

'What do you mean?'

'Well, who do you think killed Underhay?'

She cried:

'I don't believe it! I don't believe it!'

'Of course he killed Underhay! Who else could have done it? He was down here that day. Came down by the five-thirty. I was meeting some stuff at the station and caught sight of him in the distance.'

Lynn said sharply:

'He went back to London that evening.'

'After having killed Underhay,' said Rowley triumphantly.

'You oughtn't to say things like that, Rowley. What time was Underhay killed?'

'Well—I don't know *exactly*.' Rowley slowed up—considered. 'Don't suppose we shall know until the Inquest to-morrow. Some time between nine and ten, I imagine.'

'David caught the nine-twenty train back to London.'

'Look here, Lynn, how do *you* know?'

'I—I met him—he was running for it.'

'How do you know he ever caught it?'

'Because he telephoned me from London later.'

Rowley scowled angrily.

'What the hell should he telephone *you* for? Look here, Lynn, I'm damned if I——'

'Oh, what does it *matter* Rowley? Anyway, it shows he caught that train.'

'Plenty of time to have killed Underhay and then run for the train.'

'Not if he was killed after nine o'clock.'

'Well, he may have been killed just before nine.'

But his voice was a little doubtful.

Lynn half-closed her eyes. *Was* that the truth of it? When, breathless, swearing, David had emerged from the copse, had it been a murderer fresh from his crime who had taken her in his arms? She remembered his curious excitement—the recklessness of his mood? Was that the way that murder would affect him? It might. She had to admit it. Were David and murder so far removed from each other? *Would* he kill a man who had never done him any harm—a ghost from the past? A man whose only crime was to stand between Rosaleen and a big inheritance—between David and the enjoyment of Rosaleen's money.

She murmured:

'*Why* should he kill Underhay?'

'My God, Lynn, can you *ask*? I've just *told* you! Underhay's being alive means that *we* get Gordon's money! Anyway, Underhay was blackmailing him.'

Ah, that fell more into the pattern. David might kill a blackmailer—in fact, wasn't it just the way he *would* deal with a blackmailer? Yes, it all fell into pattern. David's haste, his excitement—his fierce, almost angry, lovemaking. And, later, his renouncement of her. 'I'd better clear out . . .' Yes, it fitted.

From a long way away, she heard Rowley's voice asking:

'What's the matter, Lynn? Are you feeling all right?'

'Yes, of course.'

'Well, for heaven's sake, don't look so glum.' He turned, looking down the hillside to Long Willows. 'Thank goodness, we can have the place smartened up a bit now—get some labour-saving gadgets put in—make it right for you. I don't want you to pig it, Lynn.'

That was to be her home—that house. Her home with Rowley . . .

And one morning at eight o'clock, David would swing by the neck until he was dead . . .

CHAPTER III

WITH A PALE determined face and watchful eyes, David had his hands on Rosaleen's shoulders.

'It will be all right, I'm telling you, it will be all right. But you must keep your head and do exactly as I tell you.'

'And if they take you away? You said that! You did say that they might take you away.'

'It's a possibility, yes. But it won't be for long. Not if you keep your head.'

'I'll do what you tell me, David.'

'There's the girl! All you have to do, Rosaleen, is to stick to your story. Hold to it that the dead man is *not* your husband, Robert Underhay.'

'They'll trap me into saying things I don't mean.'

'No—they won't. It's all right, I tell you.'

'No, it's wrong—it's been wrong all along. Taking money that doesn't belong to us. I lie awake nights thinking of it, David. Taking what doesn't belong to us. God is punishing us for our wickedness.'

He looked at her, frowning. She was cracking—yes, definitely she was cracking. There had always been that religious streak. Her conscience had never been quite stilled. Now, unless he was extremely lucky, she'd break down completely. Well, there was only one thing to be done.

'Listen, Rosaleen,' he said gently. 'Do you want me to be hanged?'

Her eyes widened in horror.

'Oh, David, you wouldn't—they couldn't——'

'There's only one person who can hang me—that's you. If you once admit, by look or sign or word, that the dead man might be Underhay, you put the rope round my neck! Do you understand that?'

Yes, that had got home. She gazed at him with wide, horrified eyes.

'I'm so stupid, David.'

'No, you're not. In any case you haven't got to be clever. You'll have to swear solemnly that the dead man is not your husband. You can do that?'

She nodded.

'Look stupid if you like. Look as if you don't understand quite what they're asking you. That will do no harm. But stand firm on the points I've gone over with you. Gaythorne will look after you. He's a very able criminal lawyer—that's why I've got him. He'll be at the Inquest and he'll protect you from any heckling. But even to him *stick to your story*. For God's sake don't try to be clever or think you can help me by some line of your own.'

'I'll do it, David. I'll do exactly what you tell me.'

'Good girl. When it's all over we'll go away—to the South of France—to America. In the meantime, take care of your health. Don't lie awake at nights fretting and working yourself up. Take those sleeping things Dr. Cloade prescribed for you—bromide or something. Take one every night, cheer up, and remember *there's a good time coming*!

'Now——' he looked at his watch. 'It's time to go to the Inquest. It's called for eleven.'

He looked round the long beautiful drawing-room. Beauty, comfort, wealth . . . He'd enjoyed it all. A fine house, Furrowbank. Perhaps this was Good-bye . . .

He'd got himself into a jam—that was certain. But even now he didn't regret. And for the future—well, he'd go on taking chances. '*And we must take the current when it serves or lose our ventures.*'

He looked at Rosaleen. She was watching him with large appealing eyes and intuitively he knew what she wanted.

'I didn't kill him, Rosaleen,' he said gently. 'I swear it to you by every saint in your calendar!'

CHAPTER IV

THE INQUEST was held in the Cornmarket.

The coroner, Mr. Pebmarsh, was a small fussy man with glasses and a considerable sense of his own importance.

Beside him sat the large bulk of Superintendent Spence. In an unobtrusive seat was a small foreign-looking man with a large black moustache. The Cloade family: the Jeremy Cloades, the Lionel Cloades, Rowley Cloade, Mrs. Marchmont and Lynn—they were all there. Major Porter sat by himself, fidgeting and ill at ease. David and Rosaleen arrived last. They sat by themselves.

The coroner cleared his throat and glancing round the jury of nine local worthies, started proceedings.

Constable Peacock . . .

Sergeant Vane . . .

Dr. Lionel Cloade . . .

'You were attending a patient professionally at the Stag, when Gladys Aitkin came to you. What did she say?'

'She informed me that the occupant of No. 5 was lying on the floor dead.'

'In consequence you went up to No. 5?'

'I did.'

'Will you describe what you found there?'

Dr. Cloade described. Body of a man . . . face downwards . . . head injuries . . . back of skull . . . fire-tongs.

'You were of opinion that the injuries were inflicted with the tongs in question?'

'Some of them unquestionably were.'

'And that several blows had been struck?'

'Yes. I did not make a detailed examination as I considered that the police should be called before the body was touched or its position altered.'

'Very proper. The man was dead?'

'Yes. He had been dead for some hours.'

'How long in your opinion had he been dead?'

'I should hesitate to be very definite about that. At least eleven hours—quite possibly thirteen or fourteen—let us say between 7.30 and 10.30 p.m. the preceding evening.'

'Thank you, Dr. Cloade.'

Then came the police surgeon—giving a full and technical description of the wounds. There was an abrasion and swelling on the lower jaw and five or six blows had been struck on the base of the skull, some of which had been delivered after death.

'It was an assault of great savagery?'

'Exactly.'

'Would great strength have been needed to inflict these blows?'

'N-no, not exactly strength. The tongs, grasped by the pincers end, could be easily swung without much exertion. The heavy steel ball which forms the head of the tongs makes them a formidable weapon. Quite a delicate person could have inflicted the injuries if, that is to say, they were struck in a frenzy of excitement.'

'Thank you, Doctor.'

Details as to the condition of the body followed—well nourished, healthy, age about forty-five. No signs of illness or disease—heart, lungs, etc., all good.

Beatrice Lippincott gave evidence of the arrival of deceased. He had registered as Enoch Arden, Cape Town.

'Did deceased produce a ration book?'

'No, sir.'

'Did you ask him for one?'

'Not at first. I did not know how long he was staying.'

'But you did eventually ask him?'

'Yes, sir. He arrived on the Friday and on Saturday I said if he was staying more than five days would he please let me have his ration book.'

'What did he say to that?'

'He said he would give it to me.'

'But he did not actually do so?'

'No.'

'He did not say that he had lost it? Or had not got one?'

'Oh, no. He just said, "I'll look it out and bring it along."'

'Miss Lippincott, did you, on the night of Saturday, overhear a certain conversation?'

With a good deal of elaborate explanation as to the necessity she was under of visiting No. 4, Beatrice Lippincott told her tale. The coroner guided her astutely.

'Thank you. Did you mention this conversation you had overheard to anybody?'

'Yes, I told Mr. Rowley Cloade.'

'Why did you tell Mr. Cloade?'

'I thought he ought to know.' Beatrice flushed.

A tall thin man (Mr. Gaythorne) rose and asked permission to put a question.

'In the course of the conversation between the deceased and Mr. David Hunter did the deceased at any time mention definitely that he himself was Robert Underhay?'

'No—no—he didn't.'

'In fact he spoke of "Robert Underhay" as though Robert Underhay was quite another person?'

'Yes—yes, he did.'

'Thank you, Mr. Coroner, that was all I wanted to get clear.'

Beatrice Lippincott stood down and Rowley Cloade was called.

He confirmed that Beatrice had repeated the story to him and then gave his account of his interview with the deceased.

'His last words to you were, "I don't think you'll prove that without *my* co-operation?" "*That*"—being the fact that Robert Underhay was still alive.'

'That's what he said, yes. And he laughed.'

'He laughed, did he? What did you take those words to mean?'

'Well—I just thought he was trying to get me to make him an offer, but afterwards I got thinking——'

'Yes, Mr. Cloade—but what you thought afterwards is hardly relevant. Shall we put it that as a result of that interview you set about trying to find some person who was acquainted with the late Robert Underhay? And that, with certain help, you were successful.'

Rowley nodded.

'That's right.'

'What time was it when you left the deceased?'

'As nearly as I can tell it was five minutes to nine.'

'What made you fix on that time?'

'As I went along the street I heard the nine o'clock chimes through an open window.'

'Did the deceased mention at what time he was expecting this client?'

'He said "At any minute."'

'He did not mention any name?'

'No.'

'David Hunter!'

There was just a faint soft buzz as the inhabitants of Warmsley Vale craned their necks to look at the tall thin bitter-looking young man who stood defiantly facing the coroner.

The preliminaries went rapidly. The coroner continued:

'You went to see the deceased on Saturday evening?'

'Yes. I received a letter from him asking for assistance and stating he had known my sister's first husband in Africa.'

'You have got that letter?'

'No, I don't keep letters.'

'You have heard the account given by Beatrice Lippincott of your conversation with the deceased. Is that a true account?'

'Quite untrue. The deceased spoke of knowing my late brother-in-law, complained of his own bad luck and of having come down in the world, and begged for some financial assistance which, as is usual, he was quite confident of being able to repay.'

'Did he tell you that Robert Underhay was still alive?'

David smiled:

'Certainly not. He said, "*If* Robert were still alive I know he would help me."'

'That is quite different from what Beatrice Lippincott tells us?'

'Eavesdroppers,' said David, 'usually hear only a portion of what goes on and frequently get the whole thing wrong owing to supplying the missing details from their own fertile imaginations.'

Beatrice flounced angrily and exclaimed, 'Well, I never—' The coroner said repressively, 'Silence, please.'

'Now, Mr. Hunter, did you visit the deceased again on the night of Tuesday——'

'No, I did not.'

'You have heard Mr. Rowley Cloade say that the deceased expected a visitor?'

'He may have expected a visitor. If so, I was not that visitor. I'd given him a fiver before. I thought that was quite enough for him. There was no proof that he'd ever known Robert Underhay. My sister, since she inherited a large income from her husband, has been the target of every begging letter-writer and every sponger in the neighbourhood.'

Quietly he let his eyes pass over the assembled Cloades.

'Mr. Hunter, will you tell us where you were on the evening of Tuesday?'

'Find out!' said David.

'Mr. Hunter!' The coroner rapped the table. 'That is a most foolish and ill-advised thing to say.'

'Why should I tell you where I was, and what I was doing? Time enough for that when you accuse me of murdering the man.'

'If you persist in that attitude it may come to that sooner than you think. Do you recognise *this*, Mr. Hunter?'

Leaning forward, David took the gold cigarette lighter into his hand. His face was puzzled. Handing it back, he said slowly: 'Yes, it's mine.'

'When did you have it last?'

'I missed it——' He paused.

'Yes, Mr. Hunter?' The coroner's voice was suave.

Gaythorne fidgeted, seemed about to speak. But David was too quick for him.

'I had it last Friday—Friday morning. I don't remember seeing it since.'

Mr. Gaythorne rose.

'With your permission, Mr. Coroner. You visited the deceased Saturday evening. Might you not have left the lighter there then?'

'I might have, I suppose,' David said slowly. 'I certainly don't remember seeing it after Friday——' He added: 'Where was it found?'

The coroner said:

'We shall go into that later. You can stand down now, Mr. Hunter.'

David moved slowly back to his seat. He bent his head and whispered to Rosaleen Cloade:

'Major Porter.'

Hemming and hawing a little, Major Porter took the stand. He stood there, an erect soldierly figure, as though on parade. Only the way he moistened his lips showed the intense nervousness from which he was suffering.

'You are George Douglas Porter, late Major of the Royal African Rifles?'

'Yes.'

'How well did you know Robert Underhay?'

In a parade-ground voice Major Porter barked out places and dates.

'You have viewed the body of the deceased?'

'Yes.'

'Can you identify that body?'

'Yes. It is the body of Robert Underhay.'

A buzz of excitement went round the court.

'You state that positively and without the least doubt?'

'I do.'

'There is no possibility of your being mistaken?'

'None.'

'Thank you, Major Porter. Mrs. Gordon Cloade.'

Rosaleen rose. She passed Major Porter. He looked at her with some curiosity. She did not even glance at him.

'Mrs. Cloade, you were taken by the police to see the body of the deceased?'

She shivered.

'Yes.'

'You stated definitely that it was the body of a man completely unknown to you?'

'Yes.'

'In view of the statement just made by Major Porter would you like to withdraw or amend your own statement?'

'No.'

'You still assert definitely that the body was not that of your husband, Robert Underhay?'

'It was not my husband's body. It was a man I had never seen in my life.'

'Come now, Mrs. Cloade, Major Porter has definitely recognised it as the body of his friend Robert Underhay.'

Rosaleen said expressionlessly:

'Major Porter is mistaken.'

'You are not under oath in this court, Mrs. Cloade. But it is likely that you will be under oath in another court shortly. Are you prepared then to swear that the body is not that of Robert Underhay but of an unknown stranger?'

'I am prepared to swear that it is not the body of my husband but of a man quite unknown to me.'

Her voice was clear and unfaltering. Her eyes met the coroner unshrinkingly.

He murmured: 'You can stand down.'

Then, removing his pince-nez, he addressed the jury.

They were there to discover how this man came to his death. As to that, there could be little question. There could be no idea of accident or suicide. Nor could there be any suggestion of manslaughter. There remained only one verdict—wilful murder. As to the identity of the dead man, that was not clearly established.

They had heard one witness, a man of upright character and probity whose word could be relied upon, say that the body was that of a former friend of his, Robert Underhay. On the other hand Robert Underhay's death from fever in Africa had been established apparently to the satisfaction of the local authorities and no question had then been raised. In contradiction of Major Porter's statement, Robert Underhay's widow, now Mrs. Gordon Cloade, stated positively that the body was *not* that of Robert Underhay. These were diametrically opposite statements. Passing from the question of identity they would have to decide if there was any evidence to show whose hand had murdered the deceased. They might think that the evidence pointed to a certain person, but a good deal of evidence was needed before a case could be made out—evidence and motive and opportunity. The person must have been seen by someone in the vicinity of the crime at the appropriate time. If there was not such evidence the best verdict was that of Wilful Murder without sufficient evidence to show by whose hand. Such a verdict would leave the police free to pursue the necessary inquiries.

He then dismissed them to consider their Verdict.

They took three quarters of an hour.

They returned a Verdict of Wilful Murder against David Hunter.

CHAPTER V

'I WAS AFRAID they'd do it,' said the coroner apologetically. 'Local prejudice! Feeling rather than logic.'

The coroner, the Chief Constable, Superintendent Spence and Hercule Poirot were all in consultation together after the inquest.

'You did your best,' said the Chief Constable.

'It's premature, to say the least of it,' said Spence frowning. 'And it hampers us. Do you know M. Hercule Poirot? He was instrumental in bringing Porter forward.'

The coroner said graciously:

'I have heard of you, M. Poirot,' and Poirot made an unsuccessful attempt to look modest.

'M. Poirot's interested in the case,' said Spence with a grin.

'Truly, that is so,' said Poirot. 'I was in it, as you might say, before there *was* a case.'

And in answer to their interested glances he told of the queer little scene in the club when he had first heard a mention of Robert Underhay's name.

'That's an additional point in Porter's evidence when the case comes to trial,' said the Chief Constable thoughtfully. 'Underhay actually *planned* a pretended death—and spoke of using the name of Enoch Arden.'

The Chief Constable murmured: 'Ah, but will that be admissible as evidence? Words spoken by a man who is now dead?'

'It may not be admissible as evidence,' said Poirot thoughtfully. 'But it raises a very interesting and suggestive line of thought.'

'What *we* want,' said Spence, 'is not suggestion, but a few concrete facts. Someone who actually saw David Hunter at the Stag or near it on Tuesday evening.'

'It ought to be easy,' said the Chief Constable, frowning.

'If it was abroad in my country it would be easy enough,' said Poirot. 'There would be a little café where someone takes the evening coffee—but in provincial England!' He threw up his hands.

The Superintendent nodded.

'Some of the folks are in the pubs, and will stay in the pubs till closing time, and the rest of the population are inside their houses listening to the nine o'clock news. If you ever go along the main street here between eight-thirty and ten it's completely deserted. Not a soul.'

'He counted on that?' suggested the Chief Constable.

'Maybe,' said Spence. His expression was not a happy one.

Presently the Chief Constable and the coroner departed. Spence and Poirot were left together.

'You do not like the case, no?' asked Poirot sympathetically.

'That young man worries me,' said Spence. 'He's the kind that you never know where you are with them. When they're most innocent of a business, they act as though they were guilty. And when they're guilty—why, you'd take your oath they were angels of light!'

'*You* think he *is* guilty?' asked Poirot.

'Don't you?' Spence countered.

Poirot spread out his hands.

'I should be interested to know,' he said, 'just exactly how much you have against him?'

'You don't mean legally? You mean in the way of probability?'

Poirot nodded.

'There's the lighter,' said Spence.

'Where did you find it?'

'Under the body.'

'Fingerprints on it?'

'None.'

'Ah,' said Poirot.

'Yes,' said Spence. 'I don't like that too much myself. Then the dead man's watch had stopped at 9.10. That fits in with the medical evidence quite nicely—and with Rowley Cloade's evidence that Underhay was expecting his client at any minute—presumably that client was almost due.'

Poirot nodded.

'Yes—it is all very neat.'

'And the thing you can't get away from, to my mind, M. Poirot, is that he's the only person (he and his sister, that is to say) who has the ghost or shadow of a motive. Either David Hunter killed Underhay—or else Underhay was killed by some outsider who followed him here for some reason that we know nothing about—and that seems wildly improbable.'

'Oh, I agree, I agree.'

'You see, there's no one in Warmsley Vale who could possibly have a motive—unless by a coincidence someone is living here (other than the Hunters) who had a connection with Underhay in the past. I never rule out coincidence, but there hasn't been a hint or suggestion of anything of the kind. The man was a stranger to every one but that brother and sister.'

Poirot nodded.

'To the Cloade family Robert Underhay would be the apple of their eye to be kept alive by every possible precaution. Robert Underhay, alive and kicking, means the certainty of a large fortune divided amongst them.'

'Again, *mon ami*, I agree with you enthusiastically. Robert Underhay, alive and kicking, is what the Cloade family needs.'

'So back we come—Rosaleen and David Hunter are the only two people who have a motive. Rosaleen Cloade was in London. But David, we know, was in Warmsley Vale that day. He arrived at 5.30 at Warmsley Heath station.'

'So now we have Motive, written very big and the fact that at 5.30 and onward to some unspecified time, he was on the spot.'

'Exactly. Now take Beatrice Lippincott's story. I believe that story. She overheard what she says she overheard, though she may have gingered it up a little, as is only human.'

'Only human as you say.'

'Apart from knowing the girl, I believe her because she couldn't have invented some of the things. She'd never heard of Robert Underhay before, for instance. So I believe her story of what passed between the two men and not David Hunter's.'

'I, too,' said Poirot. 'She strikes me as a singularly truthful witness.'

'We've confirmation that her story is true. What do you suppose the brother and sister went off to London for?'

'That is one of the things that has interested me most.'

'Well, the money position's like this. Rosaleen Cloade has only a life interest in Gordon Cloade's estate. She can't touch the capital —except, I believe, for about a thousand pounds. But jewellery, etc., is hers. The first thing she did on going to town was to take some of the most valuable pieces round to Bond Street and sell them. She wanted a large sum of cash quickly—in other words she had to pay a blackmailer.'

'You call that evidence against David Hunter?'

'Don't you?'

Poirot shook his head.

'Evidence that there was blackmail, yes. Evidence of intent to commit murder, no. You cannot have it both ways, *mon cher*. Either that young man was going to pay up, or else he was planning to kill. You have produced evidence that he was planning to *pay*.'

'Yes—yes, perhaps that is so. But he may have changed his mind.'

Poirot shrugged his shoulders.

'I know his type,' said the Superintendent thoughtfully. 'It's a type that's done well during the war. Any amount of physical courage. Audacity and a reckless disregard of personal safety. The sort that will face any odds. It's the kind that is likely to win the V.C.—though, mind you, it's often a posthumous one. Yes, in wartime, a man like that is a hero. But in peace—well, in peace such men usually end up in prison. They like excitement and they can't run straight, and they don't give a damn for society—and finally they've no regard for human life.'

Poirot nodded.

'I tell you,' the Superintendent repeated, 'I *know* the type.'

There was some few minutes of silence.

'*Eh bien*,' said Poirot at last. 'We agree that we have here the *type* of a killer. But that is all. It takes us no further.'

Spence looked at him with curiosity.

'You're taking a great interest in this business, M. Poirot?'

'Yes.'

'Why, if I may ask?'

'Frankly,' Poirot spread out his hands, 'I do not quite know. Perhaps it is because when two years ago, I am sitting very sick in my stomach (for I did not like Air Raids, and I am not very brave though I endeavour to put up the good appearance) when, as I say, I am sitting with a sick feeling here,' Poirot clasped his stomach expressively, 'in the smoking-room of my friend's club, there, droning away, is the club bore, the good Major Porter, recounting a long history to which nobody listens; but me, I listen, because I am wishful to distract myself from the bombs, and because the facts he is relating seem to me interesting and suggestive. And I think to myself that it is possible that some day something may come of the situation he recounts. And now something *has* come of it.'

'The unexpected has happened, eh?'

'On the contrary,' Poirot corrected him. 'It is the *expected* that has happened—which in itself is sufficiently remarkable.'

'You expected murder?' Spence asked sceptically.

'No, no, no! But a wife remarries. Possibility that first husband is still alive? He *is* alive. He may turn up? He *does* turn up! There may be blackmail. There *is* blackmail! Possibility, therefore, that blackmailer may be silenced? *Ma foi*, he is silenced!'

'Well,' said Spence, eyeing Poirot rather doubtfully. 'I suppose these things run pretty close to type. It's a common sort of crime—blackmail resulting in murder.'

'Not interesting, you would say? Usually, no. But this case is interesting, because, you see,' said Poirot placidly, *'it is all wrong.'*

'All wrong? What do you mean by all wrong?'

'None of it is, how shall I put it, *the right shape?*'

Spence stared. 'Chief Inspector Japp,' he remarked, 'always said you have a tortuous mind. Give me an instance of what you call wrong?'

'Well, the dead man, for instance, *he* is all wrong.'

Spence shook his head.

'You do not feel that?' Poirot asked. 'Oh, well, perhaps I am fanciful. Then take this point. Underhay arrives at the Stag. He writes to David Hunter. Hunter receives that letter the next morning—at breakfast time?'

'Yes, that's so. He admits receiving a letter from Arden then.'

'That was the first intimation, was it not, of the arrival of Underhay in Warmsley Vale? What is the first thing he does—*bundles his sister off to London!*'

'That's quite understandable,' said Spence. 'He wants a clear hand to deal with things his own way. He may have been afraid the woman would have been weak. He's the leading spirit, remember. Mrs. Cloade is entirely under his thumb.'

'Oh, yes, that shows itself plainly. So he sends her to London and calls on this Enoch Arden. We have a pretty clear account of their conversation from Beatrice Lippincott, and the thing that sticks out, a mile, as you say, is that David Hunter *was not sure whether the man he was talking to was Robert Underhay or not. He suspected* it, but he didn't *know.*'

'But there's nothing odd about that, M. Poirot. Rosaleen Hunter married Underhay in Cape Town and went with him straight to Nigeria. Hunter and Underhay never met. Therefore though, as you say, Hunter *suspected* that Arden was Underhay, he couldn't *know* it for a fact—because he had never met the man.'

Poirot looked at Superintendent Spence thoughtfully.

'So there is nothing there that strikes you as—peculiar?' he asked.

'I know what you're driving at. Why didn't Underhay say straight out that he *was* Underhay? Well, I think that's understandable, too. Respectable people who are doing something crooked like to preserve appearances. They like to put things in such a way that it keeps them in the clear—if you know what I mean. No—I don't think that that is so very remarkable. You've got to allow for human nature.'

'Yes,' said Poirot. 'Human nature. That, I think, is perhaps the real answer as to why I am interested in this case. I was looking round the Coroner's Court, looking at all the people, looking particularly at the Cloades—so many of them, all bound by a common interest, all so different in their characters, in their thoughts and feelings. All of them dependent for many years on the strong man, the power in the family, on Gordon Cloade! I do not mean, perhaps, directly dependent. They had all their independent means of existence. But they had come, they must have come, consciously or unconsciously, to lean on him. And what happens—I will ask you this, Superintendent—*What happens to the ivy when the oak round which it clings is struck down?*'

'That's hardly a question in my line,' said Spence.

'You think not? I think it is. Character, *mon cher*, does not stand still. It can gather strength. It can also deteriorate. What a person really *is*, is only apparent when the test comes—that is, the moment when you stand or fall on your own feet.'

'I don't really know what you are getting at, M. Poirot.' Spence looked bewildered. 'Anyway, the Cloades are all right now. Or will be, once the legal formalities are through.'

'That, Poirot reminded him, might take some time. 'There is still Mrs. Gordon Cloade's evidence to shake. After all, a woman should know her own husband when she sees him?'

He put his head a little on one side and gazed inquiringly at the big Superintendent.

'Isn't it worth while to a woman *not* to recognise her husband if the income of a couple of million pounds depends on it?' asked the Superintendent cynically. 'Besides, if he wasn't Robert Underhay, why was he killed?'

'That,' murmured Poirot, 'is indeed the question.'

CHAPTER VI

POIROT left the police station frowning to himself. His steps grew slower as he walked. In the market square he paused, looking about him. There was Dr. Cloade's house with its worn brass plate, and a little way along was the post office. On the other side was Jeremy Cloade's house. In front of Poirot, set back a little, was the Roman Catholic Church of the Assumption, a small modest affair, a shrinking violet compared to the aggressiveness of St. Mary's which stood arrogantly in the middle of the square facing the Cornmarket, and proclaiming the dominance of the Protestant religion.

Moved by an impulse Poirot went through the gate and along the path to the door of the Roman Catholic building. He removed his hat, genuflected in front of the altar and knelt down behind one of the chairs. His prayers were interrupted by the sound of stifled heart-broken sobs.

He turned his head. Across the aisle a woman in a dark dress was kneeling, her head buried in her hands. Presently she got up and, still sobbing under her breath, went towards the door. Poirot, his eyes wide with interest, got up and followed her. He had recognised Rosaleen Cloade.

She stood in the porch, fighting her control, and there Poirot spoke to her, very gently:

'Madame, can I help you?'

She showed no signs of surprise, but answered with the simplicity of an unhappy child.

'No,' she said. 'No one can help me.'

'You are in very bad trouble. That is it, is it not?'

She said: 'They've taken David away . . . I'm all alone. They say he killed—— But he didn't! He didn't!'

She looked at Poirot and said: 'You were there to-day? At the inquest. I saw you!'

'Yes. If I can help you, Madame, I shall be very glad to do so.'

'I'm frightened. David said I'd be safe as long as he was there to look after me. But now they've taken him away—I'm afraid. He said—they all wanted me dead. That's a dreadful thing to say. But perhaps it's true.'

'Let me help you, Madame.'

She shook her head.

'No,' she said. 'No one can help me. I can't go to confession, even. I've got to bear the weight of my wickedness all alone. I'm cut off from the mercy of God.'

'Nobody,' said Hercule Poirot, 'is cut off from the mercy of God. You know that well, my child.'

Again she looked at him—a wild unhappy look.

'I'd have to confess my sins—to confess. If I could confess——'

'Can't you confess? You came to the church for that, did you not?'

'I came to get comfort—comfort. But what comfort is there for me? I'm a sinner.'

'We are all sinners.'

'But you'd have to repent—I'd have to say—to tell——' Her hands went up to her face. 'Oh, the lies I've told—the lies I've told.'

'You told a lie about your husband? About Robert Underhay? It *was* Robert Underhay who was killed here, wasn't it?'

She turned sharply on him. Her eyes were suspicious, wary. She cried out sharply:

'I tell you it was *not* my husband. It wasn't the least like him!'

'The dead man was not in the least like your husband?'

'No,' she said defiantly.

'Tell me,' said Poirot, 'what *was* your husband like?'

Her eyes stared at him. Then her face hardened into alarm. Her eyes grew dark with fear.

She cried out:

'I'll not talk to you any more!'

Going swiftly past him, she ran down the path and passed through the gate out into the market square.

Poirot did not try and follow her. Instead he nodded his head with a good deal of satisfaction.

'Ah,' he said. 'So that is *that*!'

He walked slowly out into the square.

After a momentary hesitation he followed the High Street until he came to the Stag, which was the last building before the open country.

In the doorway of the Stag he met Rowley Cloade and Lynn Marchmont.

Poirot looked at the girl with interest. A handsome girl, he thought, and intelligent also. Not the type he himself admired. He preferred something softer, more feminine. Lynn Marchmont, he thought, was essentially a modern type—though one might, with equal accuracy, call it an Elizabethan type. Women who thought for themselves, who were free in language, and who admired enterprise and audacity in men.

'We're very grateful to you, M. Poirot,' said Rowley. 'By Jove, it really was quite like a conjuring trick.'

Which was exactly what it had been, Poirot reflected! Asked a question to which you knew the answer, there was no difficulty whatsoever in performing a trick with the requisite frills. He quite appreciated that to the simple Rowley, the production of Major Porter out of the blue, so to speak, had been as breathtaking as any amount of rabbits produced from the conjurer's hat.

'How you go about these things beats me,' said Rowley.

Poirot did not enlighten him. He was, after all, only human. The conjurer does not tell his audience how the trick was done.

'Anyway, Lynn and I are no end grateful,' Rowley went on.

Lynn Marchmont, Poirot thought, was not looking particularly grateful. There were lines of strain round her eyes, her fingers had a nervous trick of twining and intertwining themselves.

'It's going to make a lot of difference to our future married life,' said Rowley.

Lynn said sharply:

'How do you know? There are all sorts of formalities and things, I'm sure.'

'You are getting married, when?' asked Poirot politely.

'June.'

'And you have been engaged since when?'

'Nearly six years,' said Rowley. 'Lynn's just come out of the Wrens.'

'And is it forbidden to marry in the Wrens, yes?'

Lynn said briefly, 'I've been overseas.'

Poirot noticed Rowley's swift frown. He said shortly:

'Come on, Lynn. We must get going. I expect M. Poirot wants to get back to town.'

Poirot said smilingly:

'But I'm not going back to town.'

'What?'

Rowley stopped dead, giving a queer wooden effect.

'I am staying here, at the Stag, for a short while.'

'But—but why?'

'*C'est un beau paysage*,' Poirot said placidly.

Rowley said uncertainly:

'Yes, of course . . . But aren't you—well, I mean, busy?'

'I have made my economies,' said Poirot, smiling. 'I do not need to occupy myself unduly. No, I can enjoy my leisure and spend my time where the fancy takes me. And my fancy inclines to Warmsley Vale.'

He saw Lynn Marchmont raise her head and gaze at him intently. Rowley, he thought, was slightly annoyed.

'I suppose you play golf?' he said. 'There's a much better hotel at Warmsley Heath. This is a very one-horse sort of place.'

'My interests,' said Poirot, 'lie entirely in Warmsley Vale.'

Lynn said:

'Come along, Rowley.'

Half reluctantly, Rowley followed her. At the door, Lynn paused and then came swiftly back. She spoke to Poirot in a quiet low voice.

'They arrested David Hunter after the inquest. Do you—do you think they were right?'

'They had no alternative, Mademoiselle, after the verdict.'

'I mean—do you think he did it?'

'Do *you*?' said Poirot.

But Rowley was back at her side. Her face hardened to a poker smoothness. She said:

'Good-bye, M. Poirot. I—I hope we meet again.'

'Now, I wonder,' said Poirot to himself.

Presently, after arranging with Beatrice Lippincott about a room, he went out again. His steps led him to Dr. Lionel Cloade's house.

'Oh!' said Aunt Kathie, who opened the door, taking a step or two backwards. 'M. Poirot!'

'At your service, Madame.' Poirot bowed. 'I came to pay my respects.'

'Well, that's very nice of you, I'm sure. Yes—well—I suppose you'd better come in. Sit down—I'll move Madame Blavatsky—and perhaps a cup of tea—only the cake is terribly stale. I meant to go to Peacocks for some, they do have Swiss roll sometimes on a Wednesday—but an inquest puts one's household routine out, don't you think so?'

Poirot said that he thought that was entirely understandable.

He had fancied that Rowley Cloade was annoyed by the announcement of his stay in Warmsley Vale. Aunt Kathie's manner, without any doubt, was far from welcoming. She was looking at him with something not far from dismay. She said, leaning forward and speaking in a hoarse conspiratorial whisper:

'You won't tell my husband, will you, that I came and consulted you about—well, about we know what?'

'My lips are sealed.'

'I mean—of course I'd no idea at the time—that Robert Underhay, poor man, so *tragic*—was actually *in* Warmsley Vale. That seems to me still a most *extraordinary* coincidence!'

'It would have been simpler,' agreed Poirot, 'if the Ouija board had directed you straight to the Stag.'

Aunt Kathie cheered up a little at the mention of the Ouija board.

'The way things come about in the spirit world seem quite incalculable,' she said. 'But I do feel, M. Poirot, that there is a *purpose* in it all? Don't you feel that in life? That there is always a *purpose?*'

'Yes, indeed, Madame. Even that I should sit here, now, in your drawing-room, there is a purpose in that.'

'Oh, is there?' Mrs. Cloade looked rather taken aback. 'Is there, really? Yes, I suppose so . . . You're on your way back to London, of *course?*'

'Not at present. I stay for a few days at the Stag.'

'At the *Stag*? Oh—at the Stag! But that's where—oh, M. Poirot, do you think you are *wise?*'

'I have been guided to the Stag,' said Poirot solemnly.

'*Guided?* What do you mean?'

'Guided by *you*.'

'Oh, but I never meant—I mean, I had no *idea*. It's all so dreadful, don't you think so?'

Poirot shook his head sadly, and said:

'I have been talking to Mr. Rowley Cloade and Miss Marchmont. They are getting married, I hear, quite soon?'

Aunt Kathie was immediately diverted.

'Dear Lynn, she is such a sweet girl—and so very good at figures. Now, I have no head for figures—no head at all. Having Lynn home is an absolute blessing. If I get in a terrible muddle she always straightens things out for me. Dear girl, I do hope she will be happy. Rowley, of course, is a splendid person, but possibly—well, a little *dull*. I mean dull to a girl who has seen as much of the world as Lynn has. Rowley, you see, has been here on his farm all through the war—oh, quite rightly, of course—I mean the Government wanted him to—that side of it is *quite* all right—not white feathers or things like that as they did in the Boer War—but what I mean is, it's made him rather limited in his ideas.'

'Six years' engagement is a good test of affection.'

'Oh, it *is*! But I think these girls, when they come home, they get rather restless—and if there is someone else about—someone, perhaps, who has led an adventurous life——'

'Such as David Hunter?'

'There isn't anything between them.' Aunt Kathie said anxiously. 'Nothing *at all*. I'm *quite* sure of that! It would have been dreadful if there had been, wouldn't it, with his turning out a *murderer*? His own brother-in-law, too! Oh, no, M. Poirot, please don't run away with the idea that there's any kind of an understanding between Lynn and David. Really, they seemed to quarrel more than anything else every time they met. What I feel is that—oh, dear, I think that's my husband coming. You will remember, won't you, M. Poirot, *not* a word about our first meeting? My poor dear husband gets so annoyed if he thinks that—oh, Lionel dear, here is M. Poirot who so cleverly brought that Major Porter down to see the body.'

Dr. Cloade looked tired and haggard. His eyes, pale blue, with pin-point pupils, wandered vaguely round the room.

'How do you do, M. Poirot; on your way back to town?'

'*Mon Dieu*, another who packs me back to London!' thought Poirot. Aloud he said patiently:

'No, I remain at the Stag for a day or so.'

'The Stag?' Lionel Cloade frowned. 'Oh? Police want to keep you here for a bit?'

'No. It is my own choice.'

'Indeed?' The doctor suddenly flashed a quick intelligent look. 'So you're not satisfied?'

'Why should you think that, Dr. Cloade?'

'Come, man, it's true, isn't it?' Twittering about tea, Mrs. Cloade left the room. The doctor went on: 'You've a feeling, haven't you, that something's wrong?'

Poirot was startled.

'It is odd that you should say that. Do you, then, feel that yourself?'

Cloade hesitated.

'N-n-o. Hardly that . . . perhaps it's just a feeling of *unreality*. In books the blackmailer gets slugged. Does he in real life? Apparently the answer is Yes. But it seems unnatural.'

'Was there anything unsatisfactory about the medical aspect of the case? I ask unofficially, of course.'

Dr. Cloade said thoughtfully:

'No, I don't think so.'

'Yes—there is something. I can see there is something.'

When he wished, Poirot's voice could assume an almost hypnotic quality. Dr. Cloade frowned a little, then he said hesitatingly:

'I've no experience, of course, of police cases. And anyway medical evidence isn't the hard-and-fast, cast-iron business that laymen or novelists seem to think. We're fallible—medical science is fallible. What's diagnosis? A guess, based on a very little knowledge, and some indefinite clues which point in more than one direction. I'm pretty sound, perhaps, at diagnosing measles because, at my time of life, I've seen hundreds of cases of measles and I know an extraordinary wide variation of signs and symptoms. You hardly ever get what a text book tells you is a "typical case" of measles. But I've known some queer things in my time—I've seen a woman practically on the operating table ready for her appendix to be whipped out—and paratyphoid diagnosed just in time! I've seen a child with skin trouble pronounced as a case of serious vitamin deficiency by an earnest and conscientious young doctor—and the local vet. comes along and mentions to the mother that the cat the child is hugging has got ringworm and that the child has caught it!

'Doctors, like every one else, are victims of the preconceived idea. Here's a man, obviously murdered, lying with a bloodstained pair of fire-tongs beside him. It would be nonsense to say he was hit with anything else, and yet, speaking out of complete inexperience of people with their heads smashed in, I'd have suspected something rather different—something not so smooth and round—something—oh, I don't know, something with a more cutting edge—a brick, something like that.'

'You did not say so at the inquest?'

'No—because I don't really know. Jenkins, the police surgeon, was satisfied, and he's the fellow who counts. But there's the preconceived idea—weapon lying beside the body. *Could* the wound have been inflicted with that? Yes, it *could*. But if you were shown the wound and asked what made it—well, I don't know whether you'd say it, because it really doesn't make sense—I mean if you had two fellows, one hitting him with a brick and one with the tongs——' The doctor stopped, shook his head in a dissatisfied way. 'Doesn't make sense, does it?' he said to Poirot.

'Could he have fallen on some sharp object?'

Dr. Cloade shook his head.

'He was lying face down in the middle of the floor—on a good thick old-fashioned Axminster carpet.'

He broke off as his wife entered the room.

'Here's Kathie with the cat-lap,' he remarked.

Aunt Kathie was balancing a tray covered with crockery, half a loaf of bread and some depressing-looking jam in the bottom of a 2-lb. pot.

'I *think* the kettle was boiling,' she remarked doubtfully as she raised the lid of the teapot and peered inside.

Dr. Cloade snorted again and muttered: 'Cat-lap,' with which explosive word he left the room.

'Poor Lionel, his nerves are in a terrible state since the war. He worked much too hard. So many doctors away. He gave himself no rest. Out morning, noon, and night. I wonder he didn't break down completely. Of course he looked forward to retiring as soon as peace came. That was all fixed up with Gordon. His hobby, you know, is botany with special reference to medicinal herbs in the Middle Ages. He's writing a book on it. He was looking forward to a quiet life and doing the necessary research. But then, when Gordon died like that—well, you know what things are, M. Poirot, nowadays. Taxation and everything. He can't afford to retire and it's made him very bitter. And really it *does* seem unfair. Gordon's dying like that, without a will—well, it really quite shook my faith. I mean, I really couldn't see the *purpose* in that. It seemed, I couldn't help feeling, a *mistake*.'

She sighed, then cheered up a little.

'But I get some lovely reassurances from the other side. "Courage and patience and a way will be found." And really, when that nice Major Porter stood up to-day and said in such a firm manly way that the poor murdered man was Robert Underhay—well, I saw that a way *had* been found! It's wonderful, isn't it, M. Poirot, how things do turn out for the best?'

'Even murder,' said Hercule Poirot.

CHAPTER VII

POIROT entered the Stag in a thoughtful mood, and shivering slightly for there was a sharp east wind. The hall was deserted. He pushed open the door of the Lounge on the right. It smelt of stale smoke and the fire was nearly out. Poirot tiptoed along to the door at the end of the hall labelled 'Residents Only.' Here there was a good fire, but in a large arm-chair, comfortably toasting her toes, was a monumental old lady who glared at Poirot with such ferocity that he beat an apologetic retreat.

He stood for a moment in the hall looking from the glass-enclosed empty office to the door labelled in firm old-fashioned style COFFEE-ROOM. By experience of country hotels Poirot knew well that the only time coffee was served there was somewhat grudgingly for breakfast and that even then a good deal of watery hot milk was its principal component. Small cups of a treacly and muddy liquid called Black Coffee were served not in the COFFEE-ROOM but in the Lounge. The Windsor Soup, Vienna Steak and Potatoes, and Steamed Pudding which comprised Dinner would be obtainable in the COFFEE-ROOM at seven sharp. Until then a deep peace brooded over the residential area of the Stag.

Poirot went thoughtfully up the staircase. Instead of turning to the left where his own room, No. 11, was situated, he turned to the right and stopped before the door of No. 5. He looked round him. Silence and emptiness. He opened the door and went in.

The police had done with the room. It had clearly been freshly cleaned and scrubbed. There was no carpet on the floor. Presumably the 'old-fashioned Axminster' had gone to the cleaners. The blankets were folded on the bed in a neat pile.

Closing the door behind him, Poirot wandered round the room. It was clean and strangely barren of human interest. Poirot took in its furnishings—a writing-table, a chest of drawers of good old-fashioned mahogany, an upright wardrobe of the same (the one presumably that masked the door into No. 4), a large brass double bed, a basin with hot and cold water—tribute to modernity and the servant shortage—a large but rather uncomfortable arm-chair, two small chairs, an old-fashioned Victorian grate with a poker and a pierced shovel belonging to the same set as the fire-tongs; a heavy marble mantel-piece and a solid marble fire-curb with squared corners.

It was at these last that Poirot bent and looked. Moistening his finger he rubbed it along the right-hand corner and then inspected the result. His finger was slightly black. He repeated the performance with another finger on the left-hand corner of the curb. This time his finger was quite clean.

'Yes,' said Poirot thoughtfully to himself. 'Yes.'

He looked at the fitted washbasin. Then he strolled to the window. It looked out over some leads—the roof of a garage, he fancied, and then to a small back alley. An easy way to come and go unseen from room No. 5. But then it was equally easy to walk upstairs to No. 5 unseen. He had just done it himself.

Quietly, Poirot withdrew, shutting the door noiselessly behind him. He went along to his own room. It was decidedly chilly. He went downstairs again, hesitated, and then, driven by the chill of the evening, boldly entered the Residents Only, drew up a second arm-chair to the fire and sat down.

The monumental old lady was even more formidable seen close at hand. She had iron-grey hair, a flourishing moustache and, when presently she spoke, a deep and awe-inspiring voice.

'This Lounge,' she said, 'is Reserved for Persons staying in the hotel.'

'I am staying in the Hotel,' replied Hercule Poirot.

The old lady meditated for a moment or two before returning to the attack. Then she said accusingly:

'You're a foreigner.'

'Yes,' replied Hercule Poirot.

'In my opinion,' said the old lady, 'you should all Go Back.'

'Go back where?' inquired Poirot.

'To where you came from,' said the old lady firmly.

She added as a kind of rider, *sotto voce*: 'Foreigners!' and snorted.

'That,' said Poirot mildly, 'would be difficult.'

'Nonsense,' said the old lady. 'That's what we fought the war for, isn't it? So that people could go back to their proper places and stay there.'

Poirot did not enter into a controversy. He had already learnt that every single individual had a different version of the theme, 'What did we fight the war for?'

A somewhat hostile silence reigned.

'I don't know what things are coming to,' said the old lady. 'I really don't. Every year I come and stay in this place. My husband died here sixteen years ago. He's buried here. I come every year for a month.'

'A pious pilgrimage,' said Poirot politely.

'And every year things get worse and worse. No service! Food uneatable! Vienna steaks indeed! A steak's either Rump or Fillet steak—not chopped-up horse!'

Poirot shook his head sadly.

'One good thing—they've shut down the aerodrome,' said the old lady. 'Disgraceful it was, all those young airmen coming in here with those dreadful girls. Girls, indeed! I don't know what their mothers are thinking of nowadays. Letting them gad about as they do. I blame the Government. Sending the mothers to work in factories. Only let 'em off if they've got young children. Young children, stuff and nonsense! Any one can look after a baby! A baby doesn't go running round after soldiers. Girls from fourteen to eighteen, they're the ones that need looking after! Need their mothers. It takes a mother to know just what a girl is up to. Soldiers! Airmen! That's all they think about. Americans! Niggers! Polish riff-raff!'

Indignation at this point made the old lady cough. When she had recovered, she went on, working herself into a pleasurable frenzy and using Poirot as a target for her spleen.

'Why do they have barbed wire round their camps? To keep the soldiers from getting at the girls? No, to keep the girls from getting at the soldiers! Man-mad, that's what they are! Look at the way they dress. Trousers! Some poor fools wear shorts—they wouldn't if they knew what they looked like from behind!'

'I agree with you, Madame, indeed I agree with you.'

'What do they wear on their heads? Proper hats? No, a twisted up bit of stuff, and faces covered with paint and powder. Filthy stuff, all over their mouths. Not only red nails—but red *toe*-nails!'

The old lady paused explosively and looked at Poirot expectantly. He sighed and shook his head.

'Even in church,' said the old lady. 'No hats. Sometimes not even those silly scarves. Just that ugly crimped, permanently waved hair. Hair? Nobody knows what hair is nowadays. *I* could *sit* on my hair when I was young.'

Poirot stole a glance at the iron-grey bands. It seemed impossible that this fierce old woman could ever have been young!

'Put her head in here the other night, one of them did,' the old lady went on. 'Tied up in an orange scarf and painted and powdered. I looked at her. I just LOOKED at her! She soon went away!

'*She* wasn't a Resident,' went on the old lady. 'No one of *her* type staying here, I'm glad to say! So what was she doing coming out of a man's bedroom? Disgusting, I call it. I spoke about it to that Lippincott girl—but she's just as bad as any of them—go a mile for anything that wears trousers.'

Some faint interest stirred in Poirot's mind.

'Coming out of a man's bedroom?' he queried.

The old lady fell upon the topic with zest.

'That's what I said. Saw her with my own eyes. No. 5.'

'What day was that, Madame?'

'The day before there was all that fuss about a man being murdered. Disgraceful that such a thing could happen *here*! This used to be a very decent old-fashioned type of place. But *now*——'

'And what hour of the day was this?'

'Day? It wasn't day at all. Evening. Late evening, too. Perfectly disgraceful. Past ten o'clock. I go up to bed at a quarter-past ten. Out she comes from No. 5 as bold as brass, stares at me, then dodges back inside again, laughing and talking with the man there.'

'You heard *him* speak?'

'Aren't I telling you so? She dodges back inside and he calls out, "Oh, go on, get out of here. I'm fed up." That's a nice way for a man to talk to a girl! But they ask for it! Hussies!'

Poirot said, 'You did not report this to the police?'

She fixed him with a basilisk stare and totteringly rose out of her chair. Standing over him and glaring down on him, she said:

'I have never had *anything* to do with the police. The police indeed! *I*, in a *police* court?'

Quivering with rage and with one last malevolent glance at Poirot she left the room.

Poirot sat for a few minutes thoughtfully caressing his moustache, then he went in search of Beatrice Lippincott.

'Oh, yes, M. Poirot, you mean old Mrs. Leadbetter? Canon Leadbetter's widow. She comes here every year, but of course between ourselves she is rather a trial. She's really frightfully rude to people sometimes, and she doesn't seem to understand that things are different nowadays. She's nearly eighty, of course.'

'But she is clear in her mind? She knows what she is saying?'

'Oh, yes. She's quite a sharp old lady—rather too much so sometimes.'

'Do you know who a young woman was who visited the murdered man on Tuesday night?'

Beatrice looked astonished.

'I don't remember a young woman coming to visit him at any time. What was she like?'

'She was wearing an orange scarf round her head and I should fancy a good deal of make-up. She was in No. 5 talking to Arden at a quarter past ten on Tuesday night.'

'Really, M. Poirot, I've no idea whatsoever.'

Thoughtfully Poirot went along in search of Superintendent Spence.

Spence listened to Poirot's story in silence. Then he leaned back in his chair and nodded his head slowly.

'Funny, isn't it?' he said. 'How often you come back to the same old formula. *Cherchez la femme*.'

The Superintendent's French accent was not as good as Sergeant Graves', but he was proud of it. He got up and went across the room. He came back holding something in his hand. It was a lipstick in a gilt cardboard case.

'We had this indication all along that there *might* be a woman mixed up in it,' he said.

Poirot took the lipstick and smeared a little delicately on the back of his hand. 'Good quality,' he said. 'A dark cherry red—worn by a brunette probably.'

'Yes. It was found on the floor of No. 5. It had rolled under the chest of drawers and of course just possibly it might have been there some time. No fingerprints on it. Nowadays, of course, there isn't the range of lipsticks there used to be—just a few standard makes.'

'And you have no doubt made your inquiries?'

Spence smiled.

'Yes,' he said; 'as you put it, we have made our inquiries. Rosaleen Cloade uses this type of lipstick. So does Lynn Marchmont. Frances Cloade uses a more subdued colour. Mrs. Lionel Cloade doesn't use lipstick at all. Mrs. Marchmont uses a pale mauve shade. Beatrice Lippincott doesn't appear to use anything as expensive as this—nor does the chambermaid, Gladys.'

He paused.

'You have been thorough,' said Poirot.

'Not thorough enough. It looks now as though an outsider is mixed up in it—some woman, perhaps, that Underhay knew in Warmsley Vale.'

'And who was with him at a quarter past ten on Tuesday evening?'

'Yes,' said Spence. He added with a sigh, 'This lets David Hunter out.'

'It *does?*'

'Yes. His lordship has consented to make a statement at last. After his solicitor had been along to make him see reason. Here's his account of his own movements.'

Poirot read a neat typed memorandum.

Left London 4.16 *train for Warmsley Heath. Arrived there* 5.30. *Walked to Furrowbank by footpath.*

'His reason for coming down,' the Superintendent broke in, 'was, according to him, to get certain things he'd left behind, letters and papers, a cheque-book, and to see if some shirts had come back from the laundry—which, of course, they hadn't! My word, laundry's a problem nowadays. Four ruddy weeks since they've been to our place—not a clean towel left in our house, and the wife washes all my things herself now.'

After this very human interpolation the Superintendent returned to the itinerary of David's movements.

'*Left Furrowbank at* 7.25 *and states he went for a walk as he had missed the* 7.20 *train and there would be no train until the* 9.20.'

'In what direction did he go for a walk?' asked Poirot.

The Superintendent consulted his notes.

'Says by Downe Copse, Bats Hill and Long Ridge.'

'In fact, a complete circular tour round the White House!'

'My word, you pick up local geography quickly, M. Poirot!'

Poirot smiled and shook his head.

'No, I did not know the places you named. I was making a guess.'

'Oh, you were, were you?' The Superintendent cocked his head on one side.

'Then, according to him, when he was up on Long Ridge, he realised he was cutting it rather fine and fairly hared it for Warmsley Heath station, going across country. He caught the train by the skin of his teeth, arrived at Victoria 10.45, walked to Shepherd's Court, arriving there at eleven o'clock, which latter statement is confirmed by Mrs. Gordon Cloade.'

'And what confirmation have you of the rest of it?'

'Remarkably little—but there is some. Rowley Cloade and others saw him arrive at Warmsley Heath. The maids at Furrowbank were out (he had his own key of course) so they didn't see him, but they found a cigarette stump in the library which I gather intrigued them and also found a good deal of confusion in the linen cupboard. Then one of the gardeners was there working late—shutting up greenhouses or something and he caught sight of him. Miss Marchmont met him up by Mardon Wood—when he was running for the train.'

'Did any one see him catch the train?'

'No—but he telephoned from London to Miss Marchmont as soon as he got back—at 11.05.'

'That is checked?'

'Yes, we'd already put through an inquiry about calls from that number. There was a Toll call out at 11.4 to Warmsley Vale 36. That's the Marchmonts' number.'

'Very, very interesting,' murmured Poirot.

But Spence was going on painstakingly and methodically.

'Rowley Cloade left Arden at five minutes to nine. He's quite definite it wasn't earlier. About 9.10 Lynn Marchmont sees Hunter up at Mardon Wood. Granted he's run all the way from the Stag, would he have had time to meet Arden, quarrel with him, kill him and get to Mardon Wood? We're going into it and I don't think it can be done. However, now we're starting again. Far from Arden being killed at nine o'clock, he was alive at *ten minutes past ten*—that is unless your old lady is dreaming. He was either killed by the woman who dropped the lipstick, the woman in the orange scarf—or by somebody who came in *after* that woman left. And whoever did it, deliberately put the hands of the watch back to nine-ten.'

'Which if David Hunter had not happened to meet Lynn Marchmont in a very unlikely place would have been remarkably awkward for him?' said Poirot.

'Yes, it would. The 9.20 is the last train up from Warmsley Heath. It was growing dark. There are always golfers going back by it. Nobody would have noticed Hunter—indeed the station people don't know him by sight. And he didn't take a taxi at the other end. So we'd only have his sister's word for it that he arrived back at Shepherd's Court when he said he did.'

Poirot was silent and Spence asked:

'What are you thinking about, M. Poirot?'

Poirot said, 'A long walk round the White House. A meeting in

Mardon Woods. A telephone call later . . . And Lynn Marchmont is engaged to Rowley Cloade . . . I should like very much to know what was said over that telephone call.'

'It's the human interest that's getting you?'

'Yes,' said Poirot. 'It is always the human interest.'

CHAPTER VIII

IT WAS GETTING LATE, but there was still one more call that Poirot wanted to make. He went along to Jeremy Cloade's house.

There he was shown into Jeremy Cloade's study by a small, intelligent-looking maid.

Left alone, Poirot gazed interestedly round him. All very legal and dry as dust, he thought, even in his home. There was a large portrait of Gordon Cloade on the desk. Another faded one of Lord Edward Trenton on a horse, and Poirot was examining the latter when Jeremy Cloade came in.

'Ah, pardon,' Poirot put the photo-frame down in some confusion.

'My wife's father,' said Jeremy, a faint self-congratulatory note in his voice. 'And one of his best horses, Chestnut Trenton. Ran second in the Derby in 1924. Are you interested in racing?'

'Alas, no.'

'Runs away with a lot of money,' said Jeremy dryly. 'Lord Edward came a crash over it—had to go and live abroad. Yes, an expensive sport.'

But there was still the note of pride in his voice.

He himself, Poirot judged, would as soon throw his money in the street as invest it in horseflesh, but he had a secret admiration and respect for those who did.

Cloade went on:

'What can I do for you, M. Poirot? As a family, I feel we owe you a debt of gratitude—for finding Major Porter to give evidence of identification.'

'The family seems very jubilant about it,' said Poirot.

'Ah,' said Jeremy dryly. 'Rather premature to rejoice. Lot of water's got to pass under the bridge yet. After all, Underhay's death was accepted in Africa. Takes years to upset a thing of this kind—and Rosaleen's evidence was very positive—very positive indeed. She made a good impression you know.'

It seemed almost as though Jeremy Cloade was unwilling to bank upon any improvement in his prospects.

'I wouldn't like to give a ruling one way or the other,' he said. 'Couldn't say how a case would go.'

Then, pushing aside some papers with a fretful, almost weary gesture, he said:

'But you wanted to see me?'

'I was going to ask you, Mr. Cloade, if you are really quite certain your brother did not leave a will? A will made subsequent to his marriage, I mean?'

Jeremy looked surprised.

'I don't think there's ever been any idea of such a thing. He certainly didn't make one before leaving New York.'

'He might have made one during the two days he was in London.'

'Gone to a lawyer there?'

'Or written one out himself.'

'And got it witnessed? Witnessed by whom?'

'There were three servants in the house,' Poirot reminded him. 'Three servants who died the same night he did.'

'H'm—yes—but if by any chance he *did* do what you suggest, well, the will was destroyed too.'

'That is just the point. Lately a great many documents believed to have perished completely have actually been deciphered by a new process. Incinerated inside home safes, for instance, but not so destroyed that they cannot be read.'

'Well, really, M. Poirot, that is a most remarkable idea of yours . . . Most remarkable. But I don't think—no, I really don't believe there is anything in it . . . So far as I know there was no safe in the house in Sheffield Terrace. Gordon kept all valuable papers, etc., at his office—and there was certainly no will there.'

'But one might make inquiries?' Poirot was persistent. 'From the A.R.P. officials, for instance? You would authorise me to do that?'

'Oh, certainly—certainly. Very kind of you to offer to undertake such a thing. But I haven't any belief whatever, I'm afraid, in your success. Still—well, it is an offchance, I suppose. You—you'll be going back to London at once, then?'

Poirot's eyes narrowed. Jeremy's tone had been unmistakably

eager. Going back to London . . . Did they *all* want him out of the way? Before he could answer, the door opened and Frances Cloade came in.

Poirot was struck by two things. First, by the fact that she looked shockingly ill. Secondly, by her very strong resemblance to the photograph of her father.

'M. Hercule Poirot has come to see us, my dear,' said Jeremy rather unnecessarily.

She shook hands with him and Jeremy Cloade immediately outlined to her Poirot's suggestion about a will.

Frances looked doubtful.

'It seems a very outside chance.'

'M. Poirot is going up to London and will very kindly make inquiries.'

'Major Porter, I understand, was an Air Raid Warden in that district,' said Poirot.

A curious expression passed over Mrs. Cloade's face. She said:

'Who is Major Porter?'

Poirot shrugged his shoulders.

'A retired Army Officer, living on his pension.'

'He really *was* in Africa?'

Poirot looked at her curiously.

'Certainly, Madame. Why not?'

She said almost absently, 'I don't know. He puzzled me.'

'Yes, Mrs. Cloade,' said Poirot. 'I can understand that.'

She looked sharply at him. An expression almost of fear came into her eyes.

Turning to her husband she said:

'Jeremy, I feel very much distressed about Rosaleen. She is all alone at Furrowbank and she must be frightfully upset over David's arrest. Would you object if I asked her to come here and stay?'

'Do you really think that is advisable, my dear?' Jeremy sounded doubtful.

'Oh—advisable? I don't know! But one is human. She is such a helpless creature.'

'I rather doubt if she will accept.'

'I can at any rate make the offer.'

The lawyer said quietly: 'Do so if it will make you feel happier.'

'Happier!'

The word came out with a strange bitterness. Then she gave a quick doubtful glance at Poirot.

Poirot murmured formally:

'I will take my leave now.'

She followed him out into the hall.

'You are going up to London?'

'I shall go up to-morrow, but for twenty-four hours at most. And then I return to the Stag—where you will find me, Madame, if you want me.'

She demanded sharply:

'Why should I want you?'

Poirot did not reply to the question, merely said:

'I shall be at the Stag.'

Later that night out of the darkness Frances Cloade spoke to her husband.

'I don't believe that man is going to London for the reason he said. I don't believe all that about Gordon's having made a will. Do you believe it, Jeremy?'

A hopeless, rather tired voice answered her:

'No, Frances. No—he's going for some other reason.'

'What reason?'

'I've no idea.'

Frances said, 'What are we going to do, Jeremy? What are we going to *do*?'

Presently he answered:

'I think, Frances, there's only one thing to be done——'

CHAPTER IX

ARMED WITH the necessary credentials from Jeremy Cloade, Poirot had got the answers to his questions. They were very definite. The house was a total wreck. The site had been cleared only quite recently in preparation for rebuilding. There had been no survivors except for David Hunter and Mrs. Cloade. There had been three servants in the house: Frederick Game, Elizabeth Game and Eileen Corrigan. All three had been killed instantly. Gordon Cloade had been brought out alive, but had died on the way to hospital without recovering consciousness. Poirot took the names and addresses of the three servants' next-of-kin. 'It is possible,' he said, 'that they may have spoken to their friends something in the way of gossip or comment that might give me a pointer to some information I badly need.'

The official to whom he was speaking looked sceptical. The Games had come from Dorset, Eileen Corrigan from County Cork.

Poirot next bent his steps towards Major Porter's rooms. He remembered Porter's statement that he himself was a Warden and he wondered whether he had happened to be on duty on that particular night and whether he had seen anything of the incident in Sheffield Terrace.

He had, besides, other reasons for wanting a word with Major Porter.

As he turned the corner of Edge Street he was startled to see a policeman in uniform standing outside the particular house for which he was making. There was a ring of small boys and other people standing staring at the house. Poirot's heart sank as he interpreted the signs.

The constable intercepted Poirot's advance.

'Can't go in here, sir,' he said.

'What has happened?'

'You don't live in the house, do you, sir?' Poirot shook his head. 'Who was it you were wishing to see?'

'I wished to see a Major Porter.'

'You a friend of his, sir?'

'No, I should not describe myself as a friend. What has happened?'

'Gentleman has shot himself, I understand. Ah, here's the Inspector.'

The door had opened and two figures came out. One was the local Inspector, the other Poirot recognised as Sergeant Graves from Warmsley Vale. The latter recognised him and promptly made himself known to the Inspector.

'Better come inside,' said the latter.

The three men re-entered the house.

'They telephoned through to Warmsley Vale,' Graves explained. 'And Superintendent Spence sent me up.'

'Suicide?'

The Inspector answered:

'Yes. Seems a clear case. Don't know whether having to give evidence at the inquest preyed upon his mind. People are funny that way sometimes, but I gather he's been depressed lately. Financial difficulties and one thing and another. Shot himself with his own revolver.'

Poirot asked: 'Is it permitted that I go up?'

'If you like, M. Poirot. Take M. Poirot up, Sergeant.'

'Yes, sir.'

Graves led the way up to the first-floor room. It was much as Poirot remembered it: the dim colours of the old rugs, the books. Major Porter was in the big arm-chair. His attitude was almost natural, just the head slumped forward. His right arm hung down at his side—below it, on the rug, lay the revolver. There was still a very faint smell of acrid gunpowder in the air.

'About a couple of hours ago, they think,' said Graves.' 'Nobody heard the shot. The woman of the house was out shopping.'

Poirot was frowning, looking down on the quiet figure with the small scorched wound in the right temple.

'Any idea why he should do it, M. Poirot?' asked Graves.

He was respectful to Poirot because he had seen the Superintendent being respectful—though his private opinion was that Poirot was one of these frightful old dug-outs.

Poirot replied absently: 'Yes—yes, there was a very good reason. That is not the difficulty.'

His glance shifted to a small table at Major Porter's left hand. There was a big solid glass ashtray on it, with a pipe and a box of matches. Nothing there. His eye roamed round the room. Then he crossed to an open roll-top desk.

It was very tidy. Papers neatly pigeon-holed. A small leather blotter in the centre, a pen-tray with a pen and two pencils, a box of paper-clips and a book of stamps. All very neat and orderly. An ordinary life and an orderly death—of course—that was it—that was what was missing!

He said to Graves:

'Didn't he leave any note—any letter for the coroner?'

Graves shook his head.

'No, he didn't—sort of thing one would have expected an ex-Army man to do.'

'Yes, that is very curious.'

Punctilious in life, Major Porter had not been punctilious in death. It was all wrong, Poirot thought, that Porter had left no note.

'Bit of a blow for the Cloades this,' said Graves. 'It will set them back.

They'll have to hunt about for someone else who knew Underhay intimately.'

He fidgeted slightly. 'Anything more you want to see, M. Poirot?'

Poirot shook his head and followed Graves from the room.

On the stairs they met the landlady. She was clearly enjoying her own state of agitation and started a voluble discourse at once. Graves adroitly detached himself and left Poirot to receive the full spate.

'Can't seem to catch my breath properly. 'Eart, that's what it is. Angina Pectoria, my mother died of—fell down dead as she was crossing the Caledonian Market. Nearly dropped down myself when I found him—oh, it did give me a turn! Never suspected anything of the kind, though 'e 'ad been low in 'is spirits for a long time. Worried over money, I think, and didn't eat enough to keep himself alive. Not that he'd ever accept a bite from us. And then yesterday he 'ad to go down to a place in Oastshire—Warmsley Vale—to give evidence in an inquest. Preyed on his mind, that did. He come back looking *awful.* Tramped about all last night. Up and down—up and down. A murdered gentleman it was and a friend of his, by all accounts. Poor dear, it did upset him. Up and down—up and down. And when I was out doing my bit of shopping—and 'aving to queue ever so long for the fish, I went up to see if he'd like a nice cuppa tea—and there he was, poor gentleman, the revolver dropped out of his hand, leaning back in his chair. Gave me an awful turn it did. 'Ad to 'ave the police in and everything. What's the world coming to, that's what I say?'

Poirot said slowly:

'The world is becoming a difficult place to live in—except for the strong.'

CHAPTER X

IT WAS PAST EIGHT O'CLOCK when Poirot got back to the Stag. He found a note from Frances Cloade asking him to come and see her. He went out at once.

She was waiting for him in the drawing-room. He had not seen that room before. The open windows gave on a walled garden with pear trees in bloom. There were bowls of tulips on the tables. The old furniture shone with beeswax and elbow-grease and the brass of the fender and coal-scuttle were brightly gleaming.

It was, Poirot thought, a very beautiful room.

'You said I should want you, M. Poirot. You were quite right. There is something that must be told—and I think you are the best person to tell it to.'

'It is always easier, Madame, to tell a thing to someone who already has a very good idea of what it is.'

'You think you know what I am going to say?'

Poirot nodded.

'Since when——'

She left the question unfinished, but he replied promptly:

'Since the moment when I saw the photograph of your father. The features of your family are very strongly marked. One could not doubt that you and he were of the same family. The resemblance was equally strong in the man who came here calling himself Enoch Arden.'

She sighed—a deep unhappy sigh.

'Yes—yes, you're right—although poor Charles had a beard. He was my second cousin, M. Poirot, somewhat the black sheep of the family. I never knew him very well, but we played together as children—and now I've brought him to his death—an ugly sordid death——'

She was silent for a moment or two. Poirot said gently:

'You will tell me——'

She roused herself.

'Yes, the story has got to be told. We were desperate for money—that's where it begins. My husband—my husband was in serious trouble—the worst kind of trouble. Disgrace, perhaps imprisonment lay ahead of him—still lies ahead of him for that matter. Now understand this, M. Poirot, the plan I made and carried out was *my* plan; my husband had nothing to do with it. It wasn't his sort of plan in any case—it would have been far too risky. But I've never minded taking risks. And I've always been, I suppose, rather unscrupulous. First of all, let me say, I applied to Rosaleen Cloade for a loan. I don't know whether, left to herself, she would have given it to me or not. But her brother stepped in. He was in an ugly mood and he was, or so I thought, unnecessarily insulting. When I thought of this scheme I had no scruples at all about putting it into operation.

'To explain matters, I must tell you that my husband had repeated to me last year a rather interesting piece of information which he had heard at his club. You were there, I believe, so I needn't repeat it in detail. But it opened up the possibility that Rosaleen's first husband might not be dead—and of course in that case she would have no right at all to any of Gordon's money. It was, of course, only a vague possibility, but it was there at the back of our minds, a sort of outside chance that might possibly come true. And it flashed into my mind that something could be done by *using* that possibility. Charles, my cousin, was in this country, down on his luck. He's been in prison, I'm afraid, and he wasn't a scrupulous person, but he did well in the war. I put the proposition before him. It was, of course, blackmail, neither more nor less. But we thought that we had a good chance of getting away with it. At worst, I thought, David Hunter would refuse to play. I didn't think that he would go to the police about it—people like him aren't fond of the police.'

Her voice hardened.

'Our scheme went well. David fell for it better than we hoped. Charles, of course, could not definitely pose as "Robert Underhay." Rosaleen could give that away in a moment. But fortunately she went up to London and that left Charles a chance of at least suggesting that he might be Robert Underhay. Well, as I say, David appeared to be falling for the scheme. He was to bring the money on Tuesday evening at nine o'clock. Instead——'

Her voice faltered.

'We should have known that David was—a dangerous person. Charles is dead—murdered—and but for me he would be alive. I sent him to his death.'

After a little she went on in a dry voice:

'You can imagine what I have felt like ever since.'

'Nevertheless,' said Poirot, 'you were quick enough to see a further development of the scheme? It was you who induced Major Porter to identify your cousin as "Robert Underhay"?'

But at once she broke out vehemently:

'No, I swear to you, no. Not that! No one was more astonished . . . Astonished? We were dumbfounded! when this Major Porter came down and gave evidence that Charles—*Charles!*—was Robert Underhay. I couldn't understand it—I *still* can't understand it!'

'But *someone* went to Major Porter. Someone persuaded him or bribed him—to identify the dead man as Underhay?'

Frances said decisively:

'It was not I. And it was not Jeremy. Neither of us would do such a thing. Oh, I dare say that sounds absurd to you! You think that because I was ready to blackmail, that I would stoop just as easily to fraud. But in my mind the two things are worlds apart. You must understand that I felt—indeed I still feel—that we have a *right* to a portion of Gordon's money. What I had failed to get by fair means I was prepared to get by foul. But deliberately to swindle Rosaleen out of everything, by manufacturing evidence that she was not Gordon's wife at all—oh, no, indeed, M. Poirot, I would not do a thing like that. Please, *please*, believe me.'

'I will at least admit,' said Poirot slowly, 'that every one has their own particular sins. Yes, I will believe that.'

Then he looked at her sharply.

'Do you know, Mrs. Cloade, that Major Porter shot himself this afternoon?'

She shrank back, her eyes wide and horrified.

'Oh, no, M. Poirot—*no*!'

'Yes, Madame. Major Porter, you see, was *au fond*, an honest man. Financially he was in very low water, and when temptation came he, like many other men, failed to resist it. It may have seemed to him, he can have made himself feel, that his life was almost morally justified. He was already deeply prejudiced in his mind against the woman his friend Underhay had married. He considered that she had treated his friend disgracefully. And now this heartless little gold-digger had married a millionaire and had got away with her second husband's fortune to the detriment of his own flesh and blood. It must have seemed tempting to him to put a spoke in her wheel—no more than she deserved. And merely by identifying a dead man he himself would be made secure for the future. When the Cloades got their rights, he would get his cut . . . Yes—I can see the temptation . . . But like many men of his type he lacked imagination. He was unhappy, very unhappy, at the inquest. One could see that. In the near future he would have to repeat his lie upon oath. Not only that; a man was now arrested, charged with murder—and the identity of the dead man supplied a very potent motive for that charge.

'He went back home and faced things squarely. He took the way out that seemed best to him.'

'He shot himself?'

'Yes.'

Frances murmured: 'He didn't say who—who——'

Slowly Poirot shook his head.

'He had his code. There was no reference whatever as to who had instigated him to commit perjury.'

He watched her closely. Was there an instant flash of relief, of relaxed tension? Yes, but that might be natural enough in any case . . .

She got up and walked to the window. She said:

'So we are back where we were.'

Poirot wondered what was passing in her mind.

CHAPTER XI

SUPERINTENDENT SPENCE, the following morning, used almost Frances' words:

'So we're back where we started,' he said with a sigh. 'We've got to find out who this fellow Enoch Arden really was.'

'I can tell you that, Superintendent,' said Poirot. 'His name was Charles Trenton.'

'Charles Trenton!' The Superintendent whistled. 'H'm! One of the Trentons—I suppose *she* put him up to it—Mrs. Jeremy, I mean . . . However, we shan't be able to prove her connection with it. *Charles* Trenton? I seem to remember——'

Poirot nodded.

'Yes. He has a record.'

'Thought so. Swindling hotels if I remember rightly. Used to arrive at the Ritz, go out and buy a Rolls, subject to a morning's trial, go round in the Rolls to all the most expensive shops and buy stuff—and I can tell you a man who's got his Rolls outside waiting to take his purchases back to the Ritz doesn't get his cheques queried! Besides, he had the manner and the breeding. He'd stay a week or so and then, just when suspicions began to arise, he'd quietly disappear, selling the various items cheap to the pals he'd picked up. Charles Trenton. H'm——' He looked at Poirot. 'You find out things, don't you?'

'How does your case progress against David Hunter?'

'We shall have to let him go. There *was* a woman there that night with Arden. It doesn't only depend on that old tartar's word. Jimmy Pierce was going home, got pushed out of the Load of Hay—he gets quarrelsome after a glass or two. He saw a woman come out of the Stag and go into the telephone box outside the post office—that was just after ten. Said it wasn't any one he knew, thought it was someone staying at the Stag. "A tart from London," is what *he* called her.'

'He was not very near her?'

'No, right across the street. Who the devil *was* she, M. Poirot?'

'Did he say how she was dressed?'

'Tweed coat, he said, orange scarf round her head. Trousers and a lot of make-up. Fits with the old lady's description.'

'Yes, it fits.' Poirot was frowning.

Spence asked:

'Well, who was she, where did she come from, where did she go? You know our train service. The 9.20's the last train up to London—and the 10.3 the other way. Did that woman hang about all night and go up on the 6.18 in the morning? Had she got a car? Did she hitch-hike? We've sent out all over the place—but no results.'

'What about the 6.18?'

'It's always crowded—mostly men, though. I think they'd have noticed a woman—that type of woman, that's to say. I suppose she might have come and left by car, but a car's noticed in Warmsley Vale nowadays. We're off the main road, you see.'

'No cars noticed out that night?'

'Only Dr. Cloade's. He was out on a case—over Middlingham way. You'd think someone would have noticed a strange woman in a car.'

'It need not have been a stranger,' Poirot said slowly. 'A man slightly drunk and a hundred yards away might not recognise a local person whom he did not know very well. Someone, perhaps, dressed in a different way from their usual way.'

Spence looked at him questioningly.

'Would this young Pierce recognise, for instance, Lynn Marchmont? She has been away for some years.'

'Lynn Marchmont was at the White House with her mother at that time,' said Spence.

'Are you sure?'

'Mrs. Lionel Cloade—that's the scatty one, the doctor's wife—says she telephoned to her there at ten minutes past ten. Rosaleen Cloade was in London. Mrs. Jeremy—well, I've never seen her in slacks and she doesn't use much make-up. Anyway, she isn't young.'

'Oh, *mon cher*,' Poirot leaned forward. 'On a dim night, with feeble street lights, can one tell youth or age under a mask of make-up?'

'Look here, Poirot,' said Spence, 'what are you getting at?'

Poirot leaned back and half-closed his eyes.

'Slacks, a tweed coat, an orange scarf enveloping the head, a great deal of make-up, a dropped lipstick. It is suggestive.'

'Think you're the oracle at Delphi,' growled the Superintendent. 'Not that I know what the oracle at Delphi was—sort of thing young Graves gives himself airs about knowing—doesn't help his police work any. Any more cryptic pronouncements, M. Poirot?'

'I told you,' said Poirot, 'that this case was the wrong shape. As an instance I said to you that the dead man was all wrong. So he was, as Underhay. Underhay was clearly an eccentric, chivalrous individual, old-fashioned and reactionary. The man at the Stag was a blackmailer; he was neither chivalrous, old-fashioned, nor reactionary, nor was he particularly eccentric—therefore he was not Underhay. He could not be Underhay, for *people do not change*. The interesting thing was that Porter said he was Underhay.'

'Leading you to Mrs. Jeremy?'

'The likeness led me to Mrs. Jeremy. A very distinctive cast of countenance, the Trenton profile. To permit myself a little play on words, as Charles Trenton the dead man *is* the right shape. But there are still questions to which we require answers. Why did David Hunter permit himself to be blackmailed so readily? Is he the kind of man who lets himself be blackmailed? One would say very decidedly, no. So he too acts out of character. Then there is Rosaleen Cloade. Her whole behaviour is incomprehensible—but there is one thing I should like to know very much. Why is she afraid? Why does she think that something will happen to her now that her brother is no longer there to protect her? Someone—or something has given her that fear. And it is not that she fears losing her fortune—no, it is more than that. It is for her *life* that she is afraid . . .'

'Good Lord, M. Poirot, you don't think——'

'Let us remember, Spence, that as you said just now, we are back where we started. That is to say, the Cloade family are back where they started. Robert Underhay died in Africa. And Rosaleen Cloade's life stands between them and the enjoyment of Gordon Cloade's money——'

'Do you honestly think that one of them would do that?'

'I think this. Rosaleen Cloade is twenty-six, and though mentally somewhat unstable, physically she is strong and healthy. She may live to be seventy, she may live longer still. Forty-four years, let us say. Don't you think, Superintendent, that forty-four years may be too long for someone to contemplate?'

CHAPTER XII

WHEN POIROT left the police station he was almost at once accosted by Aunt Kathie. She had several shopping-bags with her and came up to him with a breathless eagerness of manner.

'So terrible about poor Major Porter,' she said. 'I can't help feeling that his outlook on life must have been very materialistic. Army life, you know. Very narrowing, and though he had spent a good deal of his life in India, I'm afraid he never took advantage of the spiritual opportunities. It would be all *pukka* and *chota hazri* and *tiffin* and pig-sticking—the narrow Army round. To think that he might have sat as a *chela* at the feet of some *guru*! Ah, the missed opportunities, M. Poirot, how sad they are!'

Aunt Kathie shook her head and relaxed her grip on one of the shopping-bags. A depressed-looking bit of cod slipped out and slithered into the gutter. Poirot retrieved it and in her agitation Aunt Kathie let a second bag slip, whereupon a tin of golden syrup began a gay career rolling along the High Street.

'Thank you so much, M. Poirot.' Aunt Kathie grasped the cod. He ran after the golden syrup. 'Oh, thank you—so clumsy of me—but really I have been so upset. That unfortunate man—yes, it *is* sticky, but really I don't like to use your clean handkerchief. Well, it's very kind of you—as I was saying, in life we are in death—and in death we are in life—I should never be surprised to see the astral body of any of my dear friends who have passed over. One might, you know, just pass them in the street. Why—only the other night I——'

'You permit?' Poirot rammed the cod firmly into the depths of the bag. 'You were saying—yes?'

'Astral bodies,' said Aunt Kathie. 'I asked, you know, for twopence —because I only had halfpennies. But I thought at the time the face was familiar—only I couldn't *place* it. I still can't—but I think now it must be someone who has Passed Over—perhaps some time ago— so that my remembrance was very uncertain. It is wonderful the way people are *sent* to one in one's need—even if it's only a matter of pennies for telephones. Oh, dear, quite a queue at Peacocks—they must have got either trifle or Swiss roll! I hope I'm not too late!'

Mrs. Lionel Cloade plunged across the road and joined herself to the tail end of a queue of grim-faced women outside the confectioner's shop.

Poirot went on down the High Street. He did not turn in at the Stag. Instead he bent his steps towards the White House.

He wanted very much to have a talk with Lynn Marchmont, and he suspected that Lynn Marchmont would not be averse to having a talk with him.

It was a lovely morning—one of those summer mornings in spring that have a freshness denied to a real summer's day.

Poirot turned off from the main road. He saw the footpath leading up past Long Willows to the hillside above Furrowbank. Charles Trenton had come that way from the station on the Friday before his death. On his way down the hill, he had met Rosaleen Cloade coming up. He had not recognised her, which was not surprising since he was not Robert Underhay, and she, naturally, had not recognised him for the same reason. But she had sworn when shown the body that she had never seen that man before. Did she say that for safety's sake? Or had she been, that day, so lost in thought, that she had not even glanced at the face of the man she had passed on the footpath? If so, what had she been thinking about? Had she, by any chance, been thinking of Rowley Cloade?

Poirot turned along the small side road which led to the White House. The garden of the White House was looking very lovely. It held many flowering shrubs, lilacs and laburnums, and in the centre of the lawn was a big old gnarled apple tree. Under it, stretched out in a deck-chair, was Lynn Marchmont.

She jumped nervously when Poirot, in a formal voice, wished her 'Good morning!'

'You did startle me, M. Poirot. I didn't hear you coming across the grass. So you are still here—in Warmsley Vale?'

'I am still here—yes.'

'Why?'

Poirot shrugged his shoulders.

'It is a pleasant out-of-the-world spot where one can relax. I relax.'

'I'm glad you are here,' said Lynn.

'You do not say to me like the rest of your family, "When do you go back to London, M. Poirot?" and wait anxiously for the answer.'

'Do they want you to go back to London?'

'It would seem so.'

'I don't.'

'No—I realise that. Why, Mademoiselle?'

'Because it means that you're not satisfied. Not satisfied, I mean, that David Hunter did it.'

'And you want him so much—to be innocent?'

He saw a faint flush creep up under her bronzed skin.

'Naturally, I don't want to see a man hanged for what he didn't do.'

'Naturally—oh, yes!'

'And the police are simply prejudiced against him because he's got their backs up. That's the worst of David—he likes antagonising people.'

'The police are not so prejudiced as you think, Miss Marchmont. The prejudice against him was in the minds of the jury. They refused to follow the coroner's guidance. They gave a verdict against him and so the police had to arrest him. But I may tell you that they are very far from satisfied with the case against him.'

She said eagerly:

'Then they may let him go?'

Poirot shrugged his shoulders.

'Who do they think did do it, M. Poirot?'

Poirot said slowly: 'There was a woman at the Stag that night.'

Lynn cried:

'I don't understand *anything*. When we thought the man was Robert Underhay it all seemed so simple. Why did Major Porter say it was Underhay if it wasn't? Why did he shoot himself? We're back now where we started.'

'You are the third person to use that phrase!'

'Am I?' She looked startled. 'What are *you* doing, M. Poirot?'

'Talking to people. That is what I do. Just talk to people.'

'But you don't ask them things about the murder?'

Poirot shook his head.

'No, I just—what shall we say—pick up gossip.'

'Does that help?'

'Sometimes it does. You would be surprised how much I know of the everyday life of Warmsley Vale in the last few weeks. I know who walked where, and who they met, and sometimes what they said. For instance, I know that the man Arden took the footpath to the village passing by Furrowbank and asking the way of Mr. Rowley Cloade, and that he had a pack on his back and no luggage. I know that Rosaleen Cloade had spent over an hour at the farm with Rowley Cloade and that she had been happy there, unlike her usual self.'

'Yes,' said Lynn, 'Rowley told me that. He said she was like someone having an afternoon out.'

'Aha, he said that?' Poirot paused and went on, 'Yes, I know a lot of the comings and goings. And I have heard a lot about people's difficulties—yours and your mother's, for example.'

'There's no secret about any of us,' said Lynn. 'We've all tried to cadge money off Rosaleen. That's what you mean, isn't it?'

'I did not say so.'

'Well, it's true! And I suppose you've heard things about me and Rowley and David.'

'But you are going to marry Rowley Cloade?'

'Am I? I wish I knew . . . That's what I was trying to decide that day—when David burst out of the wood. It was like a great question mark in my brain. Shall I? Shall I? Even the train in the valley seemed to be asking the same thing. The smoke made a fine question mark in the sky.'

Poirot's face took on a curious expression. Lynn misunderstood it. She cried out:

'Oh, don't you see, M. Poirot, it's all so difficult. It isn't a question of David at all. It's *me*! I've changed. I've been away for three—four years. Now I've come back I'm not the same person who went away. That's the tragedy everywhere. People coming home changed, having to readjust themselves. You can't go away and lead a different kind of life and *not* change!'

'You are wrong,' said Poirot. 'The tragedy of life is that *people do not change*.'

She stared at him, shaking her head. He insisted:

'But yes. It is so. Why did you go away in the first place?'

'Why? I went into the Wrens. I went on service.'

'Yes, yes, but why did you join the Wrens in the first place? You were engaged to be married. You were in love with Rowley Cloade. You could have worked, could you not, as a land girl, here in Warmsley Vale?'

'I could have, I suppose, but I wanted——'

'*You wanted to get away*. You wanted to go abroad, to see life. You wanted, perhaps, *to get away from Rowley Cloade* . . . And now you are restless, you still want—to get away! Oh, no, Mademoiselle, people do not change!'

'When I was out East, I longed for home,' Lynn cried defensively.

'Yes, yes, where you are not, there you will want to be! That will always be so, perhaps, with you. You make a picture to yourself, you see, a picture of Lynn Marchmont coming home . . . But the picture does not come true, because the Lynn Marchmont whom you imagine is not the real Lynn Marchmont. She is the Lynn Marchmont you would like to be.'

Lynn asked bitterly:

'So, according to you, I shall never be satisfied anywhere?'

'I do not say that. But I do say that, when you went away, you were dissatisfied with your engagement, and that now you have come back, you are still dissatisfied with your engagement.'

Lynn broke off a leaf and chewed it meditatively.

'You're rather a devil at knowing things, aren't you, M. Poirot?'

'It is my *métier*,' said Poirot modestly. 'There is a further truth, I think, that you have not yet recognised.'

Lynn said sharply:

'You mean David, don't you? You think I am in love with David?'

'That is for you to say,' murmured Poirot discreetly.

'And I—don't know! There's something in David that I'm afraid of—but there's something that draws me, too. . .' She was silent a moment and then went on: 'I was talking yesterday to his Brigadier. He came down here when he heard David was arrested to see what he could do. He's been telling me about David, how incredibly daring he was. He said David was one of the bravest people he'd ever had under him. And yet, you know, M. Poirot, in spite of all he said and his praise, I had the feeling that he wasn't sure, not absolutely sure that David hadn't done this!'

'And are you not sure, either?'

Lynn gave a crooked, rather pathetic smile.

'No—you see, I've never trusted David. *Can* you love someone you don't trust?'

'Unfortunately, yes.'

'I've always been unfair to David—because I didn't trust him. I've believed quite a lot of the beastly local gossip—hints that David wasn't David Hunter at all—but just a boy friend of Rosaleen's. I was ashamed when I met the Brigadier and he talked to me about having known David as a boy in Ireland.'

'*C'est épatant*,' murmured Poirot, 'how people can get hold of the wrong end of a stick!'

'What do you mean?'

'Just what I say. Tell me, did Mrs. Cloade—the doctor's wife, I mean—did she ring up on the night of the murder?'

'Aunt Kathie? Yes, she did.'

'What about?'

'Some incredible muddle she had got into over some accounts.'

'Did she speak from her own house?'

'Why no, actually her telephone was out of order. She had to go out to a call-box.'

'At ten minutes past ten?'

'Thereabouts. Our clocks never keep particularly good time.'

'Thereabouts,' said Poirot thoughtfully. He went on delicately:

'That was not the only telephone call you had that evening?'

'No.' Lynn spoke shortly.

'David Hunter rang you up from London?'

'Yes.' She flared out suddenly, 'I suppose you want to know what *he* said?'

'Oh, indeed I should not presume——'

'You're welcome to know! He said he was going away—clearing out of my life. He said he was no good to me and that he never would run straight—not even for my sake.'

'And since that was probably true you did not like it,' said Poirot.

'I hope he will go away—that is, if he gets acquitted all right . . . I hope they'll both go away to America or somewhere. Then, perhaps, we shall be able to stop thinking about them—we'll learn to stand on our own feet. We'll stop feeling ill will.'

'Ill will?'

'Yes. I felt it first one night at Aunt Kathie's. She gave a sort of party. Perhaps it was because I was just back from abroad and rather on edge—but I seemed to feel it in the air eddying all round us. Ill will to her—to Rosaleen. Don't you see, *we were wishing her dead*—all of us! Wishing her dead . . . And that's awful, to wish that someone who's never done you any harm—may die——'

'Her death, of course, is the only thing that can do you any practical good.' Poirot spoke in a brisk and practical tone.

'You mean do us good financially? Her mere being here has done us harm in all the ways that matter! Envying a person, resenting them, cadging off them—it isn't *good* for one. Now, there she is, at Furrowbank, all alone. She looks like a ghost—she looks scared to death—she looks—oh! she looks as though she's going off her head. And she won't let us help! Not one of us. We've all tried. Mums asked her to come and stay with us, Aunt Frances asked her there. Even Aunt Kathie went along and offered to be with her at Furrowbank. But she won't have anything to do with us now and I don't blame her. She wouldn't even see Brigadier Conroy. I think she's ill, ill with worry and fright and misery. And we're doing nothing about it because she won't let us.'

'Have *you* tried? You, yourself?'

'Yes,' said Lynn. 'I went up there yesterday. I said, was there anything I could do? She looked at me——'

Suddenly she broke off and shivered. 'I think she hates me. She said, "*You, least of all.*" David told her, I think, to stop on at Furrowbank, and she always does what David tells her. Rowley took her up eggs and butter from Long Willows. I think he's the only one of us she likes. She thanked him and said he'd always been kind. Rowley, of course, *is* kind.'

'There are people,' said Poirot, 'for whom one has great sympathy—great pity, people who have too heavy a burden to bear. For Rosaleen Cloade I have great pity. If I could, I would help her. Even now, if she would listen——'

With sudden resolution he got to his feet.

'Come, Mademoiselle,' he said, 'let us go up to Furrowbank.'

'You want me to come with you?'

'If you are prepared to be generous and understanding——'

Lynn cried:

'I am—indeed I am——'

CHAPTER XIII

IT TOOK THEM only about five minutes to reach Furrowbank. The drive wound up an incline through carefully massed banks of rhododendrons. No trouble or expense had been spared by Gordon Cloade to make Furrowbank a show-place.

The parlourmaid who answered the front door looked surprised to see them and a little doubtful as to whether they could see Mrs. Cloade. Madam, she said, wasn't up yet. However, she ushered them into the drawing-room and went upstairs with Poirot's message.

Poirot looked round him. He was contrasting this room with Frances Cloade's drawing-room—the latter such an intimate room, so characteristic of its mistress. The drawing-room at Furrowbank was strictly impersonal—speaking only of wealth tempered by good taste. Gordon Cloade had seen to the latter—everything in the room was of good quality and of artistic merit, but there was no sign of any selectiveness, no clue to the personal tastes of the room's mistress. Rosaleen, it seemed, had not stamped upon the place any individuality of her own.

She had lived in Furrowbank as a foreign visitor might live at the Ritz or at the Savoy.

'I wonder,' thought Poirot, 'if the other——'

Lynn broke the chain of his thought by asking him of what he was thinking, and why he looked so grim.

'The wages of sin, Mademoiselle, are said to be death. But sometimes the wages of sin seem to be luxury. Is that any more endurable, I wonder? To be cut off from one's own home life. To catch, perhaps, a single glimpse of it when the way back to it is barred——'

He broke off. The parlourmaid, her superior manner laid aside, a mere frightened middle-aged woman, came running into the room, stammering and choking with words she could hardly get out.

'Oh, Miss Marchmont! Oh, sir, the mistress—upstairs—she's very bad—she doesn't speak and I can't rouse her and her hand's so cold.'

Sharply, Poirot turned and ran out of the room. Lynn and the maid came behind him. He raced up to the first floor. The parlourmaid indicated the open door facing the head of the stairs.

It was a large beautiful bedroom, the sun pouring in through the open windows on to pale beautiful rugs.

In the big carved bedstead Rosaleen was lying—apparently asleep. Her long dark lashes lay on her cheeks, her head turned naturally into the pillow. There was a crumpled-up handkerchief in one hand. She looked like a sad child who had cried itself to sleep.

Poirot picked up her hand and felt for the pulse. The hand was ice-cold and told him what he already guessed.

He said quietly to Lynn:

'She has been dead some time. She died in her sleep.'

'Oh, sir—oh—what shall we do?' The parlourmaid burst out crying.

'Who was her doctor?'

'Uncle Lionel,' said Lynn.

Poirot said to the parlourmaid: 'Go and telephone to Dr. Cloade.' She went out of the room, still sobbing. Poirot moved here and there about the room. A small white cardboard box beside the bed bore a label, 'One powder to be taken at bedtime.' Using his handkerchief, he pushed the box open. There were three powders left. He moved across to the mantelpiece, then to the writing-table. The chair in front of it was pushed aside, the blotter was open. A sheet of paper was there, with words scrawled in an unformed childish hand.

'I don't know what to do . . . I can't go on . . . I've been so wicked. I must tell someone and get peace . . . I didn't mean to be so wicked to begin with. I didn't know all that was going to come of it. I must write down——'

The words sprawled off in a dash. The pen lay where it had been flung down. Poirot stood looking down at those written words. Lynn still stood by the bed looking down at the dead girl.

Then the door was pushed violently open and David Hunter strode breathlessly into the room.

'David,' Lynn started forward. 'Have they released you? I'm so glad——'

He brushed her words aside, as he brushed her aside, thrusting her almost roughly out of the way as he bent over the still white figure.

'Rosa! Rosaleen . . .' He touched her hand, then he swung round on Lynn, his face blazing with anger. His words came high and deliberate!

'*So you've killed her, have you?* You've got rid of her at last! You got rid of *me*, sent me to gaol on a trumped-up charge, and then, amongst you all, you put *her* out of the way! All of you? Or just one of you? I don't care which it is! You killed her! You wanted the damned money—now you've got it! Her death gives it to you! You'll all be out of Queer Street now. You'll all be rich—a lot of dirty murdering thieves, that's what you are! You weren't able to touch her so long as I was by. I knew how to protect my sister—she was never one to be able to protect herself. But when she was alone here, you saw your chance and you took it.' He paused, swayed slightly, and said in a low quivering voice '*Murderers.*'

Lynn cried out:

'No, David. No, you're wrong. None of us would kill her. We wouldn't do such a thing.'

'One of you killed her, Lynn Marchmont. And you know that as well as I do!'

'I swear we didn't, David. I swear we did nothing of the kind.'

The wildness of his gaze softened a little.

'Maybe it wasn't *you*, Lynn——'

'It wasn't, David, I swear it wasn't——'

Hercule Poirot moved forward a step and coughed. David swung round on him.

'I think,' said Poirot, 'that your assumptions are a little over-dramatic. Why jump to the conclusion that your sister was murdered?'

'You say she wasn't murdered? Do you call *this*'—he indicated the figure on the bed—'a natural death? Rosaleen suffered from nerves, yes, but she had no organic weakness. Her heart was sound enough.'

'Last night,' said Poirot, 'before she went to bed, she sat writing here——'

David strode past him, bent over the sheet of paper.

'Do not touch it,' Poirot warned him.

David drew back his hand, and read the words as he stood motionless.

He turned his head sharply and looked searchingly at Poirot.

'Are you suggesting suicide? Why should Rosaleen commit suicide?'

The voice that answered the question was not Poirot's. Superintendent Spence's quiet Oastshire voice spoke from the open doorway:

'Supposing that last Tuesday night Mrs. Cloade wasn't in London, but in Warmsley Vale? Suppose she went to see the man who had been blackmailing her? Suppose that in a nervous frenzy she killed him?'

David swung round on him. His eyes were hard and angry.

'My sister was in London on Tuesday night. She was there in the flat when I got in at eleven o'clock.'

'Yes,' said Spence, 'that's your story, Mr. Hunter. And I dare say you'll stick to it. But I'm not obliged to believe that story. And in any case, isn't it a little late'—he gestured towards the bed—'the case will never come to court now.'

CHAPTER XIV

'HE WON'T ADMIT IT,' said Spence. 'But I think he knows she did it.' Sitting in his room at the police station he looked across the table at Poirot. 'Funny how it was *his* alibi we were so careful about checking. We never gave much thought to *hers*. And yet there's no corroboration at all for her being in the flat in London that night. We've only got his word that she was there. We knew all along that only two people had a motive for doing away with Arden—David

Hunter and Rosaleen Cloade. I went bald-headed for *him* and passed *her* by. Fact is, she seemed such a gentle thing—even a bit half-witted—but I dare say that partly explains it. Very likely David Hunter hustled her up to London for just that reason. He may have realised that she'd lose her head, and he may have known that she's the kind who gets dangerous when they panic. Another funny thing: I've often seen her going about in an orange linen frock—it was a favourite colour of hers. Orange scarves—a striped orange frock, an orange beret. And yet, even when old Mrs. Leadbetter described a young woman with her head tied up in an orange scarf I still didn't tumble to it that it must have been Mrs. Gordon herself. I still think the girl wasn't quite all there—wasn't wholly responsible. The way you describe her as haunting the R.C. church here sounds as though she was half off her head with remorse and a sense of guilt.'

'She had a sense of guilt, yes,' said Poirot.

Spence said thoughtfully, 'She must have attacked Arden in a kind of frenzy. I don't suppose he had the least idea of what was coming to him. He wouldn't be on his guard with a slip of a girl like that.' He ruminated for a moment or two in silence, then he remarked, 'There's still one thing I'm not quite clear about. *Who got at Porter?* You say it wasn't Mrs. Jeremy? Bet you it was all the same!'

'No,' said Poirot. 'It was not Mrs. Jeremy. She assured me of that and I believe her. I have been stupid over that. I should have known who it was. Major Porter himself told me.'

'He told you?'

'Oh, indirectly, of course. He did not know that he had done so.'

'Well, who was it?'

Poirot put his head a little on one side.

'Is it permitted, first, that I ask you two questions?'

The Superintendent looked surprised.

'Ask anything you like.'

'Those sleeping-powders in a box by Rosaleen Cloade's bed. What were they?'

The Superintendent looked more surprised.

'Those? Oh, they were quite harmless. Bromide. Soothing to the nerves. She took one every night. We analysed them, of course. They were quite all right.'

'Who prescribed them?'

'Dr. Cloade.'

'When did he prescribe them?'

'Oh, some time ago.'

'What poison was it that killed her?'

'Well, we haven't actually got the report yet, but I don't think there's much doubt about it. Morphia and a pretty hefty dose of it.'

'Was any morphia found in her possession?'

Spence looked curiously at the other man.

'No. What are you getting at, M. Poirot?'

'I will pass now to my second question,' said Poirot evasively. 'David Hunter put through a call from London to Lynn Marchmont at 11.5 on that Tuesday night. You say you checked up on calls. That was the only outgoing call from the flat in Shepherd's Court. Were there any incoming calls?'

'One. At 10.15. Also from Warmsley Vale. It was put through from a public call box.'

'I see.' Poirot was silent for a moment or two.

'What's the big idea, M. Poirot?'

'That call was answered? The operator, I mean, got a response from the London number.'

'I see what you mean,' said Spence slowly. 'There must have been *someone* in the flat. It couldn't be David Hunter—he was in the train on his way back. It looks, then, as if it must have been Rosaleen Cloade. And if so, Rosaleen Cloade couldn't have been at the Stag a few minutes earlier. What you're getting at, M. Poirot, is that the woman in the orange scarf *wasn't* Rosaleen Cloade. And if so, it wasn't Rosaleen Cloade who killed Arden. But then why did she commit suicide?'

'The answer to that,' said Poirot, 'is very simple. She did not commit suicide. Rosaleen Cloade was killed!'

'*What?*'

'She was deliberately and cold-bloodedly murdered.'

'But who killed Arden? We've eliminated David——'

'It was not David.'

'And now you eliminate Rosaleen? But dash it all, those two were the only ones with a shadow of motive!'

'Yes,' said Poirot. '*Motive*. It was that which has led us astray. If A has a motive for killing C and B has a motive for killing D—well, it does not seem to make sense, does it, that A should kill D and B should kill C?'

Spence groaned. 'Go easy, M. Poirot, go easy. I don't even begin to understand what you are talking about with your A's and B's and C's.'

'It is complicated,' said Poirot, 'it is very complicated. Because, you see, you have here *two different kinds of crime*—and consequently you have, you *must* have, two different murderers. Enter First Murderer, and enter Second Murderer.'

'Don't quote Shakespeare,' groaned Spence. 'This isn't Elizabethan drama.'

'But yes, it is very Shakespearian—there are here all the emotions—the human emotions—in which Shakespeare would have revelled—the jealousies, the hates—the swift passionate actions. And here, too, is successful opportunism. "*There is a tide in the affairs of men which taken at its flood leads on to fortune . . .*" Someone acted on that, Superintendent. To seize opportunity and turn it to one's own ends—that has been triumphantly accomplished—under your nose so to speak!'

Spence rubbed his nose irritably.

'Talk sense, M. Poirot,' he pleaded. 'If it's possible, just say what you mean.'

'I will be very clear—clear as the crystal. We have here, have we not, three deaths? You agree to that, do you not? Three people are dead.'

Spence looked at him curiously.

'I should certainly say so . . . You're not going to make me believe that one of the three is still alive?'

'No, no,' said Poirot. 'They are dead. But *how* did they die? How, that is to say, would you classify their deaths?'

'Well, as to that, M. Poirot, you know my views. One murder, and two suicides. But according to you the last suicide isn't a suicide. It's another murder.'

'According to me,' said Poirot, '*there has been one suicide*, one accident and one murder.'

'Accident? Do you mean Mrs. Cloade poisoned herself by accident? Or do you mean Major Porter's shooting himself was an accident?'

'No,' said Poirot. 'The accident was the death of Charles Trenton—otherwise Enoch Arden.'

'Accident!' The Superintendent exploded. '*Accident?* You say that a particularly brutal murder, where a man's head is stove in by repeated blows, is an *accident*!'

Quite unmoved by the Superintendent's vigour, Poirot replied calmly:

'When I say an accident, I mean that there was no intent to kill.'

'No intent to kill—when a man's head is battered in! Do you mean that he was attacked by a lunatic?'

'I think that that is very near the truth—though not quite in the sense you mean it.'

'Mrs. Gordon was the only batty woman in this case. I've seen her looking very queer sometimes. Of course, Mrs. Lionel Cloade is a bit bats in the belfry—but she'd never be violent. Mrs. Jeremy has got her head screwed on the right way if any one has! By the way, you say that it was *not* Mrs. Jeremy who bribed Porter?'

'No. I know who it was. As I say, it was Porter himself who gave it away. One simple little remark—ah, I could kick myself, as you say, all round the town, for not noticing it at the time.'

'And then your anonymous A B C lunatic murdered Rosaleen Cloade?' Spence's voice was more and more sceptical.

Poirot shook his head vigorously.

'By no means. This is where the First Murderer exits and Second Murderer enters. Quite a different type of crime this, no heat, and no passion. Cold deliberate murder and I intend, Superintendent Spence, to see that her murderer is hanged for that murder.'

He got up as he spoke and moved towards the door.

'Hi!' cried Spence. 'You've got to give me a few names. You can't leave it like this.'

'In a very little while—yes, I will tell you. But there is something for which I wait—to be exact, a letter from across the sea.'

'Don't talk like a ruddy fortune-teller! Hi—Poirot.'

But Poirot had slipped away.

He went straight across the square and rang the bell of Dr. Cloade's house. Mrs. Cloade came to the door and gave her usual gasp at seeing Poirot. He wasted no time.

'Madame, I must speak to you.'

'Oh, of course—do come in—I'm afraid I haven't had much time to dust, but——'

'I want to ask you something. How long has your husband been a morphia addict?'

Aunt Kathie immediately burst into tears.

'Oh dear, oh dear—I did so hope nobody would ever know—it began in the war. He was so dreadfully overtired and had such dreadful neuralgia. And since then he's been trying to lessen the dose—he has indeed. But that's what makes him so dreadfully irritable sometimes——'

'That is one of the reasons why he has needed money, is it not?'

'I suppose so. Oh, dear, M. Poirot. He has promised to go for a cure——'

'Calm yourself, Madame, and answer me one more little question. On the night when you telephoned to Lynn Marchmont, you went out to the call-box outside the post office, did you not? Did you meet anybody in the square that night?'

'Oh, no, M. Poirot, not a *soul*.'

'But I understood you had to borrow tuppence because you had only halfpennies.'

'Oh, yes. I had to ask a woman who came out of the box. She gave me two pennies for one halfpenny——'

'What did she look like, this woman?'

'Well, rather actressy, if you know what I mean. An orange scarf round her head. The funny thing was that I'm almost sure I'd met her somewhere. Her face seemed very familiar. She must, I think, have been someone who had passed over. And yet, you know, I couldn't remember where and how I had known her.'

'Thank you, Mrs. Cloade,' said Hercule Poirot.

CHAPTER XV

LYNN came out of the house and glanced up at the sky.

The sun was getting low, there was no red in the sky but a rather unnatural glow of light. A still evening with a breathless feel about it. There would be, she thought, a storm later.

Well, the time had come now. She couldn't put things off any longer. She must go to Long Willows and tell Rowley. She owed him that at least—to tell him herself. Not to choose the easy way of the written word.

Her mind was made up—quite made up—she told herself and yet she felt a curious reluctance. She looked round her and thought: 'It's good-bye to all this—to my own world—my own way of life.'

For she had no illusions. Life with David was a gamble—an adventure that was as likely to turn out badly as to turn out well. He himself had warned her . . .

The night of the murder, over the telephone.

And now, a few hours ago, he had said:

'I meant to go out of your life. I was a fool—to think I could leave you behind me. We'll go to London and be married by special licence—oh, yes, I'm not going to give you the chance of shilly-shallying about. You've got roots here, roots that hold you down. I've got to pull you up by the roots.' He had added: 'We'll break it to Rowley when you're actually Mrs. David Hunter. Poor devil, it's the best way to break it to him.'

But to that she did not agree, though she had not said so at the time. No, she must tell Rowley herself.

It was to Rowley she was going now!

The storm was just starting as Lynn tapped at the door of Long Willows. Rowley opened it and looked astonished to see her.

'Hallo, Lynn, why didn't you ring up and say you were coming? I might have been out.'

'I want to talk to you, Rowley.'

He stood aside to let her pass and followed her into the big kitchen. The remains of his supper were on the table.

'I'm planning to get an Aga or an Esse put in here,' he said. 'Easier for you. And a new sink—steel——'

She interrupted. 'Don't make plans, Rowley.'

'You mean because that poor kid isn't buried yet? I suppose it does seem rather heartless. But she never struck me as a particularly happy person. Sickly, I suppose. Never got over that damned Air Raid. Anyway, there it is. She's dead and in her grave and oh the difference to me—or rather to us——'

Lynn caught her breath.

'No, Rowley. There isn't any "us." That's what I came to tell you.'

He stared at her. She said quietly, hating herself, but steadfast in her purpose:

'*I'm going to marry David Hunter, Rowley.*'

She did not know quite what she expected—protests, perhaps an angry outburst—but she certainly did not expect Rowley to take it as he did.

He stared at her for a minute or two, then he went across and poked at the stove, turning at last in an almost absentminded manner.

'Well,' he said, 'let's get it clear? You're going to marry David Hunter. Why?'

'Because I love him.'

'You love me.'

'No. I did love you—when I went away. But it's been four years and I've—I've changed. We've both changed.'

'You're wrong . . .' he said quietly. 'I haven't changed.'

'Well, perhaps you haven't changed so much.'

'I haven't changed at all. I haven't had much chance to change. I've just gone plodding on here. *I* haven't dropped from parachutes or swarmed up cliffs by night or wound an arm round a man in the darkness and stabbed him——'

'Rowley——'

'*I* haven't been to the war. *I* haven't fought. *I* don't know what war is! I've led a nice safe life here, down on the farm. Lucky Rowley! But as a husband, you'd be ashamed of me!'

'No, Rowley—oh, no! It isn't that at all.'

'But I tell you it is!' He came nearer to her. The blood was welling up in his neck, the veins of his forehead were starting out. That look in his eyes—she had seen it once as she passed a bull in a field. Tossing its head, stamping its foot, slowly lowering its head with the great horns. Goaded to a dull fury, a blind rage . . .

'*Be quiet*, Lynn, *you*'ll listen to *me* for a change. I've missed what I ought to have had. I've missed my chance of fighting for my country. I've seen my best friend go and be killed. I've seen my girl—*my* girl—dress up in uniform and go overseas. I've been Just the Man She Left Behind Her. *My* life's *been hell*—don't you understand, Lynn? It's been Hell. And then you came back—and since then it's been worse Hell. Ever since that night at Aunt Kathie's when I saw you looking at David Hunter across the table. But *he's not going to have you, do you hear?* If you're not for me, then no one shall have you. What do you think I am?'

'Rowley——'

She had risen, was retreating a step at a time. She was terrified. This man was not a man any longer, he was a brute beast.

'*I've killed two people*,' said Rowley Cloade. '*Do you think I shall stick at killing a third?*'

'Rowley——'

He was upon her now, his hands round her throat . . .

'I can't bear any more, Lynn——'

The hands tightened round her neck, the room whirled, blackness, spinning blackness, suffocation—everything going dark . . .

And then, suddenly, a cough. A prim, slightly artificial cough.

Rowley paused, his hands relaxed, fell to his sides. Lynn, released, sank in a crumpled heap on the floor.

Just inside the door, Hercule Poirot stood apologetically coughing.

'I hope,' he said, 'that I do not intrude? I knocked. Yes, indeed, I knocked, but no one answered . . . I suppose you were busy?'

For a moment the air was tense, electric. Rowley stared. It looked for a moment as though he might fling himself on Hercule Poirot, but finally he turned away. He said in a flat empty voice:

'You turned up—just in the nick of time.'

CHAPTER XVI

INTO AN ATMOSPHERE quivering with danger Hercule Poirot brought his own atmosphere of deliberate anti-climax.

'The kettle, is it boiling?' he inquired.

Rowley said heavily—stupidly—'Yes, it's boiling.'

'Then you will, perhaps, make some coffee? Or some tea if it is easier.'

Like an automaton Rowley obeyed.

Hercule Poirot took a large clean handkerchief from his pocket; he soaked it in cold water, wrung it out and came to Lynn.

'There, Mademoiselle, if you fasten that round your throat—so. Yes, I have the safety-pin. There, that will at once ease the pain.'

Croaking hoarsely, Lynn thanked him. The kitchen of Long Willows, Poirot fussing about—it all had for her the quality of a nightmare. She felt horribly ill, and her throat was paining her badly. She staggered to her feet and Poirot guided her gently to a chair and put her into it.

'There,' he said, and over his shoulder:

'The coffee?' he demanded.

'It's ready,' said Rowley.

He brought it. Poirot poured out a cup and took it to Lynn.

'Look here,' said Rowley, 'I don't think you understand. I tried to strangle Lynn.'

'Tscha, tscha,' said Poirot in a vexed voice. He seemed to be deploring a lapse of bad taste on Rowley's part.

'Two deaths I've got on my conscience,' said Rowley. 'Hers would have been the third—if you hadn't arrived.'

'Let us drink up our coffee,' said Poirot, 'and not talk of deaths. It is not agreeable for Mademoiselle Lynn.'

'My God!' said Rowley. He stared at Poirot.

Lynn sipped her coffee with difficulty. It was hot and strong. Presently she felt her throat less painful, and the stimulant began to act.

'There, that is better, yes?' said Poirot.

She nodded.

'Now we can talk,' said Poirot. 'When I say that, I mean, really, that *I* shall talk.'

'How much do you know?' said Rowley heavily. 'Do you know that I killed Charles Trenton?'

'Yes,' said Poirot. 'I have known that for some time.'

The door burst open. It was David Hunter.

'Lynn,' he cried. 'You never told me——'

He stopped, puzzled, his eyes going from one to the other.

'*What's the matter with your throat?*'

'Another cup,' said Poirot. Rowley took one from the dresser. Poirot received it, filled it with coffee and handed it to David. Once more, Poirot dominated the situation.

'Sit down,' he said to David. 'We will sit here and drink coffee, and you shall all three listen to Hercule Poirot while he gives you a lecture on crime.'

He looked round on them and nodded his head.

Lynn thought:

'This is some fantastic nightmare. It isn't *real*!'

They were all, it seemed, under the sway of this absurd little man with the big moustaches. They sat there, obediently—Rowley the killer; she, his victim; David, the man who loved her—all holding cups of coffee, listening to this little man who in some strange way dominated them all.

'What causes crime?' Hercule Poirot demanded rhetorically. 'It is a question, that. What stimulus is needed? What inbred predisposition does there have to be? Is *every one* capable of crime—of *some* crime? And what happens—that is what I have asked myself from the beginning, what happens when people who have been protected from real life—from its assaults and ravages—are suddenly deprived of that protection?'

'I am speaking, you see, of the Cloades. There is only one Cloade here, and so I can speak very freely. From the beginning the problem has fascinated me. Here is a whole family whom circumstances have prevented from ever having to stand on their own feet. Though each one of the family had a life of his or her own, a profession, yet really they have never escaped from the shadow of a beneficent protection. They have had, always, freedom from fear. They have lived in security—and a security which was unnatural and artificial. Gordon Cloade was always there behind them.

'What I say to you is this, there is no telling what a human character is, until the test comes. To most of us the test comes early in life. A man is confronted quite soon with the necessity to stand on his own feet, to face dangers and difficulties and to take his own line of dealing with them. It may be the straight way, it may be the crooked way—whichever it is, a man usually learns early just what he is made of.

'But the Cloades had no opportunity of knowing their own weaknesses until the time when they were suddenly shorn of protection and were forced, quite unprepared, to face difficulty. One thing, and one thing only, stood between them and the resumption of security, the life of Rosaleen Cloade. I am quite certain in my own mind that every single one of the Cloades thought at one time or another, "If Rosaleen was to die——"'

Lynn shivered. Poirot paused, letting the words sink in, then went on:

'The thought of death, *her* death, passed through every mind—of that I am certain. Did the further thought of murder pass through also? And did the thought, in one particular instance, go beyond thinking and become action.'

Without a change of voice he turned to Rowley:

'Did *you* think of killing her?'

'Yes,' said Rowley. 'It was the day she came to the farm. There was no one else there. I thought then—I could kill her quite easily. She looked pathetic—and very pretty—like the calves I'd sent to market. You can see how pathetic they are—but you send them off just the same. I wondered, really, that she wasn't afraid . . . She would have been, if she'd known what was in my mind . . . Yes, it was in my mind when I took the lighter from her to light her cigarette.'

'She left it behind, I suppose. That's how you got hold of it.'

Rowley nodded.

'I don't know why I *didn't* kill her,' he said wonderingly. 'I thought of it. One could have faked it up as an accident, or something.'

'It was not your type of crime,' said Poirot. 'That is the answer. The man you did kill, you killed in a rage—and you did not really *mean* to kill him, I fancy?'

'Good Lord, no. I hit him on the jaw. He went over backwards and hit his head on that marble fender. I couldn't believe it when I found he was dead.'

Then suddenly he shot a startled glance at Poirot:

'How did you know that?'

'I think,' said Poirot, 'that I have reconstructed your actions fairly accurately. You shall tell me if I am wrong. You went to the Stag, did you not, and Beatrice Lippincott told you about the conversation she had overheard? Thereupon you went, as you have said, to your uncle's, Jeremy Cloade, to get his opinion as a solicitor upon the position. Now something happened there, something that made you change your mind about consulting him. I think I know what that something was. *You saw a photograph*——'

Rowley nodded.

'Yes, it was on the desk. I suddenly realised the likeness. I realised too why the fellow's face had seemed so familiar. I tumbled to it that Jeremy and Frances were getting some relation of hers to put up a stunt and get money out of Rosaleen. It made me see red. I went headlong back to the Stag and up to No. 5 and accused the fellow of being a fraud. He laughed and admitted it—said David Hunter was going to come across all right with the money that very evening. I just saw red when I realised that my own family was, as I saw it, double-crossing me. I called him a swine and hit him. He went down as I said.'

There was a pause. Poirot said: 'And then?'

'It was the lighter,' said Rowley slowly. 'It fell out of my pocket. I'd been carrying it about meaning to give it back to Rosaleen when I saw her. It fell down on the body, and I saw the initials, D.H. It was David's, not hers.

'Ever since that party at Aunt Kathie's I'd realised—well, never mind all that. I've sometimes thought I'm going mad—perhaps I *am* a bit mad. First Johnny going—and then the war—I—I can't talk about things but sometimes I'd feel blind with rage—and now Lynn—and this fellow. I dragged the dead man into the middle of the room and turned him over on his face. Then I picked up those heavy steel tongs—well, I won't go into details. I wiped off fingerprints, cleaned up the marble curb—then I deliberately put the hands of the wrist-watch at ten minutes past nine and smashed it. I took away his ration book and his papers—I thought his identity might be traced through them. Then I got out. It seemed to me that with Beatrice's story of what she'd overheard, David would be for it all right.'

'Thanks,' said David.

'And then,' said Poirot, 'you came to *me*. It was a pretty little comedy that you played there, was it not, asking me to produce some witness that knew Underhay? It was already clear to me that Jeremy Cloade had repeated to his family the story that Major Porter had told. For nearly two years all the family had cherished a secret hope that Underhay might turn up. That wish influenced Mrs. Lionel Cloade in her manipulation of the Ouija board—unconsciously, but it was a very revealing incident.

'*Eh bien*, I perform my "conjuring trick." I flatter myself that I impress you and really it is *I* who am the complete mug. Yes and there in Major Porter's room, he says, after he offers me a cigarette, he says to you, "You don't, do you?"

'*How did he know that you did not smoke?* He is supposed only that moment to have met you. Imbecile that I am, I should have seen the truth then—that already you and Major Porter, you had made your little arrangement together! No wonder he was nervous that morning. Yes, *I* am to be the mug, *I* am to bring Major Porter down to identify the body. But I do not go on being the mug for ever—no, I am not the mug now, am I?'

He looked round angrily and then went on:

'But then, Major Porter went back on that arrangement. He does not care to be a witness upon oath in a murder trial, and the strength of the case against David Hunter depends very largely upon the identity of the dead man. So Major Porter backs out.'

'He wrote to me he wouldn't go through with it,' said Rowley thickly. 'The damned fool. Didn't he see we'd gone too far to stop? I came up to try to drive some sense into him. I was too late. He'd said he'd rather shoot himself than perjure himself when it was a question of murder. The front door wasn't locked—I went up and found him.

'I can't tell you what I felt like. It was as though I was a murderer twice over. If only he'd waited—if he'd only let me talk to him.'

'There was a note there?' Poirot asked. 'You took it away?'

'Yes—I was in for things now. Might as well go the whole hog. The note was to the coroner. It simply said that he'd given perjured evidence at the inquest. The dead man was *not* Robert Underhay. I took the note away and destroyed it.'

Rowley struck his fist on the table. 'It was like a bad dream—a horrible nightmare! I'd begun this thing and I'd got to go on with it. I wanted the money to get Lynn—and I wanted Hunter to hang. And then—I couldn't understand it—the case against him broke down. Some story about a woman—a woman who was with Arden later. I couldn't understand, I *still* can't understand. What woman? How could a woman be in there talking to Arden after he was dead?'

'There was no woman,' said Poirot.

'But, M. Poirot,' Lynn croaked. 'That old lady. She *saw* her. She heard her.'

'Aha,' said Poirot. 'But what did she see? And what did she hear? She saw someone in trousers, with a light tweed coat. She saw a head completely enveloped in an orange scarf arranged turbanwise and a face covered with make-up and a lipsticked mouth. She saw that in a dim light. And what did she hear? She saw the "hussy" draw back into No. 5 and from within the room she heard a man's voice saying, "Get out of here, my girl." *Eh bien*, it was a *man* she saw and a *man* she heard! But it was a very ingenious idea, Mr. Hunter,' Poirot added, turning placidly to David.

'What do you mean?' David asked sharply.

'It is now to *you* that I will tell a story. You come along to the Stag at nine o'clock or thereabouts. You come not to murder, but to *pay*. What do you find? You find the man who had been blackmailing you lying on the floor, murdered in a particularly brutal manner. You can think fast, Mr. Hunter, and you realise at once that you are in imminent danger. You have not been seen entering the Stag by any one as far as you know and your first idea is to clear out as soon as possible, catch the 9.20 train back to London and swear hard that you have not been near Warmsley Vale. To catch the train your only chance is to run across country. In doing so you run unexpectedly into Miss Marchmont and you also realise that you cannot catch the train. You see the smoke of it in the valley. She too, although you do not know it, has seen the smoke, but she has not consciously realised that it indicates *that you cannot catch the train*, and when you tell her that the time is *nine-fifteen* she accepts your statement without any doubt.

'To impress on her mind that you do catch the train, you invent a very ingenious scheme. In fact, you now have to plan an entirely new scheme to divert suspicion from yourself.

'You go back to Furrowbank, letting yourself in quietly with your key and you help yourself to a scarf of your sister's, you take one of her lipsticks, and you also proceed to make up your face in a highly theatrical manner.

'You return to the Stag at a suitable time, impress your personality on the old lady who sits in the Residents Only room and whose peculiarities are common gossip at the Stag. Then you go up to No. 5. When you hear her coming to bed, you come out into the passage, then withdraw hurriedly inside again, and proceed to say loudly, "You'd better get out of here, my girl."'

Poirot paused.

'A very ingenious performance,' he observed.

'Is that true, David?' cried Lynn. 'Is it true?'

David was grinning broadly.

'I think a good deal of myself as a female impersonator. Lord, you should have seen that old gorgon's face!'

'But how could you be here at ten o'clock and yet telephone to me from London at eleven?' demanded Lynn perplexedly.

David Hunter bowed to Poirot.

'All explanations by Hercule Poirot,' he remarked. 'The man who knows everything. How did I do it?'

'Very simply,' said Poirot. 'You rang up your sister at the flat from the public call-box and gave her certain precise instructions. At eleven-four exactly she put through a toll call to Warmsley Vale 34. When Miss Marchmont came to the phone the operator verified the number, then saying no doubt "A call from London," or "Go ahead London," something of that kind?'

Lynn nodded.

'Rosaleen Cloade then replaced the receiver. *You*,' Poirot turned to David, 'carefully noting the time, dialled 34, got it, pressed Button A, said "London wants you" in a slightly disguised voice and then spoke. The lapse of a minute or two would be nothing strange in a telephone call these days, and would only strike Miss Marchmont as a reconnection.'

Lynn said quietly:

'So *that's* why you rang me up, David?'

Something in her tone, quiet as it was, made David look at her sharply.

He turned to Poirot and made a gesture of surrender.

'No doubt about it. You *do* know everything! To tell the truth I was scared stiff. I had to think up something. After I'd rung Lynn, I walked five miles to Dasleby and went up to London by the early milk train. Slipped into the flat in time to rumple the bed and have breakfast with Rosaleen. It never entered my head that the police would think *she'd* done it.

'And of course *I* hadn't the remotest idea who *had* killed him! I simply couldn't imagine who could have *wanted* to kill him. Absolutely nobody had a motive as far as I could see, except for myself and Rosaleen.'

'That,' said Poirot, 'has been the great difficulty. *Motive*. You and your sister had a motive for killing Arden. Every member of the Cloade family had a motive for killing Rosaleen.'

David said sharply:

'She *was* killed, then? It wasn't suicide?'

'No. It was a carefully-premeditated well-thought-out crime. Morphia was substituted for bromide in one of her sleeping-powders—one towards the bottom of the box.'

'In the *powders*.' David frowned. 'You don't mean—you *can't* mean *Lionel Cloade*?'

'Oh, no,' said Poirot. 'You see, practically *any* of the Cloades could have substituted the morphia. Aunt Kathie could have tampered with the powders before they left the surgery. Rowley here came up to Furrowbank with butter and eggs for Rosaleen. Mrs. Marchmont came there. So did Mrs. Jeremy Cloade. Even Lynn Marchmont came. And one and all they had a motive.'

'Lynn didn't have a motive,' cried David.

'We all had motives,' said Lynn. 'That's what you mean?'

'Yes,' said Poirot. 'That is what has made the case difficult. David Hunter and Rosaleen Cloade had a motive for killing Arden—but they did *not* kill him. All of you Cloades had a motive for killing Rosaleen Cloade and yet none of you killed her. This case is, always has been, *the wrong way round*. Rosaleen Cloade was killed by the person who had *most to lose* by her death.' He turned his head slightly, '*You* killed her, Mr. Hunter . . .'

'I?' David cried. 'Why on earth should I kill my own sister?'

'You killed her because she wasn't your sister. Rosaleen Cloade died by enemy action in London nearly two years ago. The woman you killed was a young Irish housemaid, Eileen Corrigan, whose photograph I received from Ireland to-day.'

He drew it from his pocket as he spoke. With lightning swiftness David snatched it from him, leapt to the door, jumped through it, and banging it behind him, was gone. With a roar of anger Rowley charged headlong after him.

Poirot and Lynn were left alone.

Lynn cried out, 'It's not true. It can't be true.'

'Oh, yes, it is true. You saw half the truth once when you fancied David Hunter was not her brother. Put it the other way and it all falls into shape. This Rosaleen was a Catholic (Underhay's wife was *not* a Catholic), troubled by conscience, wildly devoted to David. Imagine his feelings on that night of the Blitz, his sister dead, Gordon Cloade dying—all that new life of ease and money snatched away from him, and then he sees this girl, very much the same age, the only survivor except for himself, blasted and unconscious. Already no doubt he has made love to her and he has no doubt he can make her do what he wants.

'He had a way with women,' Poirot added dryly, without looking at Lynn who flushed.

'He is an opportunist, he snatches his chance of fortune. He identifies her as his sister. She returns to consciousness to find him at her bedside. He persuades and cajoles her into accepting the role.

'But imagine their consternation when the first blackmailing letter arrives. All along I have said to myself, "Is Hunter really the type of man to let himself be blackmailed so easily?" It seemed, too, that he was actually uncertain whether the man blackmailing him was Underhay or not. But how *could* he be uncertain? Rosaleen Cloade could tell him at once if the man were her husband or not? Why hurry her up to London before she has a chance to catch a glimpse of the man? Because—there could only be one reason—because he could not risk the man getting a glimpse of *her*. If the man *was* Underhay, he must not discover that Rosaleen Cloade was not Rosaleen Cloade at all. No, there was only one thing to be done. Pay up enough to keep the blackmailer quiet, and then—do a flit—go off to America.

'And then, unexpectedly, the blackmailing stranger is murdered—and Major Porter identifies him as Underhay. Never in his life has David Hunter been in a tighter place! Worse still, the girl herself is beginning to crack. Her conscience is becoming increasingly active. She is showing signs of mental breakdown. Sooner or later she will confess, give the whole thing away, render him liable to criminal prosecution. Moreover, he finds her demands on him increasingly irksome. He has fallen in love with you. So he decides to cut his losses. Eileen must die. He substitutes morphia for one of the powders prescribed for her by Dr. Cloade, urges her on to take them every night, suggests to her fears of the Cloade family. David Hunter will not be suspected since the death of his sister means that her money passes back to the Cloades.

'That was his trump card: lack of motive. As I told you—this case was always the wrong way round.'

The door opened and Superintendent Spence came in.

Poirot said sharply, '*Eh bien?*'

Spence said, 'It's all right. We've got him.'

Lynn said in a low voice:

'Did he—say anything?'

'Said he'd had a good run for his money——'

'Funny,' added the Superintendent, 'how they always talk at the wrong moment . . . We cautioned him, of course. But he said, "Cut it out, man. I'm a gambler—but I know when I've lost the last throw."'

Poirot murmured:

'"There is a tide in the affairs of men
Which, taken at the flood, leads on to fortune . . ."

'Yes, the tide sweeps in—but it also ebbs—and may carry you out to sea.'

CHAPTER XVII

IT WAS A SUNDAY MORNING when Rowley Cloade, answering a knock at the farm door, found Lynn waiting outside.

He stepped back a pace.

'Lynn!'

'Can I come in, Rowley?'

He stood back a little. She passed him and went into the kitchen.

She had been at church and was wearing a hat. Slowly, with an almost ritual air, she raised her hands, took off the hat and laid it down on the window-sill.

'*I've come home, Rowley.*'

'What on earth do you mean?'

'Just that. I've come home. This is home—here, with you. I've been a fool not to know it before—not to know journey's end when I saw it. Don't you understand, Rowley, I've come *home*!'

'You don't know what you're saying, Lynn. I—I tried to kill you.'

'I know.' Lynn gave a grimace and put her fingers gingerly to her throat. 'Actually, it was just when I thought you *had* killed me, that I began to realise what a really thundering fool I'd been making of myself!'

'I don't understand,' said Rowley.

'Oh, don't be stupid. I always wanted to marry you, didn't I? And then I got out of touch with you—you seemed to me so tame—so *meek*—I felt life would be so safe with you—so dull. I fell for David because he was dangerous and attractive—and, to be honest, because he knows women much too well. But none of that was *real*. When you caught hold of me by the throat and said if I wasn't for you, no one should have me—well—I knew then that I was *your* woman! Unfortunately it seemed that I was going to know it—just too late . . . Luckily Hercule Poirot walked in and saved the situation. And I *am* your woman, Rowley!'

Rowley shook his head.

'It's impossible, Lynn. I've killed two men—murdered them——'

'Rubbish,' cried Lynn. 'Don't be pigheaded and melodramatic. If you have a row with a hulking big man and hit him and he falls down and hits his head on a fender—*that* isn't murder. It's not even legally murder.'

'It's manslaughter. You go to prison for it.'

'Possibly. If so, I shall be on the step when you come out.'

'And there's Porter. I'm morally responsible for his death.'

'No, you're not. He was a fully adult responsible man—he could have turned down your proposition. One can't blame any one else for the things one decides to do with one's eyes open. You suggested dishonesty to him, he accepted it and then repented and took a quick way out. He was just a weak character.'

Rowley shook his head obstinately.

'It's no good, old girl. You can't marry a gaol-bird.'

'I don't think you're going to gaol. A policeman would have been round for you before now if so.'

Rowley stared.

'But damn it all, manslaughter—bribing Porter——'

'What makes you think the police know anything about all that or ever will.'

'That fellow Poirot knows.'

'He isn't the police. I'll tell you what the police think. They think David Hunter killed Arden as well as Rosaleen, now they know he was in Warmsley Vale that evening. They won't charge him with it because it isn't necessary—and besides, I believe you can't be arrested twice on the same charge. But as long as they *think* he did it, they won't look for any one else.'

'But that chap Poirot——'

'He told the Superintendent it was an accident, and I gather the Superintendent just laughed at him. If you ask me I think Poirot will say nothing to any one. He's rather a dear——'

'No, Lynn. I can't let you risk it. Apart from anything else I—well, I mean, can I trust myself? What I mean is, it wouldn't be *safe* for you.'

'Perhaps not . . . But you see, Rowley, I *do* love you—and you've had such a hell of a time—and I've never, really, *cared* very much for being safe——'

The Seven Dials Mystery

1. *On early rising*

THAT AMIABLE YOUTH, Jimmy Thesiger, came racing down the big staircase at Chimneys two steps at a time. So precipitate was his descent that he collided with Tredwell, the stately butler, just as the latter was crossing the hall bearing a fresh supply of hot coffee. Owing to the marvellous presence of mind and masterly agility of Tredwell, no casualty occurred.

'Sorry,' apologised Jimmy. 'I say, Tredwell, am I the last down?'

'No, sir, Mr. Wade has not come down yet.'

'Good,' said Jimmy, and entered the breakfast-room.

The room was empty save for his hostess, and her reproachful gaze gave Jimmy the same feeling of discomfort he always experienced on catching the eye of a defunct codfish exposed on a fishmonger's slab. Yet, hang it all, why should the woman look at him like that? To come down at a punctual nine-thirty when staying in a country house simply wasn't done. To be sure, it was now a quarter past eleven which was, perhaps, the outside limit, but even then——

'Afraid I'm a bit late, Lady Coote. What?'

'Oh it doesn't matter,' said Lady Coote in a melancholy voice.

As a matter of fact, people being late for breakfast worried her very much. For the first ten years of her married life, Sir Oswald Coote (then plain Mr.) had, to put it baldly, raised hell if his morning meal were even a half-minute later than eight o'clock. Lady Coote had been disciplined to regard unpunctuality as a deadly sin of the most unpardonable nature. And habit dies hard. Also, she was an earnest woman, and she could not help asking herself what possible good these young people would ever do in the world without early rising. As Sir Oswald so often said, to reporters and others: 'I attribute my success entirely to my habits of early rising, frugal living, and methodical habits.'

Lady Coote was a big, handsome woman in a tragic sort of fashion. She had large, dark, mournful eyes and a deep voice. An artist looking for a model for 'Rachel mourning for her children' would have hailed Lady Coote with delight. She would have done well, too, in melodrama, staggering through the falling snow as the deeply wronged wife of the villain.

She looked as though she had some terrible secret sorrow in her life, and yet if the truth be told, Lady Coote had had no trouble in her life whatever, except the meteoric rise to prosperity of Sir Oswald. As a young girl she had been a jolly flamboyant creature, very much in love with Oswald Coote, the aspiring young man in the bicycle shop next to her father's hardware store. They had lived very happily, first in a couple of rooms, and then in a tiny house, and then in a larger house, and then in successive houses of increasing magnitude, but always within a reasonable distance of 'the Works,' until now Sir Oswald had reached such an eminence that he and 'the Works' were no longer interdependent, and it was his pleasure to rent the very largest and most magnificent mansions available all over England. Chimneys was a historic place, and in renting it from the Marquis of Caterham for two years, Sir Oswald felt that he had attained the top notch of his ambition.

Lady Coote was not nearly so happy about it. She was a lonely woman. The principal relaxation of her early married life had been talking to 'the girl'—and even when 'the girl' had been multiplied by three, conversation with her domestic staff had still been the principal distraction of Lady Coote's day. Now, with a pack of housemaids, a butler like an archbishop, several footmen of imposing proportions, a bevy of scuttling kitchen and scullery maids, a terrifying foreign chef with a 'temperament,' and a housekeeper of immense proportions who alternately creaked and rustled when she moved, Lady Coote was as one marooned on a desert island.

She sighed now, heavily, and drifted out through the open window, much to the relief of Jimmy Thesiger, who at once helped himself to more kidneys and bacon on the strength of it.

Lady Coote stood for a few moments tragically on the terrace and then nerved herself to speak to MacDonald, the head gardener, who was surveying the domain over which he ruled with an autocratic eye. MacDonald was a very chief and prince among head gardeners. He knew his place—which was to rule. And he ruled—despotically.

Lady Coote approached him nervously.

'Good-morning, MacDonald.'

'Good-morning, m'lady.'

He spoke as head gardeners should speak—mournfully, but with dignity—like an emperor at a funeral.

'I was wondering—could we have some of those late grapes for dessert to-night?'

'They're no fit for picking yet,' said MacDonald.

He spoke kindly but firmly.

'Oh!' said Lady Coote.

She plucked up courage.

'Oh! but I was in the end house yesterday, and I tasted one and they seemed very good.'

MacDonald looked at her, and she blushed. She was made to feel that she had taken an unpardonable liberty. Evidently the late Marchioness of Caterham had never committed such a solecism as to enter one of her own hothouses and help herself to grapes.

'If you had given orders, m'lady, a bunch should have been cut and sent in to you,' said MacDonald severely.

'Oh! thank you,' said Lady Coote. 'Yes, I will do that another time.'

'But they're no properly fit for picking yet.'

'No,' murmured Lady Coote, 'no, I suppose not. We'd better leave it then.'

MacDonald maintained a masterly silence. Lady Coote nerved herself once more.

'I was going to speak to you about the piece of lawn at the back of the rose garden. I wondered if it could be used as a bowling green. Sir Oswald is very fond of a game of bowls.'

'And why not?' thought Lady Coote to herself. She had been instructed in her history of England. Had not Sir Francis Drake and his knightly companions been playing a game of bowls when the Armada was sighted? Surely a gentlemanly pursuit and one to which MacDonald could not reasonably object. But she had reckoned without the predominant trait of a good head gardener, which is to oppose any and every suggestion made to him.

'Nae doot it could be used for that purpose,' said MacDonald noncommittally.

He threw a discouraging flavour into the remark, but its real object was to lure Lady Coote on to her destruction.

'If it was cleared up and—er—cut—and—er—all that sort of thing,' she went on hopefully.

'Aye,' said MacDonald slowly. 'It could be done. But it would mean taking William from the lower border.'

'Oh!' said Lady Coote doubtfully. The words 'lower border'

conveyed absolutely nothing to her mind—except a vague suggestion of a Scottish song—but it was clear that to MacDonald they constituted an insuperable objection.

'And that would be a pity,' said MacDonald.

'Oh! of course,' said Lady Coote. "It *would*.' And wondered why she agreed so fervently.

MacDonald looked at her very hard.

'Of course,' he said, 'if it's your *orders*, m'lady——'

He left it like that. But his menacing tone was too much for Lady Coote. She capitulated at once.

'Oh, no,' she said. 'I see what you mean, MacDonald. N—no—William had better get on with the lower border.'

'That's what I thocht meself, m'lady.'

'Yes,' said Lady Coote. 'Yes. Certainly.'

'I thocht you'd agree, m'lady,' said MacDonald.

'Oh, certainly,' said Lady Coote again.

MacDonald touched his hat and moved away.

Lady Coote sighed unhappily and looked after him. Jimmy Thesiger, replete with kidneys and bacon, stepped out on to the terrace beside her, and sighed in quite a different manner.

'Topping morning, eh?' he remarked.

'Is it?' said Lady Coote absently. 'Oh, yes, I suppose it is. I hadn't noticed.'

'Where are the others? Punting on the lake?'

'I expect so. I mean, I shouldn't wonder if they were.'

Lady Coote turned and plunged abruptly into the house again. Tredwell was just examining the coffee pot.

'Oh, dear,' said Lady Coote. 'Isn't Mr.—Mr.——'

'Wade, m'lady?'

'Yes, Mr. Wade. Isn't he down *yet*?'

'No, m'lady.'

'It's very late.'

'Yes, m'lady.'

'Oh, dear. I suppose he will come down *sometime*. Tredwell?'

'Oh, undoubtedly, m'lady. It was eleven-thirty yesterday morning when Mr. Wade came down, m'lady.'

Lady Coote glanced at the clock. It was now twenty minutes to twelve. A wave of human sympathy rushed over her.

'It's very hard luck on you, Tredwell. Having to clear and then get lunch on the table by one o'clock.'

'I am accustomed to the ways of young gentlemen, m'lady.'

The reproof was dignified, but unmistakable. So might a prince of the Church reprove a Turk or an infidel who had unwittingly committed a solecism in all good faith.

Lady Coote blushed for the second time that morning. But a welcome interruption occurred. The door opened and a serious, spectacled young man put his head in.

'Oh, there you are, Lady Coote. Sir Oswald was asking for you.'

'Oh, I'll go to him at once, Mr. Bateman.'

Lady Coote hurried out.

Rupert Bateman, who was Sir Oswald's private secretary, went out the other way, through the window where Jimmy Thesiger was still lounging amiably.

''Morning, Pongo,' said Jimmy. 'I suppose I shall have to go and make myself agreeable to those blasted girls. You coming?'

Bateman shook his head and hurried along the terrace and in at the library window. Jimmy grinned pleasantly at his retreating back. He and Bateman had been at school together, when Bateman had been a serious, spectacled boy, and had been nicknamed Pongo for no earthly reason whatever.

Pongo, Jimmy reflected, was very much the same sort of ass now that he had been then. The words 'Life is real, life is earnest' might have been written specially for him.

Jimmy yawned and strolled slowly down to the lake. The girls were there, three of them—just the usual sort of girls, two with dark shingled heads and one with a fair shingled head. The one that giggled most was (he thought) called Helen—and there was another called Nancy—and the third one was, for some reason, addressed as Socks. With them were his two friends, Bill Eversleigh and Ronny Devereux, who were employed in a purely ornamental capacity at the Foreign Office.

'Hallo,' said Nancy (or possibly Helen). 'It's Jimmy. Where's what's his name?'

'You don't mean to say,' said Bill Eversleigh, 'that Gerry Wade's not up *yet*? Something ought to be done about it.'

'If he's not careful,' said Ronny Devereux,' he'll miss his breakfast altogether one day—find it's lunch or tea instead when he rolls down.'

'It's a shame,' said the girl called Socks. 'Because it worries

Lady Coote so. She gets more and more like a hen that wants to lay an egg and can't. It's too bad.'

'Let's pull him out of bed,' suggested Bill. 'Come on, Jimmy.'

'Oh! let's be more subtle than that,' said the girl called Socks. Subtle was a word of which she was rather fond. She used it a great deal.

'I'm not subtle,' said Jimmy. 'I don't know how.'

'Let's get together and do something about it to-morrow morning,' suggested Ronny vaguely. 'You know, get him up at seven. Stagger the household. Tredwell loses his false whiskers and drops the tea urn. Lady Coote has hysterics and faints in Bill's arms—Bill being the weight carrier. Sir Oswald says 'Ha!" and steel goes up a point and five eighths. Pongo registers emotion by throwing down his spectacles and stamping on them.'

'You don't know Gerry,' said Jimmy. 'I daresay enough cold water *might* wake him—judiciously applied, that is. But he'd only turn over and go to sleep again.'

'Oh! we must think of something more subtle than cold water,' said Socks.

'Well, what?' asked Ronny bluntly. And nobody had any answer ready.

'We ought to be able to think of something,' said Bill. 'Who's got any brains?'

'Pongo,' said Jimmy. 'And here he is, rushing along in a harried manner as usual. Pongo was always the one for brains. It's been his misfortune from his youth upwards. Let's turn Pongo on to it.'

Mr. Bateman listened patiently to a somewhat incoherent statement. His attitude was that of one poised for flight. He delivered his solution without loss of time.

'I should suggest an alarum clock,' he said briskly. 'I always use one myself for fear of oversleeping. I find that early tea brought in in a noiseless manner is sometimes powerless to awaken one.'

He hurried away.

'An alarum clock.' Ronny shook his head. '*One* alarum clock. It would take about a dozen to disturb Gerry Wade.'

'Well, why not?' Bill was flushed and earnest. 'I've got it. Let's all go into Market Basing and buy an alarum clock each.'

There was laughter and discussion. Bill and Ronny went off to get hold of cars. Jimmy was deputed to spy upon the dining-room. He returned rapidly.

'He's there right enough. Making up for lost time and wolfing down toast and marmalade. How are we going to prevent him coming along with us?'

It was decided that Lady Coote must be approached and instructed to hold him in play. Jimmy and Nancy and Helen fulfilled this duty. Lady Coote was bewildered and apprehensive.

'A rag? You will be careful, won't you, my dears? I mean, you won't smash the furniture and wreck things or use too much water. We've got to hand this house over next week, you know. I shouldn't like Lord Caterham to think——'

Bill, who had returned from the garage, broke in reassuringly.

'That's all right, Lady Coote. Bundle Brent—Lord Caterham's daughter—is a great friend of mine. And there's nothing she'd stick at—absolutely nothing! You can take it from me. And anyway there's not going to be any damage done. This is quite a quiet affair.'

'Subtle,' said the girl called Socks.

Lady Coote went sadly along the terrace just as Gerald Wade emerged from the breakfast-room. Jimmy Thesiger was a fair, cherubic young man, and all that could be said of Gerald Wade was that he was fairer and more cherubic, and that his vacuous expression made Jimmy's face quite intelligent by contrast.

'Morning, Lady Coote,' said Gerald Wade. 'Where are all the others?'

'They've all gone to Market Basing,' said Lady Coote.

'What for?'

'Some joke,' said Lady Coote in her deep, melancholy voice.

'Rather early in the morning for jokes,' said Mr. Wade.

'It's not so very early in the morning,' said Lady Coote pointedly.

'I'm afraid I was a bit late coming down,' said Mr. Wade with engaging frankness. 'It's an extraordinary thing, but wherever I happen to be staying, I'm always last to be down.'

'Very extraordinary,' said Lady Coote.

'I don't know why it is,' said Mr. Wade, meditating. 'I can't think, I'm sure.'

'Why don't you just get up?' suggested Lady Coote.

'Oh!' said Mr. Wade. The simplicity of the solution rather took him aback.

Lady Coote went on earnestly.

'I've heard Sir Oswald say so many times that there's nothing for getting a young man on in the world like punctual habits.'

'Oh, I know,' said Mr. Wade. 'And I have to when I'm in town. I mean, I have to be round at the jolly old Foreign Office by eleven o'clock. You mustn't think I'm always a slacker, Lady Coote. I say, what awfully jolly flowers you've got down in that lower border. I can't remember the names of them, but we've got some at home—those mauve thingummybobs. My sister's tremendously keen on gardening.'

Lady Coote was immediately diverted. Her wrongs rankled within her.

'What kind of gardeners do you have?'

'Oh, just one. Rather an old fool, I believe. Doesn't know much, but he does what he's told. And that's a great thing, isn't it?'

Lady Coote agreed that it was with a depth of feeling in her voice that would have been invaluable to her as an emotional actress. They began to discourse on the iniquities of gardeners.

Meanwhile the expedition was doing well. The principal emporium of Market Basing had been invaded and the sudden demand for alarum clocks was considerably puzzling the proprietor.

'I wish we'd got Bundle here,' murmured Bill. 'You know her, don't you, Jimmy? Oh, you'd like her. She's a splendid girl—a real good sport—and mark you, she's got brains too. You know her, Ronny?'

Ronny shook his head.

'Don't know Bundle? Where have you been vegetating? She's simply it.'

'Be a bit more subtle, Bill,' said Socks. 'Stop blethering about your lady friends and get on with the business.'

Mr. Murgatroyd, owner of Murgatroyd's Stores, burst into eloquence.

'If you'll allow me to advise you, Miss, I should say—*not* the 7/11 one. It's a good clock—I'm not running it down, mark you, but I should strongly advise this kind at 10/6. Well worth the extra money. Reliability, you understand. I shouldn't like you to say afterwards——'

It was evident to everybody that Mr. Murgatroyd must be turned off like a tap.

'We don't want a reliable clock,' said Nancy.

'It's got to go for one day, that's all,' said Helen.

'We don't want a subtle one,' said Socks. 'We want one with a good loud ring.'

'We want——' began Bill, but was unable to finish, because Jimmy, who was of a mechanical turn of mind, had at last grasped the mechanism. For the next five minutes the shop was hideous with the loud raucous ringing of many alarum clocks.

In the end six excellent starters were selected.

'And I'll tell you what,' said Ronny handsomely, 'I'll get one for Pongo. It was his idea, and it's a shame that he should be out of it. He shall be represented among those present.'

'That's right,' said Bill. 'And I'll take an extra one for Lady Coote. The more the merrier. And she's doing some of the spade work. Probably gassing away to old Gerry now.'

Indeed at this precise moment Lady Coote was detailing a long story about MacDonald and a prize peach and enjoying herself very much.

The clocks were wrapped up and paid for. Mr. Murgatroyd watched the cars drive away with a puzzled air. Very spirited the young people of the upper classes nowadays, very spirited indeed, but not at all easy to understand. He turned with relief to attend to the vicar's wife, who wanted a new kind of dripless teapot.

2. *Concerning alarum clocks*

'NOW WHERE shall we put them?'

Dinner was over. Lady Coote had been once more detailed for duty. Sir Oswald had unexpectedly come to the rescue by suggesting bridge—not that suggesting is the right word. Sir Oswald, as became one of 'Our Captains of Industry' (No. 7 of Series I), merely expressed a preference and those around him hastened to accommodate themselves to the great man's wishes.

Rupert Bateman and Sir Oswald were partners against Lady Coote and Gerald Wade, which was a very happy arrangement. Sir Oswald played bridge, like he did everything else, extremely well, and liked a partner to correspond. Bateman was as efficient a bridge player as he was a secretary. Both of them confined themselves strictly to the matter in hand, merely uttering in curt short barks, 'Two no trumps,' 'Double,' 'Three spades.' Lady Coote and Gerald Wade were amiable and discursive, and the young man never failed to say at the conclusion of each hand, 'I say, partner, you played that simply splendidly,' in tones of simple admiration which Lady Coote found both novel and extremely soothing. They also held very good cards.

The others were supposed to be dancing to the wireless in the big ballroom. In reality they were grouped around the door of Gerald Wade's bedroom, and the air was full of subdued giggles and the loud ticking of clocks.

'Under the bed in a row,' suggested Jimmy in answer to Bill's question.

'And what shall we set them at? What time, I mean? All together so that there's one glorious what not, or at intervals?'

The point was hotly disputed. One party argued that for a champion sleeper like Gerry Wade the combined ringing of eight alarum clocks was necessary. The other party argued in favour of steady and sustained effort.

In the end the latter won the day. The clocks were set to go off one after the other, starting at 6.30 a.m.

'And I hope,' said Bill virtuously, 'that this will be a lesson to him.'

'Hear, hear,' said Socks.

The business of hiding the clocks was just being begun when there was a sudden alarm.

'Hist,' cried Jimmy. 'Somebody's coming up the stairs.'

There was a panic.

'It's all right,' said Jimmy. 'It's only Pongo.'

Taking advantage of being dummy, Mr. Bateman was going to his room for a handkerchief. He paused on his way and took in the situation at a glance. He then made a comment, a simple and practical one.

'He will hear them ticking when he goes to bed.'

The conspirators looked at each other.

'What did I tell you?' said Jimmy in a reverent voice. 'Pongo always *did* have brains'

The brainy one passed on.

'It's true,' admitted Ronny Devereux, his head on one side. 'Eight clocks all ticking at once do make a devil of a row. Even old Gerry, ass as he is, couldn't miss it. He'll guess something's up.'

'I wonder if he is,' said Jimmy Thesiger.

'Is what?'

'Such an ass as we all think.'

Ronny stared at him.

'We all know old Gerald.'

'Do we?' said Jimmy. 'I've sometimes thought that—well, that it isn't possible for any one to be quite the ass old Gerry makes himself out to be.'

They all stared at him. There was a serious look on Ronny's face.

'Jimmy,' he said, 'you've got brains.'

'A second Pongo,' said Bill encouragingly.

'Well, it just occurred to me, that's all,' said Jimmy, defending himself.

'Oh! don't let's all be subtle,' cried Socks. 'What are we to do about these clocks?'

'Here's Pongo coming back again. Let's ask him,' suggested Jimmy.

Pongo, urged to bring his great brain to bear upon the matter, gave his decision.

'Wait till he's gone to bed and got to sleep. Then enter the room very quietly and put the clocks down on the floor.'

'Little Pongo's right again,' said Jimmy. 'On the word one all park clocks, and then we'll go downstairs and disarm suspicion.'

Bridge was still proceeding—with a slight difference. Sir Oswald was now playing with his wife and was conscientiously pointing out to her the mistakes she had made during the play of each hand. Lady Coote accepted reproof good-humouredly, and with a complete lack of any real interest. She reiterated, not once but many times:

'I see, dear. It's so kind of you to tell me.'

And she continued to make exactly the same errors.

At intervals, Gerald Wade said to Pongo:

'Well played, partner, jolly well played.'

Bill Eversleigh was making calculations with Ronny Devereux.

'Say he goes to bed about twelve—what do you think we ought to give him—about an hour?'

He yawned.

'Curious thing—three in the morning is my usual time for bye-bye, but to-night, just because I know we've got to sit up a bit, I'd give anything to be a mother's boy and turn in right away.'

Every one agreed that they felt the same.

'My dear Maria,' rose the voice of Sir Oswald in mild irritation. 'I have told you over and over again not to hesitate when you are wondering whether to finesse or not. You give the whole table information.'

Lady Coote had a very good answer to this—namely that as Sir Oswald was dummy, he had no right to comment on the play of the hand. But she did not make it. Instead she smiled kindly, leaned her ample chest well forward over the table, and gazed firmly into Gerald Wade's hand where he sat on her right.

Her anxieties lulled to rest by perceiving the queen, she played the knave and took the trick and proceeded to lay down her cards.

'Four tricks and the rubber,' she announced. 'I think I was very lucky to get four tricks there.'

'Lucky,' murmured Gerald Wade, as he pushed back his chair and came over to the fireplace to join the others. 'Lucky, she calls it. That woman wants watching.'

Lady Coote was gathering up notes and silver.

'I know I'm not a good player,' she announced in a mournful tone which nevertheless held an undercurrent of pleasure in it. 'But I'm really very lucky at the game.'

'You'll never be a bridge player, Maria,' said Sir Oswald.

'No, dear,' said Lady Coote. 'I know I shan't. You're always telling me so. And I do try so hard.'

'She does,' said Gerald Wade *sotto voce*. 'There's no subterfuge about it. She'd put her head right down on your shoulder if she couldn't see into your hand any other way.'

'I know you try,' said Sir Oswald. 'It's just that you haven't any card sense.'

'I know, dear,' said Lady Coote. 'That's what you're always telling me. And you owe me another ten shillings, Oswald.'

'Do I?' Sir Oswald looked surprised.

'Yes. Seventeen hundred—eight pounds ten. You've only given me eight pounds.'

'Dear me,' said Sir Oswald. 'My mistake.'

Lady Coote smiled at him sadly and took up the extra ten shilling note. She was very fond of her husband, but she had no intention of allowing him to cheat her out of ten shillings.

Sir Oswald moved over to a side table and became hospitable with whisky and soda. It was half past twelve when general good-nights were said.

Ronny Devereux, who had the room next door to Gerald Wade's was told off to report progress. At a quarter to two he crept round tapping at doors. The party, pyjamaed and dressing-gowned, assembled with various scuffles and giggles and low whispers.

'His light went out about twenty minutes ago,' reported Ronny in a hoarse whisper. 'I thought he'd never put it out. I opened the door just now and peeped in, and he seems sound off. What about it?'

Once more the clocks were solemnly assembled. Then another difficulty arose.

'We can't all go barging in. Make no end of a row. One person's got to do it and the others can hand him the what-nots from the door.'

Hot discussion then arose as to the proper person to be selected. The three girls were rejected on the grounds that they would giggle. Bill Eversleigh was rejected on the grounds of his height, weight and heavy tread, also for his general clumsiness, which latter clause he fiercely denied. Jimmy Thesiger and Ronny Devereux were considered possibles, but in the end an overwhelming majority decided in favour of Rupert Bateman.

'Pongo's the lad,' agreed Jimmy. 'Anyway, he walks like a cat—always did. And then, if Gerry should waken up, Pongo will be able to think of some rotten silly thing to say to him. You know, something plausible that'll calm him down and not rouse his suspicions.'

'Something subtle,' suggested the girl Socks thoughtfully.

'Exactly,' said Jimmy.

Pongo performed his job neatly and efficiently. Cautiously opening the bedroom door, he disappeared into the darkness inside bearing the two largest clocks. In a minute or two he reappeared on the threshold and two more were handed to him and then again twice more. Finally he emerged. Every one held their breath and listened. The rhythmical breathing of Gerald Wade could still be heard, but drowned, smothered and buried beneath the triumphant, impassioned ticking of Mr. Murgatroyd's eight alarum clocks.

3. *The joke that failed*

'TWELVE O'CLOCK,' said Socks despairingly.

The joke—as a joke—had not gone off any too well. The alarum clocks, on the other hand, had performed their part. *They* had gone off—with a vigour and *élan* that could hardly have been surpassed and which had sent Ronny Devereux leaping out of bed with a confused idea that the day of judgment had come. If such had been the effect in the room next door, what must it have been at close quarters? Ronny hurried out in the passage and applied his ear to the crack of the door.

He expected profanity—expected it confidently and with intelligent anticipation. But he heard nothing at all. That is to say, he heard nothing of what he expected. The clocks were ticking all right—ticking in a loud, arrogant, exasperating manner. And presently another went off, ringing with a crude, deafening note that would have aroused acute irritation in a deaf man.

There was no doubt about it; the clocks had performed their part faithfully. They did all and more than Mr. Murgatroyd had claimed for them. But apparently they had met their match in Gerald Wade.

The syndicate was inclined to be despondent about it.

'The lad isn't human,' grumbled Jimmy Thesiger.

'Probably thought he heard the telephone in the distance and rolled over and went to sleep again,' suggested Helen (or possibly Nancy).

'It seems to me very remarkable,' said Rupert Bateman seriously. 'I think he ought to see a doctor about it.'

'Some disease of the ear-drums,' suggested Bill hopefully.

'Well, if you ask me,' said Socks, 'I think he's just spoofing us. Of course they woke him up. But he's just going to do us down by pretending that he didn't hear anything.'

Everyone looked at Socks with respect and admiration.

'It's an idea,' said Bill.

'He's subtle, that's what it is,' said Socks. 'You'll see, he'll be extra late for breakfast this morning—just to show us.'

And since the clock now pointed to some minutes past twelve the general opinion was that Socks's theory was a correct one. Only Ronny Devereux demurred.

'You forget, I was outside the door when the first one went off. Whatever old Gerry decided to do later, the first one must have surprised him. He'd have let out something about it. Where did you put it, Pongo?'

'On a little table close by his ear,' said Mr. Bateman.

'That was thoughtful of you, Pongo,' said Ronny. 'Now, tell me.' He turned to Bill. 'If a whacking great bell started ringing within a few inches of your ear at half past six in the morning, what would you say about it?'

'Oh, Lord,' said Bill. 'I should say——' He came to a stop.

'Of course you would,' said Ronny. 'So should I. So would anyone. What they call the natural man would emerge. Well, it didn't. So I say that Pongo is right—as usual—and that Gerry has got an obscure disease of the eardrums.'

'It's now twenty past twelve' said one of the other girls sadly.

'I say,' said Jimmy slowly, 'that's a bit beyond anything, isn't it? I mean a joke's a joke. But this is carrying it a bit far. It's a shade hard on the Cootes.'

Bill stared at him.

'What are you getting at?'

'Well,' said Jimmy. 'Somehow or other—it's not like old Gerry.'

He found it hard to put into words just what he meant to say. He didn't want to say too much, and yet—— He saw Ronny looking at him. Ronny was suddenly alert.

It was at that moment Tredwell came into the room and looked round him hesitatingly.

'I thought Mr. Bateman was here,' he explained apologetically.

'Just gone out this minute through the window,' said Ronny. 'Can I do anything?'

Tredwell's eyes wandered from him to Jimmy Thesiger and then back again. As though singled out, the two young men left the room with him. Tredwell closed the dining-room door carefully behind him.

'Well,' said Ronny. 'What's up?'

'Mr. Wade not having yet come down, sir, I took the liberty of sending Williams up to his room.'

'Yes?'

'Williams has just come running down in a great state of agitation, sir.' Tredwell paused—a pause of preparation. 'I am afraid, sir, the poor young gentleman must have died in his sleep.'

Jimmy and Ronny stared at him.

'Nonsense,' cried Ronny at last. 'It's—it's impossible. Gerry——' His face worked suddenly. 'I'll—I'll run up and see. That fool Williams may have made a mistake.'

Tredwell stretched out a detaining hand. With a queer, unnatural feeling of detachment, Jimmy realised that the butler had the whole situation in hand.

'No, sir, Williams has made no mistake. I have already sent for Dr. Cartwright, and in the meantime I have taken the liberty of locking the door, preparatory to informing Sir Oswald of what has occurred. I must now find Mr. Bateman.'

Tredwell hurried away. Ronny stood like a man dazed.

'Gerry,' he muttered to himself.

Jimmy took his friend by the arm and steered him out through a side door on to a secluded portion of the terrace. He pushed him down on to a seat.

'Take it easy, old son,' he said kindly. 'You'll get your wind in a minute.'

But he looked at him rather curiously. He had had no idea that Ronny was such a friend of Gerry Wade's.

'Poor old Gerry,' he said thoughtfully. 'If ever a man looked fit, he did.'

Ronny nodded.

'All that clock business seems so rotten now,' went on Jimmy. 'It's odd, isn't it, why farce so often seems to get mixed up with tragedy?'

He was talking more or less at random, to give Ronny time to recover himself. The other moved restlessly.

'I wish that doctor would come. I want to know——'

'Know what?'

'What he—died of.'

Jimmy pursed up his lips.

'Heart?' he hazarded.

Ronny gave a short, scornful laugh.

'I say, Ronny,' said Jimmy.

'Well?'

Jimmy found a difficulty in going on.

'You don't mean—you aren't thinking—I mean, you haven't got it into your head that—that, well, I mean he wasn't biffed on the head or anything? Tredwell's locking the door and all that.'

It seemed to Jimmy that his words deserved an answer, but Ronny continued to stare straight out in front of him.

Jimmy shook his head and relapsed into silence. He didn't see that there was anything to do except just wait. So he waited.

It was Tredwell who disturbed them.

'The doctor would like to see you two gentlemen in the library, if you please, sir.'

Ronny sprang up. Jimmy followed him.

Dr. Cartwright was a thin, energetic young man with a clever face. He greeted them with a brief nod. Pongo, looking more serious and spectacled than ever, performed introductions.

'I understand you were a great friend of Mr. Wade's,' the doctor said to Ronny.

'His greatest friend.'

'H'm. Well, this business seems straightforward enough. Sad, though. He looked a healthy young chap. Do you know if he was in the habit of taking stuff to make him sleep?'

'Make him *sleep*.' Ronny stared. 'He always slept like a top.'

'You never heard him complain of sleeplessness?'

'Never.'

'Well, the facts are simple enough. There'll have to be an inquest, I'm afraid, nevertheless.'

'How did he die?'

'There's not much doubt; I should say an overdose of chloral. The stuff was by his bed. And a bottle and glass. Very sad, these things are.'

It was Jimmy who asked the question which he felt was trembling on his friend's lips, and yet which the other could somehow or other not get out.

'There's no question of—foul play?'

The doctor looked at him sharply.

'Why do you say that? Any cause to suspect it, eh?'

Jimmy looked at Ronny. If Ronny knew anything now was the time to speak. But to his astonishment Ronny shook his head.

'No cause whatever,' he said clearly.

'And suicide—eh?'

'Certainly not.'

Ronny was emphatic. The doctor was not so clearly convinced.

'No troubles that you know of? Money troubles? A woman?'

Again Ronny shook his head.

'Now about his relations. They must be notified.'

'He's got a sister—a half-sister rather. Lives at Deane Priory. About twenty miles from here. When he wasn't in town Gerry lived with her.'

'H'm,' said the doctor. 'Well, she must be told.'

'I'll go,' said Ronny. 'It's a rotten job, but somebody's got to do it.' He looked at Jimmy. 'You know her, don't you?'

'Slightly. I've danced with her once or twice.'

'Then we'll go in your car. You don't mind, do you? I can't face it alone.'

'That's all right,' said Jimmy reassuringly. 'I was going to suggest it myself. I'll go and get the old bus cranked up.'

He was glad to have something to do. Ronny's manner puzzled

him. What did he know or suspect? And why had he not voiced his suspicions, if he had them, to the doctor.

Presently the two friends were skimming along in Jimmy's car with a cheerful disregard for such things as speed limits.

'Jimmy,' said Ronny at last. 'I suppose you're about the best pal I have—now.'

'Well,' said Jimmy, 'what about it?'

He spoke gruffly.

'There's something I'd like to tell you. Something you ought to know.'

'About Gerry Wade?'

'Yes, about Gerry Wade.'

Jimmy waited.

'Well?' he inquired at last.

'I don't know that I ought to,' said Ronny.

'Why?'

'I'm bound by a kind of promise.'

'Oh! Well then, perhaps you'd better not.'

There was a silence.

'And yet, I'd like—— You see, Jimmy, your brains are better than mine.'

'They could easily be that,' said Jimmy unkindly.

'No, I can't' said Ronny suddenly.

'All right,' said Jimmy. 'Just as you like.'

After a long silence, Ronny said:

'What's she like?'

'Who?'

'This girl. Gerry's sister.'

Jimmy was silent for some minutes, then he said in a voice that had somehow or other altered:

'She's all right. In fact—well, she's a corker.'

'Gerry was very devoted to her, I knew. He often spoke of her.'

'She was very devoted to Gerry. It—it's going to hit her hard.'

'Yes, a nasty job.'

They were silent till they reached Deane Priory.

Miss Loraine, the maid told them, was in the garden. Unless they wanted to see Mrs. Coker——

Jimmy was eloquent that they did not want to see Mrs. Coker.

'Who's Mrs. Coker?' asked Ronny as they went round into the somewhat neglected garden.

'The old trout who lives with Loraine.'

They had stepped out into a paved walk. At the end of it was a girl with two black spaniels. A small girl, very fair, dressed in shabby old tweeds. Not at all the girl that Ronny had expected to see. Not, in fact, Jimmy's usual type.

Holding one dog by the collar, she came down the pathway to meet them.

'How do you do,' she said. 'You mustn't mind Elizabeth. She's just had some puppies and she's very suspicious.'

She had a supremely natural manner and, as she looked up smiling, the faint wild rose flush deepened in her cheeks. Her eyes were a very dark blue—like cornflowers.

Suddenly they widened—was it with alarm? As though, already, she guessed.

Jimmy hastened to speak.

'This is Ronny Devereux, Miss Wade. You must often have heard Gerry speak of him.'

'Oh, yes.' She turned a lovely, warm, welcoming smile on him. 'You've both been staying at Chimneys, haven't you? Why didn't you bring Gerry over with you?'

'We—er—couldn't,' said Ronny, and then stopped.

Again Jimmy saw the look of fear flash into her eyes.

'Miss Wade,' he said, 'I'm afraid—I mean, we've got bad news for you.'

She was on the alert in a moment.

'Gerry?'

'Yes—Gerry. He's——'

She stamped her foot with sudden passion.

'Oh! tell me—tell me——' She turned suddenly on Ronny. '*You*'ll tell me.'

Jimmy felt a pang of jealousy, and in that moment he knew what up to now he had hesitated to admit to himself. He knew why Helen and Nancy and Socks were just 'girls' to him and nothing more.

He only *half* heard Ronny's voice saying gravely:

'Yes, Miss Wade, I'll tell you. Gerry is dead.'

She had plenty of pluck. She gasped and drew back, but in a minute or two she was asking eager, searching questions. How? When?

Ronny answered her as gently as he could.

'*Sleeping* draught? Gerry?'

The incredulity in her voice was plain. Jimmy gave her a glance.

It was almost a glance of warning. He had a sudden feeling that Loraine in her innocence might say too much.

In his turn he explained as gently as possible the need for an inquest. She shuddered. She declined their offer of taking her back to Chimneys with them, but explained she would come over later. She had a two-seater of her own.

'But I want to be—be alone a little first,' she said piteously.

'I know,' said Ronny.

'That's all right,' said Jimmy.

They looked at her, feeling awkward and helpless.

'Thank you both ever so much for coming.'

They drove back in silence and there was something like constraint between them.

'My God! that girl's plucky,' said Ronny once.

Jimmy agreed.

'Gerry was my friend,' said Ronny. 'It's up to me to keep an eye on her.'

'Oh! rather. Of course.'

They said no more.

On returning to Chimneys Jimmy was waylaid by a tearful Lady Coote.

'That poor boy,' she kept repeating. 'That poor boy.'

Jimmy made all the suitable remarks he could think of.

Lady Coote told him at great length various details about the decease of various dear friends of hers. Jimmy listened with a show of sympathy and at last managed to detach himself without actual rudeness.

He ran lightly up the stairs. Ronny was just emerging from Gerald Wade's room. He seemed taken aback at the sight of Jimmy.

'I've been in to see him,' he said. 'Are you going in?'

'I don't think so,' said Jimmy, who was a healthy young man with a natural dislike to being reminded of death.

'I think all his friends ought to.'

'Oh! do you?' said Jimmy, and registered to himself an impression that Ronny Devereux was damned odd about it all.

'Yes. It's a sign of respect.'

Jimmy sighed, but gave in.

'Oh! very well,' he said, and passed in, setting his teeth a little.

There were white flowers arranged on the coverlet, and the room had been tidied and set to rights.

Jimmy gave one quick, nervous glance at the still, white face.

Could that be cherubic, pink Gerry Wade? That still peaceful figure. He shivered.

As he turned to leave the room, his glance swept the mantelshelf and he stopped in astonishment. The alarum clocks had been ranged along it neatly in a row.

He went out sharply. Ronny was waiting for him.

'Looks very peaceful and all that. Rotten luck on him,' mumbled Jimmy.

Then he said:

'I say, Ronny, who arranged all those clocks like that in a row?'

'How should I know? One of the servants, I suppose.'

'The funny thing is,' said Jimmy, 'that there are seven of them, not eight. One of them's missing. Did you notice that?'

Ronny made an inaudible sound.

'Seven instead of eight,' said Jimmy, frowning. 'I wonder why.'

4. *A Letter*

'INCONSIDERATE, that's what I call it,' said Lord Caterham.

He spoke in a gentle, plaintive voice and seemed pleased with the adjective he had found.

'Yes, distinctly inconsiderate. I often find these self-made men *are* inconsiderate. Very possibly that is why they amass such large fortunes.'

He looked mournfully out over his ancestral acres, of which he had to-day regained possession.

His daughter, Lady Eileen Brent, known to her friends and society in general as 'Bundle,' laughed.

'You'll certainly never amass a large fortune,' she observed dryly, 'though you didn't do so badly out of old Coote, sticking him for this place. What was he like? Presentable?'

'One of those large men,' said Lord Caterham, shuddering slightly, 'with a red square face and iron-gray hair. Powerful, you know. What they call a forceful personality. The kind of man you'd get if a steam-roller were turned into a human being.'

'Rather tiring?' suggested Bundle sympathetically.

'Frightfully tiring, full of all the most depressing virtues like sobriety and punctuality. I don't know which are the worst, powerful personalities or earnest politicians. I do so prefer the cheerful inefficient.'

'A cheerful inefficient wouldn't have been able to pay you the price you asked for this old mausoleum,' Bundle reminded him.

Lord Caterham winced.

'I wish you wouldn't use that word, Bundle. We were just getting away from the subject.'

'I don't see why you're so frightfully sensitive about it,' said Bundle. 'After all, people must die somewhere.'

'They needn't die in my house,' said Lord Caterham.

'I don't see why not. Lots of people have. Masses of stuffy old great grandfathers and grandmothers.'

'That's different,' said Lord Caterham. 'Naturally I expect Brents to die here—they don't count. But I do object to strangers. And I especially object to inquests. The thing will become a habit soon. This is the second. You remember all that fuss we had four years ago? For which, by the way, I hold George Lomax entirely to blame.'

'And now you're blaming poor old steam-roller Coote. I'm sure he was quite as annoyed about it as anyone.'

'Very inconsiderate,' said Lord Caterham obstinately. 'People who are likely to do that sort of thing oughtn't to be asked to stay. And you may say what you like, Bundle, I don't like inquests. I never have and I never shall.'

'Well, this wasn't the same sort of thing as the last one,' said Bundle soothingly. 'I mean, it wasn't a murder.'

'It might have been—from the fuss that thickhead of an inspector made. He's never got over that business four years ago. He thinks every death that takes place here must necessarily be a case of foul play fraught with grave political significance. You've no idea the fuss he made. I've been hearing about it from Tredwell. Tested everything imaginable for finger-prints. And of course they only found the dead man's own. The clearest case imaginable—though whether it was suicide or accident is another matter.'

'I met Gerry Wade once,' said Bundle. 'He was a friend of Bill's. You'd have liked him, Father, I never saw anyone more cheerfully inefficient than he was.'

'I don't like anyone who comes and dies in my house on purpose to annoy me,' said Lord Caterham obstinately.

'But I certainly can't imagine anyone murdering him,' continued Bundle. 'The idea's absurd.'

'Of course it is,' said Lord Caterham. 'Or would be to anyone but an ass like Inspector Raglan.'

'I daresay looking for fingerprints made him feel important,' said Bundle soothingly. 'Anyway, they brought it in "Death by misadventure," didn't they?'

Lord Caterham acquiesced.

'They had to show some consideration for the sister's feelings.'

'Was there a sister? I didn't know.'

'Half-sister, I believe. She was much younger. Old Wade ran away with her mother—he was always doing that sort of thing. No woman appealed to him unless she belonged to another man.'

'I'm glad there's one bad habit you haven't got,' said Bundle.

'I've always led a very respectable God-fearing life,' said Lord Caterham. 'It seems extraordinary, considering how little harm I do to anybody, that I can't be let alone. If only——'

He stopped as Bundle made a sudden excursion through the window.

'MacDonald,' called Bundle in a clear, autocratic voice.

The emperor approached. Something that might possibly have been taken for a smile of welcome tried to express itself on his countenance, but the natural gloom of gardeners dispelled it.

'Your ladyship?' said MacDonald.

'How are you?' said Bundle.

'I'm no verra grand,' said MacDonald.

'I wanted to speak to you about the bowling green. It's shockingly overgrown. Put someone on to it, will you?'

MacDonald shook his head dubiously.

'It would mean taking William from the lower border, m'lady.'

'Damn the lower border,' said Bundle. 'Let him start at once. And MacDonald——'

'Yes, m'lady?'

'Let's have some of those grapes in from the far house. I know it's the wrong time to cut them because it always is, but I want them all the same. See?'

Bundle re-entered the library.

'Sorry, Father,' she said, 'I wanted to catch MacDonald. Were you speaking?'

'As a matter of fact I was,' said Lord Caterham. 'But it doesn't matter. What were you saying to MacDonald?'

'Trying to cure him of thinking he's God Almighty. But that's an impossible task. I expect the Cootes have been bad for him. MacDonald wouldn't care one hoot, or even two hoots, for the largest steam-roller that ever was. What's Lady Coote like?'

Lord Caterham considered the question.

'Very like my idea of Mrs. Siddons,' he said at last. 'I should think she went in a lot for amateur theatricals. I gather she was very upset about the clock business.'

'What clock business?'

'Tredwell has just been telling me. It seems the house-party had some joke on. They bought a lot of alarum clocks and hid them about this young Wade's room. And then, of course, the poor chap was dead. Which made the whole thing rather beastly.'

Bundle nodded.

'Tredwell told me something else rather odd about the clocks,' continued Lord Caterham, who was now quite enjoying himself. 'It seems that somebody collected them all and put them in a row on the mantelpiece after the poor fellow was dead.'

'Well, why not?' said Bundle.

'I don't see why not myself,' said Lord Caterham. 'But apparently there was some fuss about it. No one would own up to having done it, you see. All the servants were questioned and swore they hadn't touched the beastly things. In fact, it was rather a mystery. And then the coroner asked questions at the inquest, and you know how difficult it is to explain things to people of that class.'

'Perfectly foul,' agreed Bundle.

'Of course,' said Lord Caterham, 'it's very difficult to get the hang of things afterwards. I didn't quite see the point of half the things Tredwell told me. By the way, Bundle, the fellow died in your room.'

Bundle made a grimace.

'Why need people die in my room?' she asked with some indignation.

'That's just what I've been saying,' said Lord Caterham, in triumph. 'Inconsiderate. Everybody's damned inconsiderate nowadays.'

'Not that I mind,' said Bundle valiantly. 'Why should I?'

'I should,' said her father. 'I should mind very much. I should dream things, you know—spectral hands and clanking chains.'

'Well,' said Bundle. 'Great Aunt Louisa died in *your* bed. I wonder you don't see her spook hovering over you.'

'I do sometimes,' said Lord Caterham, shuddering. 'Especially after lobster.'

'Well, thank heaven I'm not superstitious,' declared Bundle.

Yet that evening, as she sat in front of her bedroom fire, a slim, pyjamaed figure, she found her thoughts reverting to that cheery, vacuous young man, Gerry Wade. Impossible to believe that anyone so full of the joy of living could deliberately have committed suicide. No, the other solution must be the right one. He had taken a sleeping draught and by a pure mistake had swallowed an overdose. That *was* possible. She did not fancy that Gerry Wade had been overburdened in an intellectual capacity.

Her gaze shifted to the mantelpiece and she began thinking about the story of the clocks. Her maid had been full of that, having just been primed by the second housemaid. She had added a detail which apparently Tredwell had not thought worth while retailing to Lord Caterham, but which had piqued Bundle's curiosity.

Seven clocks had been neatly ranged on the mantelpiece; the last and remaining one had been found on the lawn outside, where it had obviously been thrown from the window.

Bundle puzzled over that point now. It seemed such an extraordinarily purposeless thing to do. She could imagine that one of the maids might have tidied the clocks and then, frightened by the inquisition into the matter, have denied doing so. But surely no maid would have thrown a clock into the garden.

Had Gerry Wade done so when its first sharp summons woke him? But no; that again was impossible. Bundle remembered hearing that his death must have taken place in the early hours of the morning, and he would have been in a comatose condition for some time before that.

Bundle frowned. This business of the clocks *was* curious. She must get hold of Bill Eversleigh. He had been there, she knew.

To think was to act with Bundle. She got up and went over to the writing desk. It was an inlaid affair with a lid that rolled back. Bundle sat down at it, pulled a sheet of note-paper towards her and wrote.

DEAR BILL,——

She paused to pull out the lower part of the desk. It had stuck half-way, as she remembered it often did. Bundle tugged at it impatiently but it did not move. She recalled that on a former occasion an envelope had been pushed back with it and had jammed it for the time being. She took a thin paper-knife and slipped it into the narrow crack. She was so far successful that a corner of white paper showed. Bundle caught hold of it and drew it out. It was the first sheet of a letter, somewhat crumpled.

It was the date that first caught Bundle's eye. A big flourishing date that leaped out from the paper. Sept. 21st.

'September 21st,' said Bundle slowly. 'Why, surely that was——'

She broke off. Yes, she was sure of it. The 22nd was the day Gerry Wade was found dead. This, then, was a letter he must have been writing on the very evening of the tragedy.

Bundle smoothed it out and read it. It was unfinished.

'MY DARLING LORAINE,—I will be down on Wednesday. Am feeling awfully fit and rather pleased with myself all round. It will be heavenly to see you. Look here, do forget what I said about that Seven Dials business. I thought it was going to be more or less of a joke, but it isn't—anything but. I'm sorry I ever said anything about it—it's not the kind of business kids like you ought to be mixed up in. So forget about it, see?

'Something else I wanted to tell you—but I'm so sleepy I can't keep my eyes open.

'Oh, about Lurcher; I think——'

Here the letter broke off.

Bundle sat frowning. Seven Dials. Where was that? Some rather slummy district of London, she fancied. The words Seven Dials reminded her of something else, but for the moment she couldn't think of what. Instead her attention fastened on two phrases. 'Am feeling awfully fit . . .' and 'I'm so sleepy I can't keep my eyes open.'

That didn't fit in. That didn't fit in at all. For it was that very night that Gerry Wade had taken such a heavy dose of chloral that he never woke again. And if what he had written in that letter were true, why should he have taken it?

Bundle shook her head. She looked round the room and gave a slight shiver. Supposing Gerry Wade were watching her now. In this room he had died. . . .

She sat very still. The silence was unbroken save for the ticking of her little gold clock. That sounded unnaturally loud and important.

Bundle glanced towards the mantelpiece. A vivid picture rose before her mind's eye. The dead man lying on the bed, and seven clocks ticking on the mantelpiece—ticking loudly, ominously . . . ticking . . . ticking . . .

5. *The man in the road*

'FATHER,' said Bundle, opening the door of Lord Caterham's special sanctum and putting her head in, 'I'm going up to town in the Hispano. I can't stand the monotony down here any longer.'

'We only got home yesterday,' complained Lord Caterham.

'I know. It seems like a hundred years. I'd forgotten how dull the country could be.'

'I don't agree with you,' said Lord Caterham. 'It's peaceful, that's what it is—peaceful. And extremely comfortable. I appreciate getting back to Tredwell more than I can tell you. That man studies my comfort in the most marvellous manner. Somebody came round only this morning to know if they could hold a tally for girl guides here——'

'A rally,' interrupted Bundle.

'Rally or tally—it's all the same. Some silly word meaning nothing whatever. But it would have put me in a very awkward position—having to refuse—in fact, I probably shouldn't have refused. But Tredwell got me out of it. I've forgotten what he said—something damned ingenious which couldn't hurt anybody's feelings and which knocked the idea on the head absolutely.'

'Being comfortable isn't enough for me,' said Bundle. 'I want excitement.'

Lord Caterham shuddered.

'Didn't we have enough excitement four years ago?' he demanded plaintively.

'I'm about ready for some more,' said Bundle. 'Not that I expect I shall find any in town. But at any rate I shan't dislocate my jaw with yawning.'

'In my experience,' said Lord Caterham, 'people who go about looking for trouble usually find it.' He yawned. 'All the same,' he added, 'I wouldn't mind running up to town myself.'

'Well, come on,' said Bundle. 'But be quick, because I'm in a hurry.'

Lord Caterham, who had begun to rise from his chair, paused.

'Did you say you were in a hurry?' he asked suspiciously.

'In the devil of a hurry,' said Bundle.

'That settles it,' said Lord Caterham. 'I'm not coming. To be driven by you in the Hispano when you're in a hurry—no, it's not fair on any elderly man. I shall stay here.'

'Please yourself,' said Bundle, and withdrew.

Tredwell took her place.

'The vicar, my lord, is most anxious to see you, some unfortunate controversy having arisen about the status of the Boys' Brigade.'

Lord Caterham groaned.

'I rather fancied, my lord, that I had heard you mention at breakfast that you were strolling down to the village this morning to converse with the vicar on the subject.'

'Did you tell him so?' asked Lord Caterham eagerly.

'I did, my lord. He departed, if I may say so, hot foot. I hope I did right, my lord?'

'Of course you did, Tredwell. You are always right. You couldn't go wrong if you tried.'

Tredwell smiled benignly and withdrew.

Bundle meanwhile was sounding the Klaxon impatiently before the lodge gates, while a small child came hastening out with all speed from the lodge, admonishment from her mother following her.

'Make haste, Katie. That be her ladyship in a mortal hurry as always.'

It was indeed characteristic of Bundle to be in a hurry, especially when driving a car. She had skill and nerve and was a good driver; had it been otherwise her reckless pace would have ended in disaster more than once.

It was a crisp October day, with a blue sky and a dazzling sun. The sharp tang of the air brought the blood to Bundle's cheeks and filled her with the zest of living.

She had that morning sent Gerald Wade's unfinished letter to Loraine Wade at Deane Priory, enclosing a few explanatory lines. The curious impression it had made upon her was somewhat dimmed in the daylight, yet it still struck her as needing explanation. She intended to get hold of Bill Eversleigh sometime and extract from him fuller details of the house-party which had ended so tragically.

In the meantime, it was a lovely morning and she felt particularly well and the Hispano was running like a dream.

Bundle pressed her foot down on the accelerator and the Hispano responded at once. Mile after mile vanished, traffic was few and far between and Bundle had a clear stretch of road in front of her.

And then, without any warning whatever, a man reeled out of the hedge and on to the road right in front of the car. To stop in time was out of the question. With all her might Bundle wrenched at the steering wheel and swerved out to the right. The car was nearly in the ditch—nearly, but not quite. It was a dangerous manœuvre; but it succeeded. Bundle was almost certain that she had missed the man.

She looked back and felt a sickening sensation in the middle of her anatomy. The car had not passed over the man, but nevertheless it must have struck him in passing. He was lying face downwards on the road, and he lay ominously still.

Bundle jumped out and ran back. She had never yet run over anything more important than a stray hen. The fact that the accident was hardly her fault did not weigh with her at the minute. The man had seemed drunk, but drunk or not, she had killed him. She was quite sure she had killed him. Her heart beat sickeningly in great pounding thumps, sounding right up in her ears.

She knelt down by the prone figure and turned him very gingerly over. He neither groaned nor moaned. He was young, she saw, rather a pleasant-faced young man, well dressed and wearing a small toothbrush moustache.

There was no external mark of injury that she could see, but she was quite positive that he was either dead or dying. His eyelids flickered and the eyes half opened. Piteous eyes, brown and suffering, like a dog's. He seemed to be struggling to speak. Bundle bent right over.

'Yes,' she said. 'Yes?'

There was something he wanted to say, she could see that. Wanted to say badly. And she couldn't help him, couldn't do anything.

At last the words came, a mere sighing breath:

'*Seven Dials* . . . tell . . .'

'Yes,' said Bundle again. It was a name he was trying to get out—trying with all his failing strength. 'Yes. Who am I to tell?'

'*Tell . . . Jimmy Thesiger. . . .*' He got it out at last, and then suddenly, his head fell back and his body went limp.

Bundle sat back on her heels, shivering from head to foot. She could never have imagined that anything so awful could have happened to her. He was dead—and she had killed him.

She tried to pull herself together. What must she do now? A doctor—that was her first thought. It was possible—just possible—that the man might only be unconscious, not dead. Her instinct cried out against the possibility, but she forced herself to act upon it. Somehow or other she must get him into the car and take him to the nearest doctor's. It was a deserted stretch of country road and there was no one to help her.

Bundle, for all her slimness, was strong. She had muscles of whipcord. She brought the Hispano as close as possible, and then, exerting all her strength, she dragged and pulled the inanimate figure into it. It was a horrid business, and one that made her set her teeth, but at last she managed it.

Then she jumped into the driver's seat and started off. A couple of miles brought her into a small town and on inquiry she was quickly directed to the doctor's house.

Dr. Cassell, a kindly, middle-aged man, was startled to come into his surgery and find a girl there who was evidently on the verge of collapse.

Bundle spoke abruptly.

'I—I think I've killed a man. I ran over him. I brought him along in the car. He's outside now. I—I was driving too fast, I suppose. I've always driven too fast.'

The doctor cast a practised glance over her. He stepped over to a shelf and poured something into a glass. He brought it over to her.

'Drink this down,' he said, 'and you'll feel better. You've had a shock.'

Bundle drank obediently and a tinge of colour came into her pallid face. The doctor nodded approvingly.

'That's right. Now I want you to sit quietly here. I'll go out and attend to things. After I've made sure there's nothing to be done for the poor fellow, I'll come back and we'll talk about it.'

He was away some time. Bundle watched the clock on the mantelpiece. Five minutes, ten minutes, a quarter of an hour, twenty minutes—would he never come?

Then the door opened and Dr. Cassell reappeared. He looked different—Bundle noticed that at once—grimmer and at the same time more alert. There was something else in his manner that she did not quite understand, a suggestion of repressed excitement.

'Now then, young lady,' he said. 'Let's have this out. You ran over this man, you say. Tell me just how the accident happened?'

Bundle explained to the best of her ability. The doctor followed her narrative with keen attention.

'Just so; the car didn't pass over his body?'

'No. In fact, I thought I'd missed him altogether.'

'He was reeling, you say?'

'Yes, I thought he was drunk.'

'And he came from the hedge?'

'There was a gate just there, I think. He must have come through the gate.'

The doctor nodded, then he leaned back in his chair and removed his pince-nez.

'I've no doubt at all,' he said, 'that you're a very reckless driver, and that you'll probably run over some poor fellow and do for him one of these days—but you haven't done it this time.'

'But——'

'The car never touched him. *This man was shot.*'

6. *Seven Dials again*

BUNDLE stared at him. And very slowly the world, which for the last three quarters of an hour had been upside down, shifted till it stood once more the right way up. It was quite two minutes before Bundle spoke, but when she did it was no longer the panic-stricken girl but the real Bundle, cool, efficient and logical.

'How could he be shot?' she said.

'I don't know how he could,' said the doctor dryly. 'But he was. He's got a rifle bullet in him all right. He bled internally, that's why you didn't notice anything.'

Bundle nodded.

'The question is,' the doctor continued, 'who shot him? You saw nobody about?'

Bundle shook her head.

'It's odd,' said the doctor. 'If it was an accident, you'd expect the fellow who did it would come running to the rescue—unless just possibly he didn't know what he'd done.'

'There was no one about,' said Bundle. 'On the road, that is.'

'It seems to me,' said the doctor, 'that the poor lad must have been running—the bullet got him just as he passed through the gate and he came reeling on to the road in consequence. You didn't hear a shot?'

Bundle shook her head.

'But I probably shouldn't anyway,' she said, 'with the noise of the car.'

'Just so. He didn't say anything before he died?'

'He muttered a few words.'

'Nothing to throw light on the tragedy?'

'No. He wanted something—I don't know what—told to a friend of his. Oh! yes, and he mentioned Seven Dials.'

'H'm,' said Doctor Cassell. 'Not a likely neighbourhood for one of his class. Perhaps his assailant came from there. Well, we needn't worry about that now. You can leave it in my hands. I'll notify the police. You must, of course, leave your name and address, as the police are sure to want to question you. In fact, perhaps you'd better come round to the police station with me now. They might say I ought to have detained you.'

They went together in Bundle's car. The police inspector was a slow-speaking man. He was somewhat overawed by Bundle's name and address when she gave it to him, and he took down her statement with great care.

'Lads!' he said. 'That's what it is. Lads practising! Cruel stupid, them young varmints are. Always loosing off at birds with no consideration for anyone as may be the other side of a hedge.'

The doctor thought it a most unlikely solution, but he realised that the case would soon be in abler hands and it did not seem worth while to make objections.

'Name of deceased?' asked the sergeant, moistening his pencil.

'He had a card-case on him. He appears to have been a Mr. Ronald Devereux, with an address in the Albany.'

Bundle frowned. The name Ronald Devereux awoke some chord of remembrance. She was sure she had heard it before.

It was not until she was half-way back to Chimneys in the car that it came to her. Of course! Ronny Devereux. Bill's friend in the Foreign Office. He and Bill and—yes—Gerald Wade.

As this last realisation came to her, Bundle nearly went into the hedge. First Gerald Wade—then Ronny Devereux. Gerry Wade's death might have been natural—the result of carelessness—but Ronny Devereux's surely bore a more sinister interpretation.

And then Bundle remembered something else. Seven Dials! When the dying man had said it, it had seemed vaguely familiar. Now she knew why. Gerald Wade had mentioned Seven Dials in the last letter of his written to his sister on the night before his death. And that again connected up with something else that escaped her.

Thinking all these things over, Bundle had slowed down to such a sober pace that nobody would have recognised her. She drove the car round to the garage and went in search of her father.

Lord Caterham was happily reading a catalogue of a forthcoming sale of rare editions and was immeasurably astonished to see Bundle.

'Even you,' he said, 'can't have been to London and back in this time.'

'I haven't been to London,' said Bundle. 'I ran over a man.'

'What?'

'Only I didn't really. He was shot.'

'How could he have been?'

'I don't know how he could have been, but he was.'

'But why did you shoot him?'

'*I* didn't shoot him.'

'You shouldn't shoot people,' said Lord Caterham in a tone of mild remonstrance. 'You shouldn't really. I daresay some of them richly deserve it—but all the same it will lead to trouble.'

'I tell you I didn't shoot him.'

'Well, who did?'

'Nobody knows,' said Bundle.

'Nonsense,' said Lord Caterham. 'A man can't be shot and run over without anyone having done it.'

'He wasn't run over,' said Bundle.

'I thought you said he was.'

'I said I thought I had.'

'A tyre burst, I suppose,' said Lord Caterham. 'That does sound like a shot. It says so in detective stories.'

'You really are perfectly impossible, Father. You don't seem to have the brains of a rabbit.'

'Not at all,' said Lord Caterham. 'You come in with a wildly impossible tale about men being run over and shot and I don't know what, and then you expect me to know all about it by magic.'

Bundle sighed wearily.

'Just attend,' she said. 'I'll tell you all about it in words of one syllable.'

'There,' she said when she had concluded. 'Now have you got it?'

'Of course. I understand perfectly, now. I can make allowances for your being a little upset, my dear. I was not far wrong when I remarked to you before starting out that people looking for trouble usually found it. I am thankful,' finished Lord Caterham with a slight shiver, 'that I stayed quietly here.'

He picked up the catalogue again.

'Father, where is Seven Dials?'

'In the East End somewhere, I fancy. I have frequently observed buses going there—or do I mean Seven Sisters? I have never been there myself, I am thankful to say. Just as well, because I don't fancy it is the sort of spot I should like. And yet, curiously enough, I seem to have heard of it in some connection just lately.'

'You don't know a Jimmy Thesiger, do you?'

Lord Caterham was now ingrossed in his catalogue once more. He had made an effort to be intelligent on the subject of Seven Dials. This time he made hardly any effort at all.

'Thesiger,' he murmured vaguely. 'Thesiger. One of the Yorkshire Thesigers?'

'That's what I'm asking you. Do attend, Father. This is important.'

Lord Caterham made a desperate effort to look intelligent without really having to give his mind to the matter.

'There *are* some Yorkshire Thesigers,' he said earnestly. 'And unless I am mistaken some Devonshire Thesigers also. Your Great Aunt Selina married a Thesiger.'

'What good is that to me?' cried Bundle.

Lord Caterham chuckled.

'It was very little good to her, if I remember rightly.'

'You're impossible,' said Bundle, rising. 'I shall have to get hold of Bill.'

'Do, dear,' said her father absently as he turned a page. 'Certainly. By all means. Quite so.'

Bundle rose to her feet with an impatient sigh.

'I wish I could remember what that letter said,' she murmured more to herself than aloud. 'I didn't read it very carefully. Something about a joke, that the Seven Dials business wasn't a joke.'

Lord Caterham emerged suddenly from his catalogue.

'Seven Dials?' he said. 'Of course. I've got it now.'

'Got what?'

'I know why it sounded so familiar. George Lomax has been over. Tredwell failed for once and let him in. He was on his way up to town. It seems he's having some political party at the Abbey next week and he got a warning letter.'

'What do you mean by a warning letter?'

'Well, I don't really know. He didn't go into details. I gather it said "Beware" and "Trouble is at hand," and all those sort of things. But anyway it was written from Seven Dials, I distinctly remember his saying so. He was going up to town to consult Scotland Yard about it. You know George?'

Bundle nodded. She was well acquainted with that public-spirited Cabinet Minister, George Lomax, His Majesty's Permanent Under Secretary of State for Foreign Affairs, who was shunned by many because of his inveterate habit of quoting from his public speeches in private. In allusion to his bulging eyeballs, he was known to many—Bill Eversleigh among others—as Codders.

'Tell me,' she said, 'was Codders interested at all in Gerald Wade's death?'

'Not that I ever heard of. He may have been, of course.'

Bundle said nothing for some minutes. She was busily engaged in trying to remember the exact wording of the letter she had sent on to Loraine Wade, and at the same time she was trying to picture the girl to whom it had been written. What sort of a girl was this to whom, apparently, Gerald Wade was so devoted? The more she thought over it, the more it seemed to her that it was an unusual letter for a brother to write.

'Did you say the Wade girl was Gerry's half-sister?' she asked suddenly.

'Well, of course, strictly speaking, I suppose she isn't—wasn't, I mean—his sister at all.'

'But her name's Wade?'

'Not really. She wasn't old Wade's child. As I was saying, he ran away with his second wife, who was married to a perfect blackguard. I suppose the Courts gave the rascally husband the custody of the child, but he certainly didn't avail himself of the privilege. Old Wade got very fond of the child and insisted that she should be called by his name.'

'I see,' said Bundle. 'That explains it.'

'Explains what?'

'Something that puzzled me about that letter.'

'She's rather a pretty girl, I believe,' said Lord Caterham. 'Or so I've heard.'

Bundle went upstairs thoughtfully. She had several objects in view. First she must find this Jimmy Thesiger. Bill, perhaps, would be helpful there. Ronny Devereux had been a friend of Bill's. If Jimmy Thesiger was a friend of Ronny's, the chances were that Bill would know him too. Then there was the girl, Loraine Wade. It was possible that she could throw some light on the problem of Seven Dials. Evidently Gerry Wade had said something to her about it. His anxiety that she should forget the fact had a sinister suggestion.

7. *Bundle pays a call*

GETTING HOLD OF BILL presented few difficulties. Bundle motored up to town on the following morning—this time without adventures by the way—and rang him up. Bill responded with alacrity, and made various suggestions as to lunch, tea, dinner and dancing. All of which suggestions Bundle turned down as made.

'In a day or two, I'll come and frivol with you, Bill. But for the moment I'm up on business.'

'Oh,' said Bill. 'What a beastly bore.'

'It's not that kind,' said Bundle. 'It's anything but boring. Bill, do you know anyone called Jimmy Thesiger?'

'Of course. So do you.'

'No, I don't,' said Bundle.

'Yes, you do. You must. Everyone knows old Jimmy.'

'Sorry,' said Bundle. 'Just for once I don't seem to be everyone.'

'Oh! but you must know Jimmy—pink-faced chap. Looks a bit of an ass. But really he's got as many brains as I have.'

'You don't say so,' said Bundle. 'He must feel a bit top heavy when he walks about.'

'Was that meant for sarcasm?'

'It was a feeble effort at it. What does Jimmy Thesiger do?'

'How do you mean, what does he do?'

'Does being at the Foreign Office prevent you from understanding your native language?'

'Oh! I see, you mean, has he got a job? No, he just fools around. Why should he do anything?'

'In fact, more money than brains?'

'Oh! I wouldn't say that. I told you just now that he had more brains than you'd think.'

Bundle was silent. She was feeling more and more doubtful. This gilded youth did not sound a very promising ally. And yet it was his name that had come first to the dying man's lips. Bill's voice chimed in suddenly with singular appropriateness.

'Ronny always thought a lot of his brains. You know, Ronny Devereux. Thesiger was his greatest pal.'

'Ronny——'

Bundle stopped, undecided. Clearly Bill knew nothing of the other's death. It occurred to Bundle for the first time that it was odd the morning papers had contained nothing of the tragedy. Surely it was the kind of spicy item of news that would never be passed over. There could be one explanation, and one explanation only. The police, for reasons of their own, were keeping the matter quiet.

Bill's voice was continuing.

'I haven't seen Ronny for an age—not since that week-end down at your place. You know, when poor old Gerry Wade passed out.'

He paused and then went on.

'Rather a foul business that altogether. I expect you've heard about it. I say, Bundle—are you there still?'

'Of course I'm here.'

'Well, you haven't said anything for an age. I began to think that you had gone away.'

'No, I was just thinking over something.'

Should she tell Bill of Ronny's death? She decided against it—it was not the sort of thing to be said over the telephone. But soon, very soon, she must have a meeting with Bill. In the meantime——

'Bill?'

'Hullo.'

'I might dine with you to-morrow night.'

'Good, and we'll dance afterwards. I've got a lot to talk to you about. As a matter of fact I've been rather hard hit—the foulest luck——

'Well, tell me about it to-morrow,' said Bundle, cutting him short rather unkindly. 'In the meantime, what is Jimmy Thesiger's address?'

'Jimmy Thesiger?'

'That's what I said.'

'He's got rooms in Jermyn Street—do I mean Jermyn Street or the other one?'

'Bring that class A brain to bear upon it.'

'Yes, Jermyn Street. Wait a bit and I'll give you the number.'

There was a pause.

'Are you there still?'

'I'm always there.'

'Well, one never knows with these dashed telephones. The number is 103. Got it?'

'103. Thank you, Bill.'

'Yes, but I say—what do you want it for? You said you didn't know him.'

'I don't, but I shall in half an hour.'

'You're going round to his rooms?'

'Quite right, Sherlock.'

'Yes, but, I say—well, for one thing he won't be up.'

'Won't be up?'

'I shouldn't think so. I mean, who would if they hadn't got to? Look at it that way. You've no idea what an effort it is for me to get here at eleven every morning, and the fuss Codders makes if I'm behind time is simply appalling. You haven't the least idea, Bundle, what a dog's life this is——'

'You shall tell me all about it to-morrow night,' said Bundle hastily.

She slammed down the receiver and took stock of the situation. First she glanced at the clock. It was five and twenty minutes to twelve. Despite Bill's knowledge of his friend's habits, she inclined to the belief that Mr. Thesiger would by now be in a fit state to receive visitors. She took a taxi to 103 Jermyn Street.

The door was opened by a perfect example of the retired gentleman's gentleman. His face, expressionless and polite, was such a face as may be found by the score in that particular district of London.

'Will you come this way, madam?'

He ushered her upstairs into an extremely comfortable sitting-room containing leather-covered arm-chairs of immense dimensions. Sunk in one of those monstrosities was another girl, rather younger than Bundle. A small, fair girl, dressed in black.

'What name shall I say, madam?'

'I won't give any name,' said Bundle. 'I just want to see Mr. Thesiger on important business.'

The grave gentleman bowed and withdrew, shutting the door noiselessly behind him.

There was a pause.

'It's a nice morning,' said the fair girl timidly.

'It's an awfully nice morning,' agreed Bundle.

There was another pause.

'I motored up from the country this morning,' said Bundle, plunging once more into speech. 'And I thought it was going to be one of those foul fogs. But it wasn't.'

'No,' said the other girl. 'It wasn't.' And she added: 'I've come up from the country too.'

Bundle eyed her more attentively. She had been slightly annoyed at finding the other there. Bundle belonged to the energetic order of people who like 'to get on with it,' and she foresaw that the second visitor would have to be disposed of and got rid of before she could broach her own business. It was not a topic she could introduce before a stranger.

Now, as she looked more closely, an extraordinary idea rose in her brain. Could it be? Yes, the girl was in deep mourning; her black, silk-clad ankles showed that. It was a long shot, but Bundle was convinced that her idea was right. She drew a long breath.

'Look here,' she said. 'Are you by any chance Loraine Wade?'

Loraine's eyes opened wide.

'Yes, I am. How clever of you to know. We've never met, have we?'

Bundle shook her head.

'I wrote to you yesterday, though. I'm Bundle Brent.'

'It was so very kind of you to send me Gerry's letter,' said Loraine. 'I've written to thank you. I never expected to see you here.'

'I'll tell you why I'm here,' said Bundle. 'Did you know Ronny Devereux?'

Loraine nodded.

'He came over the day that Gerry—you know. And he's been to see me two or three times since. He was one of Gerry's greatest friends.'

'I know. Well—he's dead.'

Loraine's lips parted in surprise.

'*Dead!* But he always seemed so fit.'

Bundle narrated the events of the preceding day as briefly as possible. A look of fear and horror came into Loraine's face.

'Then it *is* true. It *is* true.'

'What's true?'

'What I've thought—what I've been thinking all these weeks. Gerald didn't die a natural death. He was killed.'

'You've thought that, have you?'

'Yes. Gerry would never have taken things to make him sleep.' She gave the little ghost of a laugh. 'He slept much too well to need them. I always thought it queer. And *he* thought so too—I know he did.'

'Who?'

'Ronny. And now this happens. Now he's killed too.' She paused and then went on: 'That's what I came for to-day. That letter of Gerry's you sent me—as soon as I read it, I tried to get hold of Ronny, but they said he was away. So I thought I'd come and see Jimmy—he was Ronny's other great friend. I thought perhaps he'd tell me what I ought to do.'

'You mean——' Bundle paused. 'About—Seven Dials.'

Loraine nodded.

'You see——' she began.

But at that moment Jimmy Thesiger entered the room.

8. *Visitors for Jimmy*

WE MUST AT THIS POINT go back to some twenty minutes earlier. To a moment when Jimmy Thesiger, emerging from the mists of sleep, was conscious of a familiar voice speaking unfamiliar words.

His sleep-ridden brain tried for a moment to cope with the situation, but failed. He yawned and rolled over again.

'A young lady, sir, has called to see you.'

The voice was implacable. So prepared was it to go on repeating the statement indefinitely that Jimmy resigned himself to the inevitable. He opened his eyes and blinked.

'Eh, Stevens?' he said. 'Say that again.'

'A young lady, sir, has called to see you.'

'Oh!' Jimmy strove to grasp the situation. 'Why?'

'I couldn't say, sir.'

'No, I suppose not. No,' he thought it over. 'I suppose you couldn't.'

Stevens swooped down upon a tray by the bedside.

'I will bring you some fresh tea, sir. This is cold.'

'You think that I ought to get up and—er—see the lady?'

Stevens made no reply, but he held his back very stiff and Jimmy read the signs correctly.

'Oh! very well,' he said. 'I suppose I'd better. She didn't give her name?'

'No, sir.'

'H'm. She couldn't be by any possible chance my Aunt Jemima, could she? Because if so, I'm damned if I'm going to get up.'

'The lady, sir, could not possibly be anyone's aunt, I should say, unless the youngest of a large family.'

'Aha,' said Jimmy. 'Young and lovely. Is she—what kind is she?'

'The young lady, sir, is most undoubtedly strictly *comme il faut*, if I may use the expression.'

'You may use it,' said Jimmy graciously. 'Your French pronunciation, Stevens, if I may say so, is very good. Much better than mine.'

'I am gratified to hear it, sir. I have lately been taking a correspondence course in French.'

'Have you really? You're a wonderful chap, Stevens.'

Stevens smiled in a superior fashion and left the room. Jimmy lay trying to recall the names of any young and lovely girls strictly *comme il faut* who might be likely to come and call upon him.

Stevens re-entered with fresh tea, and as Jimmy sipped it he felt a pleasurable curiosity.

'You've given her the paper and all that, I hope, Stevens,' he said.

'I supplied her with the *Morning Post* and *Punch*, sir.'

A ring at the bell took him away. In a few minutes he returned.

'Another young lady, sir.'

'What?'

Jimmy clutched his head.

'Another young lady; she declines to give her name, sir, but says her business is important.'

Jimmy stared at him.

'This is damned odd, Stevens. Damned odd. Look here, what time did I come home last night?'

'Just upon five o'clock, sir.'

'And was I—er—how was I?'

'Just a little cheerful, sir—nothing more. Inclined to sing "Rule Britannia."'

'What an extraordinary thing,' said Jimmy. '"Rule Britannia," eh? I cannot imagine myself in a sober state ever singing "Rule Britannia." Some latent patriotism must have emerged under the stimulus of—er—just a couple too many. I was celebrating at the "Mustard and Cress," I remember. Not nearly such an innocent spot as it sounds, Stevens.' He paused. 'I was wondering——'

'Yes, sir?'

'I was wondering whether under the aforementioned stimulus I had put an advertisement in a newspaper asking for a nursery governess or something of that sort.'

Stevens coughed.

'*Two* girls turning up. It looks odd. I shall eschew the "Mustard and Cress" in future. That's a good word, Stevens—*eschew*—I met it in a crossword the other day and took a fancy to it.'

Whilst he was talking Jimmy was rapidly apparelling himself. At the end of ten minutes he was ready to face his unknown guests. As he opened the door of his sitting-room the first person he saw was a dark, slim girl who was totally unknown to him. She was standing by the mantelpiece, leaning against it. Then his glance went on to the big leather-covered arm-chair, and his heart missed a beat. Loraine!

It was she who rose and spoke first a little nervously.

'You must be very surprised to see me. But I had to come. I'll explain in a minute. This is Lady Eileen Brent.'

'Bundle—that's what I'm usually known as. You've probably heard of me from Bill Eversleigh.'

'Oh, rather, of course I have,' said Jimmy, endeavouring to cope with the situation. 'I say, do sit down and let's have a cocktail or something.'

But both girls declined.

'As a matter of fact,' continued Jimmy, 'I'm only just out of bed.'

'That's what Bill said,' remarked Bundle. 'I told him I was coming round to see you, and he said you wouldn't be up.'

'Well, I'm up now,' said Jimmy encouragingly.

'It's about Gerry,' said Loraine. 'And now about Ronny——'

'What do you mean by "and now about Ronny"?'

'He was shot yesterday.'

'What?' cried Jimmy.

Bundle told her story for the second time. Jimmy listened like a man in a dream.

'Old Ronny—shot,' he murmured. 'What *is* this damned business?'

He sat down on the edge of a chair, thinking for a minute or two, and then spoke in a quiet, level voice.

'There's something I think I ought to tell you.'

'Yes,' said Bundle encouragingly.

'It was on the day Gerry Wade died. On the way over to break the news to *you*'—he nodded at Loraine—'in the car Ronny said something to me. That is to say, he started to tell me something. There was something he wanted to tell me, and he began about it, and then he said he was bound by a promise and couldn't go on.'

'Bound by a promise,' said Loraine thoughtfully.

'That's what he said. Naturally I didn't press him after that. But he was odd—darned odd—all through. I got the impression then that he suspected—well, foul play. I thought he'd tell the doctor so. But no, not even a hint. So I thought I'd been mistaken. And afterwards, with the evidence and all—well, it seemed such a very clear case. I thought my suspicions had been all bosh.'

'But you think Ronny still suspected?' asked Bundle.

Jimmy nodded.

'That's what I think now. Why, none of us have seen anything of him since. I believe he was playing a lone hand—trying to find out the truth about Gerry's death, and what's more, I believe he *did* find out. That's why the devils shot him. And then he tried to send word to me, but could only get out those two words.'

'Seven Dials,' said Bundle, and shivered a little.

'Seven Dials,' said Jimmy gravely. 'At any rate we've got that to go on with.'

Bundle turned to Loraine.

'You were just going to tell me——'

'Oh! yes. First, about the letter.' She spoke to Jimmy. 'Gerry left a letter. Lady Eileen——'

'Bundle.'

'Bundle found it.' She explained the circumstances in a few words.

Jimmy listened, keenly interested. This was the first he had heard of the letter. Loraine took it from her bag and handed it to him. He read it, then looked across at her.

'This is where you can help us. What was it Gerry wanted you to forget?'

Loraine's brows wrinkled a little in perplexity.

'It's so hard to remember exactly now. I opened a letter of Gerry's by mistake. It was written on cheap sort of paper, I remember, and very illiterate handwriting. It had some address in Seven Dials at the head of it. I realised it wasn't for me, so I put it back in the envelope without reading it.'

'Sure?' asked Jimmy very gently.

Loraine laughed for the first time.

'I know what you think, and I admit that women *are* curious. But, you see, this didn't even look interesting. It was a kind of list of names and dates.'

'Names and dates,' said Jimmy thoughtfully.

'Gerry didn't seem to mind much,' continued Loraine. 'He laughed. He asked me if I had ever heard of the Mafia, and then said it would be queer if a society like the Mafia started in England—but that that kind of secret society didn't take on much with English people. "Our criminals," he said, "haven't got a picturesque imagination."'

Jimmy pursed up his lips into a whistle.

'I'm beginning to see,' he said. 'Seven Dials must be the headquarters of some secret society. As he says in his letter to you, he thought it rather a joke to start with. But evidently it wasn't a joke—he says as much. And there's something else: his anxiety that you should forget what he'd told you. There can be only one reason for that—if that society suspected that you had any knowledge of its activity, you too would be in danger. Gerald realised the peril, and he was terribly anxious—for you.'

He stopped, then he went on quietly:

'I rather fancy that we're all going to be in danger—if we go on with this.'

'If——?' cried Bundle indignantly.

'I'm talking of you two. It's different for me. I was poor old Ronny's pal.' He looked at Bundle. 'You've done your bit. You've delivered the message he sent me. No; for God's sake keep out of it, you and Loraine.'

Bundle looked questioningly at the other girl. Her own mind was definitely made up, but she gave no indication of it just then. She had no wish to push Loraine Wade into a dangerous undertaking.

But Loraine's small face was alight at once with indignation.

'You say that! Do you think for one minute I'd be content to keep out of it—when they killed Gerry—my own dear Gerry, the best and dearest and kindest brother any girl ever had. The only person belonging to me I had in the whole world'

Jimmy cleared his throat uncomfortably. Loraine, he thought, was wonderful; simply wonderful.

'Look here,' he said awkwardly. 'You mustn't say that. About being alone in the world—all that rot. You've got lots of friends—only too glad to do what they can. See what I mean?'

It is possible that Loraine did, for she suddenly blushed, and to cover her confusion began to talk nervously.

'That's settled,' she said. 'I'm going to help. Nobody's going to stop me.'

'And so am I, of course,' said Bundle.

They both looked at Jimmy.

'Yes,' he said slowly. 'Yes, quite so.'

They looked at him inquiringly.

'I was just wondering,' said Jimmy, 'how we were going to begin.'

9. *Plans*

JIMMY'S WORDS lifted the discussion at once into a more practical sphere.

'All things considered,' he said, 'we haven't got much to go on. In fact, just the words Seven Dials. As a matter of fact I don't even know exactly where Seven Dials is. But, anyway, we can't very well comb out the whole of that district, house by house.'

'We could,' said Bundle.

'Well, perhaps we could eventually—though I'm not so sure. I imagine it's a well-populated area. But it wouldn't be very subtle.'

The word reminded him of the girl Socks and he smiled.

'Then, of course, there's the part of the country where Ronny was shot. We could nose around there. But the police are probably doing everything we could do, and doing it much better.'

'What I like about you,' said Bundle sarcastically, 'is your cheerful and optimistic disposition.'

'Never mind her, Jimmy,' said Loraine softly. 'Go on.'

'Don't be so impatient,' said Jimmy to Bundle. 'All the best sleuths approach a case this way, by eliminating unnecessary and unprofitable investigation. I'm coming now to the third alternative—Gerald's death. Now that we know it was murder—by the way, you do both believe that, don't you?'

'Yes,' said Loraine.

'Yes,' said Bundle.

'Good. So do I. Well, it seems to me that there we do stand some faint chance. After all, if Gerry didn't take the chloral himself, someone must have got into his room and put it there—dissolved it in the glass of water, so that when he woke up he drank it off. And of course left the empty box or bottle or whatever it was. You agree with that?'

'Ye—es,' said Bundle slowly. 'But——'

'Wait. And that someone must have been in the house at the time. It couldn't very well have been someone from outside.'

'No,' agreed Bundle, more readily this time.

'Very well. Now, that narrows down things considerably. To begin with, I suppose a good many of the servants are family ones—they're your lot, I mean.'

'Yes,' said Bundle. 'Practically all the staff stayed when we let it. All the principal ones are there still—of course there have been changes among the under-servants.'

'Exactly—that's what I am getting at. *You*'—he addressed Bundle—'must go into all that. Find out when new servants were engaged—what about footmen, for instance?'

'One of the footmen is new. John, his name is.'

'Well, make inquiries about John. And about any others who have only come recently.'

'I suppose,' said Bundle slowly, 'it must have been a servant. It couldn't have been one of the guests?'

'I don't see how that's possible.'

'Who were there exactly?'

'Well, there were three girls—Nancy and Helen and Socks——'

'Socks Daventry? I know her.'

'May have been. Girl who was always saying things were subtle.'

'That's Socks all right. Subtle is one of her words.'

'And then there was Gerry Wade and me and Bill Eversleigh and Ronny. And, of course, Sir Oswald and Lady Coote. Oh! and Pongo.'

'Who's Pongo?'

'Chap called Bateman—secretary to old Coote. Solemn sort of cove but very conscientious. I was at school with him.'

'There doesn't seem anything very suspicious there,' remarked Loraine.

'No, there doesn't,' said Bundle. 'As you say, we'll have to look amongst the servants. By the way, you don't suppose that clock being thrown out of the window had anything to do with it.'

'A clock thrown out of the window,' said Jimmy, staring. It was the first he had heard of it.

'I can't see how it can have anything to do with it,' said Bundle. 'But it's odd somehow. There seems no sense in it.'

'I remember,' said Jimmy slowly. 'I went in to—to see poor old Gerry, and there were the clocks ranged along the mantelpiece. I remember noticing there were only seven—not eight.'

He gave a sudden shiver and explained himself apologetically.

'Sorry. But somehow those clocks have always given me the shivers. I dream of them sometimes. I'd hate to go into that room in the dark and see them there in a row.'

'You wouldn't be able to see them if it was dark,' said Bundle practically. 'Not unless they had luminous dials—Oh!' She gave a sudden gasp and the colour rushed into her cheeks. 'Don't you see? *Seven Dials!*'

The others looked at her doubtfully, but she insisted with increasing vehemence.

'It must be. It can't be a coincidence.'

There was a pause.

'You may be right,' said Jimmy Thesiger at last. 'It's—it's dashed odd.'

Bundle started questioning him eagerly.

'Who bought the clocks?'

'All of us.'

'Who thought of them?'

'All of us.'

'Nonsense, somebody must have thought of them first.'

'It didn't happen that way. We were discussing what we could do to get Gerry up, and Pongo said an alarum clock, and somebody said one would be no good, and somebody else—Bill Eversleigh, I think—said why not get a dozen. And we all said good egg and hoofed off to get them. We got one each and an extra one for Pongo and one for Lady Coote—just out of the generosity of our hearts. There was nothing premeditated about it—it just happened.'

Bundle was silenced, but not convinced.

Jimmy proceeded to sum up methodically.

'I think we can say we're sure of certain facts. There's a secret society, with points of resemblance to the Mafia, in existence. Gerry Wade came to know about it. At first he treated it as rather a joke—as an absurdity, shall we say. He couldn't believe in its being really dangerous. But later something happened to convince him, and then he got the wind up in earnest. I rather fancy he must have said something to Ronny Devereux about it. Anyway, when he was put out of the way, Ronny suspected, and he must have known enough to get on the same track himself. The unfortunate thing is that we've got to start quite from the outer darkness. We haven't got the knowledge the other two had.'

'Perhaps that's an advantage,' said Loraine coolly. 'They won't suspect us and therefore they won't be trying to put us out of the way.'

'I wish I felt sure about that,' said Jimmy in a worried voice. 'You know, Loraine, old Gerry himself wanted you to keep out of it. Don't you think you could——'

'No, I couldn't,' said Loraine. 'Don't let's start discussing that again. It's only a waste of time.'

At the mention of the word time, Jimmy's eyes rose to the clock and he uttered an exclamation of astonishment. He rose and opened the door.

'Stevens.'

'Yes, sir?'

'What about a spot of lunch, Stevens? Could it be managed?'

'I anticipated that it would be required, sir. Mrs. Stevens has made preparations accordingly.'

'That's a wonderful man,' said Jimmy, as he returned, heaving a sigh of relief. 'Brain, you know. Sheer brain. He takes correspondence courses. I sometimes wonder if they'd do any good to me.'

'Don't be silly,' said Loraine.

Stevens opened the door and proceeded to bring in a most recherché meal. An omelette was followed by quails and the very lightest thing in soufflés.

'Why are men so happy when they're single,' said Loraine tragically. 'Why are they so much better looked after by other people than by us?'

'Oh! but that's rot, you know,' said Jimmy. 'I mean, they're not. How could they be? I often think——'

He stammered and stopped. Loraine blushed again.

Suddenly Bundle let out a whoop and both the others started violently.

'Idiot,' said Bundle. 'Imbecile. Me, I mean. I knew there was something I'd forgotten.'

'What?'

'You know Codders—George Lomax, I mean?'

'I've heard of him a good deal,' said Jimmy. 'From Bill and Ronny, you know.'

'Well, Codders is giving some sort of a dry party next week—and he's had a warning letter from Seven Dials.'

'What?' cried Jimmy excitedly, leaning forward. 'You can't mean it?'

'Yes, I do. He told Father about it. Now what do you think that points to?'

Jimmy leant back in his chair. He thought rapidly and carefully. At last he spoke. His speech was brief and to the point.

'Something's going to happen at that party,' he said.

'That's what I think,' said Bundle.

'It all fits in,' said Jimmy almost dreamily.

He turned to Loraine.

'How old were you when the war was on?' he asked unexpectedly.

'Nine—no, eight.'

'And Gerry, I suppose, was about twenty. Most lads of twenty fought in the war. Gerry didn't.'

'No,' said Loraine, after thinking a minute or two. 'No, Gerry wasn't a soldier. I don't know why.'

'I can tell you why,' said Jimmy. 'Or at least I can make a very shrewd guess. He was out of England from 1915 to 1918. I've taken the trouble to find that out. And nobody seems to know exactly where he was. I think he was in Germany.'

The colour rose in Loraine's cheeks. She looked at Jimmy with admiration.

'How clever of you.'

'He spoke German well, didn't he?'

'Oh, yes, like a native.'

'I'm sure I'm right. Listen, you two. Gerry Wade was at the Foreign Office. He appeared to be the same sort of amiable idiot—excuse the term, but you know what I mean—as Bill Eversleigh and Ronny Devereux. A purely ornamental excrescence. But in reality he was something quite different. I think Gerry Wade was the real thing. Our secret service is supposed to be the best in the world. I think Gerry Wade was pretty high up in that service. And that explains everything! I remember saying idly that last evening at Chimneys that Gerry couldn't be quite such an ass as he made himself out to be.'

'And if you're right?' said Bundle, practical as ever.

'Then the thing's bigger than we thought. This Seven Dials business isn't merely criminal—it's international. One thing's certain, somebody has got to be at this house-party of Lomax's.'

Bundle made a slight grimace.

'I know George well—but he doesn't like me. He'd never think of asking me to a serious gathering. All the same, I might——'

She remained a moment lost in thought.

'Do you think *I* could work it through Bill?' asked Jimmy. 'He's bound to be there as Codder's right hand man. He might bring me along somehow or other.'

'I don't see why not,' said Bundle. 'You'll have to prime Bill and make him say the right things. He's incapable of thinking of them for himself.'

'What do you suggest?' asked Jimmy humbly.

'Oh! it's quite easy. Bill describes you as a rich young man—interested in politics, anxious to stand for Parliament. George will fall at once. You know what these political parties are: always looking for new, rich young men. The richer Bill says you are, the easier it will be to manage.'

'Short of being described as Rothschild, I don't mind,' said Jimmy.

'Then I think that's practically settled. I'm dining with Bill to-morrow night, and I'll get a list of who is to be there. That will be useful.'

'I'm sorry you can't be there,' said Jimmy. 'But on the whole I think it's all for the best.'

'I'm not so sure I shan't be there,' said Bundle. 'Codders hates me like poison—but there are other ways.'

She became meditative.

'And what about me?' asked Loraine in a small, meek voice.

'You're not on in this act,' said Jimmy instantly. 'See? After all, we've got to have someone outside to—er——'

'To what?' said Loraine.

Jimmy decided not to pursue this tack. He appealed to Bundle.

'Look here,' he said. 'Loraine must keep out of this, mustn't she?'

'I certainly think she'd better.'

'Next time,' said Jimmy kindly.

'And suppose there isn't a next time,' said Loraine.

'Oh, there probably will be. Not a doubt of it.'

'I see. I'm just to go home and—wait.'

'That's it,' said Jimmy, with every appearance of relief. 'I thought you'd understand.'

'You see,' explained Bundle, 'three of us forcing our way in might look rather suspicious. And you would be particularly difficult. You do see that, don't you?'

'Oh, yes,' said Loraine.

'Then it's settled—you do nothing,' said Jimmy.

'I do nothing,' said Loraine meekly.

Bundle looked at her in sudden suspicion. The tameness with which Loraine was taking it seemed hardly natural. Loraine looked at her. Her eyes were blue and guileless. They met Bundle's without a quiver even of the lashes. Bundle was only partly satisfied. She found the meekness of Loraine Wade highly suspicious.

10. *Bundle visits Scotland Yard*

NOW IT MAY BE SAID at once that in the foregoing conversation each one of the three participants had, as it were, held something in reserve. That 'Nobody tells everything' is a very true motto.

It may be questioned, for instance, if Loraine Wade was perfectly sincere in her account of the motives which had led her to seek out Jimmy Thesiger.

In the same way, Jimmy Thesiger himself had various ideas and plans connected with the forthcoming party at George Lomax's which he had no intention of revealing to—say, Bundle.

And Bundle herself had a fully-fledged plan which she proposed to put into immediate execution and which she had said nothing whatever about.

On leaving Jimmy Thesiger's rooms, she drove to Scotland Yard, where she asked to see Superintendent Battle.

Superintendent Battle was rather a big man. He worked almost entirely on cases of a delicate political nature. On such a case he had come to Chimneys four years ago, and Bundle was frankly trading on his remembering this fact.

After a short delay, she was taken along several corridors and into the Superintendent's private room. Battle was a stolid-looking man with a wooden face. He looked supremely unintelligent and more like a commissionaire than a detective.

He was standing by the window when she entered, gazing in an expressionless manner at some sparrows.

'Good-afternoon, Lady Eileen,' he said. 'Sit down, won't you?'

'Thank you,' said Bundle. 'I was afraid you mightn't remember me.'

'Always remember people,' said Battle. He added: 'Got to in my job.'

'Oh!' said Bundle, rather damped.

'And what can I do for you?' inquired the Superintendent.

Bundle came straight to the point.

'I've always heard that you people at Scotland Yard have lists of all secret societies and things like that that are formed in London.'

'We try to keep up to date,' said Superintendent Battle cautiously.

'I suppose a great many of them aren't really dangerous.'

'We've got a very good rule to go by,' said Battle. 'The more they talk, the less they'll do. You'd be surprised how well that works out.'

'And I've heard that very often you let them go on?'

Battle nodded.

'That's so. Why shouldn't a man call himself a Brother of Liberty and meet twice a week in a cellar and talk about rivers of blood—it won't hurt either him or us. And if there *is* trouble any time, we know where to lay our hands on him.'

'But sometimes, I suppose,' said Bundle slowly, 'a society may be more dangerous than anyone imagines?'

'Very unlikely,' said Battle.

'But it *might* happen,' persisted Bundle.

'Oh, it *might*,' admitted the Superintendent.

There was a moment or two's silence. Then Bundle said quietly:

'Superintendent Battle, could you give me a list of secret societies that have their headquarters in Seven Dials?'

It was Superintendent Battle's boast that he had never been seen to display emotion. But Bundle could have sworn that just for a moment his eyelids flickered and he looked taken aback. Only for a moment, however. He was his usual wooden self as he said:

'Strictly speaking, Lady Eileen, there's no such place as Seven Dials nowadays.'

'No?'

'No. Most of it is pulled down and rebuilt. It was rather a low quarter once, but it's very respectable and high class nowadays. Not at all a romantic spot to poke about in for mysterious secret societies.'

'Oh!' said Bundle, rather nonplussed.

'But all the same I should very much like to know what put that neighbourhood into your head, Lady Eileen.'

'Have I got to tell you?'

'Well, it saves trouble, doesn't it? We know where we are, so to speak.'

Bundle hesitated for a minute.

'There was a man shot yesterday,' she said slowly. 'I thought I had run over him——'

'Mr. Ronald Devereux?'

'You know about it, of course. Why has there been nothing in the papers?'

'Do you really want to know that, Lady Eileen?'

'Yes, please.'

'Well, we just thought we should like to have a clear twenty-four hours—see? It will be in the papers to-morrow.'

'Oh!' Bundle studied him, puzzled.

What was hidden behind that immovable face? Did he regard the shooting of Ronald Devereux as an ordinary crime or as an extraordinary one?

'He mentioned Seven Dials when he was dying,' said Bundle slowly.

'Thank you,' said Battle. 'I'll make a note of that.'

He wrote a few words on the blotting pad in front of him.

Bundle started on another tack.

'Mr. Lomax, I understand, came to see you yesterday about a threatening letter he had had.'

'He did.'

'And that was written from Seven Dials?'

'It had Seven Dials written at the top of it, I believe.'

Bundle felt as though she was battering hopelessly on a locked door.

'If you'll let me advise you, Lady Eileen——'

'I know what you're going to say.'

'I should go home and—well, think no more about these matters.'

'Leave it to you, in fact?'

'Well,' said Superintendent Battle, 'after all, we *are* the professionals.'

'And I'm only an amateur? Yes, but you forget one thing—I mayn't have your knowledge and skill—but I have one advantage over you. I can work in the dark.'

She thought that the Superintendent seemed a little taken aback, as though the force of her words struck home.

'Of course,' said Bundle, 'if you won't give me a list of secret societies——'

'Oh! I never said that. You shall have a list of the whole lot.'

He went to the door, put his head through and called out something, then came back to his chair. Bundle, rather unreasonably, felt baffled. The ease with which he acceded to her request seemed to her suspicious. He was looking at her now in a placid fashion.

'Do you remember the death of Mr. Gerald Wade?' she asked abruptly.

'Down at your place, wasn't it? Took an overdraught of sleeping mixture.'

'His sister says he never took things to make him sleep.'

'Ah!' said the Superintendent. 'You'd be surprised what a lot of things there are that sisters don't know.'

Bundle again felt baffled. She sat in silence till a man came in with a typewritten sheet of paper, which he handed to the Superintendent.

'Here you are,' said the latter when the other had left the room. 'The Blood Brothers of St. Sebastian. The Wolf Hounds. The Comrades of Peace. The Comrades Club. The Friends of Oppression. The Children of Moscow. The Red Standard Bearers. The Herrings. The Comrades of the Fallen—and half a dozen more.'

He handed it to her with a distinct twinkle in his eye.

'You give it to me,' said Bundle, 'because you know it's not going to be the slightest use to me. Do you want me to leave the whole thing alone?'

'I should prefer it,' said Battle. 'You see—if you go messing round all these places—well, it's going to give us a lot of trouble.'

'Looking after me, you mean?'

'Looking after you, Lady Eileen.'

Bundle had risen to her feet. Now she stood undecided. So far the honours lay with Superintendent Battle. Then she remembered one slight incident, and she based a last appeal upon it.

'I said just now that an amateur could do some things which a professional couldn't. You didn't contradict me. That's because you're an honest man, Superintendent Battle. You knew I was right.'

'Go on,' said Battle quietly.

'At Chimneys you let me help. Won't you let me help now?'

Battle seemed to be turning the thing over in his mind. Emboldened by his silence, Bundle continued.

'You know pretty well what I'm like, Superintendent Battle. I butt into things. I'm a Nosy Parker. I don't want to get in your way or to try and do things that you're doing and can do a great deal better. But if there's a chance for an amateur, let me have it.'

Again there was a pause, and then Superintendent Battle said quietly:

'You couldn't have spoken fairer than you have done, Lady Eileen. But I'm just going to say this to you. What you propose is dangerous. And when I say dangerous, I *mean* dangerous.'

'I've grasped that,' said Bundle. 'I'm not a fool.'

'No,' said Superintendent Battle. 'Never knew a young lady who was less so. What I'll do for you, Lady Eileen, is this. I'll just give you one little hint. And I'm doing it because I never have thought much of the motto "Safety First." In my opinion half the people who spend their lives avoiding being run over by buses had much better be run over and put safely out of the way. They're no good.'

This remarkable utterance issuing from the conventional lips of Superintendent Battle quite took Bundle's breath away.

'What was the hint you were going to give me?' she asked at last.

'You know Mr. Eversleigh, don't you?'

'Know Bill? Why, of course. But what——'

'I think Mr. Bill Eversleigh will be able to tell you all you want to know about Seven Dials.'

'Bill knows about it? *Bill?*'

'I didn't say that. Not at all. But I think, being a quick-witted young lady, you'll get what you want from him.

'And now,' said Superintendent Battle firmly, 'I'm not going to say another word.'

11. *Dinner with Bill*

BUNDLE SET OUT to keep her appointment with Bill on the following evening full of expectation.

Bill greeted her with every sign of elation.

'Bill really *is* rather nice,' thought Bundle to herself. 'Just like a large, clumsy dog that wags its tail when it's pleased to see you.'

The large dog was uttering short staccato yelps of comment and information.

'You look tremendously fit, Bundle. I can't tell you how pleased I am to see you. I've ordered oysters—you do like oysters, don't you? And how's everything? What did you want to go mouldering about abroad so long? Were you having a very gay time?'

'No, deadly,' said Bundle. 'Perfectly foul. Old diseased colonels creeping about in the sun, and active, wizened spinsters running libraries and churches.'

'Give me England,' said Bill. 'I bar this foreign business—except Switzerland. Switzerland's all right. I'm thinking of going this Christmas. Why don't you come along?'

'I'll think of it,' said Bundle. 'What have you been doing with yourself lately, Bill?'

It was an incautious query. Bundle had merely made it out of politeness and as a preliminary to introducing her own topics of conversation. It was, however, the opening for which Bill had been waiting.

'That's just what I've been wanting to tell you about. You're brainy, Bundle, and I want your advice. You know that musical show, "Damn Your Eyes"?'

'Yes.'

'Well, I'm going to tell you about one of the dirtiest pieces of work imaginable. My God! the theatrical crowd. There's a girl—a Yankee girl—a perfect stunner——'

Bundle's heart sank. The grievances of Bill's lady friends were always interminable—they went on and on and there was no stemming them.

'This girl, Babe St. Maur her name is——'

'I wonder how she got that name?' said Bundle sarcastically.

Bill replied literally.

'She got it out of *Who's Who*. Opened it and jabbed her finger down on a page without looking. Pretty nifty, eh? Her real name's Goldschmidt or Abrameier—something quite impossible.'

'Oh, quite,' agreed Bundle.

'Well, Babe St. Maur is pretty smart. And she's got muscles. She was one of the eight girls who made the living bridge——'

'Bill,' said Bundle desperately. 'I went to see Jimmy Thesiger yesterday morning.'

'Good old Jimmy,' said Bill. 'Well, as I was telling you, Babe's pretty smart. You've got to be nowadays. She can put it over on most theatrical people. If you want to live, be high-handed, that's what Babe says. And mind you, she's the goods all right. She can act—it's marvellous how that girl can act. She'd not much chance in "Damn Your Eyes"—just swamped in a pack of good-looking girls. I said why not try the legitimate stage—you know, Mrs. Tanqueray—that sort of stuff—but Babe just laughed——'

'Have you seen Jimmy at all?'

'Saw him this morning. Let me see, where was I? Oh, yes, I hadn't got to the rumpus yet. And mind you it was jealousy—sheer, spiteful jealousy. The other girl wasn't a patch on Babe for looks and she knew it. So she went behind her back——'

Bundle resigned herself to the inevitable and heard the whole story of the unfortunate circumstances which had led up to Babe St. Maur's summary disappearance from the cast of 'Damn Your Eyes.' It took a long time. When Bill finally paused for breath and sympathy, Bundle said:

'You're quite right, Bill, it's a rotten shame. There must be a lot of jealousy about——'

'The whole theatrical world's rotten with it.'

'It must be. Did Jimmy say anything to you about coming down to the Abbey next week?'

For the first time, Bill gave his attention to what Bundle was saying.

'He was full of a long rigmarole he wanted me to stuff Codders with. About wanting to stand in the Conservative interest. But you know, Bundle, it's too damned risky.'

'Stuff,' said Bundle. 'If George *does* find him out, he won't blame you. You'll just have been taken in, that's all.'

'That's not it at all,' said Bill. 'I mean it's too damned risky for Jimmy. Before he knows where he is, he'll be parked down somewhere like Tooting West, pledged to kiss babies and make speeches. You don't know how thorough Codders is and how frightfully energetic.'

'Well, we'll have to risk that,' said Bundle. 'Jimmy can take care of himself all right.'

'You don't know Codders,' repeated Bill.

'Who's coming to this party, Bill? Is it anything very special?'

'Only the usual sort of muck. Mrs. Macatta for one.'

'The M.P.?'

'Yes, you know, always going off the deep end about Welfare and Pure Milk and Save the Children. Think of poor Jimmy being talked to by her.'

'Never mind Jimmy. Go on telling me.'

'Then there's a Hungarian, what they call a Young Hungarian. Countess something unpronounceable. She's all right.'

He swallowed as though embarrassed and Bundle observed that he was crumbling his bread nervously.

'Young and beautiful?' she inquired delicately.

'Oh, rather.'

'I didn't know George went in for female beauty much.'

'Oh, he doesn't. She runs baby feeding in Buda Pesth—something like that. Naturally she and Mrs. Macatta want to get together.'

'Who else?'

'Sir Stanley Digby——'

'The Air Minister?'

'Yes. And his secretary, Terence O'Rourke. He's rather a lad, by the way—or used to be in his flying days. Then there's a perfectly poisonous German chap called Herr Eberhard. I don't know who he is, but we're all making the hell of a fuss about him. I've been twice told off to take him out to lunch, and I can tell you, Bundle, it was no joke. He's not like the Embassy chaps, who are all very decent. This man sucks in soup and eats peas with a knife. Not only that, but the brute is always biting his finger-nails—positively gnaws at them.'

'Pretty foul.'

'Isn't it? I believe he invents things—something of the kind. Well, that's all. Oh, yes, Sir Oswald Coote.'

'And Lady Coote?'

'Yes, I believe she's coming too.'

Bundle sat lost in thought for some minutes. Bill's list was suggestive, but she hadn't time to think out various possibilities just now. She must get on to the next point.

'Bill?' she said. 'What's all this about Seven Dials?'

Bill at once looked horribly embarrassed. He blinked and avoided her glance.

'I don't know what you mean,' he said.

'Nonsense,' said Bundle. 'I was told you know all about it.'

'About what?'

This was rather a poser. Bundle shifted her ground.

'I don't see what you want to be so secretive for,' she complained.

'Nothing to be secretive about. Nobody goes there much now. It was only a craze.'

This sounded puzzling.

'One gets so out of things when one is away,' said Bundle in a sad voice.

'Oh, you haven't missed much,' said Bill. 'Everyone went there just to say they had been. It was boring really, and, my God, you *can* get tired of fried fish.'

'Where did everyone go?'

'To the Seven Dials Club, of course,' said Bill, staring. 'Wasn't that what you were asking about?'

'I didn't know it by that name,' said Bundle.

'Used to be a slummy sort of district round about Tottenham Court Road way. It's all pulled down and cleaned up now. But the Seven Dials Club keeps to the old atmosphere. Fried fish and chips. General squalor. Kind of East End stunt, but awfully handy to get at after a show.'

'It's a night club, I suppose,' said Bundle. 'Dancing and all that?'

'That's it. Awfully mixed crowd. Not a posh affair. Artists, you know, and all sorts of odd women and a sprinkling of our lot. They say quite a lot of things, but I think that that's all bunkum myself, just said to make the place go.'

'Good,' said Bundle. 'We'll go there to-night.'

'Oh! I shouldn't do that,' said Bill. His embarrassment had returned. 'I tell you it's played out. Nobody goes there now.'

'Well, we're going.'

'You wouldn't care for it, Bundle. You wouldn't really.'

'You're going to take me to the Seven Dials Club and nowhere else, Bill. And I should like to know why you are so unwilling?'

'I? Unwilling?'

'Painfully so. What's the guilty secret?'

'Guilty secret?'

'Don't keep repeating what I say. You do it to give yourself time.'

'I don't,' said Bill indignantly. 'It's only——'

'Well? I know there's something. You never can conceal anything.'

'I've got nothing to conceal. It's only——'

'Well?'

'It's a long story—— You see, I took Babe St. Maur there one night——'

'Oh! Babe St. Maur again.'

'Why not?'

'I didn't know it was about her——' said Bundle, stifling a yawn.

'As I say, I took Babe there. She rather fancied a lobster. I had a lobster under my arm——'

The story went on—— When the lobster had been finally dismembered in a struggle between Bill and a fellow who was a rank outsider, Bundle brought her attention back to him.

'I see,' she said. 'And there was a row?'

'Yes, but it was *my* lobster. I'd bought it and paid for it. I had a perfect right——'

'Oh, you had, you had,' said Bundle hastily. 'But I'm sure that's all forgotten now. And I don't care for lobsters anyway. So let's go.'

'We may be raided by the police. There's a room upstairs where they play baccarat.'

'Father will have to come and bail me out, that's all. Come on, Bill.'

Bill still seemed rather reluctant, but Bundle was adamant, and they were soon speeding to their destination in a taxi.

The place, when they got to it, was much as she imagined it would be. It was a tall house in a narrow street, 14 Hunstanton Street; she noted the number.

A man whose face was strangely familiar opened the door. She thought he started slightly when he saw her, but he greeted Bill with respectful recognition. He was a tall man, with fair hair, a rather weak, anæmic face and slightly shifty eyes. Bundle puzzled to herself where she could have seen him before.

Bill had recovered his equilibrium now and quite enjoyed doing showman. They danced in the cellar, which was very full of smoke—so much so that you saw everyone through a blue haze. The smell of fried fish was almost overpowering.

On the wall were rough charcoal sketches, some of them executed with real talent. The company was extremely mixed. There were portly foreigners, opulent Jewesses, a sprinkling of the really smart, and several ladies belonging to the oldest profession in the world.

Soon Bill led Bundle upstairs. There the weak-faced man was on guard, watching all those admitted to the gambling room with a lynx eye. Suddenly recognition came to Bundle.

'Of course,' she said. 'How stupid of me. It's Alfred, who used to be second footman at Chimneys. How are you, Alfred?'

'Nicely, thank you, your ladyship.'

'When did you leave Chimneys, Alfred? Was it long before we got back?'

'It was about a month ago, m'lady. I got a chance of bettering myself, and it seemed a pity not to take it.'

'I suppose they pay you very well here,' remarked Bundle.

'Very fair, m'lady.'

Bundle passed in. It seemed to her that in this room the real life of the club was exposed. The stakes were high, she saw that at once, and the people gathered round the two tables were of the true type. Hawk-eyed, haggard, with the gambling fever in their blood.

She and Bill stayed there for about half an hour. Then Bill grew restive.

'Let's get out of this place, Bundle, and go on dancing.'

Bundle agreed. There was nothing to be seen here. They went down again. They danced for another half-hour, had fish and chips, and then Bundle declared herself ready to go home.

'But it's so early,' Bill protested.

'No, it isn't. Not really. And, anyway, I've got a long day in front of me to-morrow.'

'What are you going to do?'

'That depends,' said Bundle mysteriously. 'But I can tell you this, Bill, the grass is not going to grow under my feet.'

'It never does,' said Mr. Eversleigh.

12. *Inquiries at Chimneys*

BUNDLE'S TEMPERAMENT was certainly not inherited from her father, whose prevailing characteristic was a wholly amiable inertia. As Bill Eversleigh had very justly remarked, the grass never did grow under Bundle's feet.

On the morning following her dinner with Bill, Bundle woke full of energy. She had three distinct plans which she meant to put into operation that day, and she realised that she was going to be slightly hampered by the limits of time and space.

Fortunately she did not suffer from the affliction of Gerry Wade, Ronny Devereux and Jimmy Thesiger—that of not being able to get up in the morning. Sir Oswald Coote himself would have had no fault to find with her on the score of early rising. At half-past eight Bundle had breakfasted and was on her way to Chimneys in the Hispano.

Her father seemed mildly pleased to see her.

'I never know when you're going to turn up,' he said. 'But this will save me ringing up, which I hate. Colonel Melrose was here yesterday about the inquest.'

Colonel Melrose was Chief Constable of the county, and an old friend of Lord Caterham.

'You mean the inquest on Ronny Devereux? When is it to be?'

'To-morrow. Twelve o'clock. Melrose will call for you. Having found the body, you'll have to give evidence, but he said you needn't be at all alarmed.'

'Why on earth should I be alarmed?'

'Well, you know,' said Lord Caterham apologetically, 'Melrose is a bit old-fashioned.'

'Twelve o'clock,' said Bundle. 'Good. I shall be here, if I'm still alive.'

'Have you any reason to anticipate not being alive?'

'One never knows,' said Bundle. 'The strain of modern life—as the newspapers say.'

'Which reminds me that George Lomax asked me to come over to the Abbey next week. I refused, of course.'

'Quite right,' said Bundle. 'We don't want you mixed up in any funny business.'

'Is there going to be any funny business?' asked Lord Caterham with a sudden awakening of interest.

'Well—warning letters and all that, you know,' said Bundle.

'Perhaps George is going to be assassinated,' said Lord Caterham hopefully. 'What do you think, Bundle—perhaps I'd better go after all.'

'You curb your bloodthirsty instincts and stay quietly at home,' said Bundle. 'I'm going to talk to Mrs. Howell.'

Mrs. Howell was the housekeeper, that dignified, creaking lady who had struck such terror to the heart of Lady Coote. She had no terrors for Bundle, whom, indeed, she always called Miss Bundle, a relic of the days when Bundle had stayed at Chimneys, a long-legged, impish child, before her father had succeeded to the title.

'Now, Howelly,' said Bundle, 'let's have a cup of rich cocoa together, and let me hear all the household news.'

She gleaned what she wanted without much difficulty, making mental notes as follows:

'Two new scullery maids—village girls—doesn't seem much there. New third housemaid—head housmaid's niece. That sounds all right. Howelly seems to have bullied poor Lady Coote a good deal. She would.'

'I never thought the day would come when I should see Chimneys inhabited by strangers, Miss Bundle.'

'Oh! one must go with the times,' said Bundle. 'You'll be lucky, Howelly, if you never see it converted into desirable flats with use of superb pleasure grounds.'

Mrs. Howell shivered all down her reactionary aristocratic spine.

'I've never seen Sir Oswald Coote,' remarked Bundle.

'Sir Oswald is no doubt a very clever gentleman,' said Mrs. Howell distantly.

Bundle gathered that Sir Oswald had not been liked by his staff.

'Of course, it was Mr. Bateman who saw to everything,' continued the housekeeper. 'A very efficient gentleman. A very efficient gentleman indeed, and one who knew the way things ought to be done.'

Bundle led the talk on to the topic of Gerald Wade's death. Mrs. Howell was only too willing to talk about it, and was full of pitying ejaculations about the poor young gentleman, but Bundle gleaned nothing new. Presently she took leave of Mrs. Howell and came downstairs again where she promptly rang for Tredwell.

'Tredwell, when did Alfred leave?'

'It would be about a month ago now, my lady.'

'Why did he leave?'

'It was by his own wish, my lady. I believe he has gone to London. I was not dissatisfied with him in any way. I think you will find the new footman, John, very satisfactory. He seems to know his work and to be most anxious to give satisfaction.'

'Where did he come from?'

'He had excellent references, my lady. He had lived last with Lord Mount Vernon.'

'I see,' said Bundle thoughtfully.

She was remembering that Lord Mount Vernon was at present on a shooting trip in East Africa.

'What's his last name, Tredwell?'

'Bower, my lady.'

Tredwell paused for a minute or two and then, seeing that Bundle had finished, he quietly left the room. Bundle remained lost in thought.

John had opened the door to her on her arrival that day, and she had taken particular notice of him without seeming to do so. Apparently, he was the perfect servant, well trained with an expressionless face. He had, perhaps, a more soldierly bearing than most footmen and there was something a little odd about the shape of the back of his head.

But these details, as Bundle realised, were hardly relevant to the situation. She sat frowning down at the blotting paper in front of her. She had a pencil in her hand and was idly tracing the name Bower over and over again.

Suddenly an idea struck her and she stopped dead, staring at the word. Then she summoned Tredwell once more.

'Tredwell, how is the name Bower spelt?'

'B-A-U-E-R, my lady.'

'That's not an English name.'

'I believe he is of Swiss extraction, my lady.'

'Oh! That's all, Tredwell, thank you.'

Swiss extraction? No. German! That martial carriage, that flat back to the head. And he had come to Chimneys a fortnight before Gerry Wade's death.

Bundle rose to her feet. She had done all she could here. Now to get on with things! She went in search of her father.

'I'm off again,' she said. 'I've got to go and see Aunt Marcia.'

'Got to see Marcia?' Lord Caterham's voice was full of astonishment. 'Poor child, how did you get let in for that?'

'Just for once,' said Bundle. 'I happen to be going of my own free will.'

Lord Caterham looked at her in amazement. That anyone could have a genuine desire to face his redoubtable sister-in-law was quite incomprehensible to him. Marcia, Marchioness of Caterham, the widow of his late brother Henry, was a very prominent personality. Lord Caterham admitted that she had made Henry an admirable wife and that but for her in all probability he would never have held the office of Secretary of State for Foreign Affairs. On the other hand, he had always looked upon Henry's early death as a merciful release.

It seemed to him that Bundle was foolishly putting her head into the lion's mouth.

'Oh! I say,' he said. 'You know, I shouldn't do that. You don't know what it may lead to.'

'I know what I hope it's going to lead to,' said Bundle. 'I'm all right, Father, don't you worry about me.'

Lord Caterham sighed and settled himself more comfortably in his chair. He went back to his perusal of the *Field*. But in a minute or two Bundle suddenly put her head in again.

'Sorry,' she said. 'But there's one other thing I wanted to ask you. What is Sir Oswald Coote?'

'I told you—a steam-roller.'

'I don't mean your personal impression of him. How did he make his money—trouser buttons or brass beds or what?'

'Oh, I see. He's steel. Steel and iron. He's got the biggest steel works, or whatever you call it, in England. He doesn't, of course, run the show personally now. It's a company or companies. He got me in as a director of something or other. Very good business for me—nothing to do except go down to the city once or twice a year to one of those hotel places—Cannon Street or Liverpool Street—and sit round a table where they have very nice new blotting paper. Then Coote or some clever Johnny makes a speech simply bristling with figures, but fortunately you needn't listen to it—and I can tell you, you often get a jolly good lunch out of it.'

Uninterested in Lord Caterham's lunches, Bundle had departed again before he had finished speaking. On the way back to London, she tried to piece together things to her satisfaction.

As far as she could see, steel and infant welfare did not go together. One of the two, then, was just padding—presumably the latter. Mrs. Macatta and the Hungarian countess could be ruled out of court. They were camouflage. No, the pivot of the whole thing seemed to be the unattractive Herr Eberhard. He did not seem the type of man whom George Lomax would normally invite. Bill had said vaguely that he invented. Then there was the Air Minister and Sir Oswald Coote, who was steel. Somehow that seemed to hang together.

Since it was useless speculating further, Bundle abandoned the attempt and concentrated on her forthcoming interview with Lady Caterham.

The lady lived in a large gloomy house in one of London's higher class squares. Inside it smelt of sealing wax, bird seed and slightly decayed flowers. Lady Caterham was a large woman—large in every way. Her proportions were majestic, rather than ample. She had a large beaked nose, wore gold rimmed pince-nez and her upper lip bore just the faintest suspicion of a moustache.

She was somewhat surprised to see her niece, but accorded her a frigid cheek, which Bundle duly kissed.

'This is quite an unexpected pleasure, Eileen,' she observed coldly.

'We've only just got back, Aunt Marcia.'

'I know. How is your father? Much as usual?'

Her tone conveyed disparagement. She had a poor opinion of Alastair Edward Brent, ninth Marquis of Caterham. She would have called him, had she known the term, a 'poor fish.'

'Father is very well. He's down at Chimneys.'

'Indeed. You know, Eileen, I never approved of the letting of Chimneys. The place is in many ways a historical monument. It should not be cheapened.'

'It must have been wonderful in Uncle Henry's day,' said Bundle with a slight sigh.

'Henry realised his responsibilities,' said Henry's widow.

'Think of the people who stayed there,' went on Bundle ecstatically. 'All the principal statesmen of Europe.'

Lady Caterham sighed.

'I can truly say that history has been made there more than once,' she observed. 'If only your father——'

She shook her head sadly.

'Politics bore Father,' said Bundle, 'and yet they are about the most fascinating study there is, I should say. Especially if one knew about them from the inside.'

She made this extravagantly untruthful statement of her feelings without even a blush. Her aunt looked at her with some surprise.

'I am pleased to here you say so,' she said. 'I always imagined. Eileen, that you cared for nothing but this modern pursuit of pleasure.'

'I used to,' said Bundle.

'It is true that you are still very young,' said Lady Caterham thoughtfully. 'But with your advantages, and if you were to marry suitably, you might be one of the leading political hostesses of the day.'

Bundle felt slightly alarmed. For a moment she feared that her aunt might produce a suitable husband straight away.

'But I feel such a fool,' said Bundle. 'I mean, I know so little.'

'That can easily be remedied,' said Lady Caterham briskly. 'I have any amount of literature I can lend you.'

'Thank you, Aunt Marcia,' said Bundle, and proceeded hastily to her second line of attack.

'I wondered if you knew Mrs. Macatta, Aunt Marcia?'

'Certainly I know her. A most estimable woman with a brilliant brain. I may say that as a general rule I do not hold with women standing for Parliament. They can make their influence felt in a more womanly fashion.' She paused, doubtless to recall the womanly way in which she had forced a reluctant husband into the political arena and the marvellous success which had crowned his and her efforts. 'But still, times change. And the work Mrs. Macatta is doing is of truly national importance, and of the utmost value to all women. It is, I think I may say, true womanly work. You must certainly meet Mrs. Macatta.'

Bundle gave a rather dismal sigh.

'She's going to be at a house-party at George Lomax's next week. He asked Father, who, of course, won't go, but he never thought of asking me. Thinks I'm too much of an idiot, I suppose.'

It occurred to Lady Caterham that her niece was really wonderfully improved. Had she, perhaps, had an unfortunate love affair? An unfortunate love affair, in Lady Caterham's opinion, was often highly beneficial to young girls. It made them take life seriously.

'I don't suppose George Lomax realises for a moment that you have—shall we say, grown up? Eileen dear,' she said, 'I must have a few words with him.'

'He doesn't like me,' said Bundle. 'I know he won't ask me.'

'Nonsense,' said Lady Caterham. 'I shall make a point of it. I knew George Lomax when he was so high.' She indicated a quite impossible height. 'He will be only too pleased to do me a favour. And he will be sure to see for himself that it is vitally important that the present-day young girls of our own class should take an intelligent interest in the welfare of their country.'

Bundle nearly said: 'Hear, hear,' but checked herself.

'I will find you some literature now,' said Lady Caterham, rising. She called in a piercing voice: 'Miss Connor.'

A very neat secretary with a frightened expression came running. Lady Caterham gave her various directions. Presently Bundle was driving back to Brook Street with an armful of the driest looking literature imaginable.

Her next proceeding was to ring up Jimmy Thesiger. His first words were full of triumph.

'I've managed it,' he said. 'Had a lot of trouble with Bill, though. He'd got it into his thick head that I should be a lamb among the wolves. But I made him see sense at last. I've got a lot of thingummy-bobs now and I'm studying them. You know, blue books and white papers. Deadly dull—but one must do the thing properly. Have you ever heard of the Santa Fé boundary dispute?'

'Never,' said Bundle.

'Well, I'm taking special pains with that. It went on for years and was very complicated. I'm making it my subject. Nowadays one has to specialise.'

'I've got a lot of the same sort of things,' said Bundle. 'Aunt Marcia gave them to me.'

'Aunt who?'

'Aunt Marcia—Father's sister-in-law. She's very political. In fact, she's going to get me invited to George's party.'

'No? Oh, I say, that will be splendid.' There was a pause and then Jimmy said:

'I say, I don't think we'd better tell Loraine that—eh?'

'Perhaps not.'

'You see, she mayn't like being out of it. And she really must be kept out of it.'

'Yes.'

'I mean you can't let a girl like that run into danger!'

Bundle reflected that Mr. Thesiger was slightly deficient in tact. The prospect of *her* running into danger did not seem to give him any qualms whatever.

'Have you gone away?' asked Jimmy.

'No, I was only thinking.'

'I see. I say, are you going to the inquest to-morrow?'

'Yes, are you?'

'Yes. By the way, it's in the evening papers. But tucked away in a corner. Funny—I should have thought they'd have made rather a splash about it.'

'Yes—so should I.'

'Well,' said Jimmy, 'I must be getting on with my task. I've just got to where Bolivia sent us a Note.'

'I suppose I must get on with my little lot,' said Bundle. 'Are you going to swot at it all the evening?'

'I think so. Are you?'

'Oh, probably. Good-night.'

They were both liars of the most unblushing order. Jimmy Thesiger knew perfectly well that he was taking Loraine Wade out to dinner.

As for Bundle, no sooner had she rung off than she attired herself in various nondescript garments belonging, as a matter of fact, to her maid. And having donned them, she sallied out on foot deliberating whether bus or tube would be the best route by which to reach the Seven Dials Club.

13. *The Seven Dials Club*

BUNDLE reached 14 Hunstanton Street about six p.m. At that hour, as she rightly judged, the Seven Dials Club was a dead spot. Bundle's aim was a simple one. She intended to get hold of the ex-footman Alfred. She was convinced that once she had got hold of him the rest would be easy. Bundle had a simple autocratic method of dealing with retainers. It seldom failed, and she saw no reason why it should fail now.

The only thing of which she was not certain was how many people inhabited the club premises. Naturally she wished to disclose her presence to as few people as possible.

Whilst she was hesitating as to her best line of attack, the problem was solved for her in a singularly easy fashion. The door of No. 14 opened and Alfred himself came out.

'Good-afternoon, Alfred,' said Bundle pleasantly.

Alfred jumped.

'Oh! good-afternoon, your ladyship. I—I didn't recognise your ladyship just for a moment.'

Paying a tribute in her own mind to her maid's clothing, Bundle proceeded to business.

'I want a few words with you, Alfred. Where shall we go?'

'Well—really, my lady—I don't know—it's not what you might call a nice part round here—I don't know, I'm sure——'

Bundle cut him short.

'Who's in the club?'

'No one at present, my lady.'

'Then we'll go in there.'

Alfred produced a key and opened the door. Bundle passed in. Alfred, troubled and sheepish, followed her. Bundle sat down and looked straight at the uncomfortable Alfred.

'I suppose you know,' she said crisply, 'that what you're doing here is dead against the law?'

Alfred shifted uncomfortably from one foot to the other.

'It's true as we've been raided twice,' he admitted. 'But nothing compromising was found, owing to the neatness of Mr. Mosgorovsky's arrangements.'

'I'm not talking of the gambling only,' said Bundle. 'There's more than that—probably a great deal more than you know. I'm going to ask you a direct question, Alfred, and I should like the truth, please. *How much were you paid for leaving Chimneys?*'

Alfred looked twice round the cornice as though seeking for inspirations, swallowed three or four times, and then took the inevitable course of a weak will opposed to a strong one.

'It was this way, your ladyship. Mr. Mosgorovsky, he come with a party to visit Chimneys on one of the show days. Mr. Tredwell, he was indisposed like—an ingrowing toe-nail as a matter of fact—so it fell to me to show the parties over. At the end of the tour, Mr. Mosgorovsky, he stays behind the rest, and after giving me something handsome, he falls into conversation.'

'And the long and the short of it was,' said Alfred, with a sudden acceleration of his narrative, 'that he offers me a hundred pound down to leave that instant minute and to look after this here club. He wanted someone as was used to the best families—to give the place a tone, as he put it. And, well, it seemed flying in the face of providence to refuse—let alone that the wages I get here are just three times what they were as second footman.'

'A hundred pounds,' said Bundle. 'That's a very large sum, Alfred. Did they say anything about who was to fill your place at Chimneys?'

'I demurred a bit, my lady, about leaving at once. As I pointed out, it wasn't usual and might cause inconvenience. But Mr. Mosgorovsky he knew of a young chap—been in good service and ready to come any minute. So I mentioned his name to Mr. Tredwell and everything was settled pleasant like.'

Bundle nodded. Her own suspicions had been correct and the *modus operandi* was much as she had thought it to be. She essayed a further inquiry.

'Who is Mr. Mosgorovsky?'

'Gentleman as runs this club. Russian gentleman. A very clever gentleman too.'

Bundle abandoned the getting of information for the moment and proceeded to other matters.

'A hundred pounds is a very large sum of money, Alfred.'

'Larger than I ever handled, my lady,' said Alfred with simple candour.

'Did you never suspect that there was something wrong?'

'Wrong, my lady?'

'Yes. I'm not talking about the gambling. I mean something far more serious. You don't want to be sent to penal servitude, do you, Alfred?'

'Oh, Lord! my lady, you don't mean it?'

'I was at Scotland Yard the day before yesterday,' said Bundle impressively. 'I heard some very curious things. I want you to help me, Alfred, and if you do, well—if things go wrong, I'll put in a good word for you.'

'Anything I can do, I shall be only too pleased, my lady. I mean, I would anyway.'

'Well, first,' said Bundle, 'I want to go all over this place—from top to bottom.'

Accompanied by a mystified and scared Alfred, she made a very thorough tour of inspection. Nothing struck her eye till she came to the gaming room. There she noticed an inconspicuous door in a corner, and the door was locked.

Alfred explained readily.

'That's used as a getaway, your ladyship. There's a room and a door on to a staircase what comes out in the next street. That's the way the gentry goes when there's a raid.'

'But don't the police know about it?'

'It's a cunning door, you see, my lady. Looks like a cupboard, that's all.'

Bundle felt a rising excitement.

'I must get in here,' she said.

Alfred shook his head.

'You can't, my lady; Mr. Mosgorovsky, he has the key.'

'Well,' said Bundle, 'there are other keys.'

She perceived that the lock was a perfectly ordinary one which probably could be easily unlocked by the key of one of the other doors. Alfred, rather troubled, was sent to collect likely specimens. The fourth that Bundle tried fitted. She turned it, opened the door and passed through.

She found herself in a small, dingy apartment. A long table occupied the centre of the room with chairs ranged round it. There was no other furniture in the room. Two built-in cupboards stood on either side of the fireplace. Alfred indicated the nearer one with a nod.

'That's it,' he explained.

Bundle tried the cupboard door, but it was locked, and she saw at once that this lock was a very different affair. It was of the patent kind that would only yield to its own key.

''Ighly ingenious, it is,' explained Alfred. 'It looks all right when opened. Shelves, you know, with a few ledgers and that on 'em. Nobody'd ever suspect, but you touch the right spot and the whole thing swings open.'

Bundle had turned round and was surveying the room thoughtfully. The first thing she noticed was that the door by which they had entered was carefully fitted round with baize. It must be completely sound-proof. Then her eyes wandered to the chairs. There were seven of them, three each side and one rather more imposing in design at the head of the table.

Bundle's eyes brightened. She had found what she was looking for. This, she felt sure, was the meeting place of the secret organisation. The place was almost perfectly planned. It looked so innocent—you could reach it just by stepping through from the gaming room, or you could arrive there by the secret entrance—and any secrecy, any precautions were easily explained by the gaming going on in the next room.

Idly, as these thoughts passed through her mind, she drew a finger across the marble of the mantelpiece. Alfred saw and misinterpreted the action.

'You won't find no dirt, not to speak of,' he said. 'Mr. Mosgorovsky, he ordered the place to be swept out this morning, and I did it while he waited.'

'Oh!' said Bundle, thinking very hard. 'This morning, eh?'

'Has to be done sometimes,' said Alfred. 'Though the room's never what you might call used.'

Next minute he received a shock.

'Alfred,' said Bundle, 'you've got to find me a place in this room where I can hide.'

Alfred looked at her in dismay.

'But it's impossible, my lady. You'll get me into trouble and I'll lose my job.'

'You'll lose it anyway when you go to prison,' said Bundle unkindly. 'But as a matter of fact, you needn't worry, nobody will know anything about it.'

'And there ain't no place,' wailed Alfred. 'Look round for yourself, your ladyship, if you don't believe me.'

Bundle was forced to admit that there was something in this argument. But she had the true spirit of one undertaking adventures.

'Nonsense,' she said with determination. 'There has *got* to be a place.'

'But there ain't one,' wailed Alfred.

Never had a room shown itself more unpropitious for concealment. Dingy blinds were drawn down over the dirty window panes, and there were no curtains. The window sill outside, which Bundle examined was about four inches wide! Inside the room there were the table, the chairs and the cupboards.

The second cupboard had a key in the lock. Bundle went across and pulled it open. Inside were shelves covered with an odd assortment of glasses and crockery.

'Surplus stuff as we don't use,' explained Alfred. 'You can see for yourself, my lady, there's no place here as a cat could hide.'

But Bundle was examining the shelves.

'Flimsy work,' she said. 'Now then, Alfred, have you got a cupboard downstairs where you could shove all this glass? You have? Good. Then get a tray and start to carry it down at once. Hurry—there's no time to lose.'

'You can't, my lady. And it's getting late, too. The cooks will be here any minute now.'

'Mr. Mosgo—what not doesn't come till later, I suppose?'

'He's never here much before midnight. But oh, my lady——'

'Don't talk so much, Alfred,' said Bundle. 'Get that tray. If you stay here arguing, you *will* get into trouble.'

Doing what is familiarly known as 'wringing his hands,' Alfred departed. Presently he returned with a tray, and having by now realised that his protests were useless, he worked with a nervous energy quite surprising.

As Bundle had seen, the shelves were easily detachable. She took them down, ranged them upright against the wall, and then stepped in.

'H'm,' she remarked. 'Pretty narrow. It's going to be a tight fit. Shut the door on me carefully, Alfred—that's right. Yes, it can be done. Now I want a gimlet.'

'A gimlet, my lady?'

'That's what I said.'

'I don't know——'

'Nonsense, you must have a gimlet—perhaps you've got an auger as well. If you haven't got what I want, you'll have to go out and buy it, so you'd better try hard to find the right thing.'

Alfred departed and returned presently with quite a creditable assortment of tools. Bundle seized what she wanted and proceeded swiftly and efficiently to bore a small hole at the level of her right eye. She did this from the outside so that it should be less noticeable, and she dared not make it too large lest it should attract attention.

'There, that'll do,' she remarked at last.

'Oh, but, my lady, my lady——'

'Yes?'

'But they'll find you—if they should open the door.'

'They won't open the door,' said Bundle. 'Because you are going to lock it and take the key away.'

'And if by any chance Mr. Mosgorovsky should ask for the key?'

'Tell him it's lost,' said Bundle briskly. 'But nobody's going to worry about this cupboard—it's only here to attract attention from the other one and make a pair. Go on, Alfred, someone might come at any time. Lock me in and take the key and come and let me out when everyone's gone.'

'You'll be taken bad, my lady. You'll faint——'

'I never faint,' said Bundle. 'But you might as well get me a cocktail. I shall certainly need it. Then lock the door of the room again—don't forget—and take all the door keys back to their proper doors. And Alfred—don't be too much of a rabbit. Remember, if anything goes wrong, I'll see you through.'

'And that's that,' said Bundle to herself when, having served the cocktail, Alfred had finally departed.

She was not nervous lest Alfred's nerve should fail and he should give her away. She knew that his sense of self-preservation was far too strong for that. His training alone helped him to conceal private emotions beneath the mask of a well-trained servant.

Only one thing worried Bundle. The interpretation she had chosen to put upon the cleaning of the room that morning might be all wrong. And if so—Bundle sighed in the narrow confines of the cupboard. The prospect of spending long hours in it for nothing was not attractive.

14. *The meeting of the Seven Dials*

IT WOULD BE AS WELL to pass over the sufferings of the next four hours as quickly as possible. Bundle found her position extremely cramped. She had judged that the meeting, if meeting there was to be, would take place at a time when the club was in full swing—somewhere probably between the hours of midnight and two a.m.

She was just deciding that it must be at least six o'clock in the morning when a welcome sound came to her ears, the sound of the unlocking of a door.

In another minute the electric light was switched on. The hum of voices, which had come to her for a minute or two, rather like the far-off roar of sea waves, ceased as suddenly as it had begun, and Bundle heard the sound of a bolt being shot. Clearly someone had come in from the gaming room next door, and she paid tribute to the thoroughness with which the communicating door had been rendered sound proof.

In another minute the intruder came into her line of vision—a line of vision that was necessarily somewhat incomplete but which yet answered its purpose. A tall man, broad shouldered and powerful looking, with a long black beard. Bundle remembered having seen him sitting at one of the baccarat tables on the preceding night.

This, then, was Alfred's mysterious Russian gentleman, the proprietor of the club, the sinister Mr. Mosgorovsky. Bundle's heart beat faster with excitement. So little did she resemble her father that at this minute she fairly gloried in the extreme discomfort of her position.

The Russian remained for some minutes standing by the table, stroking his beard. Then he drew a watch from his pocket and glanced at the time. Nodding his head as though satisfied, he again thrust his hand into his pocket and, pulling out something that Bundle could not see, he moved out of her line of vision.

When he reappeared again, she could hardly help giving a gasp of surprise.

His face was now covered by a mask—but hardly a mask in the conventional sense. It was not shaped to the face. It was a mere piece of material hanging in front of the features like a curtain in which two slits were pierced for the eyes. In shape it was round and on it was the representation of a clock face, with the hands pointing to six o'clock.

'The Seven Dials!' said Bundle to herself.

And at that minute there came a new sound—seven muffled taps.

Mosgorovsky strode across to where Bundle knew was the other cupboard door. She heard a sharp click, and then the sound of greetings in a foreign tongue.

Presently she had a view of the newcomers.

They also wore clock masks, but in their case the hands were in a different position—four o'clock and five o'clock respectively. Both men were in evening dress—but with a difference. One was an elegant, slender young man wearing evening clothes of exquisite cut. The grace with which he moved was foreign rather than English. The other man could be better described as wiry and lean. His clothes fitted him sufficiently well, but no more, and Bundle guessed at his nationality even before she heard his voice.

'I reckon we're the first to arrive at this little meeting.'

A full pleasant voice with a slight American drawl, and an inflection of Irish behind it.

The elegant young man said in good, but slightly stilted English:

'I had much difficulty in getting away to-night. These things do not always arrange themselves fortunately. I am not, like No. 4 here, my own master.'

Bundle tried to guess at his nationality. Until he spoke, she had thought he might be French, but the accent was not a French one. He might possibly, she thought be an Austrian, or a Hungarian, or even a Russian.

The American moved to the other side of the table, and Bundle heard a chair being pulled out.

'One o'clock's being a great success,' he said. 'I congratulate you on taking the risk.'

Five o'clock shrugged his shoulders.

'Unless one takes risks——' He left the sentence unfinished.

Again seven taps sounded and Mosgorovsky moved across to the secret door.

She failed to catch anything definite for some moments since the whole company were out of sight, but presently she heard the bearded Russian's voice upraised.

'Shall we begin proceedings?'

He himself came round the table and took the seat next to the arm-chair at the top. Sitting thus, he was directly facing Bundle's cupboard. The elegant five o'clock took the place next to him. The third chair that side was out of Bundle's sight, but the American, No. 4, moved into her line of vision for a moment or two before he sat down.

On the near side of the table also, only two chairs were visible, and as she watched a hand turned the second—really the middle chair—down. And then with a swift movement, one of the newcomers brushed past the cupboard and took the chair opposite Mosgorovsky. Whoever sat there had, of course, their back directly turned to Bundle—and it was at that back that Bundle was staring with a good deal of interest, for it was the back of a singularly beautiful woman very much *décolleté*.

It was she who spoke first. Her voice was musical, foreign—with a deep seductive note in it. She was glancing towards the empty chair at the head of the table.

'So we are not to see No. 7 to-night?' she said. 'Tell me, my friends, shall we ever see him?'

'That's darned good,' said the American. 'Darned good! As for seven o'clock—*I'm* beginning to believe there is no such person.'

'I should not advise you to think that, my friend,' said the Russian pleasantly.

There was a silence—rather an uncomfortable silence, Bundle felt.

She was still staring as though fascinated at the beautiful back in front of her. There was a tiny black mole just below the right shoulder blade that enhanced the whiteness of the skin. Bundle felt that at last the term 'beautiful adventuress,' so often read, had a real meaning for her. She was quite certain that this woman had a beautiful face—a dark Slavonic face with passionate eyes.

She was recalled from her imaginings by the voice of the Russian, who seemed to act as master of ceremonies.

'Shall we get on with our business? First to our absent comrade! No. 2!'

He made a curious gesture with his hand towards the turned down chair next to the woman, which everyone present imitated, turning to the chair as they did so.

'I wish No. 2 were with us to-night,' he continued. 'There are many things to be done. Unsuspected difficulties have arisen.'

'Have you had his report?' It was the American who spoke.

'As yet—I have nothing from him.' There was a pause. 'I cannot understand it.'

'You think it may have—gone astray?'

'That is—a possibility.'

'In other words,' said five o'clock softly, 'there is—danger.'

He spoke the word delicately—and yet with relish.

The Russian nodded emphatically.

'Yes—there's danger. Too much is getting known about us—about this place. I know of several people who suspect.' He added coldly: 'They must be silenced.'

Bundle felt a little cold shiver pass down her spine. If she were to be found, would she be silenced? She was recalled suddenly to attention by a word.

'So nothing has come to light about Chimneys?'

Mosgorovsky shook his head.

'Nothing.'

Suddenly No. 5 leant forward.

'I agree with Anna; where is our president—No. 7? He who called us into being. Why do we never see him?'

'No. 7,' said the Russian, 'has his own ways of working.'

'So you always say.'

'I will say more,' said Mosgorovsky. 'I pity the man—or woman —who comes up against him.'

There was an awkward silence.

'We must get on with our business,' said Mosgorovsky quietly. 'No. 3, you have the plans of Wyvern Abbey?'

Bundle strained her ears. So far she had neither caught a glimpse of No. 3, nor had she heard his voice. She heard it now and recognised it as unmistakable. Low, pleasant, indistinct—the voice of a well-bred Englishman.

'I've got them here, sir.'

Some papers were shoved across the table. Everyone bent forward. Presently Mosgorovsky raised his head again.

'And the list of guests?'

'Here.'

The Russian read them.

'Sir Stanley Digby. Mr. Terence O'Rourke. Sir Oswald and Lady Coote. Mr. Bateman. Countess Anna Radzky. Mrs. Macatta. Mr. James Thesiger——' He paused and then asked sharply:

'Who is Mr. James Thesiger?'

The American laughed.

'I guess you needn't worry any about him. The usual complete young ass.'

The Russian continued reading.

'Herr Eberhard and Mr. Eversleigh. That completes the list.'

'Does it?' said Bundle silently. 'What about that sweet girl, Lady Eileen Brent?'

'Yes, there seems nothing to worry about there,' said Mosgorovsky. He looked across the table. 'I suppose there's no doubt whatever about the value of Eberhard's invention?'

Three o'clock made a laconic British reply.

'None whatever.'

'Commercially it should be worth millions,' said the Russian. 'And internationally—well, one knows only too well the greed of nations.'

Bundle had an idea that behind his mask he was smiling unpleasantly.

'Yes,' he went on. 'A gold mine.'

'Well worth a few lives,' said No. 5, cynically, and laughed.

'But you know what inventors are,' said the American. 'Sometimes these darned things won't work.'

'A man like Sir Oswald Coote will have made no mistake,' said Mosgorovsky.

'Speaking as an aviator myself,' said No. 5, 'the thing is perfectly feasible. It has been discussed for years—but it needed the genius of Eberhard to bring it to fruition.'

'Well,' said Mosgorovsky, 'I don't think we need discuss matters any further. You have all seen the plans. I do not think our original scheme can be bettered. By the way, I hear something about a letter of Gerald Wade's that has been found—a letter that mentions this organisation. Who found it?'

'Lord Caterham's daughter—Lady Eileen Brent.'

'Bauer should have been on to that,' said Mosgorovsky. 'It was careless of him. Who was the letter written to?'

'His sister, I believe,' said No. 3.

'Unfortunate,' said Mosgorovsky. 'But it cannot be helped. The inquest on Ronald Devereux is to-morrow. I suppose that has been arranged for?'

'Reports as to local lads having been practising with rifles have been spread everywhere,' said the American.

'That should be all right then. I think there is nothing further to be said. I think we must all congratulate our dear one o'clock and wish her luck in the part she has to play.'

'Hurrah!' cried No. 5. 'To Anna!'

All hands flew out in the same gesture which Bundle had noticed before.

'To Anna!'

'One o'clock acknowledged the salutation with a typically foreign gesture. Then she rose to her feet and the others followed suit. For the first time, Bundle caught a glimpse of No. 3 as he came to put Anna's cloak round her—a tall, heavily built man.

Then the party filed out through the secret door. Mosgorovsky secured it after them. He waited a few moments and then Bundle heard him unbolt the other door and pass through, after extinguishing the electric light.

It was not until two hours later that a white and anxious Alfred came to release Bundle. She almost fell into his arms and he had to hold her up.

'Nothing,' said Bundle. 'Just stiff, that's all. Here, let me sit down.'

'Oh, Gord, my lady, it's been awful.'

'Nonsense,' said Bundle. 'It all went off splendidly. Don't get the wind up now it's all over. It might have gone wrong, but thank goodness it didn't.'

'Thank goodness, as you say, my lady. I've been in a twitter all the evening. They're a funny crowd, you know.'

'A damned funny crowd,' said Bundle, vigorously massaging her arms and legs. 'As a matter of fact, they're the sort of crowd I always imagined until to-night only existed in books. In this life, Alfred, one never stops learning.'

15. *The inquest*

BUNDLE REACHED HOME about six a.m. She was up and dressed by half past nine, and rang up Jimmy Thesiger on the telephone.

The promptitude of his reply somewhat surprised her, till he explained that he was going down to attend the inquest.

'So am I,' said Bundle. 'And I've got a lot to tell you.'

'Well, suppose you let me drive you down and we can talk on the way. How about that?'

'All right. But allow a bit extra because you'll have to take me to Chimneys. The Chief Constable's picking me up there.'

'Why?'

'Because he's a kind man,' said Bundle.

'So am I,' said Jimmy. 'Very kind.'

'Oh! you—you're an ass,' said Bundle. 'I heard somebody say so last night.'

'Who?'

'To be strictly accurate—a Russian Jew. No, it wasn't. It was ——'

But an indignant protest drowned her words.

'I may be an ass,' said Jimmy. 'I daresay I am—but I won't have Russian Jews saying so. What were you doing last night, Bundle?'

'That's what I'm going to talk about,' said Bundle. 'Good-bye for the moment.'

She rang off in a tantalising manner which left Jimmy pleasantly puzzled. He had the highest respect for Bundle's capabilities, though there was not the slightest trace of sentiment in his feeling towards her.

'She's been up to something,' he opined, as he took a last hasty drink of coffee. 'Depend upon it, she's been up to something.'

Twenty minutes later, his little two-seater drew up before the Brook Street house and Bundle, who had been waiting, came tripping down the steps. Jimmy was not ordinarily an observant young man, but he noticed that there were black rings round Bundle's eyes and that she had all the appearance of having had a late night the night before.

'Now then,' he said, as the car began to nose her way through the suburbs, 'what dark deeds have you been up to?'

'I'll tell you,' said Bundle. 'But don't interrupt until I've finished.'

It was a somewhat long story, and Jimmy had all he could do to keep sufficient attention on the car to prevent an accident. When Bundle had finished he sighed—then looked at her searchingly.

'Bundle?'

'Yes?'

'Look here, you're not pulling my leg?'

'What do you mean?'

'I'm sorry,' apologised Jimmy, 'but it seems to me as though I'd heard it all before—in a dream, you know.'

'I know,' said Bundle sympathetically.

'It's impossible,' said Jimmy, following out his own train of thought. 'The beautiful foreign adventuress, the international gang, the mysterious No. 7, whose identity nobody knows—I've read it all a hundred times in books.'

'Of course you have. So have I. But it's no reason why it shouldn't really happen.'

'I suppose not,' admitted Jimmy.

'After all—I suppose fiction is founded on the truth. I mean unless things did happen, people couldn't think of them.'

'There is something in what you say,' agreed Jimmy. 'But all the same I can't help pinching myself to see if I'm awake.'

'That's how I felt.'

Jimmy gave a deep sigh.

'Well, I suppose we are awake. Let me see, a Russian, an American, an Englishman—a possible Austrian or Hungarian—and the lady who may be any nationality—for choice Russian or Polish—that's a pretty representative gathering.'

'And a German,' said Bundle. 'You've forgotten the German.'

'Oh!' said Jimmy slowly. 'You think——'

'The absent No. 2. No. 2 is Bauer—our footman. That seems to me quite clear from what they said about expecting a report which hadn't come in—though what there can be to report about Chimneys, I can't think.'

'It must be something to do with Gerry Wade's death,' said Jimmy. 'There's something there we haven't fathomed yet. You say they actually mentioned Bauer by name?'

Bundle nodded.

'They blamed him for not having found that letter.'

'Well, I don't see what you could have clearer than that. There's no going against it. You'll have to forgive my first incredulity, Bundle—but you know, it was rather a tall story. You say they knew about my going down to Wyvern Abbey next week?'

'Yes, that's when the American—it was him, not the Russian—said they needn't worry—you were only the usual kind of ass.'

'Ah!' and Jimmy. He pressed his foot down on the accelerator viciously and the car shot forward. 'I'm very glad you told me that. It gives me what you might call a personal interest in the case.'

He was silent for a minute or two and then he said:

'Did you say that German inventor's name was Eberhard?'

'Yes. Why?'

'Wait a minute. Something's coming back to me. Eberhard, Eberhard—yes, I'm sure that was the name.'

'Tell me.'

'Eberhard was a Johnny who'd got some patent process he applied to steel. I can't put the thing properly because I haven't got the scientific knowledge—but I know the result was that it became so toughened that a wire was as strong as a steel bar had previously been. Eberhard had to do with aeroplanes and his idea was that the weight would be so enormously reduced that flying would be practically revolutionised—the cost of it, I mean. I believe he offered his invention to the German Government, and they turned it down, pointed out some undeniable flaw in it—but they did it rather nastily. He set to work and circumvented the difficulty, whatever it was, but he'd been offended by their attitude and swore they shouldn't have his ewe lamb. I always thought the whole thing was probably bunkum, but now—it looks differently.'

'That's it,' said Bundle eagerly. 'You must be right, Jimmy. Eberhard must have offered his invention to our Government. They've been taking, or are going to take, Sir Oswald Coote's expert opinion on it. There's going to be an unofficial conference at the Abbey. Sir Oswald, George, the Air Minister and Eberhard. Eberhard will have the plans or the process or whatever you call it——'

'Formula,' suggested Jimmy. 'I think "formula" is a good word myself.'

'He'll have the formula with him, and the Seven Dials are out to steal the formula. I remember the Russian saying it was worth millions.'

'I suppose it would be,' said Jimmy.

'And well worth a few lives—that's what the other man said.'

'Well, it seems to have been,' said Jimmy, his face clouding over. 'Look at this damned inquest to-day. Bundle, are you sure Ronny said nothing else?'

'No,' said Bundle. 'Just that. *Seven Dials. Tell Jimmy Thesiger*. That's all he could get out, poor lad.'

'I wish we knew what he knew,' said Jimmy. 'But we've found out one thing. I take it that the footman, Bauer, must almost certainly have been responsible for Gerry's death. You know, Bundle——'

'Yes?'

'Well, I'm a bit worried sometimes. Who's going to be the next one! It really isn't the sort of business for a girl to be mixed up in.'

Bundle smiled in spite of herself. It occurred to her that it had taken Jimmy a long time to put her in the same category as Loraine Wade.

'It's far more likely to be you than me,' she remarked cheerfully.

'Hear, hear,' said Jimmy. 'But what about a few casualties on the other side for a change? I'm feeling rather bloodthirsty this morning. Tell me, Bundle, would you recognise any of these people if you saw them?'

Bundle hesitated.

'I think I should recognise No. 5,' she said at last. 'He's got a queer way of speaking—a kind of venomous, lisping way—that I think I'd know again.'

'What about the Englishman?'

Bundle shook her head.

'I saw him least—only a glimpse—and he's got a very ordinary voice. Except that he's a big man, there's nothing much to go by.'

'There's the woman, of course,' continued Jimmy. 'She ought to be easier. But then, you're not likely to run across her. She's probably putting in the dirty work, being taken out to dinner by amorous Cabinet Ministers and getting State secrets out of them when they've had a couple. At least, that's how it's done in books. As a matter of fact, the only Cabinet Minister I know drinks hot water with a dash of lemon in it.'

'Take George Lomax, for instance, can you imagine him being amorous with beautiful foreign women?' said Bundle with a laugh.

Jimmy agreed with her criticism.

'And now about the man of mystery—No. 7,' went on Jimmy. 'You've no idea who he could be?'

'None whatever.'

'Again—by book standard, that is—he ought to be someone we all know. What about George Lomax himself?'

Bundle reluctantly shook her head.

'In a book it would be perfect,' she agreed. 'But knowing Codders——' And she gave herself up to sudden uncontrollable mirth. 'Codders, the great criminal organiser,' she gasped. 'Wouldn't it be marvellous?'

Jimmy agreed that it would. Their discussion had taken some time and his driving had slowed down involuntarily once or twice. They arrived at Chimneys, to find Colonel Melrose already there waiting. Jimmy was introduced to him and they all three proceeded to the inquest together.

As Colonel Melrose had predicted, the whole affair was very simple. Bundle gave her evidence. The doctor gave his. Evidence was given of rifle practice in the neighbourhood. A verdict of death by misadventure was brought in.

After the proceedings were over, Colonel Melrose volunteered to drive Bundle back to Chimneys, and Jimmy Thesiger returned to London.

For all his light-hearted manner, Bundle's story had impressed him profoundly. He set his lips closely together.

'Ronny, old boy,' he murmured, 'I'm going to be up against it. And you're not here to join in the game.'

Another thought flashed into his mind. Loraine! Was she in danger?

After a minute or two's hesitation, he went over to the telephone and rang her up.

'It's me—Jimmy. I thought you'd like to know the result of the inquest. Death by misadventure.'

'Oh, but——'

'Yes, but I think there's something behind that. The coroner had had a hint. Someone's at work to hush it up. I say, Loraine——'

'Yes?'

'Look here. There's—there's some funny business going about. You'll be very careful, won't you? For my sake.'

He heard the quick note of alarm that sprang into her voice.

'Jimmy—but then it's dangerous—for *you*.'

He laughed.

'Oh, *that's* all right. I'm the cat that had nine lives. Bye-bye, old thing.'

He rang off and remained a minute or two lost in thought. Then he summoned Stevens.

'Do you think you could go out and buy me a pistol, Stevens?'

'A pistol, sir?'

True to his training, Stevens betrayed no hint of surprise.

'What kind of a pistol would you be requiring?'

'The kind where you put your finger on the trigger and the thing goes on shooting until you take it off again.'

'An automatic, sir.'

'That's it,' said Jimmy. 'An automatic. And I should like it to be a blue-nosed one—if you and the shopman know what that is. In American stories, the hero always takes his blue-nosed automatic from his hip pocket.'

Stevens permitted himself a faint, discreet smile.

'Most American gentlemen that I have known, sir, carry something very different in their hip pockets,' he observed.

Jimmy Thesiger laughed.

16. *The house party at the Abbey*

BUNDLE DROVE OVER to Wyvern Abbey just in time for tea on Friday afternoon. George Lomax came forward to welcome her with considerable *impressement*.

'My dear Eileen,' he said, 'I can't tell you how pleased I am to see you here. You must forgive my not having invited you when I asked your father, but to tell the truth I never dreamed that a party of this kind would appeal to you. I was both—er—surprised and—er—delighted when Lady Caterham told me of your—er—interest in—er—politics.'

'I wanted to come so much,' said Bundle in a simple, ingenuous manner.

'Mrs. Macatta will not arrive till the later train,' explained George. 'She was speaking at a meeting in Manchester last night. Do you know Thesiger? Quite a young fellow, but a remarkable grasp of foreign politics. One would hardly suspect it from his appearance.'

'I know Mr. Thesiger,' said Bundle, and she shook hands solemnly with Jimmy, who she observed had parted his hair in the middle in the endeavour to add earnestness to his expression.

'Look here,' said Jimmy in a low hurried voice, as George temporarily withdrew. 'You mustn't be angry, but I've told Bill about our little stunt.'

'Bill?' said Bundle, annoyed.

'Well, after all,' said Jimmy, 'Bill is one of the lads, you know. Ronny was a pal of his and so was Gerry.'

'Oh! I know,' said Bundle.

'But you think it's a pity? Sorry.'

'Bill's all right, of course. It isn't that,' said Bundle. 'But he's—well, Bill's a born blunderer.'

'Not mentally very agile?' suggested Jimmy. 'But you forget one thing—Bill's got a very hefty fist. And I've an idea that a hefty fist is going to come in handy.'

'Well, perhaps you're right. How did he take it?'

'Well, he clutched his head a good bit, but—I mean the facts took some driving home. But by repeating the thing patiently in words of one syllable I at last got it into his thick head. And, naturally, he's with us to the death, as you might say.'

George reappeared suddenly.

'I must make some introductions, Eileen. This is Sir Stanley Digby—Lady Eileen Brent. Mr. O'Rourke.' The Air Minister was a little round man with a cheerful smile. Mr. O'Rourke, a tall young man with laughing blue eyes and a typical Irish face, greeted Bundle with enthusiasm.

'And I thinking it was going to be a dull political party entirely,' he murmured in an adroit whisper.

'Hush,' said Bundle. 'I'm political—very political.'

'Sir Oswald and Lady Coote you know,' continued George.

'We've never actually met,' said Bundle, smiling.

She was mentally applauding her father's descriptive powers.

Sir Oswald took her hand in an iron grip and she winced slightly.

Lady Coote, after a somewhat mournful greeting, had turned to Jimmy Thesiger, and appeared to be registering something closely akin to pleasure. Despite his reprehensible habit of being late for breakfast, Lady Coote had a fondness for this amiable, pink-faced young man. His air of irrepressible good nature fascinated her. She had a motherly wish to cure him of his bad habits and form him into one of the world's workers. Whether, once formed, he would be as attractive was a question she had never asked herself. She began now to tell him of a very painful motor accident which had happened to one of her friends.

'Mr. Bateman,' said George briefly, as one who would pass on to better things.

A serious, pale-faced young man bowed.

'And now,' continued George, 'I must introduce you to Countess Radzky.'

Countess Radzky had been conversing with Mr. Bateman. Leaning very far back on a sofa, with her legs crossed in a daring manner, she was smoking a cigarette in an incredibly long turquoise-studded holder.

Bundle thought she was one of the most beautiful women she had ever seen. Her eyes were very large and blue, her hair was coal black, she had a matte skin, the slightly flattened nose of the Slav, and a sinuous, slender body. Her lips were reddened to a degree with which Bundle was sure Wyvern Abbey was totally unacquainted.

She said eagerly: 'This is Mrs. Macatta—yes?'

On George's replying in the negative and introducing Bundle, the countess gave her a careless nod, and at once resumed her conversation with the serious Mr. Bateman.

Bundle heard Jimmy's voice in her ear:

'Pongo is absolutely fascinated by the lovely Slav,' he said. 'Pathetic, isn't it? Come and have some tea.'

They drifted once more into the neighbourhood of Sir Oswald Coote.

'That's a fine place of yours, Chimneys,' remarked the great man.

'I'm glad you liked it,' said Bundle meekly.

'Wants new plumbing,' said Sir Oswald. 'Bring it up to date, you know.'

He ruminated for a minute or two.

'I'm taking the Duke of Alton's place. Three years. Just while I'm looking round for a place of my own. Your father couldn't sell if he wanted to, I suppose?'

Bundle felt her breath taken away. She had a nightmare vision of England with innumerable Cootes in innumerable counterparts of Chimneys—all, be it understood, with an entirely new system of plumbing installed.

She felt a sudden violent resentment which, she told herself, was absurd. After all, contrasting Lord Caterham with Sir Oswald Coote, there was no doubt as to who would go to the wall. Sir Oswald had one of those powerful personalities which make all those with whom they come in contact appear faded. He was, as Lord Caterham had said, a human steamroller. And yet, undoubtedly, in many ways, Sir Oswald was a stupid man. Apart from his special line of knowledge and his terrific driving force, he was probably intensely ignorant. A hundred delicate appreciations of life which Lord Caterham could and did enjoy were a sealed book to Sir Oswald.

Whilst indulging in these reflections Bundle continued to chat pleasantly. Herr Eberhard, she heard, had arrived, but was lying down with a nervous headache. This was told her by Mr. O'Rourke, who managed to find a place by her side and keep it.

Altogether, Bundle went up to dress in a pleasant mood of expectation, with a slight nervous dread hovering in the background whenever she thought of the imminent arrival of Mrs. Macatta. Bundle felt that dalliance with Mrs. Macatta was going to prove no primrose path.

Her first shock was when she came down, demurely attired in a black lace frock, and passed along the hall. A footman was standing there—at least a man dressed as a footman. But that square, burly figure lent itself badly to the deception. Bundle stopped and stared.

'Superintendent Battle,' she breathed.

'That's right, Lady Eileen.'

'Oh!' said Bundle uncertainly. 'Are you here to—to——'

'Keep an eye on things.'

'I see.'

'That warning letter, you know,' said the Superintendent, 'fairly put the wind up Mr. Lomax. Nothing would do for him but that I should come down myself.'

'But don't you think——' began Bundle, and stopped. She hardly liked to suggest to the Superintendent that his disguise was not a particularly efficient one. He seemed to have 'police officer' written all over him, and Bundle could hardly imagine the most unsuspecting criminal failing to be put on his guard.

'You think,' said the Superintendent stolidly, 'that I might be recognised?'

He gave the final word a distinct capital letter.

'I did think so—yes——' admitted Bundle.

Something that might conceivably have been intended for a smile crossed the woodenness of Superintendent Battle's features.

'Put them on their guard, eh? Well, Lady Eileen, why not?'

'Why not?' echoed Bundle—rather stupidly, she felt.

Superintendent Battle was nodding his head slowly.

'We don't want any unpleasantness, do we?' he said. 'Don't want to be too clever—just show any light-fingered gentry that may be about—well, just show them that there's somebody on the spot, so to speak.'

Bundle gazed at him in some admiration. She could imagine that the sudden appearance of so renowned a personage as Superintendent Battle might have a depressing effect on any scheme and the hatchers of it.

'It's a great mistake to be too clever,' Superintendent Battle was repeating. 'The great thing is not to have any unpleasantness this week-end.'

Bundle passed on, wondering how many of her fellow guests had recognised or would recognise the Scotland Yard detective. In the drawing-room George was standing with a puckered brow, holding an orange envelope in his hand.

'Most vexatious,' he said. 'A telegram from Mrs. Macatta to say she will be unable to be with us. Her children are suffering from mumps.'

Bundle's heart gave a throb of relief.

'I especially feel this on your account, Eileen,' said George kindly. 'I know how anxious you were to meet her. The Countess too will be sadly disappointed.'

'Oh, never mind,' said Bundle. 'I should hate it if she'd come and given me mumps.'

'A very distressing complaint,' agreed George. 'But I do not think that infection could be carried that way. Indeed, I am sure that Mrs. Macatta would have run no risk of that kind. She is a most highly principled woman, with a very real sense of her responsibilities to the community. In these days of national stress, we must all take into account——'

On the brink of embarking on a speech, George pulled himself up short.

'But it must be for another time,' he said. 'Fortunately there is no hurry in your case. But the Countess, alas, is only a visitor to our shores.'

'She's a Hungarian, isn't she?' said Bundle, who was curious about the Countess.

'Yes. You have heard, no doubt, of the Young Hungarian party. The Countess is a leader in that party. A woman of great wealth, left a widow at an early age, she has devoted her money and her talents to the public service. She has especially devoted herself to the problem of infant mortality—a terrible one under present conditions in Hungary. I—Ah! here is Herr Eberhard.'

The German inventor was younger than Bundle had imagined him. He was probably not more than thirty-three or four. He was boorish and ill at ease, and yet his personality was not an unpleasing one. His blue eyes were more shy than furtive, and his more unpleasant mannerisms, such as the one that Bill had described of gnawing his finger-nails, arose, she thought, more from nervousness than from any other cause. He was thin and weedy in appearance and looked anæmic and delicate.

He conversed rather awkwardly with Bundle in stilted English and they both welcomed the interruption of the joyous Mr. O'Rourke.

Presently Bill bustled in—there is no other word for it; in the same such way does a favoured Newfoundland dog make his entrance—and at once came over to Bundle. He was looking perplexed and harassed.

'Hullo, Bundle. Heard you'd got here. Been kept with my nose to the grindstone all the blessed afternoon or I'd have seen you before.'

'Cares of State heavy to-night?' suggested O'Rourke sympathetically.

Bill groaned.

'I don't know what your fellow's like,' he complained. 'Looks a good-natured, tubby little chap. But Codders is absolutely impossible. Drive, drive, drive, from morning to night. Everything you do is wrong, and everything you haven't done you ought to have done.'

'Quite like a quotation from the prayer book,' remarked Jimmy, who had just strolled up.

Bill glanced at them reproachfully.

'Nobody knows,' he said pathetically, 'what I have to put up with.'

'Entertaining the Countess, eh?' suggested Jimmy. 'Poor Bill, that must have been a sad strain—to a woman hater like yourself.'

'What's this?' asked Bundle.

'After tea,' said Jimmy with a grin, 'the Countess asked Bill to show her round the interesting old place.'

'Well, I couldn't refuse, could I?' said Bill, his countenance assuming a brick-red tint.

Bundle felt faintly uneasy. She knew, only too well, the susceptibility of Mr. William Eversleigh to female charms. In the hands of a woman like the Countess, Bill would be as wax. She wondered once more whether Jimmy Thesiger had been wise to take Bill into their confidence.

'The Countess,' said Bill, 'is a very charming woman. And no end intelligent. You should have seen her going round the house. All sorts of questions she asked.'

'What kind of questions?' asked Bundle suddenly.

Bill was vague.

'Oh! I don't know. About the history of it. And old furniture. And—oh! all sorts of things.'

At that moment the Countess swept into the room. She seemed a shade breathless. She was looking magnificent in a close-fitting black velvet gown. Bundle noticed how Bill gravitated at once into her immediate neighbourhood. The serious, spectacled young man joined him.

'Bill and Pongo have both got it badly,' observed Jimmy Thesiger with a laugh.

Bundle was by no means so sure that it was a laughing matter.

17. *After dinner*

GEORGE was not a believer in modern innovations. The Abbey was innocent of anything so up to date as central heating. Consequently, when the ladies entered the drawing-room after dinner, the temperature of the room was woefully inadequate to the needs of modern evening clothes. The fire that burnt in the well-furnished steel grate became as a magnet. The three women huddled round it.

'Brrrrrrrrrrrr!' said the Countess, a fine, exotic foreign sound.

'The days are drawing in,' said Lady Coote, and drew a flowered atrocity of a scarf closer about her ample shoulders.

'Why on earth doesn't George have the house properly heated?' said Bundle.

'You English, you never heat your houses,' said the Countess.

She took out her long cigarette holder and began to smoke.

'That grate is old-fashioned,' said Lady Coote. 'The heat goes up the chimney instead of into the room.'

'Oh!' said the Countess.

There was a pause. The Countess was so plainly bored by her company that conversation became difficult.

'It's funny,' said Lady Coote, breaking the silence, 'that Mrs. Macatta's children should have mumps. At least, I don't mean exactly funny——'

'What,' said the Countess, 'are mumps?'

Bundle and Lady Coote started simultaneously to explain. Finally, between them, they managed it.

'I suppose Hungarian children have it?' asked Lady Coote.

'Eh?' said the Countess.

'Hungarian children. They suffer from it?'

'I do not know,' said the Countess. 'How should I?'

Lady Coote looked at her in some surprise.

'But I understood that you worked——'

'Oh, that!' The Countess uncrossed her legs, took her cigarette holder from her mouth and began to talk rapidly.

'I will tell you some horrors,' she said. 'Horrors that I have seen. Incredible! You would not believe!'

And she was as good as her word. She talked fluently and with a graphic power of description. Incredible scenes of starvation and misery were painted by her for the benefit of her audience. She spoke of Buda Pesth shortly after the war and traced its vicissitudes to the present day. She was dramatic, but she was also, to Bundle's mind, a little like a gramophone record. You turned her on, and there you were. Presently, just as suddenly, she would stop.

Lady Coote was thrilled to the marrow—that much was clear. She sat with her mouth slightly open and her large, sad, dark eyes fixed on the Countess. Occasionally, she interpolated a comment of her own.

'One of my cousins had three children burned to death. Awful, wasn't it?'

The Countess paid no attention. She went on and on. And she finally stopped as suddenly as she had begun.

'There!' she said. 'I have told you. We have money—but no organisation. It is organisation we need.'

Lady Coote sighed.

'I've heard my husband say that nothing can be done without regular methods. He attributes his own success entirely to that. He declares he would have never got on without them.'

She sighed again. A sudden fleeting vision passed before her eyes of a Sir Oswald who had not got on in the world. A Sir Oswald who retained, in all essentials, the attributes of that cheery young man in the bicycle shop. Just for a second it occurred to her how much pleasanter life might have been for her if Sir Oswald had *not* had regular methods.

By a quite understandable association of ideas she turned to Bundle.

'Tell me, Lady Eileen,' she said; 'do you like that head gardener of yours?'

'MacDonald? Well——' Bundle hesitated. 'One couldn't exactly *like* MacDonald,' she explained apologetically. 'But he's a first-class gardener.'

'Oh! I know he is,' said Lady Coote.

'He's all right if he's kept in his place,' said Bundle.

'I suppose so,' said Lady Coote.

She looked enviously at Bundle, who appeared to approach the task of keeping MacDonald in his place so lightheartedly.

'I'd just adore a high-toned garden,' said the Countess dreamily.

Bundle stared, but at that moment a diversion occurred. Jimmy Thesiger entered the room and spoke directly to her in a strange, hurried voice.

'I say, will you come and see those etchings now? They're waiting for you.'

Bundle left the room hurriedly, Jimmy close behind her.

'What etchings?' she asked, as the drawing-room door closed behind her.

'No etchings,' said Jimmy. 'I'd got to say something to get hold of you. Come on, Bill is waiting for us in the library. There's nobody there.'

Bill was striding up and down the library, clearly in a very perturbed state of mind.

'Look here,' he burst out, 'I don't like this.'

'Don't like what?'

'You being mixed up in this. Ten to one there's going to be a rough house and then——'

He looked at her with a kind of pathetic dismay that gave Bundle a warm and comfortable feeling.

'She ought to be kept out of it, oughtn't she, Jimmy?'

He appealed to the other.

'I've told her so,' said Jimmy.

'Dash it all, Bundle, I mean—someone might get hurt.'

Bundle turned round to Jimmy.

'How much have you told him?'

'Oh! everything.'

'I haven't got the hang of it all yet,' confessed Bill. 'You in that place in Seven Dials and all that.' He looked at her unhappily. 'I say, Bundle, I wish you wouldn't.'

'Wouldn't what?'

'Get mixed up in these sort of things.'

'Why not?' said Bundle. 'They're exciting.'

'Oh, yes—exciting. But they may be damnably dangerous. Look at poor old Ronny.'

'Yes,' said Bundle. 'If it hadn't been for your friend Ronny, I don't suppose I should ever have got what you call "mixed up" in this thing. But I am. And it's no earthly use your bleating about it.'

'I know you're the most frightful sport, Bundle, but——'

'Cut out the compliments. Let's make plans.'

To her relief, Bill reacted favourably to the suggestion.

'You're right about the formula,' he said. 'Eberhard's got some sort of formula with him, or rather Sir Oswald has. The stuff has been tested out at his works—very secretly and all that. Eberhard has been down there with him. They're all in the study now—what you might call coming down to brass tacks.'

'How long is Sir Stanley Digby staying?' asked Jimmy.

'Going back to town to-morrow.'

'H'm,' said Jimmy. 'Then one thing's quite clear. If, as I suppose, Sir Stanley will be taking the formula with him, any funny business there's going to be will be to-night.'

'I suppose it will.'

'Not a doubt of it. That narrows the thing down very comfortably. But the bright lads will have to be their very brightest. We must come down to details. First of all, where will the sacred formula be to-night? Will Eberhard have it, or Sir Oswald Coote?'

'Neither. I understand it's to be handed over to the Air Minister this evening, for him to take to town to-morrow. In that case O'Rourke will have it. Sure to.'

'Well, there's only one thing for it. If we believe someone's going to have a shot at pinching that paper, we've got to keep watch to-night, Bill, my boy.'

Bundle opened her mouth as though to protest, but shut it again without speaking.

'By the way,' continued Jimmy, 'did I recognise the commissionaire from Harrods in the hall this evening, or was it our old friend Lestrade from Scotland Yard?'

'Scintillating, Watson,' said Bill.

'I suppose,' said Jimmy, 'that we are rather butting in on his preserves.'

'Can't be helped,' said Bill. 'Not if we mean to see this thing through.'

'Then it's agreed,' said Jimmy. 'We divide the night into two watches?'

Again Bundle opened her mouth, and again shut it without speaking.

'Right you are,' agreed Bill. 'Who'll take first duty?'

'Shall we spin for it?'

'Might as well.'

'All right. Here goes. Heads you first and I second. Tails, vice versa.'

Bill nodded. The coin spun in the air. Jimmy bent to look at it.

'Tails,' he said.

'Damn,' said Bill. 'You get first half and probably any fun that's going.'

'Oh, you never know,' said Jimmy. 'Criminals are very uncertain. What time shall I wake you? Three-thirty?'

'That's about fair, I think.'

And now, at last, Bundle spoke:

'What about *me*?' she asked.

'Nothing doing. You go to bed and sleep.'

'Oh!' said Bundle. 'That's not very exciting.'

'You never know,' said Jimmy kindly. 'You may be murdered in your sleep whilst Bill and I escape scot-free.'

'Well, there's always that possibility. Do you know, Jimmy, I don't half like the look of that countess. I suspect her.'

'Nonsense,' cried Bill hotly. 'She's absolutely above suspicion.'

'How do you know?' retorted Bundle.

'Because I do. Why, one of the fellows at the Hungarian Embassy vouched for her.'

'Oh!' said Bundle, momentarily taken aback by his fervour.

'You girls are all the same,' grumbled Bill. 'Just because she's a jolly good-looking woman——'

Bundle was only too well acquainted with this unfair masculine line of argument.

'Well, don't you go and pour confidences into her shell-pink ear,' she remarked. 'I'm going to bed. I was bored stiff in that drawing-room and I'm not going back.'

She left the room. Bill looked at Jimmy.

'Good old Bundle,' he said. 'I was afraid we might have trouble with her. You know how keen she is to be in everything. I think the way she took it was just wonderful.'

'So did I,' said Jimmy. 'It staggered me.'

'She's got some sense, Bundle has. She knows when a thing's plumb impossible. I say, oughtn't we to have some lethal weapons? Chaps usually do when they're going on this sort of stunt.'

'I have a blue-nosed automatic,' said Jimmy with gentle pride. 'It weighs several pounds and looks most murderous. I'll lend it to you when the time comes.'

Bill looked at him with respect and envy.

'What made you think of getting that?' he said.

'I don't know,' said Jimmy carelessly. 'It just came to me.'

'I hope we shan't go and shoot the wrong person,' said Bill with some anxiety.

'That would be unfortunate,' said Mr. Thesiger gravely.

18. *Jimmy's adventures*

OUR CHRONICLE must here split into three separate and distinct portions. The night was to prove an eventful one and each of the three persons involved saw it from his or her own individual angle.

We will begin with that pleasant and engaging youth, Mr. Jimmy Thesiger, at a moment when he has at last exchanged final goodnights with his fellow conspirator, Bill Eversleigh.

'Don't forget,' said Bill, 'three a.m. If you're still alive, that is,' he added kindly.

'I may be an ass,' said Jimmy, with rancorous remembrance of the remark Bundle had repeated to him, 'but I'm not nearly so much of an ass as I look.'

'That's what you said about Gerry Wade,' said Bill slowly. 'Do you remember? And that very night he——'

'Shut up, you damned fool,' said Jimmy. 'Haven't you got *any* tact?'

'Of course I've got tact,' said Bill. 'I'm a budding diplomatist. All diplomatists have tact.'

'Ah!' said Jimmy. 'You must be still in what they call the larval stage.'

'I can't get over Bundle,' said Bill, reverting abruptly to a former topic. 'I should certainly have said that she'd be—well, difficult. Bundle's improved. She's improved very much.'

'That's what your Chief was saying,' said Jimmy. 'He said he was agreeably surprised.'

'I thought Bundle was laying it on a bit thick myself,' said Bill. 'But Codders is such an ass he'd swallow anything. Well, night-night. I expect you'll have a bit of a job waking me when the time comes—but stick to it.'

'It won't be much good if you've taken a leaf out of Gerry Wade's book,' said Jimmy maliciously.

Bill looked at him reproachfully.

'What the hell do you want to go and make a chap uncomfortable for?' he demanded.

'You're only getting your own back,' said Jimmy. 'Toddle along.'

But Bill lingered. He stood uncomfortably, first on one foot and then on the other.

'Look here,' he said.

'Yes?'

'What I mean to say is—well, I mean you'll be all right and all that, won't you? It's all very well ragging, but when I think of poor old Gerry—and then poor old Ronny——'

Jimmy gazed at him in exasperation. Bill was one of those who undoubtedly meant well, but the result of his efforts would not be described as heartening.

'I see,' he remarked, 'that I shall have to show you Leopold.'

He slipped his hand into the pocket of the dark blue suit into which he had just changed and held out something for Bill's inspection.

'A real, genuine, blue-nosed automatic,' he said, with modest pride.

'No, I say,' said Bill. 'Is it really?'

He was undoubtedly impressed.

'Stevens, my man, got him for me. Warranted clean and methodical in his habits. You press the button and Leopold does the rest.'

'Oh!' said Bill. 'I say, Jimmy?'

'Yes?'

'Be careful, won't you? I mean, don't go loosing that thing off at anybody. Pretty awkward if you shot old Digby walking in his sleep.'

'That's all right,' said Jimmy. 'Naturally, I want to get value out of Leopold now I've bought him, but I'll curb my bloodthirsty instincts as far as possible.'

'Well, night-night,' said Bill for the fourteenth time, and this time really did depart.

Jimmy was left alone to take up his vigil.

Sir Stanley Digby occupied a room at the extremity of the west wing. A bathroom adjoined it on one side, and on the other a communicating door led into a small room, which was tenanted by Mr. Terence O'Rourke. The doors of these three rooms gave on to a short corridor. The watcher had a simple task. A chair placed inconspicuously in the shadow of an oak press just where the corridor ran into the main gallery formed a perfect vantage ground. There was no other way into the west wing, and anyone going to or from it could not fail to be seen. One electric light was still on.

Jimmy ensconced himself comfortably, crossed his legs and waited. Leopold lay in readiness across his knee.

He glanced at his watch. It was twenty minutes to one—just an hour since the household had retired to rest. Not a sound broke the stillness, except for the far-off ticking of a clock somewhere.

Somehow or other, Jimmy did not much care for that sound. It recalled things. Gerald Wade—and those seven ticking clocks on the mantelpiece. . . . Whose hand had placed them there, and why? He shivered.

It was a creepy business, this waiting. He didn't wonder that things happened at spiritualistic séances. Sitting in the gloom, one got all worked up—ready to start at the least sound. And unpleasant thoughts came crowding in on a fellow.

Ronny Devereux! Ronny Devereux and Gerry Wade! Both young, both full of life and energy; ordinary, jolly, healthy young men. And now, where were they? Dank earth . . . worms getting them. . . . Ugh! why couldn't he put these horrible thoughts out of his mind?

He looked again at his watch. Twenty minutes past one only. How the time crawled.

Extraordinary girl, Bundle! Fancy having the nerve and the daring actually to get into the midst of that Seven Dials place. Why hadn't he had the nerve and initiative to think of that? He supposed because the thing *was* so fantastic.

No. 7. Who the hell could No. 7 be? Was he, perhaps, in the house at this minute? Disguised as a servant. He couldn't, surely, be one of the guests. No, that was impossible. But then, the whole thing was impossible. If he hadn't believed Bundle to be essentially truthful—well, he would have thought she had invented the whole thing.

He yawned. Queer, to feel sleepy, and yet at the same time strung up. He looked again at his watch. Ten minutes to two. Time was getting on.

And then, suddenly, he held his breath and leaned forward, listening. He had heard something.

The minutes went past. . . . There it was again. The creak of a board. . . . But it came from downstairs somewhere. There it was again! A slight, ominous creak. Somebody was moving stealthily about the house.

Jimmy sprang noiselessly to his feet. He crept silently to the head of the staircase. Everything seemed perfectly quiet. Yet he was quite certain he had really heard that stealthy sound. It was not imagination.

Very quietly and cautiously he crept down the staircase, Leopold clasped tightly in his right hand. Not a sound in the big hall. If he had been correct in assuming that the muffled sound came from directly beneath him, then it must have come from the library.

Jimmy stole to the door of it, listened, but heard nothing; then, suddenly flinging open the door, he switched on the lights.

Nothing! The big room was flooded with light. But it was empty.

Jimmy frowned.

'I could have sworn——' he murmured to himself.

The library was a large room with three windows which opened on to the terrace. Jimmy strode across the room. The middle window was unlatched.

He opened it and stepped out on the terrace, looking from end to end of it. Nothing!

'Looks all right,' he murmured to himself. 'And yet——'

He remained for a minute lost in thought. Then he stepped back into the library. Crossing to the door, he locked it and put the key in his pocket. Then he switched off the light. He stood for a minute listening, then crossed softly to the open window and stood there, Leopold ready in his hand.

Was there, or was there not, a soft patter of feet along the terrace? No—his imagination. He grasped Leopold tightly and stood listening. . . .

In the distance a stable clock chimed two.

19. *Bundle's adventures*

BUNDLE BRENT was a resourceful girl—she was also a girl of imagination. She had foreseen that Bill, if not Jimmy, would make objections to her participation in the possible dangers of the night. It was not Bundle's idea to waste time in argument. She had laid her own plans and made her own arrangements. A glance from her bedroom window shortly before dinner had been highly satisfactory. She had known that the gray walls of the Abbey were plentifully adorned with ivy, but the ivy outside her window was particularly solid looking and would present no difficulties to one of her athletic propensities.

She had no fault to find with Bill's and Jimmy's arrangements as far as they went. But in her opinion they did not go far enough. She offered no criticism, because she intended to see to that side of things herself. Briefly, while Jimmy and Bill were devoting themselves to the inside of the Abbey, Bundle intended to devote her attentions to the outside.

Her own meek acquiescence in the tame rôle assigned to her gave her an infinity of pleasure, though she wondered scornfully how either of the two men could be so easily deceived. Bill, of course, had never been famous for scintillating brain power. On the other hand, he knew, or should know, his Bundle. And she considered that Jimmy Thesiger, though only slightly acquainted with her, ought to have known better than to imagine that she could be so easily and summarily disposed of.

Once in the privacy of her own room, Bundle set rapidly to work. First she discarded her evening dress and the negligible trifle which she wore beneath it, and started again, so to speak, from the foundations. Bundle had not brought her maid with her, and she had packed herself. Otherwise, the puzzled Frenchwoman might have wondered why her lady took a pair of riding breeches and no further equine equipment.

Arrayed in riding breeches, rubber-soled shoes, and a dark-coloured pullover, Bundle was ready for the fray. She glanced at the time. As yet, it was only half past twelve. Too early by far. Whatever was going to happen would not happen for some time yet. The occupants of the house must all be given time to get off to sleep. Half past one was the time fixed by Bundle for the start of operations.

She switched off her light and sat down by the window to wait. Punctually at the appointed moment, she rose, pushed up the sash and swung her leg over the sill. The night was a fine one, cold and still. There was starlight but no moon.

She found the descent very easy. Bundle and her two sisters had run wild in the park at Chimneys as small children, and they could all climb like cats. Bundle arrived on a flower-bed, rather breathless, but quite unscathed.

She paused a minute to take stock of her plans. She knew that the rooms occupied by the Air Minister and his secretary were in the west wing; that was the opposite side of the house from where Bundle was now standing. A terrace ran along the south and west side of the house, ending abruptly against a walled fruit garden.

Bundle stepped out of her flower-bed and turned the corner of the house to where the terrace began on the south side. She crept very quietly along it, keeping close to the shadow of the house. But, as she reached the second corner, she got a shock, for a man was standing there, with the clear intention of barring her way.

The next instant she had recognised him.

'Superintendent Battle! You did give me a fright!'

'That's what I'm here for,' said the Superintendent pleasantly.

Bundle looked at him. It struck her now, as so often before, how remarkably little camouflage there was about him. He was large and solid and noticeable. He was, somehow, very English. But of one thing Bundle was quite sure. Superintendent Battle was no fool.

'What are you really doing here?' she asked, still in a whisper.

'Just seeing,' said Battle, 'that nobody's about who shouldn't be.'

'Oh!' said Bundle, rather taken aback.

'You, for instance, Lady Eileen. I don't suppose you usually take a walk at this time of night.'

'Do you mean,' said Bundle slowly, 'that you want me to go back?'

Superintendent Battle nodded approvingly.

'You're very quick, Lady Eileen. That's just what I do mean. Did you—er—come out of a door, or the window?'

'The window. It's easy as anything climbing down this ivy.'

Superintendent Battle looked up at it thoughtfully.

'Yes,' he said. 'I should say it would be.'

'And you want me to go back?' said Bundle. 'I'm rather sick about that. I wanted to go round on to the west terrace.'

'Perhaps you won't be the only one who'll want to do that,' said Battle.

'Nobody could miss seeing you,' said Bundle rather spitefully.

The Superintendent seemed rather pleased than otherwise.

'I hope they won't,' he said. '*No unpleasantness*. That's my motto. And if you'll excuse me, Lady Eileen, I think it's time you were going back to bed.'

The firmness of his tone admitted of no parley. Rather crestfallen, Bundle retraced her steps. She was half-way up the ivy when a sudden idea occurred to her, and she nearly relaxed her grip and fell.

Supposing Superintendent Battle suspected *her*.

There had been something—yes, surely there had been something in his manner that vaguely suggested the idea. She couldn't help laughing as she crawled over the sill into her bedroom. Fancy the solid Superintendent suspecting *her!*

Though she had so far obeyed Battle's orders as to return to her room, Bundle had no intention of going to bed and sleeping. Nor did she think that Battle had really intended her to do so. He was not a man to expect impossibilities. And to remain quiescent when something daring and exciting might be going on was a sheer impossibility to Bundle.

She glanced at her watch. It was ten minutes to two. After a moment or two of irresolution, she cautiously opened her door. Not a sound. Everything was still and peaceful. She stole cautiously along the passage.

Once she halted, thinking she heard a board creak somewhere, but then convinced that she was mistaken, she went on again. She was now in the main corridor, making her way to the west wing. She reached the angle of intersection and peered cautiously round—then she stared in blank surprise.

The watcher's post was empty. Jimmy Thesiger was not there.

Bundle stared in complete amazement. What had happened? Why had Jimmy left his post? What did it mean?

And at that moment she heard a clock strike two.

She was still standing there, debating what to do next, when suddenly her heart gave a leap and then seemed to stand still.

The door handle of Terence O'Rourke's room was slowly turning.

Bundle watched, fascinated. But the door did not open. Instead the knob returned slowly to its original position. What did it mean?

Suddenly Bundle came to a resolution. Jimmy, for some unknown reason, had deserted his post. She must get hold of Bill.

Quickly and noiselessly, Bundle fled along the way she had come. She burst unceremoniously into Bill's room.

'Bill, wake up! Oh, do wake up!'

It was an urgent whisper she sent forth, but there came no response to it.

'Bill,' breathed Bundle.

Impatiently she switched on the lights, and then stood dumbfounded.

The room was empty, and the bed had not even been slept in.

Where then was Bill?

Suddenly she caught her breath. *This was not Bill's room.* The dainty negligée thrown over a chair, the feminine knick-knacks on the dressing-table, the black velvet evening dress thrown carelessly over a chair—— Of course, in her haste she had mistaken the doors. This was the Countess Radzky's room.

But where, oh where, was the countess?

And just as Bundle was asking herself this question, the silence of the night was suddenly broken, and in no uncertain manner.

The clamour came from below. In an instant Bundle had sped out of the Countess's room and downstairs. The sounds came from the library—a violent crashing of chairs being overturned.

Bundle rattled vainly at the library door. It was locked. But she could clearly hear the struggle that was going on within—the panting and scuffling, curses in manly tones, the occasional crash as some light piece of furniture came into the line of battle.

And then, sinister and distinct, breaking the peace of the night for good and all, two shots in rapid succession.

20. *Loraine's adventures*

LORAINE WADE sat up in bed and switched on the light. It was exactly ten minutes to one. She had gone to bed early—at half past nine. She possessed the useful art of being able to wake herself up at the required time, so she had been able to enjoy some hours of refreshing sleep.

Two dogs slept in the room with her, and one of these now raised his head had looked at her inquiringly.

'Quiet, Lurcher,' said Loraine, and the big animal put his head down again obediently, watching her from between his shaggy eyelashes.

It is true that Bundle had once doubted the meekness of Loraine Wade, but that brief moment of suspicion had passed. Loraine had seemed so entirely reasonable, so willing to be kept out of everything.

And yet, if you studied the girl's face, you saw that there was strength of purpose in the small, resolute jaw and the lips that closed together so firmly.

Loraine rose and dressed herself in a tweed coat and skirt. Into one pocket of the coat she dropped an electric torch. Then she opened the drawer of her dressing table and took out a small ivory-handled pistol—almost a toy in appearance. She had bought it the day before at Harrods and she was very pleased with it.

She gave a final glance round the room to see if she had forgotten anything, and at that moment the big dog rose and came over to her, looking up at her with pleading eyes and wagging his tail.

Loraine shook her head.

'No, Lurcher. Can't go. Missus can't take you. Got to stay here and be a good boy.'

She dropped a kiss on the dog's head, made him lie down on his rug again, and then slipped noiselessly out of the room, closing the door behind her.

She let herself out of the house by a side door and made her way round to the garage, where her little two-seater car was in readiness. There was a gentle slope, and she let the car run silently down it, not starting the engine till she was some way from the house. Then she glanced at the watch on her arm and pressed her foot down on the accelerator.

She left the car at a spot she had previously marked down. There was a gap there in the fencing that she could easily get through. A few minutes later, slightly muddy, Loraine stood inside the grounds of Wyvern Abbey.

As noiselessly as possible, she made her way towards the venerable ivy-covered building. In the distance a stable clock chimed two.

Loraine's heart beat faster as she drew near to the terrace. There was no one about—no sign of life anywhere. Everything seemed peaceful and undisturbed. She reached the terrace and stood there, looking about her.

Suddenly, without the least warning, something from above fell with a flop almost at her feet. Loraine stooped to pick it up. It was a brown paper packet, loosely wrapped. Holding it, Loraine looked up.

There was an open window just above her head, and even as she looked a leg swung over it and a man began to climb down the ivy.

Loraine waited for no more. She took to her heels and ran, still clasping the brown paper packet.

Behind her, the noise of a struggle suddenly broke out. A hoarse voice: 'Lemme go'; another that she knew well: 'Not if I know it—ah, you would, would you?'

Still Loraine ran—blindly, as though panic stricken—right round the corner of the terrace—and slap into the arms of a large, solidly built man.

'There, there,' said Superintendent Battle kindly.

Loraine was struggling to speak.

'Oh, quick—oh, quick! They're killing each other. Oh, do be quick!'

There was a sharp crack of a revolver shot—and then another.

Superintendent Battle started to run. Loraine followed. Back round the corner of the terrace and along to the library window. The window was open.

Battle stopped and switched on an electric torch. Loraine was close beside him, peering over his shoulder. She gave a little sobbing gasp.

On the threshold of the window lay Jimmy Thesiger in what looked like a pool of blood. His right arm lay dangling in a curious position.

Loraine gave a sharp cry.

'He's dead,' she wailed. 'Oh, Jimmy—Jimmy—he's dead!'

'Now, now,' said Superintendent Battle soothingly. 'Don't you take on so. The young gentleman isn't dead, I'll be bound. See if you can find the lights and turn them on.'

Loraine obeyed. She stumbled across the room, found the switch by the door and pressed it down. The room was flooded with light. Superintendent Battle uttered a sigh of relief.

'It's all right—he's only shot in the right arm. He's fainted through loss of blood. Come and give me a hand with him.'

There was a pounding on the library door. Voices were heard, asking, expostulating, demanding.

Loraine looked doubtfully at it.

'Shall I——?'

'No hurry,' said Battle. 'We'll let them in presently. You come and give me a hand.'

Loraine came obediently. The Superintendent had produced a large, clean pocket-handkerchief and was neatly bandaging the wounded man's arm. Loraine helped him.

'He'll be all right,' said the Superintendent. 'Don't you worry. As many lives as cats, these young fellows. It wasn't the loss of blood knocked him out either. He must have caught his head a crack on the floor as he fell.'

Outside the knocking on the door had become tremendous. The voice of George Lomax, furiously upraised, came loud and distinct:

'Who is in there? Open the door at once.'

Superintendent Battle sighed.

'I suppose we shall have to,' he said. 'A pity.'

His eyes darted round, taking in the scene. An automatic lay by Jimmy's side. The Superintendent picked it up gingerly, holding it very delicately, and examined it. He grunted and laid it on the table. Then he stepped across and unlocked the door.

Several people almost fell into the room. Nearly everybody said something at the same minute. George Lomax, spluttering with obdurate words which refused to come with sufficient fluency, exclaimed:

'The—the—the meaning of this? Ah! It's you, Superintendent; what's happened? I say—what has—happened?'

Bill Eversleigh said: 'My God! Old Jimmy!' and stared at the limp figure on the ground.

Lady Coote, clad in a resplendent purple dressing gown, cried out: 'The poor boy!' and swept past Superintendent Battle to bend over the prostrate Jimmy in a motherly fashion.

Bundle said: 'Loraine!'

Herr Eberhard said: 'Gott im Himmel!' and other words of that nature.

Sir Stanley Digby said: 'My God, what's all this?'

A housemaid said: 'Look at the blood,' and screamed with pleasurable excitement.

A footman said: 'Lor!'

The butler said, with a good deal more bravery in his manner than had been noticeable a few minutes earlier: 'Now then, this won't do!' and waved away under-servants.

The efficient Mr. Rupert Bateman said to George: 'Shall we get rid of some of these people, sir?'

Then they all took fresh breath.

'Incredible!' said George Lomax. 'Battle, what has *happened?*'

Battle gave him a look, and George's discreet habits assumed their usual sway.

'Now then,' he said, moving to the door, 'Everyone go back to bed, please. There's been a—er——'

'A little accident,' said Superintendent Battle easily.

'A—er—an accident. I shall be much obliged if everyone will go back to bed.'

Everyone was clearly reluctant to do so.

'Lady Coote—please——'

'The poor boy,' said Lady Coote in a motherly fashion.

She rose from a kneeling position with great reluctance. And as she did so, Jimmy stirred and sat up.

'Hallo!' he said thickly. 'What's the matter?'

He looked round him vacantly for a minute or two and then intelligence returned to his eye.

'Have you got him?' he demanded eagerly.

'Got who?'

'The man. Climbed down the ivy. I was by the window there. Grabbed him and we had no end of a set-to——'

'One of those nasty, murderous cat burglars,' said Lady Coote. 'Poor boy.'

Jimmy was looking round him.

'I say—I'm afraid we—er—have made rather a mess of things. Fellow was as strong as an ox and we went fairly waltzing around.'

The condition of the room was clear proof of this statement. Everything light and breakable within a range of twelve feet that could be broken *had* been broken.

'And what happened then?'

But Jimmy was looking round for something.

'Where's Leopold? The pride of the blue-nosed automatics?'

Battle indicated the pistol on the table.

'Is this yours, Mr. Thesiger?'

'That's right. That's little Leopold. How many shots have been fired?'

'One shot.'

Jimmy looked chagrined.

'I'm disappointed in Leopold,' he murmured. 'I can't have pressed the button properly, or he'd have gone on shooting.'

'Who shot first?'

'I did, I'm afraid,' said Jimmy. 'You see, the man twisted himself out of my grasp suddenly. I saw him making for the window and I closed my finger down on Leopold and let him have it. He turned in the window and fired at me and—well, I suppose after that I took the count.'

He rubbed his head rather ruefully.

But Sir Stanley Digby was suddenly alert.

'Climbing down the ivy, you said? My God, Lomax, you don't think they've got away with it?'

He rushed from the room. For some curious reason nobody spoke during his absence. In a few minutes Sir Stanley returned. His round, chubby face was white as death.

'My God, Battle,' he said, 'they've got it. O'Rourke's fast asleep—drugged, I think. I can't wake him. And the papers have vanished.'

21. *The recovery of the formula*

'DER LIEBE GOTT!' said Herr Eberhard in a whisper.

His face had gone chalky white.

George turned a face of dignified reproach on Battle.

'Is this true, Battle? I left all arrangements in your hands.'

The rock-like quality of the Superintendent showed out well. Not a muscle of his face moved.

'The best of us are defeated sometimes, sir,' he said quietly.

'Then you mean—you really mean—that the document is gone?'

But to everyone's intense surprise Superintendent Battle shook his head.

'No, no, Mr. Lomax, it's not so bad as you think. Everything's all right. But you can't lay the credit for it at my door. You've got to thank this young lady.'

He indicated Loraine, who stared at him in surprise. Battle stepped across to her and gently took the brown paper parcel which she was still clutching mechanically.

'I think, Mr. Lomax,' he said, 'that you will find what you want here.'

Sir Stanley Digby, quicker in action than George, snatched at the package and tore it open, investigating its contents eagerly. A sigh of relief escaped him and he mopped his brow. Herr Eberhard fell upon the child of his brain and clasped it to his heart, whilst a torrent of German burst from him.

Sir Stanley turned to Loraine, shaking her warmly by the hand.

'My dear young lady,' he said, 'we are infinitely obliged to you, I am sure.'

'Yes, indeed,' said George. 'Though I—er——'

He paused in some perplexity, staring at a young lady who was a total stranger to him. Loraine looked appealingly at Jimmy, who came to the rescue.

'Er—this is Miss Wade,' said Jimmy. 'Gerald Wade's sister.'

'Indeed,' said George, shaking her warmly by the hand. 'My dear Miss Wade, I must express my deep gratitude to you for what you have done. I must confess that I do not quite see——'

He paused delicately and four of the persons present felt that explanations were going to be fraught with much difficulty. Superintendent Battle came to the rescue.

'Perhaps we'd better not go into that just now, sir,' he suggested tactfully.

The efficient Mr. Bateman created a further diversion.

'Wouldn't it be wise for someone to see to O'Rourke? Don't you think, sir, that a doctor had better be sent for?'

'Of course,' said George. 'Of course. Most remiss of us not to have thought of it before.' He looked towards Bill. 'Get Dr. Cartwright on the telephone. Ask him to come. Just hint, if you can, that—er—discretion should be observed.'

Bill went off on his errand.

'I will come up with you, Digby,' said George. 'Something, possibly, could be done—measures should, perhaps, be taken—whilst awaiting the arrival of the doctor.'

He looked rather helplessly at Rupert Bateman. Efficiency always makes itself felt. It was Pongo who was really in charge of the situation.

'Shall I come up with you, sir?'

George accepted the offer with relief. Here, he felt, was someone on whom he could lean. He experienced that sense of complete trust in Mr. Bateman's efficiency which came to all those who encountered that excellent young man.

The three men left the room together. Lady Coote, murmuring in deep rich tones: 'The poor young fellow. Perhaps I could do something——' hurried after them.

'That's a very motherly woman,' observed the Superintendent thoughtfully. 'A very motherly woman. I wonder——'

Three pairs of eyes looked at him inquiringly.

'I was wondering,' said Superintendent Battle slowly, 'where Sir Oswald Coote may be.'

'Oh!' gasped Loraine. 'Do you think he's been murdered?'

Battle shook his head at her reproachfully.

'No need for anything so melodramatic,' he said. 'No—I rather think——'

He paused, his head on one side, listening—one large hand raised to enjoin silence.

In another minute they all heard what his sharper ears had been the first to notice. Footsteps coming along the terrace outside. They rang out clearly with no kind of subterfuge about them. In another minute the window was blocked by a bulky figure which stood there regarding them and who conveyed, in an odd way, a sense of dominating the situation.

Sir Oswald, for it was he, looked slowly from one face to another. His keen eyes took in the details of the situation. Jimmy, with his roughly bandaged arm; Bundle, in her somewhat anomalous attire; Loraine, a perfect stranger to him. His eyes came last to Superintendent Battle. He spoke sharply and crisply:

'What's been happening here, officer?'

'Attempted robbery, sir.'

'*Attempted*—eh?'

'Thanks to this young lady, Miss Wade, the thieves failed to get away with it.'

'Ah!' he said again, his scrutiny ended. 'And now, officer, what about *this*?'

He held out a small Mauser pistol which he carried delicately by the butt.

'Where did you find that, Sir Oswald?'

'On the lawn outside. I presume it must have been thrown down by one of the thieves as he took to his heels. I've held it carefully, as I thought you might wish to examine it for fingerprints.'

'You think of everything, Sir Oswald,' said Battle.

He took the pistol from the other, handling it with equal care, and laid it down on the table beside Jimmy's Colt.

'And now, if you please,' said Sir Oswald, 'I should like to hear exactly what occurred.'

Superintendent Battle gave a brief résumé of the events of the night. Sir Oswald frowned thoughtfully.

'I understand,' he said sharply. 'After wounding and disabling Mr. Thesiger, the man took to his heels and ran, throwing away the pistol as he did so. What I cannot understand is why no one pursued him.'

'It wasn't till we heard Mr. Thesiger's story that we knew there was anyone to pursue,' remarked Superintendent Battle dryly.

'You didn't—er—catch sight of him making off as you turned the corner of the terrace?'

'No, I missed him by just about forty seconds, I should say. There's no moon and he'd be invisible as soon as he'd left the terrace. He must have leapt for it as soon as he'd fired the shot.'

'H'm,' said Sir Oswald. 'I still think that a search should

have been organised. Someone else should have been posted——'

'There are three of my men in the grounds,' said the Superintendent quietly.

'Oh!' Sir Oswald seemed rather taken aback.

'They were to hold and detain anyone attempting to leave the grounds.'

'And yet—they haven't done so?'

'And yet they haven't done so,' agreed Battle gravely.

Sir Oswald looked at him as though something in the words puzzled him. He said sharply:

'Are you telling me all that you know, Superintendent Battle?'

'All that I *know*—yes, Sir Oswald. What I think is a different matter. Maybe I think some rather curious things—but until thinking's got you somewhere it's no use talking about it.'

'And yet,' said Sir Oswald slowly, 'I should like to know what you think, Superintendent Battle.'

'For one thing, sir, I think there's a lot too much ivy about this place—excuse me, sir, you've got a bit on your coat—yes, a great deal too much ivy. It complicates things.'

Sir Oswald stared at him, but any reply he might have contemplated making was arrested by the entrance of Rupert Bateman.

'Oh, there you are, Sir Oswald. I'm so glad. Lady Coote has just discovered that you were missing—and she has been insisting upon it that you had been murdered by the thieves. I really think, Sir Oswald, that you had better come to her at once. She is terribly upset.'

'Maria is an incredibly foolish woman,' said Sir Oswald. 'Why should I be murdered? I'll come with you, Bateman.'

He left the room with his secretary.

'That's a very efficient young man,' said Battle, looking after them. 'What's his name—Bateman?'

Jimmy nodded.

'Bateman—Rupert,' he said. 'Commonly known as Pongo. I was at school with him.'

'Were you? Now, that's interesting, Mr. Thesiger. What was your opinion of him in those days?'

'Oh, he was always the same sort of ass.'

'I shouldn't have thought,' said Battle mildly, 'that he was an ass.'

'Oh, you know what I mean. Of course he wasn't really an ass.

Tons of brains and always swotting at things. But deadly serious. No sense of humour.'

'Ah!' said Superintendent Battle. 'That's a pity. Gentlemen who have no sense of humour get to taking themselves too seriously—and that leads to mischief.'

'I can't imagine Pongo getting into mischief,' said Jimmy. 'He's done extremely well for himself so far—dug himself in with old Coote and looks like being a permanency in the job.'

'Superintendent Battle,' said Bundle.

'Yes, Lady Eileen?'

'Don't you think it very odd that Sir Oswald didn't say what he was doing wandering about in the garden in the middle of the night?'

'Ah!' said Battle. 'Sir Oswald's a great man—and a great man always knows better than to explain unless an explanation is demanded. To rush into explanations and excuses is always a sign of weakness. Sir Oswald knows that as well as I do. He's not going to come in explaining and apologising—not he. He just stalks in and hauls *me* over the coals. He's a big man, Sir Oswald.'

Such a warm admiration sounded in the Superintendent's tones that Bundle pursued the subject no further.

'And now,' said Superintendent Battle, looking round with a slight twinkle in his eye, 'now that we're together and friendly like—I *should* like to hear just how Miss Wade happened to arrive on the scene so pat.'

'She ought to be ashamed of herself,' said Jimmy. 'Hoodwinking us all as she did.'

'Why should I be kept out of it all?' cried Loraine passionately. 'I never meant to be—no, not the very first day in your rooms when you both explained how the best thing for me to do was to stay quietly at home and keep out of danger. I didn't say anything, but I made up my mind then.'

'I half suspected it,' said Bundle. 'You were so surprisingly meek about it. I might have known you were up to something.'

'I thought you were remarkably sensible,' said Jimmy Thesiger.

'You would, Jimmy dear,' said Loraine. 'It was easy enough to deceive you.'

'Thank you for these kind words,' said Jimmy. 'Go on, and don't mind me.'

'When you rang up and said there might be danger, I was more determined than ever,' went on Loraine. 'I went to Harrods and I bought a pistol. Here it is.'

She produced the dainty weapon, and Superintendent Battle took it from her and examined it.

'Quite a deadly little toy, Miss Wade,' he said. 'Have you had much—er—practice with it?'

'None at all,' said Loraine. 'But I thought if I took it with me—well, that it would give me a comforting feeling.'

'Quite so,' said Battle gravely.

'My idea was to come over here and see what was going on. I left the car in the road and climbed through the hedge and came up to the terrace. I was just looking about me when—plop—something fell right at my feet. I picked it up and then looked to see where it could have come from. And then I saw the man climbing down the ivy and I ran.'

'Just so,' said Battle. 'Now, Miss Wade, can you describe that man at all?'

The girl shook her head.

'It was too dark to see much. I think he was a big man—but that's about all.'

'And now you, Mr. Thesiger.' Battle turned to him. 'You struggled with the man—can you tell me anything about him?'

'He was a pretty hefty individual—that's all I can say. He gave a few hoarse whispers—that's when I had him by the throat. He said "Lemme go, guvnor," something like that.'

'An uneducated man, then?'

'Yes, I suppose he was. He spoke like one.'

'I still don't quite understand about the packet,' said Loraine. 'Why should he throw it down as he did? Was it because it hampered him climbing?'

'No,' said Battle. 'I've got an entirely different theory about that. That packet, Miss Wade, was deliberately thrown down to you—or so I believe.'

'To *me*?'

'Shall we say—to the person the thief thought you were.'

'This is getting very involved,' said Jimmy.

'Mr. Thesiger, when you came into this room, did you switch on the light at all?'

'Yes.'

'And there was no one in the room?'

'No one at all.'

'But previously you thought you heard someone moving about down here?'

'Yes.'

'And then, after trying the window, you switched off the light again and locked the door?'

Jimmy nodded.

Superintendent Battle looked slowly round him. His glance was arrested by a big screen of Spanish leather which stood near one of the bookcases.

Brusquely he strode across the room and looked behind it.

He uttered a sharp ejaculation, which brought the three young people quickly to his side.

Huddled on the floor, in a dead faint, lay the Countess Radzky.

22. *The Countess Radzky's story*

THE COUNTESS'S RETURN to consciousness was very different from that of Jimmy Thesiger. It was more prolonged and infinitely more artistic.

Artistic was Bundle's word. She had been zealous in her ministrations—largely consisting of the application of cold water—and the Countess had instantly responded, passing a white, bewildered hand across her brow and murmuring faintly.

It was at this point that Bill, at last relieved from his duties with telephone and doctors, had come bustling into the room and had instantly proceeded to make (in Bundle's opinion) a most regrettable idiot of himself.

He had hung over the Countess with a concerned and anxious face and had addressed a series of singularly idiotic remarks to her:

'I say, Countess. It's all right. It's really all right. Don't try to talk. It's bad for you. Just lie still. You'll be all right in a minute. It'll all come back to you. Don't say anything till you're quite all right. Take your time. Just lie still and close your eyes.

You'll remember everything in a minute. Have another sip of water. Have some brandy. That's the stuff. Don't you think, Bundle, that some brandy . . . ?'

'For God's sake, Bill, leave her alone,' said Bundle crossly. 'She'll be all right.'

And with an expert hand she flipped a good deal of cold water on to the exquisite make-up of the Countess's face.

The Countess flinched and sat up. She looked considerably more wide awake.

'Ah!' she murmured. 'I am here. Yes, I am here.'

'Take your time,' said Bill. 'Don't talk till you feel quite all right again.'

The Countess drew the folds of a very transparent negligée closer around her.

'It is coming back to me,' she murmured. 'Yes, it is coming back.'

She looked at the little crowd grouped around her. Perhaps something in the attentive faces struck her as unsympathetic. In any case she smiled deliberately up at the one face which clearly displayed a very opposite emotion.

'Ah, my big Englishman,' she said very softly, 'do not distress yourself. All is well with me.'

'Oh! I say, but are you sure?' demanded Bill anxiously.

'Quite sure.' She smiled at him reassuringly. 'We Hungarians, we have nerves of steel.'

A look of intense relief passed over Bill's face. A fatuous look settled down there instead—a look which made Bundle earnestly long to kick him.

'Have some water,' she said coldly.

The Countess refused water. Jimmy, kindlier to beauty in distress, suggested a cocktail. The Countess reacted favourably to this suggestion. When she had swallowed it, she looked round once more, this time with a livelier eye.

'Tell me, what has happened?' she demanded briskly.

'We were hoping you might be able to tell us that,' said Superintendent Battle.

The Countess looked at him sharply. She seemed to become aware of the big, quiet man for the first time.

'I went to your room,' said Bundle. 'The bed hadn't been slept in and you weren't there.'

She paused—looking accusingly at the Countess. The latter closed her eyes and nodded her head slowly.

'Yes, yes, I remember it all now. Oh, it was horrible!' She shuddered. 'Do you want me to tell you?'

Superintendent Battle said, 'If you please' at the same moment that Bill said, 'Not if you don't feel up to it.'

The Countess looked from one to the other, but the quiet, masterful eye of Superintendent Battle won the game.

'I could not sleep,' began the Countess. 'The house—it oppressed me. I was all, as you say, on wires, the cat on the hot bricks. I knew that in the state I was in it was useless to think of going to bed. I walked about my room. I read. But the books placed there did not interest me greatly. I thought I would come down here and find something more absorbing.'

'Very natural,' said Bill.

'Very often done, I believe,' said Battle.

'So as soon as the idea occurred to me, I left my room and came down. The house was very still——'

'Excuse me,' interrupted the Superintendent, 'but can you give me an idea of the time when this occurred?'

'I never know the time,' said the Countess superbly, and swept on with her story.

'The house was very quiet. One could even hear the little mouse run, if there had been one. I come down the stairs—very quietly——'

'Very quietly?'

'Naturally I do not want to disturb the household,' said the Countess reproachfully. 'I come in here. I go into this corner and I search the shelves for a suitable book.'

'Having, of course, switched on the light?'

'No, I did not switch on the light. I had, you see, my little electric torch with me. With that, I scanned the shelves.'

'Ah!' said the Superintendent.

'Suddenly,' continued the Countess dramatically, 'I hear something. A stealthy sound. A muffled footstep. I switch out my torch and listen. The footsteps draw nearer—stealthy, horrible footsteps. I shrink behind the screen. In another minute the door opens and the light is switched on. The man—the burglar is in the room.'

'Yes, but I say——' began Mr. Thesiger.

A large-sized foot pressed his, and realising that Superintendent Battle was giving him a hint, Jimmy shut up.

'I nearly died of fear,' continued the Countess. 'I tried not to breathe. The man waited for a minute, listening. Then, still with that horrible, stealthy tread——'

Again Jimmy opened his mouth in protest, and again shut it.

'——he crossed to the window and peered out. He remained there for a minute or two, then he recrossed the room and turned out the lights again, locking the door. I am terrified. He is in the room, moving stealthily about in the dark. Ah, it is horrible. Suppose he should come upon me in the dark! In another minute I hear him again by the window. Then silence. I hope that perhaps he may have gone out that way. As the minutes pass and I hear no further sound, I am almost sure that he has done so. Indeed I am in the very act of switching on my torch and investigating when—*prestissimo!*—it all begins.'

'Yes?'

'Ah! But it was terrible—never—never shall I forget it! Two men trying to murder each other. Oh, it was horrible! They reeled about the room, and furniture crashed in every direction. I thought, too, that I heard a woman scream—but that was not in the room. It was outside somewhere. The criminal had a hoarse voice. He croaked rather than spoke. He kept saying "Lemme go—lemme go." The other man was a gentleman. He had a cultured, English voice.'

Jimmy looked gratified.

'He swore—mostly,' continued the Countess.

'Clearly a gentleman,' said Superintendent Battle.

'And then,' continued the Countess, 'a flash and a shot. The bullet hit the bookcase beside me. I—I suppose I must have fainted.'

She looked up at Bill. He took her hand and patted it.

'You poor dear,' he said. 'How rotten for you.'

'Silly idiot,' thought Bundle.

Superintendent Battle had moved on swift, noiseless feet over to the bookcase a little to the right of the screen. He bent down, searching. Presently he stooped and picked something up.

'It wasn't a bullet, Countess,' he said. 'It's the shell of the cartridge. Where were you standing when you fired, Mr. Thesiger?'

Jimmy took up a position by the window.

'As nearly as I can see, about here.'

Superintendent Battle placed himself in the same spot.

'That's right,' he agreed. 'The empty shell would throw right rear. It's a .455. I don't wonder the Countess thought it was a bullet in the dark. It hit the bookcase about a foot from her. The bullet itself grazed the window frame and we'll find it outside to-morrow—unless your assailant happens to be carrying it about in him.'

Jimmy shook his head regretfully.

'Leopold, I fear, did not cover himself with glory,' he remarked sadly.

The Countess was looking at him with most flattering attention.

'Your arm!' she exclaimed. 'It is all tied up! Was it you then——'

Jimmy made her a mock bow.

'I'm so glad I've got a cultured, English voice,' he said. 'And I can assure you that I wouldn't have dreamed of using the language I did if I had had any suspicion that a lady was present.'

'I did not understand all of it,' the Countess hastened to explain. 'Although I had an English governess when I was young——'

'It isn't the sort of thing she'd be likely to teach you,' agreed Jimmy. 'Kept you busy with your uncle's pen, and the umbrella of the gardener's niece. I know the sort of stuff.'

'But what has happened?' asked the Countess. 'That is what I want to know. I demand to know what has happened.'

There was a moment's silence whilst everybody looked at Superintendent Battle.

'It's very simple,' said Battle mildly. 'Attempted robbery. Some political papers stolen from Sir Stanley Digby. The thieves nearly got away with them, but thanks to this young lady'—he indicated Loraine—'they didn't.'

The Countess flashed a glance at the girl—rather an odd glance.

'Indeed,' she said coldly.

'A very fortunate coincidence that she happened to be there,' said Superintendent Battle, smiling.

The Countess gave a little sigh and half closed her eyes again.

'It is absurd, but I still feel extremely faint,' she murmured.

'Of course you do,' cried Bill. 'Let me help you up to your room. Bundle will come with you.'

'It is very kind of Lady Eileen,' said the Countess, 'but I should prefer to be alone. I am really quite all right. Perhaps you will just help me up the stairs?'

She rose to her feet, accepted Bill's arm and, leaning heavily on it, went out of the room. Bundle followed as far as the hall but, the Countess reiterating her assurance—with some tartness—that she was quite all right, she did not accompany them upstairs.

But as she stood watching the Countess's graceful form, supported by Bill, slowly mounting the stairway, she stiffened suddenly to acute attention. The Countess's negligée, as previously mentioned, was thin—a mere veil of orange chiffon. Through it Bundle saw distinctly below the right shoulder blade a *small black mole*.

With a gasp, Bundle swung impetuously round to where Superintendent Battle was just emerging from the library. Jimmy and Loraine had preceded him.

'There,' said Battle. 'I've fastened the window and there will be a man on duty outside. And I'll lock this door and take the key. In the morning we'll do what the French call reconstruct the crime —— Yes, Lady Eileen, what is it?'

'Superintendent Battle, I must speak to you—at once.'

'Why, certainly, I——'

George Lomax suddenly appeared, Dr. Cartwright by his side.

'Ah, there you are, Battle. You'll be relieved to hear that there's nothing seriously wrong with O'Rourke.'

'I never thought there would be much wrong with Mr. O'Rourke,' said Battle.

'He's had a strong hypnotic administered to him,' said the doctor. 'He'll wake perfectly all right in the morning. Perhaps a bit of a head, perhaps not. Now then, young man, let's look at this bullet wound of yours.'

'Come on, nurse,' said Jimmy to Loraine. 'Come and hold the basin or my hand. Witness a strong man's agony. You know the stunt.'

Jimmy, Loraine and the doctor went off together. Bundle continued to throw agonised glances in the direction of Superintendent Battle, who had been buttonholed by George.

The Superintendent waited patiently till a pause occurred in George's loquacity. He then swiftly took advantage of it.

'I wonder, sir, if I might have a word privately with Sir Stanley? In the little study at the end there.'

'Certainly,' said George. 'Certainly. I'll go and fetch him at once.'

He hurried off upstairs again. Battle drew Bundle swiftly into the drawing-room and shut the door.

'Now, Lady Eileen, what is it?'

'I'll tell you as quickly as I can—but it's rather long and complicated.'

As concisely as she could, Bundle related her introduction to the Seven Dials Club and her subsequent adventures there. When she had finished, Superintendent Battle drew a long breath. For once, his facial woodenness was laid aside.

'Remarkable,' he said. 'Remarkable. I wouldn't have believed it possible—even for you, Lady Eileen. I ought to have known better.'

'But you did give me a hint, Superintendent Battle. You told me to ask Bill Eversleigh.'

'It's dangerous to give people like you a hint, Lady Eileen. I never dreamt of your going to the lengths you have.'

'Well, it's all right, Superintendent Battle. My death doesn't lie at your door.'

'Not yet, it doesn't,' said Battle grimly.

He stood as though in thought, turning things over in his mind. 'What Mr. Thesiger was about, letting you run into danger like that, I can't think,' he said presently.

'He didn't know till afterwards,' said Bundle. 'I'm not a complete mug, Superintendent Battle. And, anyway, he's got his hands full looking after Miss Wade.'

'Is that so?' said the Superintendent. 'Ah!'

He twinkled a little.

'I shall have to detail Mr. Eversleigh to look after you, Lady Eileen.'

'Bill!' said Bundle contemptuously. 'But, Superintendent Battle, you haven't heard the end of my story. The woman I saw there—Anna—No. 1. Yes, No. 1 is the Countess Radzky.'

And rapidly she went on to describe her recognition of the mole.

To her surprise the Superintendent hemmed and hawed.

'A mole isn't much to go upon, Lady Eileen. Two women might have an identical mole very easily. You must remember that the Countess Radzky is a very well-known figure in Hungary.'

'Then this isn't the real Countess Radzky. I tell you I'm sure this is the same woman I saw there. And look at her to-night—the way we found her. I don't believe she ever fainted at all.'

'Oh, I shouldn't say that, Lady Eileen. That empty shell striking the bookcase beside her might have frightened any woman half out of her wits.'

'But what was she doing there anyway? One doesn't come down to look for a book with an electric torch.'

Battle scratched his cheek. He seemed unwilling to speak. He began to pace up and down the room, as though making up his mind. At last he turned to the girl.

'See here, Lady Eileen, I'm going to trust you. The Countess's conduct *is* suspicious. I know that as well as you do. It's very suspicious—but we've got to go carefully. There mustn't be any unpleasantness with the Embassies. One has got to be *sure*.'

'I see. If you were *sure* . . .'

'There's something else. During the war, Lady Eileen, there was a great outcry about German spies being left at large. Busybodies wrote letters to the papers about it. We paid no attention. Hard words didn't hurt us. The small fry were left alone. Why? Because through them, sooner or later, *we got the big fellow—the man at the top*.'

'You mean?'

'Don't bother about what I mean, Lady Eileen. But remember this. *I know all about the Countess*. And I want her let alone.'

'And now,' added Superintendent Battle ruefully, 'I've got to think of something to say to Sir Stanley Digby!'

23. *Superintendent Battle in charge*

IT WAS TEN O'CLOCK on the following morning. The sun poured in through the windows of the library, where Superintendent Battle had been at work since six. On a summons from him, George Lomax, Sir Oswald Coote and Jimmy Thesiger had just joined him, having repaired the fatigues of the night with a substantial breakfast. Jimmy's arm was in a sling, but he bore little other trace of the night's affray.

The Superintendent eyed all three of them benevolently, somewhat with the air of a kindly curator explaining a museum to little boys. On the table beside him were various objects, neatly labelled. Amongst them Jimmy recognised Leopold.

'Ah, Superintendent,' said George, 'I have been anxious to know how you have progressed. Have you caught the man?'

'He'll take a lot of catching, he will,' said the Superintendent easily.

His failure in that respect did not appear to rankle with him.

George Lomax did not look particularly well pleased. He detested levity of any kind.

'I've got everything taped out pretty clearly,' went on the detective.

He took up two objects from the table.

'Here we've got the two bullets. The largest is a .455, fired from Mr. Thesiger's Colt automatic. Grazed the window sash and I found it embedded in the trunk of that cedar tree. This little fellow was fired from the Mauser .25. After passing through Mr. Thesiger's arm, it embedded itself in this armchair here. As for the pistol itself——'

'Well?' said Sir Oswald eagerly. 'Any fingerprints?'

Battle shook his head.

'The man who handled it wore gloves,' he said slowly.

'A pity,' said Sir Oswald.

'A man who knew his business would wear gloves. Am I right in thinking, Sir Oswald, that you found this pistol just about twenty yards from the bottom of the steps leading up to the terrace?'

Sir Oswald stepped to the window.

'Yes, almost exactly, I should say.'

'I don't want to find fault, but it would have been wiser on your part, sir, to leave it exactly as you found it.'

'I am sorry,' said Sir Oswald stiffly.

'Oh, it doesn't matter. I've been able to reconstruct things. There were your footprints, you see, leading up from the bottom of the garden, and a place where you had obviously stopped and stooped down, and a kind of dent in the grass which was highly suggestive. By the way, what was your theory of the pistol being there?'

'I presumed that it had been dropped by the man in his flight.'

Battle shook his head.

'Not dropped, Sir Oswald. There are two points against that. To begin with, there are only one set of footprints crossing the lawn just there—your own.'

'I see,' said Sir Oswald thoughtfully.

'Can you be sure of that, Battle?' put in George.

'Quite sure, sir. There are one other set of tracks crossing the lawn, Miss Wade's, but they are a good deal farther to the left.'

He paused, and then went on: 'And there's the dent in the ground. The pistol must have struck the ground with some force. It all points to its having been thrown.'

'Well, why not?' said Sir Oswald. 'Say the man fled down the path to the left. He'd leave no footprints on the path and he'd hurl the pistol away from him into the middle of the lawn, eh, Lomax?'

George agreed by a nod of the head.

'It's true that he'd leave no footprints on the path,' said Battle, 'but from the shape of the dent and the way the turf was cut, I don't think the pistol was thrown from that direction. I think it was thrown from the terrace here.'

'Very likely,' said Sir Oswald. 'Does it matter, Superintendent?'

'Ah, yes, Battle,' broke in George. 'Is it—er—strictly relevant?'

'Perhaps not, Mr. Lomax. But we like to get things just so, you know. I wonder now if one of you gentlemen would take this pistol and throw it. Will you, Sir Oswald? That's very kind. Stand just here in the window. Now fling it into the middle of the lawn.'

Sir Oswald complied, sending the pistol flying through the air with a powerful sweep of his arm. Jimmy Thesiger drew near with breathless interest. The Superintendent lumbered off after it like a well-trained retriever. He reappeared with a beaming face.

'That's it, sir. Just the same kind of mark. Although, by the way, you sent it a good ten yards farther. But then, you're a very powerfully built man, aren't you, Sir Oswald? Excuse me, I thought I heard someone at the door.'

The Superintendent's ears must have been very much sharper than anyone else's. Nobody else had heard a sound, but Battle was proved right, for Lady Coote stood outside, a medicine glass in her hand.

'Your medicine, Oswald,' she said, advancing into the room. 'You forgot it after breakfast.'

'I'm very busy, Maria,' said Sir Oswald. 'I don't want my medicine.'

'You would never take it if it wasn't for me,' said his wife serenely, advancing upon him. 'You're just like a naughty little boy. Drink it up now.'

And meekly, obediently, the great steel magnate drank it up!

Lady Coote smiled sadly and sweetly at everyone.

'Am I interrupting you? Are you very busy? Oh, look at those revolvers. Nasty, noisy, murdering things. To think, Oswald, that you might have been shot by the burglar last night.'

'You must have been alarmed when you found he was missing, Lady Coote,' said Battle.

'I didn't think of it at first,' confessed Lady Coote. 'This poor boy here'—she indicated Jimmy—'being shot—and everything so dreadful, but so exciting. It wasn't till Mr. Bateman asked me where Sir Oswald was that I remembered he'd gone out half an hour before for a stroll.'

'Sleepless, eh, Sir Oswald?' asked Battle.

'I am usually an excellent sleeper,' said Sir Oswald. 'But I must confess that last night I felt unusually restless. I thought the night air would do me good.'

'You came out through this window, I suppose?'

Was it his fancy, or did Sir Oswald hesitate for a moment before replying?

'Yes.'

'In your pumps too,' said Lady Coote, 'instead of putting thick shoes on. What would you do without me to look after you?'

She shook her head sadly.

'I think, Maria, if you don't mind leaving us—we have still a lot to discuss.'

'I know, dear, I'm just going.'

Lady Coote withdrew, carrying the empty medicine glass as though it were a goblet out of which she had just administered a death potion.

'Well, Battle,' said George Lomax, 'it all seems clear enough. Yes, perfectly clear. The man fires a shot, disabling Mr. Thesiger, flings away the weapon, runs along the terrace and down the gravel path.'

'Where he ought to have been caught by my men,' put in Battle.

'Your men, if I may say so, Battle, seem to have been singularly remiss. They didn't see Miss Wade come in. If they could miss her coming in, they could easily miss the thief going out.'

Superintendent Battle opened his mouth to speak, then seemed to think better of it. Jimmy Thesiger looked at him curiously. He would have given a lot to know just what was in Superintendent Battle's mind.

'Must have been a champion runner,' was all the Scotland Yard man contented himself with saying.

'How do you mean, Battle?'

'Just what I say, Mr. Lomax. I was round the corner of the terrace myself not fifty seconds after the shot was fired. And for a man to run all that distance towards me and get round the corner of the path before I appeared round the side of the house—well, as I say, he must have been a champion runner.'

'I am at a loss to understand you, Battle. You have some idea of your own which I have not yet—er—grasped. You say the man did not go across the lawn, and now you hint—— What exactly do you hint? That the man did not go down the path? Then in your opinion —er—where *did* he go?'

For answer, Superintendent Battle jerked an eloquent thumb upwards.

'Eh?' said George.

The Superintendent jerked harder than ever. George raised his hand and looked at the ceiling.

'Up there,' said Battle. 'Up the ivy again.'

'Nonsense, Superintendent. What you are suggesting is impossible.'

'Not at all impossible, sir. He'd done it once. He could do it twice.'

'I don't mean impossible in that sense. But if the man wanted to escape, he'd never bolt back into the house.'

'Safest place for him, Mr. Lomax.'

'But Mr. O'Rourke's door was still locked on the inside when we came to him.'

'And how did you get to him? Through Sir Stanley's room. That's the way our man went. Lady Eileen tells me she saw the door knob of Mr. O'Rourke's room move. That was when our friend was up there the first time. I suspect the key was under Mr. O'Rourke's pillow. But his exit is clear enough the second time—through the communicating door and through Sir Stanley's room, which, of course, was empty. Like everyone else, Sir Stanley is rushing downstairs to the library. Our man's got a clear course.'

'And where did he go then?'

Superintendent Battle shrugged his burly shoulders and became evasive.

'Plenty of ways open. Into an empty room on the other side of the house and down the ivy again—out through a side door—or, just possibly, if it was an inside job, he—well, stayed in the house.'

George looked at him in shocked surprise.

'Really, Battle, I should—I should feel it very deeply if one of my servants—er—I have the most perfect reliance on them—it would distress me very much to have to suspect——'

'Nobody's asking you to suspect anyone, Mr. Lomax. I'm just putting all the possibilities before you. The servants may be all right—probably are.'

'You have disturbed me,' said George. 'You have disturbed me greatly.'

His eyes appeared more protuberant than ever.

To distract him, Jimmy poked delicately at a curious blackened object on the table.

'What's this?' he asked.

'That's exhibit Z,' said Battle. 'The last of our little lot. It is, or rather it has been, a glove.'

He picked it up, the charred relic, and manipulated it with pride.

'Where did you find it?' asked Sir Oswald.

Battle jerked his head over his shoulder.

'In the grate—nearly burnt, but not quite. Queer; looks as though it had been chewed by a dog.'

'It might possibly be Miss Wade's,' suggested Jimmy. 'She has several dogs.'

The Superintendent shook his head.

'This isn't a lady's glove—no, not even the large kind of loose glove ladies wear nowadays. Fit it on, sir, a moment.'

He adjusted the blackened object over Jimmy's hand.

'You see—it's large even for you.'

'Do you attach importance to this discovery?' inquired Sir Oswald coldly.

'You never know, Sir Oswald, what's going to be important or what isn't.'

'There was a sharp tap at the door and Bundle entered.

'I'm so sorry,' she said apologetically. 'But Father has just rung up. He says I must come home because everybody is worrying him.'

She paused.

'Yes, my dear Eileen?' said George encouragingly, perceiving that there was more to come.

'I wouldn't have interrupted you—only that I thought it might perhaps have something to do with all this. You see, what has upset Father is that one of our footmen is missing. He went out last night and hasn't come back.'

'What is the man's name?' It was Sir Oswald who took up the cross-examination.

'John Bauer.'

'An Englishman?'

'I believe he calls himself a Swiss—but I think he's a German. He speaks English perfectly, though.'

'Ah!' Sir Oswald drew in his breath with a long, satisfied hiss. 'And he has been at Chimneys—how long?'

'Just under a month.'

Sir Oswald turned to the other two.

'Here is our missing man. You know, Lomax, as well as I do, that several foreign Governments are after the thing. I remember the man now perfectly—tall, well-drilled fellow. Came about a fortnight before we left. A clever move. Any new servants here would be closely scrutinised, but at Chimneys, five miles away——' He did not finish the sentence.

'You think the plan was laid so long beforehand?'

'Why not? There are millions in that formula, Lomax. Doubtless Bauer hoped to get access to my private papers at Chimneys, and to learn something of forthcoming arrangements from them. It seems likely that he may have had an accomplice in this house—someone who put him wise to the lie of the land and who saw to the doping of O'Rourke. But Bauer was the man Miss Wade saw climbing down the ivy—the big, powerful man.'

He turned to Superintendent Battle.

'Bauer was your man, Superintendent. And, somehow or other, you let him slip through your fingers.'

24. *Bundle wonders*

THERE WAS NO DOUBT that Superintendent Battle was taken aback. He fingered his chin thoughtfully.

'Sir Oswald is right, Battle,' said George. 'This is the man. Any hope of catching him?'

'There may be, sir. It certainly looks—well, suspicious. Of course the man may turn up again—at Chimneys, I mean.'

'Do you think it likely?'

'No, it isn't,' confessed Battle. 'Yes, it certainly looks as though Bauer were the man. But I can't quite see how he got in and out of these grounds unobserved.'

'I have already told you my opinion of the men you posted,' said George. 'Hopelessly inefficient—I don't want to blame you, Superintendent, but——' His pause was eloquent.

'Ah, well,' said Battle lightly, 'my shoulders are broad.'

He shook his head and sighed.

'I must get to the telephone at once. Excuse me, gentlemen. I'm sorry, Mr. Lomax—I feel I've rather bungled this business. But it's been puzzling, more puzzling than you know.'

He strode hurriedly from the room.

'Come into the garden,' said Bundle to Jimmy. 'I want to talk to you.'

They went out together through the window. Jimmy stared down at the lawn, frowning.

'What's the matter?' asked Bundle.

Jimmy explained the circumstances of the pistol throwing.

'I'm wondering,' he ended, 'what was in old Battle's mind when he got Coote to throw the pistol. Something, I'll swear. Anyhow, it landed up about ten yards farther than it should have done. You know, Bundle, Battle's a deep one.'

'He's an extraordinary man,' said Bundle. 'I want to tell you about last night.'

She retailed her conversation with the Superintendent. Jimmy listened attentively.

'So the Countess is No. 1,' he said thoughtfully. 'It all hangs together very well. No. 2—Bauer—comes over from Chimneys. He climbs up into O'Rourke's room, knowing that O'Rourke has had a sleeping draught administered to him—by the Countess somehow or other. The arrangement is that he is to throw down the papers to the Countess, who will be waiting below. Then she'll nip back through the library and up to her room. If Bauer's caught leaving the grounds, they'll find nothing on him. Yes, it was a good plan—but it went wrong. No sooner is the Countess in the library than she hears me coming and has to jump behind the screen. Jolly awkward for her, because she can't warn her accomplice. No. 2 pinches the papers, looks out of the window, sees, as he thinks, the Countess waiting, pitches the papers down to her and proceeds to climb down the ivy, where he finds a nasty surprise in the shape of me waiting for him. Pretty nervy work for the Countess waiting behind her screen. All things considered, she told a pretty good story. Yes, it all hangs together very well.'

'Too well,' said Bundle decidedly.

'Eh?' said Jimmy, surprised.

'What about No. 7—No. 7, who never appears, but lives in the background. The Countess and Bauer? No, it's not so simple as that. Bauer was here last night, yes. But he was only here in case things went wrong—as they have done. His part is the part of scapegoat; to draw all attention from No. 7—the boss.'

'I say, Bundle,' said Jimmy anxiously, 'you haven't been reading too much sensational literature, have you?'

Bundle threw him a glance of dignified reproach.

'Well,' said Jimmy, 'I'm not yet like the Red Queen. I can't believe six impossible things before breakfast.'

'It's after breakfast,' said Bundle.

'Or even after breakfast. We've got a perfectly good hypothesis which fits the facts—and you won't have it at any price, simply because, like the old riddle, you want to make things more difficult.'

'I'm sorry,' said Bundle, 'but I cling passionately to a mysterious No. 7 being a member of the house-party.'

'What does Bill think?'

'Bill,' said Bundle coldly, 'is impossible.'

'Oh!' said Jimmy. 'I suppose you've told him about the Countess? He ought to be warned. Heaven knows what he'll go blabbing about otherwise.'

'He won't hear a word against her,' said Bundle. 'He's—oh, simply idiotic. I wish you'd drive it home to him about that mole.'

'You forget I wasn't in the cupboard,' said Jimmy. 'And anyway I'd rather not argue with Bill about his lady friend's mole. But surely he can't be such an ass as not to see that everything fits in?'

'He's every kind of ass,' said Bundle bitterly. 'You made the greatest mistake, Jimmy, in ever telling him at all.'

'I'm sorry,' said Jimmy. 'I didn't see it at the time—but I do now. I was a fool, but dash it all, old Bill——'

'You know what foreign adventuresses are,' said Bundle. 'How they get hold of one.'

'As a matter of fact, I don't,' said Jimmy. 'One has never tried to get hold of me.' And he sighed.

For a moment or two there was silence. Jimmy was turning things over in his mind. The more he thought about them, the more unsatisfactory they seemed.

'You say that Battle wants the Countess let alone,' he said at last.

'Yes.'

'The idea being that through her he will get at someone else?'

Bundle nodded.

Jimmy frowned deeply as he tried to see where this led. Clearly Battle had some very definite idea in his mind.

'Sir Stanley Digby went up to town early this morning, didn't he?' he said.

'Yes.'

'O'Rourke with him?'

'Yes, I think so.'

'You don't think—no, that's impossible.'

'What?'

'That O'Rourke can be mixed up in this in any way.'

'It's possible,' said Bundle thoughtfully. 'He's got what one calls a very vivid personality. No, it wouldn't surprise me if—oh, to tell the truth, nothing would surprise me! In fact, there's only one person I'm really sure isn't No. 7.'

'Who's that?'

'Superintendent Battle.'

'Oh! I thought you were going to say George Lomax.'

'Ssh, here he comes.'

George was, indeed, bearing down upon them in an unmistakable manner. Jimmy made an excuse and slipped away. George sat down by Bundle.

'My dear Eileen, must you really leave us?'

'Well, Father seems to have got the wind up rather badly. I think I'd better go home and hold his hand.'

'This little hand will indeed be comforting,' said George, taking it and pressing it playfully. 'My dear Eileen, I understand your reasons and I honour you for them. In these days of changed and unsettled conditions——'

'He's off,' thought Bundle desperately.

'——when family life is at a premium—all the old standards falling!—It becomes our class to set an example to show that we, at least, are unaffected by modern conditions. They call us the Die Hards—I am proud of the term—I repeat I am proud of the term! There are things that *should* die hard—dignity, beauty, modesty, the sanctity of family life, filial respect—who dies if these shall live? As I was saying, my dear Eileen, I envy you the privileges of your youth. Youth! What a wonderful thing! What a wonderful word! And we do not appreciate it until we grow to—er—maturer years. I confess, my dear child, that I have in the past been disappointed by your levity. I see now it was but the careless and charming levity of a child. I perceive now the serious and earnest beauty of your mind. You will allow me, I hope, to help you with your reading?'

'Oh, thank you,' said Bundle faintly.

'And you must never be afraid of me again. I was shocked when

Lady Caterham told me that you stood in awe of me. I can assure you that I am a very humdrum sort of person.'

The spectacle of George being modest struck Bundle spell-bound. George continued:

'Never be shy with me, dear child. And do not be afraid of boring me. It will be a great delight to me to—if I may say so—form your budding mind. I will be your political mentor. We have never needed young women of talent and charm in the Party more then we need them to-day. You may well be destined to follow in the footsteps of your aunt, Lady Caterham.'

This awful prospect knocked Bundle out completely. She could only stare helplessly at George. This did not discourage him—on the contrary. His main objection to women was that they talked too much. It was seldom that he found what he considered a really good listener. He smiled benignantly at Bundle.

'The butterfly emerging from the chrysalis. A wonderful picture. I have a very interesting work on political economy. I will look it out now, and you can take it to Chimneys with you. When you have finished it, I will discuss it with you. Do not hesitate to write to me if any point puzzles you. I have many public duties, but by unsparing work I can always make time for the affairs of my friends. I will look for the book.'

He strode away. Bundle gazed after him with a dazed expression. She was roused by the unexpected advent of Bill.

'Look here,' said Bill. 'What the hell was Codders holding your hand for?'

'It wasn't my hand,' said Bundle wildly. 'It was my budding mind.'

'Don't be an ass, Bundle.'

'Sorry, Bill, but I'm a little worried. Do you remember saying that Jimmy ran a grave risk coming down here?'

'So he does,' said Bill. 'It's frightfully hard to escape from Codders once he's got interested in you. Jimmy will be caught in the toils before he knows where he is.'

'It's not Jimmy who's got caught—it's me,' said Bundle wildly. 'I shall have to meet endless Mrs. Macattas, and read political economy and discuss it with George, and heaven knows where it will end!'

Bill whistled.

'Poor old Bundle. Been laying it on a bit thick, haven't you?'

'I must have done. Bill, I feel horribly entangled.'

'Never mind,' said Bill consolingly. 'George doesn't really believe in women standing for Parliament, so you won't have to stand up on platforms and talk a lot of junk, or kiss dirty babies in Bermondsey. Come and have a cocktail. It's nearly lunch time.'

Bundle got up and walked by his side obediently.

'And I do so hate politics,' she murmured piteously.

'Of course you do. So do all sensible people. It's only people like Codders and Pongo who take them seriously and revel in them. But all the same,' said Bill, reverting suddenly to a former point, 'you oughtn't to let Codders hold your hand.'

'Why on earth not?' said Bundle. 'He's known me all my life.'

'Well, I don't like it.'

'Virtuous William—Oh, I say, look at Superintendent Battle.'

They were just passing in through a side door. A cupboard-like room opened out of the little hallway. In it were kept golf clubs, tennis racquets, bowls and other features of country house life. Superintendent Battle was conducting a minute examination of various golf clubs. He looked up a little sheepishly at Bundle's exclamation.

'Going to take up golf, Superintendent Battle?'

'I might do worse, Lady Eileen. They say it's never too late to start. And I've got one good quality that will tell at any game.'

'What's that?' asked Bill.

'I don't know when I'm beaten. If everything goes wrong, I turn to and start again!'

And with a determined look on his face, Superintendent Battle came out and joined them, shutting the door behind him.

25. *Jimmy lays his plans*

JIMMY THESIGER was feeling depressed. Avoiding George, whom he suspected of being ready to tackle him on serious subjects, he stole quietly away after lunch. Proficient as he was in details of the Santa Fé boundary dispute, he had no wish to stand an examination on it this minute.

Presently what he hoped would happen came to pass. Loraine Wade, also unaccompanied, strolled down one of the shady garden paths. In a moment Jimmy was by her side. They walked for some minutes in silence and then Jimmy said tentatively:

'Loraine?'

'Yes?'

'Look here, I'm a bad chap at putting things—but what about it? What's wrong with getting a special licence and being married and living together happy ever afterwards?'

Loraine displayed no embarrassment at this surprising proposal. Instead she threw back her head and laughed frankly.

'Don't laugh at a chap,' said Jimmy reproachfully.

'I can't help it. You were so funny.'

'Loraine—you are a little devil.'

'I'm not. I'm what's called a thoroughly nice girl.'

'Only to those who don't know you—who are taken in by your delusive appearance of meekness and decorum.'

'I like your long words.'

'All out of crossword puzzles.'

'So educative.'

'Loraine, dear, don't beat about the bush. Will you or won't you?'

Loraine's face sobered. It took on its characteristic appearance of determination. Her small mouth hardened and her little chin shot out aggressively.

'No, Jimmy. Not while things are as they are at present—all unfinished.'

'I know we haven't done what we set out to do,' agreed Jimmy. 'But all the same—well, it's the end of a chapter. The papers are safe at the Air Ministry. Virtue triumphant. And—for the moment—nothing doing.'

'So—let's get married?' said Loraine with a slight smile.

'You've said it. Precisely the idea.'

But again Loraine shook her head.

'No, Jimmy. Until this thing's rounded up—until we're safe——'

'You think we're in danger?'

'Don't you?'

Jimmy's cherubic pink face clouded over.

'You're right,' he said at last. 'If that extraordinary rigmarole of Bundle's is true—and I suppose, incredible as it sounds, it must be true—then we're not safe till we've settled with—No. 7!'

'And the others?'

'No—the others don't count. It's No. 7 with his own ways of

working that frightens me. Because I don't know who he is or where to look for him.'

Loraine shivered.

'I've been frightened,' she said in a low voice. 'Ever since Gerry's death. . . .'

'You needn't be frightened. There's nothing for you to be frightened about. You leave everything to me. I tell you, Loraine—*I'll get No. 7 yet*. Once we get him—well, I don't think there'll be much trouble with the rest of the gang, whoever they are.'

'*If* you get him—and suppose he gets you?'

'Impossible,' said Jimmy cheerfully. 'I'm much too clever. Always have a good opinion of yourself—that's my motto.'

'When I think of the things that might have happened last night ——' Loraine shivered.

'Well, they didn't,' said Jimmy. 'We're both here, safe and sound—though I must admit my arm is confoundedly painful.'

'Poor boy.'

'Oh, one must expect to suffer in a good cause. And what with my wounds and my cheerful conversation, I've made a complete conquest of Lady Coote.'

'Oh! Do you think that important?'

'I've an idea it may come in useful.'

'You've got some plan in your mind, Jimmy. What is it?'

'The young hero never tells his plans,' said Jimmy firmly. 'They mature in the dark.'

'You are an idiot, Jimmy.'

'I know. I know. That's what everyone says. But I can assure you, Loraine, there's a lot of brain-work going on underneath. Now what about your plans? Got any?'

'Bundle has suggested that I should go to Chimneys with her for a bit.'

'Excellent,' said Jimmy approvingly. 'Nothing could be better. I'd like an eye kept on Bundle anyway. You never know what mad thing she won't be up to next. She's so frightfully unexpected. And the worst of it is, she's so astonishingly successful. I tell you, keeping Bundle out of mischief is a whole-time job.'

'Bill ought to look after her,' suggested Loraine.

'Bill's pretty busy elsewhere.'

'Don't you believe it,' said Loraine.

'What? Not the Countess? But the lad's potty about her.'

Loraine continued to shake her head.

'There's something there I don't quite understand. But it's not the Countess with Bill—it's Bundle. Why, this morning, Bill was talking to me when Mr. Lomax came out and sat down by Bundle. He took her hand or something, and Bill was off like—like a rocket.'

'What a curious taste some people have,' observed Mr. Thesiger. 'Fancy anyone who was talking to you wanting to do anything else. But you surprise me very much, Loraine. I thought our simple Bill was enmeshed in the toils of the beautiful foreign adventuress. Bundle thinks so, I know.'

'Bundle may,' said Loraine. 'But I tell you, Jimmy, it isn't so.'

'Then what's the big idea?'

'Don't you think it possible that Bill is doing a bit of sleuthing on his own?'

'Bill? He hasn't got the brains.'

'I'm not so sure. When a simple, muscular person like Bill does set out to be subtle, no one ever gives him credit for it.'

'And in consequence he can put in some good work. Yes, there's something in that. But all the same I'd never have thought it of Bill. He's doing the Countess's little woolly lamb to perfection. I think you're wrong, you know, Loraine. The Countess is an extraordinarily beautiful woman—not my type of course,' put in Mr. Thesiger hastily—'and old Bill has always had a heart like an hotel.'

Loraine shook her head, unconvinced.

'Well,' said Jimmy, 'have it your own way. We seem to have more or less settled things. You go back with Bundle to Chimneys, and for heaven's sake keep her from poking about in that Seven Dials place again. Heaven knows what will happen if she does.'

Loraine nodded.

'And now,' said Jimmy, 'I think a few words with Lady Coote would be advisable.'

Lady Coote was sitting on a garden seat doing wool-work. The subject was a disconsolate and somewhat misshapen young woman weeping over an urn.

Lady Coote made room for Jimmy by her side, and he promptly, being a tactful young man, admired her work.

'Do you like it?' said Lady Coote, pleased. 'It was begun by my Aunt Selina the week before she died. Cancer of the liver, poor thing.'

'How beastly,' said Jimmy.

'And how is the arm?'

'Oh, it's feeling quite all right. Bit of a nuisance and all that, you know.'

'You'll have to be careful,' said Lady Coote in a warning voice. 'I've known blood-poisoning set in—and in that case you might lose your arm altogether.'

'Oh! I say, I hope not.'

'I'm only warning you,' said Lady Coote.

'Where are you hanging out now?' inquired Mr. Thesiger. 'Town—or where?'

Considering that he knew the answer to his query perfectly well, he put the question with a praiseworthy amount of ingenuousness.

Lady Coote sighed heavily.

'Sir Oswald has taken the Duke of Alton's place. Letherbury. You know it, perhaps?'

'Oh, rather. Topping place, isn't it?'

'Oh, I don't know,' said Lady Coote. 'It's a very large place, and gloomy, you know. Rows of picture galleries with such forbidding looking people. What they call Old Masters are very depressing, I think. You should have seen a little house we had in Yorkshire, Mr. Thesiger. When Sir Oswald was plain Mr. Coote. Such a nice lounge hall and a cheerful drawing-room with an ingle-nook—a white striped paper with a frieze of wistaria I chose for it, I remember. Satin stripe, you know, not moiré. Much better taste, I always think. The dining-room faced north-east, so we didn't get much sun in it, but with a good bright scarlet paper and a set of those comic hunting prints—why, it was as cheerful as Christmas.'

In the excitement of these reminiscences, Lady Coote dropped several little balls of wool, which Jimmy dutifully retrieved.

'Thank you, my dear,' said Lady Coote. 'Now, what was I saying? Oh!—about houses—yes, I do like a cheerful house. And choosing things for it gives you an interest.'

'I suppose Sir Oswald will be buying a place of his own one of these days,' suggested Jimmy. 'And then you can have it just as you like.'

Lady Coote shook her head sadly.

'Sir Oswald talks of a firm doing it—and you know what that means.'

'Oh! But they'd consult you!'

'It would be one of those grand places—all for the antique. They'd look down on the things I call comfortable and homey. Not but that

Sir Oswald wasn't very comfortable and satisfied in his home always, and I daresay his tastes are just the same underneath. But nothing will suit him now but the best! He's got on wonderfully, and naturally he wants something to show for it, but many's the time I wonder where it will end.'

Jimmy looked sympathetic.

'It's like a runaway horse,' said Lady Coote. 'Got the bit between its teeth and away it goes. It's the same with Sir Oswald. He's got on, and he's got on, till he can't stop getting on. He's one of the richest men in England now—but does that satisfy him? No, he wants still more. He wants to be—I don't know what he wants to be! I can tell you, it frightens me sometimes!'

'Like the Persian Johnny,' said Jimmy, 'who went about wailing for fresh worlds to conquer.'

Lady Coote nodded acquiescence without much knowing what Jimmy was talking about.

'What I wonder is—will his stomach stand it?' she went on tearfully. 'To have him an invalid—with his ideas—oh, it won't bear thinking of.'

'He looks very hearty,' said Jimmy, consolingly.

'He's got something on his mind,' said Lady Coote. 'Worried, that's what he is. *I* know.'

'What's he worried about?'

'I don't know. Perhaps something at the works. It's a great comfort for him having Mr. Bateman. Such an earnest young man—and so conscientious.'

'Marvellously conscientious,' agreed Jimmy.

'Oswald thinks a lot of Mr. Bateman's judgment. He says that Mr. Bateman is always right.'

'That was one of his worst characteristics years ago,' said Jimmy feelingly.

Lady Coote looked slightly puzzled.

'That was an awfully jolly week-end I had with you at Chimneys,' said Jimmy. 'I mean it would have been awfully jolly if it hadn't been for poor old Gerry kicking the bucket. Jolly nice girls.'

'I find girls very perplexing,' said Lady Coote. 'Not romantic, you know. Why, I embroidered some handkerchiefs for Sir Oswald with my own hair when we were engaged.'

'Did you?' said Jimmy. 'How marvellous. But I suppose girls haven't got long enough hair to do that nowadays.'

'That's true,' admitted Lady Coote. 'But, oh, it shows in lots of other ways. I remember when I was a girl, one of my—well, my young men—picked up a handful of gravel, and a girl who was with me said at once that he was treasuring it because my feet had trodden on it. Such a pretty idea, I thought. Though it turned out afterwards that he was taking a course of mineralogy—or do I mean geology?—at a technical school. But I liked the idea—and stealing a girl's handkerchief and treasuring it—all those sort of things.'

'Awkward if the girl wanted to blow her nose,' said the practical Mr. Thesiger.

Lady Coote laid down her wool-work and looked searchingly but kindly at him.

'Come now,' she said. 'Isn't there some nice girl that you fancy? That you'd like to work and make a little home for?'

Jimmy blushed and mumbled.

'I thought you got on very well with one of those girls at Chimneys that time—Vera Daventry.'

'Socks?'

'They do call her that,' admitted Lady Coote. 'I can't think why. It isn't pretty.'

'Oh, she's a topper,' said Jimmy. 'I'd like to meet her again.'

'She's coming down to stay with us next week-end.'

'Is she?' said Jimmy, trying to infuse a large amount of wistful longing into the two words.

'Yes. Would—would you like to come?'

'I *would*,' said Jimmy heartily. 'Thanks ever so much, Lady Coote.'

And reiterating fervent thanks, he left her.

Sir Oswald presently joined his wife.

'What has that young Jackanapes been boring you about?' he demanded. 'I can't stand that young fellow.'

'He's a dear boy,' said Lady Coote. 'And so brave. Look how he got wounded last night.'

'Yes, messing around where he'd no business to be.'

'I think you're very unfair, Oswald.'

'Never done an honest day's work in his life. A real waster if there ever was one. He'd never get on if he had his way to make in the world.'

'You must have got your feet damp last night,' said Lady Coote. 'I hope you won't get pneumonia. Freddie Richards died of it the other day. Dear me, Oswald, it makes my blood run cold to think of you wandering about with a dangerous burglar loose in the grounds. He might have shot you. I've asked Mr. Thesiger down for next week-end, by the way.'

'Nonsense,' said Sir Oswald. 'I won't have that young man in my house, do you hear, Maria?'

'Why not?'

'That's my business.'

'I'm so sorry, dear,' said Lady Coote placidly. 'I've asked him now, so it can't be helped. Pick up that ball of pink wool, will you, Oswald?'

Sir Oswald complied, his face black as thunder. He looked at his wife and hesitated. Lady Coote was placidly threading her wool needle.

'I particularly don't want Thesiger down next week-end,' he said at last. 'I've heard a good deal about him from Bateman. He was at school with him.'

'What did Mr. Bateman say?'

'He'd no good to say of him. In fact, he warned me very seriously against him.'

'He did, did he?' said Lady Coote thoughtfully.

'And I have the highest respect for Bateman's judgment. I've never known him wrong?'

'Dear me,' said Lady Coote. 'What a mess I seem to have made of things. Of course, I should never have asked him if I had known. You should have told me all this before, Oswald. It's too late now.'

She began to roll up her work very carefully. Sir Oswald looked at her, made as if to speak, then shrugged his shoulders. He followed her into the house. Lady Coote, walking ahead, wore a very faint smile on her face. She was fond of her husband, but she was also fond—in a quiet, unobtrusive, wholly womanly manner—of getting her own way.

26. *Mainly about golf*

'THAT FRIEND OF YOURS is a nice girl, Bundle,' said Lord Caterham.

Loraine had been at Chimneys for nearly a week, and had earned the high opinion of her host—mainly because of the charming readiness she had shown to be instructed in the science of the mashie shot.

Bored by his winter abroad, Lord Caterham had taken up golf. He was an execrable player and in consequence was profoundly enthusiastic over the game. He spent most of his mornings lofting mashie shots over various shrubs and bushes—or, rather, essaying to loft them, hacking large bits out of the velvety turf and generally reducing MacDonald to despair.

'We must lay out a little course,' said Lord Caterham, addressing a daisy. 'A sporting little course. Now then, just watch this one, Bundle. Off the right knee, slow back, keep the head still and use the wrists.'

The ball, heavily topped, scudded across the lawn and disappeared into the unfathomed depths of a great bank of rhododendrons.

'Curious,' said Lord Caterham. 'What did I do then, I wonder? As I was saying, Bundle, that friend of yours is a very nice girl. I really think I am inducing her to take quite an interest in the game. She hit some excellent shots this morning—really quite as good as I could do myself.'

Lord Caterham took another careless swing and removed an immense chunk of turf. MacDonald, who was passing, retrieved it and stamped it firmly back. The look he gave Lord Caterham would have caused anyone but an ardent golfer to sink through the earth.

'If MacDonald has been guilty of cruelty to Cootes, which I strongly suspect,' said Bundle, 'he's being punished now.'

'Why shouldn't I do as I like in my own garden?' demanded her father. 'MacDonald ought to be interested in the way my game is coming on—the Scotch are a great golfing nation.'

'You poor old man,' said Bundle. 'You'll never be a golfer—but at any rate it keeps you out of mischief.'

'Not at all,' said Lord Caterham. 'I did the long sixth in five the other day. The pro was very surprised when I told him about it.'

'He would be,' said Bundle.

'Talking of Cootes, Sir Oswald plays a fair game—a very fair game. Not a pretty style—too stiff. But straight down the middle every time. But curious how the cloven hoof shows—won't give you a six inch putt! Makes you put it in every time. Now I don't like that.'

'I suppose he's a man who likes to be sure,' said Bundle.

'It's contrary to the spirit of the game,' said her father. 'And he's not interested in the theory of the thing either. Says he just plays for exercise and doesn't bother about style. Now, that secretary chap,

Bateman, is quite different. It's the theory interests him. I was slicing badly with my spoon; and he said it all came from too much right arm; and he evolved a very interesting theory. It's all left arm in golf—the left arm is the arm that counts. He says he plays tennis left handed but golf with ordinary clubs because there his superiority with the left arm tells.'

'And did he play very marvellously?' inquired Bundle.

'No, he didn't,' confessed Lord Caterham. 'But then he may have been off his game. I see the theory all right and I think there's a lot in it. Ah! Did you see that one, Bundle? Right over the rhododendrons. A perfect shot. Ah! If one could be sure of doing that every time—— Yes, Tredwell, what is it?'

Tredwell addressed Bundle.

'Mr. Thesiger would like to speak to you on the telephone, my lady.'

Bundle set off at full speed for the house, yelling 'Loraine, Loraine,' as she did so. Loraine joined her just as she was lifting the receiver.

'Hallo, is that you, Jimmy?'

'Hallo. How are you?'

'Very fit, but a bit bored.'

'How's Loraine?'

'She's all right. She's here. Do you want to speak to her?'

'In a minute. I've got a lot to say. To begin with, I'm going down to the Cootes for the week-end,' he said significantly. 'Now, look here, Bundle, you don't know how one gets hold of skeleton keys, do you?'

'Haven't the foggiest. Is it really necessary to take skeleton keys to the Cootes?'

'Well, I had a sort of idea they'd come in handy. You don't know the sort of shop one gets them at?'

'What you want is a kindly burglar friend to show you the ropes.'

'I do, Bundle, I do. And unfortunately I haven't got one. I thought perhaps your bright brain might grapple successfully with the problem. But I suppose I shall have to fall back upon Stevens as usual. He'll be getting some funny ideas in his head soon about me—first a blue-nosed automatic—and now skeleton keys. He'll think I've joined the criminal classes.'

'Jimmy?' said Bundle.

'Yes?'

'Look here—be careful, won't you? I mean if Sir Oswald finds you nosing around with skeleton keys—well, I should think he could be very unpleasant when he likes.'

'Young man of pleasing appearance in the dock! All right, I'll be careful. Pongo's the fellow I'm really frightened of. He sneaks around so on those flat feet of his. You never hear him coming. And he always did have a genius for poking his nose in where he wasn't wanted. But trust to the boy here.'

'Well, I wish Loraine and I were going to be there to look after you.'

'Thank you, nurse. As a matter of fact, though, I have a scheme——'

'Yes?'

'Do you think you and Loraine might have a convenient car breakdown near Letherbury to-morrow morning? It's not so very far from you, is it?'

'Forty miles. That's nothing.'

'I thought it wouldn't be—to you! Don't kill Loraine though. I'm rather fond of Loraine. All right, then—somewhere round about quarter to half-past twelve.'

'So that they invite us to lunch?'

'That's the idea. I say, Bundle, I ran into that girl Socks yesterday, and what do you think—Terence O'Rourke is going to be down there this week-end!'

'Jimmy, do you think he——'

'Well—suspect everyone, you know. That's what they say. He's a wild lad, and daring as they make them. I wouldn't put it past him to run a secret society. He and the Countess might be in this together. He was out in Hungary last year.'

'But he could pinch the formula any time.'

'That's just what he couldn't. He'd have to do it under circumstances where he couldn't be suspected. But the retreat up the ivy and into his own bed—well, that would be rather neat. Now for instructions. After a few polite nothings to Lady Coote, you and Loraine are to get hold of Pongo and O'Rourke by hook or by crook and keep them occupied till lunch time. See? It oughtn't to be difficult for a couple of beautiful girls like you.'

'You're using the best butter, I see.'

'A plain statement of fact.'

'Well, at any rate, your instructions are duly noted. Do you want to talk to Loraine now?'

Bundle passed over the receiver and tactfully left the room.

27. *Nocturnal adventure*

JIMMY THESIGER arrived at Letherbury on a sunny autumn afternoon and was greeted affectionately by Lady Coote and with cold dislike by Sir Oswald. Aware of the keen match-making eye of Lady Coote upon him, Jimmy took pains to make himself extremely agreeable to Socks Daventry.

O'Rourke was there in excellent spirits. He was inclined to be official and secretive about the mysterious events at the Abbey, about which Socks catechised him freely, but his official reticence took a novel form—namely that of embroidering the tale of events in such a fantastic manner that nobody could possibly guess what the truth might have been.

'Four masked men with revolvers? Is that really so?' demanded Socks severely.

'Ah! I'm remembering now that there was the round half-dozen of them to hold me down and force the stuff down my throat. Sure, and I thought it was poison, and I done for entirely.'

'And what was stolen, or what did they try and steal?'

'What else but the crown jewels of Russia that were brought to Mr. Lomax secretly to deposit in the Bank of England.'

'What a bloody liar you are,' said Socks without emotion.

'A liar? I? And the jewels brought over by aeroplane with my best friend as pilot. This is secret history I'm telling you, Socks. Will you ask Jimmy Thesiger there if you don't believe me. Not that I'd be putting any trust in what he'd say.'

'Is it true,' said Socks, 'that George Lomax came down without his false teeth? That's what I want to know.'

'There were two revolvers,' said Lady Coote. 'Nasty things. I saw them myself. It's a wonder this poor boy wasn't killed.'

'Oh, I was born to be hanged,' said Jimmy.

'I hear that there was a Russian countess there of subtle beauty,' said Socks. 'And that she vamped Bill.'

'Some of the things she said about Buda Pesth were too dreadful,' said Lady Coote. 'I shall never forget them. Oswald, we must send a subscription.'

Sir Oswald grunted.

'I'll make a note of it, Lady Coote,' said Rupert Bateman.

'Thank you, Mr. Bateman. I feel one ought to do something as a thank offering. I can't imagine how Sir Oswald escaped being shot—let alone dying of pneumonia.'

'Don't be foolish, Maria,' said Sir Oswald.

'I've always had a horror of cat burglars,' said Lady Coote.

'Think of having the luck to meet one face to face. How thrilling!' murmured Socks.

'Don't you believe it,' said Jimmy. 'It's damned painful.' And he patted his right arm gingerly.

'How is the poor arm?' inquired Lady Coote.

'Oh, pretty well all right now. But it's been the most confounded nuisance having to do everything with the left hand. I'm no good whatever with it.'

'Every child should be brought up to be ambidexterous,' said Sir Oswald.

'Oh!' said Socks, somewhat out of her depth. 'Is that like seals?'

'Not amphibious,' said Mr. Bateman. 'Ambidexterous means using either hand equally well.'

'Oh!' said Socks, looking at Sir Oswald with respect. 'Can you?'

'Certainly; I can write with either hand.'

'But not with both at once?'

'That would not be practical,' said Sir Oswald shortly.

'No,' said Socks thoughtfully. 'I suppose that would be a bit too subtle.'

'It would be a grand thing now in a Government department,' observed Mr. O'Rourke, 'if one could keep the right hand from knowing what the left hand was doing.'

'Can you use both hands?'

'No, indeed. I'm the most right-handed person that ever was.'

'But you deal cards with your left hand,' said the observant Bateman. 'I noticed the other night.'

'Oh, but that's different entirely,' said Mr. O'Rourke easily.

A gong with a sombre note pealed out and everyone went upstairs to dress for dinner.

After dinner Sir Oswald and Lady Coote, Mr. Bateman and Mr. O'Rourke played bridge and Jimmy passed a flirtatious evening with Socks. The last words Jimmy heard as he retreated up the staircase that night were Sir Oswald saying to his wife:

'You'll never make a bridge player, Maria.'

And her reply:

'I know, dear. So you always say. You owe Mr. O'Rourke another pound, Oswald. That's right.'

It was some two hours later that Jimmy crept noiselessly (or so he hoped) down the stairs. He made one brief visit to the dining-room and then found his way to Sir Oswald's study. There, after listening intently for a minute or two, he set to work. Most of the drawers of the desk were locked, but a curiously shaped bit of wire in Jimmy's hand soon saw to that. One by one the drawers yielded to his manipulations.

Drawer by drawer he sorted through methodically, being careful to replace everything in the same order. Once or twice he stopped to listen, fancying he heard some distant sound. But he remained undisturbed.

The last drawer was looked through. Jimmy now knew—or could have known had he been paying attention—many interesting details relating to steel; but he had found nothing of what he wanted—a reference to Herr Eberhard's invention or anything that could give him a clue to the identity of the mysterious No. 7. He had, perhaps, hardly hoped that he would. It was an off-chance and he had taken it—but he had not expected much result—except by sheer luck.

He tested the drawers to make sure that he had relocked them securely. He knew Rupert Bateman's powers of minute observation and glanced round the room to make sure that he had left no incriminating trace of his presence.

'That's that,' he muttered to himself softly. 'Nothing there. Well, perhaps I'll have better luck to-morrow morning—if the girls only play up.'

He came out of the study, closing the door behind him and locking it. For a moment he thought he heard a sound quite near him, but decided he had been mistaken. He felt his way noiselessly along the great hall. Just enough light came from the high vaulted windows to enable him to pick his way without stumbling into anything.

Again he heard a soft sound—he heard it quite certainly this time and without the possibility of making a mistake. He was not alone in the hall. Somebody else was there, moving as stealthily as he was. His heart beat suddenly very fast.

With a sudden spring he jumped to the electric switch and turned on the lights. The sudden glare made him blink—but he saw plainly enough. Not four feet away stood Rupert Bateman.

'My goodness, Pongo,' cried Jimmy, 'you did give me a start. Slinking about like that in the dark.'

'I heard a noise,' explained Mr. Bateman severely. 'I thought burglars had got in and I came down to see.'

Jimmy looked thoughtfully at Mr. Bateman's rubber-soled feet.

'You think of everything, Pongo,' he said genially. 'Even a lethal weapon.'

His eye rested on the bulge in the other's pocket.

'It's as well to be armed. One never knows whom one may meet.'

'I am glad you didn't shoot,' said Jimmy. 'I'm a bit tired of being shot at.'

'I might easily have done so,' said Mr. Bateman.

'It would be dead against the law if you did,' said Jimmy. 'You've got to make quite sure the beggar's house-breaking, you know, before you pot at him. You mustn't jump to conclusions. Otherwise you'd have to explain why you shot a guest on a perfectly innocent errand like mine.'

'By the way, what did you come down for?'

'I was hungry,' said Jimmy. 'I rather fancied a dry biscuit.'

'There are some biscuits in a tin by your bed,' said Rupert Bateman.

He was staring at Jimmy very intently through his horn-rimmed spectacles.

'Ah! That's where the staff work has gone wrong, old boy. There's a tin there with "Biscuits for Starving Visitors" on it. But when the starving visitor opened it—nothing inside. So I just toddled down to the dining-room.'

And with a sweet, ingenuous smile, Jimmy produced from his dressing-gown pocket a handful of biscuits.

There was a moment's pause.

'And now I think I'll toddle back to bed,' said Jimmy. 'Night-night, Pongo.'

With an affectation of nonchalance, he mounted the staircase. Rupert Bateman followed him. At the doorway of his room, Jimmy paused as if to say good-night once more.

'It's an extraordinary thing about these biscuits,' said Mr. Bateman. 'Do you mind if I just——'

'Certainly, laddie, look for yourself.'

Mr. Bateman strode across the room, opened the biscuit box and stared at its emptiness.

'Very remiss,' he murmured. 'Well, good-night.'

He withdrew. Jimmy sat on the edge of his bed listening for a minute.

'That was a narrow shave,' he murmured to himself. 'Suspicious sort of chap, Pongo. Never seems to sleep. Nasty habit of his prowling around with a revolver.'

He got up and opened one of the drawers of the dressing-table. Beneath an assortment of ties lay a pile of biscuits.

'There's nothing for it,' said Jimmy. 'I shall have to eat all the damned things. Ten to one, Pongo will come prowling round in the morning.'

With a sigh, he settled down to a meal of biscuits for which he had no inclination whatever.

28. *Suspicions*

IT WAS JUST ON the appointed hour of twelve o'clock that Bundle and Loraine entered the park gates, having left the Hispano at an adjacent garage.

Lady Coote greeted the two girls with surprise, but distinct pleasure, and immediately pressed them to stay to lunch.

O'Rourke, who had been reclining in an immense armchair, began at once to talk with great animation to Loraine, who was listening with half an ear to Bundle's highly technical explanation of the mechanical trouble which had affected the Hispano.

'And we said,' ended Bundle, 'how marvellous that the brute should have broken down just here! Last time it happened was on a Sunday at a place called Little Speddlington under the Hill. And it lived up to its name, I can tell you.'

'That would be a grand name on the films,' remarked O'Rourke.

'Birthplace of the simple country maiden,' suggested Socks.

'I wonder now,' said Lady Coote, 'where Mr. Thesiger is?'

'He's in the billiard-room, I think,' said Socks. 'I'll fetch him.'

She went off, but had hardly gone a minute when Rupert Bateman appeared upon the scene, with the harassed and serious air usual to him.

'Yes, Lady Coote? Thesiger said you were asking for me. How do you do, Lady Eileen——'

He broke off to greet the two girls, and Loraine immediately took the field.

'Oh, Mr. Bateman! I've been wanting to see you. Wasn't it you who was telling me what to do for a dog when he is continually getting sore paws?'

The secretary shook his head. 'It must have been someone else, Miss Wade. Though, as a matter of fact, I do happen to know——'

'What a wonderful man you are,' interrupted Loraine. 'You know about everything.'

'One should keep abreast of modern knowledge,' said Mr. Bateman seriously. 'Now about your dog's paws——'

Terence O'Rourke murmured *sotto voce* to Bundle:

''Tis a man like that that writes all those little paragraphs in the weekly papers. "It is not generally known that to keep a brass fender uniformly bright, etc.;" "The dorper beetle is one of the most interesting characters in the insect world;" "The marriage customs of the Fingalese Indians," and so on.'

'General information, in fact.'

'And what more horrible two words could you have?' said Mr. O'Rourke, and added piously: 'Thank the heavens above I'm an educated man and know nothing whatever upon any subject at all.'

'I see you've got clock golf here,' said Bundle to Lady Coote.

'I'll take you on at it, Lady Eileen,' said O'Rourke.

'Let's challenge those two,' said Bundle. 'Loraine, Mr. O'Rourke and I want to take you and Mr. Bateman on at clock golf.'

'Do play, Mr. Bateman,' said Lady Coote, as the secretary showed a momentary hesitation. 'I'm sure Sir Oswald doesn't want you.'

The four went out on the lawn.

'Very cleverly managed, what?' whispered Bundle to Loraine. 'Congratulations on our girlish tact.'

The round ended just before one o'clock, victory going to Bateman and Loraine.

'But I think you'll agree with me, partner,' said Mr. O'Rourke 'that we played a more sporting game.'

He lagged a little behind with Bundle.

'Old Pongo's a cautious player—he takes no risks. Now, with me it's neck or nothing. And a fine motto through life, don't you agree, Lady Eileen?'

'Hasn't it ever landed you in trouble?' asked Bundle, laughing.

'To be sure it has. Millions of times. But I'm still going strong. Sure, it'll take the hangman's noose to defeat Terence O'Rourke.'

Just then Jimmy Thesiger strolled round the corner of the house.

'Bundle, by all that's wonderful!' he exclaimed.

'You've missed competing in the Autumn Meeting,' said O'Rourke.

'I'd gone for a stroll,' said Jimmy. 'Where did these girls drop from?'

'We came on our flat feet,' said Bundle. 'The Hispano let us down.' And she narrated the circumstances of the breakdown.

Jimmy listened with sympathetic attention.

'Hard luck,' he vouchsafed. 'If it's going to take some time, I'll run you back in my car after lunch.'

A gong sounded at that moment and they all went in. Bundle observed Jimmy covertly. She thought she had noticed an unusual note of exultance in his voice. She had the feeling that things had gone well.

After lunch they took a polite leave of Lady Coote, and Jimmy volunteered to run them down to the garage in his car. As soon as they had started the same word burst simultaneously from both girls' lips:

'Well?'

Jimmy chose to be provoking.

'Well?'

'Oh, pretty hearty, thanks. Slight indigestion owing to over indulgence in dry biscuits.'

'But what has happened?'

'I tell you. Devotion to the cause made me eat too many dry biscuits. But did our hero flinch? No, he did not.'

'Oh, Jimmy,' said Loraine reproachfully, and he softened.

'What do you really want to know?'

'Oh, everything. Didn't we do it well? I mean, the way we kept Pongo and Terence O'Rourke in play.'

'I congratulate you on the handling of Pongo. O'Rourke was probably a sitter—but Pongo is made of other stuff. There's only one word for that lad—it was in the *Sunday Newsbag* crossword last week. Word of ten letters meaning everywhere at once. Ubiquitous. That describes Pongo down to the ground. You can't go anywhere without running into him—and the worst of it is you never hear him coming.'

'You think he's dangerous?'

'Dangerous? Of course he's not dangerous. Fancy Pongo being dangerous. He's an ass. But, as I said just now, he's an ubiquitous ass. He doesn't even seem to need sleep like ordinary mortals. In fact, to put it bluntly, the fellow's a damned nuisance.'

And, in a somewhat aggrieved manner, Jimmy described the events of the previous evening.

Bundle was not very sympathetic.

'I don't know what you think you're doing anyway, mooching round here.'

'No. 7,' said Jimmy crisply. 'That's what I'm after. No. 7.'

'And you think you'll find him in this house?'

'I thought I might find a clue.'

'And you didn't?'

'Not last night—no.'

'But this morning,' said Loraine, breaking in suddenly. 'Jimmy, you did find something this morning. I can see it by your face.'

'Well, I don't know if it is anything. But during the course of my stroll——'

'Which stroll didn't take you far from the house, I imagine.'

'Strangely enough, it didn't. Round trip in the interior, we might call it. Well, as I say, I don't know whether there's anything in it or not. But I found this.'

With the celerity of a conjurer he produced a small bottle and tossed it over to the girls. It was half full of a white powder.

'What do you think it is?' asked Bundle.

'A white crystalline powder, that's what it is,' said Jimmy. 'And to any reader of detective fiction those words are both familiar and suggestive. Of course, if it turns out to be a new kind of patent tooth-powder, I shall be chagrined and annoyed.'

'Where did you find it?' asked Bundle sharply.

'Ah!' said Jimmy, 'that's my secret.'

And from that point he would not budge in spite of cajolery and insult.

'Here we are at the garage,' he said. 'Let's hope the high-mettled Hispano has not been subjected to any indignities.'

The gentleman at the garage presented a bill for five shillings and made a few vague remarks about loose nuts. Bundle paid him with a sweet smile.

'It's nice to know we all get money for nothing sometimes,' she murmured to Jimmy.

The three stood together in the road, silent for the moment as they each pondered the situation.

'I know,' said Bundle suddenly.

'Know what?'

'Something I meant to ask you—and nearly forgot. Do you remember that glove that Superintendent Battle found—the half-burnt one?'

'Yes.'

'Didn't you say that he tried it on your hand?'

'Yes—it was a shade big. That fits in with the idea of its being a big, hefty man who wore it.'

'That's not at all what I'm bothering about. Never mind the size of it. George and Sir Oswald were both there too, weren't they?'

'Yes.'

'He could have given it to either of them to fit on?'

'Yes, of course——'

'But he didn't. He chose you. Jimmy, don't you see what that means?'

Mr. Thesiger stared at her.

'I'm sorry, Bundle. Possibly the jolly old brain isn't functioning as well as usual, but I haven't the faintest idea what you're talking about.'

'Don't you see, Loraine?'

Loraine looked at her curiously, but shook her head.

'Does it mean anything in particular?'

'Of course it does. Don't you see—Jimmy had his right hand in a sling.'

'By Jove, Bundle,' said Jimmy slowly. 'It was rather odd now I come to think of it; its being a left-hand glove, I mean. Battle never said anything.'

'He wasn't going to draw attention to it. By trying it on you it might pass without notice being drawn to it, and he talked about the size just to put everybody off. But surely it must mean that the man who shot at you held the pistol in his *left* hand.'

'So we've got to look for a left-handed man,' said Loraine thoughtfully.

'Yes, and I'll tell you another thing. That was what Battle was doing looking through the golf clubs. He was looking for a left-handed man's.'

'By Jove,' said Jimmy suddenly.

'What is it?'

'Well, I don't suppose there's anything in it, but it's rather curious.'

He retailed the conversation at tea the day before.

'So Sir Oswald Coote is ambidexterous?' said Bundle.

'Yes. And I remember now on that night at Chimneys—you know, the night Gerry Wade died—I was watching the bridge and thinking idly how awkwardly someone was dealing—and then realising that it was because they were dealing with the left hand. Of course, it must have been Sir Oswald.'

They all three looked at each other. Loraine shook her head.

'A man like Sir Oswald Coote! It's impossible. What could he have to gain by it?'

'It seems absurd,' said Jimmy. 'And yet——'

'No. 7 has his own ways of working,' quoted Bundle softly. 'Supposing this is the way Sir Oswald has really made his fortune?'

'But why stage all that comedy at the Abbey when he'd had the formula at his own works?'

'There might be ways of explaining that,' said Loraine. 'The same line of argument you used about Mr. O'Rourke. Suspicion had to be diverted from him and placed in another quarter.'

Bundle nodded eagerly.

'It all fits in. Suspicion is to fall on Bauer and the Countess. Who on earth would ever dream of suspecting Sir Oswald Coote?'

'I wonder if Battle does,' said Jimmy slowly.

Some chord of memory vibrated in Bundle's mind. *Superintendent Battle plucking an ivy leaf off the millionaire's coat.*

Had Battle suspected all the time?

29. *Singular behaviour of George Lomax*

'MR. LOMAX is here, my lord.'

Lord Caterham started violently, for, absorbed in the intricacies of what not to do with the left wrist, he had not heard the butler approach over the soft turf. He looked at Tredwell more in sorrow than in anger.

'I told you at breakfast, Tredwell, that I should be particularly engaged this morning.'

'Yes, my lord, but——'

'Go and tell Mr. Lomax that you have made a mistake, that I am out in the village, that I am laid up with the gout, or, if all else fails, that I am dead.'

'Mr. Lomax, my lord, has already caught sight of your lordship when driving up the drive.'

Lord Caterham sighed deeply.

'He would. Very well, Tredwell, I am coming.'

In a manner highly characteristic, Lord Caterham was always most genial when his feelings were in reality the reverse. He greeted George now with a heartiness quite unparalleled.

'My dear fellow, my dear fellow. Delighted to see you. Absolutely delighted. Sit down. Have a drink. Well, well, this is splendid!'

And having pushed George into a large arm-chair, he sat down opposite him and blinked nervously.

'I wanted to see you very particularly,' said George.

'Oh!' said Lord Caterham faintly, and his heart sank, whilst his mind raced actively over all the dread possibilities that might lie behind that simple phrase.

'*Very* particularly,' said George with heavy emphasis.

Lord Caterham's heart sank lower than ever. He felt that something was coming worse than anything he had yet thought of.

'Yes?' he said, with a courageous attempt at nonchalance.

'Is Eileen at home?'

Lord Caterham felt reprieved, but slightly surprised.

'Yes, yes,' he said. 'Bundle's here. Got that friend of hers with her—the little Wade girl. Very nice girl—*very* nice girl. Going to be quite a good golfer one day. Nice easy swing——'

He was chatting garrulously on when George interrupted with ruthlessness:

'I am glad Eileen is at home. Perhaps I might have an interview with her presently?'

'Certainly, my dear fellow, certainly.' Lord Caterham still felt very surprised, but was still enjoying the sensation of reprieve. 'If it doesn't bore you.'

'Nothing could bore me less,' said George. 'I think, Caterham, if I may say so, that you hardly appreciate the fact that Eileen is grown up. She is no longer a child. She is a woman, and, if I may say so, a very charming and talented woman. The man who succeeds in winning her love will be extremely lucky. I repeat it—extremely lucky.'

'Oh, I daresay,' said Lord Caterham. 'But she's very restless, you know. Never content to be in one place for more than two minutes together. However, I daresay young fellows don't mind that nowadays.'

'You mean that she is not content to stagnate. Eileen has brains, Caterham; she is ambitious. She interests herself in the questions of the day, and brings her fresh and vivid young intellect to bear upon them.'

Lord Caterham stared at him. It occurred to him that what was so often referred to as 'the strain of modern life' had begun to tell upon George. Certainly his description of Bundle seemed to Lord Caterham ludicrously unlike.

'Are you sure you are feeling quite well?' he asked anxiously.

George waved the inquiry aside impatiently.

'Perhaps, Caterham, you begin to have some inkling of my purpose in visiting you this morning. I am not a man to undertake fresh responsibilities lightly. I have a proper sense, I hope, of what is due to the position I hold. I have given this matter my deep and earnest consideration. Marriage, especially at my age, is not to be undertaken without full—er—consideration. Equality of birth, similarity of tastes, general suitability, and the same religious creed—all these things are necessary and the pros and cons have to be weighed and considered. I can, I think, offer my wife a position in society that is not to be despised. Eileen will grace that position admirably. By birth and breeding she is fitted for it, and her brains and her acute political sense cannot but further my career to our mutual advantage. I am aware, Caterham, that there is—er—some disparity in years. But I can assure you that I feel full of vigour—in my prime. The balance of years should be on the husband's side. And Eileen has serious tastes—an older man will suit her better than some young jackanapes without either experience or *savoir-faire*. I can assure you, my dear Caterham, that I will cherish her—er—exquisite youth; I will cherish it—er—it will be appreciated. To watch the exquisite flower of her mind unfolding—what a privilege! And to think that I never realised——' He shook his head deprecatingly and Lord Caterham; finding his voice with difficulty, said blankly:

'Do I understand you to mean—ah, my dear fellow, you can't want to marry Bundle?'

'You are surprised. I suppose to you it seems sudden. I have your permission, then, to speak to her?'

'Oh, yes,' said Lord Caterham. 'If it's permission you want—of course you can. But you know, Lomax, I really shouldn't if I were you.

Just go home and think it over like a good fellow. Count twenty. All that sort of thing. Always a pity to propose and make a fool of yourself.'

'I daresay you mean your advice kindly, Caterham, though I must confess that you put it somewhat strangely. But I have made up my mind to put my fortune to the test. I may see Eileen?'

'Oh, it's nothing to do with me,' said Lord Caterham hastily; 'Eileen settles her own affairs. If she came to me to-morrow and said she was going to marry the chauffeur, I shouldn't make any objections. It's the only way nowadays. Your children can make life damned unpleasant if you don't give in to them in every way. I say to Bundle, "Do as you like, but don't worry me," and really, on the whole, she is amazingly good about it.'

George stood up, intent upon his purpose.

'Where shall I find her?'

'Well, really, I don't know,' said Lord Caterham vaguely. 'She might be anywhere. As I told you just now, she's never in the same place for two minutes together. No repose.'

'And I suppose Miss Wade will be with her? It seems to me, Caterham, that the best plan would be for you to ring the bell and ask your butler to find her, saying that I wish to speak to her for a few minutes.'

Lord Caterham pressed the bell obediently.

'Oh, Tredwell,' he said, when the bell was anwered, 'just find her ladyship, will you? Tell her Mr. Lomax is anxious to speak to her in the drawing-room.'

'Yes, my lord.'

Tredwell withdrew. George seized Lord Caterham's hand and wrung it warmly, much to the latter's discomfort.

'A thousand thanks,' he said. 'I hope soon to bring you good news.'

He hastened from the room.

'Well,' said Lord Caterham. 'Well!'

And after a long pause:

'What *has* Bundle been up to?'

The door opened again.

'Mr. Eversleigh, my lord.'

As Bill hastened in, Lord Caterham caught his hand and spoke earnestly.

'Hullo, Bill. You're looking for Lomax, I suppose? Look here, if you want to do a good turn, hurry into the drawing-room and tell him the Cabinet have called an immediate meeting, or get him away somehow. It's really not fair to let the poor devil make an ass of himself all for some silly girl's prank.'

'I've not come for Codders,' said Bill. 'Didn't know he was here. It's Bundle I want to see. Is she anywhere about?'

'You can't see her,' said Lord Caterham. 'Not just now, at any rate. George is with her.'

'Well—what does it matter?'

'I think it does rather,' said Lord Caterham. 'He's probably spluttering horribly at this minute, and we mustn't do anything to make it worse for him.'

'But what is he saying?'

'Heaven knows,' said Lord Caterham. 'A lot of damned nonsense, anyway. Never say too much, that was always my motto. Grab the girl's hand and let events take their course.'

Bill stared at him.

'But look here, sir, I'm in a hurry. I must talk to Bundle——'

'Well, I don't suppose you'll have to wait long. I must confess I'm rather glad to have you here with me—I suppose Lomax will insist on coming back and talking to me when it's all over.'

'When what's all over? What is Lomax supposed to be doing?'

'Hush,' said Lord Caterham. 'He's proposing.'

'Proposing? Proposing what?'

'Marriage. To Bundle. Don't ask me why. I suppose he's come to what they call the dangerous age. I can't explain it any other way.'

'Proposing to Bundle? The dirty swine. At his age.'

'Bill's face grew crimson.

'He says he's in the prime of life,' said Lord Caterham cautiously.

'He? Why, he's decrepit—senile! I——' Bill positively choked.

'Not at all,' said Lord Caterham coldly. 'He's five years younger than I am.'

'Of all the damned cheek! Codders and Bundle! A girl like Bundle! You oughtn't to have allowed it.'

'I never interfere,' said Lord Caterham.

'You ought to have told him what you thought of him.'

'Unfortunately modern civilisation rules that out,' said Lord Caterham regretfully. 'In the Stone Age now—but, dear me, I suppose even then I shouldn't be able to do it—being a small man.'

'Bundle! Bundle! Why, I've never dared to ask Bundle to marry me because I knew she'd only laugh. And George—a disgusting wind-bag, an unscrupulous, hypocritical old hot-air merchant—a foul, poisonous self-advertiser——'

'Go on,' said Lord Caterham. 'I'm enjoying this.'

'My God!' said Bill simply and with feeling. 'Look here, I must be off.'

'No, no, don't go. I'd much rather you stayed. Besides, you want to see Bundle.'

'Not now. This has driven everything else out of my head. You don't know where Jimmy Thesiger is by any chance? I believe he was staying with the Cootes. Is he there still?'

'I think he went back to town yesterday. Bundle and Loraine were over there on Saturday. If you'll only wait——'

But Bill shook his head energetically and rushed from the room. Lord Caterham tiptoed out into the hall, seized a hat and made a hurried exit by the side door. In the distance he observed Bill streaking down the drive in his car.

'That young man will have an accident,' he thought.

Bill, however, reached London without any mischance, and proceeded to park his car in St. James's Square. Then he sought out Jimmy Thesiger's rooms. Jimmy was at home.

'Hullo, Bill. I say, what's the matter? You don't look your usual bright little self.'

'I'm worried,' said Bill. 'I was worried anyway, and then something else turned up and gave me a jolt.'

'Oh!' said Jimmy. 'How lucid! What's it all about? Can I do anything?'

Bill did not reply. He sat staring at the carpet and looking so puzzled and uncomfortable that Jimmy felt his curiosity aroused.

'Has anything very extraordinary occurred, William?' he asked gently.

'Something damned odd. I can't make head or tail of it.'

'The Seven Dials business?'

'Yes—the Seven Dials business. I got a letter this morning.'

'A letter? What sort of a letter?'

'A letter from Ronny Devereux's executors.'

'Good Lord! After all this time!'

'It seems he left instructions. If he was to die suddenly, a certain sealed envelope was to be sent to me exactly a fortnight after his death.'

'And they've sent it to you?'

'Yes.'

'You've opened it?'

'Yes.'

'Well—what did it say?'

Bill turned a glance upon him such a strange and uncertain one that Jimmy was startled.

'Look here,' he said. 'Pull yourself together, old man. It seems to have knocked the wind out of you, whatever it is. Have a drink.'

He poured out a stiff whisky and soda and brought it over to Bill, who took it obediently. His face still bore the same dazed expression.

'It's what's in the letter,' he said. 'I simply can't believe it, that's all.'

'Oh, nonsense,' said Jimmy. 'You must get into the habit of believing six impossible things before breakfast. I do it regularly. Now then, let's hear all about it. Wait a minute.'

He went outside.

'Stevens!'

'Yes, sir?'

'Just go out and get me some cigarettes, will you? I've run out.'

'Very good, sir.'

Jimmy waited till he heard the front door close. Then he came back into the sitting-room. Bill was just in the act of setting down his empty glass. He looked better, more purposeful and more master of himself.

'Now then,' said Jimmy. 'I've sent Stevens out so that we can't be overheard. Are you going to tell me all about it?'

'It's so incredible.'

'Then it's sure to be true. Come on, out with it.'

Bill drew a deep breath.

'I will. I'll tell you everything.'

30. *An urgent summons*

LORAINE, playing with a small and delectable puppy, was somewhat surprised when Bundle rejoined her after an absence of twenty minutes, in a breathless state and with an indescribable expression on her face.

'Whoof,' said Bundle, sinking on to a garden seat. 'Whoof.'

'What's the matter?' asked Loraine, looking at her curiously.

'George is the matter—George Lomax.'

'What's he been doing?'

'Proposing to me. It was awful. He spluttered and he stuttered, but he would go through with it–he must have learnt it out of a book, I think. There was no stopping him. Oh, how I hate men who splutter! And, unfortunately, I didn't know the reply.'

'You must have known what you wanted to do.'

'Naturally I'm not going to marry an apoplectic idiot like George. What I mean is, I didn't know the correct reply from the book of etiquette. I could only just say flatly: "No, I won't." What I ought to have said was something about being very sensible of the honour he had done me and so on and so on. But I got so rattled that in the end I jumped out of the window and bolted.'

'Really, Bundle, that's not like you.'

'Well, I never dreamt of such a thing happening. George—who I always thought hated me—and he did too. What a fatal thing it is to pretend to take an interest in a man's pet subject. You should have heard the drivel George talked about my girlish mind and the pleasure it would be to form it. My mind! If George knew one quarter of what was going on in my mind, he'd faint with horror!'

Loraine laughed. She couldn't help it.

'Oh, I know it's my own fault. I let myself in for this. There's Father dodging round that rhododendron. Hallo, Father.'

Lord Caterham approached with a hangdog expression.

'Lomax gone, eh?' he remarked with somewhat forced geniality.

'A nice business you let me in for,' said Bundle. 'George told me he had your full approval and sanction.'

'Well,' said Lord Caterham, 'what did you expect me to say? As a matter of fact, I didn't say that at all, or anything like it.'

'I didn't really think so,' said Bundle. 'I assumed that George had talked you into a corner and reduced you to such a state that you could only nod your head feebly.'

'That's very much what happened. How did he take it? Badly?'

'I didn't wait to see,' said Bundle. 'I'm afraid I was rather abrupt.'

'Oh, well,' said Lord Caterham. 'Perhaps that was the best way. Thank goodness in the future Lomax won't always be running over as he has been in the habit of doing, worrying me about things. Everything is for the best they say. Have you seen my jigger anywhere?'

'A mashie shot or two would steady my nerves, I think,' said Bundle. 'I'll take you on for sixpence, Loraine.'

An hour passed very peacefully. The three returned to the house in a harmonious spirit. A note lay on the hall table.

'Mr. Lomax left that for you, my lord,' explained Tredwell. 'He was much disappointed to find that you had gone out.'

Lord Caterham tore it open. He uttered a pained ejaculation and turned upon his daughter. Tredwell had retired.

'Really, Bundle, you might have made yourself clear, I think.'

'What do you mean?'

'Well, read this.'

Bundle took it and read:

'MY DEAR CATERHAM,—I am sorry not to have had a word with you. I thought I made it clear that I wanted to see you again after my interview with Eileen. She, dear child, we evidently quite unaware of the feelings I entertained towards her. She was, I am afraid, much startled. I have no wish to hurry her in any way. Her girlish confusion was very charming, and I entertain an even higher regard for her, as I much appreciate her maidenly reserve. I must give her time to become accustomed to the idea. Her very confusion shows that she is not wholly indifferent to me and I have no doubts of my ultimate success.

'Believe me, dear Caterham,

'Your sincere friend,

'GEORGE LOMAX.'

'Well,' said Bundle. 'Well, I'm damned!'

Words failed her.

'The man must be mad,' said Lord Caterham. 'No one could write those things about you, Bundle, unless they were slightly touched in the head. Poor chap, poor chap. But what persistence! I don't wonder he got into the Cabinet. It would serve him right if you did marry him, Bundle.'

The telephone rang and Bundle moved forward to answer it. In another minute George and his proposal were forgotten, and she was beckoning eagerly to Loraine. Lord Caterham went off to his own sanctum.

'It's Jimmy,' said Bundle. 'And he's tremendously excited about something.'

'Thank goodness I've caught you,' said Jimmy's voice. 'There's no time to be lost. Loraine's there, too?'

'Yes, she's here.'

'Well, look here, I haven't got time to explain everything—in fact, I can't through the telephone. But Bill has been round to see me with the most amazing story you ever heard. If it's true—well, if it's true, it's the biggest scoop of the century. Now, look here, this is what you've got to do. Come up to town at once, both of you. Garage the car somewhere and go straight to the Seven Dials Club. Do you think that when you get there you can get rid of that footman fellow?'

'Alfred? Rather. You leave that to me.'

'Good. Get rid of him and watch out for me and Bill. Don't show yourselves at the windows, but when we drive up, let us in at once. See?'

'Yes.'

'That's all right then. Oh, Bundle, don't let on that you're going up to town. Make some other excuse. Say you're taking Loraine home. How would that do?'

'Splendidly. I say, Jimmy, I'm thrilled to the core.'

'And you might as well make your will before starting.'

'Better and better. But I wish I knew what it was all about.'

'You will as soon as we meet. I'll tell you this much. We're going to get ready the hell of a surprise for No. 7!'

Bundle hung up the receiver and turned to Loraine, giving her a rapid résumé of the conversation. Loraine rushed upstairs and hurriedly packed her suitcase, and Bundle put her head round her father's door.

'I'm taking Loraine home, Father.'

'Why? I had no idea she was going to-day.'

'They want her back,' said Bundle vaguely. 'Just telephoned. Bye-bye.'

'Here, Bundle, wait a minute. When will you be home?'

'Don't know. Expect me when you see me.'

With this unceremonious exit Bundle rushed upstairs, put a hat on, slipped into her fur coat and was ready to start. She had already ordered the Hispano to be brought round.

The journey to London was without adventure, except such as was habitually provided by Bundle's driving. They left the car at a garage and proceeded direct to the Seven Dials Club.

The door was opened to them by Alfred. Bundle pushed her way past him without ceremony and Loraine followed.

'Shut the door, Alfred,' said Bundle. 'Now, I've come here especially to do you a good turn. The police are after you.'

'Oh, my lady!'

Alfred turned chalk white.

'I've come to warn you because you did me a good turn the other night,' went on Bundle rapidly. 'There's a warrant out for Mr. Mosgorovsky, and the best thing you can do is to clear out of here as quick as you can. If you're not found here, they won't bother about you. Here's ten pounds to help you get away somewhere.'

In three minutes' time an incoherent and badly scared Alfred had left 14 Hunstanton Street with only one idea in his head—never to return.

'Well, I've managed that all right,' said Bundle with satisfaction.

'Was it necessary to be so—well, drastic?' Loraine demurred.

'It's safer,' said Bundle. 'I don't know what Jimmy and Bill are up to, but we don't want Alfred coming back in the middle of it and wrecking everything. Hallo, here they are. Well, they haven't wasted much time. Probably watching round the corner to see Alfred leave. Go down and open the door to them, Loraine.'

Loraine obeyed. Jimmy Thesiger alighted from the driving seat.

'You stop there for a moment, Bill,' he said. 'Blow the horn if you think anyone's watching the place.'

He ran up the steps and banged the door behind him. He looked pink and elated.

'Hallo, Bundle, there you are. Now then, we've got to get down to it. Where's the key of the room you got into last time?'

'It was one of the downstairs keys. We'd better bring the lot up.'

'Right you are, but be quick. Time's short.'

The key was easily found, the baize-lined door swung back and the three entered. The room was exactly as Bundle had seen it before, with the seven chairs grouped round the table. Jimmy surveyed it for a minute or two in silence. Then his eye went to the two cupboards.

'Which is the cupboard you hid in, Bundle?'

'This one.'

Jimmy went to it and flung the door open. The same collection of miscellaneous glassware covered the shelves.

'We shall have to shift all this stuff,' he murmured. 'Run down and get Bill, Loraine. There's no need for him to keep watch outside any longer.'

Loraine ran off.

'What are you going to do?' inquired Bundle impatiently.

Jimmy was down on his knees, trying to peer through the crack of the other cupboard door.

'Wait till Bill comes and you shall hear the whole story. This is his staff work—and a jolly creditable bit of work it is. Hallo—what's

Loraine flying up the stairs for as though she'd got a mad bull after her?'

Loraine was indeed racing up the stairs as fast as she could. She burst in upon them with an ashen face and terror in her eyes.

'Bill—Bill—Oh, Bundle—Bill!'

'What about Bill?'

Jimmy caught her by the shoulder.

'For God's sake, Loraine, what's happened?'

Loraine was still gasping.

'Bill—I think he's dead—he's in the car still—but he doesn't move or speak. I'm sure he's dead.'

Jimmy muttered an oath and sprang for the stairs, Bundle behind him, her heart pounding unevenly and an awful feeling of desolation spreading over her.

Bill—dead? Oh, no! Oh, no! Not that. Please God—not that.

Together she and Jimmy reached the car, Loraine behind them.

Jimmy peered under the hood. Bill was sitting as he had left him, leaning back. But his eyes were closed and Jimmy's pull at his arm brought no response.

'I can't understand it,' muttered Jimmy. 'But he's not dead. Cheer up, Bundle. Look here, we've got to get him into the house. Let's pray to goodness no policeman comes along. If anybody says anything, he's our sick friend we're helping into the house.'

Between the three of them they got Bill into the house without much difficulty, and without attracting much attention, save for an unshaven gentleman, who said sympathetically:

'Genneman's 'ad a couple, I shee,' and nodded his head sapiently.

'Into the little back room downstairs,' said Jimmy. 'There's a sofa there.'

They got him safely on to the sofa and Bundle knelt down beside him and took his limp wrist in her hand.

'His pulse is beating,' she said. 'What *is* the matter with him?'

'He was all right when I left him just now,' said Jimmy. 'I wonder if someone's managed to inject some stuff into him. It would be easily done—just a prick. The man might have been asking him the time. There's only one thing for it. I must get a doctor at once. You stay here and look after him.'

He hurried to the door, then paused.

'Look here—don't be scared, either of you. But I'd better leave you my revolver. I mean—just in case. I'll be back just as soon as I possibly can.'

He laid the revolver down on the little table by the sofa, then hurried off. They heard the front door bang behind him.

The house seemed very still now. The two girls stayed motionless by Bill. Bundle still kept her finger on his pulse. It seemed to be beating very fast and irregularly.

'I wish we could do something,' she whispered to Loraine. 'This is awful.'

Loraine nodded.

'I know. It seems ages since Jimmy went and yet it's only a minute and a half.'

'I keep hearing things,' said Bundle. 'Footsteps and boards creaking upstairs—and yet I know it's only imagination.'

'I wonder why Jimmy left us the revolver,' said Loraine 'There can't really be danger.'

'If they could get Bill——' said Bundle and stopped.

Loraine shivered.

'I know—but we're in the house. Nobody can get in without our hearing them. And anyway we've got the revolver.'

Bundle turned her attention back again to Bill.

'I wish I knew what to do. Hot coffee. You give them that sometimes.'

'I've got some smelling-salts in my bag,' said Loraine. 'And some brandy. Where is it? Oh, I must have left it in the room upstairs.'

'I'll get it,' said Bundle. 'They might do some good.'

She sped quickly up the stairs, across the gaming room and through the open door into the meeting place. Loraine's bag was lying on the table.

As Bundle stretched out her hand to take it, she heard a noise from behind her. Hidden behind the door a man stood ready with a sandbag in his hand. Before Bundle could turn her head, he had struck.

With a faint moan, Bundle slipped down, an unconscious heap, upon the floor.

31. *The Seven Dials*

VERY SLOWLY Bundle returned to consciousness. She was aware of a dark, spinning blackness, the centre of which was a violent, throbbing ache. Punctuating this were sounds. A voice that she knew very well saying the same thing over and over again.

The blackness span less violently. The ache was now definitely located as being in Bundle's own head. And she was sufficiently herself to take an interest in what the voice was saying.

'Darling, darling Bundle, Oh, darling Bundle. She's dead; I know she's dead. Oh, my darling. Bundle, darling, darling Bundle. I do love you so. Bundle—darling—darling——'

Bundle lay quite still with her eyes shut. But she was now fully conscious. Bill's arms held her closely.

'Bundle darling—Oh, dearest, darling Bundle. Oh, my dear love. Oh, Bundle—Bundle. What shall I do? Oh, darling one—my Bundle—my own dearest, sweetest Bundle. Oh, God, what shall I do? I've killed her. I've killed her.'

Reluctantly—very reluctantly—Bundle spoke.

'No, you haven't, you silly idiot,' she said.

Bill gave a gasp of utter amazement.

'Bundle—you're alive?'

'Of course I'm alive.'

'How long have you been—I mean when did you come to?'

'About five minutes ago.'

'Why didn't you open your eyes—or say something?'

'Didn't want to. I was enjoying myself.'

'Enjoying yourself?'

'Yes. Listening to all the things you were saying. You'll never say them so well again. You'll be too beastly self-conscious.'

Bill had turned a dark brick-red.

'Bundle—you really didn't mind? You know, I *do* love you so. I have for ages. But I never have dared tell you so.'

'You silly juggins,' said Bundle. 'Why?'

'I thought you'd only laugh at me. I mean—you've got brains and all that—you'll marry some bigwig.'

'Like George Lomax?' suggested Bundle.

'I don't mean a fatuous ass like Codders. But some really fine chap who'll be worthy of you—though I don't think anyone could be that,' ended Bill.

'You're rather a dear, Bill.'

'But, Bundle, seriously, could you ever? I mean, could you ever bring yourself to?'

'Could I ever bring myself to do what?'

'Marry me. I know I'm awfully thick-headed—but I do love you, Bundle. I'd be your dog or your slave or your anything.'

'You're very like a dog,' said Bundle. 'I like dogs. They're so friendly and faithful and warm-hearted. I think that perhaps I could just bring myself to marry you, Bill—with a great effort, you know.'

Bill's response to this was to relinquish his grasp of her and recoil violently. He looked at her with amazement in his eyes.

'Bundle—you don't mean it?'

'There's nothing for it,' said Bundle. 'I see I shall have to relapse into unconsciousness again.'

'Bundle—darling——' Bill caught her to him. He was trembling violently. 'Bundle—do you really mean it—do you?—you don't know how much I love you.'

'Oh, Bill,' said Bundle.

There is no need to describe in detail the conversation of the next ten minutes. It consisted mostly of repetitions.

'And do you really love me?' said Bill, incredulously, for the twentieth time as he at last released her.

'Yes—yes—yes. Now do let's be sensible. I've got a racking head still, and I've been nearly squeezed to death by you. I want to get the hang of things. Where are we and what's happened?'

For the first time, Bundle began to take stock of her surroundings. They were in the secret room, she noted, and the baize door was closed and presumably locked. They were prisoners, then!

Bundle's eyes came back to Bill. Quite oblivious of her question he was watching her with adoring eyes.

'Bill, darling,' said Bundle, 'pull yourself together. We've got to get out of here.'

'Eh?' said Bill. 'What? Oh, yes. That'll be all right. No difficulty about that.'

'It's being in love makes you feel like that,' said Bundle. 'I feel rather the same myself. As though everything's easy and possible.'

'So it is,' said Bill. 'Now that I know you care for me——'

'Stop it,' said Bundle. 'Once we begin again any serious conversation will be hopeless. Unless you pull yourself together and become sensible, I shall very likely change my mind.'

'I shan't let you,' said Bill. 'You don't think that once having got you I'd be such a fool as to let you go, do you?'

'You would not coerce me against my will, I hope,' said Bundle grandiloquently.

'Wouldn't I?' said Bill. 'You just watch me do it, that's all.'

'You really are rather a darling, Bill. I was afraid you might be to meek, but I see there's going to be no danger of that. In another half-hour you'd be ordering me about. Oh, dear, we're getting silly again. Now, look here, Bill, we've got to get out of here.'

'I tell you that'll be quite all right. I shall——'

He broke off, obedient to a pressure from Bundle's hand. She was leaning forward, listening intently. Yes, she had not been mistaken. A step was crossing the outer room. The key was thrust into the lock and turned. Bundle held her breath. Was it Jimmy coming to rescue them—or was it someone else?

The door opened and the black-bearded Mr. Mosgorovsky stood on the threshold.

Immediately Bill took a step forward, standing in front of Bundle.

'Look here,' he said, 'I want a word with you privately.'

The Russian did not reply for a minute or two. He stood stroking his long, silky, black beard and smiling quietly to himself.

'So,' he said at last, 'it is like that. Very well. The lady will be pleased to come with me.'

'It's all right, Bundle,' said Bill. 'Leave it to me. You go with this chap. Nobody's going to hurt you. I know what I'm doing.'

Bundle rose obediently. That note of authority in Bill's voice was new to her. He seemed absolutely sure of himself and confident of being able to deal with the situation. Bundle wondered vaguely what it was that Bill had—or thought he had—up his sleeve.

She passed out of the room in front of the Russian. He followed her, closing the door behind him and locking it.

'This way, please,' he said.

He indicated the staircase and she mounted obediently to the floor above. Here she was directed to pass into a small, frowsy room, which she took to be Alfred's bedroom.

Mosgorovsky said: 'You will wait here quietly, please. There must be no noise.'

Then he went out, closing the door behind him and locking her in.

Bundle sat down on a chair. Her head was aching badly still and she felt incapable of sustained thought. Bill seemed to have the situation well in hand. Sooner or later, she supposed, someone would come and let her out.

The minutes passed. Bundle's watch had stopped, but she judged that over an hour had passed since the Russian had brought her here. What was happening? What, indeed, *had* happened?

At last she heard footsteps on the stairs. It was Mosgorovsky once more. He spoke very formally to her.

'Lady Eileen Brent, you are wanted at an emergency meeting of the Seven Dials Society. Please follow me.'

He led the way down the stairs and Bundle followed him. He opened the door of the secret chamber and Bundle passed in, catching her breath in surprise as she did so.

She was seeing for the second time what she had only had a glimpse of the first time through her peep-hole. The masked figures were sitting round the table. As she stood there, taken aback by the suddenness of it, Mosgorovsky slipped into his place, adjusting his clock mask as he did so.

But this time the chair at the head of the table was occupied. No. 7 was in his place.

Bundle's heart beat violently. She was standing at the foot of the table directly facing him and she stared and stared at the mocking piece of hanging stuff, with the clock dial on it, that hid his features.

He sat quite immovable and Bundle got an odd sensation of power radiating from him. His inactivity was not the inactivity of weakness —and she wished violently, almost hysterically, that he would speak —that he would make some sign, some gesture—not just sit there like a gigantive spider in the middle of its web waiting remorselessly for its prey.

She shivered and as she did so Mosgorovsky rose. His voice, smooth, silky, persuasive, seemed curiously far away.

'Lady Eileen, you have been present unasked at the secret councils of this society. It is therefore necessary that you should identify yourself with our aims and ambitions. The place 2 o'clock, you may notice, is vacant. It is that place that is offered to you.'

Bundle gasped. The thing was like a fantastic nightmare. Was it possible that she, Bundle Brent, was being asked to join a murderous secret society? Had the same proposition been made to Bill, and had he refused indignantly?

'I can't do that,' she said bluntly.

'Do not answer precipitately.'

She fancied that Mosgorovsky, beneath his clock mask, was smiling significantly into his beard.

'You do not as yet know, Lady Eileen, what it is you are refusing.'

'I can make a pretty good guess,' said Bundle.

'Can you?'

It was the voice of 7 o'clock. It awoke some vague chord of memory in Bundle's brain. Surely she knew that voice?

Very slowly No. 7 raised a hand to his head and fumbled with the fastening of the mask.

Bundle held her breath. At last—she was going to *know*.

The mask fell.

Bundle found herself looking into the expressionless, wooden face of Superintendent Battle.

32. *Bundle is dumbfounded*

'THAT'S RIGHT,' said Battle, as Mosgorovsky leapt up and came round to Bundle. 'Get a chair for her. It's been a bit of a shock, I can see.'

Bundle sank down on a chair. She felt limp and faint with surprise. Battle went on talking in a quiet, comfortable way wholly characteristic of him.

'You didn't expect to see me, Lady Eileen. No, and no more did some of the others sitting round this table. Mr. Mosgorovsky's been my lieutenant in a manner of speaking. He's been in the know all along. But most of the others have taken their orders blindly from him.'

Still Bundle said no word. She was—a most unusual state of affairs for her—simply incapable of speech.

Battle nodded at her comprehendingly, seeming to understand the state of her feelings.

'You'll have to get rid of one or two preconceived ideas of yours, I'm afraid, Lady Eileen. About this society, for instance—I know it's common enough in books—a secret organisation of criminals with a mysterious super-criminal at the head of it whom no one ever sees. That sort of thing may exist in real life, but I can only say that I've never come across anything of the sort, and I've had a good deal of experience one way or another.

'But there's a lot of romance in the world, Lady Eileen. People, especially young people, like reading about such things, and they like still better really *doing* them. I'm going to introduce you now to a very creditable band of amateurs that has done remarkably fine work for my Department, work that nobody else could have done. If they've chosen rather melodramatic trappings, well, why shouldn't they? They've been willing to face real danger—danger of the very worst kind—and they've done it for these reasons: love of danger for its own sake—which to my mind is a very healthy sign in these Safety First days—and an honest wish to serve their country.

'And now, Lady Eileen, I'm going to introduce you. First of all, there's Mr. Mosgorovsky, whom you already know in a manner of speaking. As you're aware, he runs the club and he runs a host of other things too. He's our most valuable Secret Anti-Bolshevist Agent in England. No. 5 is Count Andras of the Hungarian Embassy, a very near and dear friend of the late Mr. Gerald Wade. No. 4 is Mr. Hayward Phelps, an American journalist, whose British sympathies are very keen and whose aptitude for scenting "news" is remarkable. No. 3——'

He stopped, smiling, and Bundle stared dumbfounded into the sheepish, grinning face of Bill Eversleigh.

'No. 2,' went on Battle in a graver voice, 'can only show an empty place. It is the place belonging to Mr. Ronald Devereux, a very gallant young gentleman who died for his country if any man ever did. No. 1—well, No. 1 was Mr. Gerald Wade, another very gallant gentleman who died in the same way. His place was taken—not without some grave misgivings on my part—by a lady—a lady who has proved her fitness to have it and who has been a great help to us.'

The last to do so, No. 1, removed her mask, and Bundle looked without surprise into the beautiful, dark face of Countess Radzky.

'I might have known,' said Bundle resentfully, 'that you were too completely the beautiful foreign adventuress to be anything of the kind really.'

'But you don't know the real joke,' said Bill. '*Bundle, this is Babe St. Maur*—you remember my telling you about her and what a ripping actress she was—and she's about proved it.'

'That's so,' said Miss St. Maur in pure transatlantic nasal. 'But it's not a terrible lot of credit to me, because Poppa and Momma came from that part of Yurrup—so I got the patter fairly easy. Gee, but I nearly gave myself away once at the Abbey, talking about gardens.'

She paused and then said abruptly:

'It's—it's not been just fun. You see, I was kinder engaged to Ronny, and when he handed in his checks—well, I had to do something to track down the skunk who murdered him. That's all.'

'I'm completely bewildered,' said Bundle. 'Nothing is what it seems.'

'It's very simple, Lady Eileen,' said Superintendent Battle. 'It began with some of the young people wanting a bit of excitement. It was Mr. Wade who first got on to me. He suggested the formation of a band of what you might call amateur workers to do a bit of secret service work. I warned him that it might be dangerous—but he wasn't the kind to weigh that in the balance. I made it plain to him that anyone who came in must do so on that understanding. But, bless you, that wasn't going to stop any of Mr. Wade's friends. And so the thing began.'

'But what was the object of it all?' asked Bundle.

'We wanted a certain man—wanted him badly. He wasn't an ordinary crook. He worked in Mr. Wade's world, a kind of Raffles, but much more dangerous than any Raffles ever was or could be. He was out for big stuff, international stuff. Twice already valuable secret inventions had been stolen, and clearly stolen by someone who had inside knowledge. The professionals had had a try—and failed. Then the amateurs took on—and succeeded.'

'Succeeded?'

'Yes—but they didn't come out of it unscathed. The man was dangerous. Two lives fell victim to him and he got away with it. But the Seven Dials stuck to it. And as I say they succeeded. Thanks to Mr. Eversleigh, the man was caught at last red-handed.'

'Who was he?' asked Bundle. 'Do I know him?'

'You know him very well, Lady Eileen. His name is Mr. Jimmy Thesiger, and he was arrested this afternoon.'

33. *Battle explains*

SUPERINTENDENT BATTLE settled down to explain. He spoke comfortably and cosily.

'I didn't suspect him myself for a long time. The first hint of it

I had was when I heard what Mr. Devereux's last words had been. Naturally, you took them to mean that Mr. Devereux was trying to send word to Mr. Thesiger that the Seven Dials had killed him. That's what the words seemed to mean on their face value. But of course I knew that that couldn't be so. It was the Seven Dials that Mr. Devereux wanted told—and what he wanted them told was something about Mr. Jimmy Thesiger.

'The thing seemed incredible, because Mr. Devereux and Mr. Thesiger were close friends. But I remembered something else—that these thefts must have been committed by someone who was absolutely in the know. Someone who, if not in the Foreign Office himself, was in the way of hearing all its chit-chat. And I found it very hard to find out where Mr. Thesiger got his money. The income his father left him was a small one, yet he was able to live at a most expensive rate. Where did the money come from?

'I knew that Mr. Wade had been very excited by something that he had found out. He was quite sure that he was on the right track. He didn't confide in anyone about what he thought that track was, but he did say something to Mr. Devereux about being on the point of making sure. That was just before they both went down to Chimneys for that week-end. As you know, Mr. Wade died there—apparently from an overdose of a sleeping draught. It seemed straightforward enough, but Mr. Devereux did not accept that explanation for a minute. He was convinced that Mr. Wade had been very cleverly put out of the way and that someone in the house must actually be the criminal we were all after. He came, I think, very near confiding in Mr. Thesiger, for he certainly had no suspicions of him at that moment. But something held him back.

'Then he did rather a curious thing. He arranged seven clocks upon the mantelpiece, throwing away the eighth. It was meant as a symbol that the Seven Dials would revenge the death of one of their members—and he watched eagerly to see if anyone betrayed themselves or showed signs of perturbation.'

'And it was Jimmy Thesiger who poisoned Gerry Wade?'

'Yes, he slipped the stuff into a whisky and soda which Mr. Wade had downstairs before retiring to bed. That's why he was already feeling sleepy when he wrote that letter to Miss Wade.'

'Then the footman, Bauer, hadn't anything to do with it?' asked Bundle.

'Bauer was one of our people, Lady Eileen. It was thought likely that our crook would go for Herr Eberhard's invention and Bauer was got into the house to watch events on our behalf. But he wasn't able to do much. As I say, Mr. Thesiger administered the fatal dose easily enough. Later, when everyone was asleep, a bottle, glass and empty chloral bottle were placed by Mr. Wade's bedside by Mr. Thesiger. Mr. Wade was unconscious then, and his fingers were probably pressed round the glass and the bottle so that they should be found there if any questions should arise. I don't know what effect the seven clocks on the mantelpiece made on Mr. Thesiger. He certainly didn't let on anything to Mr. Devereux. All the same, I think he had a bad five minutes now and again thinking of them. And I think he kept a pretty wary eye on Mr. Devereux after that.

'We don't know exactly what happened next. No one saw much of Mr. Devereux after Mr. Wade's death. But it is clear that he worked along the same lines that he knew Mr. Wade had been working on and reached the same result—namely, that Mr. Thesiger was the man. I fancy, too, that he was betrayed in the same way.'

'You mean?'

'Through Miss Loraine Wade. Mr. Wade was devoted to her—I believe he hoped to marry her—she wasn't really his sister, of course—and there is no doubt that he told her more than he should have done. But Miss Loraine Wade was devoted body and soul to Mr. Thesiger. She would do anything he told her. She passed on information to him. In the same way, later, Mr. Devereux was attracted to her, and probably warned her against Mr. Thesiger. So Mr. Devereux in turn was silenced—and died trying to send word to the Seven Dials that his murderer was Mr. Thesiger.'

'How ghastly,' cried Bundle. 'If I had only known.'

'Well, it didn't seem likely. In fact, I could hardly credit it myself. But then we came to the affair at the Abbey. You will remember how awkward it was—specially awkward for Mr. Eversleigh here. You and Mr. Thesiger were hand in glove. Mr. Eversleigh had already been embarrassed by your insisting on being brought to this place, and when he found that you had actually overheard what went on at a meeting, he was dumbfounded.'

The Superintendent paused and a twinkle came into his eye.

'So was I, Lady Eileen. I never dreamed of such a thing being possible. You put one over on me there all right.

'Well, Mr. Eversleigh was in a dilemma. He couldn't let you into the secret of the Seven Dials without letting Mr. Thesiger in also—

and that would never do. It all suited Mr. Thesiger very well, of course, for it gave him a bona fide reason for getting himself asked to the Abbey, which made things much easier for him.

'I may say that the Seven Dials had already sent a warning letter to Mr. Lomax. That was to ensure his applying to me for assistance, so that I should be able to be on the spot in a perfectly natural manner. I made no secret of my presence, as you know.'

And again the Superintendent's eyes twinkled.

'Well, ostensibly, Mr. Eversleigh and Mr. Thesiger were to divide the night into two watches. Really, Mr. Eversleigh and Miss St. Maur did so. She was on guard at the library window when she heard Mr. Thesiger coming and had to dart behind the screen.

'And now comes the cleverness of Mr. Thesiger. Up to a point he told a perfectly true story, and I must admit that with the fight and everything, I was distinctly shaken—and began to wonder whether he had had anything to do with the theft at all, or whether we were completely on the wrong track. There were one or two suspicious circumstances that pointed in an entirely different direction, and I can tell you I didn't know what to make of things, when something turned up to clinch matters.

'I found the burnt glove in the fireplace with the teeth marks on it—and then—well—I knew that I'd been right after all. But, upon my word, he was a clever one.'

'What actually happened?' said Bundle. 'Who was the other man?'

'There wasn't any other man. Listen, and I'll show you how in the end I reconstructed the whole story. To begin with, Mr. Thesiger and Miss Wade are in this together. And they have a rendezvous for an exact time. Miss Wade comes over in her car, climbs through the fence and comes up to the house. She's got a perfectly good story if anyone stops her—the one she told eventually. But she arrived unmolested on the terrace just after the clock had struck two.

'Now, I may say to begin with that she was seen coming in. My men saw her, but they had orders to stop nobody coming in—only going out. I wanted, you see, to find out as much as possible. Miss Wade arrives on the terrace, and at that minute a parcel falls at her feet and she picks it up. A man comes down the ivy and she starts to run. What happens next? The struggle—and presently the revolver shots. What will everyone do? Rush to the scene of the fight. And Miss Loraine Wade could have left the grounds and driven off with the formula safely in her possession.

'But things don't happen quite like that. Miss Wade runs straight into my arms. And at that moment the game changes. It's no longer attack but defence. Miss Wade tells her story. It is perfectly true and perfectly sensible.

'And now we come to Mr. Thesiger. One thing struck me at once. The bullet wound alone couldn't have caused him to faint. Either he had fallen and hit his head—or—well, he hadn't fainted at all. Later we had Miss St. Maur's story. It agreed perfectly with Mr. Thesiger's—there was only one suggestive point. Miss St. Maur said that after the lights were turned out and Mr. Thesiger went over to the window, he was so still that she thought he must have left the room and gone outside. Now, if anyone is in the room, you can hardly help hearing their breathing if you are listening for it. Supposing, then, that Mr. Thesiger *had* gone outside. Where next? Up the ivy to Mr. O'Rourke's room—Mr. O'Rourke's whisky and soda having been doped the night before. He gets the papers, throws them down to the girl, climbs down the ivy again, and—starts the fight. That's easy enough when you come to think of it. Knock the tables down, stagger about, speak in your own voice and then in a hoarse half-whisper. And then, the final touch, the two revolver shots. His own Colt automatic, bought openly the day before, is fired at an imaginary assailant. Then, with his left gloved hand, he takes from his pocket the small Mauser pistol and shoots himself through the fleshy part of the right arm. He flings the pistol through the window, tears off the glove with his teeth, and throws it into the fire. When I arrive he is lying on the floor in a faint.'

Bundle drew a deep breath.

'You didn't realise all this at the time, Superintendent Battle?'

'No, that I didn't. I was taken in as much as anyone could be. It wasn't till long afterwards that I pieced it all together. Finding the glove was the beginning of it. Then I made Sir Oswald throw the pistol through the window. It fell a good way farther on than it should have done. But a man who is right-handed doesn't throw nearly as far with the left hand. Even then it was only suspicion—and a very faint suspicion at that.

'But there was one point struck me. The papers were obviously thrown down for someone to pick up. If Miss Wade was there by accident, who was the real person? Of course, for those who weren't in the know, that question was answered easily enough—the Countess. But there I had the pull over you. *I knew the Countess was all right.* So what follows? Why, the idea that the papers had actually been picked up by the person they were meant for. And the more I thought of it, the more it seemed to me a very remarkable coincidence that Miss Wade should have arrived at the exact moment she did.'

'It must have been very difficult for you when I came to you full of suspicion about the Countess.'

'It was, Lady Eileen. I had to say something to put you off the scent. And it was very difficult for Mr. Eversleigh here, with the lady coming out of a dead faint and no knowing what she might say.'

'I understand Bill's anxiety now,' said Bundle. 'And the way he kept urging her to take time and not talk till she felt quite all right.'

'Poor old Bill,' said Miss St. Maur. 'That poor baby had to be vamped against his will—getting madder'n a hornet every minute.'

'Well,' said Superintendent Battle, 'there it was. I suspected Mr. Thesiger—but I couldn't get definite proof. On the other hand, Mr. Thesiger himself was rattled. He realised more or less what he was up against in the Seven Dials—but he wanted badly to know who No. 7 was. He got himself asked to the Cootes under the impression that Sir Oswald Coote was No. 7.'

'I suspected Sir Oswald,' said Bundle, 'especially when he came in from the garden that night.'

'I never suspected him,' said Battle. 'But I don't mind telling you that I *did* have my suspicions of that young chap, his secretary.'

'Pongo?' said Bill. 'Not old Pongo?'

'Yes, Mr. Eversleigh, old Pongo as you call him. A very efficient gentleman and one that could have put anything through if he'd a mind to. I suspected him partly because he'd been the one to take the clocks into Mr. Wade's room that night. It would have been easy for him to put the bottle and glass by the bedside then. And then, for another thing, he was left-handed. That glove pointed straight to him—if it hadn't been for one thing——'

'What?'

'The teeth marks—only a man whose right hand was incapacitated would have needed to tear off that glove with his teeth.'

'So Pongo was cleared?'

'So Pongo was cleared, as you say. I'm sure it would be a great surprise to Mr. Bateman to know he was ever suspected.'

'It would,' agreed Bill. 'A solemn card—a silly ass like Pongo. How you could ever think——'

'Well, as far as that goes, Mr. Thesiger was what you might describe as an empty-headed young ass of the most brainless description. One of the two was playing a part. When I decided that it was Mr. Thesiger, I was interested to get Mr. Bateman's opinion of him. All along, Mr. Bateman had the gravest suspicions of Mr. Thesiger and frequently said as much to Sir Oswald.'

'It's curious,' said Bill, 'but Pongo always is right. It's maddening.'

'Well, as I say,' went on Superintendent Battle, 'we got Mr. Thesiger fairly on the run, badly rattled over this Seven Dials business and uncertain just where the danger lay. That we got him in the end was solely through Mr. Eversleigh. He knew what he was up against, and he risked his life cheerfully. But he never dreamt that you would be dragged into it, Lady Eileen.'

'My God, no,' said Bill with feeling.

'He went round to Mr. Thesiger's rooms with a cooked-up tale,' continued Battle. 'He was to pretend that certain papers of Mr. Devereux's had come into his hands. Those papers were to suggest a suspicion of Mr. Thesiger. Naturally, as the honest friend, Mr. Eversleigh rushed round, sure that Mr. Thesiger would have an explanation. We calculated that if we were right, Mr. Thesiger would try and put Mr. Eversleigh out of the way, and we were fairly certain as to the way he'd do it. Sure enough, Mr. Thesiger gave his guest a whisky and soda. During the minute or two that his host was out of the room, Mr. Eversleigh poured that into a jar on the mantelpiece, but he had to pretend, of course, that the drug was taking effect. It would be slow, he knew, not sudden. He began his story, and Mr. Thesiger at first denied it all indignantly, but as soon as he saw (or thought he saw) that the drug was taking effect, he admitted everything and told Mr. Eversleigh that he was the third victim.

'When Mr. Eversleigh was nearly unconscious, Mr. Thesiger took him down to the car and helped him in. The hood was up. He must already have telephoned to you unknown to Mr. Eversleigh. He made a clever suggestion to you. You were to say that you were taking Miss Wade home.

'You made no mention of a message from him. Later, when your body was found here, Miss Wade would swear that you had driven her home and gone up to London with the idea of penetrating into this house by yourself.

'Mr. Eversleigh continued to play his part, that of the unconscious man. I may say that as soon as the two young men had left Jermyn Street, one of my men gained admission and found the doctored whisky, which contained enough hydrochloride of morphia to kill two men. Also the car they were in was followed. Mr. Thesiger drove out of town to a well-known golf course, where he showed himself for a few minutes, speaking of playing a round. That, of course, was for an alibi, should one be needed. He left the car with Mr. Eversleigh in it a little way down the road. Then he drove back to town and to the Seven Dials Club. As soon as he saw Alfred leave, he drove up to the door, spoke to Mr. Eversleigh as he got out in case you might be listening and came into the house and played his little comedy.

'When he pretended to go for a doctor, he really only slammed the door and then crept quietly upstairs and hid behind the door of this room, where Miss Wade would presently send you up on some excuse. Mr. Eversleigh, of course, was horror-struck when he saw you, but he thought it best to keep up the part he was playing. He knew our people were watching the house, and he imagined that there was no immediate danger intended to you. He could always "come to life" at any moment. When Mr. Thesiger threw his revolver on the table and apparently left the house it seemed safer than ever. As for the next bit——' He paused, looking at Bill. 'Perhaps you'd like to tell that, sir.'

'I was still lying on that bally sofa,' said Bill, 'trying to look done in and getting the fidgets worse and worse. Then I heard someone run down the stairs, and Loraine got up and went to the door. I heard Thesiger's voice, but not what he said. I heard Loraine say: "That's all right—it's gone splendidly." Then he said: "Help me carry him up. It will be a bit of a job, but I want them both together there—a nice little surprise for No. 7." I didn't quite understand what they were jawing about, but they hauled me up the stairs somehow or other. It *was* a bit of a job for them. I made myself a dead weight all right. They heaved me in here, and then I heard Loraine say: "You're sure it's all right? She won't come round?" And Jimmy said —the damned blackguard: "No fear. I hit with all my might."

'They went away and locked the door, and then I opened my eyes and saw you. My God, Bundle, I shall never feel so perfectly awful again. I thought you were dead.'

'I suppose my hat saved me,' said Bundle.

'Partly,' said Superintendent Battle. 'But partly it was Mr. Thesiger's wounded arm. He didn't realise it himself—but it had only half its usual strength. Still, that's all no credit to the Department. We didn't take the care of you we ought to have done, Lady Eileen—and it's a black blot on the whole business.'

'I'm very tough,' said Bundle. 'And also rather lucky. What I can't get over is Loraine being in it. She was such a gentle little thing.'

'Ah!' said the Superintendent. 'So was the Pentonville murderess that killed five children. You can't go by that. She's got bad blood in her—her father ought to have seen the inside of a prison more than once.'

'You've got her too?'

Superintendent Battle nodded.

'I daresay they won't hang her—juries are soft-hearted. But young Thesiger will swing all right—and a good thing too—a more utterly depraved and callous criminal I never met.'

'And now,' he added, 'if your head isn't aching too badly, Lady Eileen, what about a little celebration? There's a nice little restaurant round the corner.'

Bundle heartily agreed.

'I'm starving, Superintendent Battle. Besides,' she looked round, 'I've got to get to know all my colleagues.'

'The Seven Dials,' said Bill. 'Hurrah! Some fizz is what we need. Do they run to fizz at this place, Battle?'

'You won't have anything to complain of, sir. You leave it to me.'

'Superintendent Battle,' said Bundle, 'you are a wonderful man. I'm sorry you're married already. As it is, I shall have to put up with Bill.'

34. *Lord Caterham approves*

'FATHER,' said Bundle, 'I've got to break a piece of news to you. You're going to lose me.'

'Nonsense,' said Lord Caterham. 'Don't tell me that you're suffering from galloping consumption or a weak heart or anything like that, because I simply don't believe it.'

'It's not death,' said Bundle. 'It's marriage.'

'Very nearly as bad,' said Lord Caterham. 'I suppose I shall have to come to the wedding, all dressed up in tight, uncomfortable clothes, and give you away. And Lomax may think it necessary to kiss me in the vestry.'

'Good heavens! You don't think I'm going to marry George, do you?' cried Bundle.

'Well, something like that seemed to be in the wind last time I saw you,' said her father. 'Yesterday morning, you know.'

'I'm going to be married to someone a hundred times nicer than George,' said Bundle.

'I hope so, I'm sure,' said Lord Caterham. 'But one never knows. I don't feel you're really a good judge of character, Bundle. You told me that young Thesiger was a cheerful inefficient, and from all I hear now it seems that he was one of the most efficient criminals of the day. The sad thing is that I never met him. I was thinking of writing my reminiscences soon—with a special chapter on murderers I have met—and by a purely technical oversight, I never met this young man.'

'Don't be silly,' said Bundle. 'You know you haven't got the energy to write reminiscences or anything else.'

'I wasn't actually going to write them myself,' said Lord Caterham. 'I believe that's never done. But I met a very charming girl the other day and that's her special job. She collects the material and does all the actual writing.'

'And what do you do?'

'Oh, just give her a few facts for half an hour every day. Nothing more than that.' After a slight pause, Lord Caterham said: 'She was a nice-looking girl—very restful and sympathetic.'

'Father,' said Bundle, 'I have a feeling that without me you will run into deadly danger.'

'Different kinds of danger suit different kinds of people,' said Lord Caterham.

He was moving away, when he turned back and said over his shoulder:

'By the way, Bundle, who *are* you marrying?'

'I was wondering,' said Bundle, 'when you were going to ask me that. I'm going to marry Bill Eversleigh.'

The egoist thought it over for a minute. Then he nodded in complete satisfaction.

'Excellent,' he said. 'He's scratch, isn't he? He and I can play together in the foursomes in the Autumn Meeting.'